ELFLING OF VANDIKAR

The Seven Lost Swords Of Arias
BOOK 1

written by
DARYL HANSON

Cover illustration drawn by diAnne Gregorius

For all those who dream —

No matter how old you become,
never stop dreaming.

For God is in the business
of making dreams come true!

Map of Ythira, the eastern continent

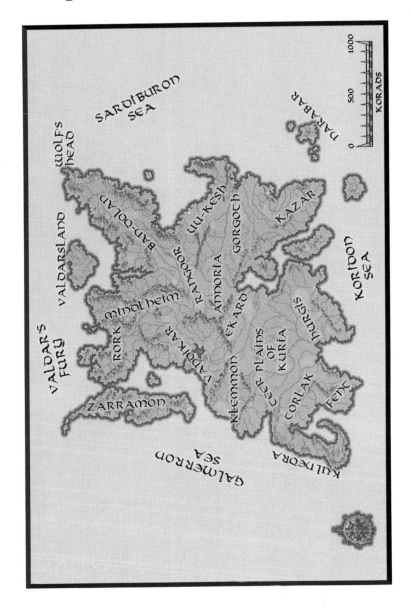

Map of Shan's Journey

Map of the Forest of Draydin

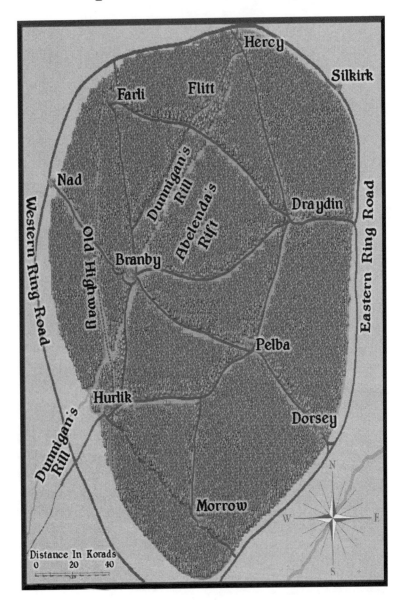

Table of Contents

− 1 −
The Beast
[12th of Kaligath, 4534 C.R.]

Shan was suddenly awake.

He lay on his back upon a broad, feather mattress, and after blinking several times in the darkness, stared up at the ceiling. Flickering shadows danced among the polished beams as torchlight from the courtyard splashed in through an open window.

He found himself listening.

The air was cool and still. He did not hear the usual rustle of wind in the forest trees or the gentle slap of the curtains against the sill. And the clicking of insects that had lulled him to sleep was gone. He listened for a moment, his head cradled on a lump of pillow, but there was not a single stray whisper of conversation to be heard from those usually about their business in the great hall. He strained with every fiber of his being for several long *mira*, yet he still could not catch any sounds of the guards laughing or talking softly among themselves in the courtyard.

That's odd, he thought.

Shan sat up in bed. He clutched the warm blankets absently about himself with one hand, his gaze settling upon a curious play of shadows along the far wall of his room. He watched them with a dull fascination as he continued to listen. Then, with a sudden start, he realized he could not even hear the coughing and sneezing of the watchbeasts. They could almost always be heard prowling the perimeter of the compound each night, jerking guards about by their neck chains as they sniffed and clawed over a swath of some thirty or forty *kora* of cleared ground between the broad, outer wall of sharpened logs and the fringe of forest trees beyond. The shifting mosaic of darkness and light on the far wall was suddenly forgotten as Shan became instantly aware that Draydin had never seemed so still.

An eerie chill quickly shivered through him.

Shan swallowed hard twice. He remained motionless for some time, his mouth hanging half-open, probing the stillness with his senses, listening, smelling, *feeling*. Slowly he unruffled the covers. There was a dryness in his throat that would not go away. Sucking air through his teeth, he flipped his feet over the side of the mattress and slid off the edge of the bed. The wooden floor was cool against his bare feet as he crept noiselessly toward the window. He paused momentarily by the curtain and listened once more.

The silence was overpowering. It hung like a thickness in the air. The soft hiss of his own breath was unusually loud in his ears. His heart raced and a tingling of fear gnawed at his innards.

Cautiously, Shan pulled the nearest flap of the drapes aside and peered down into the courtyard—and then gasped in astonishment. There was no one in sight! Without thinking, he leaned as far out over the sill as he could and quickly looked in all directions, and nearly tumbled from the second floor window.

The great gate of the palisade had been thrown open, offering a wide view of deepest night under the forest trees. On the right side of the yard, huddled against the thick barrier of iron-banded logs, the workers' barracks appeared deserted. Darkness gaped from the small open doorway of the rough-hewn, plank building. Across the yard, fringing nearly two hundred paces of trampled earth, the steel cage of the watchbeasts was empty and the heavy, metal door left ajar.

Panic tingled at Shan's heart. His hands throbbed as he gripped the window sill with a sudden fierceness. He forced himself to breathe slowly, deeply. He closed his eyes and shook his head stiffly, as if to clear the remnants of a horrifying nightmare from the cobwebs of his mind. But each time he blinked his eyes the scene below remained unchanged.

He swept his gaze back and forth across the yard with agonizing slowness, meticulously scanning every *hob* of boot-scarred ground. Many of the torches had burned low in their brackets; some had even sputtered and gone out. Ropey wisps of smoke rose up from them, leaving much of the court in thick shadow. The few that remained lit offered little more than a pale glow, and their tiny flames sent thin, wraith-like figures into the night, quivering in confusion. The elven lad stood riveted at the window as another torch let off a sizzling *pop* and suddenly went dark. A slender trail of gray smoke rose from it in irregular swirls.

Shan turned abruptly away from the window and hurried to the large chest next to his bed. He propped the heavy lid against the wall. Plunging both hands into its gloomy depths he quickly fished about for several long *biri*. He drew out a crumpled tunic and a pair of leather britches. He wriggled into these quickly in the darkness, then started to pull on a soft pair of hide boots he'd kicked off by one of the thick bedposts. The supple leather came almost to his knees. He ran back to the window, struggling with a belt which had somehow gotten twisted in his haste.

There was still no movement in the yard below. He stood there for several heartbeats, scanning the scene once more, before finally managing to straighten the belt.

He cocked an eye at the night sky. It must have been well past midnight. The faintest, almost reddish-gold sickle of Kiara offered only a feeble glow. The pale sliver of the smaller moon was low in the sky and could just be seen above the dark line of the trees. The larger, azure curve of Sheera had already completely disappeared. Stars twinkled faintly through a thin blanket of mist overhead. It was all so still. *Too still,* he thought.

Suddenly, from way off in the trees, a wild howl pierced the silence. Shan's heart froze instantly within his chest. Icy fingers of fear prickled in his gut. They spread quickly outward to all his extremities, chilling him clear to the bone. He was terrified by the moaning call, yet his face was somehow drawn to the sound. It was unlike anything he'd ever heard before. Almost against his will, he listened. It was a kind of strange, high-pitched keening, a long, weird cry that juddered through the depths of the forest. It seemed to beckon him, to tug at the edges of his mind. He could not shake the unmistakable feeling of fear that arose in the pit of his stomach as the eerie call snaked out through the stillness of the trees and seemed somehow to grasp for him. The shrill, deathlike wail brought a ripple of goose-flesh rushing over him and seemed to hover on the air for an eternity. Abruptly the cry broke apart and melted into the night like a thousand moaning whispers of the wind.

Shan stood there like a figure of stone. An overpowering sense of terror crushed down on him. He felt as if a great, clutching hand had reached down deep inside of him and snatched ruthlessly for his heart. He could sense the taint of its icy cold touch as it had grasped for him. He drew back into the deepest recesses of his mind, cowering somewhere alone in the darkness and fear. Eyes clamped tightly shut, he waited. After a moment, the great hand seemed to move on, and he was left shivering from its burning cold embrace.

It was some time before he could breathe without the sharp tightening of his stomach and a good deal longer before he could bring himself to move. In awkward, almost wooden movements, Shan opened his eyes and peeled his fingers loose from the sill. He brushed back long strands of brownish-blonde hair where it tickled at his eyes. He cupped his hands and raised them to his mouth to cry out, but then, inexplicably, did not do so. He swallowed at a hardness in his throat and slowly dropped his hands. He wheeled for the door in sudden determination, but then stopped abruptly in the center of the room.

He caught his breath, listening.

He was almost certain he had heard movement somewhere in the hallway outside his room. *Probably just one of the kitchen drudges still up and about at this late ahr,* he thought, yet something whispered in the back of his mind for him to be cautious. If there was someone there he should go out and have a word with them. Maybe they would know what had happened. Shan pivoted for the door but his leaden feet just would not respond. He waited, it seemed, for the longest time, sucking air in short, ragged gasps. His heart pounded in his throat, and he felt as if his chest would explode at any moment. His legs began to stiffen as he forced himself to wait, yet he remained motionless, straining to pick up any hint of noise in the hallway beyond.

"Fool!" he mumbled to himself after a time. "Something seems to have happened outside and you start hearing things. Some soldier you'd make!" Wiping a trickle of sweat from his forehead, he managed a wry grin at himself in the darkness.

In one corner of the room stood a large fireplace, now dark and quiet. The great, flame-blackened stones jutting out from the wall gave it the look of a huge, gaping mouth. A dying gleam of torchlight drifted in through the window and played from the hilt of a dagger upon the massive wooden mantel. Shan slipped over to the gloomy hearth, his legs tingling from the long moments he had stood motionless. He quickly stuffed the sheathed blade into his belt. If indeed there was some sort of trouble, then at least he would be armed, he reasoned. He scooped up a hooded cloak from the chair by the bed, then finally turned stiffly for the door.

The hint of heavy shuffling and a faint clicking sound in the hall outside froze his hand on the latch. He pressed himself cautiously against the portal and listened with an ear at the jamb. He was almost certain he could hear sniffling. His heart skipped a beat. The soft creak of floorboards in the hallway seemed to draw closer. With one hand Shan reached up and quietly slid the heavy iron bolt slowly into place. He listened once more at the jamb and he felt his skin start to crawl. There was no mistaking it now. Someone—some*thing*—was slowly moving nearer, and the floorboards in the hall groaned softly with its passing. Silently, he backed away from the door.

The low clicking sounds stopped abruptly outside the heavy wooden portal to his room. Then came the unmistakable whisper of something sniffing noisily at the floor. The quick hiss of breath strangely reminded Shan of a watchbeast on a hunt, its large, wet nose puffing up little jets of dust as it slithered eagerly across the ground. The memory was oddly disturbing and forced a shudder from him in the darkness. Forgotten, the cloak slipped from his fingers and curled softly into a heap on the floor as Shan continued to back away. He was unable to tear his eyes away from the darkened slit at the bottom of the door. He flinched as he bumped into a small chair that sent flares of jittery flesh down one leg and across his back. Reaching back cautiously, he felt for the obstacle with his hands and slowly maneuvered around it.

The sound of snuffling grew louder and more determined. Shan thought he caught a glimpse of moving shadows from under the door. All at once there was a scraping and clawing at the heavy wooden obstacle. The boy stumbled suddenly backwards in panic and fell against the far wall. The jolt caused a low table to tip over. A small glass figurine, perched on its small surface, was thrown into the air. It struck the floor with a *crash*, filling the room with its echoing explosion. The thing at the door immediately went into a frenzy. It tore at the wood, clawing and biting with unbridled fury. It growled and hissed and threw itself against the portal with incredible strength. The heavy iron hinges began to creak and groan under the strain and large, twisting cracks appeared suddenly in the surrounding stone wall.

Shan threw the table aside and struggled to his feet. He slipped on a shard of the scattered glass, felt it grind into the wood of the floor as he skated over it. "Guards!" he started screaming wildly, stumbling over to the window. He clamped his hands tightly onto the sill for balance. "Help! Guards!" he shouted. "Weeson! Ulfiir! Help! Help!"

The creature without bellowed in fury. It hammered at the wall and the thick wooden barrier with huge, powerful feet. The door seemed to buckle and bend like a sapling, yet somehow would not yield. Shan could hear the click and rasp of its claws as it tore at the hardened, wooden surface. The awesome wrenching and rattling of the heavy iron hinges and the cracking and splintering of the stone walls mingled crazily with the creature's maddened howls. It drenched the room with the sounds of its muffled roar. The impassioned growls caromed wildly about the thick, stone walls. The boy threw his hands over his ears to shut out the rising jumble of noise. The entire stone building seemed to shake and jounce beneath his feet.

Shan looked down through the window into the empty courtyard. Confusion creased his sweaty brow. Where *was* everyone? There had always been someone stirring in the hall, somewhere, no matter how late.

Yet, for the first time in his life, for the first time in all his remembrance, Draydin remained absolutely still. And he could not quite explain it.

"Guards!" he managed to croak out. "Guards!" He cupped his hands and hollered till his chest was sore. "Help! Guards!" *Why can't anyone else hear the commotion?* he thought with an anguished moan. *All this racket could practically raise the dead!* A sudden thought arrowed through him. *Dead? Could they all be . . . dead?* Had they already been butchered in their sleep by that thing at his door? He blinked back a sting of wetness in his eyes and slumped heavily against the window frame. *Am I the only one left alive in all of Draydin?* He slammed his fist on the sill. *What's happened to the guards?*

Behind him Shan could hear the heavy door buckle and groan on its hinges. He shot a wild glance over his shoulder. Crumbling bits of stone clunked to the floor with a rain of plaster and dust. With a last strangled cry for help he turned away from the window and hurriedly looked about the room. He ran to the great chest along the wall. He latched onto it with one hand on the thick leather handle, the other clamped firmly on a scuffed corner, and heaved. By dragging and sliding it, he managed to wedge it against the buckling doorway. He raced over to the desk and snatched up a couple of chairs. He stacked them quickly across the chest, fumbling to interlace the wooden legs tightly on the pile. The desk itself was next, followed almost immediately by a heavy stuffed chair. It took Shan several attempts before he could manage to roll the bulky chair onto the rising mound. The makeshift barrier rattled and thumped with each crash of huge claws on the door. Shan retreated to the window once more and looked out, puffing from his efforts.

Unbelievably, the yard below remained empty and still.

He thought suddenly about jumping, but it was much too far and he feared he might shatter a leg in the attempt. The creature at the door, he felt sure, would not be likely to suffer a similar fate. Once it had broken through his makeshift barrier, it could easily leap upon him as he tried to hobble away. He brushed a flap of drapes with his fingertips. He might be able to fashion a rope from the curtains and bed sheets, but one furious glance at the door told him there probably would not be enough time.

"Guards!" he screamed hoarsely again and again. "Guards, come quickly! I need your help!"

He collapsed against the window frame with a whimper. He could not stifle his own gasp as the heavy sounds of splintering wood cascaded noisily around him. He snapped his eyes shut and breathed a silent prayer.

Athiliel! Please help me! Almost immediately dim lights began flickering to life in several windows throughout the village. Even amid the clamor of ferocious hammering, he was certain he heard distant cries and shouts of confusion. *Human* cries. And after a moment, the courtyard swarmed suddenly with activity. A tangle of men came racing out of the blackness of the forest, huffing and wheezing, their fiery torches shooting off tiny sparks as they ran. They kicked up fine clouds of dust as they bolted into the compound through the abandoned gate of the palisade. Before them more than half a dozen watchbeasts tore at their long neck chains. The ferocious sleeth hissed and clawed wildly at the earth with their six powerful legs. At the same moment nearly a dozen other soldiers came tripping out of the great hall and several of the houses lining the street. They stumbled about half-dressed, shouting at each other in confusion. Torches flared wildly in the rush of wind, throwing shards of yellowish light from the stark edges of their weapons as the two groups narrowly kept from colliding in the yard. They clanked and rattled about each other in near chaos amid streams of angry curses. Several of them raised clenched fists at one another.

Deep within the building Shan could hear the shrill blast of an alarm horn and the frenzied call to arms.

"What's going on?" he heard someone scream over the harsh sea of voices. "The gate's been left wide open and it's completely unguarded!" The man was answered by a chorus of garbled explanations and angry shouts from the gathering mob.

"Up here!" Shan yelled down at them as he leaned carelessly out over the window frame. "Help! Help! It's up here!" The knots of men paused in their haste. Snapping torches washed their startled faces in an eerie glow as they lifted bloodshot eyes to stare at his window. "It's outside my door right now!" he called in a reedy voice. *"Hurry!"*

"Sounds like that elven boy's in trouble!" bellowed a stocky figure. He stopped for a moment to point a pudgy hand in the air. Glints of light sparked off the great axe in his hand.

"There's an intruder in the compound!" cried another. "Secure the gate! To arms!"

The alarm bell rang with a deep, hollow thrum. It tolled again and again as the sleeth leapt high in the air and jerked at their chains. They hissed and snarled as the call was taken up by every mouth across the courtyard. *"To arms! To arms!"*

The turmoil of shouting men and leathery-scaled bodies suddenly seemed to organize itself. Blades flashed sharply in the blaze of torchlight. There was a sudden howl as one of the watchbeasts seemed to catch the strange scent. The others joined it in a frenzied whine as they sniffed and clawed at the dry ground. It was all their keepers could do to keep up with them. The remainder of the men hastened after them, their weapons lifted up in anger. Ripples of dust thickened in the air amid the rhythm of stamping feet.

"Hurry!" the Elfling screamed at them from the window. He threw a last wild look behind him.

Shan was suddenly thrown back in a spray of shattering rock. He fell hard to the floor as the heavy door was ripped loose from its hinges. It crashed inward with a terrible jolt, crushing the chest and the pile of chairs like a chorus of snapping twigs. He ducked awkwardly as the interior of the room was showered in a thousand flying splinters of wood and rock. Shan scrambled quickly to his feet amid the debris. He swiped at the clouds of dust ringing his face, and coughed. Dimly, he felt a stinging trickle of blood down his left cheek.

It was difficult to see in the thick swirls of dust and darkness. His eyes stung from the grit. It tasted in his mouth like ash and it made him cough even more. He blinked and swatted at the dust until it slowly began to settle. After a moment he could make out ragged slivers of light leaking into the room. The low glimmer of torches in the corridor framed a huge, dark form in the ruined portal. Fear caught in his throat with a strangled gasp. The menacing thing slowly shouldered its way into the room, tearing away large chunks of wood and stone from the wall as it lumbered forward. It clawed at the tangle of broken furniture twisting out through fragments of the massive door and batted the remnants of the great chest aside with no apparent effort.

Shan quickly drew the dagger from his belt and held it out in shaking fists. He moved to his right cautiously, sliding along the wall. He kicked aside a worn pair of sandals, a carved hunk of wood and scattered bits of glass from the shattered figurine. *Don't let your feet get tangled,* he thought with great effort. He fought to remain calm. *It won't help if you slip on the floor.* Stiffly, he assumed a half-crouch.

Shan looked up at the shaggy mountain of fur. He swallowed fiercely as it settled on its haunches just inside the doorway. It snarled softly, surveying the room with dark, deep-set eyes. It sniffed noisily at the air as it peered into the darkened corners, its great head swiveling from side to side. Its enormous mouth gaped open, revealing several rows of long, yellowish teeth dripping heavily with saliva. The fur around its muzzle was wet, and a thin, dark stream dribbled slowly to the floor. The creature stretched its long neck downward and snapped out twice with its powerful jaws, then licked at its snout with a thick, foul tongue.

It rose at last onto its huge clawed feet with a soft growl. The floorboards groaned loudly as it shifted its incredible weight. It shook its great head and sneezed loudly at the heavy dust. Thick runnels of spittle flew in all directions. Then it swung around to face Shan where he cringed against the wall. It sniffed at him for several long moments, its large, black nose moist at the end of its great muzzle. Finally, it snorted loudly. It immediately bared its yellowish fangs at him, and hissed. The great clawed feet scraped noisily on the polished boards as it started to lumber forward. Shan backed away from it, sliding along the wall into the corner. It growled softly as it moved, a heavy sort of rumbling deep in its throat.

Shan gripped the knife handle tightly. He held the tapered metal blade nervously out in front of his chest, and the dull gleam of his own steel danced erratically a hob from his face. He licked at his dry lips, still tasting of dust and ash, and managed to focus his eyes on the beast's measured approach. It ambled forward in long, deliberate strides, the huge head weaving back and forth and side to side. Thick, corded muscles in its great shoulders rippled with each step. The long, dark tongue snaked out and wiped drool from its dripping muzzle.

The Elfling backed up as far as he could into the corner. The tips of his fingers whitened on the blade, numbing. Then, reversing the dagger suddenly in his hand, he threw it at the creature's face with all his strength. The great head flashed swiftly to the side and the blur of steel sank deeply into the beast's shoulder. It stopped in the center of the room and sat back on its haunches. Blood darkened the thick black fur where the knife stuck out. It sat for a moment, blinking down at the boy, and coughed once in irritation. It snarled hoarsely, with just the barest glimmer of its fangs visible from the corner of its lip. It reached up with one large claw and tore the tiny blade from its flesh almost mockingly. Then, with what looked almost like a grim, twisting smile, it held the dripping weapon up to its mouth and bit the knife blade in two. The gnarled chunks of metal fell to the floorboards with a hollow *thump*.

Shan gulped quickly in amazement. He shifted his weight uneasily, painfully swallowing at an intense raspiness in his throat. He clenched his sweaty palms into slippery fists, uncomfortably aware that he was now totally unarmed. His chest hammered with effort as he sucked air in loud, rapid puffs of agony.

The thing seemed to leer at him with an evil grin. Its wicked, dark eyes narrowed, and the sudden snap of its jaws was loud and expectant. It dropped back onto all fours with a heavy snarl and began to shuffle forward once more. The creature's steamy-hot breath choked Shan with its foul stench. The foam-lathered folds of its thick lips ruffled in a steady rhythm with each reeking blast of its mouth. His pulse became like rapid cannon fire in his ears. Shan tried to shrink even further into the corner, but there was just nowhere to go.

The sudden clatter of running feet nearby broke the heavy stillness. A jumble of gruff, shouting voices and the anxious whimper of the sleeth echoed wildly down the hallway. The soft glint of torchlight played dimly off the lacquered boards as the sounds converged rapidly on his ruined doorway.

The beast seemed to hesitate for a moment at the sound of the voices. It cocked its great head to the side, listening to the approach of the guards, to the frenzied whine of the watchbeasts. One large, tufted ear swung in their direction. It extended its long snout and sniffed noisily at the air. The black, deep-set eyes blinked several times, then snapped open to form luminous dark pools. Shan watched it warily as the thing sat back on its haunches in the middle of the room, its huge nose twitching. Slowly, its eyes began to narrow and an ominous growl broke from the depths of its shaggy chest.

"Shan! *Shan!*" he could hear someone shouting down the hall. "Are you alright, lad?"

"Yes!" he found himself croaking. He swallowed convulsively, shifting his weight nervously from one foot to the other. He could feel his calves beginning to cramp once again. "Please, hurry!" he muttered through clenched teeth. *Or I'll wind up as this thing's dinner,* he thought wildly to himself. Without taking his eyes from the monster he rubbed at the marks in his palms where his fingernails had torn the skin. *I'm hardly more than a mouthful, anyway.*

There was a sudden gasp of astonishment from the doorway as bright tongues of fire suddenly splashed the chamber in a wavering yellow light. A line of hastily clad soldiers jammed through the ruined portal, their startled faces washed with a sickly color in the glowing torches. The flames hissed and sizzled, licking hungrily at the shafts of oil-soaked wood in the heavy silence.

"By the blood of all that's holy!" someone burst out.

Daryl Hanson

"What in the name of Gar . . . is *that?*" he heard another man mutter. Several others cursed softly to themselves. They all gulped convulsively, their eyes blinking wide in abject fear.

Shan peered around the enormous bulk of the creature as the soldiers stepped carefully over the splintered rubble and quickly fanned out along the back wall of his room. Several of them held bows, their knuckles white, arrows already nocked and trained on the back of the creature. A few others gripped heavy, double-bladed axes. Another man held a large black, iron mace firmly in his thick fingers. The remainder of the company nervously brandished a combination of swords or spears. Two men stood apart from the rest, each holding the neck chains of four vicious sleeth, and it was all they could do to keep the eight leathery-scaled creatures from tearing across the floorboards at the sight of the horrid thing hunkered down in the center of the room.

The monster's low snarl was almost human-like as it turned to regard them, its great head angled oddly to the side. It coughed at them hoarsely, and it seemed to Shan as if the sound was tinged with amusement. It sounded for all the world like a kind of deep, low chuckling. Even in his fear Shan found himself wondering at the beast.

"What is it?" one of the men demanded in a harsh whisper.

"Never mind that!" snapped another with a spit at the littered floor. "What's it doing here?" He cocked a wary eye as he tightly fingered his weapon.

After regarding them curiously for a moment the beast swung away, its dark eyes glittering. It took one huge step toward the boy and growled menacingly. In that same instant several arrows hissed through the air and shuddered into the monster's back. The hideous thing spun about to face them, hissing furiously. Saliva coursed down its jaw and moistened its throat and chest. It flexed its claws together like the sharp scraping of steel. It started to chuckle in low, throaty tones. Reaching back with one razored claw, it ripped a feathered shaft from its hide as a runnel of dark blood dribbled to the floor. The watchbeasts went mad with fury, hissing and whining as they yanked at their chains at the closeness of their prey. The beast held the arrow up to its face and sniffed at it. It licked at the blood dripping from the tip, then chewed the slender length of wood into several pieces. The soldiers watched in silence, unable to move or tear their eyes from the strange spectacle as the thing slowly repeated the same performance six more times.

Suddenly a tall man charged into the room and pushed his way in front of the other men. He puffed lightly from a long run, a glowing torch held in one hand.

"Weeson!" Shan cried out, unconsciously edging toward his friend. The beast's large, furry head spun around to glare at him. Its devilish eyes flashed brightly as it swung about to intercept him. It shuffled quickly to the side, snarling in a throaty bark as if in warning, and forced the boy to retreat into the corner.

"It's okay, lad," the man huffed. He gestured for the boy to remain calm with his free hand, palm out. "Are you hurt?" Shan could only shake his head slightly. "Good," Weeson told him softly, edging a step closer. "Take it easy, Shan. There's nothing to worry about. We'll get you out of this. I promise." He watched the creature warily as he spoke, but managed to cast a reassuring nod to the youth. "Just stay still."

The beast shuffled about, glowering at Weeson as he drew a step closer. It snarled and rose upon its hind feet, its ears laid back. It towered nearly three *kora* in height, the large curve of its skull nearly scraping the wooden beams of the ceiling. It raked the air with its huge, flashing claws. Throwing back its head, it growled a mighty challenge to the puny gathering of humans. Saliva glistened from its fangs, the great, shaggy throat suddenly exposed. With a swift whistling snap several long, feathered shafts appeared in the beast's fur as if by magic. The monster clamped its jaws together with a sputtering of blood, then bellowed once in a strange, piercing howl. Intense shivers leapt across Shan's spine in cold rivulets of prickling skin. He cowered in the corner, paralyzed by the same weird cry he had heard just moments before as he had looked out from the window.

He had a sudden terrifying thought that more of these hellish beasts lurked hungrily somewhere out there in the darkness. Almost against his will, his eyes sought the open window. His fingers dug into the chipped paint of the wall as he stared out into the night, half-cringing with the fear he might hear a wild, answering call. He swallowed slowly, then held his breath. After a few agonized moments he pulled his eyes from the window, almost swooning with relief as the night air outside remained cool and still.

The gigantic creature lowered its head, narrowing its fiendish eyes upon Weeson. The young officer stood apart from his fellows, his chin held high, the fiery brand still clutched tightly in one fist. It seemed that the creature's eyes began to glow with a sudden, unnatural fire. They shimmered a bright red like a trapped animal on a night hunt when it's caught with the light just right. Weeson felt the tingle of hair on his scalp. He fought down the rising fear that suddenly burned in his stomach. He shrugged it off with a rough cough and a shaky step forward. The monster seemed to sense his momentary panic and *laughed* at him again in deep, coarse rumbles. With a diabolical grin it tore the pitiful barbs from its neck, one at a time, and threw them at the soldiers with great force. One of the men screamed as an arrow creased his arm. The remainder of the projectiles skipped off a hastily raised wall of shields and clattered harmlessly from the walls of the room like little cracks of thunder.

The men stood their ground nervously, shuffling about restlessly amidst the splinters of wood. Slowly they lowered their shields, but tensely held them ready for anything. They cast dark looks at one another and whispered harshly under their breaths. Uncertainly, each man watched the face of their young commander.

Weeson fought the unreasoning fear that gnawed at his insides as he stood there. The great beast looked down at him with a hideous sneer. The large, dark eyes seemed to change, to burn into him with a crimson fire. Small dribbles of wetness stained the fur around the little wounds in its neck and glistened darkly in the light of the torches. Weeson felt himself sinking, drawn into the depths of the creature's shimmering eyes. Their pulsing, unearthly glow grew to fill his entire vision. He felt himself being pulled down into a ring of darkness and fire.

"Weeson!" Shan cried. He watched in fear as the captain began to sway slowly, then his whole body began to shake with a flurry of violent tremors. His arm went limp and the torch fell from his grasp. A man raced over to stamp out the hungry yellow sparks that licked at the wood. He sought to pull the captain away, but without success. "Weeson!" the Elfling shouted.

The man heard only a tiny voice filtering down through a swirling shroud of darkness and light. *Weeson!* The voice seemed to drift towards him from far off. *Look away!* urged the voice. *Look away!*

Weeson's head lolled to one side. He felt his legs begin to buckle beneath him.

Weeson! the voice screamed with a sudden fierceness. *Weeson, pull your eyes free. You must look away!* The man somehow managed to close his eyes for a few long *biri*, and the spell was broken. The room became a reality around him once more as Weeson fought to pull his eyes from the dark pools of flame glaring down at him from the looming mountain of fur. The man's neck and shoulder muscles exploded in angry surges with every attempt. He blinked his eyelids rapidly several more times, and each time the shimmering scarlet afterimage grew less and less.

He took two steps back and wiped at a trickle of sweat on his brow. He drew several long, deep breaths before carefully focusing his eyes on the beast once more, careful this time not to look directly into its strange eyes. With sudden resolve, Weeson drew his sword. There was a slither of steel as he cautiously picked his way through the piles of splintered wood surrounding the beast. The keen blade shone with a dull, yellowish-white gleam in the torchlight.

The creature watched him approach through the narrow slits of its deep eyes. It snarled softly, amused. The great lips drew back in a snarl. The man began to circle to his left, weaving the tip of his weapon in a slow arc before him. With surprising speed the beast shuffled heavily to the side, effectively cutting Weeson off from the boy. The captain feinted left again then circled back to the right. Once again the beast easily lumbered into position to block the way between them.

It looked strangely like some exotic dance ritual, played out cruelly in slow motion. The man would move and the creature would react quickly, almost effortlessly, casually displaying its fangs and wicked claws in the eerie light. Helplessly, the boy watched the spectacle slowly unfold less than a dozen steps away. Shan fought the pounding in his chest. He tugged at his shirt, now soaked with sweat, as it clung tenaciously against his body.

Suddenly weary of the game, the beast crashed forward, its great jaws snapping out. Weeson ducked and swerved easily to one side. The sword flashed brightly as he slashed quickly left, then right. Huge claws closed on empty air as the man danced away, a bright splash of red on the blade, a crimson wet stream slowly darkening the creature's fur along both huge forearms.

The beast merely grinned as it stalked after the darting figure. It licked at the heavy flow of drool around its own muzzle and gurgled once softly in annoyance. The captain leaped forward, the weapon a blur in his hands. The monster raked both its claws in nasty swaths at Weeson's head. The bobbing swordsman fended off one wicked swipe with the keen edge of his steel and dodged quickly away from the other. But he shouted suddenly in pain as a spout of blood flew out from the angry red line that appeared along his left arm.

Weeson leaped away and cast a hasty glance at the wound. A small stream of blood colored his shirt scarlet and ran sluggishly down the torn sleeve. It felt much worse than it looked. The beast gnashed its teeth together and grinned, waiting for the man to approach once more. It slurped blood from its own wounded claw, the large, deep-set eyes still gleaming like fire. Weeson pranced closer.

Heads lowered, circling, they engaged.

The beast bellowed in a series of husky roars and the man answered with a fierce war cry. They swirled about each other, hacking and snapping, sweeping and weaving, as wild streams of blood trailed through the air. Torchlight played from the slashing blade like dazzling streaks of gold. Suddenly Weeson was down, slipping in the thick puddles spewed across the polished floor. The thing was on him in an instant, the powerful jaws striking out.

The captain drove a *kor* of steel into the yawning pit of sharpened teeth. He tried to wriggle away, but the deadly blur of slashing claws kept him dodging and sliding in the sticky mess. A rain of arrows sizzled into the creature's hide and several of the soldiers raced forward.

"Save the captain!" someone was shouting, and the man flourished an axe in a wide, sweeping arc.

The beast reared up to its full stature, towering nearly four *kora* in height. It shrugged off the puny attacker with ease. The demonic eyes blazed in hatred, a warning snarl escaping from its thick curled lips. It threw back its enormous head then and roared a chilling blast that rattled the rafters. Feeling as if his heart would certainly fail him completely, Shan grabbed futilely at the wall for support. The men hesitated in their advance, gulping back their fear.

"We've got to get the captain!" another man finally screamed, stepping up at last and swinging his mace.

Others regained their nerve as well and leapt in to do battle. They hacked and chopped at the shifting monstrosity. Weeson was quickly pulled free by two of the men as the fight swung away from them. The grunts and cursing of the soldiers were lost amid a chorus of wild howls and screams of pain.

The frenzy of the watchbeasts became unbearable as they sucked in the strong scent of close, hot blood. They jerked at their neck chains and tore jagged chunks out of the floorboards with their splayed talons. They yelped and tugged wildly at the chains until the keepers could control them no longer. They sprang forward in great bounds.

The men fell back as the eight large reptiles slid and surged over each other in their haste, tearing and snapping at the air. Flecks of foam shot out from their leathery muzzles in all directions. The creatures leapt upon their towering adversary in a snarling rage. Shan watched in grisly fascination as the sleeth sank their razor-edged teeth into its hide. The thing yowled in fury. It spun and tore at its scaly antagonists in a flurry of vicious swipes, knocking five of them sprawling in a knot of teeth and claws. It gripped two other sleeth in huge clawed fists and ripped them from its body, bleeding chunks of its own flesh still clamped tightly in their jaws. It swung them about and threw them, with a sickening crunch, against the wall. They collapsed on the floor in howls of pain.

The other watchbeasts recovered quickly and feverishly clattered after their prey once more. The beast spun rapidly on all fours, swatting them aside with little effort. It tore loose the one creature still clutching desperately to its flesh, then cast the wretched animal out the window in a wild tangle of legs and scaly hide. The others wheeled on the slippery surface, their six legs a blur of motion, and attacked again, with loud snarls of rage. They were met by the crunch of snapping jaws and a lightning-like barrage of raking talons. In a matter of heartbeats the last of the sleeth lay in a mound of bloodied hides on the littered floor. The monster severed its head with one snapping bite.

The men stood in awed silence, some of their weapons even slipping from bloodless fingers to thump hollowly across the floor. The beast shook back its head and roared in triumph. It glared down upon the ring of soldiers, its fierce eyes still glowing unnaturally, and seemed to laugh, its great, shaggy frame shaking. Weeson stood back from the others. He leaned unsteadily on his sword and patted gingerly at the burning gash on his arm with a tatter of his shirt. The beast rocked on its haunches, cackling in harsh spasms. It pivoted slowly to gaze down at the boy huddled against the wall. It sidled its great bulk slowly closer to claim its prize.

Shan felt crushed. He cowered in the corner, his head bowed.

The thing moved heavily toward him. Dark, wet streams of blood pulsed from numerous wounds at each lumbering step.

"No!" Weeson screamed, raising his sword weakly and wobbling forward. "No! Not the boy!" Some of the other soldiers rushed forward to join him. They rattled their weapons to draw it back in their direction.

"STOP!"

The command crackled through the air like thunder. The men fell back in confusion and the great monstrosity paused near the boy. It twisted to look over its great shoulder. The bloody scimitars of its fists hovered near Shan's head and clicked together once in annoyance. A rush of whispers thickened the air as all eyes turned to stare at the source of the voice.

"Ulfiir!" Shan breathed, looking up.

The creature swung fully about and glowered at the pitiful old man standing amongst the splintered ruins of the doorway. It twisted its thick lips into a wicked grin, squaring its huge shoulders to face the wizened little figure, and growled. It bared its yellowish fangs and raked the air with its deadly claws in challenge.

"Get back, men," Ulfiir spoke quietly. He waved them aside with a feeble nod, his gray eyes sparkling within the hood of his cloak. A heavy stillness settled over the room as he stepped delicately over the rubble and stopped beside Weeson. He placed a wrinkled hand lightly on the young man's arm. "Naked steel will not harm this beast, my friend," he said softly. "I am afraid you cannot help me."

The soldiers crept back, snatching up any discarded weapons from the littered flooring. The beast was oblivious to everything now save the old man. Its blazing, red eyes narrowed to creases of scarlet flame as it lowered its wet, dripping muzzle towards him, growling softly in challenge. The crimson pools seemed to bore into the withered old man leaning innocently on his twisted staff. The beast clucked hoarsely under its breath as the wrinkled figure stood there unmoving.

The boy shuddered uncontrollably.

With a sudden chill Shan understood that this enormous creature had wanted this confrontation from the very beginning. Somehow it knew his uncle, had come looking for him, and it had caused enough trouble throughout the village to draw him out. *But why?*

In a sudden rush, Weeson raced past the beast and slid quickly up to the boy's side. He whirled to face an expected charge, the tip of his sword dancing a few *hobbin* from his eyes. He was startled to find the monster still standing calmly before the old man, the shaggy curve of its back turned towards them. It snarled softly at Ulfiir, baring its great yellowish fangs. It rocked heavily forward to meet him. Weeson shot a quick glance over the boy. There were no signs of any wounds that he could see. "Are you alright?" he asked.

Shan nodded without looking up to meet the man's searching gaze. Weeson threw an arm around the Elfling's shoulders and gave him a strong hug. The pressure and warm contact were reassuring to the boy, especially after what had seemed like an eternity separated from the others. But Shan could not tear his eyes away from the strange scene. The two unlikely opponents faced one another across his ruined bedroom floor.

Ulfiir planted the butt of his staff on the wooden floor and swung it into the hands of the nearest fellow. He flexed long, stiff fingers together and shuffled a bit closer, mumbling a series of odd-sounding words under his breath. Wisps of bluish smoke rose from the floor about him, curling in gentle braids to the ceiling. The old man held out his gnarled hands. Shan gaped as sparks of blue light rippled into existence out of the very air and ran about his wrinkled skin in erratic patterns. The fire crackled and hissed in the dusty air, circling down each of Ulfiir's long, bony fingers.

"Don't worry, Shan," Weeson was whispering in his ear. "Everything's going to be fine now." The boy hovered there with his mouth hanging open, hardly noticing when the captain pulled his arm from about his shoulder. Weeson stepped in front of him to shield the boy with his own body. But deprived of the riveting spectacle, Shan quickly peered around the arm of his friend.

The beast threw wide its great jaws and bellowed at the old man. It bounded forward on all four of its powerful legs, snarling hellishly, its claws flashing out in the torchlight. Shan cried out in fear, but Ulfiir stood impassively, arms calmly extended. The tips of his fingers glowed in dazzling streaks of sapphire.

"Athiliel!" he cried in a booming voice. "Athiliel, erith calytus vanova aneem tiri adyn'dor!" Blue fire erupted from his fingers as he spoke and shot out in rippling bands. "Tiri adyn'dor!"

The crackling wave of energy enveloped the beast in a sheet of iridescence. The huge creature howled in fury as it was thrown back. It skidded across the polished boards, huge claws wildly scraping deep gouges from the wood. It lifted itself on its massive haunches, roaring in anger and pain. It furiously raked at the air, at the interlacing swirls of fire that swam about its head. Clawing and screaming, it threw itself at the old man. But another blast of sizzling blue radiance sent it tottering awkwardly to the side. The bloodcurdling screams prickled at Shan's neck hairs, sent rushes of icy tendrils over many a terrified heart. The enormous beast writhed in obvious pain, spluttering slimy trails of ooze from its lips. It clawed savagely at its own face, at its eyes, at the curling flames of agony lancing through its skull.

The soldiers shielded themselves from the thick red spray of foam. Dark rivers of blood drizzled down the creature's muzzle to stick in the heavy fur of its chest and throat. It shrieked in agony and spun about, thrashing and flailing insanely at the air with vicious swipes of its claws.

Shan saw his uncle's lips move in silent command. The bluish fire coursed up and down his outstretched arms in rambling patterns like delicate sparks of lightning. They rippled and crackled loudly, and then were suddenly gone, dissipating into the air like smoke. Ulfiir lowered his hands tiredly and took a long, deep breath.

He reached slowly for his staff and took it from the hands of the man next to him. "It is done," he said in a low, distant voice. "You may do your work now, my friends."

A dozen feathered shafts whistled instantly across the room and sank deep into the creature's chest. The beast rumbled in pain and staggered drunkenly under its own weight. Its hideous face was a ruined mass of bloodied flesh. It had torn out its own eyes in its frenzy. Now thick, black streams drained from the darkened sockets. It tottered blindly on its massive legs, snapping out and clawing at random. The men ducked warily under its maddened attack. Some of them darted in and hacked at it with their swords and axes, then sprang quickly away as the thing whirled to slash at them. One man jumped forward and drove his spear blade deeply into the beast's shoulder. He was thrown from his feet by the pivoting wall of muscle and fell back with a snapping of the wooden handle. Three men rushed over to harry the beast while two others pulled the man safely away from the huge, crashing feet. The man grinned sheepishly at them in thanks, the splintered shaft of the spear still gripped tightly in his fists.

The reactions of the beast were slow now, dulled with pain, its cries becoming pitiful and weak. It finally collapsed in the center of the room, its breathing loud and ragged. Rivers of blood oozed onto the flooring in dark pools. It lay in a heap, a massive pile of quivering fur. It dropped its wide head onto bloody forepaws and wheezed noisily.

The men edged closer.

Weeson clapped a hand on Shan's elbow and gave him a little squeeze. "Stay back," he cautioned as he stepped forward warily to join the loose ring of soldiers.

The beast lifted its head weakly. Through a runnel of slushy fluid it eerily focused the empty eye sockets upon the Elfling. With one final growl it heaved its dripping bulk to a crouch, battered several of the men from its path, and leaped toward the boy. The force drove them both to the wall as Shan disappeared under the mountain of bloody fur. Weeson hurried over and buried his sword to the hilt in the creature's steaming side. Others quickly did the same.

"Careful of the boy," Ulfiir urged them.

With a shrill, moaning whine the beast shuddered once and was still.

Between them all they managed to drag the thing from Shan's crumpled form. There was a hushed stillness in the room as the boy lay across the scattered mess, unmoving. Ignoring the stabbing fire in his arm, Weeson delicately lifted the limp body from the floor. Carefully he carried him to the bed and eased him onto the rumpled covers. Streaks of blood stained the boy's clothes and dappled his face and arms. The guards crowded around the foot of the bed, their faces long and white with concern.

Ulfiir gently nudged them aside and settled himself on the edge of the mattress. He ran a crusty hand over Shan's forehead and cautiously lifted the lid of one eye with the wrinkled tip of a long index finger. He felt about the boy's ribs and along both arms and legs. The old man looked up into the hovering swell of worried faces.

"He'll be fine," he said, the heavy creases easing on his brow. "He might have a headache though when he awakens."

Weeson detected a hint of relief in the old man's humor. He looked down on the youth and backhandedly swiped at a trickle of sweat on his own forehead. The captain sauntered over to the beast and pulled his slimy blade from the carcass with a grunt of effort. He wiped the steel on the hairy mass and quickly slammed it home in the scabbard hanging at his thigh.

In a few moments Shan began to stir. He opened his eyes slowly, clutching at his head. "Oh," he mumbled groggily. He rubbed gingerly at a bump on his forehead as they helped him to sit up. He blinked several times before focusing on Ulfiir's craggy features. A tinge of a smile played about the old man's lips. "What are all of you doing here?" Shan looked up, somewhat puzzled. His eyes settled on the group of soldiers huddled around his bed. They were sweaty and disheveled. Many of them were only half-dressed, and there were streaks of blood in the creases of their skin. The haggard looks of worry spread over their long faces caught him by surprise. A few of them turned away with quick shrugs and busied themselves about the room with faked nonchalance.

Weeson stood at the foot of the bed, the scuffed toe of his boot propped on a corner post. He was cleaning his sword with a tattered rag in long, even strokes. "Just cleaning up," the captain said with a grin as he finally slid the weapon back into its sheath with practiced ease.

Daryl Hanson

"Cleaning up?" Shan rubbed at his eye. "Cleaning what? You know Majora would never let me make a mess in here without cleaning it up before I . . ." Weeson nodded with a knowing smile. "Hey, where did this come from?" Shan demanded, thrusting his hands out accusingly. He stared at the bloodstains on his skin and shirt sleeves. Suddenly his eyes went large as they riveted on the huge hump of blood and fur in the middle of the room. Several of the soldiers knelt by the carcass and poked at it with their knives.

"I thought it was just some kind of nightmare," he managed in a strained whisper, as the recent memory lanced vividly through his head. He held his eyes shut for the longest time.

"No, I'm afraid it was very real," Ulfiir told him at last, gently, from the edge of the bed.

"Too real," Weeson added, dabbing at a stream of blood on his arm.

"Then it really happened?"

"Yes," his guardian nodded grimly.

Shan slid off the bed and wavered momentarily. His head pounded as he stood up. Circles of bright sparks tingled at the edges of his vision. "No, I'm alright," he said when several hands reached out to steady him. "Just a little dizzy." He walked slowly toward the bloody heap, careful to avoid the growing pool of dark blood.

"Don't get too close!" Weeson told him harshly.

Ulfiir hobbled up next to the lad, laid a gentle hand on his shoulder. "Don't worry, my boy," he said, "it's quite dead."

"—Now!" Weeson remarked with a tight laugh.

"I've never seen anything like it." Shan's voice was an awed whisper. "What is it?" He glanced at Weeson, who shrugged, then at each of the other men in turn. They looked at one another in ignorance and shook their heads.

"Shan," Ulfiir's voice tugged at him, "I need to speak with you in the main chamber of the hall." The old man drifted away. He halted after a few steps and swung back to the boy. "As soon as you clean yourself up a little." Shan nodded. "Oh, and Weeson, I'll want to see you, as well." The youth looked up from the steaming carcass. "There are many, many things that should have been spoken of long before this night," Ulfiir chided himself. "I am such an old man." He caught the captain's eye as he turned to go, then picked his way carefully over the splinters of wood and chunks of stone littering the ruined doorway.

Shan wondered at his uncle's words. He scratched at the back of his head and shrugged. He walked over to the beast where a man stabbed lightly at it with his sword. The polished metal slid into the dripping hide easily and gurgled softly as he pulled it out once again. Shan kicked at the thing with the toe of his boot.

"It'll have to be burned," he heard Weeson saying to a man at his left. "Bring some ropes and drag it out of the compound. Burn it beyond the walls."

"Yes, sir," the man snapped with a quick salute. He turned and hurried off.

Shan stood silently near the center of the room, staring at the carcass. He rubbed at the bump on his forehead and looked out the window. The sliver of moon was gone, and the forest was dark and mysterious. Shivering, he listened for some time, half-expecting to hear another long, frightening moan reach out to him from within its gloomy depths. But there was only silence. He stared out at the still night sky as a flutter of wind teased the curtain. Dimly, he heard the clicking of insects and the gentle swaying of tree branches. He blinked wearily and turned away. The sting had returned to his cheek. He dabbed at it tentatively with the tip of his finger and came away with a smudge of drying blood.

He looked down at the beast sprawled at his feet. "What are you?" he asked in a small voice.

"It's called a kurgoth," Ulfiir answered him dryly from some distance away.

Startled, Shan tossed a look over his shoulder. He was surprised to see Ulfiir still standing in the wreckage of the doorway, his arms folded about his staff, watching him quietly. The glow of the torches somehow gave the old man a mystical quality. His long white hair and beard fell about him in great, sweeping curls like billowing masses of approaching storm clouds. His cold gray eyes seemed to glitter with an unearthly fire of their own. Dangerous, aloof, he stood there as if he was etched out of ancient stone. A sense of subdued power coiled softly about him.

Shan fell back as if struck. It was like seeing him with completely new eyes, and the Elfling wasn't altogether certain he liked the change. He stared awkwardly at this magical visitor for several long moments.

Ulfiir sensed the boy's confusion and offered him a little smile. Abruptly, the mood was broken and the mysterious stranger was gone. There was only an old man before him, his feeble eyes twinkling in the torchlight, a bony hand poised on a twisted staff for balance.

Shan smiled weakly in return. Here was the Ulfiir he knew, the kind, thoughtful uncle he loved, the guardian he'd always known and grown up with. The old man nodded once, his eyes moist, then he swung about and hobbled slowly from the room.

– 2 –
ꓠid-Summer's Eve
[24th of Sa'ran, 4533 C.R.]

Dusk was slowly settling over the forests of Draydin. The great gate of banded logs had been shut with a *crack* as the last straggling line of villagers hurried into the compound, tugging at wooden carts jammed with large reddish-clay pots.

"Good gather today?" a man stopped in the courtyard and asked one of those hauling on a creaking cart.

"Fair," the cartman responded without slowing. He took one blistered hand from the handle and wiped at trickles of sweat on his face in two quick strokes. "Seen better," he called over his shoulder, and he swung the cart to the left along a narrow lane of packed earth.

An older woman padded along behind him, one hand braced on the low railing of the rickety wagon. "The trees are dryin' up, I tell 'e," she said in a squeaky voice. "Dryin' up! Ain't seen this little syrup in all my born days." She slapped at one of the clay pots with a small weathered hand, leaving a faint palm-shaped print on the dusty side. "An ill omen, I'd say, and that's the truth, I tell 'e. That's the truth."

"Yes, yes, Dorgana," puffed the man pulling at the cart. "I've heard it all before—a thousand times at least, if I've heard one!" And with that they were lost to sight as the cart creaked around the corner.

Lights quickly flared to life in the windows of small houses on both sides of the great hall. A man in a worker's smock methodically began lighting the torches around the yard. He reached up to the tall metal receptacles with a long, thin rod that spit pale sparkles of yellow as he touched the end to each of the oiled lengths of wood. He was rewarded by a sudden burst of flame as the yellowish-red tongues licked greedily at the oil and sent a wreath of thick, black smoke skyward.

Somewhere below his window Shan heard the chorus of laughter from a knot of villagers as they approached the great doors of the hall. He thumbed through the yellowed pages of the book a moment longer then closed the heavy cover with a thump. Gently he placed the worn copy of *The Kebbelfurd Cycle* back on the stand and got up from the desk with a stretch. He fought off a yawn with the back of his hand. He glanced quickly in the polished silver mirror on the wall and picked at a few stray tufts of his hair. He wet his fingertips on his tongue and roughly patted the unruly strands into a semblance of order. Crossing the room in a couple of long strides, he whistled carelessly to himself and poked his head out the window.

Several families converged on the tiled landing below. A wild array of children laughed and prodded at each other in an endless swirl of confusion. They darted about their unconcerned, slow-moving parents while they talked amiably among themselves in a series of smiles, nods and sweeping gestures. Trails of dust rose lightly about them like a fine mist. A woman reached out a fleshy arm as a pair of rascals swept by.

"Deezl, Mirelda," she chided mildly as her hand settled on empty air. "Now, now, children," she poked a finger in their direction, "you mustn't stir up such a cloud. Yosef, Fyrd, Karina, you're apt to choke someone with all that commotion." She coughed lightly as if to emphasize her words and *swished* at the dusty air about her with a wave of her chubby arms.

A pocket of men stood off to one side, unconcerned, talking together in brusk tones.

"He had heard a report of them, several of them, skulking through the woods to the west," one of the men was saying.

"I'm sure you're right," another of them said. "And it seems to be getting more frequent." They all nodded vigorously.

"And not just more frequent, as if that's not bad enough," a third man spoke up, "but the tales of their mischief are spreading throughout the forest."

"Come on, children," piped in a second woman as she stopped at the edge of the landing and spun around. "Eloise is right, 'specially since you're all dressed so nice." She corralled a couple of them with a deft snap of her wrist. "Don't want to get yourselves dirty before supper, do you?" She propped her hands on her hips, her eyes twinkling.

"No, ma'am," the children muttered in a series of echoes.

"Good!" Orsha smiled. "They might not let you into the hall tonight if'n you are." The youngsters dropped their heads amid a rush of groans and peeked at one another shyly through the cover of their long lashes. The woman reached down and lifted the chin of the little girl who stood by her side. "I'm certain there'll be lots of singin' tonight, you know," she said with a wink. "And story tellin', to be sure." The gaggle of childish pouts broke into broad looks of surprise.

"That's right, children," chimed in Eloise.

"Who is it?" one of the little faces wanted to know.

"Is it Shan?" another asked eagerly. "Is Shan gonna sing?"

"No, no, it's not the elven lad, far as I know," offered Orsha, "though he has got a sweet voice, I'll admit." She flicked at a stray wisp of her own hair with an absent-minded gesture of one hand. "No, after supper Master Ulfiir may have a few stories to recount. And then there's that tinker fellow. Gravelle's his name, I think. He might be persuaded to tell a tale or two from his travels, or maybe even offer us a song. He's been all across the Eastern Lands, I hear tell." She nipped the rosy lump of Deezl's cheek with the thumb and first finger of her left hand.

Eloise grabbed two of the children by the hand. "Now brush yourselves off and straighten your hair." She stooped down to whisper in their little ears. "And we'll see if we can sneak you past the guards without their noticin' the dusty condition of your clothes." The swarm of children hurried to comply, patting and smoothing at themselves and their clothing. She scrunched up her nose and shot Orsha a mischievous glance.

"Come here, Mirelda," Orsha called as she bent down. "I'll give you a hand."

Shan chuckled softly to himself as he turned from the window. He hastened across the room, pulled the door shut behind him and skipped off lightly down the hallway. Absently wondering what tales Ulfiir had in store for the evening gathering, he leaped down the twisting flight of stairs in a couple of light bounds. He almost tripped over an older man who stepped suddenly from his room at the base of the broad staircase. "Sorry, Bellor," he said, swirling quickly past him. The youth hurried on without so much as missing a stride. "See you in the dining hall," he called over his shoulder.

"That elven boy again," the man grumbled to himself with a slow shake of his head. He paused for a moment in the hallway and cocked an eye from under his bushy brows to look up the stairs to his left. He shook his head again and sauntered off down the corridor in the direction of the dwindling youth, combing his long beard with calloused fingers. "He's the quickest youngster I've ever laid eyes on," he muttered, grudgingly. "Sure footed." He scratched at a spot just above his right ear. "And probably the sneakiest, too, I'll wager." He plodded wearily down the dusty passage, his shuffling gait *shushing* like a slithering of dry leaves scattered across a barren path. "Suspect he'd make a good hunter," he mumbled to himself. "Think I'll have a chat with Ulfiir tonight. About time that boy took on some responsibilities around here." Bellor broke into a ragged smile as he ambled along. After a few moments, he softly began to whistle a lively tune, one of the many hunting songs he knew.

Shan dashed up the corridor in long, nimble strides. He swung right down the first major intersection, and headed off towards the back of the great hall. Torches flared from wall brackets spaced alternately along both walls, giving the air a smoky tang. A few townspeople, mostly off-duty servants and soldiers, hurried past him up the corridor in the opposite direction. Their clothes were simple country fare, clean, well-mended garments of dyed *sharcloth*. The inexpensive, wool-like material woven from the long, silken hair of the bounding *shart* was popular among the villagers. The evening's choice of attire, loose-fitting shirts and britches for the men and long dresses for the ladies, was perhaps a bit brighter in color than was usual, but that was to be expected. It was Mid-Summer's Eve, after all.

Shan side-stepped several small knots of laughing adults moving their way slowly up the broad corridor in the opposite direction. He smiled to himself as he ran past. Most people chose to use the front entrance of the dining hall with its broad doors and wide lobby, while he preferred to use the back way. Maybe he just didn't like drawing any undue attention to himself. He rounded a sharp corner to the right as he approached the back wall of the great hall. The gentle, rhythmic patter of his feet and the soft crackle of the torches in their wall brackets were the only sounds to dispel the heavy silence in the back hallway. He passed a few darkened storerooms before coming upon the rear freight door standing wide open. He caught a glimpse of darkening sky as he slowed to an easy trot.

"Who would be receiving goods at this time of day?" Shan wondered aloud. "Especially this late on a feast day?" He skipped to a halt in the wide doorway and peered out. The massive wooden door had been jammed open with a mallet, wedged into the dirt of the alleyway. A large wagon sat there silently in the gathering darkness and no one seemed to be about. Perhaps one of the kitchen drudges had to fetch something and would be right back. "Must be some last moment addition for the festival. Guess I'll find out soon enough." And with that, Shan started to turn away. After all, he didn't want to be late for supper. His mouth began to water with the thought of the holiday meal. He could just smell the spicy aromas drifting down the corridor.

Suddenly, there was a muffled crash from outside. Shan spun instantly on his heels and scurried through the doorway. Perhaps somebody needed help. Skidding in the dust, he looked quickly in both directions along the alley, but could see nothing in the deepening shadows. The only thing at all out of the ordinary was the large wagon. Shan stared at it for a moment before realizing he had never seen it before. The battered old thing was not a flat delivery wagon, certainly not the kind that carried goods from village to village. It was some sort of passenger wagon, perhaps the kind an itinerant salesman would use for travel. It was completely enclosed, with shuttered windows along the sides, a little door in the back, and a covered chimney pipe sticking up out of a tin-plated roof. It looked more like a small house on wheels than anything else, Shan decided.

The elven youth glided over to it curiously. Even in the dim light he could tell it had once been painted very garishly with a bright red lacquer and gold trim. The coating had long since cracked and peeled in several places. On the broad side panel, large bold letters, now faded to a pale blue, proudly proclaimed, *"Silas Gravelle: Merchant, Tinker, Historian, Bard and Magician."*

Shan walked around the entire wagon. He had never seen anything like it before, especially not this big. Tiny fragments of paint crackled and chipped off as he trailed an index finger along the worn, dusty surface. He clapped a hand on one of the huge rear wheels. He could feel the pits and gouges in the hammered metal rim. His hand slid lightly along the wheel as he ambled toward the front of the wagon. A sharp edge of the battered rim caught suddenly at his finger. Shan stifled a yelp and quickly popped the finger into his mouth. He could taste the unmistakable tang of blood as he sucked on it.

He moved slowly toward the front of the wagon. The three cutaway steps leading up to the wagon box were crusted with a thin film of dried mud. Shan pulled himself up onto the first step and peered over the edge of the box. A few parcels in oilcloth bags had been stuffed under the driver's bench. A long leather switch, not quite thick enough really to be a proper whip, was coiled loosely and jammed into a slot on the far side of the wagon box. Still sucking lightly on his finger, Shan gripped onto the tall, wooden brake lever with his other hand and leaned over the driver's bench. He sighted down the reins, imagining for a moment what it would be like to roam freely over the broad land, far away from Draydin, rolling along the hills and valleys, carefree, seeing all the wonderful sights the world had to offer.

Curiously, there were no animals present, Shan realized. No *thorka* or *bathalisk*, or any other form of draft animal, for that matter. They must have already been led away after the wagon's arrival, and were off grazing now in the stables to rest a spell before being hitched back up to the wagon to trundle off on its way somewhere down the forest road.

Daryl Hanson

Shan dropped nimbly back to the ground with a sigh. His pricked finger had stopped bleeding so he wiped away the wetness on the side of his britches. Near the front wheel he bent down and looked under the wagon. The underside was caked with dust and Shan wondered how many leagues of travel and how many exotic locations were represented there. Both axles were black with a heavy, oily grime, and as he watched, a slow runnel of grease dribbled off the front axle and plopped into the dust.

Shan was torn from his imaginings by a sudden sound from above him, from somewhere inside the wagon. He froze for a moment in fear, painfully certain that he would be caught snooping around someone else's property. He could almost hear the scoldings from his guardian already, not to mention the one he would have to endure from the owner of the wagon itself, this Gravelle person, a magician no less. What if the man turned him into some sort of animal? A toad, or a *shart*, perhaps? He straightened up, prepared to fly swiftly back into the hall, his throat all at once dry and tight, but then he heard it again.

It was soft and muffled by the layers of wood above him and yet he knew he could not be mistaken. It sounded more than anything like the snort of an animal. And then he could hear the scratching at the wood. He remained where he was, frozen, and listening. After a few moments the scraping noise was repeated, this time more urgently, and it was accompanied by a pecking sound. Shan swallowed against the feel of cotton in his mouth. He really should get out of there. Perhaps someone else had gone poking around where he shouldn't have, and as a result, had been transformed into some sort of wild beast by this Gravelle character. As if to accent the thought, the animal above shifted its weight and the wagon creaked in protest.

Shan leaned against the side of the wagon and listened with an ear at the wood. He thought he heard a grunt and then some sort of gurgling. He had to pull away as the wagon began to sway back and forth somewhat. There was a dull thump from inside, as if something had been dropped on the floor. As he listened there was another, and then another, and then all at once the sound of scraping could be heard once again, this time much more determined than before. The sound grew louder as the wagon continued to sway, groaning softly on its huge wheels.

Shan found himself moving along with the sound, pacing slowly down the length of the wagon towards the back end. He could hear a kind of mumbling and heavy breathing. The scraping sound suggested to him that something was being dragged across the floor of the wagon, something quite heavy and probably made of dried leather or wood. There was a last muffled grunt as the scratching sound suddenly stopped by the back door of the wagon. The elven youth circled around the huge rear wheel and planted himself by the rung of wooden steps. Shan leaned in to listen.

"Must find the goods, must find the goods!" he could hear in a whiny, nasal voice. "Yes. Must find the goods, Grundel! Must find the goods or Master will punish. Where did master hide them?" There was a strangled sort of snort. "Where?"

The back door suddenly popped open and slammed loudly against the outside wall of the wagon. It gouged new furrows in the wood as it rattled vigorously on its hinges. Shan was thrown back as a large wad of leather and cloth shot out at him. He stumbled back and fell into the dirt amid the loosening tangle of clothing. He fought with the interlocking bundle of arms and legs. When he could peel the remnants away from his face at last Shan looked up into the wagon's open doorway. An indignant snort was expelled from inside, and a large head peered out at him from the dim interior.

The big head seemed oddly out of shape, sort of lumpy, as it tilted to the side in consternation. Hidden at first in the shadows, the puffy face leaned closer, out into the feeble light of an alley torch. Shan could not repress a gasp as he struggled to sit up.

The grossly lopsided head was a mix of strange features. The large, knob-like nose was off center amid an avalanche of fleshly cheeks to either side. The long mouth was slanted sharply to one side, with just a tip of a thick tongue thrust out in the bottom corner through flabby lips. The whole right side of the skull was completely out of proportion, and looked as if it had been pushed and stretched out of shape by the abnormal growth of its brain. The entire thing appeared heavy and awkward. The most striking feature, though, was the great bulbous eye that dominated that side of its face. Nearly the size of a large fruit, the big, watery eye stared out, unblinking, much like a fish, while the other, more normal-sized left eye, seemed to blink and squint continually.

"What? Sneakin' up on Grundel?" the strange, sluggish voice wheezed at him. "Huh? Sneakin' up, is it?"

"Huh?" Shan stuttered. "N-No. No, I wasn't." Shan finally managed to scramble to his feet, most of the wad of brightly colored garments dropping away from his lap into the dust. He still had a few pieces of cloth inextricably tangled around his left hand. He pushed and pulled at them as he squirmed under that riveting gaze. "I-I was just w-walking by a-and . . ."

"Grundel got you good," it sneered, shuffling forward a step. "Yes. Yes, he did. Should teach you a lesson. Good lesson. Never sneak up on Grundel." He took another, much larger step forward, the bulky head swinging wildly to the side as he did. He reached out for the door jamb with his left hand, gripping onto the wood as his body seemed to rock forward. His huge right hand came up and pointed a thick, twisted finger accusingly at Shan. "No, sneakin' bad. Grundel be forced to get you back. Yes, he will." The bent finger stabbed towards him once again, then the large hand clamped onto the other door jamb.

"Grundel got you once already," he jabbered. "Got you once good." He snorted loudly in amusement.

Grundel took another step with his left foot, a short *slide-step*, as the disproportionate frame swung around and rocked wildly forward once again. The huge right hand slid from the jamb onto a rusty metal handle running down the wood just outside the doorway. The thick, stubby fingers whitened as they grasped powerfully at the metal. With a scraping *thump* Grundel's large right foot twisted around and planted itself by the first step down.

Shan watched as the misshapen creature painfully pitched and turned his body back and forth and sideways in what seemed like an awkward dance down the three wooden steps of the wagon. In the process Shan realized the entire right side of Grundel's body was completely disproportionate to the left. It was almost as if he had been formed from the bodies of two different men, the left side taken from a small weasel of a man and the right from some sort of giant. It was unbelievable how the two halves could have somehow been conformed into one hideous match. One side was completely shriveled and shrunken, dwarf-like, while the other side seemed stretched and bloated.

Shan had to look away as Grundel struggled precariously to get himself off the last step of the wagon. At first, he reached out tentatively with his much shorter left leg, fishing it about as he worked his thick tongue back and forth along his twisted lips. Next, failing to make contact with the ground, the hunchback jerked the leg back and then leaned suddenly to his right, launching himself uncertainly with his large right foot. He landed heavily on the same foot in a kind of awkward hop, kicking up sprays of dust while he fought clumsily to position his left foot for balance.

Shan bent over and scooped up the fallen garments as Grundel seemed to totter forward precariously, the frail arm waving futilely like the broken wing of a *kuulo*. Shan straightened up, took a few short steps and offered the loose bundle to Grundel without a word. The enormous fish-like eye hovered before the lad's chest as Grundel snatched the clothes away from him and cradled them in his mismatched arms. The man's crest of messy hair did not even reach the boy's chin. Grundel hissed in satisfaction as he turned back to the wagon doorway. For the first time Shan caught a glimpse of the strange little man's hunched back. Muscles beneath his loose shirt bunched and rolled across the large hump as the shriveled figure lurched over and laid the stack on the top-most step. With a grunt of effort he reached into the wagon and, using his longer right arm, dragged a large, leather-bound chest by one of its handles. He slid the chest forward and worked it back and forth until he could grab onto the other rope handle with his puny arm. He heaved and puffed noisily as he finally managed to shift it awkwardly down to the alley floor.

Shan found his voice at last.

"E-excuse me. I-I don't mean to be nosy but—just who are you a-and what are you doing here?"

The great fish-eye rotated back towards him. It studied him for a moment, the misshapen head tilting to one side, more because of the weight distribution than anything else, Shan decided. The small left eye squinted at him like a wild *bork*.

"Name's Grundel," he said, sputtering slightly. "And Grundel no answer to you. Not Grundel's master." He thrust out his lower lip and scratched at the tangled mass of dark curls at the back of his over-sized head. He spit suddenly at the Elfling, grinning with a twisted sort of smirk. Shan easily side-stepped as the glob smacked onto the ground beside him.

"Hey, now look here!" he called out angrily. "There's no call for that." Grundel only thrust out his tongue in an impish way and turned back to the clothes on the step. Shan was positive he heard the fellow sniggering amid his wheezing for air. "Look," the Elfling tried to sound diplomatic, "you're obviously not from around here, not from our village, anyway. I just want to know what you're doing here. Does anybody even know who you are?"

Grundel snapped up the bundle of clothing in his huge right hand and curled the colorful tangle into the crook of his arm. He bent over to snatch at a rope handle, grinning at Shan with an ugly gleam in his eye. The tip of his tongue slid out between his lips as he clearly thought about spitting once again. But Shan was wary this time, leaning onto his toes as if ready to spring away, so Grundel simply snickered to himself and hefted the trunk with a grunt.

At that moment two boys darted into the alley and raced up to the wagon. They would have climbed up onto the steps had not Grundel swung around to face them. They yelped in surprise when they saw him, his twisted face and body suddenly looming over them. He growled at them like an animal before they could say anything, lumbering awkwardly in their direction with a see-saw gait. They squealed in fear and bolted away, racing like the wind for the safety of the street beyond. They peeked back around the corner once, their whitened faces pressed against the back wall of the great hall. Grundel snarled at them and launched a slug of spit that fell far short of their position. They yelped again and quickly disappeared. Shan could hear their breathless cries, "Mama, Mama," as Grundel teetered back towards him, an evil sneer draped across his hideous face.

"What'd you go and do that for?" Shan exploded. "They wouldn't have hurt anything. You didn't have to frighten them!"

"Grundel like to," the hunchback wheezed. He hobbled up to Shan, the chest banging across his knees, and swung his big head towards the elven lad. He licked slowly at his puffy lips. The bulbous eye did not stir while the other tried to open up as wide as it could. Grundel's breath was warm and sour on his face. "Grundel have a scary face." The lips parted to reveal a wild row of pointed yellow teeth. "Grundel like to frighten." The smaller eye twitched spastically, then lapsed back into a squint. "Grundel frighten you?" The strange creature leaned closer.

The elven lad swallowed reflexively. Grundel's evil smile deepened.

"No," Shan said with as much conviction as he could muster. He endured Grundel's long silent stare without flinching. He leveled his chin and looked squarely into the ugly mass of flesh without so much as a blink, but his insides quivered like a dying fish. He swallowed once more as Grundel turned away with a snort and headed for the back door to the main hall. Shan let out a slow breath that he hadn't realized he was holding, spun on his heel and strode off after him.

The hunchback kicked up clouds of dust with each shambling *step-slide-step*. The large chest smacked loudly against his knees in an odd sort of rhythm.

"You didn't answer my question," Shan told him as he drew alongside. The man's tiny eye twitched once in annoyance. "Who are you and what are you doing here?"

"Told you," piped the humped figure. "Name's Grundel."

"Yes, I know," Shan retorted, irritated. "You said that already. But why are you here? Why are you in Draydin? I've never seen you before."

The hunchback didn't respond as he continued to labor towards the hall. Exasperated, Shan reached out a hand and spun the hideous little man around. Grundel's eyes flashed brightly with anger and his face twisted into even more of a horrible mask. The thick lips sucked noisily at his crooked yellow teeth, the tongue swooped out to wipe furiously at escaping drool. Grundel missed a stream of saliva and it dribbled off his lumpy chin, spattering on the dust of the alley. The knob-like nose flared suddenly, the breathing loud and labored.

"Well?" asked Shan, staring obdurately down at him.

The squinty eye snapped open and closed several times in quick succession as Grundel tried to raise himself to his full height, still a head or two well short of the undaunted Elf lad staring down at him. Shan firmly planted his hands on his hips, an angry ridge furrowed across his forehead. Grundel growled menacingly for a moment, his flabby lips twitching, then all at once, he seemed to shrink back. The fight quickly drained out of him and he bowed his head like a frightened animal. The boy remained firm. "Well?"

"Uh . . . business," Grundel finally whimpered. "Grundel here on business."

"Business? What kind of business?" asked the Elfling. Grundel only seemed to cower even more. "There's nothing around here to steal," Shan told him, "so don't even bother thinking about it."

"No-no," the hunchback gurgled. "Grundel not steal. Grundel here with master." He made a warbling sound deep in his throat. "Master has business. Master seeking—" He looked up at the elven youth suddenly, his eyes wide.

"Seeking? Seeking—*what?*" Shan wanted to know.

"Uh . . . ," Grundel hesitated, looking up at the lad with those strange eyes, the muscles of his face quivering in odd little twitches. Clearly he feared he had said too much. "Master seek—audience," he finally spluttered. He nodded quickly in affirmation. "Yes, audience. For—festival."

Shan visibly relaxed. "Oh," he said. "You're here for the festival. Mid-summer's Eve."

"That it," Grundel hurriedly replied. He nodded his bulging head

Daryl Hanson

more emphatically.

"Alright, then," Shan returned. "That makes sense." It was Grundel's turn to relax a little.

"Yes-s-s," he purred. "Nice master. Festival be good."

"Well, nothing like a big city, I'm sure," Shan offered, "but we do our best to celebrate it. And your—*master*—is going to help out, you say?"

"Yeah, yeah," slurred Grundel. "That it."

"Well, alright then," Shan said. "You can go about your *business*."

"Business, yes," the hunchback rejoined. "Uh-huh, uh-huh. Grundel do that. Thank you, kind master." He bowed awkwardly, watching Shan from under bushy brows as the youth turned and stalked away. He waited until Shan had disappeared down the corridor, listening for several moments before straightening up, his evil face darkening. "Uckh!" he muttered, and spit contemptuously into the dirt. His left eye became a slit. "Yes-s, business," he croaked thickly. "Just wait and see." He chuckled menacingly to himself as he hobbled into the doorway and up the long corridor.

A lone figure stood quietly in the thickening shadows of the alley. The wide brim of his tall, pointed hat was pulled low over his face. A soft breeze played through his long dark hair and bright clothes, delicately snapping the hem of his grey cloak against the colorful leg of his trousers. A thin, bony hand toyed with the drooping tendrils of his moustache.

He had watched most of the exchange between the hunchback and the elven boy from the shadow of the doorway. He had found the encounter to be interesting and quite enlightening. It seemed strange to him that an elven boy should be growing up in the midst of a human village isolated somewhere deep in the forest. He stroked thoughtfully at the small beard on his chin as he cupped something in his other hand. He shook it around in his palm several times, tossed it up in the air where it glinted in the torchlight, and then snatched it expertly from view with the same hand. "Hmm," he said, softly to himself, a cruel smile tugging at his thin lips as he looked down at the thing lying in his palm. He stuffed the oddment into a pocket and turned towards the wagon. His long, spidery legs covered the ground quickly and he leaped up the stairs in two bounds.

The tall man turned in the wagon doorway, pulling the little door closed behind him with a *thump*. After a moment, a soft glow could be seen through the curtained rear window. The rakish shadow moved momentarily across the opening. The wagon shifted and creaked. Crickets began to chirp in chorus as the night finally settled in.

Shan dashed into the great hall in light bounds, ducking quickly under a serving tray that spun towards him. Celina offered a shy smile in apology as she swept past him on the right. She plopped a beaker of ale and one of cider down on the end of a table with a slosh and hurried off to the kitchens for more, the dripping tray held flat against her stomach.

The large room was nearly to full capacity already, and Shan had to scan the tables for several moments before he spotted two of his friends on the far side of the hall. He whirled in their direction, weaving through a stream of serving maids who circled the tables with heaped platters of steaming meat and bread. The wafting aroma brought a surge of moisture to his mouth. He squeezed in between Laith and Keo as Celina paced by. She leveled her dark eyes on him for a moment as he sat down, then sped away with her empty tray once again.

"Good thing you showed up when you did," Laith hollered as he leaned towards the Elfling. Roars of laughter and excited snatches of conversation rose up around them in a wild jumble of noise. "We might not have been able to hold the spot much longer." Shan nodded his thanks.

"Yeah, it's nearly packed in here already," Keo added with a snort.

"You'd think it was a feast day or something," Shan hollered back with a wink.

"Well it is, sort of," Laith countered. "Mid-Summer's Eve. There's good food, and lots of it. The whole village is gathered together. And, best of all, there's no work tomorrow, so we don't have to turn in early. 'Sides, how often do we get a chance to listen to some of the old man's wonderful stories?"

"I hear there's another man spinning some tales tonight," Keo piped up. "A real bard!"

Shan could only shrug. He swept his gaze about the hall as several stragglers piled in through the wide, log-braced portal. He caught Celina eyeing him again from across three crowded tables, but she quickly spun the other way when he glanced her way.

"She's definitely got the eye for you, Shan," Laith commented in his ear. Keo only snickered through his nose.

"No, I don't think so, Laith," Shan managed with an emphatic shake of his head. "It's just that I'm a little different from all the other boys she's seen. She's probably just curious about me, that's all." Laith's face creased into a broad grin. Shan started to look for his uncle in the sea of colorful tunics. "Do you really think so?" he asked under his breath.

Daryl Hanson

"It's obvious, my friend," Laith mumbled as he shoved a slab of meat into his mouth. A stream of juice dribbled down his chin. He wiped at it with his sleeve, then grabbed for a hot, buttered roll from the serving dish. "Ouch," he cried, tearing it open. Little clouds of steam curled up out of the two halves. Still chewing on the meat, Laith thrust one of the hot buttered pieces into his mouth. Puffing out his cheek like a squirrel, he somehow managed to chew on the whole wad some more. He piled a couple more slabs of meat onto his plate, snatched up three additional rolls and several thick slices of cheese, before swallowing the enormous load in his mouth.

"Hungry?" Shan asked him with a little grin.

"Uh-huh," his large shouldered friend managed between swigs of cider from a wooden mug. He backhanded the froth from his lips and plunked the mug down near the plate. "You've no idea how hungry you can get tree farmin' all day long." Shan got in a feeble shake of his head while Laith jammed two more pieces of cheese into his mouth. "First thing in the morning there's collectin' the syrup. And scarcely a handful of dry fruit or nuts to get you going. Then comes the harvestin' of the pitch and resin. That's pretty sticky work. And then in the afternoon, after a poor helping of stale bread and moldy cheese, they make us climb all about in those thorn-infested trees on the eastern slope to pick all the blasted fiber from a million spider webs." He bit into one of the rolls without yelping. "Count yourself lucky they haven't put you on any of the gathering teams."

Shan continued to eat in silence. He wondered for the hundredth time why he had never gone out with any of the farmers. After all, tree harvesting was the primary source of livelihood for the villagers of Draydin and commanded the largest group of its workers. The next largest contingent of able bodies, those past their fifteenth yahr, were the hunters, those who stalked the great forests for wild game, for *bork*, *ur*, *alk* and *thag*. And, with as many mouths as there were to feed in the village, fresh meat was certainly a necessity. Shan hadn't been allowed to participate in any of the hunting forays, either. He shoveled a cold strip of *thag* meat into his mouth with a frown. The only other noticeable grouping of workers were those employed by the kitchen staff and cleaning crews. Of what use would he be to them?

As he looked around the great hall Shan noticed an odd character standing off to one side. He wore a brightly colored jacket and had on a tall, broad-brimmed hat. The tall spike of the hat was a bit off-kilter, as if it had been caught awkwardly in the branches of a tree. It looked severely bent out of shape. It also had several patches on it where the felt had worn through. The man had long, thin, drooping moustaches and a spiky little beard. His nose was hooked to one side, like it had been broken several times perhaps. His skin tone was ashen and perhaps slightly yellowish. He had beady, sort of devious looking eyes, Shan could tell from where he sat. They were deep-set and dark under bushy eyebrows, and were, he now noticed, a bit slanted as well. They were furtive and seemed constantly in motion, as if they were holding back some sinister secret within their smoky depths. His head swivelled this way and that, appearing to search the sea of faces within the large room in a sense of urgency. Upon a sudden impulse, Shan ducked down behind his friends to avoid the wandering gaze. He remained motionless for several long *biri*, resisting the urge to look until he sensed the questing stare had moved on. Shan peeked cautiously around his bench mates, relieved to find the man looking elsewhere. For some unknown reason, he shivered.

Shan ate the remainder of his meal pensively, thoroughly chewing each bite slowly before swallowing it at last. He glanced every now and then at the mysterious figure by the wall. At one point he was surprised to find Celina standing over him, an expectant look on her face.

"Finished?" she asked coyly.

"Yes," he stammered, offering her his empty plate. He held onto the mug of cider in one hand as she cleared away the other dishes. He took a long, slow draft once she had pivoted on her heels and hastened off. He set the mug down idly on the table, dropping his chin into his cupped hands.

Amid the clatter of those gathering up plates and utensils, and the gurgle of those replenishing drained beakers of cider and ale from huge pitchers balanced on their hips, Shan could make out the strains of a sweet little melody gradually drifting his way. It started on the far side of the hall, faintly at first and sort of flat in pitch, but stronger voices soon joined in and lifted the pitch into its normal range. It grew steadily in volume, leaping from table to table until it had been picked up by every tongue within the hall, until the boisterous tune had filled the big room with sweet sound. The added rhythms of stamping feet, clapping hands and banging mugs upon the wet tabletops rattled the rafters on their pilings. It was a tune Shan enjoyed and he eagerly lifted his own voice to sing along.

Daryl Hanson

"I am as lofty as an eagle, on feathered wing I long to fly
Flashing higher over hillsides, watch how effortlessly I glide
Sailing over patchwork pastures, painted gloriously with trees
Soaring ever, ever higher, on the kiss of the gentle breeze.

I am, I am the eagle, soaring even higher in the sun
Winging up from the valleys where the thorka love to run
Streaking above golden meadows, and fields where farmers start to sew
O'er the tallest carven mountains, glistening white with brand new snow.

I am, I am the eagle, I rise much higher on the wind
Racing, forever racing, then drifting on at my slightest whim
Flashing o'er crashing oceans, winging wildly through darkest trees
Swooping down to snatch my prey from the gentle bubbling of a stream.

We are, we are the eagles, we're fierce brothers of the wind
No earthly domain can hold us, not mountain nor forest or glen.
Winging wildly o'er green pastures painted gloriously with trees
Soaring ever, ever higher, on the kiss of the gentle breeze."

When the last echoing phrases of the song had faded away into smatterings of applause, Ulfiir rose from his place near the hearth and made his way slowly through the crowd. A hush spread swiftly through the hall as the old man lowered himself onto the ledge of a small corner platform used for the performances of visiting singers and jugglers, and the like. A few men hastened about the room to turn down the lamps on the tables. The dying glimmer of coals still glowed red in the fire pit and the semi-darkness gave the hall a dramatic feel. The air seemed close and warm.

The old man cleared his throat hoarsely and settled himself more comfortably on the wooden platform. The flare of a bracketed torch caught his eyes and gave them a sparkle. He seemed somehow mysterious as he peered out from under his bushy white brows and pursed his lips. A small child babbled somewhere in the middle of the upturned faces and was quickly shushed by his mother. The village folk leaned forward in eagerness, the snap and flutter of the torches the only sound in the chamber. Even the kitchen drudges and serving maids had quietly crowded out of the back rooms and fanned out along the serving counter.

"It's Mid-Summer's Eve," Ulfiir began softly, "as you all know."

Many in the crowd leaned even closer to catch the old man's quiet words. The voices of several small children could suddenly be heard as they all seemed to speak out at once in excitement of Ulfiir's pronouncement. They were quickly hushed by their parents. The soft patter of feet continued to scurry past as the last of the stragglers strove to find a vacant seat in the press of bodies. The rustle of excited voices finally died away until all that could be heard once more was the soft crackle of wall torches throughout the great room.

"Mid-Summer's Eve," the old man said again. "It is a time we set aside to give thanks for all the good things we have received. True, we celebrate once again and to an even greater degree at the actual Harvest in the fall, and it is appropriate for us to do so at that time. Yet now is the time when we traditionally take a step back from the long, hard work of the Summer to give thanks in *anticipation* of all the good things we will be given. Athiliel has truly blessed us, as is His way. He is the Creator and Sustainer of all things."

Out of curiosity Shan sought to observe the odd figure waiting in the shadows to the side. He noticed a brief look of anger and annoyance flash momentarily across his ferret-like features at the mention of Athiliel's name. It was there only for an instant, and then it was gone. Shan frowned in thought and turned his attention back to the old man sitting lightly on the performer's platform.

"In honor of the occasion," Ulfiir began again, "and to give your ears a well-deserved rest from my tired old voice . . ." There were murmurs of disagreement at his humble words.

"Never," Shan heard a woman in the back call out. "We never get tired of your stories." There were echoing cries from others around the hall. The old man raised a weary hand and waved them to silence.

"Thank you," Ulfiir spoke up. "I appreciate your feelings, I truly do. But there are times, maybe only once in a great while, when we all need a little change. And tonight's that night. Oh, you'll probably get to hear from me on lots of other occasions, I'm sure. But tonight, we all have the pleasure to hear from a man who has been from one end of Ythira to another. He's a world traveler, a tinker, and historian. They say he knows things that no other man could possibly know, seen things that no other eye has ever seen. Let him now entertain us with his songs and tales of adventure and intrigue, gleaned from extensive time spent bouncing along the dusty roads from one scattered village to the next throughout all the lands. Please give a warm Draydin welcome to a true bard of the people and gifted magician: Silas Gravelle." And with that, Ulfiir stood up from his perch and flung out a hand toward the man standing in the shadows by the wall.

A chorus of applause broke out all over the room as the nefarious figure stepped out into the light and strode up to the platform with a long, stalking gait. Several people in the great hall caught their breath at the sight of him. To many of them, Gravelle certainly looked more like a greasy salesman than a respected poet. Most of the people in the audience continued to clap their hands warmly for him, as he made his way forward. Yet a few, however, Shan included, sensed something much more sinister about the man, and they found their hands resting limply in their laps.

"Not, ah, exactly what I expected," Laith said in a heavy whisper, leaning close.

"I know what you mean," Shan returned in low tones. "Guess we'll just have to wait and see what happens."

"I, for one, would like to see him do a little magic," chimed in Keo in a loud voice.

Silas Gravelle took the steps up to the performer's platform in three quick bounds. He turned with a practiced movement on the ball of one foot to face the crowd. His beady eyes focused in on the young man who had spoken. "That will come in due time, my young friend," he uttered in a slithering drawl. Keo was embarrassed by the sudden attention as every face turned to look his way. He quickly lowered his eyes to the tabletop in front of him and refused to look up. And with that, Shan found himself staring into the restless eyes of the odious fellow upon the stage. A spark of mischief played about the man's face as he looked directly across at him. Shadows from a guttering torch lent him an air of mystery. "Well, well, well," he said with a greasy smile. "What have we here?"

Shan caught a glimpse of movement from the corner of his eye and realized, curiously, that Ulfiir had fled the room.

− 3 −
Ulfiir
[13th of Kaligath, 4534 C.R.]

The great hall was dark and drenched in heavy shadows. An oil lamp had been placed on one end of a long, wooden table, but the feeble, yellowish smear of light it gave off did little to chase away the chill or gloom of the large room. The tiny flame sputtered and crackled upon the small, leaf-shaped ceramic vessel, and thin slivers of smoke drifted upwards from it in slow, lazy curls.

Three figures sat hunched over the table. Their stone-like faces, bathed in the sickly glow of the lamp, were dimly mirrored on the smooth, polished surface. They remained motionless for a long while, their heads bowed, each of them intently studying the flickering wand of light from the dark pools of their eyes. The wan glow betrayed the sense of secrecy they shared, and the nervous, stilted silence managed to heighten the growing pangs of unease that seemed to crackle in the stuffy air.

Shan looked up from the table and blinked his eyes a number of times. A fuzzy after-image danced erratically through his field of vision for several moments in a thick swath of purple, pulsing larger and brighter with each flutter of his eyelids. Once the splotches had finally faded from his eyes Shan lifted his chin from the cup of his hands and glanced slowly about the large hall. A reassuring rush of warmth flooded over him and a half-smile tugged at the corners of his mouth. It broadened slowly to a grin as he swept his gaze across the inky stillness.

Even in the darkness he knew the place well.

At the back of the hall were the kitchens. They were vaguely discernable now through a buffed swath of counter space where trays of steaming food could be passed through. A narrow portal to the left opened onto the series of low rooms used for the preparation of meals. Doorways on either side of the tiny hallway led to smaller rooms, storerooms mostly, a pantry, and a worn ladder descending to a cellar for wine, cheese and cider.

In the center of the hall was a large, circular fire pit. It was dark and cold now, and the outer ring, a double row of hardened bricks scarcely a step high, was black with grease and soot. The thick metal poles and crossbar of the spit were also charred, crusted over with clinging bits of grizzled flesh and dappled remnants of burnt oil. Strewn throughout the wide pit, nestled amid mounds of grayish-black ash, were irregular chunks of blackened wood, cracked and scarred by the fire.

Daryl Hanson

Surrounding the pit and laid out in three large, concentric circles, were twelve long tables of roughened planks. These were smoothed and polished by constant use and were large enough to seat ten men to a side. There were some fifteen thick poles staggered throughout the hall. They had been hardened by fire and lathered in heavy coats of pitch. Like massive tree trunks, they rose up through the dusty patchwork flooring to support an intricate network of criss-crossing beams and rafters that disappeared into the gloom of the vaulted ceiling high above.

All about the room, strapped to the walls and ceiling poles with leather ties, hung all kinds of helmets and shields and the dusty weapons of men who had long passed on. There were also many ragged tapestries and bright paintings on polished wood dangling limply from the stout beams of the rafters high overhead. Washed now of their color by the darkness, many of these had been arranged as if to tell their history. Once proud reminders of a noble lineage, these were now mostly only forgotten dreams of glory and flecked with dust and soot. Fuzzy trailers of cobwebs swung between them like tiny bridges. In earlier, less confusing days, Shan would have been flooded with happy memories. There had been endless cold winter nights when he had listened to stories of each and every one of these dusty mementoes arrayed about the gloomy rafters, grim tales of hard fought battles told in such stark, heart-wrenching detail that he could almost visualize every hammering blow, every echoing thump of hooves as they swept across the quivering earth.

But the room held only gloom for him now. The air was crisp with a certain chill and his breath formed little patches of mist before his eyes. The fire pit was dark, the torches left unlit in their brackets, the oil lamps on the tables all extinguished save one. And with each flicker of that meager flame shadowy forms were thrown out in a shaky semblance of reality.

Shan shivered suddenly at a ripple of gooseflesh. Powerful, unbidden memories leapt at him from out of the darkness. He clamped his eyes tightly shut and gave in to the chaotic blur of emotion.

* * * * *

Lightning suddenly shot across the sky. The darkness was momentarily banished by the jagged bolt that ripped through the night. Shan jerked up from his pillow and grasped frantically for the covers displaced by his wild movements. He sat rigidly on his bed, his fingers groping fearfully for the rumpled mass of blankets, as lashing rain began to pelt the window pane. The room seemed somehow eerie as scattered bits of furniture took on monstrous shapes in the rapidly fading light. He blinked his eyes nervously, desperately trying to place his surrounding after a horrifying dream had wakened him in a clammy sweat. His frenzied breathing became more controlled when a sudden, loud crack of thunder, which seemed to grind and roll just over the ceiling of his room, sent him scurrying from the chamber in a blind panic.

Another jagged flash of light blinded him for a few ragged heartbeats and turned the long, dark corridor into a glowing serpent in his mind. He bounced heavily off the wall several times and careened into half a dozen yawning doorways. He slid wildly past them as the hammering rain rattled window after window. The next rumble of thunder found him at the top of a wide flight of stairs. He caught his foot on the upper step and tumbled crazily to the bottom. Scuffed and bruised by his wild fall, yet no worse for wear, Shan scrambled clumsily to his wavering feet. He ran haphazardly through the darkened hallway, stumbling and tripping over any number of obstacles lining the way. All the torches seemed to have burned out in their brackets, leaving shoes, small tables, wooden racks, and even scattered dishes to clutter his path.

He ran on blindly, trails of blood dribbling from numerous cuts on his arms, legs and face. He burst suddenly into the great hall and slid on the patchwork flooring. He stumbled over a table in the darkness, pitching himself forward over its polished top to land heavily on one shoulder. He tumbled end over end until he skidded to a halt against the thick bench of another table. He lay there for several long moments, his breathing hoarse and labored.

Occasional bursts of lightning still continued to lance off articles strewn along the long hallway in his frenzied flight. He could see them through the opened doorway as they loomed suddenly large in the light, then melted away into nothingness. He closed his eyes for a moment as the panic slowly began to subside, yet he could still hear the fury of the lashing rain dimly drumming upon the roof tiles outside. Once his breathing settled into something a little more normal, Shan opened his eyes and looked upwards. Several articles hanging from the rafters swayed slowly on their pegs as a result of vibrations from the wind and rain. He watched in dull fascination as they rocked and swung ever so slightly.

Suddenly a cord snapped on a large, dust-laden axe and it plummeted down towards him. Shan had no time to react before the razor sharp blade buried itself in the floor just a finger's length from his face.

Daryl Hanson

Shan shook his eyes from the darkness with a shudder. The memory of that night left him shaken. He must have been only six or seven the evening of that severe storm, yet the images still haunted him. He could never quite remember the nightmare that had woken him from sleep just as the storm hit. All he could ever conjure up were vague sensations of being hunted down like an animal by someone, some*thing*, he could never quite see. He folded his arms together and rubbed his hands over them vigorously in an attempt to restore warmth. He felt suddenly cold, very cold. It was some time before he realized that it was not a physical sensation, but one that crept upon him from the clammy depths of his soul.

He shivered savagely.

The elven youth sat uneasily on one of the long benches. Across from him, his elbows on the edges of the table, his chin resting in his hands, sat Weeson. The captain of the guards seemed mesmerized by the tiny dancing flame before him. At the head of the table, in a great chair that had been dragged from his room, reclined Ulfiir, a small metal object cupped in one bony hand. A slender run of chain dangled from his closed palm and cast minute speckles of light as he slowly opened and closed his fingers in an odd cadence.

They were no longer hastily clad. Shan had washed himself in a basin of cold water and dressed in fresh clothing. He had even managed to keep his belt from twisting this time. He combed the long strands of his hair in a way that kept the pointed tips of his ears from sticking through. He had also received a new dagger and sheath from one of the soldiers, which he thrust into his belt with a grateful jerk.

"Thanks," Shan had told the man.

"Right," the soldier responded, "you can never know when you're gonna need it. I mean, who was to think you'd be attacked in your own chamber like that?"

"I'm just glad you and all the others made it to my room in time," Shan had replied, "before I would've had to jump for it."

"No, I wouldn't fancy a broken leg and all," the man returned. "Guess it beats becoming a hasty meal for that thing, I reckon."

Shan had nodded uneasily at the reminder of the beast's flashing claws and large slathering fangs coming within arm's reach of him. He smiled wanly at the man and headed for the great hall.

"Seems like these strange sort of incidents been happening all over the forest lately," the soldier had said as he began to turn away.

"What's that?" Shan asked him as he spun about in his tracks.

"Oh," the soldier pivoted back to look Shan in the eye. "Must be some kind of trend, is all."

"What do you mean?" Shan drifted closer. "Trend?"

"Yeah," the man had licked his lips. "I was talkin' to a friend o' mine the other day. He's from Pelba, some twenty, thirty *korads* to the southwest. He says all their animals started disappearin' some time back. Gone missin' come two, three hands ago."

"What kind of animals?" Shan wanted to know. "There must be some explanation."

"You know, the domesticated kind." The soldier ticked them off on his fingers. "*Shart, kuulo, turth*. That kinda thing." Shan just looked at him for a moment. "Oh, and he heard tell of some other settlement further west, Hurlik, I think, where they was sure somethin' got one of their watchbeasts. Real close to their outer wall, I think he said."

"No fooling?" Shan had asked, his eyes widening a bit. "That's pretty serious stuff."

"By the Flame!" the soldier retorted. "Time has come when a man can't even walk out into the forest at night. Strange things are lurkin' around out there in the dark and that's no lie."

"Don't I know it," Shan had murmured under his breath. He swallowed reflexively.

"That beast sure was a bugger gettin' out past the gates, I tell 'e," the man said. "But the flames are lickin' hungrily at his mangy hide right now. Whew. Stinks to high heaven." He screwed up his nose. "Well, you have a nice rest of your night, young master." The man tossed that last comment over his shoulder as he started off down the hall. Shan nodded wearily and strode off in the opposite direction, wondering if the captain had any further news to relay.

On impulse, Shan had swung down the eastern corridor, swept past the front entrance of the great hall, and found himself in an area reserved for key village personnel. He came to a halt near the end of the passage and rapped smartly on the captain's door. It snapped open after a moment. "Ho, there," Weeson greeted him with a nod. Leaving the door ajar for Shan to enter, he turned back to a mirror on the wall to finish buttoning his collar. Weeson had returned to his quarters after the ordeal with the beast and, after allowing Madora to dress the wound on his arm properly, had donned a fresh tunic. It was dark green in color, like the forest beyond, and fell to mid-thigh. Sewn above the left breast was a stylized crest of

Daryl Hanson

Draydin. Shan thought it gave the captain a much more formidable appearance, more war-like, than his usual garb of forest cloak cast over a loose shirt and britches. The Elfling watched from the doorway as Weeson arrayed himself with the weapons of his trade. A dagger was concealed in each of his boots. A quiver of arrows had been strapped tightly to his right thigh and the bow was set aside on the tabletop within arm's reach. A short sword swung from the left hip, a long knife on his right, and along his back, criss-crossed, hung a double-bladed axe and great broadsword.

"Going to war?" the boy asked him with an uneasy glance.

"Never know when you're going to need them." He patted lightly at his array with a satisfied grin. "Ready?" the man asked, turning to the boy. He scooped up the bow from the table and stalked over to where the Elfling leaned at the doorjamb, flashing him a confident smile.

Shan could only shrug. "I hope so," he managed to say as Weeson stepped out into the corridor and pulled the door shut behind them. It was late and Shan suddenly felt very tired.

Weeson clapped him on the shoulder with a gloved hand as they started off down the passage together. "Come on," he said. "We don't want to keep the old man waiting." They came to the front door of the great hall in stride, only to find Ulfiir had not yet arrived. Weeson struck a spark to a small oil lamp he found on a stand just inside the doorway and carried it to one of the long, wooden tables in the center of the large room. The tiny flame flickered, sending quivering shadows out into the darkness as he moved. He set the small, leaf-shaped vessel on the worn wooden surface but the feeble light did little to dispel the overwhelming gloom.

Ulfiir had dressed himself in a thick, black robe, one that Shan had never seen before. He could see the creased lines where it had been folded for some time, probably tucked deeply away in the bottom of a chest, Shan decided. It gave Ulfiir a rather ceremonial look, very businesslike and official. The old man's pale skin and his long white hair and beard contrasted sharply against the dark plush fabric. He almost took on a ghostly appearance, especially in the sputtering light of the oil lamp. It had taken Shan's breath away when Ulfiir had hobbled into the dim chamber, his gray eyes twinkling. He shuffled across the floor, picking his way slowly between the tables, and plopped himself down in the cushioned chair at the end of the table where they had seated themselves. The old man sat there wrapped deeply in thought for some time before ever speaking.

Ulfiir finally lifted his weary head. "It has begun," the old one said at last, softly.

Shan's eyes shot quickly over to search the wrinkled face of the old man. There was a smoldering fire in the icy depths of his stare that gave Shan a chill. He glanced then over at Weeson, but the captain's attention was riveted solely upon his uncle.

"It has begun!" Ulfiir spoke again, this time more firmly. "There were times I thought this night would never come. I had hoped and prayed we would never have to be plunged into these dark, uncertain times. I realize now it was folly on my part to expect we could avoid them entirely." Shan leaned forward and fastened his eyes on the old man's craggy face. A stray wisp of long, gray hair danced before the lump of his nose. "The Usurper's power has grown tremendously over the last few yehrin," Ulfiir's voice was low but steady, "and with it, his greed. Many yehrin ago he was satisfied with only the one throne, one kingdom. But now I fear a whispering evil has darkened his mind, and poisoned his heart more and more, if indeed that were possible. Even now the whole continent of Ythira stands poised before him like a sparkling jewel, enticing him, luring him, and he has dared to stretch forth his hand to snatch it up."

Weeson shifted his position and the old man's gray eyes fell upon him. "Has the Regent's power truly grown so formidable?" The captain looked down upon the smooth surface of the table as if he gazed upon a map spread out before him. "There have been increasing raids to the east, to be sure, wandering skirmishes to the west, distant at first, yet drawing closer. There have even been flashes of open warfare to the south, but . . ." and he swept his hands over the worn surface of the table, almost as if conjuring up for them various clusters of tokens depicting military engagements. ". . . But I cannot see how the enemy has turned all of this to his advantage."

"Precisely!" Ulfiir spit out. "You do not see!"

The captain's face darkened momentarily. "And that's the crux of it," the old man went on. "You . . . *we* . . . see only what the enemy wants us to see. Most of what is now happening is being done in secret." Weeson nodded slowly, the angry flush fading from his cheeks.

"Khairon's nefarious agents have filtered throughout the land." Ulfiir lowered the tone of his voice, leaned forward to prop his bony elbows on the table's edge. "They have been secretly buying allegiances with stolen gold, gathering information in dark, hideous places to the west and south, insinuating themselves into every town, village and kingdom in order to complete their dark missions."

"Which is just what exactly?" the young captain asked. Ulfiir bristled momentarily at the interruption and shot him a quick look of annoyance, but then realized there was no trace of sarcasm in the man's frank stare. He was almost immediately mollified.

"His ultimate goal is power," Ulfiir went on in measured tones. "It goads him and dominates his thoughts. He is mad with the lust of it. Once, long ago, he was kind and good, or so I thought. Yet now I am not so sure." He scratched absently at his chin. "Perhaps his kindness was only a ruse to accomplish his hidden plans. Perhaps he has somehow been corrupted by the greatest of all evils. That seems likely." He shrugged. "But now it appears he will stop at nothing to possess the whole world itself, to conquer every kingdom, to bend all people to his will."

"That does sound evil," Shan offered weakly.

Ulfiir looked over at the boy, his gaze softening.

"A few of his dark agents have even ventured as far as the Spur of Grothos and enlisted the foul spawn of Kulnedra to their cause," the old man continued, solemnly. "I, like so many others, thought them to have been eradicated from the world as a result of war long ago, their accursed filth wiped away forever. It was hoped that they had been eliminated with the fall of Muurdra long ages past. But even now, under the thick veil of night, dark hordes of *gorguls* issue forth from their long dead, barren land, spreading out rapidly across the face of Anarra like a shriveling disease. They skulk about through the cover of darkness, crawling out from every foul hole, in their attempts to infiltrate the haunts of men with their devious snares. They strive, with their unwavering devotion, to accomplish their insidious tasks known only to their dark master."

"Khairon has somehow managed to maneuver all this?" Weeson asked him incredulously. "All on his own?"

"No," Ulfiir shook his head slowly. "His power is indeed growing, but in no way has he the means, the reach, the . . . *tentacles* . . . to accomplish all this on his own. At least not yet." He swung his eyes from the captain to the boy. "In his greed the Usurper has been seeking to conquer all of the eastern continent, but in the process he has unwittingly awakened an evil so dark, so foul, that even his own atrocities pale next to those of the *Sinister One*."

Shan looked about the eerie hall and shivered. In his heart he knew there was only one being the old man could possibly mean. His eyes grew wide in fear and his lips worked spastically to mouth the name. *Muurdra!*

"And so, as a result of his own greed and recklessness, the shadows begin to grow once again in the far south," the old man whispered. "The tireless servants of Muurdra even now strive with great power to bring their wicked master back into the world. He was banished by the hand of Athiliel to the Outer Darkness, imprisoned there without body or form for a thousand yehrin."

"But who are these foul servants?" Shan couldn't help asking. "Where are they now?"

Both Ulfiir and Weeson swung their faces toward the elven youth. He cringed involuntarily to see the fire burning in their eyes. Shan was surprised, though, when the old man softened his gaze and shook his head sadly.

"They are everywhere, my boy," the old man's voice dripped with menace. "Foraging parties have been combing the region for some time, quietly penetrating the borders of our very own forest. Bandits, ruffians, undesirables from every walk of life. Even bounty hunters." Shan looked down at his hands. "That tinker, for one," Ulfiir went on after a moment. The boy glanced quickly up into the craggy face. "You remember? Last Mid-Summer?"

Realization slowly dawned in the Elfling's mind. "I knew there was something peculiar about him from the first moment I laid eyes on him." Shan shivered again, as if in the movement he could somehow rid himself of the unsavory memory which still seemed to cling so tenaciously. "And that servant of his, the hunchback. Ugghh. What a vile creature he was!" Shan subconsciously wiped his hands on his britches. But before Ulfiir could go on, another thought leapt into his mind. "Ulfiir," he began, not exactly sure how to phrase it. "Ulfiir, if . . . if you knew that Gravelle was an Ag—a *spy*—why did you ever let him speak that night at the feast?" Ulfiir narrowed his bushy eyebrows on the boy. "I mean, why give him such a glowing introduction like that?"

The old man screwed up his wrinkled lips and thrust his ragged eyebrows out even further. "I had suspected him even before that night," he said evenly. "For quite some time, as a matter of fact. And it was not my decision to allow him access to the village. But by the time I realized he was coming, it was too late to do anything about it, or to make any kind of changes that would not arouse his suspicion."

"And I *suspect* you didn't want to reveal that knowledge to Gravelle, anyway," Weeson cut in. Ulfiir's small nod affirmed the truth. "Cagey old man," the captain added with a smile.

"Gravelle, and many more like him," Ulfiir went on, "either work directly for the enemy, or are being manipulated by him through nefarious means to accomplish his bidding. Khairon himself is just a powerful pawn in the Dark Master's game." He blew air out of his lips. "Together, all these fell servants seek to give him substance and shape once again. And should they succeed, the *Cyr Nilth* will seek to destroy us all!"

Shan shuddered violently, barely managing to stifle a cry.

Ulfiir focused his gray eyes on the boy, narrowing his brows. Then abruptly he shifted them to Weeson and then back again. "If Muurdra's foul hordes are successful in returning him to physical form, and he manages to escape from his prison in the Outer Darkness, he will become invincible. No one will be able to face him. Not only will he lay waste to this continent of Ythira, but all of Anarra as well. Nothing will be able to escape him, nothing living will be left to stand in the sun." Ulfiir paused a long moment, running the tip of his tongue across dry lips. "His very gaze could wither the flesh from a man's bones. He is Evil itself, an evil far greater than you could possibly imagine." The old man spoke softly once again, but neither of the two listening had trouble hearing what he said.

"Soon, Shan, very soon, you will be in grave danger." Ulfiir's words broke and crackled like the tongues of a fire. "What am I saying? You *are* in grave danger right now! Tonight has already proven it. Always has he sought you, yet never could he discern where you were hidden away. He was never really certain that you lived. But somehow there must have been rumors, stories of your birth, that made their sluggish way back to him, passed along from one vile lip to another. Echoing whispers which meandered their way through the darkness, until even his own deadly pawn, Khairon, became informed. Yet his powers were weak and his allies were few and widely scattered for the longest of times."

The old man paused for a moment, his eyes sparkling in the soft light. "But slowly his power began to grow once again, the ranks of his foul armies quickly began to swell. He has sent forth feelers and the circles of his influence gradually reached out to touch every nation. His hunger has tainted every town and village. Soon his sinister hand stretched out across the land, searching, forever searching. And still he could not find you. So, in his wrath he devastated what was left of the peaceful communities of the Elves, scattering them in his insatiable hatred, wreaking death and destruction upon the Chosen wherever he turned. Yet still you remained hidden from him, still your life seemed to slip through his grasp—*until now.*"

"Uncle," Shan interrupted, nervously. "What are you talking about?" He suppressed an urge to cough, but he could still feel the tickling itch at the back of his throat.

"Even now he knows where you may be found, my boy," uttered the old man. "His power is growing, the wheels of his devilish schemes are turning. He has waited many, many long yehrin to find you, and, if it were not for my presence tonight, you would have been killed!"

Shan gripped the edges of the table with numb fingers. "You make it sound as if you believe that . . . that thing in my room was some sort of an assassin," he cried, "not just a stray beast." He blinked in disbelief. "It . . . it must have wandered into the compound by chance. Picked my room at random." His voice had turned shrill with the unmistakable whine of one trying desperately to convince others of the truthfulness of his words, yet he did not quite believe it himself. Shan looked urgently at Weeson for support, but the young captain sat grim-faced and shook his head almost imperceptibly. Shan swung back to the old man.

"By chance, you say?" A mirthless smile played about Ulfiir's thin lips. "Is this creature so commonplace, so ordinary, that you have seen many of them lurking about in the woods?" The old man leveled his gaze on the boy. "Have you ever seen such a beast before? Even once?"

"No," Shan had to admit grudgingly.

Ulfiir glanced at Weeson. The captain shook his head slowly once again. Shan felt the growing knot in his stomach begin to tighten. "Have you ever even *heard* of such a beast?" the old man asked in a reedy voice. "Either of you?" The two listeners shook their blank faces at him. "I have!" Ulfiir told them sharply, leaning forward in his chair. There was a sudden flash of wonder in Shan's blue eyes. "I have dealt with them before, and believe me, I know what I am talking about."

The boy swallowed quickly as the knot in his stomach exploded into queasy jets of fire.

"There are forces at work here which neither one of you can understand," Ulfiir offered firmly. "Kurgoths are incredibly fearsome creatures," the old man told them as he settled back in his seat once again. "They were spawned long ago by the evil hand of Muurdra in some misguided imitation of Athiliel's creation. They are killers. You saw it." Shan could only rock back and forth in fear as the echo of its wild howling seemed to cascade around his ears. "They are wild and vicious, strong and extremely tenacious. They make unbelievable trackers. Blood hunters they are. They can follow the faint scent of their prey and pursue it for hand after hand, it is said. But they are very, very rare. In fact, I had even thought them extinct, wiped out, killed off in a vengeful war many yehrin ago." He trailed off softly and sat for a long while, staring into the single sputtering flame on the table.

"It took all seven Noble Clans of the Elves," the old man spoke to them in little more than a whisper, "united in one cause and possessing their fabled weapons of old to subdue them long ago." He turned his disquieting gaze upon them. "And to think that even just one of those foul beasts had survived to this day is frightening."

"Yet you killed it!" Shan responded in awe. "With . . . with some kind of sorcery." His eyes went wide in wonder.

"No, I didn't kill it, my boy," the old man told him. "I am not a sorcerer. I had the help of Athiliel." He looked down for a moment. "His power can do all things. I merely severed the connection it had with its controller, lurking somewhere close-by in the woods, most likely."

"Controller?"

"You saw its eyes, boy!" Ulfiir snapped. "Someone with great power was manipulating the terrible beast, guiding its actions." He shook his head. "To do that, to control a creature of such strength and size, would require incredible power. I certainly cannot do that. A Morlung perhaps, or maybe even one of the Fallen Ones himself."

"A what?" Shan's head was reeling.

"I wouldn't have guessed Khairon had that kind of power," Weeson pointed out.

"He doesn't," the old man reassured them, "but the Neffeluur . . . now that's a different matter." He trailed off once again. He even closed his eyes for several long moments, before snapping them open once again, to stare into the small flame.

It seemed to Shan that Ulfiir must have forgotten them for a time, for his eyes became misty and unfocused. It was as if he looked back across a great distance, through the thick folds of time, back to a lost era, to an age spoken of only in the heroic tales and legends of minstrels. Ulfiir sat there in silence, stroking his gray beard with knobby fingers for several long *mira*. The soft crackle of the lamp was the only sound that stirred the stillness of the room.

Shan glanced anxiously across the table at his friend. Weeson simply shrugged, then looked away, seemingly studying the creases on the back of his left hand. Shan's gaze drifted once again about the great hall. His eyes came to rest on a dusty pennon dangling from a rafter overhead. The scene depicted a mighty warrior in shining battle armor, a glittering sword held poised over the head of a vanquished foe, some dark and dreadful creature spilled before him in the dust. The age-old threads were dull and faded, and the slight ruffle in the fabric gave it the appearance of movement in the flickering light.

Ulfiir abruptly cleared his throat and blinked the mist from his eyes at last. He looked at both of them meaningfully. "There are strange things happening in the world all around us," he croaked. He held a thin hand to his lips and cleared his throat again. "There are rumors of war in the east, great unrest in the south, Weeson, just as you've said. The west is already becoming a turmoil of fighting and killing. There is no trust among the nations of the world any longer, largely due to the twisted ploys of a devilish mind who cleverly orchestrates these ever-increasing deeds of suspicion and mistrust." He gazed at Weeson through his bushy white brows as if to confirm what he had said. The captain nodded. "Dark threats of war descend on us from every side. Nation is at war with nation. Countries that have been staunch friends for centuries are now the bitterest of enemies. Even now, armies of strange creatures creep ever closer, tightening their clutches around us in a growing sea of darkness. And we will soon find ourselves, like a small island, under siege to the swelling tides of war."

Shan found himself swallowing with a dry throat.

"Okay," he said at last, "I'm not disputing that some of these things are happening. That much is obvious, even to me." Shan swung his face from one of them to the other. "But what I don't understand is how I fit into this tragic little tale." Ulfiir opened his dry lips to speak, but Shan cut him off abruptly with a wave of his hand. "I mean," the boy went on quickly, "what has all this talk of war and darkness got to do with me? What are these things, these kurgoths, and why would they be hunting me? What have I done?"

"All good questions, my boy," the old man began. He lifted an eyebrow in Weeson's direction and fingered the small, metallic object in his palm. He sighed. "When you were brought to us long ago, Shan, I knew this day would come, and I dreaded it. I did not know then how I would tell you, just what I would say. And I still do not." He tried once again to clear his throat.

Shan rose quickly from the table and paced away, suddenly angry.

Daryl Hanson

"Why didn't you tell me any of this before tonight? Was I too much of a child to understand?" He turned to face Ulfiir. "I still don't understand. Its like a riddle game, but I haven't got a clue how it all goes."

"I . . . I'm sorry for that," Ulfiir said with a bow of his head. Weeson looked on impassively, a dark cast over his face. "I knew it would be difficult, but it *was* necessary."

"Was it?" Shan stalked about nervously. "I have reached seventeen summers and not a word of this before tonight. Not an inkling!" He fidgeted with the side of his britches. "Just who are you protecting? Me or you?" Startled, Ulfiir opened his mouth to reply. "And just how long did you intend to keep me in the dark?" Shan went on in a rush. He threw up his hands in exasperation. "Shards! I'm still in the dark." He hopped over to the old man, a finger held out accusingly. "If that thing hadn't come looking for me, if it hadn't found me tonight, how long would you have waited to bring this out? How long would you have waited to tell me? How long?" Ulfiir sat in silence, unable to meet the young man's blazing eyes. Shan began to pace once again, then stopped with an abrupt whirl. "And I suppose now you're going to tell me that you're really not even my uncle?"

"No, my boy," Ulfiir said softly, "I'm not your uncle." Darkness suddenly clouded the boy's handsome features. "I'm sorry."

Shan dashed away and slumped down heavily on the bench of a neighboring table. He tossed his arms over its rough, wooden surface and buried his face. Weeson could see that Ulfiir was shaken by the ordeal, but was somewhat startled when he saw a river of tears trickle down the old man's wrinkled cheeks.

"No, I am not your uncle, Shan," Ulfiir told the boy in a shaky voice, "but I have loved you as one."

Shan got up quickly from the neighboring table and ran to him. They embraced each other fiercely for several long moments. Ulfiir patted the boy on the back before they eventually broke apart, each wiping a trail of moisture from his eyes with the back of a hand.

"Now, now," Ulfiir began, still dabbing lines of tears from his face, "we need to figure out what we are going to do with you." He sniffled softly and gave Shan a meaningful look. "And we shall try to answer all your questions. At least the ones we can." He reached out and held Shan's eyes with a soft touch under his chin. "Fair enough?"

The elven boy nodded. "Fair enough," he said, and Ulfiir gave his head an affectionate shake. The lad resumed his seat at the table, folding his hands quietly before him. Weeson glanced over and gave him a wink.

"It's a long story, Shan, to be sure." Ulfiir's voice was firm once again. "And I'm not certain where to begin, or indeed, even how much I know myself." Shan cocked an eyebrow, giving him a skeptical appearance. Ulfiir caught the look out of the corner of his eye, and changed his approach. "Shan," he stated flatly, leveling his gray eyes on the boy, "the main reason I haven't spoken to you about any of this before tonight, I suppose, was because of your own safety. The less you knew, the less you had to hide. Unfortunately," he said, looking up at the boy's ears, "there was no way to hide your true elven ancestry completely."

"But I'm proud of my heritage," Shan shot out.

"And well you should be, my boy." Ulfiir held up a wrinkled hand. "Well you should. It's just that an elven youth growing up in a human village is especially hard to keep quiet. It's not an easy thing to conceal, even in such an out of the way place like Draydin. And secrecy is something we have so desperately needed." The old man rubbed at his lips. He looked closely at the boy. "We have done the best we could without locking you away in a cell. But people are prone to talk, and even those casual remarks are often overheard, then repeated. And then the rumors spread." Shan was thoroughly confused, and his look showed it. "That little incident you had in Branby a few yehrin back nearly did us in." Ulfiir leveled his gaze on the elven youth. "It really stirred up the pot, shall we say."

Shan twisted his face into a frown. "You mean, the brawl?" he queried, softly.

The old man looked quietly at the young Elf at his side, and gave him a nod. He sat back in his chair with a sigh, his old eyes staring into the sputtering flames of the oil lamp. "It really was such a delicate matter," he muttered through his beard. "I never should have let you go. I should have forced you to remain here." He reached out and stroked Shan's arm. "Word of that scuffle between an elven boy and a bunch of angry humans must have filtered out from all those attending the fair, and somehow it found its way to those anxiously searching for just such bits of news."

Ulfiir settled himself deeper into his chair. He meticulously adjusted his robe, smoothing out folds and wrinkles with deep care as he tried to arrange his thoughts in logical order. His eyes drifted to the emblems of war overhead. When the old man did not speak at once, Shan tilted his head back and studied the network of crisscrossing beams in the high ceiling. His quick eyes leapt from helmet and spear to the dull gleam of sputtering light playing delicately from the polished surface of a lacquered shield.

"Vandikar!" The word was barely a whisper.

Shan nodded his head slowly, his gaze falling from the axes and swords, shields and lances, to alight on the old man's wizened features. The ancient eyes twinkled in the feeble glow. "Spoken of in the ballads, and in the Holy Book, as the legendary, long lost home of the Elves. Yet it was abandoned long ago, forsaken for yehrin beyond count, considered now only just a pitiful haunt of desolation. A place fit for no one. It was destroyed at the hand of Muurdra." Shan waited breathlessly until Ulfiir's smoky eyes shifted to him once again. He felt a sudden tingling touch that began at the tips of his ears, then quickly spread down his spine like a violent chill. His heart somehow felt it had been squeezed. He clasped one hand to his chest and he fought painfully to breathe.

"What is it, lad?" Weeson asked, leaning across the table toward him. "Are you alright?" Ulfiir twisted in his chair and stared out into the darkness of the hall, his eyes narrowing.

"I don't know . . ." Shan began, his face masked in concentration. Then, "Listen!"

Weeson sprang to his feet, one hand unconsciously seeking the hilt of his sword. A faint scream broke the silence. He snatched up the bow he had set aside upon entering the room.

"The village is under attack!" Shan cried out suddenly as he jumped up from the bench.

Weeson was off and running instantly, the sword leaping from its scabbard with a rasping of steel. Shan started to bolt after him, but skidded abruptly to a halt as the old man's call echoed among the rafters.

"No, Shan!" Ulfiir shouted. "It's you that they want!"

Ulfiir clamped bony hands on the table and pushed himself up out of the cushioned chair. The small object he had caressed in his hand skittered across the well worn surface. He scooped it up in an instant and turned for the door at the back of the hall. "This way!" he cried. Shan looked anxiously after Weeson, but the man had already melted from sight. The dwindling sound of his running feet was lost amid the growing chaos of screams and clattering weapons in the outer halls. Ulfiir stopped at a veil of blackness that led back into the kitchens, and whirled. "Come on, boy!" he called with an urgent wave of his hand.

Shan stood momentarily in indecision, glanced once more in the direction Weeson had taken, and then dashed quickly across the room after the old man. *Where is he going?* he thought in a moment of panic. He swept up the small oil lamp from the table as Ulfiir turned and vanished into the gloomy alcove. The lamp sputtered wildly at the sudden movement and nearly went out. The Elfling cupped one hand close to the protesting flames as he hurried after the rapidly retreating figure. The black cloak made the man hard to follow, but at one point he turned back for a moment, and the feeble pool of light glimmered faintly from his silvery hair and beard. Shan darted after his padding footsteps.

"Through here," he heard Ulfiir saying once he had nearly caught up with him. The old man turned sharply to the left, through a small preparation room, swung to the right through another small room and then left again. They hurried down a short corridor before bursting through a swinging door. The dark kitchens looked eerie to Shan in the feverishly shifting light as they maneuvered around crates and boxes and cupboards with long, faintly gleaming knives. A wild clatter of feet sounded hollowly from the main chamber behind them, then drew rapidly closer. Ulfiir paused at the end of the corridor and touched the wall lightly just above his head. Shan could not discern anything special about the spot. There was a small hiss of escaping air and a little door popped open before them. Shan could not contain his gasp of astonishment.

"I've never seen this before," he managed to say, "and I used to come back here to play quite a bit when I was younger."

"I know," Ulfiir said simply. "Only Weeson and I knew of it."

Ulfiir held the door open with the palm of one hand and indicated with a hasty nod that the boy should proceed him. The harsh sounds of stamping feet were suddenly close behind them.

"Quickly!" Ulfiir wheezed.

Shan shouldered past him. Ducking his head, he immediately found himself in a small, dark passage. The old man turned back toward the sounds of pursuit, leveled his skeletal hands, and shot a few bursts of shimmering, blue fire back through the kitchen. From within the threshold Shan could see little of what was happening, but he could hear the sudden startled cries, then afterwards a series of muffled screams. Ulfiir aimed one last blast of sparkling blue energy behind them. He bent his head and stepped quickly through the small doorway, to stand alongside the Elfling. He reached above his head and touched the wall on the inside, and the little door swung shut with a muffled snap.

They found themselves on a narrow, dirt landing. A dark hole yawned just beyond their boots where the soft glow of their lamp revealed the top rung of a ladder. They scurried down the frail wooden steps into a blanket of total darkness. The thin rungs were coated with a gritty film of mud and groaned with each step of their descent.

It was cool in the passageway. They could not make out any more sounds of their pursuers. Shan held out the lamp at arm's length and wrinkled up his nose at the sickly smell. The narrow, earthen walls were dank and glistened with some kind of colorless slime. Somewhere far ahead he heard the faltering *drip-drip-drip* of water.

"I'm sorry," Ulfiir's voice rasped in his ears. "But, under the circumstances, it was the best I could do on such short notice." The wriggling light of the lamp gave his grin a mischievous gleam. Shan was still too stunned to say anything. "Now, come quickly," he said, and slipped past the boy on the right, his dark robe scraping against the muddy wall. He hurried off down the passageway, daintily stepping over a half-buried root that crossed the path.

They walked on without speaking for some time. Only the heavy sound of their breathing, the scuff of their shoes on the damp, earthen floor and the occasional chorus of dripping water broke the heavy stillness. After they had traveled for quite a while, the floor sloped downwards for about a hundred paces, leveled off for perhaps twice that distance, then began to rise again slowly. When the passage flattened out once more Shan sensed they were near the end of the tunnel.

A blank wall suddenly loomed before them. A small flight of knobby steps ran up into the darkness and disappeared within a thick tangle of tree roots above. Ulfiir shuffled to a halt a few paces from the ladder and turned to face the boy. He placed both hands on the youth's shoulders and looked deeply into his eyes. Shan still held the oil lamp cupped in his palm and the light played mysteriously from the wrinkled face hovering near him. "This opens out into the middle of the forest," the old man told him. "Hide yourself as best you can. Make for Finger Rock in the clearing, you know the one. Get there by dusk tomorrow night. Someone will meet you there. Is that understood?"

Shan drew back slightly in disbelief. "You're not coming with me?" he asked, a knot suddenly welling up in his throat.

"No, my boy, I cannot," Ulfiir told him softly. "I must go back and see what I can do for the others, but I had to make sure you were safe first." His eyes glittered strangely in the wavering light. "Besides, it was only given to me to keep you safe until the time was upon us, then to see you off on the first leg of your journey."

"Journey?" Shan's voice cracked.

Ulfiir nodded solemnly.

"I'm sorry for the suddenness of all this. I haven't had time to explain any of this properly," the old man said, a note of genuine sorrow in his tone. "I really should have warned you ahead of time. But things did not work out as I had planned. Events came upon us much sooner than I had hoped, or expected." He wet his lips as he narrowed his twinkling eyes on the boy. "Perhaps its best this way. No long drawn-out farewells." He took the lamp from Shan's limp fingers and set it behind him on the wet stones of the passage wall. He slid his worn hands down the boy's shoulders and firmly gripped at Shan's own hands. "Make for Redhaven. Find Arris Junn. He will be able to help you, be able to answer all the things that I could not." Ulfiir pulled the youth close and gave him a rough hug. "I will miss you very much, my boy."

Things were going far too fast for Shan. He couldn't dispel the painful knot in his chest. He suddenly felt helpless and very, very vulnerable. He pulled back from the old man's embrace. "You can't just leave me," he choked out.

"I must go," Ulfiir told him softly. "Do not be angry. Our destinies lie on two different paths. Mine is winding down and yours is just now beginning. Good luck and may Athiliel keep you ever in his care." He embraced the boy once again then took out the small object he had been clutching in his palm. "Take this," he said as he pressed it into Shan's hands. "It will guide you when you desperately need it," he said, to ease the questioning look the Elfling shot at him. Shan glared down into the palm of his hand. The light spun in little rainbows from a curiously shaped medallion coiled in a fine, gold chain. The dark metal was somehow familiar to him.

"But . . ."

"Now, you must go!" Ulfiir said, firmly. He clamped Shan's fingers tightly shut around the small figure and purposefully spun him about. "Be careful," he called as Shan began to climb the ragged steps, numbly. "Trust no one. And watch out for gorguls. You must avoid their filthy clutches at all costs!"

Shan slipped the medallion into one of his pockets with his left hand and wiped tears from his eyes with the other. Ulfiir climbed up a few steps after him and touched a spot on a chipped wood panel. As Shan watched, a door appeared in the blank wall before him and hissed open. Ulfiir shielded the lamp with the folds of his robe so that it would not shine out like a beacon through the trees of the forest. He clutched at Shan's hand one more time, then pushed him out into the dark, chill air. "Good-bye!" he whispered. "May Athiliel guide you."

Shan turned for one last glimpse of the old man, but the door had already shut behind him. He found himself facing the wide trunk of a large tree. Startled, he reached out and touched the rippled bark in disbelief. The stiff, rough furrows scraped skin from his fingertips. Shan pressed the trunk firmly once, but to no avail. "Good-bye, Uncle," he breathed, after a few moments, his words little more than a croak. Then, stunned, he turned and walked off numbly into the night.

He was alone.

– 4 –
Under A Pale Moon
[13th of Kaligath, 4534 C.R.]

Shan looked down upon the rock in the clearing. Tall and slender, like a needle of stone, it thrust out of the thick, lumpy grass. It looked like a smooth, yellowish-white finger pointing at the sky and seemed strangely out of place in the quiet circle of open ground. It was almost as if a giant had reached down with one enormous fist and torn a ring of trees loose from the forest soil in a mighty scoop, leaving the spot barren of growth, save for thriving tangles of grassy weeds and roots. Perhaps then the giant had used the clearing as a target for his great, stone-tipped spear. But after casting it into the bald patch with tremendous effort, he had wandered off and left it unclaimed. The thick shaft of wood had long since decayed, returning to the soil from which it had sprung, yet the chipped stone spear blade remained, silent and unmovable, a lonely sentinel standing as a warning to visitors who might tread the dark paths of the forest unwisely.

Shan quietly brushed a branch from his face, spitting softly at the leaf that caught in his mouth. He shifted his position upon the smooth, fat branch he had been straddling, sliding closer to the broad trunk of the tree.

It was nearly dusk. Shadows were lengthening quickly in the clearing. Twisted stumps and shifting leaves weaved jagged patterns of dark green and gray. The last burnt gold rays of the sun played brilliantly for just a moment among the topmost branches of the trees as they danced in the soft sway of the breeze. Then the intense streaks were gone as the sun sank away from him.

Shan watched the clearing through broad leaves.

Thinking strongly of Ulfiir and the sudden departure from his home—*escape* was really more like it— brought the sting of tears to his eyes and a painful swell to his throat. *How are they doing?* he wondered. *Is the village still standing? Has anyone been hurt or—killed?* Dreadful thoughts lanced through his brain. His heart ached to know what had happened to everyone as horrible flashes of the charred, smoking ruins of Draydin and the sprawled figures of villagers lying face down in pools of mud and blood haunted his mind. He imagined thick swarms of black flies sinking lower over the trees and alighting on the twisted corpses to feed on the slaughter. And then he saw the carrion birds, dark feathered *jackards* with their enormous wingspan, flapping downward into what was left of the settlement to pick through the mess. "No!" Shan screamed, and the echo of his own cry bounced wildly back at him out of the trees. Startled by his own outburst, he bit at his lip and sat bolt upright. "Let's hope there aren't any unfriendly ears around to hear that," he castigated himself, under his breath. "Fool!"

He blinked away the moisture from his eyes and swallowed hard several times. His mouth was dry and tasted like sand. His stomach rumbled softly, and he unconsciously sought to quell the noise with a cupped hand across his belly. He winced suddenly in pain. Delicately, he reached one hand to his left hip and gingerly felt about his makeshift bandage. The cloth was caked with dried blood and the wound still burned if he moved too much, or too suddenly, in any direction.

Shan looked down from his vantage point. He made a slow circuit of the clearing with a steady turn of his head before scanning the surrounding trees on all sides. Shan's sharp, elven eyes could detect no signs of movement in the gathering twilight. Once the sun had dropped below the edge of the trees the shadows grew haphazardly across the area into long ghosts. The gloom quickly thickened and spread out under the murmuring branches.

The sudden screech of an owl was startling, and nearly pitched him from the tree. He grabbed desperately for a branch and scraped his arm in the process. He slid backwards on the limb but finally managed to catch a handful of creepers to pull himself back onto his perch. The flap of wings overhead forced him to duck. The creature settled on a branch hardly out of his reach. It twisted its head around to face him, ruffling long feathers upon its neck ring. The little thing cooed in his direction. Blinking large, glittering eyes several times, it danced about on the limb, snapped its wings twice, and was still.

Shan was frozen to the spot, his mouth hanging half-open as he clung fiercely to his roost.

The owl regarded him quizzically. It tilted its head to the side and blinked. The dark orbs of its eyes disappeared for a moment as it winked once again, then glittered palely at him in the faltering light. Its head rotated in a half-circle, paused there for a moment, then swung back. The owl continued to watch the boy as it shifted position once again, the claws scraping on the rough bark. It uttered another throaty rumble and then launched itself from the branch with a spring. It shot through the trees, twisting its body back and forth expertly in the air to avoid drooping limbs that rustled softly in the breeze. Shan watched it circle the clearing and disappear somewhere over the trees, mingling with the growing darkness in the east.

The sky had paled to pink on the horizon, then quickly deepened to streaks of burnt orange and midnight blue. Shan arched his neck and shoulders as tiredness seeped into his body. He yawned, blinking back fatigue. *They'll never find me if I fall asleep in the trees,* he thought. He slumped back against the thick trunk, stifling another yawn, and forced his eyes open wide.

* * * * *

The Elfling had walked for some time in the dark forest before he had gotten his bearings. He listened for sounds of struggle in Draydin, but there was nothing. He wasn't even sure in which direction it lay. The absolute silence was unnerving, and the mosaic of shadow upon shadow played uneasily on his fears. He tripped and stumbled several times on tangled roots and stumps of fallen trees. He fell heavily on his face, painfully forcing the air from his bruised chest and lungs. He lay groaning for several *mira*. He sat up at last, blinking sparks from the edges of his vision. He rubbed mud from his cheek and pulled twigs from his hair with a stifled yelp. He could feel wetness from the ground seeping through his britches. He grasped onto a low-hanging branch, pulled himself to his feet. He wavered for a moment, then trudged stubbornly on, heading in what he hoped was due south. He picked at his clothes as he walked. He could feel himself covered in dirt and slimy, half-rotting leaves.

He had not gone far when something tore at his leg. He screamed, and started to run. It clamped onto his foot and bore him to the ground, splashing his face in a large puddle of cold, mucky water. He came up screaming and sputtering as foul water dribbled into his mouth. He pulled wildly but the thing would not yield, and he could feel a sudden bite on his ankle through the soft leather of his boot. He yanked and kicked and pulled and twisted until he collapsed. Still the thing held him firmly. Shan fell back in exhaustion, his breath coming in wrenching spasms, his chest throbbing like a maddened drum.

He lay for a while, panting, waiting for the thing to spring upon him anew. He looked up at what he could see of the stars, at the stray wisps of swiftly scudding clouds. He wondered when the end would come as the fire in his throat slowly subsided. He drew on his foot experimentally, but it still would not budge. His heart quieted.

Shan finally sat up, listening.

He braced himself against a rock. He couldn't hear the growl of a wild animal, nor the stealthy slither of a snake. He blinked at the darkness.

Daryl Hanson

Tentative fingers probed along his ankle. Then he started laughing, a deep, racking howl that sent him doubling over his curled-up knees. Still chuckling, he drew his dagger and began sawing at a thick root that had gotten wedged around his boot. His attempts at twisting free had only tightened it against his ankle and driven its thorny spines more painfully into his leg through the soft leather.

"This is foolishness!" he told himself as he scrambled to his feet. "Stumbling about like this in the dark, I could wind up with a broken leg." He took a few steps gingerly. "Or possibly even break my neck!"

He stretched a kink out in his back and carefully felt his way to the trunk of a large tree. He found a niche in a mound of tangled roots, and crawled in. He fashioned a bed out of dried leaves that he scooped together with his cold fingers. He curled up as best he could and stared up at the sky. A few faint stars twinkled at him from the misty darkness. His muscles ached and throbbed, and started to stiffen as sleep avoided him. He rolled over restlessly onto his side for a few moments, then rolled onto his back once again. A stiff clump of root stabbed him along the spine and forced him to shimmy around to find relief. He lay for a long while, thinking in jumbled snatches about gorguls, kurgoths, some sort of Evil One who was apparently trying to kill him, and a strange old man, who was not his uncle after all, that he somehow loved.

When Shan finally awoke, he was cold and stiff. He crawled from his refuge among the roots and leaves, and then stood up painfully. He rubbed a fist over first one shoulder, then the other, while he attempted to study his surroundings. Broad beams of light slanted down through the leafy ceiling and splashed the forest floor in rosy-brown color. Pale traces of mist clung, here and there, among the great twisting trunks. *No wonder I had so much trouble walking about in the darkness,* Shan thought to himself as he looked around. Many of the large roots twined in and out of the ground like serpents, some of which were nearly chest high.

All at once, Shan realized he was hungry. He'd been up most of the night and hadn't eaten since much earlier the previous evening. It was now fairly late in the morning, he could tell, by the angle of the dusty streams of sunlight. He felt a queer rippling in his stomach and then an angry rumble, like the roar of a lion, burst through the folds of his tunic. He clutched one hand tightly to his middle as another rumble gurgled from his insides. He opened the catch on his belt and pulled it a notch tighter. Amid a continual flow of growls and grumbles, he started off.

He munched on berries where he could find them growing wild in dense thickets scattered throughout the forest floor. There were many different varieties, some of which he wasn't even sure were edible, but he ate them anyway. He continued to pop them in his mouth, a handful at a time, wiping the sweet juice from his face with the back of his hand as he chewed. The first few times he paid dearly for his theft. Sharp thorns, hidden by the broad swath of overlapping leaves, tore at the fleshy parts of his hands and arms. He withdrew them instantly, sucking at the wounded members. Later, Shan learned to flip the prickly vines back with a small stick in considerable ease, snap a bunch of berries from their stems with a little jerk and continue on his way, munching almost instantly on his prize. He didn't even need to break his stride in some cases. Although they weren't very filling, the berries managed to assuage the brunt of his gnawing hunger for a time. He continued moving through the undergrowth, always working his way south, picking an occasional small fruit as he walked.

He had been tramping along for a few ahrin when he spotted a familiar sight. He plopped down next to a tree which had two trunks. Their twisted roots were a jungle of dried leaves and moss. The boles shot skyward, twining together, weaving forever back and forth and around each other till they were lost in the leafy green shroud of the forest roof. Shan craned his neck and peered up into the fuzzy light as great splashes of sunlight streamed through the whispering surface.

It had been nicknamed the *Lovers* by the men of the village, Shan recalled. It always sent them off chuckling when they passed this way.

With a sour grunt he realized that he must have been traveling more to the southeast last night as he stumbled about in the darkness, for he should not have run into that particular landmark at all on his way to the clearing. *Oh, well,* he thought to himself, *at least now I know exactly where I am.* After he had rested for a few mira he struggled to his feet and started off once again. He angled slightly west to compensate for his error, still occasionally stuffing berries into his mouth as he trudged along. He licked his fingers often and wiped at his face. Feeling much more confident of himself, he began to hum. It wasn't long before he even broke into a full song.

> *"With a hip-hip-hey and a hip-hip-ho*
> *I set my steps and it's off I go*
> *A fiddle-Dee-Dee and a fiddle-Dee-do*
> *It won't be long 'fore I get back home."*

But with that he stopped short, the sudden realization of what he'd just been singing hitting him full force. He sank emotionally to his knees on the path. "Will I ever get back home?" he wondered aloud, his breath a puff of mist before his eyes. The air somehow seemed to turn chill, and the forest felt quiet and still. Gray sunlight flooded down through the trees as the sky was momentarily obscured by scudding clouds. He looked around himself slowly, warily. Behind every shadow there seemed to lurk potential danger. He had been entirely too careless up to that point, he realized. Traipsing around, making a lot of noise and singing. He knelt there, listening for the longest time, scarcely daring to breathe. At last he climbed to his feet and started off quietly through the trees. But there was no more singing, no more enjoying the trek. He just closely scrutinized the bushes, the trees, the sky, for any signs of movement and he listened carefully for faint traces of sound on the wind.

In mid-afternoon, Shan broke through the tangle of woods and found himself in the large clearing Ulfiir had specified to him. He was early, he knew, and there was no one in sight. He gazed up for a moment at the tall column of stone standing almost exactly in the middle of the wide, flat expanse.

Suddenly, there was a wild trampling and snorting in the brush on his left. A large, hairy *bork* tore out of the cover and shot towards the boy, bellowing, its wicked little eyes narrowing upon him. Shan bolted into the clearing, nearly stumbling within his first five steps. He dashed for Finger Rock, zigzagging wildly, and he could barely stay out of the maddened animal's reach. The curved tusks sliced at the air as its sharp hooves tore up patches of earth in frantic pursuit. It squealed with rage, sweeping its head at him in quick, vicious strokes.

Shan made it to the pillar, but one quick attempt at scaling it brought him only scuffed and bleeding fingers. It was not smooth or polished by any means, but there were no immediate spurs or cuts in it to serve him sufficiently as handholds. At least, not on this side. He immediately started to circle the rock, looking desperately for something to grasp. He caught his foot over a patch of weeds and he tumbled heavily to the gritty soil. He scampered quickly to his feet, a blur of movement tugging at the corner of his eye. He had to leap aside as the maddened animal charged. It thundered by, one wicked tusk ripping a burning line across his hip. He screamed in pain and clutched at his side. Warm blood flowed in a widening stain across his torn shirt. Shan pushed himself away from the stone and stumbled toward the trees. The bellowing of the *bork* was close at his heels.

He dove to his right and rolled. The humped animal whooshed by like a dark streak, its tusks flashing within a finger length of his face. He scrambled up quickly and ran, angling rapidly away from the angry terror in another direction. It tore at the ground with its hooves, twisting and sliding in its haste to reach him. It snorted and squealed, and clawed quickly after him. Shan continued to zigzag across the scrubby clumps of grass and weeds, careful now of his footing over the uneven surface. He dove and rolled when he felt the whistle of its breath too close behind him. His side pulsed with heat, burning fiercely with each movement, and his legs felt weak and unsteady.

Shan leaped for the limb of a nearby tree as the boar snapped at his heels. His hands slipped as a chunk of bark came loose, but he managed to grab quickly at another branch and swing himself up to safety. He hastily scrambled higher before looking down. The *bork* stamped and squealed and butted its head against the trunk. Steam shot from its dark snout in little jets and its sides heaved with each labored breath. Its tiny eyes were bloodshot as it peered up at him through the matted hair of its ugly face. Shan waved weakly to taunt it in his small victory, then grabbed painfully for his side. The boar grunted several times, snorted at the dust and trotted off in pursuit of easier prey.

Shan watched it wind its way through the trees. When he could see it no longer he breathed a sigh of relief and went to work on his hip. He ripped several strips of cloth from the hem of his tunic. He wadded some of these and placed them along the wound in order to staunch the trickle of blood. Then he wound several more around his waist and secured them with a knot. Once this was completed he pulled himself higher into the tree, to a leafy place that afforded him better cover than the relatively open lower branches. He sat down where the interlacing branches started to thicken, straddling a broad limb.

He peered down into the clearing and waited.

* * * * *

Shan woke sometime later with a start.

He scraped his cheek on the rough bark. He afforded himself a low curse before yawning. He blinked several times to clear the sleepiness from his eyes. He shook his head, scattering the lingering cobwebs. "Must have fallen asleep," he mumbled to himself.

The Elfling looked down into the clearing, muffling another yawn with the back of his hand. It was well past dusk by now and had actually

Daryl Hanson

grown quite dark. Neither of the two moons was up as yet, and even with his sharp elven eyes he could not distinguish one blotch of shadows from another. Overhead, banks of trailing clouds swept swiftly across the dark expanse of the sky. A cool wind stirred the branches, their gentle creak the only sound filling the broad stretch of forest. Shan brushed back the hair from his eyes and quietly changed his position on the thick limb. He glanced down, wincing slightly at his movement. He was probably a little more than six or seven kora from the ground, but in the darkness it could have been a hundred. He couldn't see a thing.

The sudden snap of a twig rifled sharply through the air.

Shan's ears immediately began to tingle. He almost called out, to let the people from the village know where he was hiding, but the cry died in his throat. An overwhelming sense of unease tickled down his back. He pressed himself hard against the bole of the tree and tightened his grip on the branch with both hands and feet. His breathing came in a hushed whisper. He gulped once softly but then remained perfectly still.

From the far side of the clearing, faintly at first, then with a gathering strength, came the gradual approach of stamping feet. *Too many to be from Draydin,* Shan thought realistically. *Doesn't quite sound like a search party, either.* The snapping and trampling of underbrush grew steadily closer. Shan thought he heard the murmur of voices too, thick, gruff voices. As the sound grew louder and louder he realized it had an odd rhythm, like some sort of singing or chanting, only he could not quite understand the words. *Perhaps a marching cadence,* he thought, but it was unlike anything he'd heard in his time in the village.

The pale sickle of the smaller moon drifted up over the tops of the trees and sent a feeble, reddish-yellow spray of light into the clearing. Almost instantly the soft glimmer was veiled by the swift flight of rushing clouds. The milky spire of Finger Rock was washed with a fuzziness that brightened and dimmed then brightened again as the clouds swept quickly past.

Shan scanned the far line of trees intently. Slowly, amid the crackling of roots and twigs, and the stomp of heavy feet, he could make out a line of large, hunched shapes weaving and lurching along to the strange beat. Every few strides Shan heard the ring of metal as some gloomy form struck at something in its path, a root, a bush or a low-hanging branch with a bite of steel. The string of marching figures suddenly burst into the clearing, and Shan, some fifty korads away, was startled at what he saw. They were roughly man-sized, walked about on two limbs, yet that was where his definition stopped. He counted twenty large, broad shapes as they drew closer.

The creatures fanned out as they swung in the direction of Finger Rock, and halted in the middle of the wide, barren swath, their rough chanting dying instantly away with a short, guttural shout from the first creature in line. He spun about and pointed a huge arm at two or three others, grunting orders in short, raspy commands. The hissing speech sounded somehow reptilian to him as the Elfling struggled to see what it was they were doing. The three brutes pounded off in different directions. Shan could hear the stomp of metal boots as they scattered. The rest of the company threw themselves down on the lumpy turf with a jingle of their weapons, broad, flat scimitars by the looks of them.

Shan would have tightened the grip on his roost if that were possible. His heart pounded in his chest and his mouth felt like it held wads of cotton. A dribble of cold sweat ran down the back of his neck. He fought the urge to sneeze and cautiously lifted a hand to rub at his nose, hardly daring to breathe.

From this distance Shan could not get a clear look at the things, especially in Kiara's fuzzy half-glow. What feeble moonlight there was felt masked by layers of rapidly rushing clouds. The things were little more than silhouettes to him, stocky figures vaguely discernible from the hardened earth. Though somewhat short in stature the creatures had thick, muscular bodies, broad across the chest and back. Their long arms dangled down to their knees and seemed oddly out of proportion to their squat frames. Their heads were large and heavy, and drooped a little between the shoulders. A pale sliver of moonlight peeked intermittently through the sweeping, dark clouds, glimmering dully from their large eyes and the long, curving scimitars draped at their sides.

With a sudden growling of his stomach, Shan became terrified he would be discovered. He tightened his belly against the trunk of the tree and hushed at it under his breath. He glanced fearfully into the clearing, but he could see no sign that he had been heard.

Most of the strange soldiers sat huddled in groups of three or four. Shan could hear them hissing at each other in a hoarse, guttural tongue as they laughed and talked amongst themselves. A few of them jabbed one of their fellows in the ribs and then cackled roughly at his expense. The burly fellow spit out something that was a half-snarl, half-hiss, then angrily edged away from them. The others laughed again in uproarious fits, hammering their large fists into the turf and cracking their metal gauntlets loudly together.

A single harsh word from their leader hushed the entire squad into silence. It stalked away from those sprawled on the matted ground, its thick-set arms jammed upon its hips. The dark, muzzle-like face scanned the surroundings. As the coarse sounds of their jesting commenced all over again, the officer whirled around and cut them off with a sharp hiss. The angry figure stood glaring over them long enough for the order to sink in this time. The leader finally spun on its heels and marched off. After a span of several heartbeats the troops picked up their conversations once again, this time in much more subdued tones.

Shan caught his breath as one of the sentries that had been sent out circled back through the trees, crashing by directly below him. The elven youth clamped his eyelids tightly shut and held his breath. He swallowed fiercely. The crunching steps withdrew rapidly and Shan mustered enough courage to pop one eye open.

The bulky figure ran up to the leader and gave a stiff salute. It croaked a report in a string of thick coughs and hisses. Trails of mist clouded its face as it spun around to indicate something off to the side with a clawed fist. The officer dismissed the scout with a rigid nod and turned to converse with the other two spies as they scrambled up moments later. They gurgled and rasped on together for a few mira, pointing frequently in various directions with their long, thick arms. No sooner had they finished and backed away than the officer growled out an order. The entire squad dragged themselves to their feet and hurriedly formed up into their marching column. With a final hiss from the commander, they lumbered off, almost instantly resuming their low, slithering chant. They plowed into the trees at right angles to their earlier line of march and were soon out of sight, swallowed easily by the leafy darkness of the forest. Shan could hear them for some time, though, crashing and stomping toward the north, toward Draydin.

The elven boy blew out air in a rush. He fell back and collapsed with the broad limb of the tree squarely between his shoulder blades. He took several long, deep breaths, expelling each like the rush of wind escaping from a blacksmith's bellows. And, as if to accent the situation, his stomach grumbled loudly. He lost track of the time as he lay back against the trunk of the tree, shaken and weak with hunger, his side still burning from the boar's attack.

Sometime later, Shan sat up quickly.

Someone was coming his way, and whistling as he approached. The boy blinked into the darkness, listening intently. It came from a long way off and sounded like the plaintive call of a bird. The shrill cry echoed oddly through the trees. At first he thought it was on his left, then he thought it came from the right, then it sounded as if it drifted lazily from both directions. It grew steadily in volume until it was almost beneath him. It seemed to invite an answer. Shan wet his lips with the tip of his tongue and whistled a feeble response. It came out as a sort of soft, mournful wail. The other voice mimicked his call, sounding somehow like a wounded bird in flight. Suddenly a rich voice called to him out of the darkness below.

"Shan?" The boy whistled again as he began to climb down. "Shan," beckoned the voice to him out of the gloom, "where are you?"

"Up here," he cried, slipping and sliding from branch to branch as he descended. He dropped painfully to the ground and slumped against the scratchy bark.

Bindar materialized out of the inky night and knelt at his side. Under the trees the pale swath of moon revealed little more than a lump of darkness with hands. "Been waiting long?" he asked lightheartedly. The man swung the cloak from his shoulders and offered it to Shan, who had begun to shiver silently in the chill night air. He gave the boy a friendly shake. Shan winced painfully at the touch. "Weeson," Bindar called out softly. "Over here. Hurry, he's hurt."

Two other shapes quietly slipped up and gathered around the tree.

"Shan, are you alright?" Weeson's face was a mask of darkness. He reached out and laid a hand on the boy's arm.

"Yeah, I'm fine," Shan had to admit. "Had a run-in with a *bork*, though. I'd have to say he got the better end of it." He touched the wrapping at his hip with numbing fingers and felt a fresh trickle of wetness inside his tunic. "I'll be alright, but I think I'm starving." As if to emphasize his statement, Shan's belly gurgled loudly.

Shan could not see Weeson's grin as the captain slipped off his pack and unlatched it with a flick of the wrist. "We'll take care of the important things first," the man said as he delved into the flap, "then we'll patch you up later." He pulled out a lump wrapped in a thin cloth and pressed the wedge into Shan's hands.

"Thanks," Shan muttered as he hurriedly peeled away the wrappings and tore into the cheese. He hardly chewed, tearing off large pieces with his teeth and swallowing great chunks at a time. Crumbs cascaded down his face and gathered in his lap. He greedily snatched them up and crammed them into his swollen mouth.

"Ho, slow down, boy!" the third man chided him. Shan looked up momentarily from his task. He could just make out Irion's profile, the hooked nose and the long, drooping moustache, as the man brushed the hood back from his face.

"I'm sorry," Shan mumbled between mouthfuls. "I found out pretty quick that berries just don't fill you up!" The three men laughed softly.

"Here," Bindar said, catching at the boy's hand and slapping a bulging wineskin into his palm with a slosh. The youth twisted the stopper from the leather bag and thrust the spigot between his teeth. He threw back his head and sucked noisily. Wild streams of *tanga* juice seeped from the corners of his mouth and dribbled down his throat. He lowered the sack long enough to stuff the last bit of cheese into his cheek, then upended it once again for another long draw. At last, he lowered the leather bottle and sank back against the tree. He wiped at his face with a dirty sleeve and belched.

"Such manners!" Irion did his best to imitate the husky tones of Madora, the plucky queen of Draydin's kitchens.

"Still hungry?" Weeson teased him. Shan's bashful silence gave him his answer.

"Oh!" Shan was suddenly excited. "There's a small company of strange men heading toward Draydin, only they weren't men. I don't know what they were!"

"Yes, I know," Weeson told him. "They're the reason we're late. We had to circle them to keep from being seen."

"Oh," Shan murmured. "What were they?"

"Those were gorguls, Shan," Bindar said after a moment.

"Gorguls?" the Elfling murmured. *Didn't Ulfiir mention them?*

"They're foul creatures from the far south, spawned by Muurdra and trained to be his soldiers. They're paid off in stolen gold to do his own black deeds." Shan could tell by the way Irion spit out the words that he had no love for them or their evil master.

"Now," said Weeson, reaching over, "let's see if we can do something about that nasty cut of yours."

The Long Trek Begins
[14th of Kaligath, 4534 C.R.]

The little company wound its way slowly through the trees. Gray streaks of light played down through the leaves, highlighting the fine dust in the air with a hazy glow.

Shan leaned forward in the saddle, stretching his back as he bobbed along. The small thorka pony shifted its weight suddenly and nearly sent him flying. He fumbled for the horn of the saddle then, grabbing firmly for the reins, sat back uneasily. The clasp at his neck had slipped and his cloak slid around till it was almost in front of him, flapping eagerly at his face. The closure began to tighten, nearly choking him. He fought with it for an embarrassing moment before finally getting the thing under control. He managed to throw the cloak back over his shoulder with a flourish.

When he looked up he realized with a relieved sigh that no one had even seemed to notice. He leaned back in the saddle and breathed easier. He adjusted the cloak and the loose clasp in a much more casual fashion, gave his thorka a tiny kick in the ribs to shorten the distance with the rider in front of him, and looked about himself with renewed interest.

Bindar led the little party on a large brown thorka, its entire right flank flecked with odd-shaped splotches. Irion drew in close behind, his prancing, gray stallion picking its way delicately among the roots and vines, its sharp, retractable claws snapping out wherever its footing was unsure. A dark, billowing tail lashed out at a small swarm of flies as it bent a long neck down to nip at some of the fine grass that grew in tiny clumps every few kora. Shan bounced along the trail on a small reddish-brown thorka with streaks of white running daintily through its thick mane. Weeson brought up the rear on a beautiful black stallion. Sleek and firm, it stamped regally along behind Shan, tirelessly stepping over rocks and stumps and roots. The six-legged animals were perfect for the rolling, uneven nature of the forest floor.

At a word from Weeson, Bindar brought his mount to rest at the top of a small rise. The others drew in alongside of him, their thorka tossing their heads back with a flurry of manes and snorting into the wind. The captain slid to the ground and walked to the edge of the mound, his animal's reins dangling free behind him. Weeson bent down on one knee, a skillful hand lightly moving among the small plants. He found some broken stems and the trampling of several steel-shod feet. His dark eyes trailed off to the left, in the direction the tracks indicated, perpendicular to their own, and stood up. He rubbed dust from the knee of his pants.

"They've already been through here," he said, turning to the others. "An ahr ago, perhaps two."

"Not far enough away, then," Irion grunted.

Weeson pointed off toward the dwindling marks, then curved his hand slowly around in front of them. "They might circle back; they're pretty tricky." He crossed to his thorka and pulled himself easily into the saddle. "I'm afraid we don't have the time for a rest." The leather stirrups squeaked softly as he swung about to look at Bindar. "I think I'll take the point for a while, if you don't mind." The other nodded and edged his mount out of the way as Weeson slipped past. The captain urged his stallion briskly down the slope. "We need to be cautious," he called out softly over his shoulder. The others fell into stride behind him, with Bindar dropping back to take the rear.

They rode on in silence for some time. The only sounds that reached them were the twittering of birds as they flitted among the branches, the soft clomp and sniffling of their thorka, the gentle wheeze of wind flapping softly at their cloaks and hair, and an occasional squeal or grunt from some small creature scurrying about in the underbrush. If it wasn't for the tenseness of the moment Shan would have thoroughly enjoyed himself. The chances for him to go out very far from the walls of Draydin had been few. He was allowed to tag along a couple of times on small trading visits with other nearby villages, but these had never been more than a day's journey in any direction, nor had he ever been allowed to wander off alone.

They angled west for several ahrin. The morning sun, now nearly halfway to its zenith, warmed their necks and arms where it peered through the lofty, green curtain. Shan wiped at a trickle of sweat on his forehead and began shedding his cloak. He rolled it up tightly and stuffed it in a pack on the right side of his saddle. He loosened the throat lacing on the front of his tunic, flapping the shirt several times as a fan.

Weeson topped another rise and reined in. His great thorka nickered faintly and sniffed at the air. The captain cocked his head and listened for a long moment, scanning the darkness through the trees on all sides. Satisfied, he started off again at last. "Let's make good time," Weeson called over his shoulder. He broke into a gallop, and the others followed quickly after him.

They rode hard for an ahr or two, dodging twisting tree trunks and stiff, claw-like branches that swayed and groped for them as they shot past. The small company raced up and down hillocks and slid down rocky ravines. They forded one small river and three smaller streams, each time stopping briefing to allow the animals a soothing drink. When the sun had climbed straight overhead, Weeson called a halt. His coal-black thorka stamped quietly as he swung about in the saddle and slid from its back. Shan gratefully wheeled his pony into a tight circle with the others. Stiffly, he pulled his legs from the stirrups and plopped to the mossy ground.

The hot rays of the sun baked down on their bodies, leaving them sweltering a bit and sticky with sweat. They flung themselves down on a tumble of rocks and struggled out of their outer tunics. Each of them wore a cool, white inner shirt, which they retained. They munched quietly on a cold meal of dried meat and small, crumbling cakes made of *lence*, a fine yellowish flour pounded from the tall stalks of grain grown in a few scattered meadows throughout the forest. The meal was washed down with a leather jug of cider, which they passed easily back and forth between them. Shan leaned against a boulder and had nearly dozed off when Weeson called them all back to their saddles. Within moments the last of the food was stuffed away and they were all up and riding once again, bumping and bounding along winding trails as elusive as they were narrow.

Already stiff, Shan was soon sore as well, in just a matter of mira. This was more riding than he had ever done in a single day, possibly in his whole life. The trees and rocks and twisting paths began to blur, and he found his mind wandering. *Who am I?* he wondered. *And why all the secrecy? I mean, where are we going? How are we going to get there? And what's going to happen once we arrive?* He looked around at the stark closeness of the trees. *If we arrive, that is.*

They stopped only one other time all that day before the swiftly descending darkness forced them to make camp. Shan dimly heard Weeson talking to Irion and Bindar as he dismounted. His back was unbelievably sore and tight, and he could feel the muscles in his legs begin to cramp. He straightened himself with effort, his fingers still curled as if they held a streamer of reins. *Is this what it's like to feel old?* He knuckled at a knot in his back as he hobbled to a stump and eased himself down onto its uneven, decaying surface with a grunt of pain.

"We can always lead the animals through the murky night if need be," the captain was saying, "but I don't feel that it's necessary, at least not yet."

Shan's mind was too numb to consider his words. He slipped from his mossy perch as Irion unslung the saddle packs from the thorka and dropped them on the leafy ground. The boy scooped up his own pack and threw himself down in a small rounded depression, the stiff leather satchel serving as a pillow. He managed to draw a wool blanket sluggishly from one of its pouches, for the night air had begun to turn cool. Though he was bone weary, Shan lay awake for some time, blinking up at the whispering treetops in the blackness above. Twinkling specks of light winked down at him through ragged gaps in the quickly shifting roof of clouds.

Bindar led the four animals to a nearby tree and tied them there by their long reins. Irion wandered off for a space, returning shortly with an armload of sticks and twigs. He dropped these in a pile near a large, flat rock and knelt to arrange them.

"I don't think a fire is wise tonight," Weeson called to him as he appeared from behind a thick trunk. "There are still too many things, too many unfriendly faces, wandering abroad tonight that we don't want to attract."

Irion nodded. "I suppose you're right," he said grimly. "I wouldn't want to wake up to some foul-faced devil trying to wedge a knife in my ribs." He gathered the bundle of wood in his arms and sauntered off, randomly dropping a twig here and tossing a stick there. He came back and thumped down next to Bindar a short time later.

They shared another cold meal between them, strips of dried meat and lumps of white cheese. They ate in silence, munching softly on their provisions and sipping sparingly from their canteens. No one seemed to want to talk and Shan found it hard to see their faces in the spreading gloom.

"You two go ahead and get some sleep," the captain told them as he propped himself against a boulder. "I'll take first watch. Irion, I'll rouse you in three ahrin. Bindar after that."

The two big men grunted in assent. They curled up among the roots, wrapping themselves in their light blankets. The deep, regular rhythm of their breathing told Shan that they were soon fast asleep. He rolled over softly and sighed, pulling up his own blanket to his chin. Sleep avoided him. He flapped and fidgeted, but couldn't seem to get comfortable. The brownish-red sickle of Kiara crept slowly into the sky, gradually melting to yellowish-gold as it lifted slowly across the heavens. Shan stared at it until sleep finally overtook him.

He woke once in the middle of the night with a start. He sat up, cold, the woolen blanket slipping down around his knees. He looked about, blinking. The forest was dark and quiet. Irion and Bindar were both still curled lightly in their sleep, nestled among the roots. The thorka stamped nearby with their faces together, a faint whisker of steam flaring at their nostrils. Weeson still sat with his back to a large rock, a silent, framed shadow. His head turned slowly from side to side, and he would pause long moments to listen, his eyes sparkling softly from within the dark hood of his cloak whenever they caught the pale glimmer of the moons.

Shan gazed up at the sky. The large, silvery-blue curve of Sheera had joined her sister in the black arch overhead, chasing the smaller moon gradually across the diamond-studded depths. The boy wrestled to his feet. He drew his folded cloak from the pouch of his pack, snuggled into it. He pulled the hood close about his face and carefully picked his way along the rocky soil. He sank down in front of Weeson. The captain's face took shape in the fuzzy wash of light, the dark eyes regarding him quizzically from the fold of the hood. After a moment the man nodded to himself, as if hearing something someone was saying. He reached over and pulled something from his pack.

Weeson tossed the Elfling a rumpled ball of cloth. Shan caught it in surprise. It was dark blue in color and made of some lightweight material. The elven youth unrolled it to reveal a square of cloth a little more than the length of his arm. He held it out curiously before him. It felt sort of like a woman's scarf against his fingertips.

"What's this?" he asked the young captain.

"Headcloth," Weeson responded. "I think it's probably a good idea to start concealing your features somewhat, mask your true heritage as much as we can." Shan raised his eyebrows a bit in surprise. "Your *elven* heritage," he continued, in answer to the youth's questioning look. "At least for now." Shan looked down at the cloth as he thoughtfully ran it through his hands. "We don't know exactly who we might come across in our journey over the next few days, and I think it's best not to stir up any undue curiosity if we can avoid it. We need to maintain a low profile."

Shan swallowed any reply he might have offered. Instead, he lifted the cloth up before his eyes and turned it all about in the low light of the moons. He looked over at the captain and scrunched up his lips. "How do you wear one of these things?"

Weeson pulled himself up from his rock backrest and settled down next to the boy. He took the cloth from Shan's open palm and folded it loosely into a triangle. He held the folded edge up to his forehead, flipping the cloth back with a flick of his wrists and applying a little pressure as he leaned slightly forward. Then he slid both hands outward to the widest parts of the cloth. The last point, opposite from the folded edge, fell away over his head behind him and settled along the back of his neck. Deftly, he tied the two ends he held in his hands into place and sat back, spreading his open hands out with a slight smile.

"Makes you look like a pirate," Shan snickered.

Weeson swept the cloth from his head with a slight bow. "At your service," he chuckled. He quickly loosened the knot and offered the dark cloth back to the boy. "You could also wear it with a little more southern flare, if you like. Just sling it over your head and tie it on with a cord."

"Like a kaffiyeh," Shan offered, smiling.

"Exactly. You can even pull one of the flaps around to conceal your face a little more." Weeson grinned. "You know, you might just be able to pull off the appearance of a desert nomad from Uu-Kesh." Shan flipped the cloth over his head and held it in place with one hand. He couldn't help gazing back at Weeson with a grin of his own.

The grin suddenly faded from his face as the man stared thoughtfully at the boy. "You could, 'cept that might create too much of a stir around these parts. Not too many nomads wandering through the forests of Draydin these days, I'm afraid." His eyes sparkled mysteriously in the light of the moons. The youth continued to experiment with the headcloth, trying to determine how best to use it. "Just remember, Shan," Weeson suddenly became solemn, "this is not a game." Shan instantly stopped playing with the scarf and looked the captain in the eyes. "You need to wear that cloth at all times from now on. Don't ever let anyone catch you without it." The man's firm gaze gave him a start. "Your life may depend upon it."

Shan pulled the cloth from his head and it slowly slid down into his lap and settled about his knees.

"Who am I, Weeson?" the boy asked, nervously. "Why is this all happening to me?" His eyes were fearful as he pleaded with the young captain.

"I can't tell you that, Shan." The boy seemed hurt and began to turn his face away. "I can't tell you," Weeson faltered, "because I don't really know myself. Ulfiir never felt it was wise to confide the whole story with me." Shan swung his eyes back around to meet those of the captain. "Probably had something to do with the fewer people who knew about it, the better." The Elfling nodded. "Believe me, you're not the only one left in the dark," Wesson told him. "All I know is that it's vital for you to remain hidden, especially from those who might wish you harm." Their eyes locked upon each other. "So don't trust anyone. Not just the people you don't know. Anyone. Keep your head down, don't draw any attention to yourself, and make absolutely sure no one ever gets a glimpse of those pointy ears of yours."

Shan self-consciously reached a hand up and softly touched the tip of one ear. *The sure marks of an Elf,* he thought. In the back of his mind he could hear the voice of Ulfiir explaining to him many yehrin ago why his ears were different than all those others living in Draydin. He had been only four or five at the time, and some of the other children had been teasing him. "Your ears are a mark in your flesh, my boy," Ulfiir had said. "Nothing to be ashamed of." Shan remembered being somewhat puzzled about it at the time. "A symbol of your race," the old man had gone on. "Long ago, when Athiliel created all things, He formed the stars in the heavens above and everything upon the surface of the world itself. With the words of His mouth Athiliel created all of Anarra. He raised up the mountains and smoothed out the plains. He carved rivers to bring fresh water to His creation. He covered the land with trees and all other kinds of growing things, and He formed all the animals we see today. He brought forth various kinds of people and placed them in many different nations. He made them all differently, and to each group He gave distinct features. To the Dwarves He granted short stature, bushy beards and great strength." Shan chuckled softly. "To the Humans He gave single-minded determination and an inquisitive nature. But to the Elves, because of His great love for them, Athiliel gave the gift of immortality." The Elfling's eyes opened wide in wonder. "Oh, don't get me wrong," the old man went on, "Elves can be killed alright, just like the rest of us. Most of the time they fall in battle. Yet if they never receive a mortal wound of some kind, the *Thuvan* would thrive here on Anarra, forever." Ulfiir had narrowed his bushy brows as he spoke. "And along with this gift, Athiliel put a sign in their flesh, an outward mark to let all other nations and races know, without a shadow of doubt, that the Elves belonged to Him."

"The ears?" Shan had asked.

"That's right, my boy," Ulfiir had stated, "the ears. It would be a sure sign of their heritage, an outward mark of their covenant relationship to the Creator."

Shan continued to trace the tip of one ear in memory of that conversation long ago. "Why does everyone hate the Elves?" Shan suddenly asked the captain.

"That," offered Weeson after a moment, a surprised look on his face, "is a very, very difficult question to answer." He picked up a small stick and idly began tracing in the dust with it as he thought. Shan waited patiently as Weeson continued to draw in the dust for several mira. When at last he spoke again, his voice was low and seemed somewhat far away. "I suppose it's more than a fact that Elves are different from all other peoples. I mean, we're all different. No two races are alike. That's what makes Athalias' creation . . ."

"Who?" Shan wanted to know.

"Athalias, the Creator of all things," Weeson went on. "You probably know Him as Athiliel, that's the *Keldarin*, ah, elvish name for Him. It means the Eternal One. He's one and the same; my people just have a different name for Him, that's all. To us He is Athalias, and it means He Who Is."

"Huh, I like that," Shan admitted.

"As I was saying, Atha . . . Athiliel's . . . creation is so incredible, so diverse, no two kinds of people are the same. Yet," he went on slowly, thoughtfully, "there is one important distinction that separates the Elves from all other peoples."

"What's that?" Shan had to ask.

Weeson looked up at him from what he had absently been scribbling in the dust. "The Elves are considered the Chosen Ones," he said with a level gaze. "They are favored by Athiliel, and set apart from all others. The apple of His eye, so to speak. And because of that, I think, all other races are jealous of their relationship with Him."

"And jealousy breeds hatred," Shan replied.

"Exactly," Weeson said with a guilty edge to his voice.

Shan sat back thoughtfully, trying to make sense of all he had learned. Weeson looked away into the darkness of the trees. "I used to feel that way myself, Shan—once upon a time." The elven youth looked up at him in surprise. "That is, before I came to know you personally." Weeson turned his face back to lock eyes with the boy. "I used to believe all the hateful talk by those around me. Like, like all the problems the people of Anarra were facing was somehow on account of the Elves. If they were simply wiped away, eradicated from the world, all the wars, all the hatred and the violence would just disappear." Weeson laughed in disgust. "Never again," he said then, with conviction. "I'll never feel that way again, Shan." He leaned forward and touched the Elfling on the knee. "Never again!" It wasn't actually a smile that escaped his lips, but rather was more like a tight grimace of pain. His face was etched with a long, solemn gaze of determination and resolve.

"Oh," Weeson broke the thick silence, "I almost forgot." He reached down and pulled a small, leather coin purse from his belt. "I should probably give you this." He tossed it lightly to the boy, who caught it neatly out of the air. It jingled softly with a handful of coins. Shan's brow furrowed in thought as he shook the small bag in his hand. "Just in case," Weeson remarked. "I don't expect us to get separated any time soon, but you can never know just what might happen. Best be prepared for anything." The boy nodded, still trying to take it all in. He squished the small pouch between his fingers for a last time, then tucked it clumsily away in his own belt.

"So," Shan ventured softly, "what's the plan? Where do we go from here?"

Weeson smiled. "More of the same," he said. "We continue to head west for the time being, maybe slightly south, till we reach the edge of the forest. We'll have to ride in the open for a little while—and that will pose a bit of a problem in itself—before we come to the banks of a great river. The Tanalorn. We'll follow it for a time until we come to a large fork. There, we'll cross at Donner's Ferry just north of Akthis. That is," and Weeson paused long enough for emphasis, "if we can keep avoiding any of those wandering patrols." Shan gulped involuntarily, felt the hint of tightness in his face. "Once we get on the other side of the river," the man continued, "things should be a lot safer for us. We'll skirt the mountains to the southwest, a pretty considerable distance, until we can join the Brittlehorn. We'll have to buy a couple of boats, or maybe fashion ourselves a raft, and float down the river all the way to Redhaven."

Shan was somewhat confused. He had never really taken the time to study the geography of foreign lands.

"Sound feasible?" Weeson asked casually, scanning the darkness all around them.

"Yeah, sure," Shan returned, but the man could tell he was still unconvinced. "What if we *do* run into patrols?" The Elfling leaned forward nervously. "What then?"

Weeson's eyes stopped drifting over the stillness and settled upon the lad. "Hopefully that will never happen," he said honestly, "but if it does, we'll just have to fight our way through, and run for it." The captain's frank look seemed to bore into him. "I doubt we'll be able to count on much assistance from the people along the way, so we'll be pretty much on our own." He flashed the boy a grim smile. "I know none of this makes any sense to you right now, or even seems very fair, and I'm sorry for that. But it's all real, I can assure you, and it's happening to you whether you like it or not." He leaned forward to clap a hand on the boy's shoulder, and squeezed firmly.

"You've got an important role to play in a very dangerous game that's just now beginning, Shan," the man told him. "It'll be a fascinating affair, as most games go, but, as I'm sure you've already seen yourself, quite a deadly one." The boy appeared to shrink before his eyes, crouching there anxiously before him. "Who knows how each of the moves will turn out, which pieces will be involved, or just how it'll all end?" He rubbed at his jaw. "Perhaps everything will erupt in outright war, perhaps not. But all of this has been brewing for a long, long time." Weeson gave Shan another friendly squeeze, then gently released his hold and withdrew the hand into his cloak. "If we can see you safely to Arris Junn, we may avoid this whole mess entirely." He sat back without another word and resumed his watchfulness.

"You mentioned dangerous," Shan began uncertainly. "You haven't told me what happened the other night in Draydin, and that makes me wonder." Weeson leveled his gaze on the boy's face. "How's Ulfiir? Is he hurt? Is he . . . ?" He couldn't bring himself to say the word.

"Dead?" Weeson ventured. "No, he's most certainly not dead." Shan's sigh of relief was audible. "No, I'm not sure anything could kill that old man. You saw him take care of that kurgoth."
The boy nodded his head firmly. "As you've probably guessed already, several gorguls attacked the compound, most likely looking for you. There was some fierce fighting for a time, some outer buildings got burned in the melee, but we eventually managed to drive them off with minimal casualties. We chased them into the woods. They scattered and melted away in the darkness. We combed the forest for several ahrin, in fact. We searched for whatever it was controlling the beast, but could find nothing." Shan found himself tense, vividly remembering the wild events of that night.

He sat with his own thoughts for a long time, not speaking. Every time he asked questions things got more and more confusing to him. He decided firmly there would be no more questions.

Weeson reached quickly for a bow at his feet, nocking an arrow with surprising speed. He drew the string back to his ear and scanned the gloom on his left. Shan started to rise to his feet, but Weeson stopped him with a hushed whisper. "Be still!"

There was a soft crunching from the brush very close at hand, then a small head peered out at them from under the loop of a hairy vine. Weeson relaxed his hold on the bowstring and lowered the weapon to his side. The little deer sniffed quietly at them, regarding them with its deep eyes. Then it lifted its head and began chewing at a leaf. They watched it in silence until it backed casually away, spun lightly on its hooves, and was gone.

The two sat watching the swaying vine, chuckling softly.

"Well now," Weeson muttered as he stood up. "It's time for sleep," he said with a yawn. Shan rose slowly. The captain moved over between the two sleeping men and shook Irion lightly. The man sputtered softly and rolled over. He shook his head and sat up.

"That time already?" he grumbled mildly. He ran a hand through his tangle of hair and forced his eyes open very wide three or four times. Tossing the blanket aside with a mumble under his breath, he clambered to a standing position. He rocked briefly on his feet before stumbling up to where the boy stood.

"Alright, alright," the man said, gruffly, "I'm awake. You can all go to sleep now."

Shan hesitated.

"Go on," Irion mumbled, nodding at Shan's bedding. "I may take a couple of moments to get myself going, but I'm usually fine after that." The young man looked at him as if unconvinced. "No, really."

Weeson chuckled as he stretched out and wrapped himself in a blanket. "He's okay," he confided to Shan. He nodded in Irion's direction, watching him as he trudged around between the trees, softly clapping at his arms for warmth. "That's not bad, considering he hasn't had his morning mug of *kabba* yet."

Shan laughed and crawled back to his pack. He plopped against it and nestled down into a ball. He watched Irion settle himself on a stump a short distance away. His own eyes grew heavy in a hurry and he was fast asleep in no time.

Ƕunted
[15th of Kaligath, 4534 C.R.]

The morning dawned bright and clear. Broad streaks of sunlight filtered down where they lay, warming them to wakefulness. Shan stirred and looked around with a tilt of his head. Irion had already risen and was talking to Bindar in low tones. The two men must have switched watches at some other point in the night, Shan realized, but for the life of him he couldn't remember hearing them do so. The captain rolled from his bed and moved easily over to the tethered thorka. They nickered softly at him as he stroked each one of their long, sleek backs.

"How are you this morning, Eru-el?" he said, brushing at the powerful neck of his own animal. The black stallion threw back its great head with a snort. It pranced about lightly on its hooves. "Good," the man said with a scratch at the tip of Eru-el's long sleek nose. "We've got plenty of riding ahead of us today." He gave the beast an affectionate slap and stalked off. "Come on, Shan," he waved at the boy, "we've got to be moving before too long."

"No *kabba* today," Irion called after him with a snicker.

Shan stifled a yawn and began stuffing his blanket and cloak into his travel pack from a cross-legged position. He brushed at some long, loose strands of his hair with the fingers of one hand. Reluctantly he drew out the head scarf and tied it awkwardly in place. He wrestled the pack over one shoulder and stood up. He crossed to his own small thorka and threw the bundle over its back with a practiced fling. He clucked his tongue at the animal reassuringly, tightening the saddle along with the pack about the thorka's middle section with a sharp tug.

"What's his name?" Shan asked Bindar as the man walked over to inspect his work.

"Roanoke," the man responded with a nod, then glanced over at Shan before pulling tight the saddle of his own thorka.

"Roanoke," Shan murmured. "Nice to meet you." He stroked the animal amicably along its glossy neck, then turned back to the others as they huddled together and passed out small portions of food. They ate a quick breakfast of *lence* cakes and cheese. Moments later, still wiping crumbs from their fingers, they climbed lightly onto their mounts and were soon galloping off to the west.

They rode for several uneventful ahrin, the sunlight slashing down through the trees upon them as they jogged along. They stopped only once to fill their leather water bottles from a bubbling brook that wound like a serpent from a large thicket of *rogin* berries. Shan couldn't resist reaching over and plucking a few of the dark sweet berries from their prickly vines. He snatched his hand back with a yelp as he came away with a nasty thorn prick. He promptly thrust his wounded finger into his mouth as Weeson gave him a small shake of his head with a knowing smile. Shan pulled his finger from his mouth, examining it for a moment in the dappled light, then triumphantly popped the purloined berries into his mouth with a smirk. Next time he'd remember the trick he learned about using a stick.

They pressed on again until mid-afternoon. The six-legged rhythm of the thorka seemed monotonous as they rose over small hills and mounds then plunged down into shallow depressions in the endless tracks of the forest. Weeson finally pulled them to a halt with a lifted hand in a small clearing. The animals pranced lightly for a few moments then settled into a cluster, their noses close together. Shan dismounted thankfully, the insides of his legs chafed raw from the long period in the saddle. He stooped awkwardly while trying to hold the fabric of his britches away from the angry skin of his inner thighs. The others swung themselves down from their animals, laughing. Shan shambled over painfully and slumped down slowly on a thick root.

Irion pulled a packet of dried meat from a stiff pouch in his saddle bag and passed it around. They eagerly dipped their hands into the packet and munched noisily on the jerky without so much as a word. They shared what was left of the cider, breaking out their own water bottles when it was gone. They continued to eat in silence, a growing feeling of urgency creeping over them.

Shan looked up from the ground. He listened for a while before he realized that there was no sound in the forest. The buzz of insects was gone, and the twittering of the birds had completely died away. Weeson suddenly noticed it as well. He lifted his head and scanned the trees in all directions. The thorka began to stamp impatiently, pulling at their neck ropes with increasing vigor. Shan stood up, the pain in his legs forgotten. His palms began to tingle. Irion and Bindar paused in mid-chew, looking questioningly at the elven youth, a handful of meat poised at their mouths.

Suddenly, there was a wild howl a long ways off. Chills lanced up Shan's spine as he listened to it slowly fade away. The cry was echoed faintly by a similar call from another direction.

"Wolves!" Bindar choked out. They were on their feet instantly, racing for their mounts.

Daryl Hanson

"Trouble," Irion corrected him.

They scrambled for their neck ropes and jerked them free from their branches with a snapping of wood. "This way!" Weeson called, swinging up into the saddle and giving his great thorka a kick. The other animals pranced and reared nervously. Shan fought his way up onto his mount and bolted after the rapidly retreating captain. Sharp branches slashed at their arms and faces, drawing painful welts. Shan managed to look back once, but could see nothing but a blur of foliage.

They flew on through a wall of wildly lashing arms of brown and green. Shan fought to stay in the saddle as they pounded up and down the rolling mounds. They raced in and out of the groping sweep of the branches, ducking and dodging in their saddles. The howling continued at their backs, and seemed to grow steadily closer with each thumping stride. Shan fought at the rush of wind in his face. His mouth was dry and his tongue stuck to the inside of his cheek. His chest was exploding and his lungs cried out for air. The howls behind him juddered through the tangle of trees.

Shan did all he could do to keep up, yet Weeson and the others, with their long-legged mounts, began to draw away from him. He soon found himself several lengths behind. He kicked his thorka in the ribs and lashed at its flanks with the end of the leather reins. He lowered his head along Roanoke's bounding neck, the long hair of its mane stinging his face in angry slaps. The wild yowling at his back was answered by fierce blasts from either side. *They're trying to box us in*, Shan thought in a panic. He shot a startled look over his shoulder as long, dark shapes crashed through the underbrush and tore after him in rapid pursuit.

"Run, Roanoke!" he cried into the wind. "Run! Run!"

The animal shot forward with new vigor, but the wolves sprang quickly after them. Dark forms seemed to arrow towards him from each side, but Roanoke bolted through them with a surge of power. A wave of snapping jaws and flashing teeth fell behind, but only for a moment, as they joined with those behind and pressed ever closer. In the tangle of running bodies behind him Shan thought he could make out a dozen or more furry heads, their vicious fangs snapping and dripping with foamy saliva. A startled look ahead told him that he was all alone; he had completely lost sight of the others. In his rising terror Shan must have taken a wrong turn in the blur of pounding branches around him.

The Elfling began jerking at the reins in order to stay ahead of the swell of bodies behind him, first right, then left, then left again in a random pattern. The thorka responded in fright at each pull, over-reacting, weaving sharply in the direction of each careless tug. The unorthodox maneuvering gained him a moment of time as they rocketed through staggered lines of trees, through long, clinging vines and over twisted tendrils of thick roots.

"Good boy, Roanoke!" Shan exclaimed. "Run!"

He had lost whatever trail he thought he was following. He couldn't catch any sign of the other animals amid the blurry flash of the forest ahead of him. He guided the pony haphazardly in a wild attempt to stay clear of the snap and slash of jaws at their heels. The shrill, piercing howls hammered in his ears, curdling his blood. A powerful claw raked Roanoke's left flank, drawing a faint spray of scarlet. The animal veered suddenly to the right in a wild panic. Shan pulled at the reins with all his strength, but Roanoke drove on recklessly without heed. The boy's frantic efforts to jerk the pony's head from side to side only seemed to add to the animal's terror.

Shan had lost all hope of catching the others when a blur from ahead sent whistling barbs singing past his ear. There were several sudden screams of pain, then he heard the sound of something crashing heavily to the floor of the forest. Shan clung helplessly to the back of his thorka as the hooded faces of Weeson and Irion shot towards him in a smear of light.

"Bindar will guide you!" he heard Weeson's breathy shout. "Keep going. We'll catch up to you later!"

Shan saw their bowstrings snap as the feathered shafts vanished with an angry hiss. A terrifying scream wrenched the air. Roanoke thundered past Eru-el and bolted toward Bindar where he rose in his stirrups and waved commandingly to him. The man's anxious mount pranced on a small rise some thirty paces off. Bindar fell in next to Shan with a quick whip of his reins, and the two thorka, their sides heaving and streaked with sweat, raced like the wind. Shan cast a worried glance back over his bouncing shoulder. He saw the two men fire their weapons once again then wheel their mounts quickly in his direction, a hideous wall of blazing eyes and snapping jaws swarming around them.

"Targs!" he could hear Bindar cry over the wind. "Very dangerous!"

"I thought they were wolves!" Shan shouted back between jarring strides.

Bindar nodded with a hard swallow for air. "They are," was his hasty return. "A special breed. They're just bigger and faster! And they've got more teeth!" He clamped his mouth shut as a line of green slashed at his face. He ducked instantly, but came back up spitting leaves.

Their two thorka raced on through the trees, their coats now heavily drenched in sweat, foam beginning to dribble from their mouths. Shan wiped wildly at sweat on his own face, then realized suddenly, some of it had actually been thrown off from the animal's glistening muzzle. Bindar thrust a stream of whipping hair over his shoulder. The immediate sounds of pursuit had died away, but still they pressed on. They rode until their thorka had nearly collapsed, stumbling heavily over the uneven ground and wheezing loudly.

They finally brought the animals to a rest, but did not dismount. The thorka stood shakily, shifting on their feet almost drunkenly. Their legs were sheathed in dirt and sweat, and flecks of green showed where branches had lashed at them, leaving grimy furrows from their impact. Their nostrils shot jets of steam flaring out in time with the rapid swell and contraction of their great chests. The thorka laid their ears back and hung their heads weakly, almost totally spent. The muscles in their legs seemed to shiver uncontrollably as they chomped noisily at the bits in their mouths.

Shan rubbed at Roanoke's warm, damp neck. He strained his vision back along the swirling path they had raced, but could see nothing. There was no sign of Weeson or Irion, only the soft rustling of a sea of green and darkening brown. He tried to stretch his back in the saddle, his own breathing finally beginning to slow. There was a sudden, distant howl that split the silence. Shan cast a startled look at his benefactor.

"They'll be alright," Bindar told him. "They're both used to taking care of themselves. Even in difficult situations." He shot a look past the elven youth and managed a weak smile. "Now, come on," he said, turning his mount with a twist of the reins, "we've got to keep moving."

"But these animals can't run anymore!" Shan was emphatic. "They're half dead already."

"I know," Bindar spoke quietly, stroking his thorka softly along the neck. "We'll have to walk them."

Content with that, Shan gave Roanoke a loving pat and urged the animal forward, picking his way slowly on the other's heels.

They had gone only a short distance when Shan realized that the normal sounds of the forest had returned. Tiny birds flashed along above their heads, chittering and scolding one another as they flapped their wings and hopped about among the branches. The loud drone of an insect zipped by his face and caused him to duck. A tiny streak of brown fur launched itself into space and landed on a thin limb that bent radically downward. The little creature scrabbled quickly up the branch and disappeared into the wavering sea of green above.

Shan began to breathe easier. The tightness in his throat and chest started to dissipate but did not depart altogether. He reached for the water bottle wrapped about the horn of his saddle on a wide, leather strap. The cool liquid washed the taste of dust from his mouth and eased the dryness of his lips and throat. Shan tossed the bag to Bindar after taking two long swigs. The soldier took three quick sips and, driving the wooden stopper home, handed the water bag back to him. Shan did not bother to tie it back on the saddle horn, but thrust his head and one arm through the strap, and the half-empty skin dangled at his hip.

"How are we ever going to meet up with the others?" Shan wanted to know after walking their animals for several mira in silence.

"We'll wait for them," Bindar informed him matter-of-factly. He never took his eyes off the trail as they picked their way through the trees.

"But how will they know where to meet us?" Shan asked.

"If nothing else we'll wait for them at the Ferry," the man replied.

"Donner's Ferry?" Shan seemed incredulous. "But isn't that still many days away?"

The big man bobbed his head in a simple nod. "We'll wait for them there," the man said, "but only for a short time. If they don't follow along directly, we'll just have to push on without them."

Shan swallowed at that little knot in the back of his throat. He didn't relish the thought of abandoning his friends somewhere behind them, perhaps somehow lost in the trackless forest, bleeding and on foot, their weapons lost somewhere in the underbrush, surrounded by ravenous monsters closing in on them with their razor-sharp teeth. He forced the lingering image of the two men from his mind. "How much time can we give them?" he asked with an awkward swallow.

"That depends on what the situation is like when we get to the Ferry." Bindar never bothered to look back at him as he continued onward. He slapped at an insect then scratched fiercely along the inside of his left arm.

"The situation?" Shan's thoughts were garbled and slow.

"Yes," Bindar stated. This time he turned to look at Shin with a level gaze. "Like who, or *what*, might be waiting for us when we get there." Shan hadn't even considered that thought. He shifted uneasily in his saddle. "And," the man continued as he turned back around, "how many bands of scaly-faced wretches we find roaming around between here and there." Somehow Bindar must have sensed the boy's puzzled stare. "Gorguls!" he said in clarification.

Shan nodded numbly, his face drained of color. He couldn't think of a response and so fell silent amid the steady click of his animal's easy pace among the roots and stones of the path. The trail wound slowly up a hill, the first of any size they had seen all that day. Here the trees did not grow quite so thickly together, and the close canopy of overhanging branches seemed to recede, at least for a time. Periodically they rode through small clearings, where the sun slanted down upon them with late afternoon warmth. Shan gazed for a time up into the sky, yet for the life of him he could not help but feel a little exposed. The trunks of the trees really seemed to thin out dramatically and he found himself wishing for a little cover to mask their movements.

There was a sudden snarl from the bushes to their right as three great wolves, their shoulders touching, leaped as one into the clearing. "Fly!" screamed Bindar. He leaned over abruptly to swat Roanoke on the flanks with the back of his hand, then he turned to do battle. Shan caught only a glimpse of the man reaching for an axe on a loop around his back as the three snarling wolves—*targs*—dove for him, their wicked jaws snapping out viciously.

It was all Shan could do to stay seated on the thorka as it bolted wearily away. The path rose immediately before him, steep and straight. The trees disappeared entirely as the ground sloped sharply away on either side, leaving them racing upward on a thin spine of rocky earth. The thorka stumbled several times as it pounded up the dusty trail. Shan lurched wildly in the saddle with each jerk of its drunken stride. He lost his hold on the reins altogether and reached out desperately for the saddle horn. He gripped onto it tightly, glancing back in terror at the sudden savage growl from close behind.

Shan let out a tight cry of alarm when he saw that all three huge wolves had gotten past Bindar and came clawing up the path at him in great bounds. There was something strange about them, Shan thought in that instant, something completely out of proportion. He had no further time to think as Roanoke stumbled weakly against a half-buried stump jutting unexpectedly out of the dirt.

The path suddenly leveled off, spreading out onto the wide, flat surface of a plateau, broken with only a scattering of bushes and small trees. Roanoke staggered on, slicing side to side through boulders, roots and random bushes. Shan fumbled for the longbow that had been slid into a leather sheath on the side of the saddle. He managed to get the thing out amid the jolting pace but nearly dropped it with a snarling howl just a few finger length's away. He was struck heavily in the back as a wolf leaped for his flapping cloak. He felt it begin to rip away as he flew off the thorka in a wild, skidding slide across the loose, rocky ground. He tumbled over several times as the wolf shot past and spun to face him. Rolling quickly to the side, Shan scrambled to his feet, startled.

It was the first time that he had a clear look at what had been chasing them. It was incredibly large for a wolf, standing nearly as tall as his thorka. As the Elfling stood trembling, he could dimly hear his mount bolting off to his right, crashing wildly away from him through some dry brush in stark terror. The great wolf snarled at him with a flash of its large, white teeth. From one set of powerful shoulders, rose three fearsome heads, their savage eyes locked upon him in hatred. The three great heads weaved about restlessly, their thick ears laid back against their skulls, their huge, snapping jaws casting foamy missiles of thick saliva in all directions.

Shan was frozen to the spot. "Targs!" he heard the word rifling through his mind. *A three-headed wolf!* No wonder the thing had seemed somehow oddly out of proportion. Three pairs of wicked, yellow eyes, blood-shot in rage, narrowed on the boy. It bared its fangs even wider, licking at its own dribbling lips with long, bright tongues. Shan noticed that there was blood on its muzzles and flecks of dark red on its splayed claws. He gulped convulsively in sorrow for Bindar, and fought at the moisture rimming his eyes. The targ curved its enormous back and threw its heads high in the air, its jaws snapping in throaty howls.

At that moment Shan suddenly found his nerve, and dashed away. His legs pumped awkwardly at the ground. His heart pounded in his throat as his legs fought to find some sort of rhythm. He looked back once to see the great targ loping easily after him. He dodged quickly through scattered rocks and bushes, cutting sharply at a right angle when he felt the slathering breath hot on his neck. His lungs were soon on fire as he twisted and spun painfully out of range of those snapping jaws. With a howl of rage the targ tore after him. The ground suddenly seemed to end as Shan came abruptly to the edge of a great ravine. One startled look over the cliff sent him scrambling wildly to the side. He cut sharply to his left, scattering a sheet of dust and rocks.

The targ loomed instantly before him like a blur of darkness. In a great, leaping bound it slammed heavily into the boy and swept him from his feet. There was a sickening moment of helplessness as Shan felt the ground rushing away from him. He flailed wildly at the air. The sky seemed to whirl first above him and then below him. They plunged downward together in a twisting curve of flailing arms and legs, snapping teeth and flashing claws.

7

ᙏiᙑ-Summer's Day
[1st of Peldyr, 4533 C.R.]

Shan stepped lightly from the great hall and looked about. He drew in a long breath of fresh, morning air and let it out slowly. The street was peaceful and relatively deserted at that early ahr. Abruptly a line of children burst around the corner of the building, laughing and crying out to one another in reckless abandon. Their shouts were loud and shrill as they tore up to him where he stood on the landing pad just outside the hall doorway. He stepped back reflexively to avoid a collision and nearly tripped over a planter behind him. "Oh," he blurted out, almost falling back.

"Sorry," several of them shouted, giggling, their makeshift column suddenly parting, as some of them veered to the right and the others to the left of him. He managed to freeze in his tracks without stepping on any of them as they raced and flashed all around him. Some of them saw the fun in what they were doing and circled around for a second time. Their laughter grew all the more louder.

The last of the children flew away from him after a moment and tore off after their playmates who had already pounded on down the street. They all met together in a heap, screeching in laughter, just as an old man hobbled out from the backside of the main building. They tripped and crashed over each other as they came skidding to a stop, tumbling about like so many large pins in a game of skittle ball. They capered about in the dust of the street, kicking up a great brown cloud and laughing hysterically. The wizened old figure didn't even seem to notice them. As they capered in the dust around his feet the old man plodded slowly along, oblivious to their shouts and cries, one gnarled hand gripped firmly onto a long wooden cane. The children raced off around the back corner of the hall after he'd passed out of range, still laughing and giggling wildly amongst themselves.

"Feast days," Shan muttered to himself with a chuckle. "I pity anyone getting in their way today." He took a hesitant step off the pad, before casting a leery eye towards the opposite corner where the children had first bolted into view. But seeing no more signs of movement from that direction, he turned to his left and sauntered up the street toward the village square. Easing across the alley at the end of the main hall, he hopped up onto the boardwalk and began peering into the shop windows.

Townspeople slowly began to appear from some of the houses on the main street. They tripped down the two or three short steps from their small front porches onto the wooden sidewalk. They turned and drifted lightly along the shady street with no sense of haste. The shops were closed for the day, in honor of the holiday, and the townsfolk were not supposed to engage in work or any other sort of financial activity which would usually take place throughout the village.

"Happy Peldrayn!" a few of those strolling down the lane called out once they noticed him peering into the windows.

"And a good Mid-Summer's Day to you!" Shan acknowledged them with an easy nod and a friendly wave of his hand. He wandered aimlessly along, stopping every so often to gaze into a particular shop at an assortment of glittering objects on display. He longed to find something unique for his uncle. His birthing day was swiftly approaching and Shan wanted to find him something small, but perhaps otherwise a little unusual. With the holiday he knew he wouldn't be able to buy anything today, but maybe something here or there might catch his eye through the window and he could come back to purchase it at another time.

"Hmm," he mumbled to himself as he carefully scanned the window displays. There were rings and knives and lockets, along with gem stones of every color and description, but nothing that really leaped out at him. His uncle didn't need a whetstone or a saddle, or some other useless trifle. He wasn't a vain man, so a mirror would definitely be unneeded. Shan leaned down and looked closer at a small pendant on a silk-lined shelf. And as he did so, he thought he caught a glimpse of movement in the mirror next to it. It was a bright flash of color from somewhere behind him.

He straightened up quickly. He whirled about and looked out across the street, but there was nothing there. He did catch the last flap of a cloak disappearing around a corner into an alleyway. Nothing unusual, exactly, but the sudden motion almost seemed like someone might be ducking away behind a building to hide from him. It was really probably nothing at all, but the fact that someone in the village could be lurking about, perhaps even spying on people, was a little disconcerting. For someone to dash about at a faster clip than anyone else on such a leisurely holiday was sure to draw attention.

He turned around and resumed his perusal of the various items on the shelf, but now with only a feigned sense of interest. Instead, he found himself watching in the mirror for any signs of movement behind him. With growing intensity, he watched the spot by the alley way for several mira, but could never catch a hint of activity amid the early morning shadows. He rose up at last from where he had been leaning upon the glass pane and moved off slowly up the street. "It was probably just my imagination," he told himself at last, the curious medallion in the window totally forgotten. By the time he had reached the next corner, his mind was once again on the task at hand. What could he find for his uncle that he didn't already have?

He looked absently up a side street as he tried to place a particular shop in his mind. The angle of the sun was still very low in the sky to the east and the small lane was still dimly clothed in shadow. He stopped suddenly in the middle of the street when he thought he saw movement in one of the small doorways. As he stood there a small figure peered out at him from the gloom, then almost immediately ducked back into cover. At first he thought it was a child simply playing hide and seek from his fellows, and so he moved on. But after a moment he realized there were no other children moving down that particular lane, and the form had seemed somehow oddly misshapen.

In sudden determination Shan wheeled back and hurried down the side street. He quickly came up to the doorway he had seen and darted in to surprise whoever was hiding there. "Hey," he said to himself when he realized the doorway was empty. There was no trace of a child, or anyone else, for that matter. He was a little chagrined. Glancing out in the street, he checked to see if someone could be seen hurrying away from him. But there was no one.

He turned back to the door after a moment, wondering if the person had gone inside. He reached out slowly to try the latch when the door abruptly opened and a woman stepped out. She cried out with a start and stopped instantly in her tracks.

"What are you doing, young master?" she asked a little breathlessly, blinking her eyes in the semi-shadows.

"I . . . ah . . . nothing," the elven youth proclaimed. He stepped quickly back to allow her to exit. "I was . . . ah . . . looking for someone," he went on a little nervously, "but I think I must've come to the wrong place." Shan continued to back peddle a bit. "I . . . I'm sorry if I disturbed you, ma'am. No . . . no offense intended."

The woman drifted out into the lane with him, apparently mollified. "That's alright, lad," she told him evenly. "No harm done. Just don't go sneakin' on old ladies no more. Might give 'em a heart attack, you might." She laughed brightly and turned back to lock the door with a loose key she held in her hand. She fell into step with him as they turned back toward the main street. "Now, just who was you tryin' to find down here?" She wanted to know, her gait somewhat quick and bouncy.

"I . . . ah, don't know," Shan replied, somewhat guiltily. "I was chasing someone this way and I thought he turned down here. I . . . must have been mistaken."

"Chasin' someone you don't know?" she wondered. "That's a little odd." She narrowed an eye at him.

"Uh . . . but it's Mid-Summer's Day," he tried to explain.

"Oh, I see how it is. Playin' a game, huh?" Her eyes twinkled a little in the fuzzy, morning light. "How fun!" They reached the main street and when Shan realized she was headed to the village square, down the road to the right, he decided to turn left.

"I'll be going this way," the boy offered. "I'm sure there's something I need to get back to."

"Oh," she said, a trifle disappointed. "Well then, you have a pleasant feast day, young man. Happy Peldrayn!"

"Thank you," he responded. "You too. Happy Mid-Summer's Day!" And with that he veered off to the left and started back toward the way he had come. The woman waved a pudgy hand at him and spun toward the village center, her bouncing step causing the edge of her skirt to bob up and down on the sidewalk planks.

Shan drifted aimlessly down the street. He regretted not finishing his search for something unusual for Ulfiir's birthing day, some unique oddment which might tickle his fancy. All at once he remembered the curious medallion he had spotted earlier in a shop on the left. He angled across the street and stepped up onto the boardwalk. He found the shop without any difficulty and looked at the piece once again.

He couldn't quite make out what it represented, but it was made from an unusual dark metal, different than anything he'd ever seen. It sort of reminded him of a thorka, but he wasn't quite so sure. The sweeping lines along one edge gave it the look of a wild mane flying back in rapid flight. The rest of the medallion seemed to give off the impression of nobility, had sort of a regal quality to it that he liked. He had just completely made up his mind about it, when he heard an obvious swish of cloth from behind him.

Shan turned about and found himself staring into a smiling face. "See anything you like?" Celina asked him lightly. He found himself with his mouth hanging open for an instant. He hadn't expected to see the young serving maid outside the kitchens, yet had the sudden realization that some of the kitchen staff probably enjoyed a little time off around the holidays like everyone else. He closed his mouth with a little snap and wiped at a trail of saliva on his chin. "The shops are closed today, you know," the girl said to him as she seemed to float a little closer.

"I-I realize that," he proclaimed with a touch of nervousness in his belly. "I-I was looking for something for my uncle. His birthing day is coming up—"

"And you wanted to find him something special which he doesn't know about," she finished for him. "That's nice."

"Exactly," Shan replied, starting to feel a little more at ease in her presence. She wasn't dressed in her usual kitchen attire, but rather had on a soft, blue dress with delicate images of what looked like clouds to him. Her long hair fell loose and free about her shoulders, instead of being bound up and tied under a greasy bonnet as he'd usually seen it. It wafted delicately on the tiny breeze and had taken his breath away for a moment when he first saw her, especially since he had expected to see a long, narrow face with an oddly hooked nose and greasy moustaches glaring down at him from under a wide-brimmed, pointed hat.

"I'm sorry for my reaction when you first came up, but I was really expecting to see someone else." He twisted his lips into a lame sort of smile and pulled a little nervously at his britches pocket.

"Oh," she asked innocently, "and who might that be?"

He looked at her a little sheepishly, wondering if he should have said anything at all. He considered for a moment before replying.

"That singer from last night," he finally said to her. "He's kind of a strange character."

"I'll agree with that," she said, sidling up to him. "He gives me the shivers."

"Right, me too," he confessed. "And everywhere I go this morning I think I keep seeing him, or that hideous servant of his. I thought I saw them following me around earlier, spying on me from around the corner or peering out at me from some darkened doorway down the street. It's quite unsettling, to say the least."

"Well, I can see what you mean," Celina replied with a little shudder. "I certainly wouldn't want them following after me. Last night after his performance he poked around the kitchen, talked to the whole staff. And now that I think about it he was asking all of us about you." She gave a small shake of her head. "I completely understand how you must feel."

Daryl Hanson

Shan felt a sudden jolt at her words. There was something definitely peculiar about the greasy fellow.

"Can I offer you a little company instead?" she asked. Her sweet smile was almost demure, and, for the first time in his life, Shan felt like he could talk to her.

The knot in his chest started to ease a little. "Sure," he said, "that would be nice." He awkwardly motioned her down the street and together they turned, unhurried, to saunter along the boardwalk. His search was completely forgotten. They drifted slowly along, engaged in light conversation, and neither of them saw the tall figure in bright clothes leaning around the corner to watch them move away. A tall, pointed hat, wide-brimmed and bent off to one side, cast a heavy shadow over the nefarious face beneath, yet dark eyes seemed to sparkle at them from its gloomy depths.

Before too long the two young people had strolled past the main building with its great hall along the right side of the lane. A huge tree towered like a sentinel before them to guard access to the main street of the village. They moved slowly into the great circle of shade underneath the spreading branches. They stopped at a bubbling fountain on the edge of the large, earthen courtyard. Celina splashed one hand in the churning water of the tiled basin and flicked sparkling droplets in all directions. Shan reached for a dipper hanging from a peg by the fountain and plunged it into the cool water. He scooped up a shimmering cupful, and turning to Celina, offered it to her with a bow.

"Why, thank-you, sir," she snickered at him, curtsying lightly in return. She took the ladle in both hands, brought it up to her lips and drank, careful not to spill any water on her dress. Celina started to hand the metal dipper back to the elven youth, then froze, her eyes locked suddenly on something off to the side. Shan followed the direction of her gaze, half expecting to see Silas Gravelle staring at them from somewhere within the large courtyard, or his ugly sidekick. But, instead, he found the girl peering over the ladle in fright, her eyes riveted upon the large cage for the watchbeasts. Water splashed and dribbled along the handle as her hands began to shake. One of the great sleeth stretched and yawned, its large fangs seeming to snap out at her, the long, dark tongue coiled restlessly like a serpent.

Shan reached up to pull the dipper from her twitching fingers. "It's alright," he told her softly. "They won't hurt you." He flung the remainder of the water to the side and replaced the handle on its peg. He guided her carefully to the side of the fountain and helped her to sit on the tiled edge.

"I've never seen them so close," she whispered. Her face had gone pale, her hands came down on either side of her lap and she gripped at the smooth tiles with shaking fingers. "I never really hear them from the kitchens. I mean, I know they're here, but . . ." Her voice trailed off.

"They're not so mean," Shan tried to soothe her, "unless, of course, you're an enemy." He laughed awkwardly, looking down at her. "Which I know you're not. You live here, after all, so they're here to protect you. To protect all of us."

"I know," she said with a little more firmness in her voice. "It's not that I doubt their loyalty . . . It's just that they're so ferocious looking, and, and so big!" She lifted her troubled eyes to the boy. "Really, really big. They're kind of like dragons, except without the wings." She swallowed.

"Huh, dragons. I never looked at them that way." He observed their tough, leathery hides and the bony ridges running from their eye sockets down the back of their necks and all along their dorsal scales. "But they're nowhere near the size of dragons," Shan tried to comfort her. "Besides, they're practically blind in the daylight. They probably can't even see you right now." His words seemed somehow to calm her fears as she rested delicately on the fountain's edge.

Not far away, concealed in the shadow of the great tree, a sinister figure crept closer. The man leaned around the huge bole and strove to listen to their conversation. He only peered out occasionally, careful not to move too quickly so as not to attract their attention. His motions were furtive yet fluid. He licked his lips, much like a thief who comes unexpectedly across a treasure beyond his wildest dreams.

"Come on," Shan said to Celina, reaching down and tugging at her hands. "Let's get you away from here." She looked up at him thankfully, allowing herself to be pulled up from her perch. Once she was gliding along beside him, he relinquished her hands, somewhat regrettably, and guided her away from the cages, heading at last for the log palisade which surrounded the entire village of Draydin. The great, iron-banded gate stood open. A tall shadow drifted along after them, slinking from cover to cover in a slow zig-zag across the yard.

The wild sounds of cheering greeted them as they exited the compound. The sun had risen quite a bit higher by now and warm rays slanted down over the cleared area between the outer wall of the palisade and the forest beyond. Twenty or thirty young people were playing a game of *Castle Siege*. Many of them laughed and cried out in encouragement as several others from their group raced around on the cleared ground.

Shan and Celina wandered in their direction, joining a tangle of spectators applauding or jeering loudly for one team or the other, one player or another. The participants streaked desperately about after a leather-wrapped, wooden ball. The leather sphere was the size of a small melon and was vital to determine who was winning or losing the game.

"Hey, Shan!" someone called from the field of play. The elven youth shielded his face from the sun with one hand. Laith waved a hand vigorously at him, beckoning him to join their team. "Come on, Shan," he hollered. "We need you." At that moment someone sent the ball rocketing past him and the boy turned immediately to scamper after it. "See," he called wildly over his shoulder as he sprinted over the roughly turned ground, "we really need you."

"Forget it, Laith!" someone on his team was shouting. "Just get the ball. And hurry!" The person looked back at the group standing in the *'castle,'* while one of their spies raced around the various safe *'outposts.'* Several of those on the *'siege'* team stood dejectedly in the field, their hands lifted in despair. The spy turned the last corner from the safe zones and hurtled recklessly down to his own *'castle walls.'* The rest of his team loudly cheered him on. Laith reached the ball, looked back to see the game was already over, then threw himself down on the turf, his sides heaving.

"That's three to nothing," the captain of the first team exclaimed. "We win!" His whole team exploded in celebration.

Celina turned to Shan with a puzzled expression. "I don't think I understand this game," she confided. "It doesn't make any sense to me. Can you teach me how to play?"

Shan regarded her in surprise. "What? In a dress?"

"No," she told him. "I don't mean I want to play it right this mur." She looked out over the field where most of the young people had already thrown themselves upon the ground to rest. Some of them sucked noisily at their water skins. Others had broken open little packets of dried sweetmeats or munched on a few handfuls of nuts. All of them were sweaty and covered with dust, but they laughed easily with each other in their comradery. "I mean, just explain it to me," Celina looked back at the Elfling, "so I can understand what's going on."

"You mean . . . like the strategy?" he asked.

"More like the rules, first," she smiled. "And then strategy after that."

"I think I can probably manage that," he returned with a smile of his own. "So, the object of the game is to score more points than your opponents."

"Really?" she teased him. "Isn't that the goal of every game?"

"I-I suppose," he stammered, put off a trifle by her sarcasm. He flushed a little, around the ears, but forced himself to go on. "Um, let's start at the beginning. First, you obviously divide up the players into even teams. The more bodies you have, of course, the better. Because then you can fill up the whole siege field with lots of players." He turned slowly to walk back towards the gate. Celina decided to head toward the forest road, instead. When Shan looked up she had already veered off, her light steps crunching softly on the turf. He followed quickly after, catching up with her in a matter of a few strides. "So next," Shan returned to his explanation, "you have to decide which of the two teams forms the castle defenders first and which team takes up the siege." Together their footsteps scuffed up tiny patches of dust as they turned their backs to the village wall.

They hadn't wandered very far down the road when a young page came running towards them from the village. "Master Shan!" the young boy called out breathlessly. Anything else he might have said was lost over the crunching impacts of his running feet. The two of them stopped on the edge of the road and turned to face him as he came pounding down the lane. After a few moments the young lad skipped to a halt next to them on the loose gravel roadway. His breathing was quick and heavy, and he had to swallow several times before he could go on. Shan looked over at Celina and the two of them shared an awkward smile. "Master Shan," the boy finally managed to speak, "Master Shan, and you too, miss." He offered this last with a slight bow.

"What is it, Roderick?" the Elfling asked of him. He had recognized him immediately as Ulfiir's young page. He had often seen him scurrying in and out of his guardian's chambers on some kind of task or other. "What brings you all the way out here, so far away from Ulfiir?"

"That's it, Master Shan," the boy spoke a little easier. "It's Master Ulfiir's orders. He sent me to find you, and bids you to come back inside the village." His wheezing started to subside. "I had to run all over the village before I even thought to look out here. Then Fallon said he saw you going this way," he said, still breathing hard. "Master Ulfiir said it was too dangerous for you to venture out beyond the walls, especially today." Shan's puzzled look was leveled upon the boy. "He said there have been too many strange things going on in the forest lately. Said the woods are completely overrun with all sorts of dangerous people these days."

Shan had to admit his uncle's reasoning was sound, as usual, but he felt a surge of disappointment course over him. He looked briefly over at Celina, then swung his gaze down the main road to stare wistfully out into the dim confines of the forest trees. He sighed almost audibly. Shan looked back at her. He ran his tongue over his teeth and finally nodded at the boy. "Alright, Roderick," he mumbled. "You can tell Ulfiir we'll be back inside directly." He turned to Celina with a sardonic smirk. "I guess we'll have to postpone our walk."

Her eyes sparkled a little mischievously as she looked up at him. "I should probably get back anyway," the girl told him. "There's another feast tonight and I have to work in the kitchens."

He would have said something in return but the boy still hovered at his elbow. "Run along now, Roderick," he cast an eye at the page. "We're coming." And with that he swung about and began to escort the girl back up the short road towards the great gate.

"Good, Master Shan," the boy spun on his heels. "I'll tell Master Ulfiir you're on your way." Shan gave him a curt nod and the boy raced off, the patter of his feet fading quickly into the background as a raucous burst of excitement swept over them from the young people playing in the field. After a quick rest they had all resumed their game.

Shan watched them absently for a moment while they trudged up the road. Laith raced outward from the 'castle gate' toward the safety of the first outpost, a wooden pole thrust into the ground about the height of a man. The ball had been struck between two of those playing in the field. They bolted quickly after the bounding leather wrapped clump as Laith reached the first post. He tapped it lightly on his way around it, his legs pumping madly. He circled the second post, his fingers barely trailing against it and dashed for the third.

One of the players finally reached the ball and, scooping it up from where it had finally rolled to a stop, hurtled it forcefully toward the 'castle gate.' Laith streaked past the third post and rounded for the waiting line of his teammates. He suddenly lost his footing, sending the large boy pitching onto the turf. He rolled wildly over and over amid a thrashing cloud of dust. He scrambled hastily to his feet and threw himself back toward the third post. One of the players smartly caught the ball out of the air near the *'castle gate.'* He rushed over the ground in pursuit of the flailing Laith. They arrived at the post together, but Laith somehow managed to slide under the player's tag. He snatched breathlessly onto the wooden piling with a broad grin splitting his face.

"Safe!" he exclaimed loudly, one hand firmly gripping the post. A cheer rose from his own teammates, while an audible groan hissed out through the other player's gritted teeth. The boy glared fiercely at Laith's grinning face, then threw the ball down into the dirt in disgust. Laith meanwhile stood there huffing and wheezing from his run. He waved at Shan and Celina as they strolled past them and back into the village.

Shan opened his mouth to explain the course of the game to the girl but she held up one of her small hands and shook her head slightly. "Not now," she said demurely. "Tell me later. When we have more time." He nodded. They came in through the huge gate and moved slowly across the courtyard in an awkward silence. The fountain gurgled faintly as they strode past. Neither of them saw the brightly clad figure peer out at them from the other side of the huge tree trunk which dominated that end of the yard. They passed out from under its enormous shadow and moved unhurriedly up the central street.

They came to a halt on the tiled pad just outside the entrance to the main hall. *Too soon,* Shan thought to himself. They stood together in silence for a moment, their eyes drifting just about everywhere except at each other. "It's been . . . fun," Shan finally managed to say.

"Yes," the girl responded, shyly.

"I'm sorry we couldn't take a walk in the woods," he retorted. "But my uncle, well, he can be a little over-protective at times."

"That's alright," Celina offered. "It just means he cares a great deal for you."

"I suppose," Shan had to admit. "But sometimes it can feel just a little . . . restrictive."

She nodded. "And now," she spoke softly, "I had better go." Shan nodded reluctantly. "I don't want to try and serve tables in this dress."

"No, I suppose not," the elven youth replied. "It's much too pretty to get splashed in all that flour and broth and cider you usually get covered with."

She twirled lightly on the pad. "You think so?" she asked coyly, the hem of the dress billowing out a little. She giggled. He just nodded dumbly as she darted away with a smile. "I'll probably see you later," she called over her shoulder, skipping down the street.

"I hope so," was all he could say before she flew lightly around the back end of the main hall and was gone. He swallowed his sudden disappointment at her departure. He stood there looking after her for quite some time, before he realized how crowded the street had become. People streamed up and down the avenue in their festive attire, stopping frequently to engage others in conversation. There were clusters of villagers along the entire length of the boardwalk. He smiled to himself and reached for the handle to the door of the main hall. His hand froze on the latch.

He glanced quickly up the street, past the tangled knots of those in conversation, to see people popping in and out of several shops. *The shops are open now?* he thought with a start. He dashed off up the lane without a moment's hesitation. *Maybe they were only closed for the morning.* To his delight the shop where he had paused to look earlier that morning was open for business. He practically ran a woman down as she exited the shop, her startled eyes thrown wide as he suddenly ran up to her. He hopped lightly to the side to let her pass, mumbling his apologies, before slipping quickly inside.

The shopkeeper looked up suddenly from a display case and perhaps would have scolded him if not for his contrite look and bowed head. The man cleared his throat, snorted once softly in his annoyance, then forced a smile. "May I help you?" he drawled, leveling his gaze on the boy.

"I'd like to purchase a medallion," Shan stated. He leaned over the window display. "That one," he offered in response to the proprietor's raised eyebrows. He pointed to the curious piece he'd spotted earlier this morning. The man swung his gaze to follow Shan's extended finger.

"Ah," he said in approval. "That's a nice piece." He shuffled over to pluck it up by its chain and turned back to the elven youth. He dangled it before the boy as the dark metal spun slowly about on the light chain.

"I like it," Shan bobbed his head in a pleased nod. The proprietor cupped it in one hand and placed it delicately on the counter in the middle of a short stack of wafer thin papers. He deftly folded the top layer over the small object and set the small packet aside on the counter top.

"Seems appropriate for you, don't you think?" the owner smiled. Shan looked at him with a puzzled expression. "It's the sigil for the house of Korell," he offered softly by way of explanation. When still no recognition stirred in the Elfling's eyes the man leaned forward almost conspiratorially. He glanced to make sure everyone else in the shop was out of earshot. "It's the symbol for one of the seven lost Clans of the

Elves," the man spoke in hushed tones.

"Oh," Shan was momentarily taken aback. "Hmm, that's interesting." *Maybe that's why I was drawn to it,* he thought. He reached into a pouch hanging from his belt and pulled out the necessary coins. The man accepted them with a slight lick of his lips, inclining his head in gratitude for the sale.

Shan was just tucking the wrapped item into his pouch when he caught a flash of movement just outside the shop window. He darted quickly into the corner of the shop, as it was shielded somewhat from the street. A broad, wide-brimmed hat could just be seen leaning into the window. A long, hooked nose poked out from under the brim and dark beady eyes hovered close to gaze for a long moment through the pane. Shan found himself holding his breath for several wild heartbeats before the hat withdrew and the brightly clad figure stalked past the shop and up the sidewalk. Another figure moved at his side.

The elven youth let out his breath slowly, the world seeming to blur slightly at the edges of his vision. He eased himself to the front door, craning his neck to follow the retreating footsteps. He waited by the door for a few more biri before slowly turning the latch to peer cautiously out. The shopkeeper noticed his reticence and pondered it for a moment before turning to another customer approaching his counter.

When Shan found the nerve at last to exit the shop, he did so very, very slowly. He swung his head and looked fearfully up the street. Standing at the corner he could just make out the long, slender form of Silas Gravelle. He leaned in close and spoke in low tones to a woman at his side. They conversed back and forth for some time. With one last furtive glance in their direction Shan launched himself from the relative safety of the shopkeeper's doorway and scurried back down the street. He consciously strove to keep as many people between himself and Gravelle as possible to avoid detection.

He looked back only once when he reached the pad outside the main hall entrance. He could just make out the worn brim of the man's hat and the dim form of the woman before he pulled the handle on the door and plunged into the relative safety of the corridor within. He was quickly tramping up the stairs to the second floor when it suddenly dawned on him the woman's identity. She had somehow seemed familiar when he first spotted them outside the shop, but in his momentary concern about not being seen he had failed to notice.

He stopped suddenly on the stairs. He looked back hastily, as if he could see them still engaged in conversation outside near the corner. He gulped reflexively.

It was the same woman he had seen earlier this morning coming out of her house when he thought he had been chasing that Grundel character. He bit at his lip and raced madly up the stairs.

8

The Web
[15th - 16th of Kaligath, 4534 C.R.]

Shan fell in a contorting curve, the swift rush of wind snapping past his face. It stung at his eyes, lashed at his cloak in sharp, little slaps. He clutched wildly at the air in a helpless frenzy. The targ continued to claw at him as they fell. It reached out and snapped at him with great swipes of its clashing fangs as they tumbled downward in a twisting, rolling rush. The Elfling fought desperately to fend off those rending jaws, flailing his arms pitifully and kicking out with his boots. The ground spun crazily and shot up at him in a dizzying blur. Shan clamped his eyelids tight and screamed one word through stiff, whitened lips in his downward plunge.

"Athiliel!" he cried.

Several times they crashed violently against rocky spurs of the cliff wall in a wild tangle. The Elfling cried out in pain with each new burning gash that tore at his arms and face. The force of one such impact suddenly broke them apart at last. Skipping painfully off the rocks, they continued to tumble and spin relentlessly downward. The targ careened away from him in a snarling knot of black fur. The twisting floor of the ravine rushed up at him with increasing speed. Shan was startled to feel the sudden thrash and slap of stinging branches. They snapped and cracked against him as he hurtled through their dark clutches. His skin was torn in several places as they thumped savagely against his arms, legs and back. *It won't be long now*, he thought with an anguished moan. Yet, if he could catch onto one of those flashing limbs in his twisting plunge, he might just have a chance.

He tried desperately to reach out and snatch at the dark rushing foliage, felt the burn of raking needles slipping helplessly through his palms with the reckless speed of his descent. He couldn't manage to get a grasp on any of them, yet somehow in the effort, the rush of his fall seemed to diminish. The branches seemed to catch at him now, give way under him, as they bent and cracked. He sputtered at a mouthful of pine needles as he found himself slowing.

Suddenly, he struck something soft and pliant. It yielded to his weight and stretched with him. His relentless plunge instantly slowed, as some sort of elastic fiber wrapped itself around him like a blanket. The fabric pulled with him, but brought him quickly to a halt—then immediately bounced back. He felt himself being lifted in the soft strands of fiber as they rose with him and clutched at his body. After a brief upward swell he felt himself being pulled inexorably downward again, yet not as far or as deep as before. And then he was raised once again. Dimly, he felt himself repeating the same short motions in a series of ever-decreasing vibrations. He finally came to rest as darkness enfolded him.

Shan awoke sometime later, stiff and sore. The rim of the sun gleamed dully at him and was just slipping away over the further edge of a great ravine. He lay mostly on his back on a glistening white sheet of lace. His arms and legs were held out from his body in awkward positions, and he tried to pull them in but found he could not. His head was throbbing. A sliver of pain shot through his neck as he tried to lift his head from the soft fiber. He slumped back and lay still for a moment, feeling somehow mysteriously constrained. Pinned down as he was, he forced his eyes to the limits of their sockets in order to look painfully around himself. He stared up through the twisted branches of pine trees, their great shafts poking up through the carpet of white lace. Delicate, feathered clouds stretched lazily across the darkening sky. Their ragged edges shimmered with the color of flames. The rugged walls of the ravine were sheer and unscalable, towering nearly two hundred kora above him.

He could hear the soft trickling of a stream somewhere far below, and he realized that he was incredibly thirsty. He smacked his lips together a couple of times, considering his predicament. He remembered he had placed his waterskin around his neck the last time he drank from the saddle. He tried reaching for it now, but found he could not move. Angry fire flared up his neck and down one arm as he tried futilely to grab at it. He struggled once again, but found himself held firmly in place. *I can't move!* he thought with a sudden start. *Have I broken my neck? Will I paralyzed for the rest of my life?* Panic started to set it as he continued to wriggle and thrash about uncontrollably. After a few more moments of frantic movement, he collapsed back against the lacy sheet beneath him. No, it wasn't a matter of paralysis, he decided. *I've got feeling in my arms and legs*, he thought. *It's as if I've been tied up, trussed up somehow like a wild kuulo on the way to the market.*

The pliant fabric moved under him. He felt it quiver slightly, then begin to bob more vigorously. Shan steeled himself for the expected stab of fire he knew would tear at his neck when he tried twisting his head around to see what had caused the movement. His muscles were definitely sore, he could tell, but the pain he felt was more from the skin along his neck, than from the actual muscles themselves. It almost seemed like his flesh was being pulled away, as if something very strong, like some strange form of glue, was adhered to it. It resisted his every tug.

He clung, or rather, he was stuck to a vast expanse of reticulated fiber that ran all along the treetops. It vibrated gently for a moment and then was still. He looked more closely at the material. Tiny, delicate strands of a glittering, silvery-white substance had been fashioned into a gigantic net all throughout his field of vision. Woven among the stronger grid-work of filaments, like milky white sheets of silk, were a myriad of finer threads. The entire gigantic structure flowed and billowed softly in the breeze.

Enormous trees shot up sporadically through the fabric as they rose up from the valley floor. The rigid cloth-like fibers stretched out as far as he could see on this side of the ravine. Hugging the sheer contours of the rocky walls, they wound, serpent-like, along the rugged seam of the cliffs. The other edge of the vast, white mass fell off at some point near the middle of the chasm as the huge trees began to thin out and then eventually ceased entirely. The huge net was honeycombed with intricate twisting, white tunnels. It reminded Shan for all the world of large, hairy cobwebs, laden heavily with dust, which he had often seen spanning the petals of flowers in the courtyard or draped across the upper reaches of the rafters in the great hall of Draydin. All at once, the realization of his predicament struck him like a heap of bricks.

The sudden horror of it sent hot tongues of bile coursing up his throat. Shan pulled firmly at the larger, rope-like strands and tried to sit up, but he found them tough and sticky. He squirmed and wriggled about with all the strength he could muster. He tore at the bands with whatever leverage he could manage, but all to no avail. The network gave and stretched with his efforts, but quickly sprang back into place. He feverishly pushed and twisted the fibers every way he could think of, but each time they simply lapsed back into shape, obdurate, intact and unyielding. He fell back at last in frustration, a rush of warmth at his cheeks. A line of perspiration dribbled down his face and along his nose. It poised there for a moment, then dove off into space. He wondered how the mesh of interlocking threads could seem so delicate, so fragile, yet at the same time feel so strong and confining so as to catch and hold him this effectively. He mustered one last attempt to free himself before falling back in total exhaustion.

The sensitive structure radiated with sudden movement. The entire network swung and rocked in increasing ripples as an angry chorus of snarls and howls erupted through the air. The piercing echos pounded from the rocks and trees all around him. Shan contorted himself on the clinging fiber to snatch a glimpse of the targ as it struggled ferociously to free itself not too far away. The three, large heads thrashed continuously and wheeled about as great droplets of saliva were flung outward from the slobbering muzzles in all directions. The Elfling narrowed his eyes across the six or seven kora of delicate lace separating him from the mindless brute. The great, black adversary tore furiously at the net in futility, howling and rending with reckless abandon. Its thick dark fur was almost completely tangled with sticky, creamy-white tatters of silk.

The targ screamed in desperation. It shot out two of its large heads to bite at the ensnaring bands. The nasty flow of mucus from its huge jaws served to prevent the fierce creature from adhering completely to the shifting fabric. But one great head had already been entrapped by the adhesive folds, yet with powerful jerks of its neck, it furiously sought to tear its own fur loose from the thread-like carpet. The other two heads continued to weave about in restless circles high in the air. Fearsome growls rumbled out from deep within its massive throats.

The entire body of the animal shook and rocked upon the net as it struggled to claw its way to its feet. Razor sharp teeth tore at the unyielding restraints which pinned its great chest and legs to the surface of the rolling fabric. At one point it fell back from its efforts, its breath coming in great, ragged gasps. It gave off a long whine of despair, sounding for all the world to Shan like the dying warble of a *thisalant*.

Night was coming on rapidly. The sky was paling to gray, and a long, dark mass of clouds was swiftly approaching from the south. The ragged line of trees running along the nearer edge of the gorge were now little more than hairy silhouettes, and succeeded in blocking out a good potion of the heavens. The rusty-colored walls of the canyon were pocked with all kinds of dark holes and deep, scarred slots where the far cliff face wound its meandering way northward. On his side of the great ravine, much higher up from his position, Shan could make out the large, black mouth of a cave. The broken hole seemed gloomy and unfriendly, and strangely reminded him of the gaping jaws of a kurgoth. The darkening veil of the sky only seemed to add to its sinister look.

Beside the Elfling the targ continued to moan and whine, yet Shan tried to ignore it as best he could. He squirmed a bit to look down through the silky mesh, to try to judge just how far he was from the rocky floor. But in the gathering darkness, he could see almost nothing through the gossamer fibers. Far down the gorge, before it curved sharply out of sight, he caught a glimpse of a hazy carpet of brown and green, beckoning him to freedom. Wistfully, the elven youth yearned to stroll down alongside the stream that bubbled somewhere softly far below him. Then, as a trickle of wetness tickled at his cheek, he lost the ability to discern one object from another in the darkness.

Pale points of light slowly winked down at him from what he could see of the dark blue curve of the western sky. The rush of swirling, dark clouds swiftly obscured the deepening array of cold, white stars above. The wind gradually picked up until it came whistling down through the gorge. It snapped at the fragile network with incredible force. Shan soon found himself being rocked and buffeted roughly about as he lay helplessly upon the buckling fabric. The chill wind sliced through his cloak and tunic as if they weren't even there. Icy blasts tore at the loose flaps of his clothing which slapped and stung at his neck and face in angry lashes. The ends of his head scarf swirled around in a wild disarray. His teeth chattered fiercely and he began to shiver uncontrollably. The skin about his face and hands began to grow numb and stiffen in the wind. He clamped his eyes shut to save them from a beating, clenching his teeth as well in the process.

A sudden gnawing within his stomach made him yearn helplessly for home. The thought of a few simple comforts of Draydin nearly sent him into madness. What he wouldn't give right now to be bundled in a nice warm blanket, nestled down in front of a roaring fire. He ached for a platter of roasted *kuulo*, mounds of steaming vegetables and hot, buttered bread, not to mention a warm mug of spicy *kabba* at his elbow. He felt a burning sensation rise up in his throat, a sour knot of hunger and greasy bile mixed strangely together in his gut. He craved for his elusive feast but was somehow sickened by it all at the same time. He had to swallow hard several times before the burning in his throat began to subside. A bitter residue of phlegm clung to the back of his tongue and left an incredibly foul taste in his mouth. His stomach continued to growl through his nightmarish ordeal, leaving him weak and extremely hungry.

At that moment, a great flash of light ripped across the sky, igniting the world in a bright, yellowish-white radiance. The tops of the trees seemed to leap up like gnarled giants in the sudden brightness, their great, humped backs looming frighteningly over him. Their thick, furry arms were oddly distorted, swaying erratically, as they groped and reached down wildly for him in the driving wind. Startled, Shan found himself fighting for breath. Then abruptly the light was gone, plunging the

Daryl Hanson

canyon, in its sudden rapid change, into a deeper gloom than before.

Clouds continued to wheel and swirl in the angry sky. He counted four heartbeats before he heard the grinding clash of thunder crackling like a loud whip over his head. Another jagged bolt of brilliance creased the darkness. It outlined the cliffs in a thousand tiny shadows. It was followed by a great, drumming roll of noise that deafened him. The thunder was a lot closer than before, and it seemed to grind and rumble across the sky like a huge, stone wheel.

And then the rain came down.

It fell in great, driving sheets of water. It hammered at the boy with tremendous force, drumming into his face and hands, and leaving his whole body numb. It formed a dark curtain around him, a black shroud even his keen eyes could not penetrate. He could no longer even see the crumpled form of the targ just a short distance away. It was completely obscured from his view, and the thrashing limbs of the trees were nothing more than outlines in the darkness. His clothing was thoroughly soaked in a matter of mira and became plastered to his body. Water pelted his limbs and ran off his body in little rivers. He shivered incessantly, chilled now completely to the bone.

Shan fought futilely against the buckling network of fiber. If he could only free himself he might be able to find some shelter from the storm. In that cave high up the cliff face, perhaps. Instead, the wind howled in his ears, hammering the cold sheets of rain onto his shivering body in steady, icy blasts. At one point he tried ducking his head under his arm as a shield against the buffeting sting of water, but both arms were pinned awkwardly and he could not quite reach. His neck muscles strained against their bonds and required too much effort against the resiliency of the strong threads. Lightning spread quickly across the darkness above like a great, white finger. Another earth-shaking rumble followed almost immediately.

After about an ahr of this, the fierce downpour began to slacken. The rain resolved itself into a soft, gray drizzle. The relentless flash of lightning moved steadily away and the echo of thunder became a distant murmur to the north. The wind finally abated sometime later; it fell to just a whisper against his cheek. After a while, through high, scudding clouds Shan caught a hint of Kiara. The pale, reddish-gold sickle of the smaller moon could just be seen as it slid up over the rim of the gorge to the east and began its slow climb. Shan lay back upon the net in utter exhaustion. The delicate strands bobbed gently, rocking him in its grip, and quickly lulled him to sleep.

Shan woke with a start. He popped his eyes open and blinked several times. He was wet and stiff in the misty morning light. Troubled dreams still haunted his thoughts. He had found himself pounding interminably through the twisting forest, chased endlessly by ferocious things with slathering jaws, and then he had been falling, forever falling, into a well of darkness. The disquieting images roiled starkly together in his mind and left him wanting to dive back under the covers of his bed. But as the unmistakable truthfulness of the last few days slowly dawned on him, his heart sank and he found himself looking around in utter despair.

A cold, gray fog hugged the land. It drifted slowly in thick swirls of pale mist and blanketed everything within his limited range of vision. Tiny droplets of moisture glistened faintly from the weave of reticulated fiber stretching away into the mist. Patches of the finer, almost silk-like material had been torn loose in the storm. These dangled limply from the main grid in tattered folds.

Shan pulled experimentally at his bonds, but found them still unyielding. He pulled and tore and scraped at them with his hands to no avail. He did notice, however, that the stringy fibers themselves seemed to be somewhat less adhesive than before. The sparkling wreath of moisture may have had something to do with it. He didn't know for sure, yet they no longer seemed to grab at his body as fiercely as they had the night before. "Well," he offered aloud, a little heartened by the discovery, "perhaps the rain has washed away some of their stickiness. If I could just get one hand free," he mumbled to himself, "I might be able to reach my knife. Then we'll see how these fibers can withstand the keen edge of my blade."

And with that he commenced to wriggle and shimmy this way and that until he felt he was making some kind of progress. He continued to pry with slow success, but he was heartened just a little by his efforts. After a few mira of diligent work, he managed to peel one hand loose with a minimum of hair torn from his forearm in the process.

Suddenly he felt it.

The network of fibers quivered almost imperceptibly at first, almost hesitantly. The fabric went still after a moment, but then moved again softly.

Shan looked up from his activities into the swirls of fog. He listened for anything unusual. He could hear the targ, but it remained fairly still, whimpering softly to itself in exhaustion. When he failed to perceive any other noises he began to reach his hand across his body with slow, deliberate motions. Weeson had given him a knife to replace the one he'd lost the night of the kurgoth's attack. The small blade hung at his belt.

He felt the tremor again almost immediately, but still far off. The silvery strands vibrated softly. He imagined a group of warriors, perhaps an entire squad of those nasty gorguls, moving about somewhere along the outer fringes of the net. Had they spotted him from the cliff face and were they even now testing the strength of the fiber? *Perhaps this is their bridge across the gorge*, he thought with sudden disquieting fear. *If they come this way, they're sure to find me. Unless they somehow get lost in the fog.* He stretched and reached for the knife at his belt with renewed determination. He finally eased his fingers around the hilt so as not to drop it in his haste. He carefully pulled it free of its sheath with his heart pounding in his chest, and began to saw at the tough strands holding his body helplessly in place.

"But what if it's Weeson and the others coming to find me?" he mumbled to himself. The blade stopped on the threads. "Well, if it really is soldiers from Draydin," he reasoned with sudden resolve, "they'll understand it if I try and hide from them." Once again he started to cut at the strange fabric.

The webbing shook again, this time somewhat stronger, and then it was still. Then came the slow, continuous vibrating movements, as if many feet delicately walked out together upon its surface. Shan began to hack more rapidly at the fiber, wondering how such a large group of men could step out upon the fragile network without becoming stuck to it as he had, as the targ had, or even just to keep themselves from falling through the delicate strands altogether. He glanced up through the heavy fog but could make out nothing except curling tendrils of mist. Far overhead he heard the sudden terrible cry of a bird as it wheeled away, sending his heart racing.

The targ lifted two of its great heads weakly from its entangled paws and began to growl softly. "That's done it!" Shan cursed in a forced whisper. He sawed at the strands with ferocious determination. The targ continued to snarl. "They're certain to hear that," he murmured angrily to himself. "And I'm sure they'll be heading this way any moment!"

The constant throbbing of the net seemed to grow stronger and the fibers soon began to jiggle and sway in a pattern which Shan found oddly rhythmical. Whoever was moving out over the fabric did so with a measured stride or kind of cadence. He thought instantly of the gorguls he had seen in the clearing near Draydin with their peculiar sing-song march, and returned to his efforts with a renewed sense of urgency.

First there was a rapid succession of short pulses on the strands, followed by a quick pause, while the quivering structure would fade into stillness. Then there was another short burst of movement, and again a pause, this time much longer than the first. In a sudden roiling of the fabric, the net erupted into a frenzy of motion. The minor vibrations continued for several heartbeats, growing steadily closer and stronger, before pausing again briefly, then resuming with renewed vigor.

Shan continued to slice away at the tough strands with his small knife. The strange substance seemed to resist the bite of the blade like it was made of steel itself. To his great frustration he could make only very slow progress. Tiny shavings of white clung to the knife, gumming it up, and reducing its overall effectiveness. The Elfling's fingers were quickly growing sticky and numb, but he eventually managed to cut and peel his other hand and arm away from the clinging material.

The great targ began to grow restless. It whined and moaned, snapping angrily at the webbing as it thrashed about. It managed to tear loose large swaths of fur from its forelegs as it frantically peered up into the swirling, gray mist. The quivering strands rippled like waves on the sea. The frightful animal laid back its ears and lowered its heads, glaring out into the mist. It growled fiercely and drew back its tightened lips, spitting foam in all directions. It bared its great, yellow fangs and snarled viciously in challenge.

By now Shan was reasonably angry at the large wolf for making such a racket. He clenched his teeth tightly together and attacked the gossamer structure with increased fervor. He gripped the knife in both of his sticky hands, carving at the tangled threads pinning his chest. His fingers slipped and smacked softly on the gooey handle. The Elfling lifted his head suddenly. His hands wavered for a moment at their work and he cocked his head to one side, listening for a moment. Through the frenzied yowling of the targ Shan could make out the sharp, steady sound of *clicking*. He frowned momentarily in confusion. The odd *clacking* noise quickly drew closer. A stray whisper of wind rippled past the boy and a great stench suddenly washed heavily over him. And if it hadn't been for its stickiness he would have dropped the knife completely through a rent in the silky fabric. The swell of revulsion hit him like a physical presence. It was like an intense rotting smell, unbearably close and persistent. It reminded him strangely of death and decay, and Shan found the foul aroma nearly overwhelming. His stomach churned in wrenching waves of nausea as spasms cascaded throughout his body. His insides heaved upwards. He clamped the back of one hand over his mouth to fight the bitter warmth that rose in his throat. If not for the lack of food, he might have retched right there on the swaying fibers.

The throbbing of the net came to an abrupt halt but the strands themselves continued to vibrate steadily in decreasing ripples. Staring up through the drifting blanket of fog, Shan sensed a hint of something incredibly large and dark weaving about just beyond the frantic hump of the targ. The huge form must have been studying the maddened creature for several long moments as it peered down through the mist just out of sight. Shan's skin crawled in the eerie calmness. The rolling network of lace under him slowly subsided but the foul reek remained overpowering and close.

A sharp *snapping* sound, like the crackling of dry bones, could be heard just above the helpless Elfling. It grew louder and more determined. The howls of the targ rose up, wild and shrill, as something immense hovered just above it. The great wolf's cry of despair echoed oddly through the heavy air. Shan looked up, unable to tear his eyes away from the scene, as a large, dark head, bulbous and hairy, reached down and snapped at the terrified animal with two, wickedly curved pincers.

Shan recoiled suddenly in horror!

The targ screamed in bloodcurdling agony as a huge, ugly maw opened up and its great lateral jaws clamped down upon one of its heads with a horrific, *clomping* sound. Then came a terrible crunching and tearing of bone and hide, the enormous head pulled back and wrenched upwards. The great mandibles clicked and ground together in a wild shower of blood. The central head of the targ was instantly gone as fountains of crimson spray shot out. The other two heads collapsed in twitching heaps of blood and gore, half-strangled howls dying in their throats. The targ's limbs shook in violent spasms. Thick runnels of dark reddish fluid poured from its wounds and ran down its matted fur. Hovering, as if out of nowhere, the large, misshapen head swept down to feast on the grisly remains, its great jaws moving from side to side.

Shan fell back hysterically against the webbing, his insides heaving. He retched and choked till he was weak and shaky. The monster continued to feed noisily on the twitching remains. Somehow the Elfling managed to slid the knife back into his sheath before he dropped it entirely. He groped for the rope-like strands to steady his spinning head. His bleary eyes burned with a fiery wetness, and his head was pounding like some enormous drum inside his skull.

The huge thing shuffled forward on its spindly legs and tore at the targ's carcass in several quick, powerful lunges of its bulbous head. Shan looked up in wild panic. He wiped a searing streak of bile from his cheek. Through his clouded vision the Elfling could finally make out the shape of the monster. It hovered over its victim like a hideous, bloated bag, black, and covered with stiff, short hair. The dark, coarse bristles dominated its ugly head, fading back along its distended abdomen almost like a gray fur. It shifted its immense bulk easily, moving about almost daintily on eight long, jointed legs. Mounted atop its grotesque face were eight or ten shiny compound eyes. These protruded from the carpet of stiff hair like glittering black bulbs.

The spider was monstrous in size. It easily towered ten or twelve kora to the high dome of its back, and measured nearly twenty kora from the tip of one hairy foreleg across the bloated body to the end of the opposite appendage. The mammoth thing filled the boy's vision and left him shaking in terror. He couldn't help watching in horror as it greedily sucked up the bloody remnants, a stream of foul, greenish-black gore dribbling down from its dark jaws. Shan caught a glimpse of sharp, chitinous teeth slashing together between the large, horny pincers. A shiver of gooseflesh rushed over him, suddenly breaking the hypnotic spell of its grisly feast.

With renewed determination he tore the blade out from his sheath once again and frantically went to work on the web. He sawed and hacked at the resilient filaments with mighty strokes. The ponderous arachnid stopped for a moment and focused its glittering eyes on the boy. Its great mandibles came to rest with a sharp *clack*. The pincers tapped noisily together once, the prodigious thing went on with its feeding. Shan watched it warily but continued his chore, feeling out to steady himself with one hand and cutting with the other. Suddenly, one of the thick bands snapped, and the giant web lurched sickeningly for an instant. The spider scuttled its massive weight quickly about on its thin, bony legs. It clung easily to the quivering surface of the silken fabric, hissing and sputtering in sudden rage. It scurried rapidly forward.

The enormous spider skittered to a halt over him, spitting and clicking noisily. Droplets of foul, dark fluid spilled from its jaws and spattered the lacy fibers near the boy's face. The strands seemed to sizzle and blacken. The hideous monster tapped the sharp tips of its pincers together and bent its massive head down to within a few hobbin of the boy's head. Shan

Daryl Hanson

stifled a scream and turned his head away, the incredible stench lancing over him in pulsating waves. When the killing blow did not come immediately, he rolled back and peered up into the devilish maw, the chitinous teeth churning laterally in a slow, drooling process. At this close distance, Shan actually caught distorted images of himself reflected in the pearly, dark depths of the spider's compound eyes.

The Elfling looked up awkwardly through the arch of one jointed leg. He could see flame-like streaks of orange run like jagged fingers up across the black dome of its back. They converged into a paler, almost brownish ring along the edges of its bloated abdomen, then faded into a circle of sickly yellow on its underbelly.

Abruptly the spider lifted its head away from the boy and looked warily about, its jewel-like eyes glittering in the morning mist. Its great jaws clacked together a few times. The bristly head swept from side to side as it shifted its prodigious bulk upon the net in swift, jittering thrusts of its spiny limbs. It shuffled backwards several paces and remained motionless. Shan was completely puzzled, but quickly took the opportunity to cut at a tangle of bands across his chest.

The spider spun quickly about then angled its huge body back to the boy, the curved, horny projections clacking loudly. The web buckled softly beneath it. Shan looked up hastily from his work as the spider's twinkling eyes settled upon him once more. It scurried heavily forward, then suddenly recoiled, its great front legs coming up before its hideous face. Shan caught a glimpse of wetness upon the creature's abdomen. A tiny, wooden projectile lay half-buried in the tough hide. A long stream of dark slime oozed from it, mingling with the thick lining of short, stiff hairs.

Shan was startled. He quickly tried to look about. The fog had begun to thin out in places, but there still were great patches of gray mist clinging to the ghosts of the trees and swirling low over the surface of the glistening web. The Elfling had sharp ears, yet he had heard nothing in the excitement. His curious thoughts were suddenly driven from his mind as the towering mass scurried forward and snapped down at him with its fearsome mandibles. He shivered as the smooth, cold touch of one large pincer slid across his arm. The wicked jaws swept closer to Shan's face and closed onto a flap of his cloak. He frantically tried to pull himself away as a section of cloth ripped loose. The jaws clashed together in powerful, lateral strokes, a thin stream of dark saliva dribbling down onto the boy's arm.

Shan took in several quivering breaths as fear forced his lungs to stiffen. His heart was hammering wildly in his chest. He clenched the knife in both fists and drove the tiny blade upward into the spider's exposed head and face. It spit the tatters of the cloak out of its mouth and pranced rapidly out of reach, nearly tearing the feeble blade from the boy's hands. The monstrous creature hissed and clicked loudly in unexpected pain. It shook its great head and crunched its jaws together several times in rapid succession. Dark splotches of fluid oozed in a thick sludge down the spider's face and over several of its eyes. Shan's knife was stained with a sticky black wetness. It drizzled down the blade and onto the hilt, burning him somewhat where it touched his skin.

The spider hissed and danced upon the web. It emitted a shrill scream, shooting forward in anger, its great jaws twitching open. This time, from behind him, Shan heard the unmistakable sharp twang of a bow, then the breathless whir of an arrow hissing by overhead. The spider screeched and stopped still in its tracks. The ropey fibers of the net lurched with the sudden movement. A small sliver of wood was buried to its feathers in one of the faceted eyes. The thing screamed in agony, its massive body rocking back on its spindly legs. Greenish-black gore coursed freely out of the wound. Again, from behind, Shan heard the snap of a bow, the whistling flash of an arrow as it found its target. The huge spider shrieked at the fresh pain of the dart. The wooden barb struck about a hob from one of its many other eyes. Already the horny ridges of its face streamed with dark, wet fluid.

Its shrill moan was deafening.

It backed uncertainly away, hissing and screaming, shaking its great, bulbous head from side to side in an attempt to dislodge the searing pain from the tiny wooden sticks lodged in its huge body. It retreated several more paces, trembling, its sack-like abdomen fading back into the billowing swirl of fog. Shan could hear it spluttering noisily to itself. Seven of its dark orbs glittered dully at him, the eighth now a mess of foul fluid.

An incredible stillness hung in the air for a moment. Shan could not hear the sound of any other living thing, just the mournful wheeze of the creature before him. The fog seemed to magnify and distort any sounds close-by, yet somehow muffled everything from any distance away. Wind kissed lightly at the boy's scarf. During his momentary respite, Shan returned to saw at the tenacious cords, one wary eye trained on the hairy monster. After a few intense moments, he finally succeeded in freeing his chest and his hips. He bent to apply himself to the fibers still binding his legs when the surface of the web exploded in movement. The spider clacked sharply and shot forward, fearful its prey might somehow escape. Its bloated bulk raced across the rippling structure. Its legs became a blur of motion, its ugly face contorted in a gleaming mask of hatred and pain.

The swift hiss of an arrow sang past, followed almost instantly with the whistle of another. The loud, double *pop* was unmistakable. Two gleaming eyes burst open in dark slime as the archer's darts thudded into the spider's head. A thick spray of inky fluid showered the web in all directions. The horrible thing shrieked in a loud, moaning wail that sent shivers running over Shan's entire body. The monstrous bulk wobbled awkwardly about on its long jointed legs, its savage contortions hurling the reticulated strands through a series of gut-wrenching vibrations.

Shan looked up.

The monster staggered almost drunkenly. Slicing waves of pain lanced through its evil little brain like searing needles of fire. It rocked and shook and collapsed on the web as two of its great legs stiffened in quivering paralysis. It tried to drag the weight of its massive abdomen around with it. Its grotesque face was streaming black rivers of pitchy fluid. Three of its eyes were ruined pools of yellowish-brown puss. Foul drizzles of gore ran down into the stiff hair of its bloated body. Its mandibles clattered wildly, opening and closing in erratic spasms. It clawed its way with the prehensile hooks of its working legs across the net toward the boy.

An arrow sizzled past Shan's ear and disappeared into the spider's abdomen with a muffled *plop*. Its horrifying scream was now just a forsaken cry. Two more feathered shafts rushed out of the fog and buried their way into the creature's thick, black hide. The numbing sting of paralysis swept quickly over the spider's enormous bulk. It bellowed once more and then the bloated form was still.

The web rocked violently for some time, slowly diminishing at last to a slight throb and sway in the light breeze. Shan's head cloth rustled softly against his cheek as sunlight fought to pierce the thinning fog. The boy scanned the surface of the web. Hairy giants' limbs began to take on the look of tree branches once again. Wispy patches of mist began to break up and drift apart. A large bird swept down out of the swirling trailers and winged its way just over his head, squawking its lonely call across the sky. Something small rustled through the branches of a nearby tree and launched itself across the intervening space to a neighboring bole. Shan grinned softly in relief as the tension slowly drained out of his body. The world seemed somehow to step back from the dark brink of destruction where he had found himself so recently poised, and things began to lighten for a change. He smiled weakly, trying so very hard to ignore the huge, oozing mound in front of him. He looked away from it and found himself watching the web for any sign of mysterious bowmen.

There was no evidence of movement for the longest time.

That's odd! he shrugged to himself. *Have they simply gone away and left me alone out here?*

Puzzled, he returned his attention to the constricting bands still holding him fast, and he was soon making good progress with the fibers along the outside of his thighs. He chopped at them until his fingers began to throb with the pressure. He sat back for a moment and temporarily slid the knife back into its sheath. It was then that he noticed the delicate trembling of the web. He reached quickly for the blade, a sickening feeling coming alive in his stomach. He glanced wildly at the spider. *Did it have any young?* he wondered in panic.

The tall form of a man stepped easily across the thin strands of the net in long, measured strides towards him. He walked up to the boy and halted at his side, just out of reach of the knife. Shan looked up at the hooded figure, shading his eyes with the hand still gripping the blade. The slant of brightening sunlight was directly behind the man and gave him a wreath of dazzling light. Darkness seemed to fill the folds of the man's hood. Shan could not make out any of his features, not even his eyes. The boy swallowed once in anticipation, realized the raised knife might easily have been perceived as a threat, and immediately lowered it. The tall figure stood in silence, an elaborately carved bow held lightly in one gloved hand.

"Sorry," Shan offered at last. "I mean you no harm. I was just trying to get out of this blasted web." The man still did not respond, but just stood there looking down at him. "It's a good thing for me you came along when you did, or I might have been spider food by now." He tried to keep his tone light, but the tall figure continued to stare down at him uncomfortably from the cover of his hood. A bright halo of sunlight wreathed the hooded figure.

"*Tanitha?*" the man finally asked him in a melodious voice. Startled by the question, the boy simply stared up into the darkness of his cowl. He was surprised to find intense green eyes studying him. "*Tanitha li'ana? Lo vashi Keldar?*"

Daryl Hanson

"I-I'm sorry," the youth stammered. "I don't know what you're asking me."

The man stood unmoving as he gazed at the helpless figure. The Elfling clamped his hands tightly into fists. His fingers felt sweaty as he reflexively clenched and unclenched them. "Do you speak common?" Shan finally blurted out.

The man lifted his head to stare past the trapped youth at the oozing, black mountain. Several of the spider's long, stilted legs had fallen through tattered holes in the silken network, and dangled down freely into the air below.

"Quite an ugly thing," the man mused at last as he stepped around the boy to take a closer look. "Don't you think?"

"Yes," Shan responded with a relieved shudder. "Never thought in my wildest dreams I'd get so close to such a thing."

The man approached the bloated husk slowly, poking at its face with the tip of the bow. Satisfied, he wheeled away. "You're a lucky boy," the man said, turning to face Shan once again. "Extremely lucky." He reached up with his right hand, the dark green glove running all the way to the elbow, and lightly brushed back the edge of his hood. A mass of dark hair fell about his face like the mane of a lion. He had wound a length of dark cloth around his head to keep the hair from hindering his vision. He shook the hair free of his face and regarded the boy with deep, emerald-green eyes. "I'd say you could use a little help," he said with a grin.

He started forward, but at that moment the massive head moved behind him. Shan screamed a warning as the huge, tusk-like pincers clamped about the man's waist. The bow flew from his grip and stuck to the web several kora away. The spider lifted the tall figure in its grasp with apparently little effort and began to draw him toward its powerful jaws. The great head moved feebly, its immense body nearly useless as it hung limply in the lattice. The man spun himself forcefully around to face the monstrous head, the lateral jaws snapping noisily out for him. With the thrust of his boots against the creature's bloody face, he kept the sharp, bony wedges of chitin at a distance. It hissed weakly at him, sputtering oozing trails of dark fluid from its mouth.

The man kicked vehemently at the slimy wounds on its face. It screamed with its diminishing strength, reaching desperately for the pesky thing causing its pain. The man dug the heel of his boot into one of the creature's eyes, splattering it into mush. The great head shook in violent spasms, thick streams of pussy fluid, like dark slush, seeping out of the wounds.

The stench from the ruined head was incredible. The closeness of its foul body and the crush of its pincers nearly drove the air from the man's lungs. He grabbed at the horny protuberances as he felt himself slipping.

Shan still held the small blade in his hand. In an instant he reversed the knife in his hand and flung it, with all the force he could manage, at the horrid face of the spider. There was a brief flash of light from the whirling blade, then a loud, slurping *thud* as it drove itself deeply into one of the sparkling facets. Completely maddened by pain, the huge spider reared back on its lame body and bellowed shrilly.

The man pushed savagely against the pincers and slipped free of their grasp. He bounced lightly on the web and rolled away from the huge thing. He jumped quickly to his feet on the buckling surface of the net, his sword leaping from its scabbard in a sudden blur. Sunlight danced along its polished length in fiery flashes. The man stepped in quickly and drove the long blade to its hilt in the creature's bulbous head. He pulled the sword loose and then leapt back.

The spider roared and threw its head back in agony. Its entire frame shook in tremendous jerks. It hissed weakly, screamed once balefully, and fell forward in a heap. It continued to twitch uncontrollably in violent shudders of its enormous bulk. A great stream of sludge poured from the wounds in its head as it shook once more, then was still.

9

Wars And Rumors Of Wars
[16th of Kaligath, 4534 C.R.]

The tall man bent over and wiped the dark fluid from the flat of his shining sword with a few quick swipes along a tattered streamer of the silky net. He withdrew a small rag from a pocket within his cloak and wiped the blade with it as well. It coated the fine metal with a light film of protective oil. The man then slid the sword into its sheath with practiced ease, and tucked the rag back away into its hidden pouch. With a last glance at the fallen hulk of the spider, he turned and strode lightly across the delicate strands of the great web, then knelt down by the boy.

Still struggling to free himself, Shan looked up at the hooded figure and smiled a bit nervously. "Thank you," he said, in a guarded fashion. "I-I don't know what I would have done if you hadn't come along when you did." The man nodded without offering a word in response. Instead he pulled a glistening knife from the inside of his right boot and held it out toward the boy. Sunlight danced from the short, bright surface. Shan swallowed at a sudden knot in his throat, painfully aware that his own knife now jutted woefully out of reach from one of the ruined eyes of the dead spider.

Shan could not take his eyes from the hovering blade. It seemed to dip and weave in front of him for the longest time. A trickle of sweat dribbled down his face as he stared fixedly at the gleaming metal tip. His eyes went suddenly wide in alarm as the small knife swept downward in a rapid blur of motion. He cried out helplessly in fright.

The flash of steel sliced quickly through the silken strands still remaining tangled about his feet. The strong, sticky fibers parted easily under the keen edge of the blade. Shan let out a rush of pent-up air as the dagger disappeared once again with a last, bright spark of sunlight, tucked expertly away in its hidden sheath. The elven youth was still sucking his breath in rapid gasps when the stranger stood up and reached into the other side of his cloak. He produced a lump of a pale, white substance about the size of his palm. He tossed the thing to Shan with a small flick of his wrist. The elven boy snatched it out of the air and looked curiously at it, twisting it about in his fingers.

"Rub that on your hands and arms," the tall man directed, turning away. "Spread it over any part of your body affected by the web. And especially coat the bottoms of your boots."

Shan felt the odd-shaped ball in his hands. It looked more or less like a chunk of wax, but it had a strange, oily quality to it that made it feel slippery. He rolled it over in his palm for a few moments. He *humphed* quietly to himself, then quickly began to rub his arms and legs with it. His jaw dropped open in utter surprise as clinging bits of adhesive residue slid easily off of his body like beaded droplets of water. He continued to smooth the lumpy ball along the soft leather of his boots and down on their soles as well.

The boy's eyes trailed off after the big man, who had by now retraced his steps back to the reeking mass of the spider, and was diligently hacking away at the spots where his feathered shafts protruded from the dripping carcass. He employed a different blade than he had used to free the boy. It was longer and broader than the dagger he carried in his boot, one much more suited for the onerous task at hand. This one must have been strapped in the empty leather sheath on the outside of his left thigh. Long streams of pitchy fluid still bubbled slowly from the wounds. The bright, clean metal was soon fouled by ribbons of dark gore.

Finished with its application, Shan tucked the greasy lump into his belt. He clamped slippery hands onto two of the larger, crisscrossing fibers. He marveled that his fingers no longer stuck to them. He rose slowly to his knees then, bracing his feet wide apart, he let go with his hands and stood up shakily on the gently swelling expanse. He wobbled for a moment, flailing his arms about as he fought for balance. The tall man shot a glance over his shoulder at the unsteady youth and smiled.

Shan trembled drunkenly on the framework. He stared down uneasily through the tattered mesh at a strip of earth far below. He air gulped convulsively, as wave-like shivers of flesh ran all over his body. Several strands of long hair hung loosely out below the bottom edge of his headcloth. Wisps of wind tickled through them and stung at his eyes. "Look, kid," the man said with a grin, as he continued to pry his protruding arrows from the corpse. "It's really pretty easy. Just forget where you are and you'll do fine."

"That's easier said than done," Shan replied as he continued to focus on the ground far below. He swallowed hard at the sudden lump in his throat. His feet felt like lead; he found himself frozen to the spot in uncertainty. The big man looked over his shoulder at him once more.

"Don't worry. You won't be able to slip through any of those strands, if that's what you're thinking." He stared frankly at the boy. "The spaces are much too narrow."

Shan looked down at the quivering web under his feet. "Really?" he

Daryl Hanson

asked.

"Well, you shouldn't be able to," came the reply as the man turned back to his grisly task of hacking at the hairy carcass. Enviously the boy noticed how naturally the man moved about on the web, chopping and tearing at the chitinous armor in one spot, then sliding to another place without so much as a peek at the intricate network below him. Shan couldn't believe how unconcerned the man seemed to be of the incredible height and was soon resolved to try and walk about for himself. He managed a few awkward strides, his arms still flapping and flailing at the empty air for balance. All the while Shan looked down at his feet and forced another wobbling step. He heard the soft chuckle of the man nearby.

The boy looked up into the grinning face and had to laugh at himself. "Not too good," he said, screwing up his lips. The big man laughed, an elbow resting idly on the joint of a long, horny leg jutting stiffly out from the massive carcass at odd angles. "I guess I never really expected to be caught in this sort of situation," Shan went on. "I mean, who would have ever thought I'd be walking about on a giant spider's web a few hundred kora from the ground?"

"A rith," the man interjected, nodding at the monstrosity. "It's called a rith. Not exactly your garden variety spider. Very large and very dangerous. You can't just stomp this one under your foot."

"Needless to say, whatever it's called, it's not the kind of thing that happens every day."

"True," the big man said, "but life tends to respect you a little bit more if you're prepared for anything it throws in your path, even something as large and ugly as this." He slapped at the hairy leg and turned to complete his work.

Shan didn't know what to say. The Elfling looked down at the glittering surface that still moved gently beneath him. He managed another faltering step.

"I've got my arrows," the tall man said as he finally turned away from the bloated carcass. He waved a bundle of thin shafts in one fist, their tips dark and drippy. He wrapped the points in a scrap of cloth and shoved them back into the quiver he had slung low over one shoulder. "Here's your knife." He handed the sticky thing to the Elfling hilt first. The boy managed to slip it into his belt a little distastefully. "I'm leaving now," the man muttered. "You can stay out here if you really like the view, but I think I've had just about enough of it for a while." The man turned away and easily began to stroll across the web away from him. Shan stood there slack jawed, watching his casual retreat. "Don't just stand there with your mouth hanging open," the man called over one shoulder without even looking back. "Come on."

"How do you do it?" the boy cried out after him, taking a few more wobbly steps.

"Look," the man called, some distance away. He stopped for an instant and spun about. "You're making it much harder than you need to. Just imagine that you're walking on the ground." Shan shot him a wild look of disbelief. The man shrugged, then turned and strode off. "I'm not going to carry you, so don't even bother to ask."

Shan closed his eyes for a couple of *biri*, gulped once dryly, and started slowly off after him. The web gave softly under him, springing quickly back into place as he shuffled along. He moved stiffly at first and made very slow progress, but he gained confidence with each new step. He grinned a little to himself after a time, the gnawing fear in his gut gradually fading away. It wasn't long until he reached the edge of the large web. The layered strands along the cliff face were certainly thicker and heavier than the rest of the net. The plastering effect of these extra fibers served to anchor the delicate structure more solidly to the rocky wall.

Shan sprang up off the expansive network at last and scampered agilely up onto a sort of flattened ledge of stone. The tall man stood there eyeing him, leaning casually against the rocks. He clapped the lad on the back and smiled. "What's your name, boy?" he asked, with a sudden twinkle in his eye.

"Shan," the elven youth replied without thinking.

The man seemed to lean in to give him a closer look. He noticed the head scarf as if for the first time. He studied the young face for several long moments. "Got a surname?" he posed with a touch of idle curiosity. His deep green eyes studied the boy's face intently.

"No, just Shan," the youth remarked innocently. "It's the only name I have."

"Hmm," the man offered flatly, "pretty common nowadays I guess. Having only one name, I mean."

But Shan seemed to catch the tiniest hint of disappointment from him, and he wondered at that. Suspicion tickled lightly at the back of his mind. "*Trust no one*," he could still hear Ulfiir warning him. After a moment, the man appeared to relax his scrutiny, then turned easily away. He picked his way effortlessly to his left along a small ledge leading upward at a slight angle against the cliff face. It twisted in and out as it wound its narrow way along the rocky wall.

"Hey," Shan called after him, "what's yours?" He hurried carefully after him, gripping tightly onto gnarled handholds and occasional lumps of jutting rock. "Your name, I mean."

"Altyrian." The big man's rich voice echoed stiffly off the curving walls of stone. "No time for talking now," he called back, reaching up and grabbing onto a jagged spur of rock. "Here's where you need to concentrate. I'll see you at the top!" He lifted himself off the ledge and deftly began climbing up the cliff face, his hands and feet expertly working as he grappled for little cracks or juts of stone.

Shan watched him slowly ascend. He shielded his eyes with the back of his arm as bits of rock and dust trickled down around him. "Why don't we just use the path?" Shan hollered up at the retreating figure, but there was no answer. He waited a moment longer, his eyes tight and the knot returning to his throat all at once. "I don't think I'm much of a climber," he said softly, still looking up. In sudden determination, he shuffled past the light flow of debris and edged further up the path. He moved slowly, feeling his way along. He hugged the cliff, his stomach tight against the wall. Carefully reaching up and over the uneven, pitted surface, he searched the rocks for any possible handholds. He kicked a stone loose from the ledge where it hindered his passage. It fell outward in a graceful curve and disappeared through a rent in the web. Shan peered over his shoulder in an effort to watch it fall, and nearly lost his footing. He pulled frantically at the cliff face, his heart pounding madly. The sudden shifting of his weight weakened the clump of rock under his left hand and it came loose with a shower of pebbles.

Shan lurched backwards crazily, hanging solely by his right hand. He grabbed wildly for the ledge with his flailing hand. The rocks tore painfully at his skin and his body swung out sickeningly. He cried out in sudden fear, his legs dangling insanely in the air. Particles of dust powdered his upturned face from the rocks above. The whole ledge began to crumble under his weight; bits of rock sifted away through his fingers. In one wild movement he let go of the dissolving ledge and leaped recklessly for a long, twisting strand of root thrusting out of the cliff face. It burned his palms as he slid helplessly down its length for several heart-stopping *biri*, scattering dirt all about. Tiny, thread-like filaments ripped loose from the thick root as he continued to slide rapidly downwards. He swung recklessly to a halt near the end of the root as several large fragments of the dissolving ledge fell away from him. He cast his eyes fearfully downward as the tumbling rocks tore a great hole in the web. It was long, heart-pounding moments before they struck a wide spur of rock far below, shattering into a thousand tiny particles of dust.

"What are you doing down there?" he could dimly hear Altyrian's echoing voice from above. Shan clung savagely to the tangle of root as it swayed back and forth against the wall of rock. He shook dirt from his face and peered upward. He could see nothing at first, but then he spotted the big man's concerned face peering down at him from far above. "Are you alright?" His cheeks pressed tightly between his arms, Shan somehow managed a small shrug.

"Yes, I think so," gasped the boy. "For the moment."

"Well, stay put!" Altyrian's head disappeared momentarily, lost to view by the curve of the rocky escarpment. Shan's fingers began to slip on the root, the stiff, hairy filaments digging painfully into his palms. He tried to coil his legs around the pliant fiber in order to take some of the strain off his hands but there was not much of it left hanging down. He shot an apprehensive look skyward.

Altyrian's face popped back into view as a long, curving section of rope snaked steadily downward. After a few moments, the slender cord slapped lightly against him. "Grab onto the rope!" the big man called down. "Wrap it around yourself if you can!" Shan tried to reach out with just one hand, but found himself sliding several handholds down the root. And in his effort to grab the rope, he actually succeeded in slapping it further away. It shifted agonizingly away from him for a time, then slowly swung back toward him. He grasped onto it and twisted the strand around his arm with a couple of quick, circular motions of his wrist. He held firmly onto the line and wriggled free from the root. He waved about with his second hand until he managed to latch it onto the rope as well. He drew himself in tightly and clutched onto it for dear life. "Now hang on!" the man cried from far above. "I'll pull you up!"

The cord flexed and slowly began to rise. Shan used his feet on the rocky face, bouncing gently out in small arcs with a light spring, to help keep himself from being torn up on the rough surface. In a couple of moments Altyrian gripped a large hand onto the hood of Shan's cloak and pulled him up lightly. The big man stood in the yawning black mouth of a cave, his feet spread out to brace himself on the stony lip. He stooped over and heaved the boy up through the low, rounded opening of the cave.

Daryl Hanson

He shoved the youth up against an inner wall. The boy found himself kneeling on a narrow strip of rusty earth just inside the cave mouth. After a few kora the bright tongue of sunlight gave way to heavy shadow and the rest of the chamber melted back into the darkness. Shan braced himself against the rocky wall, breathing in slow, deliberate intakes of air.

"What were you doing out there?" Altyrian chided him. "Trying to take the scenic route?" He leveled a stern gaze at the boy. He crouched down on one knee and began to curl up his rope. He looked over after a moment when the boy did not immediately respond.

Shan slumped to the uneven floor of the cave, his knees suddenly weak and shaky. He propped his chin in the cup of his hands and drew his knees up to his elbows. He rocked gently back and forth, his eyes squeezing shut. His head seemed light and queasy. He popped open his eyes as brightly colored streaks swam crazily about the rim of his vision.

"You'll be okay," Altyrian told the boy. "The shock won't last too long." He sat down in front of Shan with the small bundle of rope in his hands now expertly coiled. "It's an after-effect. It'll pass in a moment." He slid over a few kora in the dust and tucked the parcel deeply into a large pack which lay kicked open on the cave floor. It rested just beyond the bright swath of sunlight spilling into the chamber. There were four other dark lumps lying near the stiff flap, half buried in the dirt.

Shan tilted his head to the side, a slight frown furrowing his forehead.

"I slept here last night," the man explained in answer to the Elfling's unspoken question. "And these are my things." Shan lifted his head in understanding and looked about the small cavern. The smear of sunlight marked a long, irregular oval across the dusty floor of the cave, and anything beyond it was somewhat fuzzy and receded into heavy shadow. But along with the pack Shan thought he could make out, leaning along one wall, a couple of other weapons, an axe and a tall lance. Altyrian squatted down next to his pack and scooped the small objects from the dusty floor, shaking each free of dirt before packing it away in the heavy, canvas bag. "Dried packets of food," Altyrian told the boy when he noticed the puzzled expression.

"Food?!" Shan gasped, his stomach suddenly gurgling loudly. "You have food?" He licked his lips quickly. "I haven't had anything to eat in nearly twenty ahrin!"

"I should have guessed," the man said with a laugh. He dug back into his bag and pulled out one of the small packages. He tossed it underhanded into Shan's waiting hands. The boy leaned back against the cool stone wall and eagerly tore into the thin, translucent fiber wrapped tightly around a small cube of a dried substance. He held up the chunk of flaky brown pastry in his palm and looked closely at it in the bright sunlight. He sniffed at it uncertainly.

"*Ethulan,*" Altyrian offered. Shan broke off a piece in his fingers and stuffed it into his mouth. He mumbled with pleasure, quickly cramming another lump into his mouth and chewing greedily. The large wad bulged his cheek out like a small rodent. "You might call it a meat-cake," Altyrian explained, sitting down in front of him once again. "It's an old trick among soldiers. A combination of dried meat and flour, mixed together and baked until brown among the coals of a fire. It's really quite good." Shan nodded his head quickly in agreement. "It will last practically forever, if kept wrapped tightly in these *barsilas* leaves." Shan popped the last morsel of the meat-cake into his mouth and wiped at a cluster of crumbs sticking to his lips. He uncurled the pale leaf in his hand in idle curiosity, munching all the while. He turned it over and over in his hands. He'd never seen anything like it before. There were dark, red veins running through the almost translucent membrane, and the leaf itself, amazingly enough, wasn't dried out or brittle. It actually felt somehow soft and elastic, almost like human flesh.

"*Ethulan* is also very nourishing," Altyrian said. "It's light, but extremely satisfying." As if on cue Shan's belly rumbled once again. "I know you're probably thinking you could eat ten of those packets about now," Altyrian told him, "but you really shouldn't, even if I had that many still left in my pack." The boy peered at him hungrily. "Trust me. They have a way of expanding in your stomach. You should try to drink a little water instead."

Shan suddenly remembered just how thirsty he had felt earlier while he was hanging out there on the web. He licked his lips hastily and reached for the waterskin still hanging around his neck. He pulled the stopper loose and tossed back his head, sloshing some water down his own face in his eagerness. He gulped noisily at the nozzle for several long moments.

"Easy there!" Altyrian reached over and pulled the skin from his hands. The boy began to cough until his eyes turned red. "It's not good to overdo it at first. It'll make you sick." Shan sputtered softly and coughed once again. He wiped at his mouth with the back of one hand. After a moment Altyrian offered him the skin once again. "Easy," he said. "A little at a time." Shan nodded and took the water bag. He looked over at the man and raised it to his lips. "Easy, easy. Take it in small sips." The boy tried to comply and brought the bag down after a few light pulls on the nozzle. "That's right," Altyrian beamed at him. "Maybe you should get a little rest before you try and set out on your way."

The boy mumbled something incoherently, his eyes suddenly looking very tired. Altyrian took the skin where it had slumped down in the boy's lap. "Tell me," he asked, as he shoved the stopper back in place and set the thing aside. "Have you ever been outside of your hometown before?" He looked back at the boy when there was no answer. Shan leaned back against the wall and had already nodded off to sleep. "I really should press on this morning," Altyrian said softly to himself. He watched the youth for a few moments, clucking his tongue, and then seemed to make up his mind. "Well, perhaps it's best this way."

He busied himself with the pack for a time as the boy continued to lie against the cave wall, breathing heavily.

When Shan awoke sometime later, it was starting to get dark. The cave was bathed in the soft glow of a crackling fire. The Elfling blinked sleep from his eyes and yawned. He pulled himself to his feet and, turning towards the cave mouth, poked his head outside for a look. The silvery blue crescent of Sheera was chasing the sun from the sky, which now hung low against the far horizon. The pale blue vault of the heavens was already beginning to deepen as the sun slid lower and finally winked out behind the far wall of cliffs to the west.

Shan turned from the rocky opening and gazed throughout the chamber. The flickering flames of the fire now revealed the cave to be of fairly decent size. It was roughly circular and spanned about fifteen kora across. The low light danced from the rugged stone wall, splattering it with quivering shadows that shifted with the flames. The fire itself sat in a scooped out depression in the center of the floor. The yellowish-orange tongues licked greedily at the banked mound of dried limbs. Several other pieces of wood had been stacked to the side within easy reach. Somewhere opposite him the cave seemed to fall back into dense gloom.

With a sudden jolt, Shan realized he was completely alone in the cave. There was no sign of Altyrian. *He must have hurried off on his way*, he reasoned somewhat sadly. *At least he lit a fire for me to scare off any wandering predators. Even provided a little extra wood.* He noticed their neat placement on the cave floor next to his feet. *But he didn't leave me any food*, he noted with some disappointment. He scanned the yellowish-gray walls once again. Maybe there was something he missed.

Sure enough, his keen eyes came to rest on the large, wooden axe handle leaning against the chamber wall. The lance was gone but the axe remained. It sat in sort of a niche in the stone, where the shadows seemed thickest. He had missed it somehow in his first glance around the room. *So, the big man must still be around somewhere*, he realized with a sense of relief.

He drifted across the dusty floor to study the great axe in more detail. The thick haft of the weapon was polished from extensive handling, rubbed smooth by strong hands. The heavy tip was capped with a bronze knob, darkened from age. His eyes traveled down the haft and he knelt on one knee to study the great broad axe-head. It was double-bladed and revealed signs of heavy use. Fine scratches ran across the polished metal where it had engaged other weapons. Shan reached out and traced one finger along the regular indentations in the tarnished metal. One of the large blades even had a notch in it, a slight nick in the long, smooth curve. He could tell the thing had been lovingly honed and was very sharp.

The Elfling rose up from his knees and padded back to the fire. Hunkering down in the dust in front of it, he crossed his legs under him. He stared for a long moment into the writhing flames. Although he wasn't really cold, the warmth of the fire felt good to him. The heat washed over him and toasted his cheeks. He fished around in the dirt, coming up with a good-sized stick. Shan poked at the glowing fragments of wood, shifting them about in the pile of embers, and was rewarded by a little increase in their output of light. The tapered end of the stick began to glow softly. He smothered the tiny sparks in the dust and started to place the stick back on the floor. His hand froze.

Shan heard something scuffling in the back of the cave. He looked up warily, the stick poised in front of him if needed. The sound was still a ways off, but he still could make nothing out in the gloom. The after-image of the flames hampered his vision. He tried blinking rapidly several times, but to no avail. The rustle and scrape came steadily towards him, until it finally melted into the form of Altyrian. The large man looked up from the uneven flooring to find the boy sitting by the fire.

"Oh, you're awake," he said, moving easily into the chamber. "Good." He leaned the lance he had been carrying against the rock wall next to the axe, then gently placed the great bow alongside it. He stepped lightly over a lip of stone and sidled up to the fire. "Hungry?" he asked as he knelt by the flames.

"Yes, very," Shan had to admit. "Seems like I haven't eaten for days."

"I was afraid of that," Altyrian offered with a grin. He reached up and unslung a line from his shoulder. "That's why I was gone so long." Dangling from a slender cord he produced a couple of rabbits and three fairly good-sized fish.

"Oh-ho!" Shan exclaimed with a sudden clap of his hands. "Looks like we're going to have a feast tonight." His mouth began to water almost immediately and his belly rumbled loudly in response.

Altyrian reached into a back pocket and withdrew some long, thin sticks. "Here," he said, tossing them to the Elfling. "We'll be needing these." Shan snapped them neatly out of the air, frowning slightly as he puzzled at their purpose. "Drive them through the fishes' gills and angle them out over the fire," the man responded. "I don't know about you but I prefer my fish cooked." Shan simply grinned over at him as he bent to his task. Meanwhile, Altyrian drew his heavy knife from his belt sheath and quickly went to work skinning the rabbits with long, even strokes of the blade.

"So, tell me," Altyrian asked the boy without raising his head, "just how did you wind up in that spider's web?"

"Well," Shan stammered as he fumbled with one of the fish, "it was kind of an accident." He lowered his head a bit to hide his eyes, feeling a sudden rush of blood burn his cheeks. He was thankful for the blanket of semi-darkness to hide his embarrassment. "I was riding along the rim of the canyon yesterday when my pony got spooked," Shan continued after a time, "throwing me from the saddle. I think I was extremely lucky to fall in that web out there." He drove a stick into the ground with an impaled fish dangling from it over the little fire.

"Well, it depends on how you look at it, I guess." Altyrian spoke with a tilt of his head.

"I've never seen a web so big," the youth went on. He started working with the next fish. "I nearly broke my neck, but I never would have survived that fall otherwise." He clamped his eyelids shut as he relived that horrid moment. He could almost still see those huge, clashing mandibles in front of his eyes, still smell the fetid odor of the thing as it scuttled closer. "But then I couldn't get out!"

"You spent the entire night stuck out there?" The man's voice rang with a tone of respect. He thrust the rabbits onto a small, metal spit he had retrieved from his pack. It had a small hinge and could be folded neatly away.

"Yes," Shan offered sheepishly, "I didn't exactly have a choice!" The boy shuddered uncontrollably. "I'm just thankful you came by when you did." He stared over at the big man. "How did you even know I was there?"

"I didn't," Altyrian confessed simply. He stacked a few stones on either side of the fire. He took the spit and balanced it over the flames between the two mounds of rocks.

"There was a storm last night," Shan told him. He carefully drove another fish through the gills. He slipped the stick into a soft spot in the floor, angling the scaly thing over the fire.

"Yes, I know," Altyrian replied. He shifted the spit to provide maximum heating surface. "I found this cave just moments before the big rains came down."

"And," said the youth, "you wouldn't have been able to see or hear anything during the night. Not with all that lightning and thunder." He reached for the third fish.

"I assure you, I slept through the whole thing," Altyrian remarked with a lean grin to himself. "I've been traveling hard for some time, and it was the first chance to catch up on some of the sleep I've been missing."

"It still doesn't make sense to me, though," Shan mused. He planted the last fish over the flames and leaned back. Altyrian grabbed for the stick Shan had discarded earlier. Tiny sparks leapt up as he poked at the glowing red coals.

"What doesn't?" the man muttered, gazing across the flames at the boy. His eyes looked like dark pools in the dancing light.

"There was a heavy fog this morning, right?" the youth pointed out. "Even from the opening of this cave there's no way you could have seen me from up here."

"That's right," Altyrian agreed matter-of-factly.

"Then how could you have been down there to save me?" Shan blurted out. Altyrian opened his mouth to speak but the boy rushed on before he could answer. "I mean, what would have drawn you out of the safety of this cave to explore down there in the mist? If you weren't looking for me, something else must have drawn you down there," Shan concluded, raising his blue eyes to meet the man's steady gaze.

"Exactly," grunted Altyrian.

"So, what was it?" Shan blurted out, the suspense suddenly getting the better of him. "What brought you down to the web to have a look?"

"I heard a strange, moaning cry early this morning," the man said. "It woke me from a deep sleep and gave me chills as I sat here listening. It sounded as if there was an animal in great distress, in some kind of agony. Normally I wouldn't have paid it any mind, but for some unknown reason, I felt compelled to check it out before I continued on my way."

"Oh," Shan breathed, nodding his head thoughtfully. He was somewhat humbled to think he owed his life to the dying wail of a targ.

"You see, I've been searching for someone," Altyrian told him. He leveled his gaze on the boy. "At first, when I saw you out there on the web, I thought you might be the one I was looking for." Shan felt a sudden stab in his heart. A tingling of discovery tightened in his chest and coursed quickly up his spine. He tried to sit there calmly, but his hands shook ever so slightly and his legs felt rubbery and weak. He tried not to meet the man's piercing eyes. "I see now," he went on with an almost imperceptible toss of his head, "that just isn't possible. Anyway, I had been told I could find him somewhere in this area. In Falduin, or Draydin. Or one of the other small villages nearby." Altyrian turned the rabbits on their spit. Dribbles of juice sizzled into the fire. "But as of yet, I have had little success in locating him."

"Are you an assassin?" Shan asked rigidly, his eyes swelled in fear.

"Of course not," Altyrian was firm.

"Then what do you want with this fellow?" Shan couldn't help asking, yet unsure that he really wanted to know the answer.

Altyrian leveled his gaze on the boy. "I'd rather not say. It's strictly personal business." The Elfling looked down into the dying flames of the fire. "These woods are full of enemies and I've had to spend most of my time hiding from them, avoiding their fervent searches. They seem to be everywhere, and they're getting bolder by the day." The big man's own troubled gaze fell into the fire for a time as well. "Perhaps they've already accomplished their dark objective by now and my mission here has become fruitless." He shrugged his shoulders stiffly. "I don't know. But I think I still need to keep on searching."

The conversation lapsed for a time into silence. The popping and hissing of their small fire seemed unusually loud to Shan as he continued to gaze into what was left of the leaping flames. He looked back then over his shoulder. It was completely dark beyond the mouth of the cave by now, yet he could only make out a few faint points of light in the night sky. The silvery tail of Sheera was just beginning to slip behind the jagged edge of the canyon. He turned back to the fire, wondering if the man across from him was trying to kill him or capture him. They both feigned interest in the food for a time, turning the various pieces now and then, and occasionally stealing glances at the other across the curling flames. The shifting light glinted from the polished metal of Altyrian's weapons resting easily against the chamber wall.

"I noticed your axe over there," Shan tried to break the heavy silence. Altyrian looked up from where he turned the small spit. His eyes shifted to the heavy handled weapon leaning against the stone. "And I couldn't help noticing your other things, your sword, your lance, the bow, and your assortment of other blades."

"What of them?" Altyrian inquired dispassionately.

"I've seen a lot of weapons before," the boy began, "the soldiers back home all carry them around. But theirs always look shiny and brand new. Like they've never had to use them." Altyrian regarded the boy with a new sense of interest. "Yours, on the other hand, look well used and worn with age. They sort of remind me of the antique weapons on display in the rafters. I mean, they're not covered with dust and cobwebs like all of those. Rather, they look well seasoned, like they've seen a lot of action over the yehrin."

Altyrian swung his head to peer at his collection along the rocky wall. His eyes hovered over them almost lovingly. The great axe rested on its double-bladed head, the light gleaming dully from its polished surface. That sharpened edge was capable of cutting clean through a man. The long, slender lance, with its tapering blade-tip sparkled next to it. It was made of a stout length of wood and lacquered with a special resin to give it added strength, to help prevent it from snapping in battle. The great bow was unmatched in its craftsmanship. Only the finest, firmest staves of *telm*-wood were selected. Each shaft was sealed within a narrow cannister for over a yahr in a solution known only to the most gifted bow-smiths. This curing process gave the bow its incredible strength and flexibility. A great bow, it was said, could fire an arrow through a wooden plank at a distance of over a hundred *kora*.

Shan could see the pride mirrored in the man's eyes as he turned back to the fire. "I think these rabbits are ready to eat," Altyrian said, pulling the spit down from the rocks. A last trail of juice dripped into the embers with a sharp hiss. He laid the brace of rabbits out upon a broad leaf and carefully pulled out the spit. "What about those fish?"

Shan reached over to pluck up one of the sticks impaling the scaly morsels and withdrew his fingers with a stifled yelp. "I'd say they were done," he mumbled, sucking on his fingers.

"Good," Altyrian said with a little smack of his lips. "I think I've worked up a bit of an appetite."

"I'll say," the elven youth replied. As if on cue, the boy's stomach gurgled loudly in response. Shan grinned sheepishly as Altyrian passed him one of the rabbits wrapped in a broad leaf. He began to tear into the succulent flesh with his teeth almost immediately. He ignored the burning in his mouth as he greedily bit off tender chunks of scalding, roasted meat and nearly swallowed them whole.

"Ho there, slow down, boy!" the big man chided him humorously. "I don't think it's going to run away from you before you can bolt the whole thing down."

"Sorry," Shan mumbled between mouthfuls. "I just can't help myself. Feels like it's been days since I last ate." He tore off another large piece and chewed on it hastily before swallowing it in a gulp. Altyrian shook his head with a soft chuckle, then drew a knife out of one of his boots. He sliced a piece from his own rabbit and raised it up to his mouth on the keen edge of the blade. He blew on the morsel a couple of times before thrusting it lightly into his mouth. He chewed thoughtfully as he watched Shan over the fire. The boy continued to cram meat into his mouth, pausing after a moment to swipe at a dribble of juice down his chin. They ate in silence for some time. The man paced himself, steadily slicing tidbits from the rabbit with his knife and chewing thoroughly on each bite before swallowing. The boy, however, finished off the rabbit in short order, licking and slurping on his fingers before tossing the remains aside. He snatched up one of the fish. It was cool enough now to eat and he began to peel lumps of meat from between the tiny bones. He popped these into his mouth continually until he had quickly polished it off.

Shan looked over to see Altyrian still munching slowly on the last of his rabbit. He looked down at the two remaining fish, then looked back up at the big man's eyes with a guilty smirk on his face. "Go ahead," Altyrian told him. "I won't want more than the one fish." Shan reached out for the thing, then stopped.

"Are you sure?" he asked. "We can split the third one."

The warrior shook his head. "No, go on and take it." He smiled. "You need it more than I do." The boy snapped it up gratefully and began to peel back the thick layer of scales. Altyrian flipped the rabbit bones into the darkness behind him. He wiped his hands on a rag before reaching out for the last fish. He glanced over at the boy, noting that Shan's pace had diminished somewhat as he picked a little less ravenously at the bits of white meat.

"So," the man said slowly, turning his attention to the fish, "you want to hear a few stories from the battlefield. Is that right?" Shan looked up at him from his own fish and nodded.

"Back home, every feast day, we'd hear all kinds of wild tales," the boy murmured. "You know, bits of ancient history, all sorts of songs, epic poems, and the like. But you could always tell those were only being spun from the lips of someone who had never really been in a battle in his life." Altyrian looked at him evenly. "You could never quite tell whether what they said was actually real or it was just something they made up for the audience."

The big man nodded almost imperceptibly as he stared down into the sputtering flames of their fire. He picked up a stick and poked at the glowing coals for some time. Shan chewed slowly on a bit of fish as he watched the man's face closely. His handsome countenance had turned grim and lined with grief, and the youth sensed the man was looking back across the long reaches of time. Shan looked down at the fire by way of apology, suddenly sorry for stirring up such obviously painful memories. He steeled himself for a long stretch of silence as he listened to the *pop* and *snap* of the small fire. When at last he was convinced he would get no response the large man finally spoke.

"War is far too devastating," Altyrian said in hushed tones, "far too broad in its scope, ever to be captured in the metered lines of a poem." Shan lifted his eyes to focus in on the big man's face once again. But Altyrian kept his gaze solidly fixed on the leaping flames. "No rhyme, no matter how grand it might sound, can ever actually do it justice. And no bard, as far as I'm concerned," he said distastefully, "regardless of just how good a poet he might be, has ever been able to describe— adequately describe—both the terror and the exhilaration of combat."

"I'm sorry," the Elfling stammered. "I-I never meant for you to dredge up such terrible memories." Altyrian's expression was dark and closed in as he contemplated the fire between them. "I guess I never stopped to realize how you might feel about it . . . I-I really don't know what I was thinking." He dropped his own eyes to stare at the dirt around him.

"No need to apologize, boy," Altyrian told him. He fixed his emerald eyes upon the youth. "Pain is a part of life. How we react to it helps to make us who we are. It defines us." Shan nodded slowly, the last of the fish forgotten in his lap. "I don't mind telling you about some of the battles I've fought in over the yehrin—there have been quite a few, let me tell you—but you must understand, I'm not a poet." Shan managed to raise his head to lock eyes with the man. "I can share with you how I felt, what I did, what I saw, but don't ever expect someone like me to romanticize warfare, to fabricate some sort of flashy tale, or to embellish the truth, just to tickle the ears of an eager audience." His eyes sparkled dimly in the firelight. "Nor will I ever trivialize it, either." The Elfling shook his head in understanding.

"War is terrible, that's for sure," Altyrian went on. "It is filled with death and horror and pain. Nations should never rush into war blindly. There is an awful cost to it, a dreadful loss of life and limb which can never be repaid. We should always think first before we act, weighing the incredible cost of each campaign against the possible outcome. But, even after striving to prevent the confrontation if at all possible, there are times when the prospect of war is inevitable. And in that event, we must be prepared to face it, head on, grim-faced, weapons in hand, to engage the enemy or die in the attempt. Always consider your enemy is implacable, and unrelenting in their drive. Never expect them to extend quarter, to cut off their attack or suddenly offer you mercy."

Shan found himself studying the collection of weapons leaning against the chamber wall.

"There was a time long ago, when I served in the border guard," Altyrian proclaimed. "I was a Realmsman, a part of the Knight Watch." The boy swung his face back to his companion, his eyebrows raised in curiosity. "I was a member of a special company," the warrior said by way of explanation, "tasked to guard the border of the kingdom from any and all incursions into our territory. There were only a few of us, for we were an elite force, rigorously trained and not just common foot soldiers."

Shan leaned forward with great interest. "We were spread out along the fringes of our land," the man went on grimly, "sleeping rough, traveling unseen, unsuspected, forever blending into the shadows. It was our duty to watch and ward against the encroachment of any unwanted foreign elements into our homeland. There were skirmishes all the time, small encounters with enemy troops or solitary spies seeking to infiltrate our defenses. We would often fight single-handed against such foes, strung out as we were along the border, *korads* from our nearest brother to the left or right of us in the line."

Shan's eyes widened in surprise. He wondered suddenly what it would actually be like to be a Realmsman himself, knowing the thrill of slinking stealthily through the woods, weapons in hand, alone, constantly on the watch for intruders, forever trying to thwart the dark plans of the enemy as they sought to sneak up on him unawares. He swallowed dryly as the realization of such incredible responsibility slowly sank in. *A first line of defense*, he thought to himself. He looked at Altyrian with a new sense of wonder.

"I was young," Altyrian was saying. "It was my first solo encounter. I came suddenly upon a squad of enemy soldiers in the woods just inside the border. The early morning light was still fairly dim under the trees and it was a little hard for them to see. There were six of them, I think. They moved quietly through the brush, stopping every so often to communicate with each other in whispered tones and hand signals. I tracked them silently, moving with them as they moved, stopping whenever they paused, blending in with the foliage. I was all alone and a little nervous, yet all of my training welled up in me as I stalked them. They crept deeper and deeper into our territory and were determined to accomplish some nefarious plan, I have no doubt. They were completely unaware of my presence, yet I got close enough to them at one point to hear some of their exchanges. When I heard their leader mutter under his breath, 'To kill the King,' I attacked."

Shan's gasp seemed loud in his own ears.

"I exploded out of the underbrush like the sudden charge of a watchbeast. My sword leapt from its sheath and swept around in a blur as I burst into their midst and struck to the right and left before they ever knew what hit them. Four of them were down before they could manage to draw weapons of their own. The fifth man I engaged as he hacked clumsily at me with his blade. I struck the sword from his hand and quickly ran him through. He slumped into the layer of dead leaves as I turned to the sixth man. He bolted away without trying to engage me and I sprang instantly after him. He hadn't gone more than a dozen steps before I snatched the knife from my boot and hurled it at his retreating figure. It buried itself in his back as he collapsed with his face to the ground. I scrambled over in a hurry and caught at his shoulder. He moaned painfully as I rolled him over, the point of my sword under his chin. His eyes were screwed shut as he cried out loudly in agony. I kicked his weapons away and stood there a moment over his body as he continued to moan."

"What did you do then?" Shan wanted to know, breathlessly.

"I was about to thrust my blade into his heart, to end the encounter, when he suddenly begged me for mercy. His eyes looked up at me along the length of my sword, a stream of blood running from his lips. 'Please, please,' he cried weakly, 'let me live.' "

"And, did you?" the boy asked, totally enthralled with the story.

Altyrian nodded softly. "He was dying anyway. The knife must have pierced one of his lungs, for he was bleeding heavily from his mouth. I pulled my blade from his back and laid him back on the leaves. I helped him drink from his water bag as he sputtered and choked. He coughed weakly and spit out bloody foam for a time. I checked the other soldiers to assure myself they were no longer a threat before returning to where he lay. His eyes had begun to roll up into their sockets when I asked him what they had planned to do with their incursion. With his last breaths he told me of their plot to assassinate our King, of their people's hatred of mine, and their unreasoning desire to wipe us from the face of Anarra. I watched from a short distance away as he wheezed heavily for the last time and sank into a still heap, his eyes staring out blindly."

"What did you do with the soldiers?" Shan wanted to know. "Did you bury them or just leave them where they lay?"

"They deserved to be left as carcasses for the carrion eaters, especially in light of their wicked plans for our King," Altyrian intoned thoughtfully. "But even with their hateful attitude towards us, I somehow could not just leave them there to rot. So I buried them. But first I searched their pouches and clothing for any incriminating evidence of their mission, yet I could find nothing. Even their attire was nondescript, completely devoid of recognizable signs or markings. As if someone wanted to erase all signs of their true origins."

"But isn't that common in such a secret type of adventure?" Shan asked.

"Sometimes," the man responded, "but not always. Some kingdoms will proudly boast of their endeavors, openly displaying their insignia to create a sense of fear or loathing among their enemies. Others might try to conceal their true allegiance, hoping to sink their claws even deeper into another country's defenses, in order to further their own nefarious schemes in their tangled web of espionage. Or, better yet, they might try to cast suspicion on another country by wearing false colors. No, if those men were meant to look like common ruffians they would have had older looking clothing, patched and worn, and carried poor weaponry about them, perhaps in a sad state of repair. But these were obviously soldiers in fresh clothing and had weapons of finer quality. I cannot help but feel there was something deeper and darker in their activities than just a simple raid from a neighboring kingdom."

Shan listened intently as Altyrian turned his attention to another encounter, but he could not keep himself from yawning and blinking his eyes as his strength quickly began to sag.

"There was a later time, when I was marching in the vanguard of an incredible army," the big warrior recited. The resonant voice seemed to Shan to slip into a sort of sing-song pattern as he was lured into closing his eyes. Altyrian rose after a few moments, still carrying on with his tale. He reached down to his pack and loosened a blanket tied to it with light cords. "The northern tribes had come together for the first time in several hundred yehrin, determined to take more land for themselves by shear weight of numbers. I was part of a force sent to disperse them from our borders before they could . . ." With a soft flap of his lips Shan drifted suddenly off to sleep and heard no more.

− 10 −
The Way Through The Forest
[17th of Kaligath, 4534 C.R.]

The morning dawned bright and clear. Sunlight streamed down over the cliff edge and cast a tiny patch of brilliance upon the mouth of the cave. The fire had gone out sometime in the night, and the majority of the cave was still gripped in thick shadow. Shan rolled over and yawned. Flinging the light blanket aside, he sat up and stretched. The tall man had already lumbered to his feet. Shan could see that he had re-packed all his possessions, except for the blanket he had loaned the boy the night before. Altyrian snatched it up and rolled it quickly into a small bundle.

"Perhaps you should remain here for another day," he said as he bent down to tie the roll onto the bottom of his pack. "You're looking better this morning, but you could probably use another day of rest."

"What about you?" Shan asked, watching the man knotting light cords around the blanket.

"I really must be on my way," Altyrian responded, rising once again to his feet. "I've lost a lot of time here already."

"Wasted, you mean," Shan said a little bitterly.

"I wouldn't say that," the big man countered. "Saving a life is never a waste of time. I'm glad I was able to help you out of that mess you were in." He hesitated. "It's just that I have some very pressing business east of here, and I cannot wait any longer." He turned his emerald eyes on the boy. "I feel I might be too late already. You can understand that, can't you?" Shan was forced to nod as he rose unsteadily to his feet. He braced a hand against the stone. "So, rest here for the day and continue on your journey tomorrow." He clapped a hand on the boy's shoulder.

"No, I don't think so," Shan replied. "I must be off as well. I might still have friends wandering around in the forest looking for me. The targs' attack must have scattered us in every direction." Altyrian seemed to flinch in surprise. "Maybe I can still find them. I hope they're alright."

"Targs, you say?" the man mused thoughtfully. "Is that what carried you off the cliff?" The elven boy could only nod his head slightly. The sudden thought that there might be more of them lurking out there somewhere in the woods was a little disturbing. "I wish you had told me this yesterday," the warrior went on, "before I went out to hunt. I wouldn't have wanted to come across one of them unexpectedly. They're pretty dangerous creatures."

"Tell me about it," Shan managed with a gulp. He almost seemed to turn white.

Altyrian flashed him a wan smile. "That's really very odd, though. Targs don't normally come this far south. They usually haunt the forests and mountain crags of the northern regions. Unless game is scarce or they were somehow tracking a particular scent. When they're on a trail like that, they can be pretty relentless." The elven youth turned away and peered out the mouth of the cave, yet did not really see anything beyond his unfocused stare. "I wonder what would have driven them way down here."

Shan turned back to face him. "You've saved my life twice already, Altyrian," the boy managed a little woodenly. "I thank you for that. But I really should let you get on your way without any further delay. Besides, I need to find my friends. The sooner I find them—or they find me—the better. And my thorka is probably still out there, somewhere. If he hasn't already bolted all the way back home, that is."

"Fair enough," Altyrian spoke up. He turned toward the cave wall and started snatching up his weapons. He slipped the great axe, handle down, into a broad, leather holder strapped across his back. He wriggled his arms through the straps of the canvas pack as it nestled down over the broad head of the axe. He drew the dark cloak around his large frame with a swirl of cloth and clipped it at his neck with a small, golden chain. He hefted the slender lance in his left hand and snapped up the great bow in his right. He spun back to face the boy, an imposing figure armed for battle.

Shan scooped up his own torn cloak from where it lay across a rock. He wrapped himself in it, then reached for the waterskin resting on the dusty floor. He was surprised to find it already filled. It sloshed softly as he drew it over his shoulder. He tossed a thankful smile at the tall warrior.

"Shall we go?" Altyrian said with a level gaze.

"Back out there?" Shan blurted doubtfully. He shot one hand out and stabbed it at the stream of light slashing down through the chipped, stone opening. He backed slowly away from the cave mouth. "No thanks!" Altyrian grinned at the lad. "Even you won't be able to scale that cliff with all your equipment." The boy waved his hand at him feebly.

"Not that way," the man smiled. He tipped his head towards the darkness at the back of the cave. "Through there." Shan followed the direction of the nod. He looked down the sloping floor into a wall of gloom.

"Huh?" the youth offered with a little snort.

Daryl Hanson

"There's another way into this chamber," Altyrian said. "It winds its way under all those tons of rock above us and opens on the far side of the hill. I stumbled upon the opening sometime late yesterday as I made my way through the forest. I couldn't find any recent signs of an animal using it for a lair, and decided to crawl into it for the night. It was no more than a rocky tunnel for quite a ways, then finally sloped up to this chamber. I threw myself down and slept."

"Oh," Shan murmured. "Beats the alternative route, I guess."

"Come on then!" the big man called. He spun on his heels and sauntered down the gently slanting ground. "Just follow me!" His brisk pace made Shan hurry to catch up to him.

"But—but we don't have any torches," Shan pointed out as he caught his foot on an outcropping.

"Neither did I when I came through here the other night," Altyrian countered, "and I made it through without any difficulty." The elven youth drifted forward, staring into the blanket of darkness a little dubiously. "It's not that far," the man said, as if he could read the boy's uneasy thoughts. "And half the time I could dimly make out the rocks by the light of the opening ahead."

The boy still wasn't so sure as he struggled to catch up to the big man in the darkness. He couldn't see the rough grin on Altyrian's face as he peered over his shoulder at the faltering form behind him.

Shan stumbled slightly on the uneven floor, scattering a fine spray of dust. He listened to the echo of his own breath from the high vaulted roof somewhere far above. He reached out every so often with his right hand and felt for the stony wall he could no longer see. The other hand he held cautiously out in front of his chest to prevent himself from stumbling into any boulders or pillars of rock.

After meandering for a couple hundred kora, Shan noticed the sound of their footsteps had changed subtly. The high ceiling seemed to have dropped down close to their heads, for even the shuffling of their feet, now less hollow sounding than before, had little or no echo. And the soft sounds of their breathing seemed close and immediate.

"So, where are you from, boy?" Altyrian's voice startled him from just ahead.

An instant sense of distrust rushed over Shan as he groped through the darkness. "Uh," Shan stammered. His mind reeled furiously as he tried to think what to say. "A little place you've probably never heard of before." He swallowed at dust in his throat. "Hurlik," he managed to lie after a moment. "Not really much of a place." His boot snagged on a rock and he wavered awkwardly.

"Hurlik," the man responded. "I've heard of it." Shan had a wild thought he might have been found out and held his breath. "Never been there myself. But you're probably right, doesn't sound like anything special." Shan eased out his breath as he tried not to stumble. "Still, I think Hurlik lies south and especially west of here. Didn't you say you were traveling from the west?"

"Well, I don't know," the Elfling offered nervously. "I've been so turned around since the targs attacked I don't know which way I've been going." He swallowed convulsively, unsure if his excuse would sound plausible.

"That makes sense," Altyrian replied. "Fear sometimes distorts our perception of reality."

They trudged on in silence for some time, kicking up bits of dust as they walked. The tunnel had sloped downward at first for quite some time, then gently began to bend upwards for a short while. They picked their way through a series of bends and turns. Shan found themselves topping a rise and then the ground began to fall away once again. When the rocky floor finally leveled off a couple dozen paces later, Shan thought he could see a dim glow a short way ahead. A vague light glimmered dully from one rugged wall of rock, yet he could hardly make out the other. *The passage must still snake around a bit*, he thought. He blundered suddenly into Altyrian, who had stopped unexpectedly in the passageway. Even with the cushioning of the man's pack the jolt against the flat of one axe-blade left his head ringing. He rubbed his forehead gingerly.

"Sorry," the man told him. "Things get a little tight through here."

"Right," came the youth's soft return. He felt for any drops of blood at the corner of his mouth.

The tall man slid sideways in the rocky corridor, avoiding a large boulder imbedded deeply in the right hand wall. Under the cloak Shan could hear the heavy pack scrape against the stone with a rasp of thick canvas. Altyrian moved on in a quickened pace, the light ahead gradually getting better. Trails of light streaked past the hunched, moving figure. It gave the boy a glimpse of just how tight the passage had become. Shan squeezed around the boulder and hastened after him. The tunnel curved slowly to the right and it wasn't long before they found themselves flooded by bright sunlight slanting down at them from the mouth of the cave just ahead.

Daryl Hanson

They both plodded to a halt just inside the opening and looked out. Shan blinked at the sudden brightness, but would have ventured out into the sunlight if not for Altyrian's sudden movement. He threw an arm up across the boy's chest to halt his progress. "Hold it!" he hissed softly. The tall warrior shielded his eyes with one gloved hand, peering intently out through the interlacing branches of the trees.

The scene was quiet and still, except for the slow bob of greenery in the light breeze. "Best not be too hasty," the big fellow cautioned. Trying to follow the man's expert gaze, Shan fell back and slumped against the rock wall. After so long in the darkness of the passage his eyes stung at the overwhelming glare. Altyrian simply narrowed his eyes and studied the vast tangle of trees intently. His head pivoted slowly, scrutinizing every rock and bush, as well as some of the lower-hanging branches. Satisfied at last, the tall warrior dropped his green eyes and regarded the boy. "Looks safe enough," he proclaimed. He noted the strange expression on Shan's face and idly attributed it to nerves. He shifted the weight of his pack with a shrug. "Wait here!" he ordered curtly. He gripped the lance more firmly, leveled the shaft of his bow to parallel the ground, and stepped lightly away from the cave entrance.

Altyrian moved swiftly, stealthily, across the intervening space. He plunged noiselessly into the underbrush, gliding easily over the leaf-strewn ground. Turning quickly this way and that, he paused every so often to listen. He slapped quietly at a trailing strand of thorns as they tried to catch at his cloak. The boy watched in fascination as Altyrian zig-zagged through the gently waving fronds then scurried up a small hill to the right. The man disappeared a moment later over the low rise.

Shan slid to a crouch against the wall, wiping at a trickle of sweat down his face. He had come to like the big man, but Ulfiir's sharp words still echoed in his mind. *"Trust no one!"* And with that thought an overwhelming sense of loneliness and despair swelled over him. How was he ever going to find his way to Redhaven all by himself? *I'll have to find someone*, he consoled himself. *Somewhere.*

In a moment Altyrian was back. He slipped quietly out of the bushes on the left and loped up to the little cave opening. He knelt down for a moment and looked back over his shoulder. "There's no one about!" he spoke softly, yet Shan could feel his sense of urgency. "Come on!"

Shan edged out of the cave and fell into step behind Altyrian. They quickly moved across the small clearing and ducked under the drooping branch of the nearest tree. Sunlight from high above filtered down through the gently rustling leaves as they drifted noiselessly from dappled shadow to light and back to shadow again. The tall man lifted a hand from time to time, calling them to a halt as he listened to the sounds of the forest around them. Birds constantly flitted about in the upper canopy, chirping and squawking softly to each other. After a few moments he would beckon Shan forward and they would start off again, twisting and winding through the mossy trunks.

Altyrian moved briskly past blossoming flowers and dangling vines. Shan almost found himself running to keep up with the man's long gait. He often had to dip and duck under low hanging branches as he turned this way and that through dense undergrowth. At one point, Shan found himself puffing a bit as he halted at Altyrian's hand signal. A squirrel darted along a branch just in front of him, pausing momentarily to flick its bushy tail a few times before racing off through the greenery.

"Which way are you headed?" Shan finally thought to ask during one of their brief pauses.

Altyrian never let his shifting eyes come to rest on the boy. "North," he responded, continuing to study the shadows ahead. "North, and slightly to the east." Altyrian's face finally turned back to look at the boy. "What about you?"

"Um," the youth stammered, "I'm not going that way." Altyrian gave him a long stare. He thought the boy chafed a little uncomfortably under his gaze, but he said nothing. He swung away, casually scanning the twisted shadows splashing across the trunks of several large trees ahead. The play of sunlight from above caused them to shift and move continually. "Ah, south, I think," Shan offered after a few moments. "I'm going south."

Altyrian turned back to look at him, and nodded. "Seems like our paths lie in two different directions," he observed, but he somehow wasn't convinced the boy was actually heading that way. It was more as if he had just blurted it out at random. "Any place in particular?" he asked nonchalantly. Altyrian glanced down at the boy from the corner of his eye. Shan seemed to shift nervously from one foot to the other under his sidelong gaze. "Back to Hurlik?"

"Ahh," Shan's eyes moved quickly, his mind a blur. "N-No. At least not right away, " he said at last. "M-My pony shot off in that direction when he got frightened. I'm hoping I'll be able to find him wandering around somewhere nearby." Shan looked over at the man evenly, hoping he sounded convincing.

Daryl Hanson

Altyrian nodded his head once slowly. "It's possible," he shrugged. "But if something spooked him, a targ as you say, he might still be running." The big warrior pursed his lips. "For home, I'll wager. And wildly. Hopefully we won't find any more of those savage creatures prowling around in the woods." Shan could only blink nervously.

Altyrian was just about to start off once again, when they both noticed the lack of sound in the forest. There were no more birds darting from tree to tree in colorful bursts of feathers and their incessant chittering had stopped abruptly. A soft wind tickled through the branches with a low sighing of leaves. Shan found himself straining to hear the slightest sound, but even the crackle of rodents scurrying through the underbrush was absent.

Both of them were wary and alert as they stood hardly breathing. After a long, tense tableau, Shan thought he could make out a kind of hum drifting on the slight breeze. It was far-off at first, coming towards them from the west at a rapid clip. It sounded like a garbled song or chant. There was a flurry of stamping and bashing which grew with incredible speed. It was rhythmic in nature and had an odd cadence to it. It sounded vaguely familiar and Shan had the unmistakable sensation he had heard it somewhere before.

"Hide!" Altyrian hissed sharply at him. "Now!" He bolted for cover behind a large tree trunk that had fallen a short distance away. He crossed the space in a matter of heartbeats and lunged over the sprawling, moss-covered mass. The arms of leafy fronds parted for him as he disappeared beyond. Shan was hot on his heels as the snapping and crashing through the underbrush seemed suddenly just behind him. He flung himself over the great trunk and dropped down beside Altyrian. In the process the hood of his cloak had settled over his head, masking his face in shadow. He spit at a hairy branch that scratched at his cheek. Their eyes met briefly, the big man raising one finger to his tightly drawn lips. Shan nodded almost imperceptibly, his eyes wide in fear, his heart drumming wildly in his throat.

The pounding of heavy footsteps reverberated loudly from the forest trunks scattered all around them. Shan reached up a hand to brace himself against the moist curve of the decaying giant. A fragment of bark crumbled away through his fingers. His hand froze on the trunk as a dozen dark forms burst through a wall of foliage where he and Altyrian had stood just moments before. A sudden guttural command split the air and brought them all crashing to a halt on the opposite side of the great fallen tree. The strange song they were chanting fell raggedly away as they lapsed into silence, broken only by the hissing and gurgling of their breathing, and the clink and stomp of steel-shod boots. A thick, raspy voice barked out a terse command. The dark company fanned out and threw themselves on the ground. Many of them even thrust their backs up against the mossy giant.

Shan was shaking with fear as the great tree shifted slightly with their added weight. He flashed a look at Altyrian, who cautiously reached up a hand, palm out, to urge the boy to absolute stillness. They could hear the loathsome creatures hissing and whistling softly to one another as they drank noisily from water skins or nibbled at light rations from their packs.

The elven youth was pressed tightly against the moldy bark, listening intently. Even in his fear he was overcome with curiosity. *What do these things really look like?* he wondered. He slowly, ever so slowly, raised his head and peered out from under the cloak hood, through the thick ferns lining both sides of the great tree trunk. He felt sure he had seen these things before, that night he had clung helplessly to his perch overlooking the clearing.

The first glance almost brought a gasp from him, but he managed to clamp his lips tightly shut without so much as a sound. He allowed only his eyes to move as he stared out through his leafy covering. One of the gorguls, which he somehow felt certain these creatures must be, sprawled only three or four kora from him. It greedily devoured a chunk of rotting meat, chomping and biting at it with single-minded haste.

Its head was somewhat elongated at the crown, with greasy strands of long, dark hair pulled up into a top-knot. Its large eyes were set widely apart and were a bit slanted to the outside. Shan couldn't get a good look at the pupils, since it had narrowed its eyelids intently upon its meal, yet he thought they had a lateral look to them, sort of like the slitted stare of a cat. Its nose was broad and strangely flat, like a bull ape. Its ears were long and fleshy, and were distinctly pointed, with the outside edge serrated like the wings of a bat. A large, gold ring dangled from each lobe.

The great mouth was easily the most distinguishing feature, Shan felt sure. The lips seemed to split the sallow face from ear to ear. It had large yellowish teeth, fang-like, which dripped foul streams of saliva continuously. Protruding from the flabby bottom lip were two large tusks which curled upward near its eyes. They looked wickedly sharp, but were stained to a hideous yellowish brown.

The thing itself was broad through the shoulders. Huge arms rolled with muscle beneath a thick, scaly hide, which reminded him a little of snake skin. Its hands ended in heavy claws. These easily appeared capable of ripping a person's throat out. Shan watched in fascination as the thing finished gnawing on the meat and tossed the scrap of bone aside. It licked at its slobbering lips with a long, dark tongue, somewhat forked near the end, before pulling the stopper from a waterskin with its great teeth. It threw back its large head and sucked loudly from the spigot.

A harsh growl brought the entire squad to their feet. Some of them greedily shoved the last of their odious food into gaping mouths, while others crammed the remnants into their packs. A couple of them stoppered their botas and swung them back over their shoulders on their leather straps. A few others continued to chew on the lingering scraps in their mouths for several moments before swallowing hastily. Many of them belched fiercely amid a chorus of sniggers. Another sharp hiss from their leader goaded them all to silence. They shuffled into loose formation behind him. He glared at them in irritation then swung about and barked a throaty command. With surprising speed they charged off into the underbrush, their sing-song chant taken up again almost instantly. The jingle and rattle of their weapons was soon lost amid the heavy stamping of their steel boots.

Altyrian slowly rose to his feet. He stared off to the east, in the direction of their march, for some time. Shan popped up through the lightly weaving fronds next to him. Altyrian continued to scrutinize the forest before hopping back over the fallen log. "That was pretty close," he stated. "It's a good thing they didn't discover us or we'd have been hard pressed to fight them off."

"So, that's what a gorgul looks like up close," Shan commented, a tinge of fear shading his voice. His gaze trailed off after them, but the sounds of their passing were completely lost on the light wind. "They move pretty fast." He slid down over the top of the log and joined Altyrian.

"Not very stealthy, though," the big man looked down at him. Shan shook his head in agreement. "We're lucky this was just a short meal break," Altyrian went on. "If they had been seriously searching the area they'd have sent out some scouts."

"And then we would have been spotted for sure," the elven youth proclaimed.

"Exactly." The warrior looked off to the north and slightly east in their original direction of travel. "Come on," he said, "we'd better get going." He made to move off.

"Wait," the boy interjected. Altyrian turned and leveled his emerald eyes on the boy. "I'm not going that way," Shan continued with some insistence. "I can't."

Altyrian's brow furrowed in consternation. "Why? What's the matter?"

The elven youth swallowed with a little effort. He knew he had to give the man a reasonable story for his hesitancy. His eyes raced back and forth as he thought furiously to come up with a good excuse for not traveling along with him. "I'm not really from Hurlik," he confessed softly.

"I didn't think so," Altyrian acknowledged with a tilt to his head.

"Silkirk," Shan went on slowly. "I'm from Silkirk." He looked eastward as if to confirm his words. "There was a . . . there was this brawl, you see." He lowered his eyes to stare at his feet. He tapped the toes of his light boots together to emphasize his contrition. "Property was damaged, some people got hurt. It wasn't my fault." He hesitated. "But they all just think it was my fault. Who knows how much trouble I'd have been in if I hadn't gotten out of there." He looked up at Altyrian. "That's why I took the thorka without permission. And now he's lost out there somewhere, and I need to get him back before I can go home." He thrust out his chin in determination.

Altyrian clapped a gloved hand on the boy's shoulder. "I understand," the big man said with a grin. "I think we've all gotten into a little trouble from time to time." Shan tried to look a little sheepish and then finally offered a wan smile. "So you probably thought the village elders sent me out here to track you down and haul you back in. Huh?" Shan managed a guilty nod. "Don't worry, I won't force you to come with me if you don't want to." The boy came up with a look of measured relief on his face, but inside Shan was ecstatic. "Do you have a place to stay for a couple of days, at least until you can find that pony of yours?"

"Sure," Shan replied. "I've got some friends in Branby. It's not too far from here, I think."

"No, not too far," Altyrian returned. "About a day's walk in that direction." He pointed almost due west. Shan followed the man's gesture with a turn of his head. "Are you sure you want to travel alone?" the man asked him when Shan swung back to face him.

"I'll be fine," the elven youth said with a false tone of confidence to his voice. He bit at his lip to keep it from quivering a little. He looked

Daryl Hanson

back towards the direction of Branby and smiled.

"Well, I guess that's it," Altyrian said. He gave the boy a rough shake. "Take care of yourself then. And don't get careless. These woods are teeming with unsavory characters, the kind of riffraff you'd best not stumble into. Not just gorguls, if you know what I mean." Shan nodded. "And try to stay out of trouble," the big man chuckled. "I won't be there to cut you loose next time." The lad flashed him a wry smile.

"Oh, that reminds me," Shan said, fumbling at his belt. He pulled out a greasy lump about the size of his palm from the circlet of leather. "Here," he said, holding it out to the big man, "whatever it is."

"Keep it," Altyrian said with a grin. "You might need it again."

"Thanks," said the boy, and stuffed it back under his belt. Then, as an afterthought, he asked, "What is it?"

"*Avira* butter." The big man laughed at Shan's look of confusion. "It comes from a desert plant that grows far to the south. You have to cut open the broad stalks and drain the thick, milky fluid. Then it has to be boiled in great wooden vats for days—it stinks like you wouldn't believe—and the resulting fiber is scooped into lumps and left to dry." He clapped the boy on the arm. "Don't worry, I have another one," he said, patting at his cloak, "somewhere." He laughed.

"Thanks again!" Shan said with a broad grin.

Altyrian gripped firmly onto the boy's hands for a moment before letting go. "Be careful and watch out for more of those gorguls!" he said. "There seems to be a lot of them about these days." He turned and started off at once in long, brisk strides. "I wish you well, boy," he called over his shoulder.

"I wish you well," Shan returned, raising his right hand and waving. He watched the man disappear in the fold of undergrowth, then turned and sauntered off in the opposite direction.

Branby

[18th of Kaligath, 4534 C.R.]

Kilgar pulled back hard on the reins. The thorka lifted its great head high and thundered to a halt with a flurry of dust on the top of a small rise. The large animal pranced about for a few moments upon its six, long legs, stamping and clawing at the surface of the roadway, and kicking up even larger swirls of dust. The stallion snorted loudly through its nostrils and shook its great head. It sputtered little flecks of foam in all directions then came to rest in the middle of the road, its sides heaving lightly. Kilgar could feel the swell of the animal's breathing press outward rhythmically against his legs. The thorka threw back its head and snorted once again, its wild, thick mane flying out in ebony streamers. Small jets of steam formed tiny clouds about the animal's long muzzle.

Kilgar leaned forward in the saddle and slapped the wet neck of his mount affectionately. "Good work, Adrulax!" the boy crooned in the thorka's ear. "Good boy! You're still the best!" The stallion curled its head around and settled one dark eye on the beaming face of its rider. It nickered softly at him, then looked away with a quick dip of its head to the ground. It sniffed noisily at the dirt, inspiring little wisps of fine dust to scatter out lazily.

The boy pressed his cheek against the long, sleek neck. It felt wet and warm against his skin. "You deserve a good rub down tonight," he murmured. A tuft of mane tickled at Kilgar's face, just below his eye. He shook his head gently and brushed the stiff, black hair away with his left hand. Then he reached down with his other hand and began to stroke the animal in long, slow motions back and forth upon the glistening coat along the front of its neck. The thorka huffed softly in contentment, flicking its long ears and stamping its feet. The sharp, retractable claws flashed out momentarily from under its hooves, scratching at the soft dirt of the roadway, and then were snapped swiftly back out of sight. Kilgar gave the animal a quick hug before he sat up.

He heard the faint beat of hooves from down the road behind him. He swung about in the saddle with a creaking of leather, shading his eyes with the back of one hand. The road bore sharply downhill from the rise where Adrulax stood and was lost to view a hundred kora away, curving suddenly to the right and dipping into a series of shallow hills. Kilgar followed the fine smudge of dust rising gently above the sea of forest trees lining the undulating ribbon of roadway. The other riders weren't too far

Daryl Hanson

behind him now. The little cloud grew larger and more distinct as the sharp sound of hoof beats approached. His great thorka rested easily on its six legs, its breathing now more relaxed and even. Occasionally the muscles of one leg or another would quiver for a moment. Adrulax lashed his long, dark tail quietly at a buzzing swarm of flies.

Two wildly galloping thorka came hurtling around the bend and tore up the road toward the waiting youth. Clumps of rock and dirt flew out behind the ponies in graceful arcs amid the fierce rhythm of their hooves. The two riders were hardly discernible from Kilgar's position. They appeared as mere humps, leaning far forward in the stirrups and pressing themselves tightly to the backs of their thundering mounts. The boys' faces were lashed savagely by the animals' bristly manes.

The powerful thorka almost seemed to float toward Kilgar, their hooves barely touching the ground at the end of each long, graceful stride. Both riders strained in the saddle, urging their mounts onto greater speed. They both employed the touch of their heels, the light slap of the reins, and small cries of encouragement, which somehow seemed little more than muffled grunts.

Adrulax shifted uneasily at the swelling sound of their approach. He swung quickly about in the middle of the road and danced around on his six, long legs. He reared himself up on his two hind legs and snorted loudly with a mighty toss of his head. He came down heavily and rumbled a trumpeting challenge from deep in his chest.

"Easy, boy," Kilgar spoke lightly in his ear. The youth patted the animal on the muscular shoulder and turned his gaze to the riders quickly bearing down on them. Kilgar was sure he could feel the shivering of the ground beneath him as they hurtled rapidly closer. He swept his face away suddenly as the two thorka roared simultaneously to a halt in a shower of earth hardly a kor away from the nose of his own stallion. Adrulax snorted in agitation and lifted himself on his haunches, raking at the air with dark flashes of his front two hooves. Kilgar hung on tightly to the horn of his saddle until his great mount fell back to the surface of the road. He peered through a cloud of dust at the grinning faces of his two friends, and choked.

"I won!" bellowed a red-haired youth. He wiped a trickle of dirt and sweat from his face with the back of one hand.

"No, I won, Doornig!" yelled the other lad, a broad grin splitting his face from ear to ear. He shook dust from his sandy-brown hair as if to emphasize his words. "You'll never beat me!" he proclaimed loudly, still grinning.

"Oh yeah?" Doornig retorted stoutly. "Says who?"

"Says me!" the second boy told him with a snort. "Not on that useless nag anyway."

"Listen, Gorian," Doornig spit out, a sparkle in his eye. "It's not really the animal that makes the difference, anyway. It's the rider." Gorian rolled his eyes skyward and chuckled. "It's true!" the fiery-headed youth shot back. "Why, I've more than made up for my lack of a great steed with my expertise in the saddle," he stated flatly.

"Hah!" Gorian blurted out, exploding with laughter. He rocked forward in the saddle and slapped at his knee. "The only thing you are an expert at, Doornig," he managed to say between small fits of laughter, "is falling off your thorka. And that's no lie!"

Doornig reddened noticeably. "That only happened once!" he snapped back, scowling. "It was a brand new saddle and it was way too stiff. I couldn't cinch it up properly and that's the truth." Still chuckling, Gorian blew out air and shook his finger at the red-haired youth. "Well," Doornig offered lamely, "what about that time you—"

"Hey, hey, hey!" Kilgar cut in. "That's enough, you two." The sharp ring in his voice drew startled looks from the other two boys. It was almost as if they hadn't noticed him sitting there quietly waiting for them. They dropped their feud and peered around at him slack-jawed, another string of invective already poised on their lips. "No use getting sore at each other!" Kilgar continued with mild reproach. The two boys exchanged quick glances, then swung their faces back to stare at him, their eyes still flashing. "Besides," Kilgar ventured with a little smile, "neither of you won." Their foreheads wrinkling in protest, both of the boys opened their mouths as if to speak, but Kilgar quickly waved them off. "I did!" They glared at him for a moment, blinking in confusion. "Remember?"

The three boys remained staring at each other for the longest time, and then they slowly broke into a laugh. "He's right, you know," Gorian snickered.

"Yeah," Doornig said with reluctance. "But that doesn't really count. He always wins!"

"You noticed that too, huh?" Gorian shot a quick look at his red-haired friend.

"Yeah," responded Doornig with a playful leer in Kilgar's direction. He winked at Gorian. "What do you say? Let's get him!"

Daryl Hanson

"Yeah," Gorian agreed, "let's get him!"

The two boys slapped at their mounts with the reins. Their thorka pranced lightly forward and pressed closer to Adrulax. Kilgar wheeled his own beast as the others darted forward and managed to duck under their playful punches. But Doornig's stallion collided with Adrulax and both mounts expelled their breaths noisily. Whispers of dust, clinging to the animals' flanks, curled gently into the air. Kilgar expertly backed his thorka away as the two boys reined in their own mounts and swung about in pursuit.

"Are you two spoiling for another race?" Kilgar asked with a laugh.

"You bet!" squeaked Doornig.

"Any time!" chimed Gorian. The two boys nodded firmly together.

"Okay," Kilgar cried out, wheeling away from them with a deft flick of his wrists on the reins. The long, thin strips of leather held delicately in his fingers snaked out behind him as his thorka sped off down the road. "You asked for it!" he called back over his shoulder. With a slap of their own reins and a burst of wild yelps the other boys were after him in an instant. The three sleek animals tore rapidly back up the lane towards town. Great clumps of dirt flew out behind them and spattered the road like falling hail.

"We're gonna get you this time!" Doornig hollered at Kilgar's back. The wind snapped at his face and whipped through his unruly red hair.

"You'll have to catch me first!" Kilgar laughed amid the pounding of their hooves.

The road wound in and out of patches of the forest. Sometimes they found themselves in bright sunlight, and at others, they were plunged into the shady dimness under the great branches. Birds scolded them from the safety of the trees as they thundered past. Kilgar leaned close over the neck of his mount, the pair pounding up and down small rises on their way back to the village. Gorian and Doornig could never quite draw any closer to him as their own thorka battled shoulder to shoulder together on the bumpy roadway. Leaves slapped at them and they gritted their teeth through the rush of foliage. Their eyes watered constantly, blurring their vision. They cried out in short bursts of encouragement, occasionally flicking the loose end of their reins upon the animals' broad flanks. One mount surged forward for a couple of heartbeats, and then the other would catch up and start to pass, only to be caught a few moments later by the first. On and on they raced, forever jockeying their positions.

Far ahead, Kilgar broke out from under the closeness of the trees as the road swept in a wide curve to the left. It fell away into a large meadow where a small stream meandered through the low- lying ground. Adrulax streaked toward the wooden bridge spanning the water and was soon clattering across it. Kilgar looked back once to find no glimpse of the other two boys behind him. "Good boy," he patted the animal's glistening neck as they swept up the rising incline of the roadway on the opposite side of the meadow and bore on to the gate of the village. He eased back on the reins and allowed the great animal to slow to a canter as they drew closer. Adrulax whinnied in response, raising his head high and snorting in triumph.

Kilgar waved to the old watchman as they rode in through the gate, slowing his great animal to a walk almost instantly. Once through the broad portal, the boy immediately swung to the right at the first cross street. The creature's six legs delicately clipped at the dust-strewn cobbles of the street as they slowly rode past scattered clumps of villagers scurrying about on their late afternoon errands. They turned sharply to the right once again as they came upon the stables. Kilgar ducked into the big opening under the hayloft and emerged a few moments later through a large, sliding door, poised open, leading to a wide central courtyard. A young boy was scattering straw into the covered stalls encircling the yard of hard-packed earth. He nodded at them when they entered. Kilgar pulled up the big mount in the middle of the court and slid down off the saddle. He led the animal to the last stall on the left, one hand tenderly stroking the side of its sweaty neck. The great animal's breathing had slowed to a deep, slow whisper.

He had already unbuckled the leather saddle and pulled it down from his mount before Doornig and Gorian pranced into the open courtyard through the sliding door. Kilgar deposited the saddle on a wooden rack along one wall of the cubicle before turning to look at his friends. Their faces were still flushed and their hair was in wild disarray as they climbed down off of their thorka. They bantered among themselves as they pulled the animals along by their reins.

"I won again!" Doornig was saying, his red hair flapping about his face.

"No you didn't," Gorian came back, wiping a trickle of sweat from his own eyes. "You seem to have a way of seeing things wrong."

"I know exactly what I saw, and I saw us getting to the bridge before you did." Doornig blew at a strand of hair across his nose. "That was pretty clear."

Daryl Hanson

"I hate to burst your bubble, my hot-headed friend," Gorian returned with a twisted smile, "but we *crossed* the bridge first." He affected an air of triumph as they reached the adjacent stalls.

"Oh? Since when has that been the finish line?" Doornig snorted. "It's always been the first plank of the bridge."

"Oh, yeah? Who made up that rule?" Gorian bellowed.

Doornig scratched at his head. "Uhh . . . Kilgar, I think." He stood at the edge of the stall and glanced over at Kilgar quietly rubbing his animal down with a *bristleweed* brush. "Tell him, Kilgar. You made up the rules a long time ago. Right?" Both boys turned to glare at him as he slowly stroked Adrulax with the dried *bristleweed*. He looked back innocently at the boys and shrugged. "Oh, come on," Doornig went on. "It's always been from here to Florrin Hill. And then from the hill back to the bridge, the first piece of *wood* on the bridge." He crossed his arms with a smug look.

"It really doesn't matter, you two," Kilgar finally offered. "Neither one of you won. Either on the way to the hill—or back. We won," he continued to brush his thorka's sleek flanks. "Or have you both forgotten that already?" The two boys looked at him for a few moments, their mouths hanging open.

"Who cares?" Gorian finally blurted out. The two companions turned back to one another with a toss of their heads at Kilgar and picked up their argument where they left off.

They were still chattering back and forth as they strode all the way through the streets of the village, climbed the stairs of the inn, and pattered down the hallway to Kilgar's room. Dusk was starting to settle over Branby as they opened up the thick, wooden door and drifted inside. Kilgar eased over to a table in the center of the room where a half-burned candle sat in a low stand. He scooped up a piece of flint and struck it a few times with the edge of a small knife he found lying there. Sparks scattered briefly in the half-darkness and then quickly disappeared. On the fourth attempt a spark caught on the candle wick and slowly glowed to life. Kilgar used the flickering flame to light a couple of other candles placed throughout the chamber. He passed one to each of the boys. Splashed in the soft, warm light, the upstairs room soon took on a cozy feel.

The roof slanted down from a central beam and there were two dormer windows on either side of the long axis. A small cot was situated against the back wall, opposite the door. There was a little desk in one corner near the cot and a soft chair in the other. Kilgar set his candle down on the edge of the desk and crossed to the chair. The other boys placed their lights on small, wooden shelves, where the slanting ceiling gave way to low walls about a kor or so from the floor.

"Look," Kilgar said as he slumped down into the chair in the corner, slouching back and throwing one leg over a padded arm. "Is it possible to have one evening without the constant bickering?"

"Bickering?" Doornig questioned. "Who's bickering?" Kilgar leaned his head to the side and rolled his eyes toward the ceiling. "Okay, okay," the redheaded boy had to admit, "we do like to spar verbally—a *little*—but I wouldn't call it constant . . ."

"A little?" Kilgar was incredulous. "Try non-stop. Amid your continual stream of chatter I can hardly hear myself think sometimes."

"We are a little vocal on occasion, I have to admit," Gorian offered in their defense, "but I would hardly call it non-stop."

"No, most of the time we're practically as quiet as a *fleef*," Doornig affirmed. "*Most* of the time."

"Hah!" Kilgar shook his head and stared up into the nearest dormer. The sky was beginning to grow a deep purple outside.

"Well, most of the time, anyway," the red haired youth was adamant. Kilgar expelled his breath in a derisive laugh. "No, really." The two boys plopped down in a couple of other chairs nestled against the low walls.

Kilgar continued to stare up into the dormer for a long moment. "Hmm," he said to himself after a time. "I'm sure I locked that window when I went out." He rose to his feet and tapped at the window latch. He wiggled the tongue of the hasp back and forth with his fingertip a couple of times before snapping it into place over the staple and dropping the small metal bolt through the hole.

Kilgar looked warily around the room. He took a few steps toward the table in the center of the open area, peering into the heavy shadows in the other dormer windows. There was a bookcase in the corner to the right of the door with a little space between it and the slanted roof. It was impossible for him to see clearly in the gathering gloom. The other corner offered no hiding place, just a medium-sized chest, no higher than mid-thigh. His gaze drifted back to the shadowed corner.

By now the two other boys had noticed his scrutiny and had halted their bantering. Their heads swung to watch curiously as Kilgar moved quietly towards the corner. He stopped halfway between the table and the bookcase. Something caught his eye on the floor and he looked down.

Daryl Hanson

There was a dark splotch on the wooden floorboards. He slowly reached down and picked it up. It was a small, dark green leaf. It was wet between his fingertips.

"What is it?" Doornig wanted to know. Both boys rose to their feet and moved over to stand with him. They looked down onto his palm, the flickering light from the candles making it difficult to determine what he held cupped in his hand.

"Let me see," Gorian said, reaching out a hand to touch the crumpled, dark object. "Ahh," the boy chided him mildly, "it's only a leaf."

"Big deal," Doornig was disappointed, turning away. "We probably dragged it in with us from the forest. And here I thought it was something important."

"It might be," Kilgar retorted. "This kind of tree doesn't grow anywhere near Branby."

"Huh?" Doornig swung back around with renewed interest. "Then where does it come from?"

"I'm not sure." Kilgar turned the thing over in his hand. "Pretty far from here, I think."

"More importantly," Gorian asked thoughtfully, "how did it get here? It's still wet."

There was a sudden soft scuffling sound from the corner. All three of them looked up, trying desperately to pierce the deepening shadows. Kilgar reached out and snatched up the nearest candle and held it out before him. The tiny flame wavered wildly with the movement, then settled down to a soft, warm glow. Two toes from a pair of leather boots could just be seen around the edge of the bookcase.

"Who's there?" Kilgar called out firmly, but there was no reply. "Why are you here? What do you want?" Still there was no response. The three boys looked at each other nervously.

Kilgar backed up to the table a few steps behind him and reached down, without looking, for the small knife he had used to light his candle. He fished about for a few moments, then his hand finally settled over the small grip, and he picked it up. He returned to the other two, the little blade held firmly in one hand, the candle in the other. The three boys exchanged hesitant looks once more. Kilgar passed the candle to Doornig and indicated the other light nearby with a nod to Gorian. The sandy-haired youth nodded in return and bent to fetch the candle. With a final look at each other, they slowly moved in together on the bookcase.

With a sudden sheepish feeling, Kilgar hesitated. The others paused with him. "Rimmy," he called out, "Rimmy, is that you?" When there was still no answer he brought the knife up in an outstretched fist. Pale flickers of light glinted from its small blade. "Rimmy, this is not funny. I've got a knife." The soft scuffling sound was repeated from the shadows. "Don't make me hurt you." The trio of boys moved one step closer.

"Wait, wait!" said a voice from the corner. "I'm not here to harm anyone." Kilgar's grip on the knife relaxed. But the voice was not that of his brother. He'd heard it somewhere before, but he just couldn't quite place where, or when. "Don't be frightened," it said. "I need your help."

And with that Shan stepped lightly out from behind the bookcase and into the small glow of their candles. He held his hands out in front of him, palms open. "I'm not Rimmy," he said, his lips twisted into a odd smile.

"Then just who . . . ?" Doornig faltered. The three boys stared at him for several moments before recognition slowly dawned in Kilgar's eyes.

"Shan?" he asked after a moment. "Is that you?"

The elven youth managed a wry smile and an awkward nod of his head.

"Who?" Gorian glanced at Kilgar, a frown spreading across his face. "You know this guy?"

"Yeah," Kilgar replied with a grin. "Fezzik nearly beat him to a pulp about a yahr ago." The two boys looked over at him, their eyes wide. "Remember? Right here on Kalgurn."

Realization slowly crept onto Doornig's face. "You don't mean that big brawl, do you?" Kilgar nodded matter-of-factly. "This is that skinny elven kid?" The redhead swept his eyes toward Shan, who just stood there shuffling from one foot to the other. He stared closely at the Elfling. "But he just doesn't look the same."

"A lot of things can happen in a yahr," Kilgar said, setting the knife back down on the table behind them. "People change."

"I think I filled out some," Shan told them lightly. "Maybe put on a little weight."

"No, it's more than that," Doornig said, eyeing Shan's head scarf curiously. He tilted his head back and forth as he tried to peer under the cloth.

"I've had to hide who I am," the elven youth confessed. "I've got all kinds of people chasing me. I've been on the run for days. They even attacked my village and I barely got out alive."

"Somebody attacked Draydin?" Kilgar was astonished. Shan nodded to him through a hard swallow.

"Who?" Gorian wanted to know. "Who would attack your village? And why?"

"Gorguls," Shan struggled to spit out the word. "I've been hunted by packs of them over the last few days. They're still out there somewhere, scouring the woods for me right now."

"Gorguls?" Doornig snorted. "Hah! They're just an old woman's bedtime story." He turned to Gorian with a laugh.

"That's what I used to think, too," Shan spoke in a serious tone. "Until they came after me in the middle of the night. They tried to burn Draydin to the ground to get to me!" Doornig looked back at him with a smirk, still unconvinced.

"Why would they want you?" the redhead was curious. "Not that I believe they exist or anything." Shan could only shrug in ignorance.

"Come on," Kilgar said. "Let's all sit down around the table and you can tell us all about it." Doornig relented with another smirk as they placed all three candles on the worn tabletop. They all dragged chairs from around the room to the low, central table. Kilgar pulled his soft, padded chair out of the corner of the room and plopped down into it while Shan found himself a hard, wooden kitchen chair along one of the low walls. Doornig brought over a three-legged, round-top stool which he took from one of the dormer windows. Gorian had to kick aside a scuffed pair of boots and some other things next to a small bench along one of the low walls. He lifted the low seat out of the clutter and slid it across the floor. They all sat down in a circle around the table. Once they had gotten themselves settled, the boys all turned to regard the Elfling. The elven youth leaned forward in the wooden chair and cleared his throat. The others leaned in as well, anxious to hear his story. Doornig still held a skeptical look about his eyes.

"It all started about five, no, six days ago," Shan told them. "It's all been so crazy I've lost track of the time." Doornig and Gorian exchanged sidelong glances. "I awoke sometime in the middle of the night," the elven lad went on. "I had an eerie feeling as I looked out the window to discover the heavy village gate wide open and no one in sight. Then I heard a strange call from somewhere out in the forest, a sort of long, moaning wail. It was unlike anything I'd ever heard before and it chilled me all the way to the bone." The boys leaned in even more to listen raptly, like they were sharing a kind of ghost story around a campfire which could only be told in whispers. "I was about to run out of my room to alert someone to what was happening, when I heard something moving in the hall just outside my door. Whatever it was, it was big, and it sniffed noisily at the floor as it moved along."

"A watchbeast, perhaps," Gorian offered.

"Will you shut up," Kilgar admonished him. "Let Shan tell the story, will ya!"

"Okay, okay," the sandy-haired boy said. "I was just wondering out loud."

"Well, don't!" Gorian clamped his lips closed and Kilgar swung his eyes back to the elven boy. Shan licked at his own lips before going on.

"It wasn't a watchbeast, I can tell you," Shan stated. "It was bigger, much bigger, than any sleeth you've ever seen. When it stood up on its hind feet it was more than three kora in height." There were doubtful snickers from Doornig and Gorian. One stern look from Kilgar silenced them both immediately. "It was covered in black fur and had long, razor-sharp claws. Its eyes had turned blood-red because it was on a hunt. Ulfiir said it was a blood tracker, an evil beast from ages past. He called it a kurgoth. Said it was created by Muurdra long ago."

"Muurdra!" hissed Doornig in derision. "Puh! He doesn't even exist. That's just a fear tactic to keep wild children in line."

"Doornig!" Kilgar blasted him. "Will you keep quiet." The red-haired boy lapsed back into silence. He lowered his head between his shoulders and gave it a small shake.

"Whether you believe in Muurdra or not is beside the point," Shan told him softly. "The thing was real. I saw it. And it almost killed me." Even Doornig looked up at him then. There was something in the tone of his voice the boys could not deny. "When the soldiers finally arrived at my room, the huge creature tangled with a bunch of watchbeasts, and they were no match for it. It batted them aside as if they were playthings." There were looks of awe in the boys' eyes. "If it wasn't for Ulfiir, I'd probably be dead right now." He grunted heavily. "Come to find out the old man is really some kind of wizard. He killed the beast with sparks of blue fire which he shot out of his hands."

"Really?" Kilgar breathed out softly. Both Doornig and Gorian flashed him an angry glare. "Sorry," he said in apology. "Go on, Shan, what happened next?" They all swung their faces attentively in his direction.

"That's when the gorguls showed up," the Elfling went on in a tight voice. "Weeson ran off to roust out the guards. I could hear the clash of their weapons outside the great hall. I wanted to help, but I didn't know how. Ulfiir whisked me out the back way, but some of the attackers must have burst into the room, because I could hear their footsteps clattering loudly not too far behind us. Ulfiir even shot at a few of them with his bolts of fire. I could hear some of them screaming in the darkness."

Shan paused for a moment, licking at his dry lips. His voice had grown hoarse. Kilgar rose from his chair and scooped up a pitcher of water from the small desk. He sloshed some into a glass and passed it to the elven boy. Shan drank it down immediately, noisily. He smacked his lips together as Kilgar refilled it. The Elfling slurped a little more before looking up thankfully to the hovering youth with a little smile. He sipped at it and then placed the remainder on the table before him. Kilgar set the pitcher next to the glass and slid back into his chair. The boys all seemed to hold their breaths as Shan cleared his throat and launched himself into his tale once more.

"I thought we would be trapped in the kitchen for sure," the elven youth declared, his voice clearer. "But Ulfiir opened up some secret passage, a tunnel dug under the village walls, and we found ourselves somewhere in the forest. Only Ulfiir didn't come with me. He shoved me out of the doorway and left me standing there by myself." The boys seemed to gasp at his words. They shared a quick glance between themselves.

"You found yourself alone?" Doornig was stunned. "All alone?"

"And you've been by yourself since then?" Gorian asked, incredulously.

Kilgar flashed them a look of irritation, but let it slide as Shan continued to speak. "It was only for a day—at first," he told them. "I spent the night stumbling through the woods and all of the next day. It wasn't until after I saw for myself a squad of gorguls crashing through the trees on their way to Draydin that I ran into some of the others. Weeson and a couple of soldiers from the garrison had been sent out to find me. They had some thorka and we made our way west, away from Draydin. But we soon found ourselves running from pursuit, probably more of the gorguls I think, and then eventually we got attacked and separated by a pack of targs."

"Targs!" Doornig spit out in disbelief.

Shan nodded solemnly, the fear evident in his face. "That's right," he finally managed to say. "Large, three-headed wolves." He focused his eyes on the red-haired boy, who was bristling once again with the absurdity of the story. "I know, it probably sounds like just another creature from legend to you—kurgoths, targs, gorguls—but let me assure you, they're very real. They probably killed my friends and I barely escaped with my life. But the worse thing is, they're still out there somewhere, I'm sure."

The tension in the room was as thick as fog. Suddenly, a knock rattled at the door. The four of them exchanged quick glances like conspirators caught helplessly in a trap.

"Kilgar!" came a boy's excited voice at the door. He knocked again, loudly. "Kilgar, you'll never believe what I just saw!"

Shan had jumped up and quickly withdrawn into one of the dormer windows. It was completely dark outside by now, and that particular spot was shielded from the soft light of the candles, leaving him heavily drenched in shadows. He squeezed back into the small alcove as far as he could. "Rimmy," Kilgar said in a stiff undertone to the others. "Stay there for a moment," he called softly to the elven youth. "I'll send him away." The other two boys rose to their feet and stood nervously around the table.

Kilgar stalked over to the door and yanked it open. A smaller and younger version of himself stared back at him. Rimmy darted inside immediately, before Kilgar could say anything. His dark hair was in wild disarray and his breathing was ragged, as if he'd been running. Kilgar still held the door open but Rimmy rushed over to the table. He swung his head about quickly as he tried to look at them all at once.

"Not now, Rimmy," the older boy started to say.

"But Kilgar, you'll never believe what I just saw," the younger boy said in between breaths.

"Later," Kilgar said. "Can't you see we're busy?"

"But Kilgar," Rimmy panted. "They're here! I saw them in the stable." He looked from his brother to Doornig to Gorian and then back to Kilgar.

"Okay," Kilgar offered, thinking to humor him. The sooner his little brother spoke his mind the sooner he would go away and leave them in peace. He closed the door and moved back into the room. "So, just what exactly did you see in the stables?"

"Gorguls!" Rimmy said breathlessly. "Gorguls! I just saw a whole pack of 'em. In the village!" The other boys looked quickly at each other, alarm in their eyes.

"Wait!" Kilgar cried. "Are you trying to tell me there are gorguls here in Branby?" The younger boy nodded his head fiercely. "Right now?

Are you sure?"

"Yes," the boy said, his eyes nearly popping out of their sockets in fear. He swallowed hard between breaths. Shan listened intently from the window, his own throat growing tight.

"What exactly did you see?" Doornig questioned him, leaning forward.

"I was down by the gate," Rimmy said numbly. "I was going to see my friend, Kellen. He lives pretty close-by. We were supposed to meet up with the blacksmith." Kilgar nodded at him. "But then I heard someone arguing outside the gate, only I couldn't quite understand what they were saying. So I poked my head around the corner and found myself staring at a bunch of yellow-skinned scaly men. You know, right out of the storybooks. They were crowding around the gatekeeper and they were hissing angrily at him in a kind of raspy language. They forced their way past the old man and one of them clubbed him to the ground. I fell back and hid behind the gate as they marched into the village."

"They forced their way into town?" Gorian was incensed. "That's not good."

"Where are they now?" Kilgar questioned his brother.

"All over the village, I think," Rimmy replied. "They spread out with a grunt from their commander and started working their way up the streets. They had some very large, strange-looking animals with them. Kind of like watchbeasts, only much, much bigger. They must have been riding them, because they had large saddles strapped upon their huge backs. Two of the brutes escorted the ugly creatures down to the stables. I followed them at a distance. They sure made quite a commotion among all the thorka corralled in there. I've never seen so much stamping and bellowing in all my life."

"What do you suppose they're doing here?" Kilgar asked, turning to the others.

"Sounds like they're searching for something," Gorian responded. They looked at each other in shock.

"Or someone," a voice called from the shadows of the window. Rimmy started at the sound, and fell back a few steps. Kilgar caught him before he tumbled back over one of the chairs. He patted his younger brother on the arm as Shan moved quietly forward, seeming to materialize all at once out of the darkness.

"Who's that?" Rimmy squeaked, looking up into his brother's face in alarm.

"It's alright, Rimmy," Kilgar assured him. He turned his brother around with one hand on his shoulder. "His name is Shan. He's . . . he's a friend." He looked over at the Elfling with an ironic twist of his lips.

"Has he been here the whole time I was talking?" the boy queried, a little uncertainly.

"I'm afraid so," Shan responded, moving more into the light. "I think I'm the one they're looking for." He slipped over to the wooden chair and sat down. Doornig and Gorian plopped down next to him.

"But—but, what do they want with him?" Rimmy couldn't stop himself from asking.

Kilgar slipped past his brother and settled himself in the soft chair. "We don't know," he said. "But whatever it is, it can't be good." Rimmy made his way around the others and sat on the arm of Kilgar's chair, staring openly at the Elfling.

"So, what are we going to do about it?" Doornig leaned forward, his elbows on his knees, his chin cupped in his hands.

"We could always hide him until the gorguls go away," Gorian offered, puckering his lips.

"But what if they don't go away anytime soon?" Kilgar posed to them.

"I can't believe they'd want to hang around here for very long," Gorian countered. "I mean, aside from Shan here, what could they even want in Branby? It's not like we have any soldiers or militia to contend with them. No gold or valuables to speak of."

"No militia!" Kilgar snapped. "That could be part of our problem. Without any soldiers to force them out, who knows what they might do, how long they might stay? We could be totally at their mercy."

Doornig sprang back to his feet. "Giyah!" he spit out, clenching his fists. "I can't believe we're even talking about them like this." He paced away from the table and stormed about the room. He threw his hands at the ceiling. "A few mira ago they were just creatures of legend. Folk tales, children's fables! But now we've got them right here among us!" He collapsed, exasperated, onto the cot against the back wall. "What could possibly happen next?"

There was a sudden crash from downstairs. The walls and the floor seemed to reverberate with the sound. Water could be heard sloshing around in the little pitcher on the low table. There were ripples in the glass Shan had been drinking from, like someone had dropped a pebble into a pond. The boys exchanged wild looks as they all bounded to their feet. They huddled together in the middle of the room.

Daryl Hanson

"What was that?" mumbled Rimmy.

Kilgar rushed to the door. "Something's going on down in the common room," he cried. The other boys looked at him as if they were in shock. "Could be trouble." He cautiously turned the handle and opened the door a crack to listen. He thought he could make out someone bellowing two floors below, but the sound was muffled and indistinct. "I'm going to check it out."

"Me too," Doornig called, heading for the door.

"Don't leave me out of this," Gorian chimed in, hard on his heels. The three boys hovered at the door, trying their best to pick up any sounds from below. Kilgar pulled the door open even a little further and stepped out into the hallway. The others were close behind. Kilgar paused for a moment, looking back at the Elfling.

"Shan, you better stay here," he cautioned. The elven youth hadn't moved from his spot, but he nodded tightly to Kilgar. "Hide if you can." He looked towards the dormer windows. "Use the roof if you have to." The Elfling glided back to the heavily shadowed window. He placed one hand on the slanted ceiling and nodded once again. The darkness gave him an ethereal quality. Rimmy drifted forward as if to follow his brother downstairs. "No, Rimmy, you need to stay up here, too." Kilgar held up his hand to quash any protest. "Throw the bolt when we've gone. And don't let anyone in unless it's us."

And then they were gone.

− 12 −
The Feast Of Peldrayn
[1st of Peldyr, 4533 C.R.]

Shan sat at his desk, a half dozen old books splayed out across its worn polished surface. He was reading carefully from the yellowed pages of an extremely old volume. The fingers of his right hand were tenderly spread out over the text, his fingertips resting lightly on the fragile page to keep it open. He traced a line across the faded text with one extended finger. The Elfling propped his left elbow on the desk, his forearm raised. Dangling from his curled fingers, he held the curious dark medallion he had purchased earlier from the shop down the main street. Slowly it swung back and forth on its light chain. Every so often he would lift his eyes from the spidery script in the book and stare oddly at the dark metal piece for several long mira. And then his gaze would settle back on the ragged page and his eyes would move on.

"No, no, that's not it," he muttered to himself at several points. He wet the tip of one finger with his tongue and delicately turned the page. The boy continued to scan the faint writing a while longer, then, becoming dissatisfied with his fruitless search, he lightly closed the ragged cover and slid the book back on the desk. Shan randomly selected one of the other volumes splayed open across the desk. He pulled it a little closer and began to read mid-page. But after flipping through several of its crackling leaves, he closed the old book in irritation. The musty pages of several other books rustled lightly as a result. A swirl of fine dust lifted delicately from the cluttered desktop.

"Nothing," the Elfling said in disappointment. He leaned back in his chair and worked at a tightness in his neck. He held the mysterious pendant out in front of his eyes and stared at it for the longest time as it swung slowly about on its chain. It coiled into a spiral, eventually came to a stop, and then slowly began to spin in the opposite direction. He watched it there in fascination until it had completely lost all its momentum and hung still on its chain. The dark thing intrigued him like nothing ever before. He stared and stared at it. It still reminded him of a wild thorka in flight and, to him, the sweeping lines to one side were reminiscent of its unruly mane.

"The House of Korell," Shan murmured thoughtfully as he studied it, contemplating just what that might mean. It was painfully obvious to him that he knew nothing about his own elven heritage. And in some way, he found that disturbing. Yet Ulfiir had never said anything to him about it.

He sat there for long moments, wondering why.

He finally set the medallion down on the desk and rubbed at his eyes. Outside the window he could see the sun was slowly settling over the trees of the forest. Dusk would soon be upon them and shadows continued to deepen throughout the village. He could hear numerous voices raised in excitement as people moved briskly through the streets below.

"Happy Peldrayn!" he heard someone call out. "Happy Peldrayn," came the joyful response from several other voices at once.

Shan rose from his chair and eased over to the window. He stretched his back for a moment, then brushed aside the curtain flap as it gently stirred on the breeze.

"Happy Peldrayn! Happy Peldrayn!" he heard chorused from countless lips. The street teemed with villagers heading home for any last preparations they might have to make before the evening's feast. The smell of roasting meat even now drifted up past his window, causing his mouth to water.

"The feast!" he said to himself, with a start. "I'm going to miss the entire feast!" He had been so absorbed with what he had been doing, he totally forgot that it was the first day of Peldyr. Mid-Summer's day.

Shan started to turn for the door but then he suddenly remembered the wandering tinker. He grimaced at the immediate thought of facing that odious fellow again. The man had obviously been searching for someone among the faces in the crowd the night before while he had been waiting in the wings to take the stage. Shan had certainly felt like the man had been following him around earlier that morning, stalking about on his long legs, peering furtively at him around corners and through shop windows, just for a glimpse of the elven boy. But why? Was that how things really were, or could that all simply be due to Shan's imagination? He really didn't know for sure. But one thing he was absolutely certain of, Silas Gravelle gave him a distinctly uncomfortable feeling whenever he was around.

"So," he spoke out loud to himself, "do I go to the feast like everyone else, hoping I don't run into the man again, or do I stay here in my room and pretend I'm not feeling well?" He rubbed absently at his chin.

He eased himself back to his desk and sat down, crosswise on the chair. He dropped his left elbow onto the wooden backrest and stared off into space. *What is it about that man that makes me feel that way?* he wondered. He was unsavory, to say the least, but it had to be more than just the fact that he looked like some kind of greasy salesman. No, there was something much deeper than that, he felt sure, something much more sinister about him. But he couldn't quite place what it was that bothered him.

He shrugged off the heavy feeling of dread he felt creeping over him and looked down upon the desktop. He scooped up the metal trinket once again and held it out on his palm. The light chain dangled slowly back and forth as he scrutinized the dark metal. It definitely reminded him of a thorka's head as it galloped into the wind. He turned it this way and that in his hand, tilting his head to get a slightly different perspective. And then a thought suddenly struck him. *Maybe it's more than just a pictograph or a simple artistic rendering.*

He looked at the medallion in a whole new light. "Perhaps it's not a stylized thorka after all," Shan mused out loud. "Maybe it just looks that way to me." He squinted at the piece with a fresh set of eyes. "Could it be some type of exotic script instead, a completely foreign kind of writing?"

The idea was totally new to him. He turned the object over and over in his hand. The thought definitely intrigued him. He knew some people of Anarra had a peculiar way of forming their letters. Dwarves wrote in chiseled-looking runes most of the time, he remembered reading somewhere. The desert tribesmen of Uu-Kesh appeared like they simply made a series of odd marks and scratches running together across the page, and in the opposite direction, no less. Both of those systems were completely indecipherable to anyone who didn't speak their native tongue. There must be others, too, he reasoned, over the face of the eastern continent who wrote their individual languages down in a manner that was totally different than the way he was used to. He eyed the medallion again, his lips bunching up. "Could this be a form of elven script?" he asked himself.

He quickly deposited the pendant on the counter with a soft *clink* and spun about in his chair. A few books rested on a small stand at one end of the worn desktop. "No," he told himself after a brief scan at those titles. "Not here." He hopped up off the chair and paced over to a small bookcase along one wall, where it was nestled up against the fireplace. Leaning down, he quickly perused the few copies it contained. "Not there, either," he mumbled. He stood up and scratched at his head. "I know I've seen a book recently that taught about various writing systems. Now where was that?" He came back to the desk and stood with one hand tapping at the top of the chair. "Must have been in Ulfiir's study," he

Daryl Hanson

concluded at last. "I can't very well go and ask him for it, now can I?" he mused, staring down once more at the metal trinket. "Not if I want to keep this little gift a secret."

The sun had set by the time Shan looked out the window again. Oil lamps had been lit and hung from the end beams of some of the buildings to help illuminate the streets. The flow of villagers outside his window had almost completely ceased. There were two small families rushing down the little steps from their homes in festive attire. They converged on the side entrance to the main hall from opposite ends of the street.

"Happy Peldrayn!" they called out to each other as they stepped up from the dust of the street onto the tiled landing. One of the father's reached for the latch and pulled the side door open.

"Happy Peldrayn!" squealed the children before ducking inside.

Shan stood there a moment in indecision. If he didn't go to the feast he might not get much of anything to eat for the night, perhaps only a few odd scraps at best. That didn't sound like an appealing option, as the quantity and variety of food served on a feast night was not anything to be missed, if at all possible. Yet, on the other hand, if he went down to the great hall the likelihood of completely avoiding an encounter with Gravelle was certainly slim. Maybe he could slip in and out before the man even arrived for his evening's performance. He shifted his weight from one foot to the other, wavering in his mind just what he should do. His stomach rumbled lightly then, and his mind was finally made up. He turned quickly for the door and bolted off down the passageway.

He flew down the broad staircase and, after skirting the large front doors of the great hall, he swung quickly to his left. He dashed up the long corridor, rounded the corner at the end, and slid to a halt almost immediately. He preferred to enter and exit the great hall through a small side door just off the rear corridor, rather than trying to use the much more crowded main entrance. Most often he found it drew less attention to himself that way. He pulled easily at the handle and slipped inside.

The large room was almost nearly packed to overflowing. He couldn't see any of his friends among the sea of faces. People were jammed in amongst the tables, eagerly digging into the heaping platters of food. It took him several long moments before he could even find a space to squeeze into. He pardoned himself as he slid into the narrow spot. Awkwardly, he wrestled his legs over the bench and pulled himself up to the long table. His shoulders seemed to press into the men on both sides of him. Leaning forward, he took possession of an empty plate and looked enthusiastically around to see what foods were still readily available.

Bowls and trays were quickly being exchanged all around him. Shan deftly speared a couple of thick slabs of roast *bork* from a passing dish with a quick thrust of his fork. He slid them onto a plate before scooping up a mound of boiled *kuls* from a pan moving down the table away from him. Whether baked whole or boiled and mashed like this into a creamy texture, the tuber-like *kuls* had always been one of his favorite dishes. He drizzled the steaming pile with melted butter before reaching for a large bowl of cooked vegetables. A few hot rolls, snatched from a passing basket, finished off his holiday plate.

He bumped elbows with the man on his right as they both sought to carve off a portion of steaming *bork*. "Sorry," Shan managed to say before thrusting a generous bite into his mouth. He chewed rapidly on the meat while succeeding to snatch a pitcher of cider before its departure to the other end of the table. He splashed the juice into an empty cup, passing the decanter without even bothering to set it down. He swallowed the savory *bork* meat and tore off a piece of a buttered roll before plopping it into his mouth. A line of butter dribbled down his chin.

I'm getting as bad as Laith, he thought to himself between mouthfuls. *That's what happens when you're extremely hungry, I guess.*

He continued to eat in silence, his head down, only occasionally lifting his eyes to search about the room. So far he could see absolutely no sign of Gravelle, he noted with satisfaction. He did finally spot Laith and Keo together on a back table far off to his left. Only once did he catch a glimpse of Celina as she hurried out of the kitchen, hefting a heavy platter of steaming meat. The pretty young girl twirled around another serving maid returning to the kitchen, laden with a tray of dirty dishes balanced on her hip.

Someone set a dish of baked *thark* down in front of him. "Don't mind if I do," Shan grinned. He stabbed at a couple thick slices of the large, flightless bird before the platter was immediately snagged away. He poured a generous helping of gravy over the juicy pieces from a nearby boat. He didn't neglect to rustle up a few wedges of white and yellow cheese, as well, before that dish was whisked out of his reach. Once he had downed everything from his plate, he dished himself a fair amount of sliced fruit before finishing off the incredible meal with a thick slab of iced cake.

Shan cautiously poked his head up from between his neighbors as he finished chewing. He still could not see any signs of the traveling minstrel, but he did catch a glimpse of the woman he'd seen talking to him earlier in the day. He pulled back quickly before she noticed him, sinking down until he felt shielded between the burly shoulders of the men on either side of him. Maybe he should just duck out now, while he still had time.

The Elfling wriggled up from the table, staying hunched over to keep from sticking out as he moved quickly toward the side door. Several serving wenches darted past him as they rushed in to collect any remnants of the meal. He narrowly missed colliding with one of them, but he somehow managed to slide out the door without drawing any more attention to himself. Shan breathed a sigh of relief once he gained the outer hallway. He straightened up as he looked both ways down the dim passage. Luckily, there was no one in sight, so he turned smartly to take the back route to his room. He clapped his hands together in delight and swiftly strode to the end of the corridor. The boy swung to his left down the back passageway. He looked casually back over his shoulder to make sure he hadn't been followed. *Still no sign of him*, he said to himself in relief.

At the last *bur*, just as he started to bring his head back around, Shan caught a flash of movement from the corner of his eye. At that moment, a tall figure in bright clothes came striding quickly around the back corner, and they nearly collided. The Elfling leaped instantly aside to avoid a sudden spill. He looked up with an automatic apology poised on his lips. And froze.

"Where are you going in such a hurry, young man?" a slithery voice wanted to know.

Shan's mouth dropped open and his heart skipped a beat as he found himself standing face to face with Silas Gravelle. The tall man quickly closed the gap between them as he stalked forward with the long strides of his spindly legs. His greasy smile seemed more like an evil leer as he sidled up to the elven boy.

"You really don't want to rush away just yet," the frightful man said with a gleam in his restless, beady eyes. His words came more like a hiss as he leaned closer. "The fun is only just beginning." The long, hooked nose hovered almost in Shan's face, and the deep-set eyes were somewhat shielded in the shadow of the man's wide-brimmed hat. Yet even in the gloom those sparkling pools had a way of dredging into him. "If you leave the party early you won't ever know just how much you'd be missing." The man tilted his head back, his long, pale face suddenly washed in the flickering light of the wall torches. His eyes seemed to gleam unnaturally as they bored into Shan's handsome face.

"Well, I . . . ah," the youth stammered, feeling himself edge backwards a couple of steps. The man slid along with him, seeming to glide like smoke. "I . . . ah . . . don't feel too well," the boy had to admit, feeling suddenly warm all over. He blinked several times and pulled clumsily at his collar, his tongue growing thick in his mouth. He continued to back pedal, but the movement felt oddly sluggish and somewhat mechanical. He couldn't seem to pull his own eyes away from Gravelle's glittering orbs.

"That's such a shame," the sleazy man seemed to say in a raspy purr. His grin was slightly blurred and grew to be enormous. Gravelle made as if to place a long, bony hand on the boy's shoulder. Shan attempted to pull away from him, but his reactions were slow and awkward. There was some small object concealed in the man's skeletal hand, held deftly in place by his last two fingers. The movement was magician-like, yet Shan's head felt strangely numb. His eyes were too slow to follow the deft motion clearly, to tell just what it was he held hidden in his hand. The thumb and first two fingers came in contact with the boy's shoulder blade. "You must really take care of yourself, young man." Gravelle's grin morphed into a malicious sneer. "Or should I say— *Elfling?*"

Shan tried to turn and run but his legs wouldn't seem to move. The unsavory character leaned in close to him once again, chuckling softly to himself. His breath was sour on the boy's cheek. "Don't fret," he grinned, "I promise I won't keep you long." Shan's feet felt somehow bolted to the floor. Gravelle peered from one side of the boy's head to the other in a slow, deliberate swivel of his head. "I just need to satisfy my own curiosity," he hissed, raising up a bony hand and delicately touching the pointed tips of Shan's ears with one long, slender finger.

The man's long, hooked nose hovered near his face again for several long moments before Gravelle leaned back and pulled what looked like a coin from his pocket. He held it out for Shan to see. It glinted dully between his fingertips. He let it slide down into his palm before tossing it lightly into the air three or four times, grinning broadly. Then he seemed to throw it into his other waiting palm, but yet it had somehow completely disappeared.

The strange man reached up by the side of Shan's face and it looked as if he plucked the thing out of the boy's ear. He prominently displayed the small object in his fingertips, then bent down and pulled Shan's hand from where it hung limply at his side. The Elfling could not prevent the deed nor pull his hand away from the man's grip. His body would not seem to obey him and the movement felt stiff and oddly detached. He followed Gravelle's hand with his eyes as the man placed the coin-like object on the boy's palm.

Shan cried out immediately in pain as a lance of searing fire exploded on his skin and raced up his arm. His clenched lips could make only a grunting sound, his mouth refusing to work normally. The small thing continued to sizzle upon his palm for several long moments. The man's eyes twinkled with an evil glow as he leaned in and snatched up the small metal slab after it had completed its work. It disappeared quickly into one of Gravelle's pockets. They both looked down to see a tiny round mark on Shan's skin where the metal had touched him. It almost looked to the Elfling like the raised, calloused scar of a brand.

"Good," Silas Gravelle whispered. "I see it knows you." He licked lightly at his lips. "Good. Very, very good." Shan could still not speak or move his body, but his eyes locked on Gravelle's face as his long thin fingers stroked lightly on his greasy moustache in satisfaction. The boy then turned his focus back to stare at his own hand, which just seemed to hang in the air in front of him. He had no ability to control it on his own. The small, round mark stood out vividly upon his palm. "Oh, don't worry," the foul man purred to him. "It'll soon disappear."

Shan regarded him with a scowl.

"There's one more thing I need from you," Gravelle went on. He reached inside the flap of his coat and pulled out a thin sliver of metal. It looked for all the world like a sewing needle, Shan thought. It was slightly thicker on one end and tapered down to a sharp point on the other. Gravelle used it to prick one of the Elfling's fingers. Shan could hardly feel the light puncture, but a bright bead of his blood welled up at the tiny wound. The minstrel pulled out a clean, white handkerchief and soaked up the dribble of blood with it. He delicately folded up the little cloth and stuffed it into another pocket in his coat.

"There, there," the man said as he noticed Shan's angry stare. "You'll be glad to know we're done here." The boy tried to work his lips to say something, anything, but he only succeeded in causing streams of saliva to course down his chin. "You'll be able to speak again fairly soon," the man informed him. "You can even curse me all you want." Shan's eyes flashed. "Oh, but you won't remember any of this," the man's eyes flared evilly. He clucked his tongue as he drove a hand into another pocket.

Clutching something else in his curled, claw-like fingers, Gravelle waved his hand before the Elfling's nose.

Shan blinked sickeningly as he lurched into the passage wall. He shook the fuzziness from his brain and looked suddenly around. He could swear he had just been talking to someone, but he found he was standing all alone in the corridor. His head throbbed dimly and his stomach felt like a bubbling vat of acid.

"I really am not feeling well," he managed to say out loud. He shook his head to dispel the clinging strands of cobwebs and started down the back corridor of the main hall. He really needed to lie down. He walked somewhat drunkenly down the corridor, bumping into the walls several times and scraping his arm on the rough plaster, before turning the last corner and then pumping weakly up the steps to the second floor.

Shan finally managed to reach his room, his breathing heavy and labored. He lifted the latch with a trembling hand and dragged himself inside. He staggered immediately to the bed and fell down across it. The boy rolled onto his side and curled up his legs. He scratched absently at an irritation on his hand. The more he rubbed at the bump on his skin the more it seemed to itch. The Elfling traced the tip of one finger curiously over the raised hump on his palm. He must have burned himself somehow, he guessed, but he just didn't remember doing it.

"Maybe it happened at the feast," he mumbled, his lips still not seeming to work right. Shan was having a hard time even trying to remember the feast. His temples throbbed miserably. He had been in the great hall, he felt sure. There had been food there, lots of delicious food, he finally remembered. He must have started feeling sick at the table and had to come back to his room. He certainly felt pretty sick right now. There seemed to be something else he needed to remember, but he couldn't.

Shan lay there on the bed, groaning softly to himself. He strained for a moment at an elusive thought, but he just couldn't quite recall what it was. And then it came to him, sort of dream-like and only half-remembered. There had been the smear of a sallow, nefarious face hovering just out of his reach as he had struggled to move, he felt sure. Then his thickened lips formed the unsavory name. *Gravelle*, he told himself.

"Happy Peldrayn," he muttered out loud, feeling himself growing very weary. He closed his eyelids and was asleep almost instantly.

Plans And Preparations
[18th of Kaligath, 4534 C.R.]

Rimmy bounded quickly to the door. He watched down the hall for a moment before closing it with a rattle. The boy reached up and slammed the bolt home. He backed slowly away from the heavy portal and sank down into Kilgar's chair near the center of the room, his eyes riveted on the latch.

Shan shuffled uneasily from foot to foot. He listened intently, scarcely daring to breathe, half expecting the three boys to come tramping back at any moment. When they didn't return immediately, he leaned back into the darkness as far as he could. Rimmy just sat there like a figure cut out of stone, staring all the while at the door.

After long moments and still nothing happened the Elfling's eyes drifted slowly about the room. He noticed the covers on Kilgar's small, wooden cot were messed up, probably when Doornig had thrown himself down on the bed. There was a deep-blue jacket hanging on a peg by the door. It was the same one Kilgar had been wearing when he rescued Shan from a mob on New Yahr's Day just over a yahr ago now. He shuddered at the memory. Several boys and even some men had vehemently sought to take their animosity and their hatred of Elves out on him. Sadly, there were still people in the world who irrationally felt the Elves were the cause of all their problems. There had even been wars fought to free Anarra of its *"elven stain."*

Rimmy continued to sit motionless within the glow of the candles, seemingly unconcerned with everything. If he didn't know better, Shan would have thought the boy was asleep. He did move once, however, when he reached up with his hand and scratched just under one eye. Over the top of the boy's tousled dark hair Shan could see a large faded banner pinned upon the slanted ceiling. His gaze settled in on it.

The thing was made of a coarse cloth, almost like a ship's sail. It was about a kor and a half square. It had a pale blue background and was trimmed around the outside with a border in a deep reddish color, sort of like a rich burgundy wine. The central figure was formed in black in the shape of a thorka's head, its nostrils flared, its mane snapping out behind as if it were running. Over the top of the animal's head, stitched in bright red, were the words, *THE WILD THORKA.*

"Hmm," he murmured to himself. *Thorka again?* His hand reached automatically for the medallion he had slipped down deep into his pocket the night Ulfiir had squeezed it into his hands before pushing him out through the secret tunnel.

"Did you say something?" Rimmy asked, swiveling his face around to peer into the heavily shadowed dormer.

"No, not really," Shan replied. "Just made a noise without thinking about it, that's all."

"Oh," the boy said swinging back to watch the door. "Kilgar does that all the time." He smirked mildly. "His mouth must not be able to keep up with his thoughts, sometimes."

"Huh," grunted the Elfling. "I know just how that feels." His nose itched and he rubbed the side of his index finger over it several times. "No, I was just looking at that banner."

"Oh, that," Rimmy looked up at it for an instant before returning his attention to the latch. "That's the old sign for the inn," he said dryly. "There's a new one out front now. It's wooden, and it'll probably hold up a bit better in the wind and rain."

"I don't doubt it," Shan responded, as Rimmy lapsed back into silence. The Elfling looked at it once more. Though now obviously faded with weather and age, and perhaps a little threadbare in places, he liked it.

He knew that Kilgar's parents owned the Inn, the only one in this small village. The three storey structure figured prominently in the life of the townspeople. It was situated in the ring of buildings surrounding the central plaza of Branby where people had to pass in front of it practically every time they moved about through the streets. It had obviously become a favorite place to go for a meal when a person just didn't feel like cooking on their own, not to mention it was the only place in town to get a glass of wine or distilled spirits. Besides a kitchen and a common room, it also sported a few guestrooms to house the occasional weary travelers who might need a place to stay as they journeyed to much bigger and better locations.

All at once there was stiff knock at the door. Shan recoiled in fear, trying to squeeze himself even further into the alcove. Rimmy jumped up from the chair and dashed to the door.

"Rimmy," called Kilgar's familiar voice, tensely. "Rimmy, open up, it's me."

The boy slid the bolt free and pulled open the thick wood panel. Kilgar and the other two boys rushed into the room. The dark-haired youth quickly shut the door behind them. Kilgar pivoted and drove the bolt into place with the heel of his hand.

"So, what happened?" Rimmy was filled with excitement. They all stormed over to the table in a hurry, and Shan pulled himself reluctantly out of the shadows. The small flames of the three candles fluttered crazily as they all came together in the center of the room.

"It's gorguls, alright!" Kilgar growled.

"You saw them?" Shan asked, his voice hushed.

"We sure did!" Doornig burst out. "Bigger than life." He swallowed hastily. "I never would have believed it if I hadn't seen them with my own eyes."

"Did they hurt anyone?" Rimmy wanted to know. "Mom? Dad?"

Kilgar shook his head, much to Rimmy's relief. "Not yet, anyway," the older brother said.

"But who knows how long that will last?" Gorian chimed in. They all looked around at each other, sharing in a moment of uncertainty.

"They've gone for now, but they'll probably be hanging around town for a couple of days," Kilgar warned them. "At least until they've questioned everyone."

"B-but what do they want?" Rimmy could not help asking.

"Like we thought," Kilgar told them. "They're searching for someone. They said they had tracked him this way from the center of the forest. They even offered a reward, in gold."

"You actually heard them talk in the common tongue?" Rimmy ventured to ask.

"That's right," Gorian told him. "But I couldn't make out much of what they said. It was really hard to understand. They had a thick, choking sound to their words, almost like they were grunting."

"No," Doornig countered. "It was more reptilian sounding to me, kind of like the heavy hissing of a snake."

Shan's eyes were large as he remembered just how close they came when he and Altyrian had hidden from them behind a fallen tree in the forest.

"It's not important how they sound when they talk," Kilgar silenced them with a hard wave of his hand. "Thankfully they seem to be fairly patient right now, as they questioned all the people in the common room. We need to determine how long that will last before they decide to tear the village upside down in their search or until they just plain turn violent."

"But just who are they looking for?" Rimmy queried him.

Kilgar looked pointedly over at the Elfling. "Shan, it seems," he spoke quietly. With all their eyes settled upon him, the elven lad felt extremely vulnerable, and scared. They could all see it reflected in his eyes. His lip quivered slightly as he came to a resolve.

"I'll just have to run for it, I guess," the Elfling's words were choked and nervous.

"But where will you go?" the younger boy asked him. Shan focused in on Rimmy.

"Ulfiir told me to make for Redhaven . . . wherever that is," the Elfling managed to say.

"Redhaven!" Doornig cut him off. "On the northern sea? But—but that's hundreds of leagues from Branby. Perhaps even thousands!" The red-haired boy was nonplused and threw up his arms.

"Hundreds, yes, I'll grant you that, Doornig," Kilgar chided him mildly, "but certainly not thousands." The redheaded youth rolled his eyes and crossed his arms in exasperation.

"Suffice it to say, Kilgar," Gorian offered in defense of his friend, "it's a pretty long way from here." He slapped Doornig on the back in a gesture of solidarity. The boy nodded at him in satisfaction.

"Regardless of just how far away it is," Rimmy said thoughtfully, "it'll be an extremely dangerous journey." The other boys bobbed their heads in acknowledgment. "Especially all alone."

"Not to mention having gorguls hot on your trail every step of the way," Gorian intoned.

"Good luck with that," Doornig sputtered.

Kilgar leveled his gaze upon his friends. "He won't be going alone," he said firmly. They all swung to study his face, questioning looks in their eyes. "He won't be alone, because I'm going with him," he finished with a firm set to his jaw.

"What?" Rimmy exploded. "How could you do that? How could you just leave Mom and Dad to . . . to set out on some foolish quest? It'd be doomed from the start."

Kilgar placed his hand on his brother's shoulder and calmly looked down into his eyes. "It may seem like a fool's errand to you, Rimmy," Kilgar said softly, "but it could mean Shan's life. And I, for one, won't just turn my back and abandon him to his fate. I *cannot* let him go alone." He looked up into Shan's moist eyes and nodded.

"Thank you," the Elfling said, reaching over and grasping Kilgar's hand. "You can't imagine how much I appreciate the offer," the elven youth stammered, "but I'm not sure I should let you do that. Let you give up all the things you know and love just to keep me from getting killed out

Daryl Hanson

there somewhere far from home."

"I'd like to see you try and stop me," Kilgar came back at him with a grin.

"Well, if you two are running off into danger," Doornig proclaimed, "then I guess I'm going with you."

"And me, too!" Gorian insisted.

Kilgar turned to his two friends with a definite shake of his head. "No, I don't think you guys understand. This is not some kind of game we'll be playing. And it's not just another friendly race. This is for real." The two boys looked at him evenly, determination written on their features.

"We know that," the sandy-haired youth declared curtly.

"And we don't care," the fiery-headed boy remarked. "You're our friend, and if you're set on this course of action, then we're in this with you all the way."

"Alright," Kilgar fixed his eyes on the two boys. "If that's how you feel, then we've got a lot of things to figure out, a lot of plans to make."

"And we don't have a lot of time to do it," Shan said. He grinned weakly at the three of them.

"Right," Rimmy offered. "First, we'll have to get our supplies together." His face was shining with excitement.

"We?" Kilgar turned to him. "Who said anything about *we*?" His gaze was stern as he looked down at his younger brother. "You're not going with us!" the older boy said firmly, his dark hair flapping from the vigorous shake of his head. Rimmy looked up in protest. "Oh, no! You're staying right here in Branby." He pointed a stiff finger in his brothers's face. "And that's the end of it!" He spoke adamantly. "Mother and Father would never forgive me if I ever let anything happen to you."

"But . . . ," Rimmy could only muster a weak reply. Kilgar's eyes were fierce as they bored into him. They stared at each other for a long moment before Rimmy dropped his head at last and kicked dejectedly at the floorboards.

"Now, the first thing we're going to need," Kilgar looked around the room, before settling his search on the desk in the corner, "is a map." He hurried over to search through various items scattered about on its surface. He clamped onto a leather scroll and turned back to the others. "A good map," he declared, holding it up and returning to the central table with it. "Not something they might sell in the market. You know, the kind you most often find in the shops marked with the inscription *Land Unknown*."

The others gathered around as he pulled free the tie and unrolled it for them all to see.

"Oh, that's good," Shan perused it, impressed with the great detail he could see displayed upon it.

"Especially since you don't even know where we're going," Doornig spit out with a snort. Gorian elbowed him with a quick jab to the ribs.

"Right," Kilgar said, rolling up the map and quickly retying it. He reached for a pack on one of the pegs near the door and stuffed the tube inside. He snatched at the jacket hanging beside it on the wall, as well. He set these things on the table, then crossed back over to the corner or the room. He propped open the lid of his chest and began pulling out a couple changes of clothing, a few shirts and a spare pair of britches. "You two will have to go home and put some clothes together on your own. But keep it light, we may have to travel fast." They nodded at him seriously. He deposited these items on the central table as well. "Also, try to pick up any other supplies you think we'll need."

"Food," Doornig stated eagerly.

"Right," Kilgar agreed. "But not anything too perishable. Dried meat and beans would be best. Dried fruit and nuts, as well, as long as it'll keep. We'll probably have to rely on whatever we can find along the way with regards to fresh fruits and vegetables." The others nodded.

"We'll obviously need some cooking gear," commented Gorian.

"Agreed," Kilgar responded, "but keep it light. Too much stuff will only slow us down."

"Uh-huh," Gorian replied. "And I'm sure we'll need a couple good knives. You know, for cleaning any game we might catch, or just to use about the campsite."

"Good idea," Doornig declared. "Not to mention anything we might be able to use in defense." They all stopped for a moment and looked at him. "Those gorguls had some pretty wicked looking scimitars downstairs. We don't want to go up against them out there empty handed." Kilgar paused for a moment and then nodded solemnly.

"Don't forget a few candles or a small oil lamp," Shan chimed in. "As well as a little oil to go along with it. You never know when we're going to need a little light out there in the wild."

"True," Kilgar reasoned. "And that reminds me, we're gonna have to carry some money with us. Whatever we can scrape together. I'm sure there will come some times when we run out of supplies and we'll have to replenish our stock."

"Definitely," said Doornig with a nod.

Through all this Rimmy had listened to them and paced back and forth between the table and the door. He desperately wanted to accompany them on this wild adventure, but he knew Kilgar would never give in no matter how much he pleaded. He silently ticked off the ever increasing items in their check-list and wondered just how they were going to carry it all without dragging a wagon along with them. Suddenly he spun to face his brother.

"Are you going to walk out of Branby on foot with all that stuff strapped to your backs?" Rimmy wanted to know. ". . . Or are you going to take the animals, too?"

Kilgar swung around to look at him. "We'll need to take the thorka for sure," he spoke flatly, decisively. "We'll be able to travel faster and farther than we ever could on foot." The others nodded their agreement. Rimmy started to pace again as they turned back to their planning, and then after a moment, he stopped again.

"How are you going to get all of this equipment down to the stables without being seen?" he asked. "You think Mom and Dad will let you waltz out of here without so much as a by your leave?" He swung his face around to look at all of them. "And worse yet, what do you think will happen if caught out in the open by those slimy devils while you're traipsing all the way across the village?"

"Rimmy!" Gorian breathed out. "You're not being helpful."

"But no, he's right, Gorian," Kilgar pointed out. "I hadn't even stopped to consider that." He paused for a moment to mull it over. "I guess we'll have to carry our stuff down the back stairway. We can gather it all together in the alley under some kind of tarp. Then we'll walk the animals quietly back through the streets from the stables, one at a time, to avert any suspicion. We'll load them up in the alley, and make a run for it out through the gate before anyone knows what's happening."

"And what about Shan?" Rimmy queried. "How do we get him past the gorguls without anyone noticing?"

"With that head scarf he's not really distinguishable as an Elf," Gorian observed. "He just needs to pull up the hood of his cloak and nobody will be the wiser."

"So you say, Gorian," Doornig countered. "For all we know those gorguls might be able to smell Elves a *korad* away."

"True," Kilgar snapped, "but highly unlikely." He scratched at his nose with a forefinger. "If that really were the case, though, they would have been up here long ago, pounding that door in." Shan looked involuntarily toward the portal, holding his breath and half-expecting a momentary thump on the wood.

"You said they're gone, right?" Shan cast him a worried look.

Kilgar nodded stiffly. "From the Inn, yes. At least for now. But not from Branby altogether. They wanted to make sure they talked to everyone in the village, to see if somebody might have seen you—seen an elven boy—recently." Shan visibly relaxed. A little.

"But they said they'd be back," Doornig stated matter-of-factly. Shan's eyes swung to the red-haired boy, a nervous frown wrinkling his forehead.

"That just means we don't have a great deal of time to get this done," Kilgar replied. "So," he turned to his two friends, "both of you head home and gather whatever you think we might need as fast as you can, and we'll do the same here."

"Right," they whispered in unison. They turned and made as if to leave.

"Try not to let anyone know what you're doing," Kilgar cautioned them. "We don't want someone blabbering our plans to any of those nasty creatures about." They both nodded solemnly. Kilgar pulled back the bolt and cracked open the door far enough for them to slip through. "Better use the back stairs," he told them in a hushed tone. He closed the door quietly behind them.

He turned to his brother. "Rimmy, we're going to need your help in this, too," he said. His brother looked at him hopefully. "Gather as much dried food as you can find. Don't let Mom or Dad see what you're up to." Rimmy's face fell momentarily in obvious disappointment. Kilgar couldn't help noticing. "Look, I know you'd like to come with us, but that's just not going to happen. Understand?" Kilgar held his gaze by touching him under the chin with his fingertips. The boy nodded slowly. "Good." He pulled his hand back from his brother's face. "I'm still going to need your help, though. I cannot pull this whole thing off on my own."

"I know." Rimmy was crestfallen, yet he looked up into his brother's face with a sense of determination.

"Alright." Kilgar opened the door once again. Rimmy eased through the opening. "Oh, and see if you can find that little oil lamp." Rimmy paused on the threshold. "I think it's in the utility closet, somewhere back in the kitchen." The boy nodded and hurried off. The older brother shut the door behind him and threw the bolt with a soft *snap*.

Daryl Hanson

Kilgar turned back to Shan, who had remained standing in the middle of the room. "I hope all this doesn't take forever," he said with a mirthless smile. "We don't know how much time we'll have before those savages sweep through the whole village in order to find what they want." He blew air out of his lips in slow ripples.

"I really feel . . . I really *need* to thank you for all your help," the Elfling stated with a genuine look of gratitude. "I don't think I could ever survive out there without some loyal friends like you." The dark-haired youth was about to reply, one hand raised in dismissal, but Shan went on before he could speak. "But you really don't have to do this, you know. Come with me, I mean."

Kilgar stopped him before he could go on. "Yes, I do," he said. He held up his hand, palm out, his fingers slightly cupped, and motioned several times as if he were patting at the air. "Yes, I do," he reaffirmed, his expression hard. Shan looked closely at him for several *mira*. "And if you think otherwise, then you don't know me well enough yet." He softened his expression as he regarded the Elfling. "The time I pulled you out of that brawl should have told you that." He turned away. "Now, we'd better get busy." He strode back over to the chest, the lid still propped open against the wall. "You're going to need some clothes, I'll wager, since you don't seem to have much of a pack." Shan shook his head in agreement. Kilgar fished around before pulling out a few other articles. "You're about my size, so these are just gonna have to do." He produced a couple of shirts and another pair of britches, which he laid on the table next to his first small stack of cloths.

"How can I help?" Shan asked as he watched.

"Dig through the drawers in the desk," Kilgar replied, pointing into the corner. "See if there's anything there we can use. Knives. Money. Leather cords. Plop them all here on the table and we can sort through the pile afterwards."

"Alright," Shan said, "I think I can do that." He paced over to the desk and began poking through the various drawers. "You never did say exactly what happened down there." He paused to look over at Kilgar who was busy moving about the room and grabbing up likely items. "I mean, in the common room, after you left us here." Kilgar paused a moment before launching into a detailed recount of what they had seen and heard. They continued to work as the dark haired youth offered his recollections.

* * * * *

The three boys had dashed down the long hallway leading away from Kilgar's room. It ran the entire length of the inn and had several doors branching off of it. They flew past these without stopping and came to the stairwell running down sharply to the left. They had hesitated there for a long moment to listen, but they could hear nothing. With a short look at each other they swiftly scampered down the steps. A door slammed shut somewhere down the hall before they tore around the corner on that second floor. They scrambled past a half dozen guest rooms and hurried for the last stairwell. Here the landing split in two directions. The steps to the left led down to the common room, but those to the right ran down through a door to an alley at the back of the Inn. They halted on the landing to listen. This time they could hear someone clearly stomping about on the main floor below. A loud gurgling hiss drifted up to them as they stood there poised, scarcely daring to breath. The odd sound was quickly drowned out by the shrill keening of several women.

Kilgar held a finger to his lips for silence. The two boys with him nodded emphatically, their eyes wide. They both managed to force down dry swallows. The dark-haired youth slowly ventured down from the landing and eased himself onto the topmost steps of the run. Trying not to move too rapidly he crouched down and peered cautiously through the slats of the bannister. He stifled a gasp as he looked down into the common room.

A platter of food, together with several broken dishes, were scattered across the floor. A greasy stain was slowly spreading over the polished floorboards. *That could have been the crash we heard*, Kilgar mused. But he quickly dismissed the thought, for the heavy vibration had carried all the way up to his room. He focused in on the scene below when both Doornig and Gorian slipped silently down the stairs to join him. They both peered through the wooden slats of the bannister in surprise. Doornig had to grip a hand over his own mouth to keep from crying out in alarm.

The patrons of the Inn were huddled fearfully together in three or four wooden booths lining the back of the room. One of those individuals huddling against the tables, still in her apron, was Kilgar's mother. Several smaller, free-standing tables in the middle of the room had been hastily tipped over and were currently dripping their contents onto an area rug. A foul-looking figure circled predatorily around the room, his metal boots clattering against bits of broken dishes. One clawed hand tapped menacingly upon the metal edge of its belt where a wicked-looking scimitar hung down. Another of the slant-eyed mongrels seemed to be conversing with the terrified guests as they cowered in the booths. A few of the men tried to soothe their wives with a protective arm thrown over their shoulders. The women had their faces buried in their hands and were whimpering loudly.

"Where can we find him?" the scaly figure rasped out at them, his long forked tongue popping out through his curved tusks, as if testing the air.

"We told you," a man in the booths replied nervously, "we don't know what you're talking about. Like Firrul was saying, we haven't seen an Elf boy around here in over a yahr. And he only came around once, as far as we know."

"Yes-s-s-s," the thing hissed, "I heard what he said. But I am telling you, he was coming this way. If he hasn't shown his face around here yet, he will soon."

"Why do you want this boy?" another man had the nerve to ask.

"That," the hideous creature spit out at him, a clawed finger raised in his direction, "is none of your concern." Its large angled eyes blinked several times in rapid succession, the slit-like irises narrowing upon the man in irritation.

"What if we don't want to help you?" a third man spoke up. "Why should we listen to the likes of you?"

The circling form in the center of the room came to a sudden halt and wrapped his clawed fist about the handle of his great sword. He focused in on the man who had spoken and stalked a bit closer. Some of the women screamed out in fear and one of them even fainted in her seat. The interrogator hissed an order to his fellow, who reluctantly removed his hand from the curved handle and, after a moment, went back to pacing about the overturned tables. He seemed to gurgle frightfully under his breath as he stomped about.

"Forgive my—*associate*," the leader's voice grated in their ears. "He is a little over zealous at times." The gorgul turned its strange dark eyes back to the man who had spoken last. "We do not want to cause any trouble here, we just want the boy. If we find you are hiding him from us, things will go unpleasantly here for you, rest assured."

"Nobody's hiding anyone," the man said uneasily in return.

"That's good," the thing proclaimed in its thick, slippery voice. Its slitted eyes blinked several times before snapping them wide open. "And if any of you should see this boy, tell us immediately. We shall pay generously, in gold, for any information leading to his arrest."

The gorgul leader turned to leave.

"Um," a different man raised his hand and started to ask hesitantly, "if we should find this elven youth you're looking for, how will we be able to contact you?"

The gorgul captain swung back to face him. "We'll be close-by," it said in its distinctive grating tones. "Very close-by."

And with that they both stormed heavily out of the Inn and moved off down the street. The door latch, Kilgar noticed, had been torn loose from its brackets. *That must have been that big crash we heard*, he postulated. Perhaps someone in the Inn had seen the gorguls coming up the lane, his mother or one of the guests, and in desperation, had tried to lock them outside. It obviously hadn't worked very well, for what remained of the latch dangled feebly against the door post. The door itself rattled persistently in the light breeze.

* * * * *

"The rest," Kilgar told Shan as they were finishing up their tasks, "I think you know." The elven boy nodded. They both looked down at the mounds of gear they had accumulated on the table.

"I don't think all of this stuff is going to be feasible," Shan spoke up with a slow shake of his head. "Who knows how much the others will bring over?"

"No, you're right," Kilgar agreed with him. "It's way too much." He gave the large piles a long look. "We'll just have to sort through it all and make some hard decisions. And whatever we come up with will have to fit into our packs." He regarded the Elfling evenly. Shan nodded. "Well, then, let's get to work."

− 14 −
Over The Rooftops
[19th of Kaligath, 4534 C.R.]

"There's definitely more of them this morning," Kilgar said in low tones. He stood at the window and peered down into the street, a thin flap of curtains held between his fingertips. The sun had just risen over the rooftops and splashed a hazy brightness over the village square. He swivelled his head from side to side, watching the random trails of villagers moving idly back and forth down the dusty lane. Occasionally one or two of them would be stopped on the street by a scaly, yellowish-skinned soldier stalking about on the cobbled stones of the central square. Women and children shied nervously away from the burly figures, and sought the safety of several men scattered randomly about the square.

"How can that be?" Doornig grumbled in exasperation. "Rimmy said he only saw a squad of them last night."

"More of them must have arrived sometime in the night," Gorian responded.

"But how did they get in through the gate?" Doornig wanted to know, his face flushed. "They always close it up at night."

"Yes, usually that's true," Kilgar said as he turned away from the window. "But things have changed considerably with their arrival." He eased over to join the others in the center of the room. "I suspect they control the whole gate by now, in order to keep tabs on who comes in or who goes out."

"What?" Doornig exploded, his face turning a bright red. "What about the Gate Keeper? Wouldn't he have something to say about that?"

Gorian laughed mirthlessly at him. "Rimmy said they clubbed him when they came in. Remember? You really think one old man is going to stop a couple of squads of those filthy creatures from doing whatever they wanted?" Shan leveled an uneasy stare at Kilgar. "What good is his knobby cane going to be against all their swords and crossbows?"

"Well," the red-haired youth spluttered, "somebody's gotta do something before they overrun the whole town."

"Too late for that, I think," Kilgar said with a grim smile. Doornig's wide-eyed look was riveted upon his dark-haired friend. "Look, we don't have any soldiers here. This isn't some kind of outpost like Draydin. We really don't even have any weapons."

"Then we'll just have to scrape up whatever we can find," Doornig was adamant. "Search through every household. We can use kitchen utensils, hunting knives, shovels, pitchforks. You name it."

"And just who is supposed to wield these measly weapons?" Gorian wanted to know.

"You, me, Kilgar. Some of the men in the village. We roust out everyone, whoever we can get to join us. I'm sure there are plenty of people bothered by what's going on."

"You can stay and fight," a soft voice called out beside him, "but I've got to get out of here . . . somehow." They all turned to look at Shan. He stood there numbly for a moment, then reached down to snatch a bulky pack from the low table. "I thank you all for your help, but I'd better get out of here before it's too late." They regarded him silently as he struggled into the loose straps. He cinched up the pack and scooped up his cloak from a chair. He swirled it over his shoulders and clasped it at the neck. "Maybe they'll just leave you alone after I've gone."

"You're not going alone," Kilgar informed him. He bent down and grabbed up his own pack. "Like I said, I'm going with you." Shan made to say something, but Kilgar silenced him with a determined look. He wriggled into his own pack before turning to his two friends. "You both will have to decide for yourselves what you want to do. Like Shan said, the gorguls might simply desert Branby once we leave." He leveled his gaze on the boys. "But they may as well decide to vent their fury on the village once we manage to slip through their scaly fingers." Gorian and Doornig exchanged hesitant looks. "They may just burn the whole place to the ground in anger." He shrugged.

Doornig bit at his lower lip while Gorian flicked his eyes quickly back and forth between Shan and Kilgar.

"I'm with you," Gorian spoke at last. "For whatever reason we cannot just let them take Shan." He snagged his own pack from the tabletop and pulled it up into his arms. He gave Doornig a decisive look as he spun it around and shouldered into it.

They all settled their eyes on Doornig who was obviously struggling to make a decision. The red-haired boy pursed his lips, glanced impulsively to the door several times, then stared down at his feet where he kicked softly at the floorboards. Finally he raised his clouded eyes to his friends.

"I'm coming with you," he said with a set to his jaw. "There's no use hanging around here. I mean, what good would I be, anyway?" He managed a twisted smile. "I'd probably just wind up getting myself killed if I tried to fight." Gorian gave him a firm nod.

Kilgar clapped his hand on the boy's shoulder. "Good," he said. "Then we'd better get going." Doornig heaved at his pack and wrestled it onto his back. "I really wanted to get out of here last night," Kilgar went on, "but I guess that just wasn't possible."

"Not with all the things we had to get done," Gorian interjected.

"Yeah, I don't know about you," added Doornig, "but I had a rough time trying to keep my parents from getting suspicious. I couldn't keep from bumping around the house as I was trying to gather everything together."

Gorian nodded. "I hear you. I had to make up some lame excuse about going on a camping trip before they'd leave me alone."

The three boys pulled on their cloaks while Shan stood there nervously watching from the side.

"So, how are we going to do this?" Doornig questioned his companions. "We can't just traipse around through town with these packs and cloaks on. We're gonna draw a lot of attention to ourselves if we do. Especially from all those soldiers moving about."

"Right," Kilgar commented. "And even if we don't immediately get picked up by some of those roving goons on our way to the stables, someone else eager for a bit of reward will gladly turn us in to the nearest soldier."

"Yeah, someone like Hendon, no doubt," piped in Doornig. Kilgar turned to him with a start. "Oh, I heard how he was talkin' to that ugly commander last night in the common room. I'm sure he'd be itchin' to betray us if he could get his hands on a little gold."

"True," Gorian added. "He does seem a little greedy. Why, he'd probably turn in his own grandmother if the price was right." Doornig shared a little snicker with him as they bumped shoulders.

"Alright, you two," Kilgar called them back to task. "We've got to figure a way to get across the whole village in broad daylight without being seen, by Hendon or anyone else. Now let's think!"

"We could all do what I did," Shan offered lightly. They all turned to look at him quizzically. He shrugged slightly with the small flash of a smile. "Last night I got in here by walking over the rooftops."

"The rooftops!" Doornig was incredulous. "You want us all to break our necks?" He huffed loudly as he sank down onto a chair. He crossed his arms indignantly. "We might as well just fly out of here, for all the good that will do us."

"No, really," the Elfling confided to them. Doornig snorted in derision. "It wasn't really that difficult. I did it easily enough, even with the thick shadows of sunset."

"Puhhh," was all Doornig could say as he shook his head emphatically and swivelled away from them on the chair.

"Come on, Doornig," Kilgar ventured. "You can bet no one will think we'd ever try something so foolish." Doornig muttered something under his breath. "We've got to try something unexpected."

"No thanks!" the fiery youth proclaimed. "I can't see how we'd be able to scamper across the roofs dressed like this. If the weight of our packs doesn't drag us off the edge to begin with, we might catch our feet on our cloaks and go sailing off into space. And if we didn't die immediately from the fall we'd most likely end up breaking an arm or a leg in the process. And then where would we be?" Doornig spun back around to face them, his jaw thrust out determinedly as if to challenge any objections they might make.

Before anyone could speak there came a muffled crash from the common room downstairs.

"What was that?" Gorian queried, looking wildly around at the others.

"I don't know," Kilgar responded with a worried glance at the door. A moment later they could make out the patter of running feet in the corridor. The stamping grew steadily louder as the wild footfalls converged quickly on his room. Shan cautiously shrank back into one of the dormer windows at the abrupt hammering on the outside of the door.

"Kilgar! Kilgar!" they could make out the breathless voice of Rimmy as he pounded on the heavy wood. The dark-haired youth sprang to the latch and unbolted it with a loud *clank*. Rimmy bounded into the room as Kilgar quickly pulled open the door. The boy's face was flushed and his breathing was loud and erratic. Kilgar closed the heavy portal instantly behind him, snapping home the bolt with the slap of his hand.

"They're here!" the youth burst out, as his older brother wheeled to face him. "They're here, now! In the Inn!" Kilgar caught at Rimmy's hand as he flailed them around, struggling to breathe. His eyes were riveted open. "They're here, Kilgar! Gorguls! I saw them downstairs!"

The other boys tried to speak all at once, but Kilgar cut them off with a sharp wave of his hand. "Hush!" he commanded. Rimmy gulped air convulsively, his eyes still wild with fear. His fingers gripped fiercely at Kilgar's hand. "You're sure?" the older boy questioned him. "You actually saw them?" Rimmy's vigorous nod was his only answer.

"What do they want?" Doornig hissed at the boy. Kilgar rolled his eyes at him in obvious irritation.

"They're—they're looking for Shan," the younger boy blurted out between rapid mouthfuls of air.

Kilgar swung Rimmy's face around to look him squarely in the eyes. "How do you know they're looking for Shan specifically?" he asked his brother calmly.

"They said so," Rimmy returned. He swallowed quickly. "I heard them say something about an Elf boy. Thought he was hiding here."

"Why did they think that?" Kilgar looked evenly at his brother.

Rimmy's breathing began to slow a little. "Said someone had spotted him at the *Thorka*."

"What?" Doornig gasped. "Who?"

"Somebody named Hendon, I think they said." Rimmy looked at the circle of faces around him.

"Hendon!" Gorian sputtered.

"That villain!" Doornig ejaculated.

Rimmy continued to breathe in and out rapidly. "They've started to search the Inn. Room by room." The boys shared startled looks. "They'll probably be up here any moment."

"Well, that's it then!" Shan said fearfully from the window. "I've run out of time." And with that he thumbed open the lock and pulled at the window latch. A soft puff of wind ruffled his hair as he quickly stepped out onto the roof. He looked back for a moment at the others, frozen there in the middle of the room, before striding quickly down the tiled roof and out of their sight.

Kilgar gripped his brother's hand firmly once again. "I guess this is goodbye. Take care of Mom and Dad for me."

"But—" Rimmy started to protest.

"You can't go with us," Kilgar was adamant. Rimmy's face was crestfallen. "Besides," Kilgar said evenly as he lifted his brother's chin, "I need you to cover for us. Make them think Shan was never here." Rimmy nodded unhappily. Kilgar let go of his brother's chin and slid over to the open window. He regarded his two friends still standing by the table in the middle of the room. "It's now or never, boys."

Iron shod boots could suddenly be heard stomping down the hallway to his room. A fierce pounding reverberated from several other doors in the corridor, and then a harsh yell rang out through the slits around the thick door.

Doornig and Gorian hustled to the window. "We might have better chances on the rooftops than facing those hideous things," Doornig muttered fearfully as their packs collided.

"That's for sure," Gorian mumbled. They carefully picked their way over the window sill and out onto the clay tiles.

Rimmy's eyes were frightened as he looked at his brother. "Latch this behind me," Kilgar said softly, "and just be glad you're not an Elf." And then abruptly Kilgar was gone. Rimmy hurried to the window to push it closed. He spun the latch to lock it just as a heavy fist began hammering on the door.

Shan had climbed lightly up between the arms of the dormer windows and capered over the spine of the roof, where he crouched down for a few moments, out of sight from the street below, to wait for the others. He hunkered there, watching Doornig and Gorian totter awkwardly along the tiled surface as they rose up over the crown of the roof and slipped down in relief beside him. Kilgar was a little more confident as he picked his way up the slant and dropped down next to them. They cast worried glances back over the roof while they continued to hear the muffled thumping from somewhere beneath them. With a final nod from Kilgar they moved off slowly and quietly.

Shan led the way over the angled tiles. He stepped lightly from one smooth, ceramic piece to another. The two middle boys in their line wobbled and shook noticeably as they picked their way steadily down the entire length of the Inn. They avoided window openings whenever possible, crouching low over the roof tiles as best they could.

The Elfling waited for them at the edge of the roof. Once the others had joined him he crossed nimbly to an adjacent rooftop with a light spring. This new building was covered in wood slats that scuffed softly as they each stepped over the short gap. After making sure they had all made the successful transition, Shan moved easily off once again, keeping low so as not to be silhouetted against the blue sky.

They had carefully crossed over a dozen buildings in the same fashion as they worked their way slowly around the town square, when they came to their first large gap. Doornig and Gorian balked at the distance. They drew back from the edge uncertainly.

"That's too far!" Doornig moaned softly. "We'll never make it." He swallowed at a sudden dryness in his throat.

"You'll do just fine," Shan tried to soothe him. "It's not really as far as it looks." The two boys peered uncomfortably over the end of the roof. The flagstones between the houses seemed hard and cruel to them.

"Here's where you promised to make us fly, right?" Gorian stammered.

Without bothering to answer, Shan stood up from where he had been crouching and leaped easily over to the neighboring rooftop. He landed lightly and swirled to face them, his long cloak snapping softly in the breeze. "It's only a couple of *kora*," the elven youth told them, beckoning with his fingertips.

"Might as well be a *korad*," Doornig sniffed. He smacked his lips lightly. "With these packs we'll just fall like a bunch of stones." He looked down to emphasize his words.

Kilgar sprang up from where he knelt and launched himself across the gap. He grunted softly as he went down to his knees on the reddish tiles. He kept to a crouch as he spun to face the remaining boys. "Come on," he told them. "You can do it."

Doornig continued to look across the intervening space with a skeptical twist of his lips. He glared down again and again at the paving stones far below. Then Gorian rose from where he had been poised, his fingertips resting on the dusty tile segments. Doornig watched in unbelief as Gorian took a few hasty steps back, then raced forward and leaped across the gap with all his strength. He seemed to hover in mid-air for the longest time before crashing heavily down on the tiles next to Kilgar in an awkward landing. He steadied himself and turned back to stare at his friend, a rush of adrenaline coloring his cheeks.

Doornig looked across at them, his eyes swimming with amazement. His lip quivered slightly and he couldn't keep his gaze from straying over the edge of the roof.

"It's now or never, Doornig," Kilgar's voice drifted over to him. Doornig shook his head in disbelief. He pulled away from the edge of the drop-off and looked back over the route that had brought them there. Sensing his thoughts, Kilgar called out softly to him. "If you turn back now, you'll never forgive yourself."

"Not to mention, there are a bunch of gorguls waiting for you back there," Gorian muttered.

Doornig looked back at them once again, his face strained with anxiety. "It's too far," he mumbled. "I'll never make it." He licked his lips. "And even if I could somehow get across, there's an even bigger gap before we get to the stables." He continued to shake his head slowly back and forth, his restless eyes looking anywhere but over the drop-off.

Shan glanced over at Kilgar. "We need to keep moving or I'll never get out of Branby alive." The dark-haired boy nodded solemnly.

"Come on, Doornig," Gorian tried to coax him. "Last chance. If I can make it, so can you." He met the redheaded boy's nervous stare. "I thought you said you were better than me at everything. Show me how much of a better jumper you are. Now's the time to prove it." Doornig swallowed uneasily. He continued to hesitate and licked at his lips again.

"Oh, shards!" he cried as he rose up and launched himself across the void with a wild leap. Time seemed to stand still as Doornig hung over the paving stones forever. Then all at once his foot struck the leading edge of the tile roof. For one sickening moment the weight of his pack pulled heavily upon him and he began to reel backwards. Doornig flailed uselessly at the air with his arms as he felt himself sliding away from his friends.

Kilgar snatched out at him and managed to grab onto the boy's belt before he could plummet to the narrow lane far below. Both Gorian and Shan caught onto Kilgar from behind to help brace him. Between all of them they were able to wrestle Doornig onto the roof alongside them. They collapsed in a heap of packs and appendages on the slanting tiles. They lay in a jumble for several long moments, laughing softly to themselves in relief.

"Thanks," was all Doornig could manage to say. "Thanks."

"Someone's likely to have heard that," Shan commented matter-of-factly as he sat up beside the tangled heap.

"He's right," Kilgar said, peeling himself out of the pile. "Come on, we're not there yet. We'd better keep on moving."

Shan was up and streaking away from them in an instant. He dashed quickly across the angled surface of the roof in agile bounds. Gorian pulled Doornig up by his pack straps with a grim smile.

"See," the redhead told him, wiping a trickle of sweat from his face, "I told you. I knew I couldn't make it."

"What do you mean?" Gorian chided him. "You made it. You're standing here safe and sound, aren't you?"

"Only with your help," Doornig admitted, looking down.

"Yeah, maybe," Gorian replied. "But isn't that what friends are for? To help when you can't do it alone?" Doornig glanced up at him with a wan smile. Gorian clapped one hand on his friend's shoulder, nodding grimly. "Isn't that what we're trying to do here with Shan?"

"I have a strong feeling it won't be the last time we're going to need each other's help," Kilgar told them both. The others nodded in agreement. "Now, come on. We've got to get going."

They hurried off after Shan as well as they could, scurrying a bit unsteadily on the sloping rooftop. The Elfling had already reached the end of the building and jumped lightly across to the next roof. He waited for a moment to make sure they were coming. As they approached the little gap he turned and rushed off once again. His nimble form hopped easily over windows and vents and around chimney tops. He paused each time to ascertain their progress before leaping onto the next building.

After they had successfully negotiated another ten roof crossings the others pulled up beside the elven youth, puffing and wheezing somewhat from their exertions. The muscles in their calves had started to burn from all their bending and stooping as they had hurried along. Shan had thrown himself down onto his belly on the peak of a roof. The others silently nudged up alongside him and gazed cautiously down into the street.

The curving lane below was somewhat wider than most of those in Branby. They could clearly see the large entrance to the stables across the way. To their chagrin, two broad-shouldered gorguls stood posted just outside the wide doorway. They both had enormous scimitars hanging from their broad belts and one of them had a large crossbow strapped across his back. The four companions scooched themselves down a little on the rooftop, allowing just their eyes to peer over the tiled crown. The scaly monsters seemed fairly immobile, standing quietly to either side of the great portal. Their elongated heads swivelled slowly from side to side. Their large, slanted eyes blinked occasionally at the brightness of the sun as it glanced down off the brightly plastered walls of the buildings. But otherwise they appeared practically motionless, oblivious to all the frightened looks cast upon them by the few people who had ventured out of their homes. These few brave souls scurried past the sentinels to run last-moment errands before the noonday meal could be prepared. Most of the villagers seemed to have enough sense to stay inside.

Further up the street several teams of the foul creatures could be seen working their way from house to house. A handful of others stood clustered by the village gate. These monstrous soldiers stopped everyone who passed by them, anyone trying to get home from their morning shopping, and not just those attempting to enter or leave the village. They thoroughly examined any wagons or carts moving along the streets. Shan and the others watched anxiously as scores of people were detained and questioned.

"How long will we have to endure this?" Gorian asked in hushed tones. Doornig could be heard next to him grinding his teeth in frustration.

"Until they find what they're looking for," Kilgar whispered back.

"You mean me," Shan responded quietly. Their eyes met just over the dusty rooftop tiles.

"Regardless of who they're looking for," Doornig added softly, "we're never gonna make it down off this roof without being seen. And we're sure as shards not gonna get past those guards unnoticed to get to our thorka."

"Not without a fight, at least," Gorian offered.

"Huh, that's a pleasant thought," Doornig returned. "I'd hate to see the outcome of that."

Kilgar rolled onto his side to glance up at the sky. It was still only mid-morning. "And we certainly can't wait up here until it gets dark," he stated quietly.

"No, someone is liable to spot us sooner or later," Gorian pointed out. "Besides, we don't know how many more of those soldiers will turn up before then."

Kilgar rolled back onto his stomach. He fixed his eyes on the two thickly muscled gorguls outside the stable. They had moved closer together, he noticed, and they could be heard conversing in low, guttural tones. One of them must have said something humorous, for the two of them chuckled hoarsely and rocked about on their steel-shod boots. Their wicked laughter sounded almost like the maddened squeal of a *bork*. The second squat figure struck its mate with a mock blow on the heavily muscled shoulder as they continued to laugh sickeningly together.

"What are we going to do?" Doornig finally asked, staring down in disgust. "We can't stay up here all day, and we can't very well float across to the stable roof, either."

"No, you're right," Kilgar agreed with him. He looked up and down the street. "What we need is a diversion."

"Diversion?" Gorian asked softly. "What kind of a diversion?"

Kilgar shrugged his shoulders, but the movement was masked by the heavy pack humped under his cloak. "Search me," he offered quietly. "I'll tell you just as soon as I can figure it out." He continued to study the street below, carefully noting the positions of all the soldiers, the scattered knots of villagers, as well as any loaded wagons or carts in his range of sight. He focused in on one of the wagons loaded heavily with bales of hay. "If we can somehow cast an oil lamp in there . . ." he mused softly, pointing with just the tip of his finger. The others swung their eyes to follow where he indicated. Gorian nodded his head at the prospect.

At that moment, Kilgar caught sight of a cloaked figure moving stealthily between two of the buildings on their side of the street. He hadn't come down the lane as all the other villagers but had slipped quietly along several back fences and alleyways. The slightly built form stopped at the side of the street and looked surreptitiously up and down the lane before moving on. The face was hooded, so Kilgar could not get a good look at his features. He totally forgot about the wagon for the moment as he watched the hooded figure in growing fascination. Kilgar nudged those next to him with an elbow and they all leaned forward to stare at the mysterious figure slinking quietly along. The hooded form edged out into the street and slipped past the stables below them without seeming to draw more than a casual glance from the guards. They were still engaged in their jest of some sort. The small frame angled across the street and disappeared around the corner into an alleyway running adjacent to the animal pens.

They all continued to watch the mouth of the alleyway with interest. The guards joked quietly amongst themselves without ever bothering to look in that direction. When nothing seemed to come of it, the companions soon lost interest, all except for Kilgar. He pondered what he had just seen, but for the life of him, could not make any sense of it. The movement of the cloaked individual had seemed oddly familiar to him, but he could not really place a finger on who the person might have been. He had finally returned his attention to the hay wagon when his musing was disturbed by a burst of noise from somewhere below their vantage point.

A sudden wild clattering shattered the relative stillness of the morning. All their eyes swept down to search the street beneath them, trying desperately to pinpoint the source of the raucous sound. Their attention was riveted upon the stable entryway as a team of thorka exploded madly out through the wide portal and flashed past the startled guards.

"Make way for the Elf!" someone was shouting. "Make way for the Elf!"

The two gorguls growled out a series of harsh commands but the cloaked figure astride one of the three great beasts paid them no heed as they turned sharply on the cobblestones and bolted up the street away from them. The rattling of their hooves on the stones ricocheted furiously from the close-set buildings. Several of the hideous soldiers turned on the street to intercept them. Sunlight danced from their polished blades as many of the scaly creatures pulled out their fearsome scimitars.

But the rush of the enraged animals was too quick for them. The thorka buffeted gorguls easily aside. The burly creatures careened into a few wagons and standing carts parked along the front doorsteps by many of the houses. One of the wicked soldiers came running up the curving street. He pulled up a heavy crossbow and fired a glistening dart at the racing figure. It whistled harmlessly over the rider's head and sparked off a stone wall with a spattering of chips.

"Make way!" the hooded figure called out loudly as he raced for the gate. "Make way for the Elf!"

The stampeding team quickly reached the village gateway and swerved sharply to the left. The flurry of their many legs sent the three thorka skittering loudly across the stones. Their hooves scrambled momentarily for purchase, then the great animals shot out through the open gate, sending soldiers sprawling to either side. "Make way!" could still be heard on the breeze. "Make way!" Just before the figure had disappeared entirely from view, the hood of the cloak snatched at the wind and it snapped back. Kilgar caught a fleeting glimpse of the rider's dark blue headcloth before his team burst out past the startled yellow faces. The thunderous sound of hoof beats quickly dwindled away.

Kilgar cast a curious look at Shan who lay beside him. He still wore his own blue head scarf. He shrugged off the peculiar feeling and looked down on the wild scene below.

The street was immediately alive with activity. The gorguls all up and down the lane raced furiously for the gate. Many of them were still picking themselves up off the stones where they had been brushed forcefully aside by the wild flight. These quickly joined in with their shuffling brethren, converging rapidly into a growing mob just inside the gate. The writhing mob swarmed and reeled about each other in confusion. The shrill blast of a horn could suddenly be heard. It blared incessantly from somewhere down the street in long piercing wails, then changed abruptly into a series of sharp, staccato pips. The foul soldiers seemed to come charging from everywhere, hurriedly streaming down all the side streets until the intersection in front of the gate was virtually jammed with a hissing, seething mass of scaly bodies.

"I think this is the diversion you were looking for, Kilgar," Shan spoke in his ear. The two of them made eye contact.

"I agree," the dark-haired youth said with a nod. He looked down at the street. "The problem is, I think someone just stole our thorka."

"Huh, you noticed that too," Gorian spit out.

"Yeah," Doornig piped in. "How are we supposed to outrun those stinking gorguls now?" He shook his head ruefully. "We can't even get down off this roof!" His tone was indignant.

"Yes, we can," Shan told him. "I never thought this idea of yours was going to work out, anyway." They all eyed him dubiously.

"Then why did you even bother to lead us over here in the first place?" Doornig queried with a snort.

"Because this was your plan," Shan said evenly. "I was willing to try things your way, if it actually worked. But now I can see we need to do things a little differently."

As they conversed, a tangle of grim soldiers made their way quickly down the street to the stables. They plunged into the yawning portal without hesitation. The swarming, confusing mob by the gate somehow coalesced into ragged squads amid a loud mixture of barking and hissing from their superiors. A long, piercing wail from a lone horn sent them all lurching off through the gate in obvious pursuit. They squeezed and elbowed their way through the opening in a controlled chaos.

By the time they had almost cleared out the intersection, the handful of soldiers came riding out of the large stable doorway. They sat atop a pack of huge, lizard-like creatures. Thick leathery skin rolled underneath the riders as the ponderous mounts turned up the lane toward the gate. The enormous beasts scratched and tore at the cobblestones with their great clawed feet. They bellowed loudly as they scrambled up the street.

"Giant slors!" Kilgar breathed in a wide-eyed stare.

Shan sprang up suddenly and rushed off down the roof away from the stables. "This way," he called back over his shoulder.

Kilgar rose quickly to his feet and tugged at the other two boys. "Come on," he encouraged them, "now is our chance. Follow after Shan. He knows the way." They all turned and raced after him, no longer concerned with stooping to conceal their movements. They sped off as fast as they could, leaping roof after roof in an attempt to catch up to the fleet-footed elven youth.

Shan pulled up at the edge of the last roof on the lane. The big house was nestled against the village wall. A large, sprawling tree grew from a small patch of dirt at its base, thrusting out thick branches in all directions. Some of them hung over the rooftop while others reached out and interlaced with tree limbs on the other side of the wall.

Once the others had caught up to him Shan pulled himself up into the tree and began working his way along from branch to branch. Leaves lashed at his face as he twisted and wriggled along. With a quick look at the others Kilgar climbed up onto a limb and edged his way swiftly in pursuit. Doornig and Gorian lost no time in joining him, and they all soon passed over the top of the wall. They didn't all take the same route and found themselves swaying along the branches of a couple different trees outside the village. The bulkiness of their packs and cloaks caught constantly on interlocking twigs, forcing them to twist and turn through the tangle of leaves. They grunted and sputtered as they worked their way hand over hand down through the trees.

Before too long they found themselves on the ground outside the village. They stopped for a moment to pick leaves and twigs out of their hair and clothing. A few small welts lined their arms and faces in red where branches had scraped at their skin. They all continued to pluck leaves from their cloaks as they turned to look around themselves.

Branby sat on a hill. The road fell down from it and plunged into the line of forest trees not far away. A small cloud of dust was slowly settling over the earthen road where it disappeared in the distance, a grim reminder of the recent passage of numerous booted feet.

"We made it," Doornig stated triumphantly.

"We should be thankful to that hooded rider," Kilgar proclaimed. "He made it possible for us to get outside the village without being seen."

"We hope," Gorian chimed in.

Kilgar stepped up to them and placed a hand on their shoulders. "I really don't think we were observed," he said with a grin. "Those gorguls were too busy chasing after that rider, whoever he was." Shan looked at his dark-haired friend. The way he said it made the Elfling feel Kilgar had more than an idle suspicion as to his identity.

"So what do we do now?" Doornig asked with a bit of a whine in his voice. "He took our mounts."

"We walk," Kilgar told him flatly.

"Walk?" Doornig's cheeks reddened. "All the way to Redhaven?"

"Well, we can't very well tramp back into the village right now," Gorian interjected, "just brush past any soldiers left standing at the gate and collect another set of thorka, can we?"

"No, I suppose not," Doornig murmured in obvious disappointment. He looked down at his feet. "But . . ."

"We'll just have to walk—for now," Kilgar spoke up. "But we'll eventually need to find something else we can use, some other kind of transportation along the way. Hopefully something a little faster than just our feet." They all looked up at him. "Agreed?"

"Agreed," Doornig and Gorian spoke in unison.

"Alright then, we'd better get moving," Kilgar stated. "We'd be wise not to stand too long out in the open. There still might be some unfriendly eyes watching for anything that moves." He started to move off, and the others quickly fell into step beside him.

"Which way do we go?" Doornig wanted to know.

"Not on the road, that's for sure," Gorian pointed out. He looked cautiously over his shoulder. "Too many gorguls." Their eyes drifted back to the road as they tramped off roughly at a right angle to it. Fine dust still seemed to hang in the air from the myriads of steel-shod boots that had recently passed that way. They could still dimly hear the thunderous strides of the enormous reptiles. One by one the boys turned back to their original line of march.

"Weeson spoke once about floating down the river," Shan informed Kilgar as they walked. The dark-haired youth nodded.

"We'll take a look at the map a little bit later, once we get under some cover," Kilgar said with an eye on the sky.

They picked their way down the slope from Branby towards the line of the forest. They made easy progress over the broken sod, covering the intervening ground without speaking further. Before long they had come to the edge of the trees and disappeared into the shadows under the softly swaying branches.

Ϲbe Olδ ɦighwɑy
[19th of Kaligath, 4534 C.R.]

"We're basically here," Kilgar informed them. He tapped an index finger lightly at a spot on the map a little north and west of Branby. The four boys huddled over the wide swath of leather tossed out across the uneven surface of a large rock. They leaned in close, intent on the place Kilgar indicated. Early afternoon sunlight slashed down through the leafy canopy overhead, dappling the broad map in shifting patches of brightness and shadow. "Those brutes rushed off after the hooded rider in this direction . . ." He slid his finger toward the east, past Branby and over to the edge of the forest. The others followed his movement in the flickering light. " . . . Along the road to Draydin."

Gorian made a small clucking sound with his tongue. "They're sure to think Shan is making a run for home." Kilgar gave him a nod.

"Which means we won't have those ruffians breathing down our necks," Doornig said with the flash of a smile.

"I wouldn't count on that too long," Shan offered ruefully. The two boys looked up at him with a frown. "The woods are fairly crawling with those things. And who's to say all those soldiers we saw in town are the only ones left nearby?"

"Shan's right," Kilgar stated firmly. "We cannot assume we've seen the last of those devils."

"Nobody's saying that!" Doornig proclaimed defensively. "I don't think we can ever assume that. At least, not until we get to Redhaven." He wet his lips with his tongue. "I'm just saying, I was hoping, really, that we might get a good head start on them before they catch up to that rider and learn their mistake. That's all."

"And then once that happens they'll come looking for us in a hurry," Gorian added grimly. They all looked at each other uneasily.

"I pity that rider," Shan muttered softly, more to himself than anyone else.

"Well, one thing's for certain," Kilgar spoke up, "we can *assume* there'll be more of those foul things lurking about in the forest. We need to be careful, really careful, every step of the way." The other three boys grunted in assent.

"So," Doornig wanted to know, "where are we headed?"

"Redhaven, dummy!" Gorian spit out with a lazy roll of his eyes.

"I know that!" Doornig hissed back at him peevishly. "I mean, what route should we take to get there?" He elbowed his friend. "Hurlik? Nad?" He turned pointedly to the dark-haired youth, ignoring Gorian for the moment.

"Hurlik, I think," Kilgar responded. He bobbed his head firmly. "Nad's too much in the wrong direction." He tapped a finger on the northwest edge of the forest twice, then moved it off toward the great river and an even bigger forest which lay in that direction. "Unless, of course," he went on with a smirk, "you're thinking to cross the Tanalorn here, which would be very difficult for us, perhaps even impossible, without any boats." He looked his friends in the eye. "Then, even if we were somehow successful in getting to the other side of the river, we'd have to face the trackless reaches of Ban-Dolan. If you think Draydin Forest is pretty big, get a look at this one." They all bent closer to study the map. "Not a very promising endeavor, let me tell you. By all accounts I've ever heard we'd just wind up getting ourselves horribly lost in there." Doornig lowered his eyes to study the map once more.

"And we can't forget about the Arismas," Gorian pointed out with a small gesture at the chart. "It's on the other side of the forest, and it's almost as big as the Tanalorn."

"Right," Kilgar sided with the sandy-haired youth. "I don't think we have the means, to say nothing of the time, to cross two great rivers just now. Not in our present predicament, anyway." He looked over at Shan. "What do you think? This is your neck, after all."

The Elfling glanced down at the great map. His eyes moved up the Tanalorn until they came to rest on Donnor's Ferry, where the southern torrent split apart to create two great rivers. From that point they each began their own long, tumbling trek to the far distant sea at Wolf's Head. He scratched thoughtfully at the side of his ear. "When I had a chance to question Weeson about his intended route, he told me he wanted to cross the river at Akthis."

The boys all looked where he indicated with a tilt of his scarf-wrapped head, near the northern fringe of Rangoor.

"That would sure make things a lot easier," stated Gorian with a slight twist of his lips.

"But then what?" Doornig questioned the others. "Scale the lofty peaks of Mindlheim? Make our way north through hostile territory to Perilka Bay?"

"No, neither of those," Kilgar informed them with a firm shake of his head. He leaned forward and traced a line across Rangoor, to the gap between the forest of Essen and the southern extent of the Mindl Mountains. "I say we head for the edge of the mountains, here, slip our way around the southern edge, then push on for the Brittlehorn River on the other side of Mindlheim." Shan bobbed his head in assent.

"That was Weeson's intention, too," he said. "We could procure a boat somehow, make a raft if we have to, and float all the way down the Brittlehorn to Redhaven." He shrugged. "Seems simple enough, I guess." Kilgar locked eyes with him and nodded.

"That's seems like a long way," Doornig murmured, scanning the path with a small wag of his head.

"But you think trying to ford two major rivers, wandering through the trackless expanse of Ban-Dolan, not to mention struggling to scale those lofty peaks covered in deep blankets of snow is somehow shorter?" Gorian snorted. Doornig flashed him an angry scowl.

"You didn't let me finish," the redhead asserted with a flush to his cheeks. He paused before swallowing. "I said, that's a long way, but I think both Shan and Kilgar have it right." He looked up at the Elfling for a moment before shifting his gaze to the dark-haired youth. "The route around the mountains is probably the best course in the long run."

"Right," Gorian piped in. "I agree."

"It's settled then," Kilgar replied. "We'll make for Donnor's Ferry, best possible speed."

"Which means it's gonna be pretty slow going," Doornig offered with a bit of a whine in his voice. "Especially since we're on foot."

"We don't seem to have much of a choice," Shan told him softly. He met looks with Doornig.

"Well, look," Kilgar interjected, "no one ever said this whole thing was going to be easy. The journey will undoubtably be long and hard. But like Shan said, we've got no other choice."

"Yeah, I know," grumbled Doornig in return. "I'm just saying."

"Don't!" Gorian managed to elbow his friend.

"Okay, that's enough," Kilgar spoke up firmly. He stooped to fold the large, leather map in half, then proceeded to roll up the remainder into a tight scroll. The others picked up their packs where they had left them leaning against the side of their impromptu rock table. They buckled easily into them while Kilgar tied the rolled bundle with a leather strap. He stuffed it into his own bag before hefting the burden. He slung it over his back and turned away from the large stone. "Let's get going then," he said with determination. They all fell into step as he picked his way over a series of twisted roots which perpetually thrust their way up through the leafy floor of the forest. They tramped on for several mira, winding their way slowly through the trees, before Doornig pulled up short with a wave of his hand. The others abruptly followed suit.

"Hey," the redhead stammered, "I thought you said you wanted to head toward Hurlik."

"That's right," Kilgar confirmed to him with an irritated shrug. He made to move off again, but the fiery youth held his ground.

"But you're heading more towards Nad," Doornig pointed out.

"I know," the dark-haired boy said in friendly agreement.

"But . . . ?"

"Look," Kilgar confided a trifle impatiently, "I figure we need to move a little further west from Branby before trying to cross the road in the open. Thought it'd be safer that way. Who knows just who—or what—might be moving along the road at this time of the day? The closer we are to town the more likely we'll be to stumble into someone." The others nodded their heads in agreement. "This way, if anyone is still watching for us, they'll not be able to tell which way we're actually headed." He started off again.

"Makes sense," Gorian approved. Doornig only grunted, and the three of them hurried to catch up with him.

"Yeah," the red-haired boy agreed. "And it'll make it a lot harder for anyone to follow us if we stay off the roads."

"Agreed. That's a given. Besides that," Kilgar called softly over his shoulder, "I found a way through the trees they're unlikely to know about." His boots crunched lightly on broken off twigs and dried leaves. They trudged on in silence for a time, careful to place one foot in front of the other, as they meandered through the densely packed trees.

The forest was silent except for the mild puffing of their breaths. They looked about themselves as they twisted and turned their way between the gnarled trunks. It was not possible to see more than a few paces ahead of them in any direction on account of the broad, close-set boles. Shan wondered how they could keep any kind of direct line while tramping through the thick woods until he caught a glimpse of Kilgar drawing a compass from his pocket. The boy glanced at it from time to time, subtly altering his course to remain on track. *That's good*, he told himself as they continued to pick their way through the winding expanse.

After they had trudged along for more than an ahr without speaking Kilgar suddenly brought them up short with a raised fist. He swivelled around to make sure they were paying attention, one index finger held up to his lips. They gathered awkwardly around him, their eyes wide.

Kilgar knelt down on a small rise and pointed out through the gently rustling arms of the trees. He flashed a finger to his lips once again for emphasis. They huddled quietly together. The soft murmur of voices could just be heard drifting closer. They swallowed against the sudden dryness in their throats as they found themselves just overlooking the road. To the left the way led back to Branby, and on the right the dusty stretch turned northward toward Nad.

A small tangle of wagons rolled noisily closer. One of them seemed laden with produce, the wild profusion of greenery with all their leaves and stalks poking up over the cargo box from their various packets and crates. Another wagon carried all kinds of bales and boxes piled in neat rows and covered over with a gray tarp flapping gently in the light breeze. One of the last two in the line was heaped with chunks of raw ore, probably headed for a village blacksmith somewhere, and the other wain featured bolts of cloth along with a wide variety of other household goods.

The four wagons slowly trundled down the lane from Nad, most likely shipped originally from somewhere much further away. The men atop the wagon boxes conversed loudly over the incessant rattle of the metal-rimmed wheels and the thump of their draft animals' huge feet. Two massive bathalisks pulled docilely upon the traces of each vehicle, their great shaggy heads and huge front shoulders dwarfing their relatively smaller hind quarters and back legs. Shan stared at the strange combination of scaly hide and unruly fur running down the entire length of their powerful bodies.

A man with a small cart was the lone traveler from the opposite direction. His little beast, a *thorro*, a sort of half-cousin to the great thorka, but much smaller and more timid, tugged wearily at his task on the way up from Branby. As the old man came abreast of the first wagon in the line, he raised a bony hand and hailed the men in the driver's box. The two men offered friendly waves in return and would have continued on their way without another thought, if the little man hadn't stood up suddenly in his cart and cried out to them.

"Greetings, good teamsters," he shouted in a reedy voice. "Half a moment, if you'd be so kind. Half a moment, please."

"Ho, there," the driver of the first wagon called out loudly to his team of bathalisks. He pulled back heavily on the long reins and jammed down on the long wooden handle of the brake. The two large beasts lumbered awkwardly to a halt amid a cloud of dust. The other drivers in line quickly strove to follow his lead as their own wagons skidded precariously to a stop not far behind.

A brown haze rose thickly about them. All the mighty bathalisks shook their great shaggy heads, their broad, sharp horns catching at the sunlight. They bellowed into the dust with blasts from their wide nostrils. The pointed tufts of their ears flicked forward in mild irritation, before settling back against their ruffled manes once again. They stamped their heavily padded feet several times on the hard packed ground, kicking up even more clouds of dirt, before the enormous draft animals came to rest at last.

"Greetings, good teamsters," the old man in the cart cried once again. He sat back down on the wooden seat of his cart, the reins held gently in one wrinkled hand.

"What is it, old man?" the driver of the first wagon hollered across at him in obvious annoyance. "We've got a schedule to keep." He waved at the rising dust.

"I know, kind sir," he offered apologetically, "but I thought I'd better warn ya."

"Warn us?" the man next to the driver spoke out somewhat impatiently. "Warn us about what?"

"There's some odd goings-on in the forest these days," the gray-haired man told them in his wheezy voice. The two men in the wagon box shared an impatient look. "Foul things are abroad, good teamsters. Foul things indeed." He smacked his lips together loudly.

"We don't have time for your dramatics, old man," the driver's assistant said irritably. "Now, if you'll excuse us . . ."

The driver laid a firm hand on the man's arm. The two men looked at each other before turning back to the old fellow. "What kind of things?" the driver wanted to know.

The four boys peered down on the scene from a small rise along the edge of the road. They regarded each other in silence, mindful to remain still and unseen.

"Fell things," the old cartman was saying. He wet his lips. "Things out of the darkest night, things jumped right out of legend." The two men shared a troubled glance. "Foul creatures," the old one went on nervously, "slithered all their way up from Kulnedra, they say."

"Kulnedra?" the driver's assistant exploded in a laugh. "Are you daft, old man?" He shook his head skeptically. The driver waved a dismissive hand at the old man's words and was about to snap his reins to urge his beasts forward, but the feeble little man raised his reedy voice to them.

"Gorguls!" he cried. "There's gorguls ahead, I tell ya! I seen 'em and that ain't no lie."

The driver was startled by his words and let the straps fall loose across his knees. "Gorguls?"

"Where did you see these monsters?" the assistant demanded, humorously. "In the ale house?" And with that he started to laugh once again. He rocked back and forth in his seat, but the driver waved him to silence. He turned back to the elderly man on the cart.

"So where *did* you see them?" the driver wanted to know. He leveled his gaze on the old fellow, his thick eyebrows knitting together.

"In Branby," the little man said. "Just up the road a-ways. The whole town was completely overrun just this morning." The two men on the wagon box exchanged alarmed glances. "They tried to bottle up the whole village. Said they was lookin' for someone."

"Who?" the assistant asked in a way Shan felt sure he was still not convinced.

"Dunno," the old man coughed. "Some sort of elven boy, I hear tell." Kilgar flashed Shan a worrisome smile.

"Paw!" the assistant burst out derisively. "Elves and gorguls? You've definitely spent too much time in your cup at the bar room counter." He dug an elbow into the driver's ribs. "Elves and gorguls! Hah! What's next?"

"Hush!" the driver remonstrated sharply. He turned his attention back to the cartman. "Are they still in Branby now?" he wanted to know.

"A course!" the old man piped up. "But ain't as many as before." He smacked his lips once again. "They lit out after a rider a couple of ahrin ago. Probably that Elf boy hisself making a break for it, I bet. Reckon they'll probably be chasin' him for some time. But just in case he comes back, they left a few of their soldiers behind to keep an eye on things."

"Thank you for the information," the driver told him kindly. "We'll be well prepared if we run into any of them."

"Oh, you're sure to do that, young man," the old fellow advised him. "There's a pack of them foul creatures just up the road apiece." The startled look from the driver brought a odd smile to the little fellow's cracked face. Shan turned and shared a concerned look with Kilgar. "They be stoppin' everyone as goes through," the little old man went on, "searchin' every cart and wagon, rummaging through all the baggage."

"Thank you again, old fellow," the driver said with a nod. "We'll be better prepared to deal with them now that we know. Much obliged." He tossed the old guy a friendly wave and gave the reins a sharp snap. "Alright, boys," he called back over his shoulder to the other wagoneers in the line, "stay on your toes. We might have some need of a little muscle before this is all over."

The two great animals lurched forward and slowly began to make their way down the lane. The metal rimmed wheels churned noisily at the earth as the large cargo wagon creaked and groaned under its heavy load. The other transports rumbled stubbornly off in pursuit, another soft cloud of dust rising slowly into the air. The frail old man waved feebly after them from his cart, settled himself more comfortably on the bench and tugged lightly on the reins of his *thorro*. The little beast of burden leaned into the traces and the small cart rolled slowly forward.

The four friends waited patiently for some time, concealed in the trees along the side of the road, until the cart and all the heavy wagons were lost from sight. They rose cautiously to their feet, but remained rooted to the spot a while longer.

"He said there's a pack of them hiding in the trees just down the road," Doornig hissed incredulously. "That's way too close!"

"Shush," Kilgar warned him with a hand held out flat to the ground.

"He's right," Shan whispered. "We should keep quiet. They could be just about anywhere."

"Yeah," Gorian muttered softly. "There's no telling where they might come sneaking out from next."

"I don't think it's a matter of sneaking around so much," Shan continued to whisper. "They seem to be out in force. I'd say it was more a like they're trying to catch people unaware, so that they won't have time to conceal anything at the last buhr."

"I think you're right," Kilgar told him quietly. "Now come on," he called to the others. "Let's get across here before anything else comes into view." He quickly looked both ways before gliding down off of the rise where they'd been watching. He stepped out onto the packed earth, waving back at the others before easing fully out into the lane. His three companions hustled after him. Within the span of a few heartbeats they had all scurried across the open ground and disappeared into the wall of trees with its dappled shade on the opposite side of the road.

Kilgar led them cautiously onward for some time. They weaved in and out of narrow spaces between all the densely packed trunks. This part of the forest seemed somehow older to the Elfling. The trees here appeared more ancient, with large, hairy clumps of moss clinging tenaciously to their shriveled bark. The boys cast concerned glances at each other as they doggedly pattered along after the dark-haired youth who led the way. Their progress was much slower than they had hoped. They consistently had to scramble over large roots and around sagging trunks.

"Where are we going?" muttered Doornig under his breath. Gorian glanced over at him. "We're lost, I'd say," the redhead went on. He pulled himself to a halt, leaning wearily against a twisted trunk with a groan. Gorian came up next to him and clapped a hand on his shoulder.

"No, we're not lost," Kilgar told him confidently as he spun about to face them. "We're actually almost there." He pointed off through the branches.

"Almost where?" Doornig said a little dejectedly. "At this rate it'll take us months, no probably yehrin, to get where we need to go."

"It's not that much further," Kilgar boasted. "Then the way should get much easier."

"How?" Gorian wanted to know, his hand still resting lightly on his friend's shoulder. "Surely we can't be close enough to the edge of the forest already."

Kilgar leaned back against a broad trunk for a moment and smiled. The others took it as a sign to rest and found a few places to lean back for a few moments. "No, that's ways off yet, for sure." The burst of disgust from Doornig was a little disheartening to Shan. He was already feeling stiff and sore, and the thought that they still had an almost insurmountable distance to go was disconcerting. He tried not to think about the staggering journey lying before him, but it was becoming a little harder to remain positive with each passing step.

"Then where are we going?" the Elfling found himself saying. Kilgar flicked his eyelids at them a couple of times before replying.

"I've been leading us to an old road," Kilgar told them with a twinkle of conspiracy in his dark eyes. "I know it's not been easy to get to at first. But once we find it, our progress should get a lot easier." The three other companions settled their eyes on him.

"An old road?" Gorian asked. He cast a skeptical glance at Doornig before swinging his face back to the dark-haired boy. "What kind of road? You don't mean like some old animal trail, do you?"

Kilgar shook his head firmly. "It used to be the main road cutting through this part of the woods. It runs fairly north and south between Farli and Hurlik."

"The only road going between those two villages," Doornig stated matter-of-factly, "runs through Branby." He rolled his eyes. "You said you wanted to stay off the roads," the fiery-headed boy exclaimed. He knocked Gorian's hand from his shoulder and crossed his arms defiantly.

"I'm not talking about one of the main roads *now*," Kilgar proclaimed. "This one used to be the main road through the forest nearly a hundred yehrin ago." The gasps from the other two boys from Branby were almost explosive. He held up a hand to forestall them. "Now, hold on," Kilgar went on before they could burst in. "I know what you're thinking, but you're wrong." The two boys were bristling to speak, but bit at their tongues instead.

The dark-headed youth stepped away from the tree trunk and stood out in front of them. "It's an old road," he told them, "I admit it. And it's a little overgrown in places. But in many ways it's superior to the roads we have now." Doornig fastened a disbelieving eye on him. "It's more than just packed dirt, it's actually paved with flagstones. Really. Some of them are a little cracked and broken, you understand, but the whole road doesn't get bogged down with mud whenever it rains, like our newer ones do."

Gorian stepped up to Kilgar. "If this old road is so much better than the ones we have now, why has it been abandoned? Why doesn't anyone know about it any more?" Doornig snorted in agreement with him. "Why doesn't anyone still use it?"

Kilgar shrugged with his hands spread out wide. "I don't know. Does it really matter?" Their blank stares were fixed hard on him. "Maybe they felt it was haunted. Maybe you had to pay some kind of toll to travel on it. And who could really afford that?" He sauntered a few steps away before turning back to the others. "Maybe you had to have some sort of special permission from the king himself. Who knows?" He moved closer to them once more, lifting an index finger up for them to see. "But what I do know is this, no one uses it any more and it'll make our leg to Hurlik a good sight more direct. And not to mention more secret." He stood before them as they pondered his words. Shan bit at his lower lip.

"I'd say it's worth a shot," the Elfling spoke up, giving his head a series of tiny nods.

Gorian and Doornig eyed one another thoughtfully before turning to the other two with a slight bow of their heads. "Alright," the redheaded boy acquiesced. "How soon before we get there? I've had enough of all this stooping around for a while. My back's gettin' a little sore." He dropped his chin down firmly for emphasis.

"Me too," Gorian concurred.

"Let's get moving then," Kilgar stated. "We're almost there. It shouldn't take us more than a few mira to get to the old highway from here. And then we'll be as safe as we can be." He tilted his head a little to one side. ". . . At least for now." He looked briefly at the overhead canopy and then at his compass before shoving off.

The others grunted a bit in discomfort, having stiffened up somewhat from their brief rest. They grudgingly fell into step behind him. Shan was first on his heels, followed closely by Gorian, with Doornig taking up the rear. The redhead stifled a small yelp as he rubbed tenderly at his lower back.

"So, how'd you come across this old road, anyway?" Shan called softly to Kilgar as they picked their way over a large slimy root. Their boots slid mildly on the heavy moss. "I noticed it was not on your map."

"Bored, I guess," came the dark-haired youth's reply. "I like exploring the woods whenever I get the chance. My Dad got me interested in it when I was really young. Been taking little forays out through the trees ever since. Sometimes I take Rimmy with me. He's pretty keen on it, too. We like to camp out here once in a while."

They continued to wind their way along, slipping over occasional tree stumps and fallen logs, ducking under broken branches which hung down from the upper canopy at a sharp angle. Doornig and Gorian were not as nimble. They seemed to lack any sense of urgency and fell back a ways.

"One day, oh, a couple of yehrin ago now, I'd say," Kilgar chattered amiably, "we stumbled onto the road quite by accident. At first we didn't know what we'd found. An old road, yes, but we'd had no idea of its existence."

"Surely it must have appeared on an old map somewhere," Shan suggested lightly.

"You'd think," Kilgar came back. "But as hard as I looked, I could come up with nothing. No one living nowadays seemed to know anything about it." He glanced back over his shoulder momentarily to find the other two boys had dropped back still further. "Hey," he called to them without raising his voice, "try to keep up, will you."

"Yeah, right," Doornig intoned somewhat irritably. "Be right there." He shared a snicker with Gorian.

Kilgar pressed on steadily. "No one I talked to had ever even heard of it," he continued. "That is, until I happened to speak with old Tomar one day. He's the blacksmith's grandfather. He told me about a time long ago when there were such roads stretching out everywhere. He said there was a long period when the people of the entire continent lived together in peace and prosperity. No wars, no animosity between any of the races. The whole land lived under the wise and benevolent rule of the King of Vandikar."

"Vandikar?" Shan breathed.

Kilgar nodded. "The fabled kingdom of the Elves from long ago. The King ruled justly, it is said." He coughed softly as he stooped to slide under a low branch, but miscalculated and got a mouthful of leaves instead. Shan chuckled to himself, having done that more times than he liked to admit. Kilgar brushed the leaves aside and moved on. "It must have been an amazing time."

"Before Muurdra poisoned the hearts and minds of all the peoples to turn against the Elves," Shan muttered darkly. Kilgar trudged on in silence for a time.

"Anyhow," the boy spoke again after clearing his throat, "Tomar shared with me how those trade roads had been engineered supposedly to last for centuries."

True to his word Kilgar suddenly came out of the trees and found himself on a tiled roadway. Small pieces of broken flagstone crunched softly under his boots. He stopped in the middle of the road and twirled slowly about, laughing quietly in wonder. Shan stepped down out of the foliage to join him. He immediately looked both ways along the darkly shadowed stretch.

The area had been almost completely overgrown. It was as if the forest was trying to reclaim the land it had lost long ago. Thick, twisting branches interlaced their gnarled fingers high above. The density of the overhanging limbs obscured most of the afternoon sun, casting the whole place in a heavy veil of gloom. The way upon the forest floor was clear, for the most part, but stout weeds grew up through the fragmented stones. Many of the tiles were cracked with age and broken in numerous places.

The air along the road was cool and still, though it seemed a trifle stagnant to the Elfling. He found himself listening without realizing it. Thankfully there was no echo of metal boots to be heard anywhere, or the harsh grunting of shouted commands wafting down the darkened corridor. Shan felt he could breathe a little easier as he turned back to Kilgar. The dark-haired boy now stood motionless in the middle of the highway and offered the elven youth a broad grin.

"Whoa!" exclaimed Doornig as he burst out of the trees with Gorian. The two of them stopped at the edge of the road and gazed about in astonishment. The world around them seemed incredibly quiet and still. There were no sounds of birds to be heard, only the soft scuffling of rodents scratching about in the darkness under the trees. The red-haired youth tapped lightly with one foot on the paving stones. "It's in need of a little work, I think," he offered a little sarcastically.

"No, I'd say a lot," Gorian interrupted.

"Okay, a lot," Doornig said with a wide turn on his heel. "But it's still better than any of the main roads through the forest, I'll admit. Wagons sure wouldn't get bogged down here in the mud when it rains."

"I told you," Kilgar informed them. "But we've no time to dawdle here. The sun will be setting before too long and we need to make as much distance as we can before then."

"You don't really expect to get to Hurlik tonight, do you?" Doornig inquired incredulously.

"Of course not," the dark-headed youth told him. "In fact, it'll probably take us a few days to get there, even on the highway."

"Especially if we have to avoid any patrols we're likely to come across." They all looked at Shan with solemn eyes.

"Let's get on with it then," Kilgar spoke. And with that he turned southwest and began to make his way carefully over the broken pieces of flagstones littering the highway. The others fell into line behind him, kicking through the over-grown weeds almost immediately. Doornig hadn't gone far before he stumbled on a shard of stone and practically fell on his face.

"It's dark down here," he grumbled. "I'm gonna wind up with a broken ankle."

"If you think it's dark now," Kilgar instructed him, "wait until the sun sets." He looked up at the over-arching canopy above. "The thick branches will completely block any moonlight we might otherwise receive. So, let's make some good time, shall we?" He quickened his pace a little and the others struggled to match his long strides.

"But I'm hungry," the redhead whined after just a few more steps. As if to emphasize his statement, his stomach gurgled loud enough for all of them to hear. "See?"

"We cannot stop to eat now," Kilgar called back without turning to look.

"But . . ."

"Doornig!" Kilgar swirled to face him. It was too dark to catch the flash of anger in his eyes. "Not now!" He swung back smartly on his heel and marched off in annoyance.

Gorian patted his friend on the back. "We'll have plenty of time to eat once we camp for the night."

"Promise?" Doornig asked him.

"Yeah," the sandy-haired youth cajoled him. "Much as we want. Now come on, before Kilgar truly gets irritated with you." He swept past his friend and started to hurry after the others.

"Okay," Doornig was placated. "I'll be counting the mira." He shuffled off in pursuit, crunching and stomping over the flagstones. He thrashed through veils of taller weeds, batting them aside with renewed gusto.

They marched on for the better part of two ahrin before the failing sunlight forced them to a halt. "We'd better make camp before we cannot see any longer," their leader told them. They gathered together in the middle of the road around Kilgar. They started to pull off their packs. "Not on the road itself," he commanded. "Let's find a place somewhere under the trees a little ways off the highway. Maybe find some rocks or closely packed trunks to shield us from the highway."

They were too tired to argue with him, but managed to hold onto their bags long enough to stumble off the right shoulder of paving stones and into the trees. It didn't take them long to find a cluster of large boulders about forty kora away on a small rise of the forest floor. They threw themselves down in exhaustion, nestling down in the bowl of rocks.

Kilgar was the last to slump onto the ground inside their small barricade. "I don't think I need to tell you," he said tiredly, "that we shouldn't light a fire tonight." The other boys all nodded wearily. "Gorian, what have you got for us to eat?"

The light-haired boy pulled his pack closer and unlaced the front flap. "Well, let's see," he drawled out, plunging his hand down into the smaller pocket. He rummaged for a few moments before pulling out a couple of packets. "We've got some dried meat, a wedge of cheese and a handful of nuts for each of us."

"Sounds good," Shan responded lightly. "I had cheese the first night out from Draydin."

Gorian began passing out the small parcels to each of them. Doornig mumbled something under his breath as he accepted his ration. He tried glaring at his friend but it had already become too dark to see with any real kind of definition. Shan's elven eyes were the sharpest by far, so he watched off through the darkening branches as he munched slowly on his food. The quiet slurp of water bags could just be heard over the growing hum of night insects.

"Be careful not to drink all your water tonight," Kilgar warned them. "We have quite a ways to cover tomorrow before we'll get to Dunnigan's Rill. That's the only certain place I know to refill them before we make it to Hurlik."

"I'll trust your recollection," Shan told him. "You certainly know this part of the forest well. Probably better than anyone." After he had finished eating, the Elfling slung the water bottle over his head. He pulled himself up to peer out over the rocks. "I'll take the first watch," he informed them. "Try to get some sleep."

"Right," Kilgar said, pulling a blanket from his pack and settling himself lower against the rocks. "Wake me in a couple of ahrin."

"Will do," the Elfling returned. He pivoted around slowly, meticulously scanning the darkness. Gorian and Doornig made themselves as comfortable as they could on the ground, drawing the hoods of their cloaks up over their heads, and wrapping their arms around themselves for warmth. It wasn't long before the three of them were asleep.

Shan listened to the regular rhythm of their breathing for a while as he sat there quietly in the darkness. At one point a small forest animal pattered by. It stopped for a moment, sniffing at their little camp, then sidled quickly off in another direction.

It was almost two ahrin later, as he was beginning to feel a little sleepy, that Shan thought he heard something out of the ordinary. The faint murmur did not seem to match the regular sounds of the forest night. It was difficult to catch at first, and far off. It was severely muffled, too, by the heavy branches, yet the regular rhythm was somehow a little familiar. He strained intently as the low cadence grew closer, his mouth growing dry as he listened. It took quite some time before he recognized the metallic clanking of stamping feet. There weren't many of them, he could tell, but the rap of soldiers' boots was unmistakable.

Shan sprang quickly to Kilgar's side. He shook him roughly, careful to clamp a palm over the boy's mouth. The limp figure lurched up suddenly, his own hand reaching up to swipe the Elfling's grasp aside.

"Kilgar!" Shan hissed softly. "Shush. Gorguls are approaching. On the road."

"How far away are they?" came the soft inquiry. Kilgar shook his head forcefully to clear away the fuzziness of sleep. He slipped the blanket from his lap and spun to look out over their cradle of rocks. He could see nothing in the blackness.

"A couple of hundred kora, I'd say," Shan told him. They listened intently for a few moments, and by then even Kilgar could hear their measured approach. The clanking grew steadily nearer.

"They're keeping to the road," the native of Branby exclaimed quietly. "I can't hear them thrashing about through the trees like they're searching for someone."

"No," Shan agreed softly. "I think they're just marching past. Maybe they've got some kind of rendezvous up the road a-ways."

"We'd better wake the others," Kilgar advised. "Just in case we need to make a run for it. Besides, we don't want them crying out in their sleep to alert them to our presence here. Come on." He moved silently over to Doornig while Shan leaned down and crouched over Gorian.

"It's alright," the light-haired boy called out softly, "I'm awake." He yawned quietly. "What is it?"

"Soldiers," Shan cautioned him with a hand on his arm. Gorian came instantly to his knees, trying to poke his head up over the rocks, but soon realized it was impossible to see anything around them. Moonlight left a soft sapphire glow on the leaves far overhead, but did little to chase away the murkiness down there under the trees.

"Doornig," Kilgar whispered hoarsely. He reached out to cup the boy's mouth before he could thrash about, but just a little too late. Doornig spluttered something incoherently and wriggled about on the ground. He kicked at the clinging form to wrest himself loose, but Kilgar managed to get a hold on the lower portion of the boy's face.

"Doornig!" Gorian called in a tense whisper. "Be quiet! We've got company out there."

The boy went instantly limp. His eyes were wild over Kilgar's grasp, but no one could see. The clatter of metal boots was almost upon them, echoing strangely through the trees. The boys huddled some forty kora from the roadway, urgently hoping the gorguls would not be able to see them any more than they could see the soldiers.

Shan peered out into the inky blackness. The pale gleam of moonlight from above was just enough to cast a sort of gauziness over the scene. With his keen elven eyes he could just make out five burly forms stamping down the road. Gorguls, he had no doubt. They had almost passed them by, oblivious to their hiding place when the elven youth realized there was another figure moving along with them, only he was not squat or heavy shouldered as the others.

The sight of a tall, slender form, who almost appeared to hover above the ground as he moved, was entirely too dream-like for him. Shan held his breath. The figure's long white hair seemed to glow in the faint light. Was it just his imagination, or did the thing actually peer out suddenly into the darkness to where they were hunched down together behind their rocky vantage point? Shan couldn't quite tell, but the feeling left him shaken. He shivered faintly as the small column continued to glide past them without stopping.

What new thing is this? he asked himself in a cold sweat. *Am I going to be faced with new nameless terrors every step of the way?*

The four boys scarcely dared to breathe. They could all clearly hear the crunching of stone fragments under the soldiers' weight. As the stomping of metal boots continued to move steadily off to the northeast they all began to relax a little more. They carefully let out the air they had painfully been holding in their lungs.

"One thing's for sure," Doornig whispered once the sound of the soldiers was completely gone.

"What's that?" Gorian queried.

"I doubt any of us will be getting any more sleep tonight." The others grunted softly in assent. They slid back down behind their sanctuary of rocks and stared out into the darkness with unseeing eyes.

– 16 –
Gorguls
[20th of Kaligath, 4534 C.R.]

Dawn found them stiff and cold. They were clustered together for warmth within the circlet of stones, their backs touching. They had thrown their blankets and cloaks over themselves in a jumbled heap. It was still early Se'Kora, just barely into spring, after all, and the air remained a little chilly at night.

Shan sat quietly with the others, unmoving. His eyes stared out from under his hood, constantly roaming over the slowly brightening expanse of the forest. All of their eyes were red-rimmed and bleary from watching throughout the long night. They peered out tiredly as shadowed humps gradually took on form. Tendrils of mist trailed through pockets of underbrush in feathery streamers. The click and hum of insects which had droned in their ears throughout the night had died away, replaced now instead with the light chatter of countless tiny birds winging about through the interlacing branches.

Kilgar slipped out of his blanket, rose rigidly to his feet. He paused for a moment to listen then scanned their surroundings warily with a full pivot. As far as he could tell there was nothing in sight and no sounds of soldiers in the vicinity. Satisfied, he stretched the kinks from his back, tilting his body first to one side and then the other.

Gorian stirred slowly. He sat cross legged on the ground and began to roll his blanket into a tight bundle. He fastened it to the bottom of his pack by its attached straps. He climbed stiffly to his feet, looking about at his red-haired friend. Doornig yawned and rubbed at his eyes. He swished his tongue around in his mouth and across his teeth in an effort to wash away the sour taste.

"Who's got breakfast?" he wanted to know. He rose to his knees and began to work on his own bedding. When no one answered immediately, he looked up. The others all seemed preoccupied with their own tasks as they readied themselves for the day's upcoming march. "Huh?"

"I've got a few lence cakes," Kilgar responded at last. "Shan's got some dried fruit in his pack as well. We'll break them out once we're on the road." Doornig opened his mouth to say something, but the dark-haired boy went on. "I don't want to waste any more time this morning than we need to. We really ought to make as much distance as we can today. The sooner we get out of the forest, the more likely we are to slip through any traps the gorguls might try to set for us."

Doornig nodded grudgingly. The others hurried to put the last touches on their preparations, stowing blankets, making sure their boots were laced up, folding cloaks away across their packs. It only took them a matter of moments before they found themselves sliding down over the rocks of their makeshift campsite. They picked their way through the dense trees back to the roadway, careful not to trip over worrisome tangles of roots. Presently they came out onto the crumbling pavement, and peered in both directions. They turned immediately to their right, starting off in a primarily southerly course.

True to his word, Kilgar soon broke out a packet of cakes and began passing them around. They munched quietly as they walked, careful not to skid on loose fragments of paving. Shan pulled one arm from his pack strap while still on the move. He managed to delve down under the front flap of the sack while it hung along his side. He quickly located the dried fruit and pulled it out. He scooped several large pieces out onto his palm before passing the bag to Doornig. The red-haired boy thanked him with a grim smile, shuffling the sack to Gorian in turn after he'd grabbed a handful for himself. The light-haired boy picked out a few choice morsels then handed it along. Kilgar drove his fist into the bag before returning it to Shan. The Elfling resealed the packet and tucked it away in his pack once more. He cinched the rucksack back into place without missing a step.

They walked briskly down the highway in silence. They made good time throughout the morning, stopping only once for Doornig to dig a pebble out of his boot. "Don't know how that got in there," he mumbled, tossing it lightly aside before starting out after the others once again.

It was nearly the fourth ahr after dawn when they thought they heard someone approaching from the south. They scrambled quickly off the road, seeking shelter behind a couple of fallen trunks some twenty paces away under the trees. They didn't have long to wait as the sounds seemed to echo hollowly through the branches. It wasn't the heavy metal clomp of boots they had come to fear but was, rather, more like the soft clipping of small hooves on the stones.

Soon two men could be seen through the trees leading a thorro up the old highway. The stubborn little beast was heavily laden with goods. It hurried along, for one of the men was tapping it lightly in the flanks every so often with a switch. The poor animal bleated miserably with each stroke, laboring to increase its speed as much as possible. The two men spoke together in muted tones as they moved steadily on without so much as a glance out through the trees.

" . . . when up jumps this ugly cuss," one of them was saying, the man on the nearest side of the little animal. "Couldn't help slamming into the hideous thing. Thought he was after our stuff."

The other man let out an unruly laugh. "And then he pulled that great big scimitar of his out of his belt." He laughed again. "I thought he was gonna cut that frightful face 'a yours clean off your shoulders." He slapped at his leg.

"Yeah," the first man crooned with a low whistle. "If'n it wasn't for that other fella, the white-haired cadaver with those scary black eyes, I'd have been a goner for sure."

"Whew! He was sure a frightful one, I'll tell ya," the second man proclaimed with a shiver.

"I'll say!" the first one replied uneasily. But with that last remark they were out of earshot, as they herded their little pack animal hastily along. Once they were completely lost to sight the four companions crept stealthily back onto the old roadway.

"Huh," Doornig said with a snort, "I thought you said nobody knew about this abandoned highway. That makes two groups we've come across just since yesterday afternoon when we started." Kilgar shrugged.

"What were those two men doing in here?" Gorian wanted to know. "Why aren't they out on the main road, like everyone else?" He thrust out his lip, perplexed.

"Smugglers," Shan spoke up lightly. "Probably moving their illegal cargo from place to place without the risk of being seen." The others looked at him thoughtfully.

"Suppose you're right," Kilgar stated. "They're certainly the type to look for a secret way through the forest." He stared off after them. "But what were they talking about?"

"They obviously ran into a gorgul or two," Doornig quipped, a smug look playing abut his face. "It's too bad the devil didn't whack the poor fellow's head off. Sounds like he deserved it."

Kilgar shook his head. "He obviously had a frightening encounter of some kind, but I was actually wondering about the other one he mentioned." Doornig leveled a confused frown on him. "You know, the guy with the white hair and the scary black eyes."

"Oh, yeah," Gorian queried. "What's with that?"

Shan suddenly shivered violently. The others turned to him as he rubbed at patches of gooseflesh on his arms. "I think I saw one of them," he spoke up, oddly agitated by his memory.

"When?" Kilgar wanted to know.

"Last night," the Elfling replied. "When we were hiding."

"What?!" Doornig snapped. "It was too dark to see anything. How could you have possibly seen such a creature?"

The Elfling shrugged. "I've got keen eyesight," Shan told them. "Last night, when the gorguls came stomping up the road, I thought I saw another person with them. And he was quite a bit different in his appearance." The red-haired youth was extremely doubtful. "I can see things that you can't," the elven youth went on. "I'm an Elf, remember?"

"Right," Doornig bristled, "and next you'll be telling us you can breathe under water." He crossed his arms in disbelief.

"Elves do have incredible eyesight, Doornig," Kilgar informed him. "Don't be so obnoxious." The boy turned away with a sneer. "It's a proven fact. If Shan says he could see the soldiers last night, I believe him." The redhead could only manage a grunt.

"There were five gorguls marching together in step," the Elfling stated confidently. "But before they had completely passed us by, I saw another form traveling with them." He swallowed at a dry throat. "He seemed tall and somehow graceful, like he was almost floating when he moved, instead of walking." Even Doornig leaned in to listen. "He had long white hair which seemed to glow faintly in the moonlight."

"What moonlight?" Gorian queried. "Those branches were way too thick."

"Hush," Kilgar said with a stern look.

"I could never really see his eyes, though," the elven youth finished off. "But it sounds a lot like the smuggler's description." He debated for a moment whether he should say anything more about the creature's glance in their direction, but he thought better of it, and said nothing.

"Well," Kilgar confided with them solemnly, "it seems we've got yet another thing we should be careful to avoid."

"No problem," Doornig spoke up petulantly, "we just need to avoid all targs, spiders, gorguls, kurgoyles . . ."

"Kurgoths," Shan corrected him.

"Fine, kur*goths*," the fiery redhead continued, "and now you're saying we need to keep clear of all dead looking guys with nasty black eyes." He thrust out his lip. "Does that about cover it?"

"Yes," Shan told him evenly. "For now." Doornig shot a smug look at the Elfling. "Who knows what else we might run into along the way?"

Daryl Hanson

The elven youth swallowed uncomfortably.

"Come on," Kilgar called to them. "We need to make good time for a while."

"Right," Gorian agreed.

They fell into step behind their dark-haired leader. They shuffled steadily through the hazy gloom for some time, paying close attention to where they placed their feet. They picked their way over crumbled bits of rock and batted aside heavy clumps of weeds thrusting up through the cracks. They seemed to make steady enough progress. It brought a small smile to Kilgar's face as he looked back at the others from time to time. The boys tried to remain alert to the look and feel of the forest at all times, to the small sounds of birds flitting about through the branches, the rustling of dry leaves as tiny things scuttled about in the semi-darkness between the trunks.

After they had walked for nearly four ahrin, with scarcely a word passing between them during that time, Kilgar called them all to a halt with an upraised hand. They had heard no murmur of pursuit throughout the morning, nor had they seen any further sign of smugglers sneaking up the old highway. The trees here thinned out a little where they decided to rest, a small stream softly gurgling at their feet.

"Dunnigan's Rill," Kilgar informed them.

A small stone bridge crossed the stream, the track of the old highway was lost in the distant haze under the interminable trees. Delicate streamers of sunlight filtered down through the gently bobbing branches onto a narrow slip of sweet grass and cat-tails. They tried to make themselves comfortable under the spreading limbs, throwing themselves down eagerly on the little bank with sighs of relief.

Shan knelt down by the edge of the stream, cupping his hands and splashing cool water over his face. The others were quick to follow him, plunging their curled palms into the gentle rivulet. They eagerly dashed their sweaty faces and necks in the cascades of sparkling droplets. After drinking their fill and replenishing their half-empty water bottles, they crawled a few steps away from the lazy stream, giggling quietly to themselves. They leaned pleasantly back against the broad boles of several trees.

Doornig sloughed off his pack and dug down under the large flap. He came up with a packet of dried meat, pulled a couple of strips from the pouch and began passing it around. Gorian gratefully snatched up a few pieces of his own before offering it in turn to Kilgar. The dark-haired boy took out two blackened slabs, then handed the little bag to the Elfling. They all eased back against the thick bark, munching in contentment. A sack of nuts made its circuit around their group as well, fished out from Gorian's bag which he had thrown off to the side. They each scooped out a handful before the remainder got idly placed on a flattened root just visible through the grass. The soft sound of their crunching was interspersed with occasional slurps from their water bags.

When he had finished the small meal Doornig stretched himself out on the grassy bank. He leaned his head back against one arm, closing his eyes with a smile to himself.

"Don't fall asleep," Kilgar warned him. The redhead popped one eye open and looked at him. "We can't afford to rest here too long." Doornig's brows furrowed mildly in irritation, then he managed a small shrug before closing the eye once again. He settled himself more evenly on the grass, and sighed deeply. The others were content to rest back against the trees, their gaze wandering off under the trees.

Doornig's breathing had just started to become steady and even when Shan detected a change in the sound of the forest. The birds had ceased their twittering in the branches overhead, and the scuttling of rodents among the fallen leaves was gone. He sat up and cocked his head to one side. Kilgar noticed the movement and looked warily over at him.

"What is it?" Kilgar asked softly.

Shan shook his head almost imperceptibly, still listening intently. "Something's approaching," he said at last. Doornig sat up suddenly with a strangled snort and blinked his eyes fiercely. He ran his tongue noisily over his teeth, turning to look off in the direction of the others' scrutiny. Their hearts began to hammer within their chests, their breathing suddenly rapid and shallow. They sat frozen, the unmistakable clank of metal boots could be heard drifting their way.

"Quick, hide!" came Kilgar's hissed command.

They bolted up from their spots and quickly scrambled back into the screen of broad trees behind them. They scrabbled over several large roots and between twisted trunks in a blind rush, their arms and legs scraping and scratching at roughened bits of bark. Their boots crunched lightly on a carpet of dry leaves. Low limbs tore at their faces and hands, snagging at their cloaks, clutching for their packs. The echo of snapping twigs seemed loud in their own ears as the four boys threw themselves down behind a couple of large trees. They held their breaths as a squad of gorguls clattered up the roadway and materialized suddenly out of the heavy shadows of the woods near the small stone bridge.

The soldiers had been jogging along at a good clip but, at the sight of the stream, had abruptly slackened their pace to a walk. Then they stopped altogether on the far side of the rill at a bark from their commander. The savage men cast themselves onto the grassy bank and loudly began drinking their fill. Some of them lapped at the softly moving brook like animals, lashing their dark tongues out again and again. A few others simply plunged their entire heads into the stream, hauling their glistening faces out after a few heartbeats, the wet tangles of their top knots casting spray in all directions.

Shan counted a dozen of them in his partially obscured view. He peered carefully around the trunk of a large tree, allowing just one eye to take in the scene. One of the creatures separated itself form the rest of the squad. He clanked faintly onto the small bridge, looking up into the trees with a toss of his head. After a time he lowered his large eyes onto the surface of the water. He followed a twig as it bobbed out from under the bridge and glided down the stream in gentle little swells. The stick continued to course along through tiny wavelets, but the gorgul suddenly lost interest in it, instead fastening its gaze on the farther bank where the boys had eaten their lunch. Its great dark eyes narrowed on something on the ground. With a start of alarm, Shan realized it had spotted the small leftover bag of nuts. It lay sprawled open on a flattened root under the trees and had somehow been forgotten in their wild scramble for cover.

"Uh-oh!" Shan called softly between clenched teeth. Kilgar looked over at him, his forehead creased in query. "*The nuts!*" Shan mouthed to him. He jerked his head toward the abandoned sack. The boys shared a feverish glance.

The gorgul ambled the rest of the way across the little stone bridge, its slanting eyes burrowing into that spot on the ground. Its heavy metal boots scuffed over the paving stones of the highway before giving way to the muffled crunch of decaying leaves. The fearsome thing shuffled to a stop by the root. Extending one long, clawed hand, it lifted the little pouch up to its slitted snout. With the tips of two clawed fingers it extracted one of the nuts and held it up and examined it closely. The yellowed tusks worked up and down as it sniffed noisily at the contents.

The boys huddled behind their trees, their throats dry and tight. Hearts hammered wildly in their chests. They dared not breathe for fear their slightest movement would draw scrutiny even in the faint light of the forest.

The lone gorgul spun with the small bag clutched in one claw. It swung to face the rest of the soldiers and hissed out a loud command. Instantly the squad brought up their elongated faces from the stream, their thick hide dribbling with runnels of water. They lumbered to their feet and stomped over to their commander in a wild rush. Lifting the bag of nuts up before their inquisitive eyes, the leader barked out an order, flinging his other clawed hand to point emphatically out under the trees on that side of the stream. With a series of savage growls the troops scattered in all directions, leaping and sliding over the roots in a sort of hungry eagerness. They hooted and hissed as they fanned out, sweeping quickly closer to the boys' hiding place in a matter of moments.

"Run!" Kilgar cried out through gritted teeth.

The boys turned and fled through the densely packed trees, dragging their packs awkwardly along with them.

"Try to keep the trunks between us as a shield," Shan called softly as he cast a hurried look back over his shoulder. "Maybe we can elude them in here somehow."

The gorguls still hadn't discovered the boys yet as they stomped heavily over the uneven ground. Twisting and turning among the trees, the fearsome soldiers batted aside every branch, peered into every gloomy patch of shadows as they quickly lumbered along in their search. The raspiness of their foul breath and the warbling of their constant calls to one another seemed loud to the frightened companions. The boys soon found their throats on fire as they pushed themselves onward upon wobbly legs. They desperately managed to stay one step ahead of the gorguls until a strangled cry exploded from one of the soldiers.

Looking back as he raced around an enormous bole, Shan could see one of the savages point savagely in their direction, a vicious gleam in its eyes. The other soldiers swung their search in the boys' direction, howling in glee at the sight of their prey. The foul brutes quickly began to converge on their position.

The boys drove themselves onward in reckless haste, no longer concerned with stealth. They pushed wildly now with all their strength in a tremendous effort to outdistance their pursuers. But their reserves soon started to flag and they found themselves losing ground to the seemingly tireless enemy at their backs. The gorguls yowled and screamed in an endless cacophony of sound. Shan could hear them now slashing and chopping at low hanging branches with their great scimitars. The blades sang out loudly behind them with each ringing stroke.

Daryl Hanson

"This is useless!" Doornig wailed between ragged breaths. "I can't run in here. It's just too close."

Kilgar threw a hasty look over his shoulder. The gorguls were definitely closing in on them. He came to a sudden decision and swerved wildly to his left. "Back to the rill!" he shot out. "Maybe we can outrun them on level terrain." Shan instantly bolted off after him, and the others were soon in hot pursuit.

For a moment they twisted away from the devilish men and gained a little ground on the soldiers. The gorguls were momentarily confused by the apparent disappearance of their prey directly ahead of them, but a harsh call from the rear of their file refocused their pursuit, and they were immediately off on the chase. They soon began to close in on the boys once more.

Kilgar and Shan broke out of the tangle of trees at the same moment. They slashed instantly to their right, hurtling themselves down the bank of the quiet stream. Shan looked back once to witness Gorian and Doornig burst out of the confining branches and high tail it after them. They pounded along the grassy edge, cat-tails flapping at their faces. Before long, though, a dozen burly forms exploded onto the path behind them, bits of leaves and twigs trailing out after them in lazy spirals.

The weary boys managed to put a little distance on the soldiers for a time, but their strength soon began to wane. What little bit of cushion they had gained was quickly lost as their legs burned with their efforts. Their breathing, too, soon became labored, and they fought for each ragged gasp. The foul creatures steadily drew closer, until it seemed to the boys they were fairly breathing down their necks. One of the soldiers reached out a clawed fist and nearly latched onto Gorian's pack from behind. The sandy-haired youth swallowed painfully as he struggled to run, fire filling his lungs.

The four companions staggered doggedly onward, their leg muscles spasming painfully. It seemed like all hope was lost to them when they heard dimly through the rush of their own breathing, a wild clattering from somewhere up ahead. The pounding of feet drew rapidly closer, yet because of a slight bend in the stream, they could not see anything.

"It's useless! It's over!" Doornig huffed in defeat. "We're surrounded."

"Back in the trees!" Gorian wheezed. "Quick!"

They were just about to dash back into the trees when three great animals careened around the bend in a great drumming of noise. It took them all a moment to realize these were not more soldiers attempting to hem them in, nor their large lizard-like mounts from the far south. Three magnificent thorka galloped swiftly towards them, a sole rider perched atop one of the high sleek backs. The figure was hooded, and the end of his cloak billowed furiously out behind him.

In an instant of recognition, Kilgar realized that this was the same hooded rider who had torn down the streets of Branby the day before and had burst out through a mass of startled soldiers at the gate. The mysterious figure had raced from the village in such reckless abandon.

All three great thorka shot past the stumbling boys and skidded to a halt on the grassy path. The confused swarm of gorguls fell back at the wild rush. The large animals reared up with a shriek and lashed out with their front legs. The slight figure clung fiercely to the back of his mount as they pranced upon their hind legs. The sharp, retractable claws appeared suddenly, slashing out at the gorguls as they slid and tumbled over each other in their haste to flee. Many of the foul creatures went down, streams of thick dark blood flying out from their brutish faces.

The four boys couldn't help but turn to see the outcome of the collision. Doornig had even stopped running, his leg muscles quivering from the strain. Gorian pulled up as well, his breath coming in uncontrollable gasps.

The mighty thorka reared again, flashing their razor sharp claws in the dappled sunlight. The soldiers cowered back from the flailing barbs. The small rider wheeled the animals suddenly and darted off after the four travelers. He reined in amidst a shower of dirt next to the weary boys. The thorka danced about anxiously on the dusty path.

"Come on," a voice called out to them from under the hood. "Mount up before those things can recover." He held out the reins of the spare animals to them. "Quickly!" he cried when they seemed to hesitate. The voice was especially familiar. Kilgar accepted the proffered hand and swung himself up behind the rider. Doornig and Gorian each reached for the reins and scrambled wearily up into the saddles. Gorian settled his feet in the stirrups and held out a hand to the Elfling. Shan grabbed on tightly and pulled himself up behind the sandy-haired boy.

With a snap of the reins and a kick in the flanks the large animals were off in an instant. Their hooves tore clumps of grass from the bank as they flew away from the knots of soldiers still scrambling around in their wake. The powerful mounts thundered up the path and shot around the bend of the little channel, the evil brutes completely lost to view. The five companions raced along the shore, the six legs of each thorka nearly flying over the ground in an ever increasing gait.

The hood of the rider flapped in Kilgar's face as they galloped along. He turned his head to the side and leaned in, his arms easily encircling the small waist in front of him. "That was a dangerous stunt you pulled in Branby," he called into the wind. The rider stiffened for a moment.

"Yeah, maybe," the young voice returned a little cavalierly. He relaxed a bit. "But it worked, didn't it?" He shrugged, his hands playfully slapping at his animal's neck with the end of the reins. "You got out of town alive, I see."

"Yes, we certainly did," the dark-headed young man had to admit. "Thanks to you— *Rimmy*." The youth went rigid once again, tensing for the outburst he was expecting from his older brother. But it didn't come immediately. They continued to thunder down the small path.

"How did you know it was me?" the young fellow called back after a moment.

It was Kilgar's turn to shrug. "Wasn't very difficult," he declared. "Your movements and mannerisms were fairly distinct, I think. When we heard the voice of that escaping rider call out, it sounded oddly a lot like you."

"Oh," Rimmy offered weakly. "I thought I was pretty well disguised. I even had a head scarf like Shan in order to fool them."

"You looked the part," the older brother commented, "I'll grant you that. You really fooled the soldiers and that's what counts. They all went tearing off after you in a heartbeat." He clapped a hand on Rimmy's shoulder. "The thing that really gave you away, though," Kilgar confided to him, "you took *our* thorka. Not some other animals picked quickly at random, but our very own mounts. That was a little too coincidental, don't you think?"

Rimmy conceded the logic. "Oh," was all he could say.

"I've got to hand it to you though, little brother," Kilgar went on. Rimmy tilted his head back curiously. "Without your little stunt we probably wouldn't have made it out of town so easily."

They rode on in silence for a time. The pounding of the thorka's hooves reverberated in their ears. They chased each other along Dunnigan's Rill for the better part of an ahr before they pulled off into a small clearing just to the side of the stream. They listened cautiously for a few moments before easing themselves down out of the saddle.

"Oh, boy," Doornig was ecstatic. "I thought we were goners for sure." He slapped his thorka affectionately on the long nose. "Feels good to outrun those ugly devils for a change."

"I'll say," Gorian joined him, rubbing at his legs. "I'm still sore from all that running we had to do."

They both turned to thank their rescuer who was standing lightly with Kilgar by the head of the sleek, black thorka. The young man pulled the hood down and untied the dark blue cloth from about his head with a small tug. He shook his hair loose and scratched at his scalp.

"Rimmy?" Doornig and Gorian said in unison, their jaws falling open in surprise.

"It's me," the young man called. The two boys rushed to sweep him up in their arms. They gave him a twirl before setting him back on his feet.

"You're a lifesaver!" the redhead crooned. He reached out with both hands and patted the young boy alternately on each arm. His face was flushed with his enthusiasm.

"Great plan," Gorian added, taking the three thorka in with a glance. "I just wish you'd have caught up with us a little earlier. Might have saved us a few korads." He smiled grimly. "And we wouldn't have been scared half to death by all those filthy soldiers."

Shan watched quietly from the side as the four of them teased each other with a series of playful jabs. He praised Athiliel silently for their momentary deliverance, wondering just how long their respite would last before they stumbled onto another eager pack of soldiers scouring the area for them.

Kilgar looked over and caught his eye, saw the solemn cast to his lips. "Don't get too carried away," he said offhandedly to his friends, sensing the Elfling's thoughts. "We've still got a lot of ground to cover, and who knows how many more patrols we're gonna have to elude." The others sobered up a little, but still shook each other lightly in their appreciation. "Let's allow the animals a chance to rest for a few moments before we press on," Kilgar told them all after a pause. The others nodded agreeably before each of them turned away to organize their gear for the next leg of the journey. Now that they had mounts to carry them, they would be able to redistribute some of their supplies into the saddle bags and thereby lighten their overloaded rucksacks.

As Kilgar busied himself with Adrulax, he scratched and patted at the animal constantly. He rubbed the stallion's long, flat nose with affection. Rimmy helped him organize the load, fearful that his brother would send him packing at any moment. "Don't worry," Kilgar said to him, sensing his apprehension, "I'm not going to send you home." Relief flooded over the boy as he handed up some of his brother's things. "—*Yet*." They regarded each other briefly. "It'd be too dangerous for you to head back alone on foot, and I don't think we can spare any of the thorka right now." He grinned at his little brother. "Guess you're just gonna have to come with us."

Rimmy gave out a joyful holler, but then, realizing what he'd done, he clamped a hand over his own mouth. He froze momentarily, listening, his eyes restless over his fingers. "Sorry," he managed to whisper after detecting no sounds of pursuit back up the forest path.

They mounted up shortly afterwards. Kilgar had called a change in the riding order while they worked on their preparations. "I'll take Shan with me," he had said, "on Adrulax. Rimmy will start out with Doornig, but then transfer over to Gorian somewhere down the road." The others nodded in agreement. "That way neither Ruggles nor Hoofnail will get too tired."

The dark-haired leader eased his thorka out through the narrow opening in the trees. He scanned the little path along the softly moving stream first to the left and then to the right. Shan swung his head on a swivel, seeking to penetrate the distant gloom. Satisfied, Kilgar urged his stallion out of their brief haven and began walking him lightly in a southwesterly direction toward the forest's edge. The six legs picked almost delicately through the tall grasses. Doornig came next, with Rimmy straddling the barrel chest of the animal just back of the saddle. Rather than try to wrap his arms around the redhead he chose to grasp onto a few loose straps running off the back end of the saddle. Lastly, Gorian walked Hoofnail out onto the trail, turning to the right to follow lightly after the others.

After walking the beasts for about half an ahr, Kilgar swung around in the saddle to regard the others. "I'd like to see if we can break free of the forest before the sun sets."

"It's only mid-afternoon," Gorian pointed out. "On the thorka we should be able to do that easily enough." Doornig offered only a grunt.

"Yes," their leader told them, "but we haven't got the slightest clue what might be waiting for us at the edge of the trees. We've no way of knowing if all these bands of gorguls can stay in contact with each other. Even now they may know we're coming, might set up some sort of barricade to box us in."

"Or not," Shan offered flatly. He exchanged a look with Kilgar who peered back over his right shoulder.

"Or not," he agreed. "But I'd rather not take that chance. I'd hate to have to fight our way through at twilight. These things seem to prefer the darkness."

Shan swallowed reflexively.

"You'd rather make camp somewhere out in the open?" Doornig questioned him. "Rather than under the concealment of the trees?"

"Yes," came Kilgar's reply. "Maybe we can outflank them for a while. There's some low hills just on the other side of the river. We should be able to find some cover there."

"Alright," Doornig concurred.

"Hyah!" Kilgar called out with a clucking of his tongue. And with that Adrulax broke into a canter.

17

A Skirmish In The Hills
[20th of Kaligath, 4534 C.R.]

The three thorka huddled tightly together against the trees. They pranced lightly in place upon their long legs, whickering softly. Their riders held them steady, just off the narrow pathway. The boys peered intently down the course of the babbling rill to the edge of the forest a couple hundred kora away. Concealed well back in the rough, the young travelers pressed themselves into the heavy shadows of a small cleft in the trees. There was little chance, should anyone even be watching, for them to be seen. They studied the forest opening a little while longer. It beckoned to them. But they could detect no sign of ugly soldiers lurking about under the trees ahead. They watched, and still they waited.

After leaving the small clearing in the forest the five young companions had cantered their mounts for about half an ahr before slowing them to a walk for perhaps half that time. They didn't fear pursuit immediately from that direction, since they had left the gorgul band somewhat in disarray and traveling behind them on foot. The boys had seen no further evidence of them at all the rest of that afternoon, yet Kilgar pressed them back into a canter for another half ahr. He really wanted to reach the edge of the forest without too much further delay. They had stopped at one point for a brief rest, allowing the animals to drink their fill from the lazy stream. Rimmy had slipped over from riding in back of Doornig to slide in behind the sandy-headed youth once they had pushed off again.

"I don't see anything," Rimmy declared softly, peering over Gorian's shoulder.

"I don't either," the redhead confirmed.

"But that doesn't mean they're not up there somewhere," Gorian stated flatly. He eyed the darkness under the distant branches. "Hiding, waiting for us to come into sight before they spring out of the trees."

"I don't know," Kilgar spoke slowly. He rubbed his chin. "That's pretty close to Hurlik. I can't imagine the folks there'd be too happy with those brutes hanging around too closely."

"No, but what could they do about it?" Doornig sneered. "It's not like they have any more of a military presence than Branby."

They all watched the forest a little while longer as it seemed to taunt them. Shan cast a look back the way they had come, but he could not pick out any signs of movement coming along the dim trail behind them. The thorka sniffed softly and flicked their long ears impatiently.

Kilgar leaned back and swung his face to the side. "What do you think?" he asked the Elfling. Shan could only shrug for a moment. He glared back down the tiny stream to where it exited the tree line, forcing air noisily out through his flapping lips.

"I say we try it," the elven youth said slowly. "We can't stay here forever." Adrulax shifted somewhat under them and nickered softly.

"I think he agrees with you," Kilgar mused with a slight chuckle. "And so do I."

"If we have to we can always run for it," Shan told him. "Make for those hills you were talking about."

"Alright," the dark-haired boy said with a little flick of his reins. He coaxed the large stallion from the shallow niche in the trees and slowly began walking him forward. The light patter of his hooves rustled through the tufted grass as he edged along. Gorian spurred Hoofnail to follow close behind, and Doornig brought his steed up almost immediately. They walked the animals quietly; the boys hardly managed to breathe as the tension took hold of them. They swung their faces continually from side to side, earnestly searching the murky depths under the trees. But they saw nothing.

They drew steadily closer, their chests fairly wanting to explode. Doornig coughed mildly and they all turned to look at him. He hunched his shoulders apologetically. They turned their attention nervously back to the trail as they finally drew even with the line of trees. They paused for a moment, blinking in the late afternoon sun, which somehow seemed overly bright to them after spending the last few days in the relative gloom of the forest.

Kilgar shaded his eyes with the back of one hand and peered to his left. There was nothing moving their way from Hurlik, and the opposite direction was just as clear. They all breathed a deep sigh of relief as their eyes settled on the sparkle of water out to the west. The Tarloona River could be seen meandering slowly along the flat land spread out before them. It skirted along the edge of the forest to their right as it tripped and fell through a series of tiny waterfalls on its tireless run toward the mighty Tanalorn River to the northwest.

The low rolling hills on the far side of the Tarloona seemed enticing to them, luring them onto their journey a little more to the southwest.

"Come on," Kilgar called out as he spurred his mount forward. "What are we waiting for?" He picked his way over the gently sloping ground, turning the thorka's great head away from the track of Dunnigan's Rill. He led them in the direction of the lone bridge spanning the river in their immediate vicinity. The other riders plodded along behind him in an easy gait. They swayed lightly from side to side with their animals' gait as they worked their way, unhurried, down the gentle grade. As the ground leveled out Kilgar urged his mount into a light trot, the others easily settling into step to match his speed.

The rill quickly fell away on their right as they swung more to the left. The road leading away from Hurlik tumbled down from the forest edge and spilled toward the Tarloona Bridge. But before they could reach the old, wooden trestle, they would first have to cross the Western Ring Road. It lay some eight to ten korads in front of them.

They had just lapsed into a steady rhythm upon their beasts, when a shout rang out from somewhere behind them. It wasn't actually the call of a voice, but was more like the shrill blast from a horn. They turned their faces nervously in the direction of the sound. Racing fast along the fringe of the trees from the direction of Nad, came a party of mounted riders. They pounded quickly towards them on their large beasts.

"What!" cried Doornig as he skidded his pony to a halt and glared back over his shoulder. "Not again!"

The others circled around in a wide turn, staring intently at the rising cloud of dust kicked up by numerous hooves. Their own animals danced skittishly as they squinted into the declining sun.

"Those aren't gorguls," Shan told them, his eyes narrowing on the rapidly approaching party. The four other boys shaded their eyes against the dust and haze. "Gorguls don't ride thorka."

"What then?" Kilgar wanted to know. The ground hurriedly diminished between them and the thunder of the approaching hooves was nearly deafening.

"Looks like some sort of forest militia," the Elfling told them. "They're dressed in black and gold." He tossed a hasty look at the others, before turning back to the soldiers once again. They were still about a korad off when the cry of human voices could definitely be heard, raised in alarm. Some of the men were waving at them as they furiously bounced along in their saddles.

"Beware!" rang out the shouted command as they hurtled ever closer. "Beware! Beware!"

"Enemy soldiers!" howled another voice in a stentorian bellow. The riders thundered towards them as the boys anxiously sat upon their fidgeting mounts. "Enemy soldiers!" came the piercing cry.

More than a dozen mounted troopers swept past them upon thorka. The young companions fought to keep their own animals from spinning chaotically about in tight circles. Kilgar struggled to keep Adrulax in check, for he wanted to race after them. Then one of the men, the last rider in line, pulled back hard on his reins and brought his great beast sliding to a halt in a shower of dust all around them. They coughed at the rising cloud as the man swung about in his saddle to face them.

"Better head for cover, lads," the soldier blared at them. His thorka pranced ceaselessly on the lumpy sod. "We're hot on the heels of some hostile enemy solders."

"What? Raiders from Horrick?" Doornig queried.

The solder shook his head firmly. "No, there's a pack of gorguls, if you can actually believe it." The man's voice was raised in his excitement. He swallowed hurriedly before going on. "Didn't think they even existed any more but they've been seen skulking about in the woods for the past couple of days. Terrified reports have been filtering in from everywhere."

"We know," Kilgar informed him with a smirk. "We've been running into them all over the forest."

The soldier's eyes went wide in astonishment. "Glad to see you're no worse for wear," he told them in his high-pitched tones. "Wonder what's brought them out of their foul land after so many yehrin. And in such large numbers." He turned his head sharply and spit into the dust.

"Search me," Shan commented innocently. The man looked past the dark-haired youth in front and focused his eyes on the Elfling. Shan resisted the urge to pull back and hide behind Kilgar. He met the man's piercing stare, noted the momentary look of curiosity flicker across his reddened face, and then the soldier took in the rest of them with a sweeping glance.

"We've been rousting out the militia from all over the forest towns," the man went on in his reedy voice. His animal continued to dance under him. "Well, best get indoors, boys. I recommend you get back to Hurlik as soon as possible."

"Oh, we're not . . ." Rimmy started to say. A stern look from his older brother caused the boy's mouth to snap shut in a hurry. The soldier noticed the exchange and turned back to Kilgar. Adrulax shifted lightly beneath him. The younger boy dropped his head diffidently.

"We're not afraid," the older boy finished Rimmy's comment. The man's eyes drifted from one brother to the other. He blinked thoughtfully before backing his impatient thorka a few steps away.

"Well, that may be the case, son," he said evenly, "but those things can be extremely dangerous. It'll be much safer for all of you indoors."

"Yes, sir," Kilgar tried to sound contrite. "Right away." The soldier lifted a knuckle to the bill of his helmet before giving them all a nod and whirling his mount to spur off after the others. The squad of soldiers was just a distant smudge by now. The boys watched the rider for a few moments as he galloped hard in pursuit.

"We'd best get moving," Shan spoke into Kilgar's ear.

"Right," the dark-headed youth agreed. "We should try to get across the bridge before the sun sets." They spun their thorka in an easy circle and broke into a canter for the narrow wooden structure.

They rode fairly hard for about half an ahr, the rough ground slipping away rapidly behind them. They crossed over the western arm of the Ring Road without slowing and continued to angle closer to the small road leading to the bridge. About halfway between the ring and the wandering gleam of the Tarloona, they finally caught up to it. The wary travelers hurried along the narrow track of hardened earth. Doornig wanted to call for a rest, but Kilgar waved him off and kept on riding.

The dark-headed youth finally pulled up about three-quarters of an ahr later, easing his large stallion onto the planks of the bridge. The blazing ball of the sun was just beginning to set as Kilgar reined in and dismounted. Shan slid down to join him on the little wooden span. He looked back to see Doornig and Gorian just cresting a small rise about three hundred kora behind them. Rimmy could partially be seen bobbing along upon Hoofnail's long back.

Shan made as if to sit down on the wooden railing, then quickly changed his mind. Kilgar gave him a knowing smile. "Been sitting too long as it is," the elven youth had to admit. He flexed his back a couple of times to loosen the overall stiffness, then began rubbing firmly at the tightening muscles for a time. The three other boys clomped their way onto the bridge at last and dismounted alongside them. They groaned softly in unison as they paced around on the wooden slats for several mira to loosen their own stiff legs.

"What now?" Rimmy asked, finally leaning back against the railing and pulling one knee up to his chest to stretch it out. He looked enquiringly over at his brother who was slowly rotating his neck around because of the tightness. Rimmy pulled up his other leg, flexing it at the knee before turning completely around to face Kilgar.

"Well," the older boy told them, "it's like I said before. We find a place, a good place, in the hills across the river and camp for the night."

"Sounds fair enough," Rimmy said in return.

"Let's just hope those militiamen can take care of all those pesky gorguls for us," Doornig offered almost prayerfully, "so they won't come 'round to bother us tonight."

"That would be nice," Gorian added with a firm nod of his head. "I could use a good night's sleep."

"We all could!" Doornig grumbled.

"Nevertheless," the Elfling interjected, "we'll still need to keep a watch." The others regarded him grimly at the thought. "Just in case."

"I think that goes without saying," admitted Kilgar. "That should be our standard practice from here on out."

"Agreed," stated Gorian with a smug look.

"We'd better get to it then," Kilgar called them back to their animals. "Mount up, so we can find a good place before it gets too dark."

Together they groaned a little from their stiffness as they pulled themselves back up into their saddles. The clatter of the animals' hooves echoed lightly off of the bridge railing as they rode easily along. Shan peered over his shoulder once, and was startled to see a billow of smoke, dark and thick, rising up in the distance somewhere near the forest's edge. *Hurlik?* he wondered. *A skirmish of some kind?* He swung back around to stare past Kilgar's snapping hair. A dying gleam of sunlight glistened from the rippling surface of the river like small diamonds.

The heavy clomping over the wooden planks changed suddenly to a dull thudding of packed earth as the thorka's hooves hammered steadily onward. The land rose perceptibly before them and the road soon began to wind through clusters of low hills situated to either side of them. The light was fading fast and they were soon hard pressed to find anything suitable to fit their needs.

The silvery blue sphere of Sheera rose slowly at their backs. It glimmered softly down at them, and limned the surrounding hills in a delicate azure haze. The recently waning moon offered only a feeble glow, just enough for them to stumble their way in the gathering gloom.

They rode on for some time, searching anxiously for anything promising. It was Shan's keen eyes that spotted the little trail off to one side. He pointed it out and Kilgar eagerly swung Adrulax around in that direction. The rugged path wound for a little while through a series of

Daryl Hanson

small rises and depressions, and slowly worked its way up into the larger hills.

They came at last to a great mound of boulders piled atop a fairly tall hill. They had curved their way past the tumbled heap of stones when they came suddenly upon a cave. The entrance was reasonably sized, but because of a bend in the trail, it could only be seen from the opposite direction. Shan had been looking back along the winding trail they'd been following when he discovered it entirely by chance.

"Ho," he called out to the others. "A cave!"

They drew in and circled back to the jagged opening. Approaching it cautiously, they hoped it was not somehow occupied by any predators. Their mounts showed no immediate signs of agitation, and that was encouraging. They huddled momentarily just outside, listening. No signs of movement could be detected from within, nor could they make out the heavy sounds of breathing that might be associated with a cave bear or great cat.

Kilgar slid down off the saddle and withdrew a hunting knife from his belt. He paused by the darkened opening for a moment, gripping the hilt a little more firmly. He took a deep breath.

"Be careful," Shan called out softly.

The others watched breathlessly as he plunged into the murky interior. It seemed an eternity before he popped back out into the pale blue moonlight. Kilgar raised a thumb to them and flashed a little smile as he sheathed his knife.

"All clear," he proclaimed. "It's clean and dry." He smirked. "Well, clean enough for our needs." He sidled up to Adrulax and began pulling out some of his gear. "I think it's even big enough to bring the animals inside, as well."

"Good," Gorian stated. "But we'll probably need to light a torch to keep from banging our heads on the rocks in there."

Doornig climbed down off of his thorka, his face beaming slightly in Sheera's faint light. "Do you think we can have a fire tonight then?" he asked, a hopeful gleam in his eye.

"Sure," Kilgar responded, "I don't see why not."

"Yes!" Doornig ejaculated. He whirled one arm around in a windmill fashion, ecstatic.

"As long as it's well shielded from prying eyes," the dark-haired youth continued. The redhead nodded as if that should have been obvious.

"We couldn't see this place from the road, after all," added Shan. "If we're quiet enough and stay inside all night we should be reasonably safe."

They busied themselves setting up camp. Gorian took out a small bundle of kindling from his saddle bag, a piece of flint he carried in his pocket and his knife. He stumbled into the cave to try his luck at starting a fire. Doornig rummaged in his saddle bag to produce a medium-sized saucepan. Shan reached up and pulled an extra waterbag from Adrulax's saddle horn. He carried it with him into the cave to see if he could assist Gorian.

Meanwhile, Kilgar began to loosen his thorka's saddle. He eventually pulled it down and laid it across a rock. Rimmy started gathering a few sticks and twigs. He kicked at some dry leaves and whatever else he could find to aid with the fire.

"Nothing green," Kilgar told him. "We don't want to give off any unnecessary smoke."

"I know," his younger brother said a little defensively, "it's not my first fire." The boy trudged in and out through the rocks, stooping now and then to pick up something from the ground. The load in his arms gradually grew a little bulkier.

It wasn't long before a soft glow could be seen spilling out through the cave mouth. It lured the rest of them inside. After leading the animals single file into their shelter, they turned to inspect their surroundings.

Gorian knelt in the middle of the relatively even cave floor, a small fire crackling and popping just in front of him. He fed it constantly with small bits of wood from the pile Rimmy had provided. The chamber wasn't overly large, but it had enough room against one rocky wall to line up their animals comfortably. The jagged ceiling was tall enough in most places to stand up, but it sloped away sharply to the back of the cave some twenty kora from the opening. Other than a slight stale taste to the air it wasn't particularly musty inside.

Kilgar lowered his pack to the dust and pulled out a tightly wrapped package of butcher's paper. He tossed it to Doornig who held it up and sniffed at it.

"What's this?" the red-haired boy asked.

"Just a little sausage," Kilgar exclaimed. Doornig's eyes glinted in the firelight as he continued to drink in the scent of the meat.

"Excellent!" he crooned.

"And here's some flatbread to go with it," Shan offered, producing a bag from his own pack.

Daryl Hanson

They located a couple of rocks near the back of the cave. These they tugged forward and placed down around the fire in a rough circle. They laid their food items out across a few of them. Once the flames were crackling well enough on their own, they settled the saucepan down over the rocks. Doornig peeled open the butcher's paper, lovingly placing the sausage links down onto the rapidly warming pan. The meat began to sizzle and pop almost immediately. Gorian diligently used a knife to roll them from side to side to prevent them from being scorched. Doornig smacked his lips in anticipation.

While the two of them worked on the meal, Shan helped Kilgar carry in the rest of their stuff, the saddles, their backpacks and anything else they might have dropped outside. As they were finishing up with their task, Rimmy came strolling in with another armload of wood for the fire. These were mostly thin, twisted pieces of dried brush, but no real branches or logs. This particular section of the hills seemed to be devoid of any real trees. Rimmy stacked them neatly on the barren floor by the dwindling mound he had produced earlier, before throwing himself down next to Gorian. Shan and Kilgar joined them presently and they all leaned in eagerly to share in the meal. As each piece of meat was finished cooking Gorian speared it with his little knife. He passed it on to Doornig, who nestled it in a piece of flatbread, then handed it off in turn to the others. They were soon all smacking their lips in delight as they chewed noisily on the sausages, pausing once in a while to lick the grease from their fingers.

After they had finished eating, they shared the brief chores of cleaning up before pulling out their blankets and snuggling down around the little fire. They were extremely tired from their maddened dash through the woods, but sleep eluded them for some time. Kilgar had elected himself first watch, hunkering down on the cave floor just inside the opening. He stared out into the night for long mira, his eyes searching for any signs of movement. After a while he glanced back to where the others had settled down and noticed Rimmy's sparkling eyes still fastened on him.

"Thanks," his little brother spoke after their eyes had locked for a long time. "Thanks for not sending me home."

"I won't really say, 'You're welcome,' because I still can't help feeling responsible. You know that." Kilgar slouched his shoulders forward. "But there just might come a time when I regret my decision."

"I'll try not to let you down," the younger boy said softly.

"It's not really a matter of that," Kilgar informed him. "This is a very dangerous business, and I just don't want you to get hurt. That's all."

"I know," Rimmy replied.

Shan lay on his back with his eyes closed, but he couldn't help listening to the two boys as they talked. He wanted to castigate himself for involving so many others in his plight, tried to regret dragging everyone along with him on this fool's errand, but somehow he could not quite come around to that. He was still scared out of his wits about this whole adventure, and he was glad— *very, very glad* —he was not all alone. The Elfling just couldn't imagine what it would be like to run for his life totally on his own.

Shan settled down into his blanket, wondering with a kind of sickness in his heart if Weeson, Bindar and Irion were somehow still alive. *Are they hurt,* he asked himself, *or possibly lying torn and bleeding somewhere out there in the wild? Did they escape from the targs and manage to avoid all those marauding bands of gorguls scouring through every kor of the forest?*

Sleep did finally come upon the Elfling, but it seemed like he had just closed his eyes when something woke him with a start. His eyes fluttered open. He looked around the cave, uncertain just what it was that had awakened him. The fire had burned low but was not completely out yet. Doornig had switched places with Kilgar at the cave mouth while he slept. The Elfling could see him leaning on his side against a rocky wall, facing out into the night. His stiff back was turned to the elven youth. Shan quickly scanned the semi-darkness, heard the thorka stamping lightly near the side wall.

He was about to close his eyes once more, when he thought he heard something else, far-off. He listened intently for a moment, trying desperately to place the sound. There was nothing for the longest time, and then he heard it again. It was the unmistakable sound of a horn, and it was moving closer.

Shan scrambled up from the cave floor, tossing the blanket aside in an instant. He shuffled over to Doornig in a crouch, calling out to him as he approached. "Did you hear that?" he asked as he laid a hand lightly on the boy's shoulder. There was no answering movement from the redhead. It was then he heard the soft exhale of breath accompanied by a quiet snore.

"Doornig," the Elfling hissed out in a tight-lipped call. He gave the boy's shoulder a firm shake. "Doornig, wake up!"

The boy snorted forcefully as he bounded upright. "Wha?" he

mumbled with a wild shake of his head. He rose quickly from the wall and stumbled over his own feet. Shan steadied him with a tight grasp on the arm. "What is it?" The red-haired boy rubbed the heel of one hand over his eyes.

"I heard something," the Elfling remarked in a measured tone. He indicated the darkness outside the cave with an uplifted palm. They both peered out into the night and, as if in answer, they heard another blast of a horn, closer this time, more urgent. There was a quick series of sharp, staccato bursts which continued to draw rapidly nearer.

By now the other boys had heard the disturbance and had crawled out of their blankets. They tumbled together by the cave mouth, listening. The shrill blast of the horn arrowed through the stillness outside, seemingly on top of them. Their three thorka stamped nervously along the side wall.

"Soldiers!" Kilgar announced. They huddled by the opening, their breathing shallow, and peered keenly into the darkness. Their heads slightly cocked to the side, they waited anxiously, straining to pick up the slightest sound.

The unmistakable clang of weapons suddenly broke out through the cool night air. They could hear the heavy crash and slither of metal on metal somewhere extremely close to their hiding place. The clamor of blades echoed on the breeze with a sharp chorus of steel.

Rimmy dashed from the cave in a mad rush. "Rimmy, wait!" was all Kilgar could manage to call out before his brother had disappeared abruptly around a bend in the trail. "Wait here," he commanded the others, shoving his way out of their clinging grip. The rest of them hesitated at the threshold, staring at his back as he melted away into the darkness. The urgent sounds of fighting, pierced now and then by wild cries of anger and pain, caromed crazily over the rocks.

Doornig mumbled something under his breath and rocked impatiently from one foot to another. Gorian looked over at his friend, caught a glimpse at his anguished expression. The redhead felt the gaze and regarded the other boy. "Sorry," he said. Without warning, Doornig bolted off into the darkness, his rapid footsteps churning up bits of earth. Gorian couldn't wait any longer either and tore out after his friend, leaving Shan standing all alone by the stone entrance.

The Elfling paced about in the dust for several long moments. He was torn with concern for his friends and his fear of what lay just over the curve of the trail. He kicked softly at the dirt, looking up from time to time, as he watched for any changes. The deafening ring of swords and other bladed weapons shrieked off the rocks, broken only occasionally by a series of savage grunts and blood-curdling screams.

The thorka reared and stamped in nervousness on the rocky cave floor. Their hooves struck little sparks from the smooth stones. The Elfling rushed over to them to check on their bridle straps, making sure they wouldn't pull themselves loose and charge off down the trail. Satisfied that their reins were still securely fastened to a couple of large rocks, Shan moved calmly among them. He gave them all an affectionate slap on their long cheeks, clucking his tongue to soothe away their agitation. Turning from the animals with a final scratch at their ears, Shan returned to the mouth of the cave.

The fierce echoes of fighting had dwindled noticeably. Overcome at last by his own curiosity, the elven youth edged slowly out of the jagged cave opening, moving silently forward on the tips of his toes. He rounded the corner of the path cautiously and found the four other boys sprawled over some high rocks on the right edge of the twisting trail. He clambered noiselessly up to join them, easing himself down next to Kilgar. Peering over the rubble, he fastened his eyes on the carnage below.

The din of fighting by now had completely ceased. A handful of soldiers, dressed in their forest militia garb, stalked through a mound of tangled bodies. Their unattended thorka shied away from the overwhelming scent of blood. Half a dozen men held their dripping weapons out, turning a bloody form over from time to time. They leaned in close in the dim light, the few remaining torches they had carried into the battle were cast upon the slimy ground. The sputtering flames did little to chase the veil of gloom from the scene.

Occasionally a hideous face would moan and look up into the soldiers' grim eyes as they were sluggishly turned over. The militiamen would immediately run the brute through with their gleaming blades. With a dying gasp the last of the fallen gorguls collapsed amid the horrific pile, the slitted pupils of its eyes open wide and staring.

"I think that's it, Lieutenant," one of the men called out hoarsely. He wiped at a trail of dark blood across his face. "I'm pretty sure we got all of them." He leaned back on his sword with a tired stretch of his back, surveying their grisly handiwork. Nothing moved in the bloody mound.

"Good," another fellow hollered back. "I'd hate to have even one of these devils get away." The officer turned to reach for the reins of his mount. He latched onto the leather straps, pulling the animal reluctantly closer. He swung tiredly up into the saddle. "How many of them did you count, Peevy?" The thorka pranced uncomfortably near the large mound of corpses.

The younger soldier pointed a finger at each of the mangled bodies he could see, counting. "Nine, I think." he told the officer. "No, maybe ten." He wasn't sure in the darkness and shrugged.

"Well, make sure," the Lieutenant barked. "And drag our own men out of that filthy heap. They deserve better than this. I'll wait for you on the road."

"Yes, sir," Peevy cried with a snappy salute. Another soldier bent and retrieved one of the cast-off torches, handing it up to the officer after the Lieutenant had pointed and snapped his fingers at the man. The weary officer turned his mount and picked his way out along the trail on his way back to the road. "What do we do with all these foul creatures?" he called after the retreating figure. "Leave them where they lie?"

"Burn them," came the unmistakable command before the officer rode out of sight.

"Burn them?" spoke up the soldier who had given the torch away. "With what? We don't have any wood." He looked uncertainly at Peevy.

"Once we get our men separated out," the other man told him, "douse them with a little lamp oil and set the pile on fire."

"Alright, Sergeant," the younger man acknowledged. "Will do."

The five companions watched them for a while from the seclusion of the rocks above. The few remaining soldiers dragged the tangle of corpses into two distinct piles. The other boys seemed captivated by the process, but Shan quickly lost interest and slid back down the rocky moraine. A light spray of sand and pebbles coursed down with him as he lowered himself back to the trail. Kiara had finally risen over the rim of stones, casting its fading reddish-gold glow to light his way. It wasn't too long before he had re-entered the yawning mouth of the cave.

The fire had burned itself out, leaving only a faint dying glow of red from the embers. A thin trace of smoke spiraled softly up to the cave ceiling. The thorka still remained agitated for some reason. Shan could hear them neighing and stamping to one side. He called to them assuredly before shuffling over to their little fire pit. He threw himself down on his blanket and began to poke idly at the coals with a stick in an attempt to revive them. He leaned in and blew gently on the embers. He was rewarded with a dull gleam. He reached to the side for the last of the wood they had collected earlier and discovered it was wet. He held up his hand and could definitely detect a dark stain on his fingers in the poor light. He sniffed at it tentatively. It had the unmistakable tang of blood.

"Where could that have come from?" he questioned out loud.

Suddenly a hand reached up out of the darkness and latched onto his arm. The Elfling nearly jumped up and away, but the strong grip held him down. It was a clawed hand, he realized with a start. He fought to pull himself away but the sharp nails bit down even harder into his flesh. He felt a burning on his arm as a runnel of his own blood dribbled down his skin.

A foul breath struck him in the face as he twisted around to see his assailant. Shan spun onto his back and thrashed out with his boot. The clawed hand came loose from his arm, but clamped powerfully onto one of his legs. "*Elfling!*" the thing hissed at him as he struggled to get away. He elbowed his way backwards on the cave floor, kicking out and shaking his lower limbs wildly to dislodge the dark, clinging form. He felt skin scraped from the back of his arms as he desperately tried to shimmy loose. But he could feel the clawed fingers pawing forcibly at him even through the thick cloth of his britches.

The gorgul crawled painfully along with him, one long useless arm trailing away behind. It left a heavy trail of blood in its wake. They squirmed up against the rough cave wall together, where Shan cold no longer retreat. The foul creature used its heavier, more powerful body to pin the Elfling down. It relinquished its steel-like grip on his leg, reaching painfully for a wicked knife in its belt. It gurgled loudly in pain and dark streams of blood spewed out through its large mouth.

Shan caught at the muscular arm as it came forward. The dark, curved blade wavered about in the air just in front of his wild eyes. He grunted with the incredible strain to keep the weapon from his heart. The gorgul hissed and cursed at him in its ugly language, its thick dark tongue flicking out in small fits, barely visible between the two great tusks thrusting up from its bottom lip. The jagged blade descended slowly toward Shan's chest. A strangled cry escaped from his throat as the tip of the knife pricked at his skin through his shirt.

The Elfling suddenly let out a piercing scream as he managed to drive the heavy arm up and away with all his strength. The scaly hand shook with a tremor of pain. Shan struggled to hold the blade away with his left hand and desperately snatched for his own small knife at his belt. He finally wrestled it free, fumbling with it for a moment, before he succeeded in driving it to the hilt in the gorgul's neck. The creature stiffened atop him, its dark blood spilling down over both of them. It hissed once with a last spasm, and was still.

Shan managed to roll the bulky figure away from him. He eyed it dubiously for several long moments where it lay slumped in the dust. The Elfling was breathing heavily from the near death encounter. He continued to grasp the knife firmly in his hand, the hilt slimy and sticky under his fingers. His own erratic heartbeat finally began to subside. He lay back against the rocky wall for a time, still breathing heavily. The thorka nickered softly from the far gloom.

"Thanks for the warning," he croaked sarcastically. He peered across the murky cave at them. The animals had settled down considerably, blowing air quietly out of their nostrils. He realized then with a wry smile to himself they had actually tried to alert him to the danger, but he had failed to interpret the cause of their nervousness. He must have thought, absently, that it was somehow due to the close sounds of battle and the overwhelming smell of fresh blood spilling out just down the trail from the cave.

The other boys found him where he lay sprawled against the rough stone wall. It was hard for them to see at first, their eyes adjusting slowly from the pale moonlight to the relative blackness of the cave interior. "Shan," Kilgar called out into the stillness. "You in here?" The thorka whinnied softly in response.

"Yes," the Elfling mustered a bit weakly.

The boys dragged their feet as they fumbled about in the darkness. It was Rimmy who nearly tumbled over the corpse. He kicked it with his toe unexpectedly and recoiled a step, crying out.

"Watch out for the dead gorgul," the elven youth offered dully.

"The what?" Doornig spit out, biting at his lip.

"The gorgul," Shan repeated, sounding almost distracted. "Rimmy nearly fell over it."

"Where is it?" Gorian wanted to know.

"Right there in front of you," came the Elfling's numb reply. "Oh, I forgot, you boys can't see very well in the dark." The harsh sound of their breathing filled the little cave.

"Doornig, see if you can get that fire going again," Kilgar told him. The redhead shuffled carefully to the side to avoid the stiffening body and then felt awkwardly about for the fire pit. A faint sense of heat led him eventually to the right place. He slumped down in the dust before it and began to work on coaxing a flame from what was left of the embers.

"Are you alright, Shan?" Kilgar inquired of him. "You sound a little—*odd*." The dark-haired boy moved slowly through the darkness, a hand held out cautiously in front of his chest. He stumbled around the body and knelt down next to Shan.

"I'm fine," the elven youth responded quietly. "It must have crawled in here from the battle." His voice seemed somewhat detached. "It tried to kill me in the dark," he explained, swallowing convulsively. He still held the wet handle of the knife tightly in one hand. "Only I managed to kill it first."

18

Darkwood
[21st of Kaligath, 4534 C.R.]

"So, what's wrong with him?" Gorian asked, looking down at the Elfling seated disconsolately on the cave floor. He stood with Kilgar off to the side, watching with interest as Rimmy knelt in front of Shan, trying his best to coax him to take a little water from a leather bota he held out for him.

Doornig had managed to get their little fire going once again. It had taken a little love and a lot of patience. Huddled on the dust-strewn floor, the boy had blown gently on the coals, introducing small bits of dried moss and other tinder from time to time to bring it to life. Delicate wisps of smoke had curled up lazily to the ceiling, before he had finally been rewarded by the appearance of tiny flames. He continued to feed the growing flames with a little more kindling, and the chamber was soon bathed in a soft, yellowish glow.

Kilgar turned to the side, pulling Gorian along with him. "I think he's in shock," the dark-haired youth confided in him. He glanced thoughtfully back at the pair on the floor. "After all, he just had to kill someone, alone and in the dark. Perhaps for the first time in his life."

Gorian nodded his understanding. "I see what you mean."

"Never mind that it was an evil creature," Kilgar went on, "and that it was trying to kill him in the process." They both looked down at the elven youth. Rimmy had managed to get Shan to sip a little water. He looked up at them with a little smile. "First, let's get him out of that bloody shirt. Then we'll just try to keep him warm throughout the night," Kilgar advised. "We'll see how he's doing in the morning."

"Right," the sandy-haired boy said with a nod.

They covered the Elfling with a couple of their blankets, draping his own cloak over top of them. They left him propped against the rough rock wall and then settled themselves down around the small fire. Rimmy was elected to take the next watch. He wrapped himself in his own cloak while the others eventually drifted back off to sleep.

The remainder of the night passed uneventfully. Rimmy exchanged watches at one point with Gorian, who was later replaced by Kilgar. The boys awoke just after dawn to a pale mist creeping in through the small opening in the rocks. Shan seemed much more himself, joining in with the others to share a meager breakfast of toasted grain and dried fruit. They measured out some dried oats for the thorka, before packing up their gear and re-saddling the anxious mounts.

They led the animals out through the narrow cave mouth into an early morning fog. Mounting up in the light mist, they walked the thorka slowly along the winding trail through the canyon of large boulders. They came unexpectedly upon a large burn pile where the soldiers had dragged the bodies of their vanquished foes into a mound and set them aflame. A thick swarm of jackards had been picking through the charred remains, but scattered wildly in all directions with a flurry of their dark wings as the riders rounded the corner. The ugly carrion birds wheeled restlessly overhead as the five boys moved slowly past the smoking pile. There were no signs of militia men to be found. The soldiers had apparently collected their own dead, thrown them over the back of riderless mounts, and carted them off towards home.

A few discarded weapons littered the bloody ground just to one side, where the earth had been severely trampled by metal boots and a thrashing of thorka hooves. Rimmy quickly jumped down and retrieved one of the fallen swords. He wiped reddish mud from the blade and brandished it about.

"Good idea!" Doornig burst out, leaping down to join the younger boy on the small battleground. He kicked about in the crimson slime before discovering a blade of his own, half-submerged in the muck. It was a short sword, and the wrapped, wooden handle fit his hand nicely.

Kilgar joined them on the sodden ground. He flung a broken-off dagger aside with the toe of his boot, only to reveal a double-bladed axe sunk into the sludge. It was badly notched on one of the broad blades, but was otherwise still in good condition. He hefted it experimentally before deciding to keep it.

Gorian selected one of the wicked-looking scimitars. He brandished the heavy thing about a little awkwardly at first, but once he got the feel for it, he didn't care for anything else. Shan stared down into the gore-strewn field without moving from Adrulax' long back. Kilgar took notice of his unease and quietly collected a militia sword for him. *Maybe he'll come around eventually,* he thought. Of course, there were no sword belts to be had. Those had pretty much remained on the bodies of the fallen, having been carried home by the survivors or left to curl in the flames of the pyre. They thrust their newly acquired weapons awkwardly into their belts.

Most of the lances had been snapped off in the battle, but they did manage to find two relatively unscathed, and these they gladly carried off with them. Kilgar retained one of the lances for himself, and passed the other one to Rimmy who had been riding behind Gorian. Once they had finished their grim task they mounted up and slowly walked their way through the mud back to the road. The jackards descended anxiously in a dark cloud behind them and quickly commenced to feast on whatever grisly remnants they could find.

Once they got to the earthen track they immediately turned to the right and spurred their thorka into a light trot. There was no one else yet in sight on the road at that early ahr. They jogged along at an easy clip, but they hadn't gone very far before Rimmy issued a short outcry. They reined in the animals with a flurry of dust. The boy pointed off excitedly into another series of hills just off the road.

"I saw a thorka," Rimmy exclaimed. He started to point again. "Down there."

"Wild thorka are often known to run around through these hills," his brother told him offhandedly.

"No," Rimmy retorted. "This one had a saddle. I'm sure of it."

Kilgar gave his brother a look. "You think it might have run off during the battle last night?" he asked. The younger boy nodded vigorously.

"So what?" Doornig interjected. "We've got our own animals already."

"But if we can catch that stray," Rimmy chided him, "one more of us won't have to ride behind somebody else all the time."

"Oh," the redhead replied a little snobbishly, "that makes sense, I guess."

Kilgar wheeled Adrulax and headed off in the direction Rimmy had first indicated. Shan encircled the boy's waist with his arms in a light grip. "Let's see if we can round him up without taking too much time," Kilgar admonished. "Lead on, Rimmy."

Gorian spun to join their dark-haired leader. Rimmy shot an arm over the boy's shoulder, pointing with a rigid forefinger which way to go. Doornig was the last to turn off the roadway. Reluctantly he brought Ruggles into a brisk walk.

They found the lone thorka easily enough. It had wandered into a box canyon and was nipping eagerly at scrub grass as it slowly edged its way along. The reins trailed off its bridle and into the dust. Rimmy slipped quietly from Hoofnail's back. Slowly, he approached the animal in a non-threatening posture, easing up to it with a quiet clucking of his tongue. He held his hand out, a small scoop of oats visible on his open palm. The thorka's ears pricked up in interest and it raised its long face to stare at the boy.

"Here, boy," Rimmy called soothingly. "Easy. Nobody's gonna hurt you." He edged slowly closer, trying not to spook the animal with any sudden movements. "Here, boy. I've got something for you. Easy now. That's it. That's it."

Rimmy reached up his free hand and lightly stroked at the thorka's long, flat nose. The animal nickered softly and sniffed at the small lump of oats in the boy's open palm. It lowered its head and eagerly began to munch on the offering. Rimmy slowly reached up his other hand and tenderly patted the animal's great face in a long circular motion. He slid his hand back a bit in easy gliding strokes, latching gently onto the reins as he did. When the animal had finished eating, the boy swung himself up into the high saddle. The thorka flicked its ears forward but otherwise stood calmly as Rimmy settled his feet into the stirrups. With a little tap from his heels he trotted the animal over to where the others sat waiting for him.

"Well done," Kilgar told him. He grinned down at his little brother.

Rimmy shrugged off the compliment a little bashfully. "I guess I learned a few things from my brother," he said.

They turned the four animals together, heading back to the main road. It wasn't long before they found themselves cantering down the earthen track once again. Within an ahr or two the veil of fog had completely burned off, but the sky overhead remained somewhat hazy and overcast. They flashed past several clusters of low hills as the lane slowly weaved in and out between them. At times they climbed up over some gentle rises and then dropped down through shallow depressions, always skirting the majority of the hills in their wandering course.

They encountered only a small number of travelers throughout the morning. Most of that early traffic was of a commercial nature. A handful of wagons trundled by them on their way north-eastward, most likely en route to any of the numerous villages in Draydin Forest. But they never bothered to stop to engage anyone in conversation, and offered only a few friendly waves as they whisked along.

There was one small family they came upon unexpectedly near mid-day, struggling off the edge of the road with a thrown wheel. Shan sat alone upon Adrulax while the other boys dismounted to help the father re-attach the large wheel to their pushcart. While they worked the man recounted for them how they were fleeing from some form of unrest in the south. Several days back the man had piled his small family and their meager belongings onto the wagon in hopes of finding a new life somewhere else.

Shan watched them work for a time before staring off impatiently down the road. He carefully scanned the horizon in both directions, forever fearful of pursuit. Anxiety to be on their way gnawed continually at his heart. The husband looked up at the Elfling at one point, wondering why he wasn't helping in the repairs.

Kilgar noticed the glance and tried to diffuse any curiosity. "Sorry about our friend," he told the man. "He had an accident a while back and he just hasn't been the same since." The man gave a knowing bob of his head and turned back to their task without another look in Shan's direction.

The family thanked them once they had finished their labors. Wiping sweat from their faces, the four boys remounted and they were off with a final wave. The little pushcart lurched forward at last and slowly made its way north-eastward.

"Accident?" Gorian leaned over and teased Kilgar. "Hasn't been the same since?" He snickered in the saddle.

"It worked, didn't it?" Kilgar sounded a little irritated. The sandy-haired youth continued to chuckle. "It managed to deflect his curiosity." Their leader sniffed. "Besides, it really is the truth. I just let him think it happened a long while ago, and not just last night."

They rode on in silence for a couple more ahrin, the hard-packed road continued to angle mostly to the southwest. They found themselves heading for an open swath of land running between an approaching fringe of forest to their left and the broad sweep of the mighty Tanalorn River on their right. The dense line of trees was little more than just a dark smudge in the distance at that point, but as they kept on riding it loomed ever closer. Kilgar calculated that if they veered left completely, took the route upon the opposite side of the forest, they would be forced to travel several leagues out of their way before they could ever reach the ferry. He never bothered to estimate how much lost time that course would actually mean for them.

They stopped for a short rest once the sun had climbed high in the sky. There was a little hamlet nestled just off the road. They never heard the name. There, they managed to purchase a few fresh food items from an open air market for a couple of copper bits. Gorian counted out the small coins from a leather purse slung on his belt and placed them, one at a time, into the open palm of a middle-aged woman. She accepted them with a smile before turning away to help another customer.

The five members of their little company gathered on the lush grass at the outskirts of town. They quietly nibbled on pieces of fresh fruit they had just purchased and a chunk of spiced *osk* meat. They eagerly tore off slivers of the juicy meat in turn, passing the dwindling hunk around between them until it was all gone. They licked their fingers to savor the tang of the spicy seasoning.

"That was good," Doornig purred as he sat back on the grass, his arms thrown back to brace himself.

Shan looked up at the animals. The four thorka grazed contentedly nearby, cropping softly on the tall grass. His blue eyes settled thoughtfully on their newly acquired beast. "What are you going to name him?" he asked of Rimmy. The two of them turned to inspect the latest addition to their party.

"I don't know," the boy had to admit. "I guess I hadn't really thought about it yet." He shrugged. The dark brown animal went on munching with its fellows, unaware of their attention.

The Elfling watched the large beast for a moment, then swung to look at Rimmy. "You could call him Thimba," he said.

"Thimba?" the younger boy asked, testing the name. He crinkled up his nose slightly. "Where'd you come up with that?"

"I'm not sure," Shan had to admit. "I seem to remember reading about some heroic figure long ago with that name. It seems sort of noble to me."

"Hmm," Rimmy muttered, "Thimba." He watched the animal nipping on the grass. "I like it," he said at last. "Thimba it is." The two of them shared a smile.

Kilgar had watched the exchange with interest. He was glad to see the Elfling coming out of his malaise. He admitted to himself that he'd been a little concerned about the elven boy for a while. They really needed his sharp mind to help them along their journey, not to mention his keen sense of hearing and incredible eye sight. There would be many more dangers for them to face yet, he felt sure, and they were certainly going to need Shan at his full capacity.

Before long they were up and riding once again. The countryside fairly flew by beneath the long, smooth strides of the great thorka. They passed a few small farms cradled between the low hills. Their owners labored behind a tandem of osk. The powerful beasts shambled over the rugged soil, pulling slowly upon their rickety plows. The monotony of their trek was broken only by the occasional whine from the redhead.

"This is takin' forever," he moaned at one point. "My backside is gettin' a little sore."

Kilgar looked back at him from his lead spot. "Just think what it would have been like if we'd have had to walk all this way."

"I am," Doornig whimpered. "Believe me, I am." Kilgar shook his head and fixed his eyes back on the road. "If we were walking right now," the fiery youth went on, "you could just kill me, and have done with it."

"Hey," Gorian chided him curtly, "that's no way to be talking." The sandy-haired boy wagged a finger at his friend. *"Especially now,"* he mouthed, rolling his eyes forward in the Elfling's direction

"Oh," Doornig managed to blurt out a little awkwardly. "Oh, ah, you're right. Didn't know . . . ah . . . what I was saying." He stared across at Gorian for a moment, a grimace creasing his face. The redhead watched Shan's back for any reactions but the elven youth never bothered to look back at him. They continued to lope along in silence.

By late afternoon the dark smudge could clearly be seen ahead of them, and growing steadily closer. At first, the sweeping fringe of the trees appeared like it was directly in front of them, but the road they followed kept veering to the right, until it was obvious they would completely bypass the gloomy forest altogether.

"What is that over there?" Rimmy wanted to know, rising up a little in his stirrups to get a better view.

"Darkwood," his brother informed him without bothering to look back. When the notorious name failed to evoke a response from his younger sibling, Kilgar took a peek over his shoulder. "It's a very old forest," he went on. "Thought to be ancient, in fact. Possibly the oldest spot on Anarra, some would say. Still others might claim it's the very place where life began."

"Oh," Rimmy said with a tinge of excitement in his voice. "The Garden of Adonath? Really?" He tried scrunching his eyes up to pierce through the overwhelming distance.

"There's no such place as Adonath!" Doornig declared flatly. "That's just a fable, some old wives' tales." He snapped his head to the side and spit contemptuously into the rushing weeds.

"Regardless of what you think," their dark-haired leader stated, "Darkwood is a real place and we're soon going to pass by it on its western flank."

"It must be beautiful in there," Rimmy wanted to believe. "A paradise." He craned forward in his saddle.

"Hardly," the sandy-headed boy said with a laugh. The younger boy peeled his eyes from the thick line of dark green as it loomed ever closer, and swung back to Gorian. Confusion spread across Rimmy's wrinkled brow. "It's no paradise anymore," the boy told him, bounding along next to him on Hoofnail. "They say it's been cursed."

"Haunted, more like," Doornig added with a sneer. The rhythm of the thorka hooves drummed in their ears as they loped along.

"Haunted?" Rimmy was incredulous. "How did that happen?"

"By the hand of Athiliel," Shan spoke out in a hushed voice. The others all managed to tilt their faces his way. "Oh, you probably think of Him as Athalias, don't you? Well, the first two people He created Athiliel placed here in the Garden. Somehow they rebelled at His authority long ago. They disobeyed Him and, as a result, they incurred His wrath and He cast them out, forbidding them ever to return. It's believed the Garden itself was cursed at that time, and perhaps the rest of Anarra, as well."

Doornig laughed out loud. "You don't actually believe that fairy tale, do you?" He howled in mirth at the thought. *How could anyone fall for that silly story?* he asked himself. He shook his head in bewilderment.

Shan squared his eyes on the redhead. "Forgive me for saying this," the Elfling said with perfect seriousness, "but we have actually been chased through the woods, and now into these hills, over the last few days by creatures you categorically declared didn't even exist." They stared at each other for a few long moments. Sparks seemed to crackle between them. "Am I wrong?" Shan went on. Doornig reddened, swallowed slowly once or twice, and then he dropped his eyes completely. "So excuse me, if I don't automatically agree with your assessment." The Elfling turned away from him with a frown. The entire party strove not to make eye contact with one another, but instead, watched the countryside flash by them with feigned interest.

They rode on in silence for quite some time, the dark stretch of the forest gradually taking shape before their eyes. The thorka's hooves pounded on the hardened earth in a steady cadence. Rimmy bit at his lower lip, secretly stealing periodic glances at Doornig as they bounced along. The boy's face remained locked in a scowl and he refused to look anywhere but the gently undulating road before them. His blue eyes just seemed to bore ahead, his face flushed with the weight of his own dark thoughts.

They jogged along until the sun began to dip close to the horizon. Kilgar pulled them up near a small farmhouse just off the lane. He persuaded the owner to allow them to sleep in his barn for the night. The older man seemed reluctant at first, as his gray eyes surveyed their party in a slow sweep, but with the exchange of a few coins from Kilgar's purse, his gaze softened and he granted their request. They thanked him, gratefully pulling their mounts into the barn through a set of double doors. They threw themselves down amid a thick bed of straw, exhausted from their long day in the saddle.

Doornig was still not talking with the Elfling for the time being, refusing even to look in his direction. Shan, for his part, simply went about his business, helping the others to pull out some provisions from the saddle bags. Kilgar just shook his head sadly as he watched the two of them mutually ignore each other. Gorian had cleared a little space in the center of the barn floor, sweeping away the layers of straw with the thought of starting a fire.

"Be careful," Kilgar cautioned him. "We don't want to burn the man's barn down."

"I will," Gorian told him confidently. He had produced a pan and some cooking utensils when there came a soft knock at the little side door of the barn. They had pulled the large double doors closed against the rapid approach of night.

The light rap at the side door sounded again and they could hear an older woman's voice call out to them. "Boys," she could be heard to say, "boys, would you be interested in a little something for supper?"

Rimmy unlatched the door and opened it to reveal a kindly old woman just outside. She held a large lantern in one hand and a steaming pot in the other. The enticing aroma wafted in with the slight breeze and left their mouths watering. "Please, come in," the younger boy beckoned. "It's your barn, after all." He stepped back a pace, holding the door open for her. She padded lightly into the room, heading to a nearby workbench against the side wall. She set the pot on the pitted wood surface and placed the hefty lantern just off to the side. Steam continued to curl up out of the pan as she turned to the boys with a smile.

"Would you care for a little stew?" she asked them.

"Yes, ma'am," they chorused appreciatively, gathering in close. Kilgar located some small bowls in one of their packs and brought them over.

"Thank you," he said gratefully, handing the bowls to the kindly woman. She immediately began ladling out generous portions of savory stew into them from the large pot. Rimmy took each one in turn and passed it along.

"Thank you, ma'am," Shan said to her upon receiving his bowl. "You're very kind." She smiled at him. The old eyes lingered on him a while as he turned and found a place in the straw to eat.

She turned back to the others, wiping her hands on an apron. "You're all quite welcome, boys." She hovered near the workbench. "Please enjoy."

"Oh, we will, ma'am," Doornig crowed, a steamy spoonful poised at his lips. "We will."

"Well, eat up then," she told them with a smile. "There's plenty more where that came from. I'll just leave you the kettle." She indicated the pot left sitting on the worktable with a small wave of her hand.

"Thank you again, ma'am," Kilgar spoke out sincerely.

"I'll leave you in peace," the woman said. She turned away with a parting wave and disappeared out the side door. She pulled the panel lightly closed behind her. They could hear her soft steps retreating across the yard to the farm house. The lantern remained perched on the work table, casting its steady glow on them as they ate. Outside, the shadows deepened quickly, and the heavy drone of night insects closed around them.

The Elfling placed his empty bowl on the workbench. He gathered up the warm pot and quietly made the rounds. He spooned out a second helping to each of them, Doornig included, before retreating to the table to dish himself a little more. The redhead followed him warily with his eyes as the Elfling settled himself back on the floor once again. The boy from Draydin crossed his legs, the bowl raised up to his chin. Doornig dropped his gaze hastily to his own dish when Shan happened to look up.

They munched away contentedly for a spell. The only sounds were the clatter of their spoons against the inside of their bowls and the soft smacking of their lips as they chewed on the rich chunks of meat. But it wasn't long, however, before they had scraped their dishes clean and leaned back against the outer walls of the barn. Kilgar found a spot along the small retaining wall which separated the main room of the barn from the area used for animal pens towards the back. They could hear the unmistakable scuffling of a bull osk as it shifted its bulk around in the darkness behind them. It kicked at the dirt as it moved heavily about, followed by a soft bellow from its nostrils.

Rimmy went around to collect their bowls. He found a pail of water on the dusty floor near the side door. Using a rag from his knapsack, and a little water from the wooden pail, he began to clean the dishes. Shan joined him after a moment and between the two of them, they made short work of the task. Rimmy started drying the bowls with another cloth while the Elfling snatched up the bucket. He headed for the door, easily worked the latch and stepped out into the darkened yard. It took him a moment to find the well, then he sauntered easily in that direction.

Shan found a large bucket attached to the wooden framework rising up out of the circlet of stones. He swung the pail out over the dark shaft before lowering it hand over hand with the long rope. It splashed quietly into the water about five or six kora below ground. He let the large container sink gradually under the surface.

"You didn't have to feed them," he heard the old farmer call out angrily to his wife from within the house. "You know how growing boys eat. They're always hungry." Dimly, Shan could hear the man grumble as he paced about through one of the small rooms.

"They paid you," his wife returned lightly.

"For sleeping in the barn, they did," the man continued to complain. "Not for any food." He pulled out a chair with a scraping of its legs and settled himself wearily into it. "We cannot afford to be so generous every time a hungry face comes along," he mumbled. "We can barely feed ourselves as it is."

"Don't begrudge a little kindness, old man," the woman scolded her husband. "The money they paid you was more than enough to cover the cost of the food. Just consider sheltering those boys in the barn as a neighborly act on your part." He *humphed* loudly but said nothing else in return.

Shan pulled the large bucket back up the well shaft. He emptied its contents into the little pail from the barn. On a sudden impulse the Elfling checked to see if there were any other containers he might fill for the old couple. He found one sitting on the front porch, then topped it off from the pail in his hand. He also discovered an animal trough off to the side of the house. He poured four heaping bucketfuls into it before refilling the one from the barn once again. Finally, he returned with it to the barn to join the others where he found them lounging in the fluffy straw.

He pulled the little door closed and latched it from the inside. He set the pail back on the floor where Rimmy had found it. Someone had moved the good-sized lantern from the work bench and hung it on a hook over the little retaining wall. It bathed the room in a soft glow. Shan stepped lightly through the straw. He picked up his cloak, where it lay across one of the saddles, and swirled it around his shoulders.

"Going somewhere?" Kilgar asked him with a curious look.

"Thought I'd take the first watch tonight," the elven youth proclaimed. "I think I might have missed my round last night. I don't think I'll be able to sleep for a long time, anyway."

"Watch?" Gorian questioned him with a look over at Doornig. "Do you really think that's necessary?" He looked up from his seated position, a blanket thrown over his lap.

The Elfling regarded him seriously for a moment. "What do you think?" The sandy-headed youth could only blink a few times. "Do you really think we'll be safe in here, in this over-sized shed," and he looked around himself for emphasis, "if any of those gorguls should happen to track us down?"

"Shan's right," Kilgar interposed with a solemn nod. "We always need to stay on the alert. We should never assume we're safe, no matter where we are. At least not entirely."

"Yeah, yeah, I guess," Gorian agreed grudgingly. "But it would certainly be nice some time to get a good night sleep for a change."

"I'll agree with you there," the redheaded boy chimed in. "But I also think the others are right to set a guard. I, for one, don't mind doing what's needed, even if it is a little uncomfortable."

Kilgar turned away with a chuckle. "Right," he mumbled to himself. He eased himself down in the straw, pulling his own blanket up to his hips. "Wake me in a couple of ahrin," the dark-haired youth called. "I'll take the next watch." The Elfling acknowledged him with a firm nod. He parked himself on a stool by the work table, slid open a wooden window shutter in the near wall until it was about a hob wide. He peered silently out into the stillness. Rimmy turned down the lamp with a little wheel on the outer housing, reducing the interior of the barn to just short of pitch blackness. The young boy settled down into his blanket alongside the others.

The pale sickle of Sheera had risen in the east, Shan noted. The waning edge of the moon gave the world outside the partly open shutter a faint bluish-silver glow. The surrounding landscape had a sort of fuzzy softness to it, like that of a dream. After the others had fallen into a noiseless slumber, Shan rose up from the stool and drifted over to where he'd deposited his gear. He leaned over the little pile, drew his water bag up by the strap. Returning to the stool with it, he uncapped the bag and took a long draw. He wiped at his lips, resealing the plug. Rather than return it to his things he simply laid the leather bag on the bench top with a faint slosh of its contents. The Elfling turned to stare out into the night.

It was sometime later, just before he was due to awaken the next lookout, when he heard it. He couldn't quite place it at first. It was a kind of low jingling, like a rider's spurs or the rattling of a harness strap. The distant sound was fairly indistinct, faltering every so often, not the steady rhythm like the clomp of metal-shod feet. Shan listened intently, hoping that it was just some drover returning late with a portion of his herd. The more he listened the more he felt sure it was the rattling of a metal ring—*tap-tap-tapping*—on its leather harness.

"What is it?" Kilgar asked him in a sudden husky whisper. Shan nearly jumped when he realized the boy was standing next to him. He had ben concentrating so completely on the approaching sound that he failed to hear Kilgar slip from his blanket and slide stealthily up to him. The boys peered curiously out through the small opening.

"I'm not sure," the Elfling finally said, after swallowing with a dry throat. He gazed out into the darkness. "A jingling of some kind. Like the harness of an animal."

"Seems a little late to be herding animals around," Kilgar said in a soft undertone.

"I agree," Shan told him quietly. "I haven't been able to see anything yet."

They leaned toward the shutter opening, their ears straining to pick up the slightest sound. They couldn't make out anything for several moments, then they both heard the rattling of metal and a kind of scraping at the ground as something drew closer. Almost immediately the Elfling saw the huge shape of a giant lizard stalking into their narrow field of vision. Upon its back sat two unmistakable bulky figures.

"Gorguls!" Shan called breathlessly.

"Where?" Kilgar wanted to know. "I can't see anything."

"Coming up the lane toward the house," the elven youth declared through tight lips. "Two of them, and they're riding one of those dragon-like beasts."

"A giant *slor!*" the dark-haired boy exclaimed softly. "We'd better wake the others." Shan continued to monitor the gorguls' approach while Kilgar slipped over to their companions and began to shake them gently.

"Gorguls!" he informed them in a muted voice. "Get up. Get our things together. We may have to bolt out of here in a hurry."

"I'll saddle the thorka," Gorian murmured groggily. He shuffled lightly through the straw.

"I'll help you," Rimmy offered, breathless. Together they carefully began to ready their steeds. Doornig hurried to pack away their scattered gear.

The giant slor waddled noisily past the window shutter on a direct line to the farmhouse. Shan moved sharply to the left in order to get a better angle. His face was practically pressed against the wall, but he could see the great beast lumber to a halt by the front porch with a scuffling of its huge clawed feet. One of the soldiers swung down from the broad back, the one that had been perched to the rear of its companion, while the other rigidly held its seat upon the enormous beast.

The small farmhouse was dark as the gorgul approached. He stomped up onto the wooden porch. He hammered loudly on the door with a large clawed fist. He waited a moment, then banged forcibly on the panel once again, impatiently.

There was a long moment before anything happened. The darkness in the house was suddenly filled by the feeble glow of a lantern,. Footsteps could be heard as the light moved sluggishly to the door.

"Who is it?" barked the gruff voice of the old farmer through the closed door. "What do you want?

"Open up!" bellowed the burly figure on the porch in a harsh command. "Open up or we'll knock the door down." A low rumble escaped the throat of the large beast. It tamped at the ground with its heavy clawed feet.

"I ask again," came the old man's response. "Who are you and what do you want at this forsaken ahr of the night?"

The gorgul only pounded more fiercely on the stout wooden portal. "Open your door," he hissed loudly. "We must make a search of your dwelling."

"What?" came the startled cry from the farmer. "You have no authority here, now go away!"

The gorgul upon the restless beast growled something at his fellow. The one on the porch inclined its long head sharply. The loathsome creature backed a step, then kicked savagely at the door with its metal boot. The panel cracked open with a shattering of wood. The old man fell back behind the shattered door and collided with something solid in the house, a wall or piece of furniture. Shan couldn't tell which.

The Elfling looked back quickly to assess the progress his friends were making. Rimmy and Gorian had finished saddling two of the thorka and had immediately started in on the other two. The great animals nickered softly. Doornig, with some help from Kilgar, gathered all their blankets and dishes, stuffing them quietly away in their saddle bags. Shan turned quickly back to the scene on the porch.

"What do you want?" the old man moaned, cowering before the broad shouldered form on his porch. "What have we done?" He held his lamp out to reveal the menacing creature at his door.

"Where is he?" the gorgul rasped, taking a threatening step forward. "Are you hiding the wretched one inside?" The thing pointed a clawed finger at him.

"We're not hiding anyone," Shan could hear the frightened voice of the old man's wife. He couldn't see her but she must have been just inside the hallway. "We don't even know what you're talking about."

The gorgul clenched its fist and shook it in their faces. "He was coming this way," the thing gurgled oddly in its throat. "He was seen nearby earlier today."

"Who was seen?" the farmer stammered. He leaned back as the burly form stepped closer.

"A boy," the hideous creature hissed at them. "An Elf boy." Shan could hear the quick intake of its breath, imagined the sharp snap of its dark tongue as it slurped noisily.

"Elf boy?" the old man muttered. "There's no Elf boy around here." He wet his dry lips. "Ain't seen an Elf in these parts for pertty near fifty yehrin," the old farmer went on. " 'Sept maybe in that accursed forest off yonder." He nodded his head grudgingly to the east.

"He was seen!" the gorgul rasped out once again. "Coming this way."

"I tell you, there's no Elf here," the farmer said in a shrill tone of defiance.

"I must search," the foul thing spit at them, shouldering its way suddenly into their small home. Both the farmer and his wife cried out in fear as the soldier stomped down the hall and disappeared from Shan's view. There was a series of loud scrapes and crashes throughout the little house. The Elfling could clearly hear the banging of tables and chairs as they were thrust noisily aside.

Shan cast a worried glance over his shoulder. The boys were almost ready to ride out in a mad rush. It would only take a few more mira and they'd be fully prepared.

"I told you there wasn't anyone there," the old man was berating the soldier as it clanked back out onto the porch.

"He was seen!" it hissed at them once again. "He is not alone," it wheezed. "There were others with him." The wooden planks groaned under him. The ugly devil swung around to stare at the barn across the yard. Shan instinctively pulled himself back from the shutter opening, withdrawing deeper into the shadows. The creature flailed its clawed fist at the darkened building, one long nail pointing out. "What's in there?" it cried with a heavy rasp.

The farmer stared past the thing's burly shoulder. "Just some animals," the old man offered hoarsely. "Our bull and a few b . . ." The wizened man broke off, his wife's nervous hand pressing down hard on his arm. The man looked down at her, clamping his mouth shut at her pleading expression.

The gorgul swung back to face them. It flicked its dark tongue out through its tusks and settled its ghastly eyes on them. It blinked, then blinked again. "A few?—A few *what?*" it wanted to know. The farmer coughed nervously, a trembling hand at his mouth.

"Oh, nothing, really," he mumbled. The ugly soldier narrowed the gap between them. "It was—uh—just . . . ah . . ."

"Some bales," the old wife finished for him. "Bales of hay, wasn't it, Fergus?" the woman clutched at his arm, looking uncomfortably into the hideous face leering before them. The old man squeezed his wife's hand.

"That's right, dear," he stammered. "I put some bales of hay out there—*for the bull*." The thing just glared at them.

"We must check," it wheezed, spinning abruptly on its metal boots, and clattering loudly down the steps. The old couple exchanged a horrified look as it shuffled heavily across the yard.

"It's coming!" Shan cried tightly. He flashed a terrified look back at the others. They had all clambered quietly into their saddles.

"We're ready," Kilgar breathed out in a tight lipped grimace. He beckoned to the Elfling with his hand outstretched. Snatching out for his water bag, Shan ran to join him upon the animal's high back. He leaped up lightly onto the sleek hind end and hurriedly wrapped his arms around Kilgar's waist. They swung round and angled their mounts toward the double doors. The four great animals pranced softly in anticipation.

There was a sudden rattling at the side door. Shan whispered a momentary prayer of thanksgiving. He had inadvertently shot the bolt when he'd returned from fetching water. The door shook again, more violently this time, but then they could hear the thump of heavy footsteps moving around toward the double doors at the front of the barn. For a sickening moment Shan realized he hadn't bothered to close or lock the window shutter. The footsteps stopped abruptly at the small opening. The cold, pale light of the moon Sheera was blocked by the bulky form as it tried to peer inside. It hissed once in annoyance, then moved away, heading once again for the large front doors.

The boys steeled themselves for a breathless flight. The thorka, sensing the nervousness of their riders, became restive and bucked slightly in place. In a moment of sudden inspiration, Shan reached down and speared the darkened lantern from its hook above the retaining wall. The reservoir of oil sloshed wildly with the quick movement. A tiny glow could just be seen on the very tip of the wick.

The double doors shuddered momentarily, then creaked severely on their hinges as they were pulled open. A dark figure stood before them in the gaping doorway.

"Now!" Kilgar screamed. The mighty thorka sprang forward with all their pent-up energy. They whinnied loudly as they charged for their freedom. The dark-haired boy clutched one of their two lances and leveled it at the breast of the gorgul.

The thing shrieked horribly as the metal tip was driven through its chest. Dark blood exploded out through its lacquered breastplate as the lance snapped off in Kilgar's fist with a loud splintering of wood. The frenzy of flailing hooves buffeted the howling creature, thrusting it forcibly aside. The raging animals leaped over its collapsing body and raced out into the farmyard.

The second gorgul, still astride the giant slor, swung his mount slowly toward the barn at the first sounds of conflict. The great lizard lumbered around and pounded across the yard towards them. Shan spun the dial on the lantern and, in an instant, it flared brightly to life in his hand. The gorgul shielded its slitted eyes from the blinding glare, swinging its enormous beast around in a ponderous circle to cut them off. The slor's huge tail whipped around in an attempt to sweep them all from their saddles.

Shan raised the glowing lantern and threw it at the approaching pair with all his strength. The glass of the lantern shattered as it struck the gorgul in the chest. The hot oil erupted in a fireball, consuming both rider and mount. The wretched soldier screamed in agony, swatting futilely at the hungry flames that engulfed them. The giant slor screeched in a hideous fashion, whirling around in a maddened rage.

The five boys pelted down the road in a reckless flight. The thorka's hooves dug up large clods of dirt as they few along. Only Shan could see well enough in the dim light to guide them, and they had to trust more on their animals' instincts than anything else.

They swung onto the hard-packed lane almost immediately, only to find another couple of gorguls poised atop a second giant slor, guarding the road closely. The enormous lizard scuttled awkwardly in their direction, its great claws tearing up the earth as it slithered after them. The excited thorka quickly outdistanced the slor as it plodded heavily along in their wake. They cast frequent wild looks over their shoulders, but were satisfied to watch their pursuers fall back and disappear into the murky night air.

They soon began to breathe a little easier and turned their attention back to negotiate the winding path of the roadway. Suddenly, three more huge forms melted out of the darkness before them. The giant *slors* each carried two loathsome soldiers on their long, broad backs.

The four thorka abruptly reared up in terror, their riders clinging desperately to their saddle horns. Huge clawed feet reached out to rake the air. The boys' mounts stamped and circled furiously as the enormous lizards crashed after them.

"This way!" Kilgar yelled. He reined his black stallion in and shot off to their left, off the road. The others wheeled immediately after him without question. They raced over the uneven turf, hoping and praying the thorka wouldn't break a leg in the darkness or that they wouldn't be thrown free of their saddles in the maddened rush.

They rode on for some time, only bothering to slacken their headlong rush when they had heard no sounds of pursuit from behind them for more than half an ahr. Another ahr later they slowed their tired mounts to a walk, giving them their heads and allowing them to pick their own way through the gloom.

They were all nearly exhausted when they stumbled upon a wide black expanse that spread out before them like a wall. It dimly filled their field of vision in Sheera's waning light. They stopped their animals on a rise to stare anxiously out at the huge dark barrier. It was difficult to make out any details in the faltering light. They swung their faces in both directions, yet could see nothing but the gaping blackness looming before them. The huge obstacle seemed to repulse the silvery glow from the moon above, gathering instead the darkness around itself as a cloak.

"What *is* that?" Rimmy asked as he feebly tried to pierce the veil of gloom in front of them.

"Darkwood," Kilgar responded with a touch of dread. The others found they had knots in their throats. They stared uncertainly into the yawning mass of trees. "Come on," the dark-haired boy called grimly to them. "Might be our only hope." He urged Adrulax slowly forward. The thorka balked for a moment, snorting air noisily out through his nostrils. The great stallion kicked at the lumpy turf before finally yielding to his rider's bidding. The others trailed nervously behind them. The five boys ducked their heads as they plunged warily into the dark, cloying branches. And it wasn't long before they had disappeared completely within the murky depths of the forest.

19

Cbe Feldus Blossom
[21st of Kaligath, 4534 C.R.]

The total darkness was overwhelming. When they waved their hands in front of their own faces the boys could not see anything. They were quickly disheartened by the oppressive gloom that surrounded them. Even the thorka seemed nervous. They had to pick their way through the dense forest growth by feeling alone. Everywhere the ground was damp and soggy. Each delicate step of the large mounts puckered and gurgled as they moved slowly along. The animals' hooves sank down deeply into the muck, making it difficult for them to proceed without tottering erratically.

The little party had grudgingly ventured about a korad into the morass before coming to a halt. They huddled as close together as they could manage within the tightly packed trunks.

"We can't go on like this," Kilgar told them in a strained voice. They couldn't see the furrowed scowl worrying his face through the enveloping blackness. Even Shan had trouble distinguishing any kind of form more than a few hobbin away. Whatever meager light Sheera cast down from high above had mostly been blocked by the thick canopy of the leaves overarching the grim forest.

"We can't stay here, either," Doornig blurted out with a sneer. "I don't relish the thought of sleeping in the saddle and the ground is simply too muddy here for us to curl up under the trees. We'll just sink down into it."

"What do you suggest, then?" Gorian interjected sarcastically. "Climb up into the trees themselves?"

"That's actually not a bad idea," the Elfling told them. Doornig snorted at the notion. The very thought of trying to scramble up the damp limbs in the darkness, slipping and sliding over the slimy bark, was truly laughable to him.

"Once again we fail to get a good night sleep," the fiery youth moaned.

"If sleep is all you're worried about," snapped Kilgar out of the murky night, "then I suggest you turn around right now and head for home."

The others held their tongues, sensing the friction in the air. Doornig was too shocked to speak. The silence deepened around them as they sat dejectedly on their mounts. For their part, the great animals shifted continuously about in the mire, the soft suckling sounds from their hooves seemed to echo hollowly all about them.

Daryl Hanson

Finally Gorian thought to speak out. "Could we, maybe, light the little lantern we brought with us?" There was a long pause while everyone considered it.

"Well," Kilgar started to say. He drew out the single word, as if weighing all the possibilities, both good or bad.

"We don't need to have it wide open," the sandy-haired boy rushed on. "We can keep it low, shield the sides of it, somehow, with a cloth or something."

"That way," Shan spoke up in agreement, "it wouldn't shine out through the trees like a beacon."

"You mean, you don't want to cry out to anyone passing by," Doornig chortled, " 'Hey, here we are, come and get us?' " The others snickered softly around him, and with that the pall of doom was lifted somewhat from their heavily overburdened shoulders.

"Alright," Kilgar spoke up grudgingly. "We'll give it a try. Maybe that way we'll be able to find a little better place to spend the night."

"I'm for that," Doornig said with a little spark of enthusiasm.

They delved down into their packs for a couple of moments, fumbling about awkwardly in the darkness. Gorian produced the small object at last. He gave the lamp a little shake, only to discover it was totally empty. *Probably best*, he thought with a grunt. Bouncing along the road with an oil-filled lantern in your pack sounded like a recipe for disaster. "We need some oil," the boy announced.

"I've got some here," Doornig replied. He came across a sealed flask in his bag and had pulled it out in anticipation. It took several awkward moments to accomplish a transfer in the dark.

"Thanks," Gorian said as he balanced the lamp on one leg while trying to pull the plug from the flask. Precariously, he poured some of the oil into the lantern's small tank. He worked carefully while Rimmy located the blue head scarf he had worn in his escape from Branby. Once Gorian had finished, Rimmy passed over the bunched up cloth. The sealed oil flask was returned to Doornig for repacking. Gorian took the scarf and wound it around the back side of the small lamp's glass casing. He looped it around and tied it at the top of the lid where each end of the handle was attached. The others waited impatiently in the dark, unable to see what he was doing.

"Kilgar, let's see if you can give it a try," Gorian said, passing the wrapped bundle to their dark-haired leader.

Kilgar accepted it carefully, handing it back for Shan to hold while he thrust a hand into his pocket to retrieve a thin wedge of flint. The Elfling slid the glass door open on its tiny hinges as Kilgar struck the flint a couple of times with the edge of his knife. Every short stroke threw out a scattering of sparks. Rimmy looked up to see the gnarled branches of the trees hunched closely over them. They looked like the clutching hands of a monster with each bright flash of light. The bony fingers seemed to stretch down over them for an instant and then were gone, swallowed instantly into the shrouding gloom. The younger boy stifled a little cry with another shower of bright sparkles.

On the fifth attempt the dark-haired boy saw his brother's aim shoot a tiny firefly-like speck into the lantern housing. It caught on the oil soaked wick and suddenly burst into flame. Shan trimmed the wick slightly and swung the glass door closed. The actions brought a little cheer from the others, as a single beam of light shone out from the lamp precisely as they had hoped. The Elfling started to pass the light to Kilgar, but the youth waved him off with the back of his hand.

"You're going to have to hold that," Kilgar said. "I'll need both my hands free to maneuver Adrulax around in here." Shan held onto the lantern with a small shrug.

The Elfling experimented with how best to hold it to provide them all with at least a little bit of light. The rest of them took the brief opportunity to get a better look at their surroundings. The trees here were severely gnarled and misshapen, some even looked completely stunted. The broad trunks seemed to shoot off in every direction at once. The long, shriveled branches hung down close to the ground, grasping at them like wildly distorted claws. And the leaves were dark and slimy, and almost seemed to be rotting where they hung.

"What a pleasant place this is," Rimmy exclaimed. He eyed the unsavory forest dubiously.

"It's certainly no paradise," Gorian stated distastefully, "that's for sure."

"At least this lantern seems to be working out the way we wanted," Shan offered cheerfully.

"Just be careful not to shine it out towards the edge of the forest," their leader told him. "We wouldn't want to attract any company."

"No, that would defeat the whole purpose of our makeshift shield," the Elfling replied lightly. They shared a little chuckle between themselves.

"Alright," Kilgar turned to the others. "Now that we've got a little light, let's see if we can find ourselves some shelter. Take it nice and slow. Follow the tracks of the rider in front of you." He gave his reins a little tug, moving off with a quiet slurping of mud. Rimmy came next, followed closely by Doornig, with Gorian bringing up the rear. The effectiveness of the pale light quickly diminished down the line, forcing them to pay careful attention to the placement of each step.

The sodden ground gurgled constantly as they slogged carefully along. They bore on for three quarters of an ahr before they found a break in the trees. The little party sloshed into a small clearing where they discovered several large flat stones embedded in the damp turf. Thick roots and tangled growths twined in and out of the soggy ground between the scattered stones. The four animals pulled abreast of each other as their riders surveyed the area in the faint glow of the lantern.

"This looks like a good enough place," Doornig exclaimed happily. The clearing was roughly oval in shape. It was not much larger than Shan's room back in Draydin, measuring only about ten paces wide by fourteen paces long. But it seemed inviting enough to them. There was, however, a very strange looking tree in the center of the open space.

The weary travelers practically fell off their thorka in eagerness to stand upon their own feet once again. They rubbed unpleasantly at their sore backsides. One at a time they pulled down their packs in near exhaustion, dropping them onto several of the flat rocks.

"Hmmm," Shan murmured to himself. He scuffed his boot on one of the flat, yellowish stones, examining it in more detail, testing its strength. He still held onto the small lantern as the others busied themselves with spreading out their gear. He aimed the faint beam down upon the polished slab. His eyes drifted curiously from one large stone to another. "That's odd," he stated, his gaze finally making a complete circuit of the little clearing.

"What's odd?" Rimmy wanted to know. He stepped up next to Shan, looking down as well, trying to understand what the Elfling had discovered.

"This was no accident," Shan told him. "The placement of these stones, I mean." He indicated the one he'd been standing on with a gesture of his empty hand. "They were put here intentionally."

"Huh?" the younger boy grunted back at him.

"See how they form a pattern," the Elfling informed him. "Look here, it makes a full circle. That has to be on purpose." He pointed at the ground, ran his fingertip around in the air, forming a loop before the boy's tired gaze. "These run all the way around that dead tree." They both looked up apprehensively at the strange, desiccated husk. It looked as if it had been struck by lightning.

"That's really interesting," Rimmy said with a big yawn afterwards. He rubbed at his eyes. "What do you think they are?" he mumbled. "Tombstones?"

The elven youth shook his head. "More like an ancient henge, I'd say."

"What's that?" the young boy asked, spreading his lips in another big yawn. He held a fist up to his mouth. " 'Scuse me."

"A henge is a type of old time-keeping device," Shan told him. "It can be used as a natural calendar or employed in some archaic religious practices involved with planting or harvesting festivals." The Elfling yawned himself. "Who really knows for sure?"

"Maybe someone put these stones here as a sacrificial altar of some kind," Doornig offered as he spread himself out upon one of them. He propped his head upon his rucksack, pulled the blanket up to his chin. "All I care about right now is that it's dry." He closed his eyes before he'd finished speaking. Gorian stretched himself out on the stone next to him. He yawned loudly, his eyelids becoming too leaden to keep open. The two of them were asleep almost immediately.

Rimmy curled up on another of the flat stones, his cloak draped over him. He was out instantly as well. The regular sounds of their breathing soon filled the little clearing. The Elfling sank down on the level stone. He tried crossing his legs, but failed. Shan tilted sluggishly onto his side instead. He lay there for a few moments, blinking at his own weariness. With enormous effort he succeeded in placing the lantern on the ground next to him. Curiously, he noticed a strong, sweet smell hovering on the air around them.

The boys had left the thorka saddled this time, he realized groggily. Kilgar had managed to tie them to a couple of the thick roots running in and out of the moist ground, before slumping down in exhaustion on one of the pale, flat stones next to Shan. The dark-haired boy suddenly felt extremely tired, like his body had grown incredibly heavy all at once. Sleep tugged at his mind, but he fought the strong urgent feelings to lay his head down and rest.

Shan saw him falter as he struggled to get back up to his knees, but collapsed on the stone. "You alright?" the Elfling queried, tiredly.

"I'm fine," his friend murmured. "M'm jist havin' troubla keepin' ma

Daryl Hanson

eyez apen."

"Know what you mean," Shan called back with a fierce yawn. "I feel kind of drowsy all of a sudden myself. Like I haven't gotten enough sleep."

"Ya haven't," Kilgar mumbled, his lips feeling thick and slow. He looked over at the Elfling and yawned. "Tha's why m'm keepin' wa . . ." The boy fell back onto the stone. His eyelids flickered stubbornly a few times before closing completely.

Shan lay numbly on his side. He tried reaching out to check on his friend, but he could only manage to sprawl over onto his stomach. He struggled for a moment before rolling sluggishly onto his back. The Elfling stared blearily up into the dark canopy, noticing oddly, that he could actually see a sprinkle of stars above them. *There must be a gap in the forest ceiling*, he thought. He could faintly make out the stilted form of Ulrick pulling at his plow. He suddenly had the strange feeling of sinking, yet he was certain the large, flat stone beneath him wasn't shifting.

He continued to notice the strong, pungent odor on the light breeze. It was thick and sweet, almost sickly sweet. It seemed to permeate the whole clearing and hung oppressively over him like a blanket. It stung at his eyes and filled his lungs until he thought he might choke and cough. He tried to lift his head to look about, but the enormous effort left him extremely dizzy and weak. His head began to spin.

Shan strained fiercely to keep his eyes open, but they soon felt on fire and hot tears dribbled unhindered down his cheeks. His mouth felt like it was filled with thick wadding, and it became inordinately difficult to swallow. Something continued to grip pervasively at his lungs, some form of narcotic vapor tugging wickedly at his mind, as well as his body.

Have the gorguls somehow caught up to us? he thought with supreme effort. *Struck at us with some kind of nerve agent?*

The last glimpse Shan had before succumbing to the irresistible force was a long strained look up into the gently stirring branches of the dead tree. Only, the Elfling got the strangest feeling that it was not really dead. There was a sharp crackling sound from the stiff upper branches as little bits of wood broke off, and something seemed to ooze out from the small breaks like sap. It dribbled out and began to run unerringly down the outside of the dark wood. The gel-like substance seemed to glow faintly as it slithered slowly along the dead, dried-out branches.

Shan could force his eyes open no longer. He felt himself being pulled ceaselessly, savagely downward. He fought against the overwhelming impulse to sleep, but it was no use. He lapsed at last into an irresistible rush of blackness.

There was another sound of snapping wood, and then another. The blackened branches cracked open and spewed out sluggish runnels of slime. The oozing tendrils coursed slowly down the dead limbs and onto the twisted trunk. Several of the softly glowing rivulets merged together, forming larger streams which ran down the blackened bark in gradual stages. The thick, sluggish flow puddled at the base of the ugly tree. Pools grew slowly as more of the strange sludge continued to course down from above.

Then a finger of gel ventured out from one of the puddles and began running along the damp ground. It seemed to slither out in a serpentine course, twisting and winding itself around any obstacles in its path. It puddled in a small depression for a time, slowly widening as more of the viscous fluid ran down the tree.

Several other gleaming streamlets separated themselves from the gathering pools along the tree's gnarled base. They thrust out in several directions at once, their lazy courses spreading out as if searching for something. After a time the various runnels curved lazily around and merged together once again, now on a direct track for the sleeping figures in the clearing.

The slumbering boys were oblivious to the slow crawl of the gelatinous fingers towards them. Off to the side the four great thorka began to stamp restlessly and pull at their neck ropes. They snorted in agitation, skittishly dancing around as the sickly sweet odor continued to swirl thickly throughout the little clearing.

One of the creeping tendrils finally touched the edge of Gorian's blanket. It paused for a moment, as if trying to sense something, then slowly began to climb up the wrinkled surface of the blanket. The fine wool fibers became strangely discolored as the gel moved dauntlessly across it.

A second gel-like pod encountered Doornig's boot where it protruded from his covering. The pod widened slowly, then lazily began to engulf the heavy leather. It became stained as the slime trickled up and over it on its inexorable course toward the boy's exposed hand.

More feelers ran out from the tree in torpid lines. Two of them brushed slowly up against Kilgar's senseless form. The tendrils split into multiple jagged streamers and worked their way leisurely along one of his legs. Another pod morphed into five or six segments once they discovered the boy's other pant leg. They began to edge patiently up over its surface.

At that moment, Shan struggled up out of his enveloping blackness. It was like swimming up out of a deep, dark cold. He clawed feverishly for every painful handhold of the way. the Elfling opened his eyes with great difficulty. Crusty bits of his dried tears fell away with the effort, but the oppressive sense of darkness eventually gave way to a dim glow all about him. He stared up a little drunkenly at the dark twisted branches arching over him. They swayed about mildly, but not from any whisper of a breeze. The lantern was still sitting off to the side. It cast a wan light across the clearing.

The frail tips of a dozen dark branches had broken off above. Out of their thin, hollow tubes a faintly glowing gel had drizzled out. The runnels ran down from the ghastly tree in thick braids, forming themselves into yellowish-gold bulbs about the size of a melon. The elongated, translucent globes hung down over Shan's head and seemed to pulse with life, expanding and contracting as if they were somehow breathing. The tear-drop shaped orbs pulsed at random intervals, giving them the look and feel of a sputtering fire.

Shan blinked his eyes wide several times in an attempt to thrust back the drowsiness which still gripped at him. He swivelled his head to the side to gaze about the clearing. There were no gorguls in evidence. The thorka jerked madly at their tethers, stamping and rearing at something unseen on the ground. Groggily, he took in his four friends, huddled nearby on the ground. Nothing really seemed amiss to his bleary mind, yet his senses screamed at him in alarm. Shan struggled to rise, yet found that he could not. Something pinned him to the ground and he could not shake it loose.

He looked again at his companions as they lay prone upon the large, flat stones. It was then that he noticed the slimy exudate draped across all their lower extremities. To his horror, it looked to him as if the gel was alive in some way, for it moved slowly, extending itself further up their bodies even as he watched. Once again he fought to rise, to rush to his friends' aid, but he could only mange to lift his shoulders and his upper body away from the pale stone.

He cast a wild look down at his legs. His heart skipped a beat when he discovered the same foul slime slithering slowly up his own legs. He jerked desperately on his limbs, yet failed to tear himself loose from its tenacious grip. It felt like he was slowly being covered in thick syrup. It adhered to his body, preventing him from freeing himself. The slimy mass continued to crawl upwards onto his torso at an incredibly slow pace, yet wherever it moved, whatever it touched, it seemed to entrap, to grasp onto like thick glue.

It slithered along his hip over an exposed spot on his skin. The contact was cold at first, but then the creeping touch seemed to burn deeply into his flesh for a few moments. Then, almost immediately, his skin turned numb, and he could feel nothing except for a curious tingling sensation, like when his hand had fallen asleep. He watched in growing alarm as the wriggling mass slowly wormed its way upward onto his stomach.

The Elfling pulled and twisted and strained to squeeze himself free, yet all to no avail. In sudden desperation, he tried throwing himself to the side, but quickly found he could not budge his body even a finger-length. He flailed about wildly, trying to latch onto any rocks or roots which might give him some increased leverage. He accidentally battered the tiny lantern in one failed attempt. It rocked on its metal rim for a moment, then came to rest a bit closer to him. He thought nothing of it at first, as he sought to stretch out once more to grab onto anything within arm's length. But then he noticed the squirming tendrils of slime running along the ground begin to shy away from the warm metal casing. They slowly parted and circled around the little vessel, merging back together on the other side of it.

"Huh," he actually murmured out loud, "this stuff must not like fire."

He threw a hasty glance down as slimy fingers slowly began to wind their way up his chest. Other tiny streamers wriggled up off the flat stone on their way to join with them. *I'd hate to let those things reach my face*, he thought wildly to himself.

Before his upper body became totally pinned in its vise-like grasp, Shan threw himself to the side. He fumbled for the lantern handle and finally succeeded in pulling it towards him. But one of his hands became enmeshed in the gritty slime, and he had lost the use of it. That forced him to clamp onto the lamp handle with his teeth while he struggled to unwrap the headcloth from around its handles and upper housing. Once he had accomplished that, he attempted to open the casing with his free hand. The metal housing swung about crazily in his mouth. The thin, metal handle ground uncomfortably against his teeth, but he finally succeeded in lifting open the tiny glass door.

Shan carefully placed the lantern on the ground next to him.

Scooping up the scarf, he thrust one end of it into the lamp opening. It instantly burst into flame. He pulled it out and dabbed it at the thick slime. Immediately the gel seemed to stop its inexorable advance, and actually seemed to draw back from him a little. Encouraged by the reaction, the Elfling scraped at the goo trapping his left hand while the end of the cloth continued to burn. The softly glowing ooze started to blacken instantly, pulling back and away from his wrist until he could free it from its confinement altogether. But the burning head cloth was nearly consumed, so he dropped it onto the wriggling arm of sludge across his lap.

The viscous fluid curled and blackened almost immediately, but the cloth was totally devoured in the process. The ooze halted its advance across his body, and actually began to shrink back from him, yet much too slowly for him to help his friends before they eventually became totally entombed by the creeping fluid.

Suddenly, a fiery arrow whistled out of the darkness of the trees and struck near Gorian. Small flames licked up the shaft. The slime covering the boy's legs began to darken and blister. Several other flaming darts hissed out of the trees and stuck into the turf by Rimmy and Doornig. A moment later two more burning projectiles appeared close to Kilgar. Wherever the fiery shafts struck, small flames leaped up, licking hungrily at the softly glowing gel.

There really wasn't any sound to speak of, but the tendrils of oily slime writhed and bubbled all across the clearing, giving the Elfling the impression of a dying creature screaming out in agony. Trailers of the gel crisped and blackened rapidly, spreading the devastation throughout the entire oozing network. The unmistakable thrum of bow strings hummed in Shan's ears. Another half dozen arrows appeared miraculously across the clearing, wreathed in flame. The growing patchwork of fires sped the eventual withdrawal of all the devilish feelers. The small flames leapt from the scattered wooden shafts onto the grid work of slimy runnels. The burning gel turned instantly to ash.

Shan watched in horrid fascination as the tree stopped dribbling out the ghastly ooze. The bubbling fountains at the end of each hollow tubule clogged over. The melon-sized globes hanging down through the blackened branches began to shrivel and retract into the gnarled limbs. The strange glow they had given off was instantly extinguished. And the tiny fires from more than two dozen arrows quickly burned low. The feeble glow of their small lantern still resting on the ground was all that was left to dispel the oppressive gloom which closed in on the little clearing once again.

The Elfling was finally able to shimmy his way free of his confinement. He stood up on the flat stone as the last of the strange gel burst into ash and looked about himself anxiously. He half-expected a mad rush of foul bodies to pour out from the dark forest to surround them. But nothing happened; no gorguls came streaming out at them from the trees.

Shan swung around to scan the dim recesses of the forest, for some fleeting glimpse of their rescuers. Even his keen eyes could not pierce the dense blackness ringing the small open space. He continued to watch expectantly for some time, breathing shallowly, hoping *someone* would eventually show themselves, but they never did.

After a time, he glanced up at the hideous black tree, and shuddered. It had come close to killing them, he was quite sure. Even though he might have escaped its insidious trap on his own, he felt sure it would have been too late to save his friends. They owed their lives to a mysterious benefactor. He looked once again at the murky line of trees, silently thanking someone for rescuing them from almost certain doom.

Shan frowned to himself. Because of the variety of colorful fletchings on all the arrows around the clearing, he knew there had been several people involved in saving them from an agonizing death—and yet for some reason, they had chosen not to reveal themselves. He turned away with a last fruitless survey of the trees and hurried to check on his friends. A hasty examination of the four boys assured him they were all still breathing. He sighed audibly in relief, kneeling down at last near Kilgar.

The dark-haired boy stirred after a few moments. The others moaned softly to themselves and twitched around restlessly where they lay sprawled on the flat stones. Kilgar's dark eyes fluttered open and he looked weakly up at the Elfling. He brought one hand up to his head, rubbed hard at his temples.

"What happened?" he asked in a groggy voice. "I remember feeling overwhelmed with sleep, but then . . ."

"Don't try to puzzle it out now," Shan told him in a quiet voice. "We can talk about it later."

"But . . ." Kilgar interjected, trying to rise up. "The watch. I need to watch." The Elfling pushed him gently back down onto the ground.

"Don't fret," he said. "It's taken care of." Relieved by his friend's words, the dark-haired boy relaxed. He closed his eyes again and slept.

Shan flicked away clinging bits of black ash from Kilgar's pants. He covered the boy with a blanket, turning at last to the others. They had wiggled around a bit on the stones, moaning lightly to themselves, but did not awaken. The elven youth brushed off the last of the dark residue from their encounter, watching in curiosity as the crusty tendrils dissolved into black dust whenever he touched them. He readjusted the blankets on all the unconscious youths, tugging them up to their chins, and then stood up.

The Elfling slowly circled back to his own gear. He lightly pulled up one of the arrows from the turf before settling down on one of the flat rocks. He looked up warily at the immobile black husk of the tree looming above him. Dark and silent now, there were no signs of rustling in its dead branches. He shook his head with a shivering of gooseflesh as he re-lived the horror of the last few mira. The whole terrible experience washed over him in a sudden flash once again, and he shuddered violently. In an effort to tear his troubled mind away from the menacing shape still looming there so rigidly and silently above him, he turned his eyes to the arrow in his hands.

It was beautiful craftsmanship. The shaft was long and straight, without a hint of imperfection in the smooth wood. It seemed light, yet incredibly strong. The arrowhead was formed of some kind of ceramic material, rather than metal. It was as dark as obsidian, yet he felt certain it had been fashioned from some kind of clay and then baked. The small nock at the end of the arrow also appeared to be made of the same unusual substance. The fletchings were finely glued to the shaft in three clean rows. The feathers themselves had been taken from a bird he couldn't identify and then had been dyed expertly in a series of bright colors.

Shan twirled the arrow slowly between his fingers, puzzling over its origins, but then set it aside after a while. Absently, he closed the glass door of the small lantern resting near his knee. He trimmed the wick to reduce the overall light it cast out into the forest, ever mindful that enemies might still be lurking about. He sat there unmoving for some time, running his watchful gaze over his unconscious friends.

Unbeknownst to him another pair of eyes watched him curiously from the thick shadows under the trees.

20

Solonika
[22nd of Kaligath, 4534 C.R.]

The first hint of morning found Shan still sitting there in the clearing, cross-legged. Light began filtering down through the small rift in the trees. He leaned back and looked up at a trace of blue sky.

The dried husk of that sinister tree loomed silently over him. It looked for all the world like someone had set it afire, for the dark wood, if that indeed was what it was made of, seemed blackened and charred. The twisted tips of its frail branches appeared like bony fingers, forever stretching downward in brittle, clawed hands. The rest of the forest looked as if it had pulled away from it, leaving a tattered space at the edge of their own green branches to keep the deadly thing from touching them.

The Elfling glanced down at his friends huddled under their blankets. He sat there patiently, peering occasionally out through the forest or up into the little rifts in the trees, until the boys began to stir a short while later.

Rimmy woke first, opening his eyes as the fuzzy darkness was slowly chased away. He yawned and sat up on the flat stone. "Morning," he mumbled. The elven youth gave him a little nod. The younger boy scratched softly at his hair, and yawned again. He continued to blink for several moments before his older brother rolled over and rose up beside him. Kilgar looked over and cast Rimmy a wan smile. Shan eased over and squatted down between the two of them. He handed each of them a mug.

"Sorry it's not kabba," he said with a wry grin. "But at least it's wet."

They took the cups gratefully and sipped at the tanga juice. Kilgar eyed the strange tree, then suddenly stiffened as he noticed the profusion of slender, wooden shafts sticking up all over the soggy turf. He turned to the Elfling with a puzzled look, one eyebrow raised uncertainly.

"Arrows? What exactly happened last night?" he asked, the mug slowly dropping down into his lap. "Were we attacked?"

"You could say that," Shan offered sardonically.

Rimmy finally noticed the welter of darts bristling the ground about them. "Those don't look like any gorguls' weapons," he proclaimed, somewhat perplexed. He set his mug on the stone beside him and snatched at one of the long shafts. After closely examining it for a moment, he let out a low whistle. "These are the finest arrows I've ever seen."

Daryl Hanson

By now Doornig and Gorian had flickered open their eyes. They both sat up groggily, looking inquisitively over at the others. Gorian rubbed at his temple. "Ow, I think I've got a headache," he called out.

"Where'd all these arrows come from?" Doornig wanted to know, suddenly looking all about the clearing.

"Shan was just about to tell us," Kilgar said pertly. He sipped at the mug of juice with a smacking of his lips. He swung his gaze back to the Elfling. "Weren't you?"

"I remember feeling very sleepy," Gorian interjected. He continued to rub at the edge of his forehead. "It was almost like I'd been drugged or something."

"Me too," Rimmy spoke up. "I just couldn't keep my eyes open."

"It was that tree," the Elfling told them all evenly. His eyes shifted up to the blackened husk above them. The others followed his uneasy gaze, seeing the desiccated thing in more detail for the first time.

"Wait," Doornig began, but Kilgar cut him off before he could continue.

"Let Shan finish the story before you get all huffy and sarcastic like you usually do," their dark-haired leader commanded sharply. He leveled a meaningful look at the redhead, who quickly clamped his lips shut, before turning back to the Elfling with a nod. "Go on, Shan," Kilgar said firmly, "tell us all what happened last night."

The elven youth looked over at Gorian. "You were definitely drugged," he told the boy. "We all were. By *that!*" He indicated the strange tree looming above with a slight tilt of his head. The boys eyes grew large as he went on. "It gave off some kind of pollen, or noxious vapor. I couldn't see anything, but I could certainly feel it burning my eyes." The boys all nodded their heads, each of them vividly remembering how they had been overcome by the pungent fumes. Doornig rubbed at his itchy eyes.

"I fought the narcotic effects for as long as I could," Shan shared with them, "even after you had all fallen asleep. But I eventually passed out as well."

"So then what happened?" the red-haired youth interrupted. He swallowed quickly.

"I don't know, exactly," the elven youth confided. "I must have been out for a while." He licked softly at his lips. "When I finally came to, the dead tree had actually come to life. No, I don't mean it was stalking about through the clearing," he said to qualm their startled looks. "It exuded some strange slime through the tips of those hollow branches up there."

"Slime?" Kilgar inquired.

"It was kind of like thick sap," Shan said in response. "It oozed down the tree and started to move towards us in little rivers."

"What?" Doornig ejaculated. "Rivers of slime? Please."

"Doornig!" Kilgar snapped, flashing him a hard look.

The fiery youth recoiled a bit. "Okay, okay," he said a bit sheepishly. "Forgive me if I'm a little doubtful!" But he lapsed back into silence and nodded for Shan to continue.

"Whenever those nasty feelers reached out and came in contact with anything," the Elfling continued, swallowing lightly, "the—*pods*—slowly began to engulf it in their sticky substance." He held up a hand to forestall any more comments. "I know, seems pretty unbelievable, yet that's what it seemed to be doing." He swallowed at the dryness in his throat. "Slowly, the strange material began working its way over each of our helpless bodies, in an attempt to incapacitate us and, and then smother us, I think."

"Why?" Rimmy burst out loudly. His eyes went wide as he stared at the Elfling.

Shan could only shrug his shoulders. "To eat us, maybe, to absorb us somehow. I don't know." The boys all shuddered at the chilling thought. "I've heard some plants actually ingest organic material. You know, I could feel it tingling on my skin as it crawled up my arm." He pointed. "Look how it discolored the woolen fibers." They looked at the unusual markings on their blankets in alarm

"So, if that stuff was about to cover us in its folds, and eat us," Gorian voiced his thoughts with a shiver, "how come it didn't finish the job?" He blinked savagely. "Why are we still alive?"

"Apparently it hates fire," Shan told them. "I was able to drive it back a little with the flames from our lantern."

"Yeah, but that doesn't explain all these arrows," Gorian observed with a sweep of his hand. "They all look blackened by fire, too."

"Right," the elven youth went on. "There was someone in the trees. They shot a bunch of fire arrows into the clearing, just in time to stop the advance. Wherever the flames encountered any of the slime it was burnt immediately into ash." To illustrate his point, he traced a finger along the stone where he sat. They each could see dusty black lines running along the ground all around them. He noticed them slide a little nervously away from all the dark smudges.

"But who shot the arrows?" Kilgar asked him.

"I don't know for sure," Shan told them. "I couldn't see anyone from here, and they never bothered to show themselves." He smirked at them before looking off into the trees. "Whoever it was they decided to save us but they didn't want any actual contact with us."

"Strange," Gorian spoke out.

Doornig looked over at his friend with a puckering of his lips. "Everything seems strange to me these days." Gorian nodded knowingly in return. The redheaded youth blew air out noisily. "Let's face it, the whole world just seems to be getting stranger with every passing mur." The others all grunted in assent.

It was fully light by now. The boys all rose to relieve themselves just inside the edge of the trees. They broke out a cold meal of their leftover fruit and the remnants of a small wheel of cheese. They finished off their brief repast with a handful of nuts apiece. They allowed each of the animals a small portion of oats before freeing them from the roots where they had been thoroughly tied. The boys loaded up their things and looked out into the dark, forbidding trunks of the forest.

"Let's lead them for a bit, shall we?" Kilgar suggested. The others fell into step behind him as they plunged back into the thick shadows once again. The dark-haired youth pulled Adrulax lightly along with a hand on his bridle as they wound their way in and out of the tightly packed trunks. Dim as it was, the soft light was much easier for them to see by than what they had to endure the previous night. Sunlight filtered down in a fuzzy haze from the leafy canopy above them. The low clomping and smacking of the animals' hooves on the damp ground echoed quietly from the close boles around them.

They had only ventured about a koreb from the frightening clearing before Shan came up alongside Kilgar and whispered into his ear. "Don't look around," he told the boy, "but we're being watched."

The dark-haired youth regarded him silently for a moment. "I haven't heard anything," he whispered back. He peered cautiously through the branches in front of them from under his riddled brows. "Haven't seen anything either." He made an effort to place one step in front of the other in a consistent fashion. "Are you sure?" he asked softly.

"Positive," came back Shan's immediate response. He walked along quietly next to his friend. The Elfling looked down at his boots as they moved at an easy pace, reaching out with his senses to confirm what he *felt*. Whoever it was trailing them, they glided through the forest in the stealthiest manner he'd ever encountered. "What do you think we should do?" Shan murmured almost inaudibly.

They walked on for several paces before Kilgar deigned to reply. "Nothing for now," the dark-haired boy told him softly. "But stay on the alert. Maybe they'll show themselves once they conclude we're not really a threat to them." The Elfling offered a tight nod, before falling back a few steps. Adrulax slapped him lightly with his bushy tail.

Rimmy came close on the Elfling's heels, leading Thimba with a hand resting amiably on the thorka's sleek neck. Gorian picked his way quietly a few paces behind while Doornig brought up the rear, a few kora further back. They continued to work their way through the trees in single file in a fairly unhurried gait for more than an ahr.

"Are we gonna travel through the entire forest," Doornig's impatient voice called out a little too loudly, "or are we never coming back out again?"

Kilgar whirled to stare at him. "Hush, Doornig," he hissed in annoyance. "Are you trying to announce our presence to everyone within a hundred kora?" He glared at the redhead for a long moment before pivoting smartly on his heel and shuffling off once again in silence. Doornig, somewhat red-faced, cast an apologetic glance at Gorian, who offered a slight smile before moving off himself.

A short time later they stumbled upon a little pool. It was little more than a wide spot in the wild jumble of trees. It measured perhaps five or six paces across and maybe twice that long. The tangle of branches overarched the spot, giving it a deep, shadowed appearance. Insects droned over its placid surface in quick, darting movements. A tiny stream issued into it through a gap in the mossy trunks to their right. The water seemed to pass through the little basin, quiet and slow, before it was carried off through an outlet at its opposite end.

They halted long enough to allow the animals to drink their fill. The thorka lowered their great heads and lapped at the quiet pond. The boys spread themselves out, stretching down upon their stomachs over the tangle of roots, to splash handfuls of cool water on their sweaty necks and faces.

Something silvery darted quickly through the water in front of Shan's chin. Suddenly startled, the Elfling tried to push himself up from the edge, but he slipped on a mossy root and fell face first into the pool. He thrashed about wildly but his head struck sharply against a rock at the bottom of the small pond and his body relaxed instantly.

Daryl Hanson

In the shadowed light under the trees it was difficult for the boys to judge what had happened. They were all splashing themselves noisily with water, paying little attention to the person next to them, when the Elfling suddenly seemed to slip and plunge down into the pool. He completely disappeared into the murky water. The resulting wave sent ringlets sloshing and lapping in their faces and was the first sense that something was wrong.

Kilgar looked up instantly, noting in alarm that Shan had vanished from the edge of the water. He lashed quickly out into the widened stream, tripping over rocks and roots littering the bottom of the shallow pool. He reached out on all sides, groping about in the choppy water for any sign of his friend.

"Shan!" he screamed, growing frantic. "Shan! Shan!" The other boys jumped down into the pool as well, searching madly about for their lost companion. They dove down under the surface. The water had become so milky with silt that it was impossible to see anything in its depths. After several frenzied dives the boys resurfaced, having groped quickly their way around the entire bottom of the pool. They gasped for breath near the edge, wiping water hastily out of their faces. They looked long and searchingly at each other, still gulping for air, an overwhelming sense of dread gripping coldly at their hearts.

* * * * *

Shan slowly opened his eyes. He was lying on his back near the small stream. He had somehow been dragged clear of the water. His head ached fiercely. He reached up a hand and stroked at the tender spot on his forehead. He winced at the effort. There was a trace of fresh blood marking his fingertips. A tiny river of water trickled off his head and ran down into one of his eyes. He wiped at it with his knuckles before attempting to rise. A gentle hand held him down. Startled at the touch, he looked curiously up into the most beautiful face he'd ever seen.

A hooded figure knelt over him. She brushed the hood back and looked down at him. Her melodic voice said something lightly to him, but he didn't understand. He tilted his head and gazed up into a pair of incredibly blue eyes. They were somewhat almond shaped as they gazed down at him in anticipation. When he failed to respond to her, she spoke again, the words tripping off her tongue like a chorus of songbirds. He was completely entranced by the delicate curve of her cheek, the gentle slope of her nose, the delightful sweep of her lips. Her stunning features were framed by a mane of golden hair. Two small, pointed ears poked out through the long, silken strands.

"An Elf," Shan cried out suddenly. "You're an Elf." He rose up on his elbows, and this time she allowed it. He looked across at her, totally amazed by her appearance.

She knelt beside him on a small patch of turf just next to the little stream. His feet still dangled in the water, he realized. He pulled his boots out of the brook and crossed his legs in front of him. She arched a fine eyebrow at him while he could not help but stare at her openly in wonder.

"Who are you?" he asked excitedly. "You're absolutely beautiful." She seemed to blush softly at his words. He looked more closely at her in the shadowed light. "You can obviously understand me," he concluded. "Can't you?" She looked down shyly. "I mean, you do speak the common tongue, don't you?"

"Yes," she said in a sweet, almost musical tone. She lifted her liquid blue eyes to stare into Shan's. "Yes, I can speak the common tongue. But why do you not converse in *Keldarin*?" she asked lightly of him.

He shrugged. "Because I don't know it," he replied with a frown. "I never learned how."

Amazement at his words swam in her deep, blue eyes. "But how can that be? Surely you are Keldar. I can see that with my own eyes."

Shan raised a hand to make sure the head cloth was still in place. He was relieved to discover the scarf was dripping wet, but was still wrapped tightly around his scalp. "No," he tried to say. "You're obviously mistaken." But even his own words didn't sound very convincing to him.

She frowned prettily at him. "Why would you lie about your heritage?" she asked him in that musical voice. Shan lowered his head. "Are you ashamed of being an Elf?" He looked up at her quickly.

"No," he found himself telling her defensively. "I'm not ashamed." He dropped his eyes back to the turf. He noticed the long bow placed lightly on the grass next to her right hand.

"What then?" she coaxed him.

He found he could not lie to her. He raised his head and met her incredibly beautiful eyes. "I'm on the run," he told her at last. "I'm being hunted." Her delicate brows rose in surprise. "Maybe it's all because I'm an Elf, too," he went on. "I'm not sure. But I've been running for my life for days. I've been chased by gorguls and targs and even a kurgoth."

"A kurgoth?" she exclaimed in astonishment. "Do they even exist any longer?"

"At least one," Shan said with a tight swallow. "I saw it. Well, maybe two." he said after a moment. "I'm pretty sure I heard another one cry out somewhere deep in the forest. They almost sounded like they were calling to each other." He shuddered at the sudden, strong memory.

"You think this is only because you are Keldar?" she asked him, trying to make some sense of his story.

"I don't know," he said honestly. "Before today, before now," he looked closely at her, "I have never even seen another Elf before. At least not one I recognized. Ulfiir was trying to tell me something about them—about me—when the gorguls attacked my village, and I was forced to flee for my life."

She stood up in sudden decision. "Come," she said, offering a graceful hand to him. "We must speak with my father." Shan accepted her delicate grip and she helped him to his feet. He wavered momentarily, his head pounding fiercely. She steadied him with her hand then stooped to snatch up her bow. He was reluctant to release her hand. She turned back to him, her limpid eyes sparkling in the dim forest light. "How are you called?" she asked him lightly.

"Oh, Shan," he said, feeling suddenly a little tongue tied. "My name is Shan." The elven girl swung to lead the way through the dense trees. "What's your name?" he immediately wanted to know.

She spun lightly to face him, a little smile painting her delicate lips. "I'm called Solonika," she said shyly with a little flutter of her eyelids.

"Solonika," Shan told her. "That's a pretty name." He regarded her momentarily. "What does it mean?"

She flashed him a little smile. "Forest flower," she said coyly, and then she was off quickly, almost vanishing into the leafy background within a few light steps. Shan started to race after her, mindful of the twisting roots and thick tree trunks.

"Hey, wait!" he called out to her after a moment. He came to a halt and pointed back through the trees. She stopped gracefully in her tracks and twirled lightly to face him. "What about my friends?" he had almost forgotten to ask. "Shouldn't we go back and get them? I'm sure they're probably wondering where I am by now."

"No need, they'll be along directly," she called in a sing-song tone. "They might even be back at the city before we get there."

"City?" he exclaimed. "In this dense forest? You actually live here?"

"Of course," she sang. "Where else would we live? Now come on, Shan," she crooned softly, "we've got a little ways to go." She leveled her vivid eyes on him. "You are a little clumsy, after all." He cupped a hand over his forehead as if in his own defense and shrugged. She pirouetted nimbly on her heel and capered off through the trees.

Shan did eventually catch up to her as she paced lightly through the large boles. He admired the easy grace with which she moved. She was lithe and agile, bounding nimbly from step to step almost like a great cat. She carried the bow lightly in her left hand and she had a hunting knife strapped at her waist. Her dark green forest garb made her very difficult to spot in the heavy shadows.

She wore a jumpsuit of forest green he noticed for perhaps the first time. The material was mottled, he realized, to provide her added concealment in the dense shadows of the forest. Her greenish-gray cloak snapped lightly as she walked, the large, hooded cowl thrust back over her shoulders. Her glorious golden curls fluttered steadily in the breeze. She paced lightly over roots and stones, placing the heels of her long soft boots down surely with each step.

After a time, Solonika slung her bow over her left shoulder. A quiver of finely feathered arrows rose up behind the other shoulder near her right ear. *Situated for an easy draw*, the boy reasoned. Shan smiled in admiration of this young girl. She had been well trained as a warrior, he could tell, and was willing to venture out of the relative haven of her own village to help keep her people safe. He was thoroughly impressed.

"You're obviously well armed," the Elfling noted once he had drawn even with her. "Have you had any troubles with gorguls?"

"Not really," she intoned melodically. "They must be afraid to come in here." She scampered easily over several thick roots. "Our archers would cut them down before they advanced even just a koreb into the trees."

"That reminds me," Shan said, turning to face her. "Did you or your people save us last night from that horrible tree we stumbled across?" His forehead creased with the vivid memory. "Or whatever it was. I'm not actually sure it *was* a tree. But it certainly looked like one."

She leveled her beautiful gaze upon him and nodded. "Yes," she admitted lightly, "I was with the Watchers last night. We were informed a small party had entered the forest on the western border. We were dispatched to investigate, and we soon discovered you and those noisy humans."

"My friends," he told her as he walked along beside her. "They're my friends. They've been helping me to escape from all the patrols. I wouldn't have made it this far without them."

The girl looked thoughtfully at him. "By the time we came upon you," Solonika went on in her sing-song voice, "we discovered you had ignorantly blundered into the clearing with a Feldus blossom."

"A what?" he asked breathlessly, a look of horror etched across his face.

"Feldus blossom," she told him solemnly.

"Just what exactly is that?" Shan questioned her somewhat nervously. "It's not really a tree, is it?"

"Yes, it's actually a tree." Solonika's tone seemed heavy to him for the first time. "Yet unlike any tree the world has ever seen before. They're extremely dangerous to the unwary . . ."

"Wait, *they?*" the Elfling was incredulous. "You mean there's more than one of those deadly things?"

The elven girl squared her slim shoulders gracefully and nodded seriously at him. "I am afraid so. They have spread all throughout the forest. They're like a blight on our home, an evil curse on our existence." She walked along lightly. "But once you know about them and you learn how they try to ensnare unwary, unsuspecting travelers, you can easily avoid them."

Shan padded along with her. "Thank you," he told her sincerely. He looked her directly in the eyes. "Thank you for saving me and my friends. Without your timely assistance we would most likely be dead about now." He swallowed deeply.

"Well, now that you know about them," Solonika offered more cheerfully, "you won't be likely to make that same mistake again." He shook his head vigorously in agreement. "Now come," she said, pulling him along by the hand. "We're almost there." Shan allowed himself to be led deeper into the darkened forest. He smiled broadly at the girl. Her breathless beauty and friendly manner left him totally enchanted.

* * * * *

Kilgar rose up at last out of the water. His eyes were bloodshot from diving down into the pool countless times. The water churned and sloshed around him. He took several deep breaths.

"It's no use, Kilgar," Gorian cried out to him. "He's not down there."

The dark-haired boy continued to draw in deep breaths. "There could be a hole he slipped through down there," Kilgar explained. "Somewhere I just haven't found yet." He took in several more breaths.

"You searched the whole pond a dozen times already," Gorian told him. "You're not going to find him. He's not down there."

Kilgar flashed him an angry glare, and then slapped violently at the surface of the water in frustration. "Then where is he?" the dark-headed boy exploded. He stood at the edge of the murky pool, dropped his elbows onto a root and almost started to cry. "It can't end like this," he growled through gritted teeth. "It just can't end like this!" He lowered his forehead onto the wet loop of the root and moaned sadly to himself.

Rimmy had pulled himself over to the outlet of the little pool. The small stream seemed to tug a little more forcefully there. He looked back at his brother, his head still resting forlornly on the root. "Kilgar," the boy called, searching down the little brook for a sign, "maybe he got pulled downstream." The others all looked over at him. "There is a little drag here," he proclaimed, dropping a leaf at the edge of the pond for emphasis. They watched it for a moment as the current caught at it and hurried it away from them. "What if he was knocked unconscious? He wouldn't have been able to stop himself from floating away and in the heavy shadows we couldn't see him."

Kilgar exploded out of the pond and began racing down the rivulet, leaping over roots and around large trunks. "Rimmy," he called wildly, "you follow me! Doornig, Gorian, you've got the animals. We'll be back as soon as we can." Rimmy sped off after him.

The two remaining boys shared a worried look. They pushed themselves out of the pond and quickly began to dry themselves off with their cloaks. As soon as they pulled the damp cloths away from their faces they found themselves surrounded by a dozen hooded warriors. "Uh-oh," the red-haired youth said. The cowled figures stepped silently closer, arrows nocked and leveled upon them. The four large thorka whinnied softly in protest.

The two brothers scrambled on as fast as they could negotiate the uneven terrain. They tripped and slid continually over the slippery bark. They had gone no more than a hundred kora when Kilgar brought them up with a strangled cry. He pointed enthusiastically to the ground. They bent to examine the spot by the side of the stream. The brush along the bank was matted and wet. A few of the tall, thin stalks along the shallows had been bent or completely snapped off.

"Something's crawled out of the stream right here," the older boy said, patting at the grasses, feeling deftly along the muddy gouge in the soft bank.

"Or was pulled out," Rimmy commented. Kilgar looked down where

Daryl Hanson

his brother was pointing. Someone had clearly been lying there not too long ago. They exchanged a quick hopeful look. There were definitely two sets of footprints leading away from the water. They glanced off into the murky depths under the trees. Hopefully one set of those tracks belonged to their friend. They seemed about the right size, but as for the other, smaller set, they had no clue.

"Come on," Kilgar called quietly as he loped off after them.

"But what about the others?" his brother asked, looking briefly back up the small stream. "The thorka?"

Kilgar was intent on the tracks he was following, his eyes completely focused on the forest floor. "We'll return to the pool once we find our friend. They'll just have to wait for us." Rimmy bounced over to join him. They hadn't gone far when a handful of lithe forms suddenly materialized from the semi-darkness all around them. The hooded figures had their longbows trained upon them. The long, feathered shafts pointed threateningly at them looked somewhat familiar. The two brothers looked at each other with a resigned expression and then slowly raised their hands.

21

Wood Elves
[22nd of Kaligath, 4534 C.R.]

Solonika led Shan through the heavy shadows under the large overarching trees. The foliage under the low-hanging branches seemed especially dense here. The tangled mass of vines, creepers and stout bushes almost appeared to him like a wall of some sort. It had the feel of a berry patch, only much darker and thicker. Rather than skirting it as he had expected, the girl led him straight towards it. They approached the thick undergrowth which seemed to stretch out endlessly before them in both directions.   The Elfling regarded the barrier with a sense of trepidation. It looked to him almost as if the dense, leafy mass had been deliberately placed there, perhaps as a means to block out any casual observation from anyone passing by. Shan frowned openly at his fair companion.

Solonika smiled brightly back at him and started to step casually into the thicket of brambles and sharp thorns. He threw out a hand in sudden fear to prevent the beautiful girl from harming herself on the prickly expanse.

"Wait!" he cried. But she lightly brushed his hand aside and stepped deeper into the folds of the hedge.

"It's alright," she hummed back at him. He still had a pained look on his face as she reached back and clutched at his hand. She tried to pull him into the thorny barrier with her. He resisted her tug at first, but when she stepped nimbly forward, without the slightest hint of a scratch, he reluctantly allowed himself to be led along.

She seemed to disappear for a moment into the interlacing foliage, but then she leaned back towards him and materialized into his view once again. Her wreath of cascading golden hair framed her pretty smile as she beckoned him forward. Still a little apprehensive, the Elfling found himself being drawn, unscathed, into an apparent rift in the bracken. Shan looked around in the midst of their passage in stunned disbelief. Unless you actually knew it was there, a person would simply pass by the narrow cleft in the hedge without even noticing it.

"It's a special boma," she told him with an airy laugh. "It helps to keep out wild animals and any uninvited guests."

"Oh," was all he managed to say as they continued slowly through the heavy mass.

They stepped out of the thorn hedge at last, into a clearing of sorts.

It was not so much a single clearing, but was really a series of them. The trees were much further apart here, almost sparse, in fact. The oppressive darkness of the outer forest was completely dispelled. Sunlight filtered brightly down through gaps in the branches above to reveal an interconnected series of narrow cobblestone lanes. The little shadowed streets wound in and out through the widely spaced trunks, giving the place an expansive feel. High overhead a network of wooden bridges swung from one great bole to another. And to Shan's wonder, there were even cozy little dwellings nestled within and all around the huge trees. But best of all, the entire village was teeming with life.

The Elfling watched in astonishment as scores of brightly clad Elves moved along the shaded lanes in knots of three or four. They glided gracefully along in easy strides, their sing-song voices lifted harmoniously as they conversed happily together. He looked up as several stray shadows passed over him. Dappled rays of sunlight played through strings of nimble forms filing lightly across the gently swaying bridges above. His jaw fell open as he stopped in the middle of the street to gape all about himself in absolute wonder. Streams of people were forced to wind their way past him as he stood rooted there for several long moments. They parted like a river around him, moving rather sluggishly past an embedded rock, then swirling immediately back together again without a care, to flow ever onward.

Shan couldn't help gazing up in amazement. He tried to take it all in and his face kept leaping from one new wonder to another. He realized some of the incredible structures above seemed carved directly out of the broad trunks themselves. Others clung to the ruffled bark like barnacles. Still other dwellings wrapped themselves around entire boles like rings, yet all of them blended naturally with the leaves and trees to make it difficult to notice they were even there. These wondrous little houses occupied several different levels within the forest realm. Portions of them were cradled in the wide crotches of great trees while still more nestled high up in the strong branches. A few were even large enough to span across the space between several of the mighty trees.

The Elfling finally looked down at the girl beside him. Solonika flashed him a modest smile as she turned back to join him on the cobbles. "Welcome to Avalar," she said cheerfully. She cast a light wave of her hand at all the unbelievable surroundings. She giggled softly as he continued to stand there, staring wide-eyed at his surroundings.

"I never imagined there was any place like this in all the world," Shan murmured in awe. He turned slowly on his heel to take it all in. "No one outside the forest even knows that this place, this *world*, even exists," he said in total disbelief. "They all think this forest is cursed. Haunted. Nothing but a swamp." He still looked around himself in wonder. "But this . . ." he was at a loss for words, ". . . this is absolutely incredible. Ulfiir never even hinted that there was such a place."

Solonika reached out and grasped his hand. "Come," she said melodically, "we need to talk to my father. He'll most certainly want to speak with you." Shan let himself be pulled along by the lithe girl. She twisted through the flow of people, almost seeming to dance over the smooth cobblestone streets. She waved to a few friendly faces who turned inquisitive looks upon them as they walked. Some of the townspeople actually stopped and politely parted for them as they padded lightly past. Looks of curiosity played about all their handsome features.

After just a few mira they came to a single large tree standing alone in the morning sun. The cobblestones gently coursed around it. The broad trunk rose up to a dizzy height, its mighty branches curling up and around quite a substantial structure nestled in the huge crotch of the tree. The overlapping wooden panels of the building and the expansive upthrust of the heavy limbs merged together into one cohesive unit. The curving outer lines of the construction seemed to match perfectly with the natural shape of the tree. It was as if the two different materials had somehow been planted simultaneously and then had grown together, unhindered. The entire dwelling was covered in twisting vines, giving the whole place a kind of hidden quality. If not for the swoop of rope-lined bridges running over from several neighboring trees, Shan might have passed by without giving the entire framework a second glance.

"This is the Council Chamber," Solonika indicated in her customarily sweet voice. "Here news is shared, situations are debated, and decisions are made." Shan looked up from the shaded spot in the lane where they came to a halt. "Here you may find answers to your questions." The girl flashed him a smile, but then her beautiful face clouded briefly into a serious expression. "Always remember to tell the truth, Shan," she told him with a nod of her fair head. "My father is wise beyond his yehrin, and he will know if you lie to him."

Shan looked at her for a moment, swallowing inadvertently at the seriousness of her tone. His stomach fluttered briefly and he nodded solemnly. He looked up again at the large chamber with a sense of hesitation, but she smiled at him in her beautiful way, and all his doubts quickly faded away.

"Come," she sang to him. "He'll have already been informed of our arrival."

"Already?" the Elfling questioned her in obvious disbelief. She leveled her almond shaped eyes on him.

"He knew of your presence even before I pulled you out of the stream," Solonika proclaimed. Shan regarded her for a moment, a quizzical expression floating over his face. "Now come."

They made their way across the open space. Solonika nodded amiably to those passing by and around the huge tree. They stopped at its wide base and looked up. A series of strong wooden slats protruded from the huge trunk, parallel to the ground and spiraling upwards around the bole like steps. The girl took him by the hand and started easily up the curling staircase. Shan followed a little hesitantly at first, feeling even more uncomfortable as they rose higher. He carefully stayed close to the huge column of the great tree.

The flight of rungs wound around the trunk two or three times before they reached a railed walkway high off the ground. The narrow porch ran all the way around the expansive tree house. They stopped at a small doorway leading inside the large chamber. Two elven warriors stood alertly by the closed wooden panel, the slender butts of their ornately carved lances resting on the decking at their feet. They snapped to attention, nodding a welcome to the girl, before one of them rapped smartly on the door. The guards stepped off to the side as the door opened inwards, seemingly on its own. Solonika inclined her head slightly in gratitude to the two warriors, stooped down a bit and strode into the room. Shan followed her a little warily.

They found themselves in a wide enclosure. Coming out of the bright sunlight took Shan a few moments before he could see well enough to make out many details. The room was oddly shaped, perhaps more octagonal than anything else. It was due mostly to the natural structure of the tree, the Elfling surmised. It was actually quite airy in the room, with several broad open windows lining the walls. Awnings had been thrust out from the shuttered windows to shield the room's interior from excessive sunlight. The large number of these openings allowed the light breeze to drift pleasantly through the chamber.

Solonika glided forward in the dappled light. Her delicate gait brushed softly across the smooth planks of the floor. She came to a halt in the center of the room, looking back to find Shan taking in his surroundings with a wide, sweeping look of astonishment. He finally hurried to join her with a quick glance of apology.

"Greetings, Father," she called out melodiously in the common tongue. Shan settled his eyes on a low table at the back of the room. Three figures sat on cushions behind the long, low counter top, regarding them quietly. Their curious eyes glittered in the soft light. One of them warmly returned her smile with one of his own.

"Good morning, Child," the Elf seated in the middle of the triumvirate responded. His voice was fluid, like the gentle rush of a river. Like his daughter, Shan realized, he too had used the common speech for his benefit. "What have we here?" He raised one eyebrow, resting his gray eyes curiously upon the Elfling, who fidgeted somewhat nervously before him. On impulse, Shan managed a small bow.

"This is Shan," the girl said, taking one step forward and indicating her awkward companion with a small wave of her hand. "He stumbled into our forest with four human friends last night. They've been chased by wandering bands of gorguls, narrowly eluding capture or death for several days apparently. They ignorantly camped under a Feldus blossom last night and nearly got themselves killed." She smiled ruefully. "If it wasn't for our Border Watch, they'd most likely be feeding the wretched thing by now."

The three figures sat impassively while Solonika spoke to them, their elbows resting lightly on the low table, their gentle hands cupped out in front. They exchanged silent glances, before settling their eyes upon Shan once again.

"Please," the central figure spoke again. He lifted a hand, palm up in an invitation, inclining his head to indicate the low surface of the desk before them. Solonika placed a light grip on Shan's elbow and walked him gently forward. At a signal from the figure on the right, soft cushions were brought from the side of the room and placed neatly on the floor for them just in front of the table. Shan essayed another bow before dropping down easily on the padding next to Solonika. He felt their eyes resting curiously on him. Uneasily, he tried to find a comfortable place for his hands. They started out on his lap, moved down to lie flat on the floor, then came up to rest across the low tabletop, and then finally ended up back in his lap once again. He folded them together at last to keep from fidgeting any more. He looked up from his hands into the watchful eyes of the three wise Elves. Their thin faces regarded him silently for a time. He cleared his throat nervously and squirmed under their scrutiny.

Daryl Hanson

The middle figure leaned forward slightly, his long, silken hair falling across his shoulders in a golden shower. "I am Janerron," he intoned lightly. "I am Clanlord of House Torrano. This is Melandric," he motioned to the individual at his right. He had light brown hair and pale green eyes. He inclined his head forward a trifle. "And this is Kalandan," the Elf Lord said, indicating the darker haired Elf to his left. The fellow's blue-eyed stare was piercing. His icy countenance seemed to bore into the young Elfling. "They are two of my councilors."

Shan bobbed his head respectfully to all three of them. Janerron spoke something softly to them in *Keldarin*, but the Elfling couldn't tell what had been said. Their looks remained impassive for several long moments. The three of them seemed to share a wry grin before the Elf Lord turned back to the boy. He leveled his gray eyes upon Shan, who nervously felt the weight of his stare.

"You are somewhat of an enigma to us, young man," Janerron began slowly. His brows knit together into a golden line. "An Elf—and yet somehow not an Elf." Shan fidgeted on the cushion under the Elf Lord's riveting gaze. "A quandary indeed." He softened his expression slightly. "Please tell us something about yourself. Help us to understand how this thing has come to be."

Shan cleared his throat uncertainly. "Well, your Lordship, I grew up in the village of Draydin, some days distance from here," the Elfling began haltingly. "I'm an orphan, I guess, for I never knew my parents."

"Why Draydin?" questioned Melandric. He looked at Janerron. "Draydin is a human village, is it not?" The Elf Lord nodded firmly. "If you were orphaned when you were young as you say, why were you not entrusted to an elven family? To someone of your own kind?"

Shan could only shrug. "I do not know, noble lord. I was never consulted on the matter." He managed a wry grin. "Ulfiir, my guardian, never told me anything about my past. I'm not sure whether he ever felt the need to tell me."

"That strikes me as quite odd," Kalandan interjected. His blue eyes sparkled moodily.

"Perhaps Ulfiir didn't know anything himself," the Elfling responded, shuffling a little on his cushion. "He may have just been someone, perhaps the only one, in a long line of people who passed me along, who was even willing enough to take on another mouth to feed." Shan found it strange to talk about himself this way. Kalandan nodded lightly.

"Go on," Janerron spoke kindly. "What else can you tell us about your early life?"

"There's not much to tell," Shan went on. "I lived in an isolated village all of my life. It was a pretty boring existence, really, I can tell you. I never learned Thuvan—ah, *Keldarin*—and I'm pretty sure I've never even seen another Elf until today." He paused and looked over at Solonika. She smiled briefly at him, then he turned his attention back to the elders. "Everything was fairly normal in the village until about ten days ago."

"What happened then?" the Elf Lord questioned him softly, one elbow poised on the rim of the low table. The other hand now rested on his hip.

Shan swallowed fiercely. "I woke up in the middle of the night. Everything was still, unusually still. I couldn't even hear the mewling of the sleeth as they prowled along the perimeter wall. If you listened long enough you could always hear them coughing and sneezing at night." His breathing became a little uneasy. "But not that night." Solonika leaned over and placed her hand delicately on his arm. He looked at her momentarily with a grateful smile.

"And then I heard something creeping down the hall just outside my room. Something big." The Elfling swallowed again, then blinked savagely several times. "It was really big, bigger even than a man. It tore its way into my room, even through my barricaded door, and I swear it would have killed me if it hadn't been for Ulfiir." Solonika squeezed his arm in encouragement.

"It injured or killed six of the village watchbeasts," the boy went on, "almost like they were playthings." He sniffed noisily. "It even seemed to sneer at an entire squad of soldiers who eventually rushed to my rescue." The three Elves across the table narrowed their eyes upon him but otherwise remained still. "The thing was tall and hairy. It had enormous claws and deep-set eyes which seemed to blaze like fire."

"Fire?" the girl asked, startled.

Shan nodded nervously at her. "I've never seen anything like it before. It must have been somewhere between three and four kora in height."

"*Kora?*" Kalandan interjected with a hasty glance at Janerron. He narrowed his icy eyes on the Elfling. "You weren't imagining this?" The boy shook his head sharply. "Then it was not simply a cave bear or—a *timbercat*—or something of that sort?"

"No, no, not at all," Shan told him. "Ulfiir called it a kurgoth."

"A *kurgoth!*" Janerron exclaimed, nearly rising to his feet. He clamped both his palms down forcefully on the smooth table surface. "How could that be?" He shot a blazing look at Melandric, and then swung about to stare at Kalandan as well. "I had thought those fell beasts were completely eliminated nearly a thousand yehrin ago, sometime during the war with the Fallen Ones." He scratched suddenly at his chin. "How could even one of them possibly survive until this day without ever being seen?"

"Muurdra's hand seems somehow to be at work here," Melandric told the Elf Lord.

"Agreed," Kalandan replied grimly. "Even in his prison in the Outer Darkness the Cyr Nilth's reach has grown long indeed."

Janerron shook his head in disbelief. He settled himself back on his cushion, signaled for the Elfling to go on with his tale with a small flick of his long wrist.

"Anyway," the boy continued, "between some sort of magical fire that leapt out from Ulfiir's hands and a hail of arrows from the soldiers, they finally managed to kill the huge beast."

"Hmmm," Melandric said with a note of interest in his voice. "This Ulfiir you speak of must be a wizard. Yet I've never heard of him." He glanced at Janerron, who shook his head almost imperceptibly.

"I don't know," Shan admitted, uneasily. "It was the only time in seventeen yehrin that I ever saw him do anything unusual like that. He used to tell us such wonderful stories all the time, but that's about all." He shrugged. "Most of the time he just seemed like a kindly old man to me."

Janerron turned his attention back to the boy. "The attack of this beast was not the end of this affair, was it?"

Shan shook his head emphatically several times, adjusted himself more comfortably on the pad. "No," he said weakly. "It was just the beginning really." The three elders raised their brows in curiosity. Shan licked his lips and then launched himself into his account. "That same night a squad of gorguls attacked the village. No one had ever really seen them before either. They'd never even ventured into the forest until that night, as far as anyone could tell." He blinked at the memory. "I wanted to stay and fight them but Ulfiir shoved me out of the village through a secret passage under the walls."

The Elfling spent the rest of the ahr recounting his harrowing chase through the forest. He told them about running madly from targs, how he fell off a cliff and plunged into the giant web of a rith. Solonika shuddered when he described that horrible experience. He told them of his encounter with a mysterious hooded man. He relayed for them how the man had rescued him from certain death before quickly rushing off the next morning on a search for someone he was desperately trying to find in the vicinity. He spoke to them about his friends from Branby, how he'd snuck into Kilgar's room as it was getting dark, and how they had fled together over the rooftops to avoid capture by an invading band of gorguls.

At that point Janerron broke into Shan's narrative to reassure him that his friends were safe. "You'll be able to see them shortly," the Elf Lord told him. "We needed to speak with you first before reuniting you with them." Shan thanked him wholeheartedly before launching himself into another leg of his story.

The three wise Elves interrupted him from time to time, plying him with questions, asking him to clarify a particular detail or simply just to have him recite something for them all over again.

All in all, the Elfling was completely exhausted when their session together was over. Janerron dismissed them with a promise to speak with him further on a later occasion. The Elf Lord encouraged his daughter to take Shan home to rest and enjoy a good meal. "Have your mother look at that gash of his, as well," he told Solonika. She nodded and they rose up stiffly from their cushions. As they were departing through the narrow, chamber door Janerron turned grimly back to his councilors. Shan saw them lean their heads close together and quietly begin to discuss what they had just heard.

When they reached the bottom of the spiral stairway, Solonika laid a light hand on his forearm. "You have certainly been through a lot in the last few days, Shan," the Elf maid told him. She gave him a gentle squeeze on his arm. "And here I thought you had simply blundered off the road in the dark and gotten yourselves lost in Adonath." She smiled kindly at him. "You have shown an incredible amount of courage through all of this."

"Courage?" he protested. "You think too highly of me." He shook his head ruefully before looking directly into those deep blue eyes. "If that's courage," he asked her, "why do I feel so afraid all the time?" Her hand slid down to clasp his reassuringly. "I mean, everyone seems to want to catch me or kill me these days. But I still don't know why." He sank down suddenly on the last of the wooden rungs. "What have I done?" He propped his head in his hands.

Solonika knelt by his side and lifted his chin with a delicate hand. "There, there. It'll be alright," she soothed. "You're in Avalar. You're safe now. Nothing will threaten you in here." She dropped her hand when his anxious eyes came up to meet hers. "I'm sure you'll be able to stay here." She fluttered her long lashes at him.

"Really? Stay here?" His eyes became wide. "You mean that?"

"Certainly," she spoke up confidently. Her gaze shifted from eye to eye as she studied his face. She wiped at the dried blood over his left brow. "You might just have a little scar there," she smiled. He reached up and touched the lump on his forehead a little gingerly.

"Thank you, by the way," he said on a little more serious note. "Thank you for pulling me out of the water." He clutched at her hand for a moment. "After hitting my head like that I could have drowned."

She pulled her hand away a little shyly. "It was the least I could do for a kinsman," she said demurely. He peered into her eyes intently and she blushed. "Come," she spoke after a moment, "we need to get you something to eat."

"That sounds wonderful," he told her. They rose up from the steps and turned out onto the street, back in the direction they had come. She led the way across the cobblestones, laughing at him as he gawked once again at the beauty of the settlement.

"I'm sure my mother can find us a little food," she said sweetly. She licked her lips. "She makes the best griddle cakes in all of Avalar." Shan followed her eagerly, his mouth already beginning to water.

The Elfling stopped suddenly in the middle of the lane. Sunlight splashed down on him through the slowly swaying branches. Solonika turned back quickly to look at him, a puzzled tilt to her head. He had a sudden frown on his face.

"What is it?" she asked him, a serious crease spreading across her own silken forehead.

"It's my friends," he blurted out. "Before we eat, I really need to find them." He rocked his head slightly from side to side. "You know, to make sure they're alright."

The worried look lifted from her delicate features. "Oh, is that all?" she said to him. "I thought perhaps your head was giving you trouble." He shook his head in negation.

"It's still a bit sore," he admitted to her, "but I'm sure I'll be fine. It's not like I'm seeing double or anything."

"Good," she called out with a quick turn to her left. She pointed down another lane and strode off in that direction. Shan watched her agile tread for a moment before starting after her. She drifted daintily across the cobblestones. He caught up to the beautiful girl readily enough, and smiled at her.

* * * * *

Kilgar sat on a wooden bench set against one wall of the small room. It wasn't much of a house, he realized, looking around absently. It was more like a shack or a work shed of some kind. He leaned his head back and closed his eyes. Rimmy squatted in one of the corners, his own head pressed up against the panels of two adjacent walls. He closely followed Doornig with his eyes as he paced incessantly back and forth across the floor. Gorian leaned casually back in the opposite corner. He picked dirt from under his fingernails with a sliver of wood he'd found on the floor.

"When are they gonna let us out of here?" the redhead whined. "We didn't do anything." He stopped his pacing momentarily to glare at Kilgar, who remained motionless on the bench, his eyes coming half-open. "Can't they see we're no threat to them?"

"I'm sure it'll all be sorted out soon enough," Kilgar stated without bothering to look up at him. "Why don't you just sit down and relax?" He leaned his head back against the wall and re-closed his eyes.

"How can I?" Doornig wailed. "For all they know we killed Shan and tossed his body into that pond." He started pacing once again. The others looked at him suddenly in alarm.

"We don't know for sure he's dead," Kilgar offered, a small quaver in his voice. He closed his eyes once more, the small orbs moving restlessly under the lids.

Doornig stopped and whirled to face the older, dark-haired boy. "If he's not dead," the fiery youth stammered, "then where is he?" Kilgar's eyes finally fluttered completely open. He stared back hard at Doornig for a moment, then eventually managed a weak shrug before looking down at the floor.

"There were two sets of tracks at the edge of the stream," Rimmy told them. "We saw them. Didn't we, Kilgar? They moved off toward this village."

Doornig whirled in his direction. "Who knows if even one of those tracks belonged to Shan?" he challenged. "Maybe two other people just picked up his body and carried it off." Kilgar raised his face to look at the redheaded boy. He opened his mouth to say something, then held his tongue.

The hooded warriors they had encountered out in the forest had quickly surrounded them. They had all been quietly disarmed, passing over their scabbardless weapons without resistance. The naked blades seemed to disappear within the folds of the Elves' cloaks in an instant. The small band of warriors had herded the two little parties of boys together without uttering a single word. They guided the group of them through the twisting trees in the mottled morning light, a bristling ring of arrows held constantly in the boys' faces. Even the thorka had been easily led away. Each of their long slender neck straps had been held lightly in one of the Elf warriors' gloved hands. The animals had trotted along beside them willingly enough, nickering softly, their long tails swishing out.

In the haziness under the trees it was difficult to gauge the passage of time accurately. It could have been an ahr, perhaps two, before they had come upon a thickening in the undergrowth. Crowded below the overarching canopy of branches, the heavy growth had struck Kilgar as a form of shield wall. It consisted mostly of dense thorns and wild brambles, packed tightly together, to create a massive hedge.

The leader of their little party had stepped up to a random spot on the barrier and whistled twice. It sounded for all the world like the cry of a bird to them. An answering call had been warbled almost immediately from somewhere beyond the hedge. The throaty cry had only been given once, but then the leader of their captors had repeated his original signal, again whistling twice. After a moment he had stepped back from the thorn barrier and a portion of it seemed to open up slowly before them.

The boys watched in wonder as a section of the heavy thicket five kora wide had receded, and then it had swung off to the side. They had been prodded through the hedge opening by their captors. They watched in fascination as it had slowly returned to its original position behind them. To their surprise they had walked immediately onto a cobbled lane instead of another marshy path. Dozens of passing Elves had stared curiously at them as the soldiers urged them forward. The boys had been totally enchanted as they looked around themselves. There were many odd shaped houses nestled in the trees above their heads, with roped bridges running back and forth between them.

Doornig was positive they had actually stepped out of the real world and onto the pages of a fairy tale. His jaw went slack as he soaked in the sights all around them. "I'm never gonna doubt anything again," he called out quietly. Kilgar had simply chuckled to himself as his own eyes hungrily drank in every beautiful detail.

They had been brought to a halt outside a small building set strangely on the ground under a large tree. The elven Captain had swung the door open and ushered them inside with a gesture of his upturned palm. They had each nodded to him as they stepped through the small door one at a time. They found themselves in a prison cell of sorts, a bare cubicle really, with a lone bench inside. The door had closed immediately behind them, leaving them all alone in the room.

"Hey, wait!" Doornig had cried, pounding on the inside of the door. "You just can't lock us up in here. What about our animals?"

"Leave off," Kilgar had told him. He looked out through the lattice of thin, interwoven slats in the top part of the door. His eyes came in contact with the amber pools of the Captain. The broad cowl left the rest of his face in shadow.

"Please remain here," the gentle voice had told him.

"Wait!" Kilgar had called. The willowy figure had started to turn away but swung back to regard him through the slats. "Can you tell us about our friend?" the dark-haired youth went on hurriedly. "He's an Elf, like you. We were traveling together and we think he got swept down the forest stream. Is he here? Is he alright? Please, tell us."

The eyes regarded him compassionately for a moment. "Be patient," the hooded figure spoke quietly. "All your questions will be answered—in time." The Captain spoke melodically to his detachment in a flowing musical cadence. And then the Elf had turned from the panel and strode off down the lane. Three of the archers remained just outside their cell, relaxing the hold they'd kept on their bows the entire time. They pulled the arrows from the strings and returned the shafts to the long quivers strapped across their backs. The rest of the squad had dutifully padded off after their captain.

Kilgar had watched from the slatted window for a time before crossing the small room and dropping down onto the bench.

"Maybe two other soldiers just picked up his body and carried it off," Doornig repeated, "and they blame us for his death." Kilgar looked up at him with a sad shake of his head. They locked eyes for an instant, but they were interrupted by a sound from the door. They heard a key being inserted into the lock, then it turned with a snap.

They all sprang to the center of the room as the door swung open. Shan dashed into the small shack and hurried up to them.

"Shan!" Kilgar exclaimed in an excited voice. "You're alive!" The two of them embraced warmly, patting each other fiercely on the back. The others quickly joined in the scrum, Doornig included, and they whooped and hollered in sheer relief as they grappled together in the middle of the room. "I knew it!" Kilgar went on in a rush. "I just knew you were still alive."

They pulled themselves reluctantly apart, huge smiles splitting all their faces. They clutched and grasped at one another continually, clapping each other on the shoulders, or slapping playfully at one another's upper arms.

"How did you manage it?" Doornig wanted to know. "You must have bashed your head on the rocks pretty hard."

"I know." Shan held up a hand to show the darkening gash on his forehead. "See."

"Ooh," Rimmy remarked, "looks nasty."

"Tell me about it," the Elfling replied. "Solonika seems to think it might leave a scar."

"Who?" Gorian asked, looking past him.

"Solonika," Shan told them. "She's the one who pulled me out of the stream. Probably saved my life."

The girl had remained standing by the door, allowing the boys to enjoy their reunion. She smiled broadly when she saw how enthusiastically they greeted one another. But when the talk had turned to her life-saving rescue of the unconscious Elfling she had become a little bashful. Shan turned to indicate her by the door and the others all looked around to stare at her in surprise. She took a few steps back, blushing mildly under all their scrutiny.

"Everyone, this is Solonika." Shan lifted his hand to beckon her closer. She drifted in shyly, looking down quite often after as she made brief eye contact with each of their eager faces. They all beamed at her when she stepped up alongside the Elfling. Shan pointed to each of them in turn, giving the girl their names. They nodded individually to her as they were each introduced. "She's the daughter of Janerron, the Elf Lord here." The boys were duly impressed, smiling and nodding at her in open admiration. "I guess that kind of makes her a princess of some kind," Shan went on.

"Almost," she said shyly. Her eyes flitted up to the Elfling's face, gave him a coy smile. Their eyes locked for a moment and Shan smiled at her in return.

"So, how does a person get something to eat around here?" Doornig asked impatiently, suddenly breaking the mood. The Elfling rolled his eyes skyward.

"Yeah," Gorian chimed in. "We've been locked up in here for ahrin and we're starving." Someone's belly rumbled on cue.

"And what about a bathroom?" Rimmy added, squirming around a little. "I really need to go." The others laughed at him, which only managed to make him wiggle a little more.

"Well, Rimmy," Solonika told him with a smile, "let's see if we can do something about that." He dropped his chin in a firm nod. "And as for the rest of you, if you'll follow me to my mother's house, I'm sure she'd be happy to fix something for all of you to eat." The boys erupted in a spontaneous cheer. "We were just about to head over there ourselves." She turned lightly for the door. "Come." The boys eagerly fell into step behind her.

They were stopped abruptly by the three archers standing guard outside the small shack, their hands held out in front of them commandingly. One of the warriors called out something to Solonika in a sing-song voice, but she responded to him so the others might understand her.

"Speak the common tongue," she chided him.

"They must remain here, *Natreya*," the warrior proclaimed. "They are to be kept under watch until it is determined what is to be done with them."

"That is well and good, Varian," she called back to him, "for they shall be with me. I am Border Watch and I shall watch them." She took another light step, but the Elf did not retreat.

"Please forgive me, *Natreya*, but I cannot let them pass." The soldier nervously held his ground. "It is by the order of Bohannon that we obey." He blinked down at the much smaller figure. Her sapphire-colored eyes flashed up at him.

"Is it by the word of Bohannon that you *disobey?*" she demanded with an edge of fire to her tone.

The soldier hesitated. "No, of course not, *Natreya*," he retorted uncertainly. "I'm sure Bohannon would never think to countermand your wishes." He swallowed reflexively. "Nor would I, *Natreya*."

"Good," she purred. "Now step aside or I will speak to my father about it."

"Yes, *Natreya*," he responded quickly, stepping back to permit her a path between them. The two other archers relaxed their stance and did likewise.

"Come," she turned to Shan and his friends, her voice softening to its usual musical tones. "I hope my mother doesn't mind guests." She plodded past the startled sentries and headed cheerfully off down the cobblestone street. The five companions were on her heels in a heartbeat, greatly relieved to be out of their cell at last.

They hadn't traveled far before Shan leaned towards her and spoke quietly in her ear. "What was he calling you?" She looked up at him, her beautiful face drawn into a slight frown. "*Natreya?*" Her frown resolved into a wry smile. "What does that mean?" he asked.

"You really don't know *Keldarin*, do you?" she said with a laugh. He shook his head innocently, waiting for her response. They walked together for a few moments before she turned her stunning blue eyes on him. "Princess," she told him lightly. "It means Princess." He chuckled softly as they continued to patter along.

They weaved in and out of several quiet lanes, passing constantly from sunlight to shadow. Shan still marveled at how different the forest appeared inside Avalar. The ground here was solid under foot, without a trace of the swamp that seemed to dominate the outer fringes of Darkwood. The mighty trees were widely spaced within the boma, allowing for the easy, unhindered passage of scores of individuals, not at all like the dense, closely packed trees outside.

The other four boys trailed along behind them in a state of enchantment. They cried out with delight at each new wonder they viewed within the city. They saw houses above them shaped in very unusual patterns; some were round, others could be seen with six or more sides, some appeared to be stacked upon each other, and one great structure seemed to be balanced across three or four large trees.

They arrived at last at a rather modest dwelling compared to many of those they had just passed. It fit snugly into the crotch of a good-sized tree, but it also had a few side rooms nestled upon some of its broad, outer limbs. These were actually separate dwellings, with a narrow tread of steps seemingly carved into the large branches running down to the main building.

Solonika stopped at a dangling ladder which had been lowered from one end of the house. The stout wooden rungs were firmly attached to thick, ropy vines which had been plaited cunningly together.

"Here we are," the girl said sweetly. "Please come inside."

She clamped one hand onto the heavy vines and began to pull herself up to the house. She had nearly disappeared into a trapdoor in the floor of the structure before Shan felt comfortable enough to follow her. He feared his weight might snap the root-like cords and send the girl plunging painfully to the ground. Solonika poked her head down through the opening and gave him a little wave. He tested the strength of the vines then, satisfied with the result, began to climb up nimbly to the floor above.

Kilgar came next, followed closely by Rimmy, then Gorian, with Doornig pulling himself slowly up after. "Always last," the red-haired youth mumbled to himself as he started to ascend.

Once they had all made the climb, Solonika moved agilely into the dim living room. "Mother," she sang out. "Mother, we have some guests." She leaned her tall bow lightly in a corner.

The floor level changed several times throughout the room, they realized, as they unwittingly tottered and stumbled after her. It had been done to accommodate the natural shape of the tree, Shan correctly assumed, but it made for an interesting trek across the house, especially when you didn't know what to expect in the darkened interior.

"Mother," the girl called out musically once again. "I'm home, and I brought a few guests with me."

"There you are, dear," came another sweet voice from a side room. "Sorry, but I was in the kitchen." A beautiful woman glided into the room. "I was just putting on some water to boil. Thought I'd make some tea." She was wiping her hands on an apron when she stopped suddenly at the threshold. "Oh," she said in surprise as she saw her living room filled with young men. "We seem to have guests." They regarded her cheerfully from the dim interior. She fussed for a moment at her hair. She had bound it back with a woolen fillet, but she yanked it loose with a single graceful tug. The cascades of blond hair fell about her delicate face.

"Solonika," the woman went on, "won't you raise the blinds so our guests may see a little better."

"Yes, Mother." The girl turned obediently, gliding easily around the room to pull down on several of the dangling cords. One after another of the slatted blinds lifted up to reveal many broad windows looking out on all sides of the chamber. The stuffy atmosphere of the darkened room was quickly transformed into an open, breezy causeway. There were still some dappled shadows pouring down through the lightly shifting leaves above the house, so it was by no means excessively bright, but the room took on a much more refreshing feel.

"I'm sorry," the woman told them simply, "I was having a rest. I didn't hear you come in. I like the house fairly dark and still when I nap. Feels more like the nighttime to me, I guess."

"Mother," Solonika said upon returning to the center of the room. "This is Shan," she indicated the elven youth standing a step apart from the others. "He's . . ."

"The orphan," her mother finished for her. She fastened her twinkling eyes on him. "Yes, I know."

"Mother!" Solonika gasped. "There are times I would swear you had the gift of sight."

To forestall her daughter's surprised stare she held up a thin hand. "There's been some talk of an elven lad found by a patrol earlier this morning," the woman stated. "An outsider." She regarded Shan curiously. "Word is he cannot speak even a single word of *Keldarin*." She cocked her head slightly to the side. "News of this oddity has been running through the city like wild fire."

Solonika's relief was evident. "Word does travel pretty fast around here," she said in an aside to Shan.

"Mordana was just telling me all about it before I lay down," her mother continued. "Said she'd even spotted you escorting the boy in question to see your father." She smiled at her daughter. "Trust you to be right in the thick of things, young lady." She turned to the Elfling, offering him a sly wink. "I'm pleased to meet you, Shan," she said in an airy voice. She offered him her graceful hand. "My name is Mirithia. I'm Janerron's wife, if you haven't already figured that out."

"Pleased to meet you, ma'am, ah, milady." He fumbled with her hand before offering a small bow. He turned to the four others who had been standing quietly in the middle of the room. "These are my friends. Kilgar, his brother Rimmy, Gorian, and Doornig."

"Last again," the redhead murmured under his breath. "Last, always last."

"What's that you say?" Mirithia turned to him.

Taken off guard by the sudden attention, Doornig reddened and dropped his eyes to the floor. "Oh, nothing, ma'am," he said after a moment's hesitation. He caught her understanding smile as he looked up. "Just glad to be here at last," he stammered, "and out of that miserable little holding cell."

The woman took them all in with a sweeping glance. Her bright green eyes settled on Rimmy, who tried to hide his grimace. "Through there," she told him kindly, "you'll find what you're looking for." The boy looked up at her, startled. She nodded down a small hallway. "Second door on the left. His eyes looked back and forth between mother and daughter for an instant, then he bolted off gratefully in the direction she'd indicated.

"Thank you!" he called breathlessly over his shoulder as he scurried over the uneven flooring.

The others regarded Mirithia a little apologetically. She glided back over to Shan and dabbed tenderly at his purpling gash. "I'll want to clean that before too long," her voice came in a trill.

"Yes, ma'am," the Elfling responded. "That would be very kind of you."

"So," she purred lightly, "I suppose you'd all care for a bite of food."

"Yes, ma'am," came the delighted chorus of their voices all at once.

"If it wouldn't be too much trouble, ma'am," Doornig added reticently.

"No trouble, boys," the woman answered him with the touch of a lilt in her voice. "Just give me a few mira to see what I can find."

"Of course," Kilgar called out to her as she turned to glide from the room.

"Please make yourselves comfortable while you wait." She waved at some fluffy cushions and several padded chairs scattered around the room before she disappeared into the kitchen. "Solonika," she hummed after a moment, "can you give me a hand, dear?"

"Certainly, Mother," the girl said with a hint of a smile at Shan. She spun lightly on her heel and danced from the room.

22

The Stalker In The Night
[23rd of Kaligath, 4534 C.R.]

Dusk had settled over Avalar. A veil of shadows deepened among the village lanes. Oil lanterns were slowly winking to life where they swung from the ends of tree limbs and along the network of bridges spanning the cozy streets. A torch lighter eased gradually up the winding lanes, his shoes brushing lightly over the cobbles. He lifted up a long, slender bar to each of the unlit lanterns in turn. At its tip the tapering wand emitted a tiny burst of sparks whenever he held it up to the small openings in the glass housing. And then a light flame would spring suddenly to life.

The happy voices of villagers were lifted in traces of animated conversation, and the occasional wisp of a song would unexpectedly burst out somewhere among the quaint rows of tree houses. Shan and his friends, led by the soft, graceful steps of Solonika, were slowly making their way among the crowded avenues of the elven city. They often had to weave their way through clusters of people gathered in the streets. Their eventual destination was the large council chamber where the Elfling had conferred with some of the village elders earlier the previous day.

Janerron had invited their little company to a special dinner with several members of the elven community. The companions chatted amiably amongst themselves as they approached the elevated chamber. The steady hum of insects could be heard among the trees while the night continued to deepen all around them.

Far away, at the edge of the village, an elven sentry attentively patrolled the inside of the defensive boma. Away from the main gate, near one of the small rifts in the hedge, a strange shadow moved outside the barrier. It slid stealthily out of the trees and made its way slowly up to the concealed passage. It paused there for quite a while, listening, sniffing for something, before quietly edging its way through the twisting path in the thorn hedge.

The Elf pacing along inside the wall thought he heard a slight movement within the hedge and stopped by the opening to investigate. He held up a small shielded lantern to check the area thoroughly. He could neither hear nor see anything moving within the heavy thorn barrier. Then, satisfied when his brief inspection revealed there was nothing to be seen but shadows, he began to move off quietly, resuming his usual rounds.

It was then that one of the shadows separated itself from the others and moved phantom-like up behind the sentry. The dull gleam of a knife appeared out of the blackness, catching a stray glint of torchlight upon its small surface. It seemed to hover by itself in the air then came down quickly to slice the unsuspecting patrolman across the throat. The guard collapsed onto the turf in a darkening puddle. The bloodied knife disappeared as the shadow seemed to listen for a time. Then the shadow moved on.

The stealthy apparition slid steadily deeper into the village. It drifted slowly down the lane, passing small groups of Elves as they wandered along, talking cheerfully together under the trees. Several of them paused momentarily in their conversations, certain they had heard a quiet footstep in the lane, yet an expectant glance revealed there was no one there to be seen. Others heard the soft puff of breathing from somewhere beside them, but when they looked, they could find no one within a dozen paces of them. Many a puzzled head was shaken as villagers drifted back to their own conversations.

The ghost-like form continued its inexorable progress through the village. It moved first down one street and then another as it made its way slowly throughout the city. And yet it never appeared to find what it was searching for. It seemed to hesitate for the longest time before beginning to move on once again. The sounds of laughter from one of the raised structures somewhere ahead began to lure it. Where it had rested for a time there were droplets of blood on the smooth cobbles.

The phantom thing slithered softly down the street, its feet scuffing almost silently along. Those passing it by failed even to register its presence. It paused periodically to let others slide by unhindered, stepping quietly aside and freezing in place. After the villagers drifted heedlessly past, it continued on its way, unhurried, until it stood at last before the foot of the stairway spiraling up to the great council chamber.,

A wave of joyful voices rolled out through the unshuttered parlor windows to the street below. Slowly the wraith began to glide towards the stout slats circling the great trunk. Cautiously it ascended the steps, stopping every so often to listen for any signs of detection. About halfway up the staircase there was a slight groaning of wood.

Doornig stood on the wrap-around balcony outside the large chamber. The room had grown a little too hot and stuffy for him, and he had made his way outside to enjoy some cool, fresh air. He stood on the outer decking, leaning idly on a railing, taking in the enchanting view down the lane. He had been staring out over the incredible city in a sort of dreamy

Daryl Hanson

trance when the soft sound of creaking wood brought his head around. But when he looked there was no one there on the steps. Puzzled for a moment, he looked down the stairway, waiting for someone to round the curve of the large tree and climb up into his view. But there was absolutely no one approaching. He shook his head dismissively after a few moments and turned to gaze out over the captivating city once again.

He had nearly forgotten about it when he heard the groan of wood once more, this time much closer. He swung his face back to the spiral of slatted stairs. He slid idly along the rail to the top of the steps, a puzzled frown marking his features. He still couldn't see anything, but he could swear there was someone coming up the stairs in front of him. He scrutinized the steps, waiting until he thought he could see one of the slats move ever so slightly.

Doornig wavered for a moment on the decking, wondering if he was just imagining the sound. A burst of laughter spilled out of the opened doorway behind him. He kept staring down at the winding stairs, half-expecting to see someone there. Doornig heard the hiss of breath close to his face. Then, raising his hand to rub lightly at his cheek, he felt someone brush quickly past him. The redhead heard an unmistakable footstep on the threshold behind him. He whirled to look, but the soft scuff on the wood was already gone, merging into the general noise and laughter within the large room.

Doornig spun about and hurried into the chamber. He stopped just inside the open doorway, scanning the large, crowded room for anything which looked out of the ordinary. When he failed to discern any unusual signs, he quickly located Kilgar on the far side of the hall and hurried in his direction. The dark-haired youth was seated at a table with several young people on the edge of the chamber. He and Rimmy were sharing a joke with a half dozen young Elves around them. Doornig waved impatiently at him. The movement caught Kilgar's eyes. Excusing himself politely from the discussion, he rose up from his cushion to join the redhead by the wall.

"Alright, Doornig," he said, slightly perturbed, "this had better be good."

"It may be important or not," the fiery youth proclaimed, "I don't know." Kilgar flashed him an exasperated look. "I'm not exactly sure, but I think there might be someone here who's not supposed to be."

"Do I look like the event coordinator?" Kilgar snapped sarcastically. He started to turn away, but Doornig snagged him by one arm.

The boy licked at his lips. "I saw—no, I mean—I *didn't* see someone come in here just now."

"You're not making any sense, Doornig." Kilgar was growing irritated.

"Look, I was out on the deck just now, getting some air," Doornig tried to explain. "The stairway creaked like someone was coming up, but when I looked there was no one there."

"Does this story have a point?" the dark-haired boy questioned him impatiently.

Doornig nodded once before going on. "I thought I was only imagining it at first, until I heard it again near the top of the stairs. I looked but I couldn't see anything. Then I sensed someone's breath on my face. It was kind of sour. And then I felt a cloak rubbing up against my leg as someone walked past me. But there was nobody there."

Kilgar listened to his friend with growing interest. "And then what happened?" he asked, narrowing his eyes on Doornig's face.

"I heard a footstep right behind me, but there was still no one in sight," Doornig rushed on. "And then the sounds of scraping feet were lost in the noise of this crowd." Kilgar looked at him in sudden alarm. "What does it mean, Kilgar?"

"It can only mean two things," the dark-headed youth stated matter-of-factly. "There's someone—or something—in this room which has the power to remain unseen." It was Doornig's turn to show alarm.

"Invisible? Unbelievable!" Doornig breathed out with a sudden tightening of his chest. He turned to look around the room, still hoping to catch anything that could not be explained logically. "And what's the other thing?" he asked uncomfortably, when he failed to detect anything out of place.

Kilgar looked him in the eyes. "If someone has gone to all the time and effort it takes to become invisible, not to mention the expense, then he must certainly be up to no good." He swept his own eyes swiftly around the room. "He's most likely not just a common thief. He's probably bent on murder."

"Murder!" Doornig hissed quietly. "Who would he want to kill?" His eyes were suddenly furtive as they swept about the hall, trying to pick out likely candidates.

"With the way things have been going these past few days, I'll give you two guesses," Kilgar said flatly.

Doornig looked up at him in alarm. "Shan!" he exclaimed through clenched teeth. Kilgar nodded secretively.

"It's pretty unlikely," the dark-haired youth said softly, "but it is possible this has nothing at all to do with him. In that event there is one other possible target I can think of." He swung his gaze to the head table, where the Elf Lord was engaged in a quiet conversation with his councilors. "Janerron," he said, tilting his head in his direction.

Doornig looked up at Kilgar, puzzled. "Why would you think that?"

"Oh, some power hungry underling might not like the way his Lordship is ruling the kingdom. History is full of those kind of stories." Kilgar swept his eyes around the room. Out of the corner of his eye he thought he caught a glimpse of a glass tip on its own at the edge of a table. He turned instantly to study the spot. The small cup settled back on the wood, but the liquid inside continued to slosh mildly against the rim.

"So what are we going to do?" The redhead's face was flushed. "Should we warn them?"

Kilgar shook his head slightly. "No, if we shout out an alarm it would only serve to alert the assassin before he strikes." Doornig nodded his understanding. "If he realizes we're onto him, there's no telling what he might do, or who he might hurt, in order to get away."

"I see what you mean," Doornig had to admit. But then another thought struck him. He looked wildly up at Kilgar. "So we just let him do his dirty work?"

"No!" the other corrected him with a hiss, casting a stern eye at the redhead. "Let's plant ourselves close to our two possible targets, and hope we can somehow spot him before he chooses to strike. Watch closely for things which apparently move on their own. Glasses, plates, table cloths. That kind of thing."

"Right," Doornig agreed. He spun around and stared rudely about the tables.

"Not like that, Doornig!" Kilgar chided him. "Looking around suspiciously at everyone will probably just warn our uninvited *guest* we're onto him. Move around the room, try to look like you're enjoying someone's conversation. Only keep your eyes peeled for anything unusual."

"Okay," the redhead nodded firmly, "will do."

"I'll watch after Shan," Kilgar said with a sense of determination. "You concentrate on Janerron." Doornig nodded grimly. "Alright, let's do this." The two of them parted quickly and headed in opposite directions around the outer aisle of the chamber. Doornig moved off to the left, his eyes restlessly searching the rows of tables as he tripped hurriedly along. Kilgar swung to the right, sauntering much more slowly as he moved from table to table.

Shan wondered at the odd behavior of his friends as he sat next to Solonika. He had first noticed Doornig when he'd rushed into the room from somewhere outside. The redhead quickly located Kilgar across the crowded room, but the older boy had seemed about to wave him off in irritation. Yet with something Doornig happened to say to him, the dark-haired youth had suddenly grown extremely interested. The Elfling watched them with growing curiosity as they engaged in animated conversation along the back wall for several mira. At that moment Solonika leaned over and said something lightly in Shan's ear, but when he hadn't immediately laughed at her comment, she turned to find out what had distracted him.

She discovered him watching two of his friends with great interest. "What's the matter?" she asked in her musical voice.

"Huh?" he said, managing to pull his eyes away from them for a moment. He looked at her face, saw the first hint of a concerned expression. "I'm not sure," he told her, "but something definitely seems to be up with those two." He inclined his head at the two boys. Together, they swung their attention to Kilgar and Doornig across the large room. While they observed, the two of them finished their odd discussion and broke apart. They quietly began to circle the room in either direction, their roving eyes probing intently about the tables.

"I can't be certain," Shan informed her, "but it certainly appears like Doornig is looking for something. Only I don't think he even knows what it is. Look how's he's glaring at everyone." They watched the redhead in amusement as he moved awkwardly along the crowded tables. He kept tripping over his own feet, peering strangely over the sea of faces, a queer look in his eye.

"Did he lose something?" Solonika wondered. The Elfling could only shake his head ignorantly. "Notice the way he's searching among the tables," she pointed out. "He's not looking *at* the people, but rather seems to be focusing on their cups and plates and all the other things scattered on the tables." She frowned slightly. "How peculiar."

"Kilgar seems a lot more poised about it, whatever it is they're doing," Shan noticed. Solonika swivelled her cascade of golden locks to look where he had directed.

The dark-headed youth slunk around the left wall of the large chamber in an unhurried curve towards them. He stopped frequently at one table or another, seeming to engage the people in light conversation. Yet his eyes never stopped moving, alertly scanning the entire vicinity. He seemed to make careful note of the position of knives and forks amid the scattered plates and platters, observed the way attendants moved in and out through the tables, listened intently for the tread of their feet.

At one point Shan caught Kilgar looking over in his direction. There was a kind of anxious scowl on his face, like he was extremely worried about something but he didn't want to alarm anyone over it. *What could he be doing?* Shan tried to puzzle it out. Any sharp sound brought the boy to a halt, and he cast quick glances all around until he could identify the particular source of the clatter. And then he would relax his rigid posture, and move on.

The skin on the back of Shan's neck began to crawl. He shivered suddenly, spreading an icy chill, almost clawlike, all the way to his heart. His mouth went utterly dry and he tried to swallow. His tongue rasped against the back of his throat. His gaze came to rest absently on the table just in front of him. A white cloth folded lightly over a basket of sliced bread began to lift and move on its own. Intrigued by the odd movement, Shan watched as it slid off the small woven container and fluttered off the edge of the table. It settled into a lump on the wooden floor. Kilgar must have noticed the anomaly as well, for he suddenly rushed forward, eyes narrowing intently.

The wild cry of someone far down the street abruptly pierced the cool night air. Shan could hear the sounds of running feet pounding over the cobblestones toward the council chamber. Almost immediately a horn, then two or three others, resounded through the open windows. The people in the room exploded into action. They rose up hurriedly from their cushions in a seething mass of running bodies. Glasses tipped over wildly and dishes clattered together in the sudden chaos. The frenzied whine of horns from somewhere close-by peeled through the harsh welter of excited voices. They were immediately echoed from somewhere else further down the lane.

"Intruder!" came the cry from the streets. "Intruder! Intruder! Beware!"

Some of the guests milled about in confusion, casting worried glances around themselves in uncertainty. Most of the others simply scrambled quickly for the door.

Shan bolted up from his cushion. Solonika came up instantly beside him, a light hand on his arm. They watched in utter disbelief as their table lifted itself suddenly from the floor and was dashed aside without any apparent cause. Plates and bowls flew in all directions. The crash of clay pottery and rattling silverware was loud in their ears. Something slipped briefly in the mess on the floor as it hurtled itself forward.

The Elfling turned to shield the girl from danger. He saw Kilgar racing towards him, his lips curling into a yell. A glistening knife materialized miraculously before their startled eyes. It flashed forward in a wicked downward plunge.

"Shan!" Kilgar cried as he threw himself at the unseen threat. The boy lashed out with his arms extended, diving forward where he saw a set of creamy footprints appear on the wooden planking. The dark-haired boy seemed to grapple with an invisible foe for a moment before he lost his grip and skated off to the side.

The knife hovered before Kilgar's eyes for an instant, then swung quickly back toward the Elfling. Shan reached up to try to block the blow as the blade sliced downward.

There was a sudden *thrum* from behind them. The knife point above him wavered for an instant, seeming to hover in the torchlight, as the whistle of movement hissed past Shan's ear. A feathered shaft immediately appeared to sprout before their startled eyes. It embedded itself in the emptiness of the air with a sodden *smack*. A stream of blood poured out where the tip of the arrow danced erratically in their faces. Two more whistling snaps in quick succession sent whirling barbs sizzling past their cheeks.

The slender wooden shafts slugged loudly into an unseen form wavering somewhere in front of them. The ghost-like figure was hurled back several steps by their powerful impact. Strangled moans escaped from the phantom thing as it seemed to wriggle and twist spasmodically. Bright runnels of blood flew off the wildly shifting projectiles which seemed to dance on the air. All at once the heavy clatter of booted feet surged away from them, in the direction of the closest window, scattering fallen cups and plates everywhere. Then, abruptly, the three feathered shafts whirled quickly around to face Shan and Solonika where they could only stare in bewilderment at the macabre spectacle.

A knife suddenly came whistling toward the Elfling. He ducked reflexively as it shimmered past him, to stick, quivering, in the thick beam behind. The warrior with the bow stepped forward and sent another hissing projectile into the phantom assassin. There was an anguished shriek of pain, then the unseen foe toppled backwards through the low frame of an open window.

The people from the head tables all ran to the window to peer down into the street. A crowd of Elves hastily gathered around something that had suddenly fallen from above. The quartet of bloody arrows was the only hint to the presence of the thing which sprawled on the cobblestones below. Startled faces looked up from a pool of crimson slowly spreading out over the stones. A knot of shaken people squeezed in tightly along the chamber window, staring down at them in return.

Janerron found his daughter in the press of bodies and wrapped his arms around her. "Are you alright?" he asked after giving her a gentle embrace.

She nodded numbly. "I'm fine," she proclaimed, leaning back and gazing into her father's gray eyes. "It was Shan he was after, not me." Janerron pulled her in close, an arm circled about her waist.

"Yes, I know," he told her seriously. "But you could have been injured in the attack." He glanced thoughtfully at the elven boy standing on her other side.

Shan looked nervously down into the street. Kilgar had nudged up alongside of him. The dark-haired boy clamped a hand on his shoulder. Their eyes met for a moment.

"Thanks," Shan breathed in little more than a whisper. "I think you may have just saved my life—*again*."

"I'm not sure I'd go that far," Kilgar muttered in return. Shan's look of surprise tempered what he had been about to say. "I mean, I did manage to disrupt his attack, a little." His eyes sparkled softly. "Long enough, at least, to delay his delivery of the killing blow. That archer over there deserves most of the credit. He put four arrows into an attacker nobody could even see."

"True," the Elfling agreed. "I'm just glad Janerron didn't impose the no-weapons-allowed policy on his own personal guard." He looked back down into the lane. "Otherwise . . ."

"Come," Janerron announced to those still remaining in the council chamber. Most of the guests had filed out of the room by now and had wound their way down the spiral staircase to the street below. Some of them had rushed off for the safety of their own homes, but many of the others had spread out to merge with the growing crowd below. The Elf Lord turned from the opened window. "We need to examine this would-be assassin for ourselves," he said adamantly.

The others parted for him as he strode nimbly for the door. Melandric and Kalandan, two of his councilors in attendance, trod lightly after him. Solonika, with Shan and the others, followed eagerly along behind them.

After descending from the enormous tree, the head party approached the feathered hump. Except for the long shafts of the arrows, two of which had been snapped off in the fall, and the widening puddle of blood on the cobbles, the figure remained completely unseen. The Elf Lord reached a hand cautiously down to touch the still mound, but an elven warrior hurried over to intervene.

"Allow me, Sire," the soldier said cautiously. Janerron relented and drew back wisely. The guard shouldered in and prodded the empty space with the glistening tip of a long spear. There was no sound at all from the unseen form nor the sign of any movement. The man prodded the pile again. This time he sunk the razored edge of the weapon into the corpse. He withdrew the dripping blade with a low gurgling sound, yet there was still no response.

Carefully the warrior levered the unseen body over with the haft of his weapon. The two remaining arrows pointed up into the night sky. The Elf warrior reached down and felt around for the invisible form. His hand probed uncertainly about, seeming to grasp at nothing for a moment, then the curved span of his fingers latched onto something solid. He awkwardly patted all over the unseen thing. Finally, he looked up at Janerron and nodded in satisfaction.

"He's dead, my Lord," the warrior spoke firmly. He rose to his feet and stepped to one side. Janerron came forward and knelt down on one knee, his hand extended lightly. "I could not detect any other weapons, sire."

The Elf Lord groped about for a few moments, before settling his long fingers over a somewhat egg-sized object. He grasped at it firmly and pulled it free from the body. Immediately a crumpled form seemed to appear on the stones at their feet. Everyone in the crowd gasped and instinctively drew back a step. Then a few individuals crept closer, raising their flaming torches over the body.

Shan could see a cloaked figure, sprawled upon its back in the flickering torchlight. It looked to be a middle-aged man in very shabby clothing. The sightless eyes were open wide and staring upward, blood completely stained his patched shirt where the arrow shafts protruded. The young Elfling looked quickly over at Solonika. Their eyes locked solemnly for a time, then they turned their attention back to the corpse.

Daryl Hanson

Out of the corner of his eye Shan saw Janerron look down at something in his open palm. He swivelled his head in curiosity. It looked like a large jewel of some kind. Sparks of light from the fluttering torches shot out from the thing. The Elf Lord closed his hand over it when he realized Shan was watching him.

"Search the body," the Clanlord told the soldiers. "Bring anything of interest to me in the council room." And with that, Janerron spun lightly on his heel and strode for the winding staircase. He stopped after a few graceful strides, turned back to those hovering around the bloody heap. "Solonika, Shan," he called, looking at them in turn, "you'd best join us." He shifted his eyes to the dark-haired youth. "And you, as well, Kilgar." The young people nodded at him dutifully. "Send for the rest my councilors," he told a warrior at his side. "And make sure all the humans are present. They should have a voice in this as well." The warrior nodded respectfully and hastened off.

Janerron resumed his approach to the base of the large tree. He rose lightly up the slatted stairs, followed almost immediately by his councilors. Shan met Kilgar's quizzical expression with a reserved look of his own. They turned to observe the soldiers as they finished searching the man's pouch and pockets. They only found one other thing of interest concealed on the body, and that had actually been tightly clutched in the victim's left hand. It was a small flat disk, about the size of a large coin. It was a little thicker than an average gold piece, perhaps twice as thick, Shan could tell, but other than that it was a complete puzzle to him.

"Come on," he encouraged the others. "I'd like to hear what your father's got to say." Solonika nodded to him then led the way back upstairs to the large room.

Most of the mess in the meeting hall had already been cleared away. There were still abandoned plates and glasses in disarray along all the low tables, as well as cushions which had been kicked haphazardly aside in the sudden mass exodus. But the flipped-over table had been righted and the mounds of spilled food had been scooped away. A few attendants still hurried about the chamber, clearing and straightening as they went. But Janerron waved them aside with a mild flick of his hand. They quickly left their duties unfinished and exited out the door in single file.

Once the large room had been emptied and the wooden door shut behind them, Janerron turned to those gathered around the long head table. Shan leaning on the opposite side of the table from him, sat next to Solonika. Kilgar was to the Elfling's right, with Doornig next to him. To the left of the Elf maiden was Rimmy and then Gorian.

The Elf Lord sat with Melandric and Kalandan to either side of him, their hands resting in their laps. Seated to the right of Melandric were two grim looking elven warriors. Bohannon was the captain of the patrol which had brought the boys into the city. Next to him sat Varian, the Elf soldier who had been charged to watch the boys in their holding cell. On the other end of the table, to the left of Kalandan, were two other Elves, who Shan had never seen before. Dressed in simple loose tunics rather than forest garb, they looked more like statesmen than warriors to the young Elfling. He thought these last two were somehow older than the others, but with Elves, he had soon realized, it was virtually impossible to tell. They almost always looked young and vibrant, no matter their actual age.

One of the soldiers who'd searched the body on the street below approached the table from the side. He stopped at Janerron's left elbow and placed the coin-like object he'd found lightly on the table before his Clanlord. He whispered something in Janerron's ear. The elven leader nodded appreciatively before turning to face Shan across the table. The warrior bowed deeply, then withdrew from the chamber, closing the door quietly behind him.

All eyes were fastened on Janerron as he placed an object on the table in front of him. It was large and jewel-like, but it was smooth like an egg, not faceted as one would usually expect of a precious stone. It was deep red in color and almost seemed to pulse with an unnatural light of its own in the dancing light of several torches. The silence was heavy within the room.

"What is it?" Rimmy finally found the courage to ask. Everyone leaned in to take a closer look.

"This," the Elf Lord said to them slowly, "is a *theralon*. An invisibility stone." A hush settled heavily on those around the table. Janerron's gaze swept along the huddled faces. "As most of you have already witnessed, it can enable its bearer to move about unseen. Somehow light rays are bent around it, causing its bearer to become invisible." The eyes of all those gathered together narrowed upon the dark, slightly oblong gem resting on the table top.

"Some would call it a tear of the Creator," Janerron went on. They all continued to scrutinize the object intently. "They are extremely rare, said perhaps to be worth a king's ransom." He looked idly toward the window. Stray wisps of conversation drifted up to them from the lane below. He swept his gaze over the assemblage before continuing. "How an ordinary

Daryl Hanson

assassin, a relatively poor one judging by the condition of the man's clothing, could have come into the possession of such a priceless artifact as a *theralon*, is beyond my ability to comprehend." He leaned back from the edge of the table.

Athiliel's tear, Shan said to himself. He searched his memory but could never recall hearing of such a thing. He shuddered suddenly, realizing how devastating of a weapon it could be. Solonika peered over at him, saw the clouded look in his eyes and gently squeezed his hand. He clutched at her delicate palm with a firm grip, looking down to see their hands clasped together for a moment, then gazed up into her soft eyes.

"Someone is obviously seeking the youngling's life," the Elf Lord spoke again, leveling his handsome countenance on the boy. "They have certainly taken a great deal of effort, first to locate, and then to pursue him across this entire region. The question we must determine is: *why?*"

"That's all well and good," Melandric interposed at that moment. Janerron's furrowed brow brought him up short. The councilor settled himself on his cushion and looked his Clan leader in the face. "That is indeed something we must determine, *eventually*," he began again, "but I feel the more pressing question, my Lord, is how the assassin was able to penetrate our defenses without detection." Janerron raised an eyebrow. "As you say he was employing a magical item to remain unseen, that is given. Even so, he slipped past one of our sentries without being caught or even detected."

"Agreed," Kalandan offered solemnly. "He killed at least one individual already." He swept a hand to point out the window. "How did the assailant even know how to enter the city through the thorn hedge? Who gave him that knowledge? Who might have sold him such privileged information?"

The Elf Lord nodded slowly. "I see your point," Janerron spoke grimly, "and those questions will be answered, I swear to you. However . . ."

"With all due respect, my lord," Melandric interrupted him again, "we must secure our borders immediately." A note of deep concern rang true in his voice. "We must maintain the defense of the city first in order to guarantee our very survival." He looked past Janerron to the two other Elves seated next to Kalandan. They had remained stoic and impassive so far, their hands folded across their laps, their eyes glittering softly in the wavering light. "Arathur, Tinorian? Would you care to share any thoughts?"

The two Elves looked at one another before the furthest one leaned forward and laid his hands on the low table. The long, loose sleeves of his silken tunic dangled over his crossed knees. "I agree with Melandric and Kalandan," Arathur said slowly. "The security of the realm is paramount. If we fail to defend ourselves properly, we will be destroyed, and Avalar will cease to exist. We must prevent that at all costs. And with this task well in hand, then and only then, may we turn to the concerns of outsiders." He looked quickly across the table with a light gesture of his hand toward the young folk. "No offense intended." He tilted his head slightly to the side. "There are already too many evil forces in this world seeking our destruction."

Melandric nodded openly at his words. The boys shared a resigned look before turning back to observe those across the table.

Tinorian cleared his throat after a moment and the entire group swung to regard him. "I see wisdom on both sides of this discussion," he began slowly. "If we are overrun and perish, we will not be able to help our brethren here, who is obviously the target of some very threatening activity." He indicated the elven lad with a small flick of an index finger. "The trend in our world to wipe the Elves from our homes is long and disturbing. After all these yehrin, Vandikar still remains lost to us and the hatred of all other races could very well be our undoing." He paused to take a long, slow breath.

"I believe we must continue to be vigilant," he went on. "Tighten up our defenses. We have to remain alert and on guard at all times to the possibility of a full assault. And yet, at the same time, we must not neglect the lad in this time of great trial. He, too, is an Elf and deserves our help if we can offer it. I advise that we send a few of our warriors to lead him, to ease him on the way to his ultimate destination."

"Wise counsel, Tinorian," the Elf Lord responded soberly with a slow nod. "I would tend to agree with you."

The noble Elf folded his hands once again. "Did you not say he was journeying to Redhaven, my Lord?" Tinorian asked innocently,

"Yes," Janerron returned, "most definitely. At least," and here he looked to the Elfling for confirmation, "that is what I have been led to believe." Shan nodded solemnly. Solonika glanced at the Elfling's response before rounding on her father.

"But, Father," she interjected fearfully, "Shan needs to remain here. It's far too dangerous for him to venture outside the confines of Avalar. Foul beasts out of legend are tracking him. He's being hunted even now by evil creatures who are seeking to kill him. This assassin's failed attempt tonight proves that. Not to mention the words from Shan's very own lips. We cannot begin to fathom the scope of his pursuit. Gorguls, targs, a kurgoth, and now even humans have joined in the hunt. He must be protected." Janerron met her eyes evenly as she continued her impassioned plea. "He's never even been trained, he's not equipped to fend off such overwhelming odds. We should offer to shelter him here, to defend him against their evil clutches."

Janerron leaned back from the table, his daughter's bright eyes boring into him. The Elf Lord took in the faces of his warriors and councilors before turning at last to gaze upon Shan. The Elfling sat without squirming, a resigned look overshadowing his face. Janerron regarded him for some time before letting his gray eyes fall to the tabletop before him. He noticed the coin-like disk lying there, having forgotten all about it in the ensuing discussion. Now he scooped it up in one hand and examined it closely.

The little metal casing was covered with a thin layer of glass. A slender metal needle spun about on a central point within its shallow chamber. It looked for all the world like a small compass. Janerron turned the compact thing in his hand, watched the tiny needle swing back and forth for a few moments before settling into place. He moved it again and the thin metal spur rocked left and right once more. It eventually stopped in the same place it had before.

"That's odd," Kalandan said as he watched the Elf Lord closely. Janerron lifted his head with a grim smile. The others around the table looked on curiously.

"It's like a compass," the Clanlord said to them. "It points faithfully to one spot, no matter how you turn it about." He demonstrated it for them by sweeping his hand slowly to the side and pivoting his wrist in front of them. They all continued to stare at the small thing in his hand. Janerron held it out upon his palm. "The only problem with it," he said to them as the needle came to a stop, "is that it doesn't point north."

"Huh," Doornig spoke up without thinking, "what's it good for then? It would be completely worthless in the wild." Kilgar flashed him a warning look and the redhead clamped his lips tightly together.

"Quite right, my boy," Janerron exclaimed softly. "If you were using it to navigate your way across Ythira it would do you little good." He moved his hand ever so slightly back and forth. They all watched as the needle unerringly spun to indicate the exact same direction it had before. "But if you could set it on another entity—say, on another *person*—it would always guide you to your selected target no matter where it went."

The Elf Lord looked across the table meaningfully at Shan. One by one they all came to the realization that it was pointing directly at the elven youth. Startled by this revelation, their eyes all came up to meet Janerron's.

"Shan, if you would be so kind as to rise up from the table," the Elf Lord spoke in a hushed voice. Slowly, Shan got to his feet. "Now move about the room, slowly, so we may watch the thing at work." Janerron set the device on the low table in full view of them all.

Shan moved to his right, down the entire length of the table. They all watched, breathless, as the slender needle shifted on its own to follow his progress. The boy reached the wall and circled behind the head table, stepping lightly past the elven councilors. The tiny indicator matched his movements precisely each step of the way. The Elfling continued to navigate around the table before returning to his spot and sitting down once more. The needle spiked for a moment then froze as it pointed directly at his position across the way.

"I've heard of this before," Janerron told them. "An unusual tracking device, to be sure. But I have never seen one before with my own eyes. It's terribly insidious." They all lapsed into silence as they stared down at the little object.

Shan suddenly reached out and grabbed it up. He swung about and threw it against a nearby beam with all his strength. The thin layer of glass shattered instantly and the little metal casing cracked and split into several pieces. The elven lad sat down and lowered his eyes to the tabletop where it had lain.

"Sorry," he said quietly.

The room was deathly silent for a time. After a few mira the Elf Lord regarded Shan again before speaking.

"You realize," the Clan leader spoke evenly, "that was most likely just one of many identical devices, all of which may have been attuned to you."

"Great!" The Elfling dropped his mouth open, totally defeated. Kilgar placed a firm grip on Shan's shoulder and Solonika grasped reassuringly at his opposite hand.

"You mean, there could be any number of those things out there somewhere?" Gorian asked in a tight voice. "And all of them pointing to Shan wherever he goes?" The Elf Lord nodded solemnly. The sandy-haired boy whistled alarmingly.

"Then what do I do?" the eleven lad asked in a defeated tone of voice. "We can't very well hunt them all down and destroy them," he muttered sullenly.

"No," Janerron said firmly, shaking his head. "We must break whatever connection they have to you."

"How do we do that?" Rimmy asked, puzzled.

The Elf Lord looked thoughtfully at the youngest member in the room. "That's an excellent question, my boy," he said softly. He stared at Rimmy for a moment before turning back to the Elfling. "There must be something unique about you, Shan," the wise lord spoke slowly. "Some inherent quality that makes you different, distinct in some way from all others, in order for that device to latch onto you rather than anyone else."

"You mean, like being an Elf?" Doornig muttered. He looked quickly from Shan to Janerron.

"That's the idea," the Clanlord returned with a smile. "That would distinguish him from the four of you indeed . . ." The redhead was pleased with himself. ". . . But it must be something more than just that," Janerron finished. "More than just his elven heritage. After all, there are many, many Elves in this city, yet the assassin did not target any other one of us, did he?" His eyes sparkled faintly in the torchlight. Doornig's smile faded into a frown. He wagged his head slowly from side to side, trying to puzzle it all out.

"How about blood?" Gorian suggested hopefully. "The, the thing he described in Draydin, that kurgoth thing or whatever it was, homed in on him because of his blood." He turned to gaze at Shan. "Right?" The Elfling nodded numbly.

Janerron met Gorian's eyes thoughtfully. "I really don't think so," he said firmly. "Blood would only work well for an animal which happened to be somewhere close-by, tracking his scent. But that device would likely function over vast distances. No, it must have been something else, something simple."

"Could it be the clothes he's wearing, or, or something he's been carrying with him all the way from Draydin?" Kilgar asked with an eager look.

Janerron nodded solidly. "Yes, perhaps," the elven leader intoned.

The dark-haired boy's face fell after a moment. "It couldn't be his clothes, though," Kilgar stated, "because he lost most of them on the first leg of his journey and has had to make do with some of mine."

"That's true," Shan had to admit.

"But what about something you've been carrying?" Rimmy piped up. He regarded the Elfling querulously. "A pouch, some coins, maybe a necklace?" The group at the table all turned to gaze at the Elfling.

Shan slowly shook his head, patting at his pockets with both hands. "I had a pouch when we started out through the forest," he said uncertainly. "Weeson gave it to me. But I think I must have lost it when I tumbled into the web of the rith." Some of those at the table, hearing this news for the first time, fastened their eyes on the elven youth with a kind of wonder.

"Think, boy," Melandric retorted somewhat heavily. "There must be something."

Shan continued to shake his head gently as he searched the rest of his clothing. One hand felt along inside his belt and then he suddenly stopped. Carefully, he pulled a dark medallion out of his waistband. He held it between his thumb and index finger. The coiled chain dangled freely as he drew it out and set it on the low tabletop.

A swift hiss of breath came from the row of Elves across the counter. They leaned in close and stared down at the dark metal object as it lay coiled within the loose chain. The Elfling's four companions gazed at it without comprehension. To Shan it still looked like the head of a wild thorka in flight.

"The sign of Korell!" Kalandan spoke in a tense whisper.

"The sigil of the Royal House!" exclaimed Tinorian.

The elven councilors shared an unreadable expression before they all turned back to Shan, their eyes hard on him.

"Where did you get this?" Melandric hissed.

Shan managed a little shrug. "Ulfiir gave it to me," he stuttered defensively. "Well, I actually gave it to him first, as a gift for his birthing day last yahr." He met their steady looks with a timid wag of his head. "I don't even know what it is," he stammered. "I found it in a shop in Draydin. It looked interesting to me, and I thought my guardian would appreciate it. So, I bought it for him." He slowly looked at each of those across the table in turn.

Their hard expressions began to soften and they nodded to one another. "But if you gave it to your guardian some time ago," Arathur asked, "how is it you have it in your possession now?"

Shan shrugged. "The night our village was attacked by gorguls," he explained, "Ulfiir pressed it into my hands before shoving me out into the forest."

"That seems rather suspicious to me," Melandric declared. Janerron looked over at him, saw the seeds of uncertainty swimming in his narrowed eyes. "The kurgoth strikes, the gorguls attack, and you receive this medallion from your guardian. All in the same night?"

Shan's face suddenly darkened. "Now, wait a moment," he retorted with a rise in his voice, "if you're suggesting Ulfiir was in league with the gorguls, then you've got another thing coming!" He sputtered in anger. "If, if Ulfiir had ever wanted to kill me he would have had plenty of time, and opportunity, to do so long before that night!" His eyes flashed hotly. Solonika squeezed his hand soothingly. Shan looked over at her gratefully.

"No one is suggesting your guardian is responsible for all these attacks," Janerron said firmly. He leveled a stern look at Melandric. "Are we?" The councilor shook his head slowly in negation, before the Elf Lord swung his gaze back to the elven boy. Shan settled himself back on his cushion. "However," Janerron went on gradually, "we must consider the possibility that someone else may have put a spell upon this Clan sign."

The Elfling leaned forward thoughtfully, gently bobbing his head.

"Since the time you gave this to your guardian, was there anyone else who might have had some contact with it?" the Elf Lord asked him. "Anyone else you can think of who might wish you any harm?" Janerron watched him closely as the Elfling's brow crinkled in concentration.

"There was a girl," Shan began slowly, "a serving maid who might have known about it. She was sort of there when I bought it. I ran into her as I came out of the shop." He shook his head. "But I don't see how she could have had anything to do with it. She never even touched it as far as I know." He looked Janerron in the eye. "It was on Mid-Summer's Day. We took a little walk to get away from the sneaky pursuit of that greasy tinker."

Shan stopped short, suddenly remembering the beady eyes, the pointed chin, and a long-hooked nose poking out from under a wide-brimmed hat. He looked down for a moment at the tabletop, pursed his lips, then swallowed fiercely. His blue eyes snapped up to meet Janerron's steady gray orbs. "Gravelle," he said sullenly. He licked at his dry lips. "Silas Gravelle."

"The traveling minstrel?" Kilgar queried abruptly. Shan gave him a small nod of affirmation. "Not much of a singer, really," the dark-eyed boy proclaimed. "But he came to Branby several times over the last few yehrin." The other boys nodded their heads in agreement.

"Didn't care for him myself," Gorian stated. "He always seemed pretty sleazy to me."

"Yeah," Doornig added, "his eyes never seemed to stop moving. He kept looking around like he was searching for something, peering into every dark corner." He shuddered lightly.

"Right," Shan responded. "That's him." Shan shifted uncomfortably. "He appeared to take an unusual interest in me, followed me around the village. I just figured at the time he'd never seen an Elf before." His throat constricted at the memory. "He gave me the strangest feeling whenever he was around."

The Elf Lord perked up at this confession. Shan swallowed painfully, the ragged image of the nefarious character floating before his troubled eyes for an instant. He rubbed absently at one of his palms, unaware of what he was doing. He half-remembered a lump there some time ago. It had been some kind of raised mark, he felt sure, like he'd burned himself. But the thought was vague, almost dream-like.

Janerron had noticed his movement. He watched the boy continue to rub at his palm, without seeming to realize he was doing it. "May I see your hand?" the Elf Lord asked softly. Somewhat embarrassed, the Elfling reflexively began to pull his hand down into his lap, but the steady gaze of those calm gray eyes caused him to relent. Slowly, Shan brought his hand up onto the smooth wooden surface. He placed the fingertips of his right hand in the center of the table.

All eyes watched eagerly as Janerron reached out and gently turned the Elfling's hand over. There was nothing unusual to be seen—at first. But as the Clanlord held Shan's hand in his own he slowly moved his other hand above and over the boy's entire palm. A ring on the wise Elf Lord's finger suddenly pulsed to life. A blue gem embedded in the golden band started to glimmer softly.

Shan realized he hadn't even noticed the ring before. He searched the Elf Lord's face as he worked the softly glowing ring back and forth completely over the Elfling's palm. Janerron had closed his eyes in concentration, the shuttered orbs moving restlessly under his lids. After a few moments Shan looked down at his own hand. A spot on his palm began to itch intensely, then to burn somewhat. The ring seemed to slow its progress across his skin, settling at last over the irritating spot. It began to itch and burn a little more, yet the Elfling could see no signs of change. And then suddenly his hand felt like it was on fire and a red mark slowly rose up into a circular bump on his palm.

Janerron opened his eyes and looked fixedly into Shan's hand. He flipped his own hand over, placing the glowing blue gemstone firmly up against the upraised mark. Shan cried out momentarily in pain as the stone seemed to sear at his flesh. He tried to pull back his hand but Janerron held it solidly in place. The boy gritted his teeth at the fiery intensity that lanced through his fingers. Solonika's liquid blue eyes sought out his tortured face as his own eyes darted wildly about the large room. She gripped onto his other hand more firmly, pulling it down into her lap. He bit at his lower lip, and finally managed to relax his own rigidity as the fire slowly receded.

When he looked back at his palm, the angry red lump was gone, and so was the pain. Janerron released his hold and the Elfling quickly pulled back his arm. He looked at his hand suspiciously. The Elf maiden relinquished her grip on his left hand. Tentatively he touched at the spot with his fingertips, then looked up at the Clanlord with a flush of gratitude on his cheeks.

"I think it's gone," he said slowly. He opened and closed his hand a few times in disbelief.

"And that's how they were tracking Shan?" Rimmy asked incredulously. "With some secret mark on his hand?"

"Apparently," reasoned Janerron. He turned to the others. "Anyone with one of those devices attuned to him would be able to follow him anywhere."

"But now he's free of that, right?" Doornig wanted to know. The Elf Lord nodded confidently. "He won't attract gorguls wherever he goes?"

"I don't believe so," Janerron stated. "The spell has been broken at any rate. Now his pursuers must find him in the usual way—*without the use of sorcery.*"

"By their own senses, you mean?" Solonika asked her father. "Using their eyes and ears, their sense of smell?"

"Precisely," the Elf Lord told her. "That might give him a bit of an advantage for a change."

"Thank you," Shan said gratefully, bowing his head to Janerron.

"Now," the Clan chief said as he took in the rest of them at the table, "we need to develop a plan to enable our young friend here to reach his goal." The entire group leaned forward in anticipation. "How can we get him safely to Redhaven? And Arris Junn?"

Donnor's Ferry
[3rd-5th of Bellach, 4534 C.R.]

It had taken nearly a *hand* to iron out the details for their impending journey. Janerron had insisted on supplying them with all they would need for the trip, including food, clothing and even weapons.

Shan stood alone in the little tree house the Elves had made available to them. He balanced a sturdy little knife in his closed fist. It had a graceful hilt and he really liked the way it felt in his palm. He moved it lightly from one hand to the other, then slipped it back into its sheath with a smile of appreciation.

The Elves had provided each of them with their own type of well-crafted sword, as well as a strong knife and a small recurve bow. Shan had balked at the idea of a bow at first. He'd never handled one before and he wasn't absolutely sure it was necessary. But when Solonika had reminded him about their experience with a Feldus Blossom from the clearing, he had capitulated. Varian took the time to instruct all of them in its use. They practiced with them for a few ahrin each afternoon. Within a few days Shan and the others were able to hit a reasonably sized target most of the time. Solonika had smiled at their progress.

"I don't know if it'll ever come naturally to me," Shan observed, "but at least I have a small chance of hitting an enemy before he can reach me." He grinned wryly.

"You'll do fine." Solonika warmly returned his grin. " Just keep practicing whenever you get the time." He nodded agreeably to her. "True marksmanship doesn't come overnight. You have to develop a feel for it."

Their benefactors had also given them forest cloaks like their own. These were a greenish-gray blend, mottled somewhat to blend into the shadows of the forest. Torn in several places, Shan's old cloak had become worthless, but the replacements were even long enough to reach the ground. Should they have need, they could hide their faces within the deep cowls and then cover themselves entirely with the deceptive fabric to blend into a variety of backgrounds.

They also received dark leather gloves which nearly came up to their elbows. Their clothing was relatively plain, yet loose and comfortable, tending to darker shades, like deep green, gray or blue, so as to keep them from standing out against a darkened background.

They were given several small oil lamps to replace the one Shan had used against the ghastly tree slime. They had also received enough oil stored tightly in small flasks to last them for several days, perhaps even more if they used it sparingly.

The food the villagers provided them with reminded Shan of the stuff Altyrian had carried. The packets were wrapped tightly in heavily veined leaves. Much of it had been dried, but a few items seemed fresh and moist. The barsilas leaves had an uncanny ability to preserve food.

Kilgar climbed up the little rope ladder leading into the main floor of the tree house. He scrambled up next to Shan who was hastily finishing his packing. The dark-haired youth snatched up his notched axe and slipped the newly fashioned leather carrier across his back. Shan looked up from his preparations and smiled at his friend.

"It's amazing how they were able to create scabbards and holders for all those discarded weapons you found," he said.

"And really quickly at that," Kilgar stated agreeably. "These elven craftsmen are truly talented."

"I don't think we've even seen the half of their abilities," the Elfling offered flatly.

Kilgar collected the last of his things and turned back to the opened hatchway in the floor. "You almost finished?" he asked the elven youth. "We've got a long ways to go."

"Yes, I know," Shan said to him. "It'll probably take us a couple of days to reach the ferry, most likely." Kilgar nodded his agreement to the Elfling's assessment. "I'll be right there."

The dark-haired youth from Branby caught onto the rope hanging down from the ceiling and swung out onto a stout rung. "Okay," he called as he started to descend, "I'll see you at the bottom."

Shan finished stuffing a few last things into his pack, then bent to retrieve his new bow. His hand hesitated on the carved shaft. Twice over the past three days the Elves of Avalar had to defend their forest from gorgul attacks. Their encroachment was the first time in living memory for most of the Elves. Both times they had succeeded in killing the majority of the foul creatures within their first hundred steps of entering the trees and then had driven the few scattered survivors back out of the forest with their mighty bows. The elven guard had been stepped up considerably since the attack of the assassin, so the warriors were well prepared. Yet tension remained high throughout the forest city.

The sooner we're out of here the better for all of them, Shan thought. He gently lifted the bow and slung it across his back before latching onto the rope ladder and climbing down to the ground. His companions were waiting patiently for him, already mounted up and sitting easily on their thorka. The animals pranced lightly on the cobblestone street.

To their delight the Elves had seen fit to reunite them with their own animals. Newly fashioned bags, more like panniers than simple saddle bags, had been fitted over the long, broad backs of the thorka. Stuffed full of food and other necessities, the travelers were well equipped for the difficult journey which lay ahead of them.

Shan crossed nimbly over to where Kilgar held Adrulax in check. He reached up to take the boy's hand but was interrupted by a low call from the lane behind them. The Elfling swung about to see Janerron approaching them with a small party of his people. The leather boots of the Elves brushed softly over the stones as they came to a halt in a semicircle in front of the boys. Shan was pleased to see Solonika standing alongside her father. He gave her a little smile. She returned it after a moment, though rather sadly, he thought.

"The time has come to bid you farewell," the Elf Lord began firmly. "We have grown fond of you in our short time together." His smile was warm. "We have done all we can to prepare you, to provision you," he said a little sadly, "but I somehow feel it is not enough." He looked out under the trees, to the direction Shan knew they would be traveling. The elven boy sought Solonika's vivid blue eyes, but she held her face down as she stared at the stones about their feet.

Janerron sighed quietly. "War is brewing outside the borders of our forest," he spoke in a gloomy tone. "Several times in the past we have been drawn out of Adonath into the world of men and dwarves. Each time it has brought heartache to my people." He sighed again, louder this time. "We must remain here, hidden for as long as we can, protecting Avalar from all those who would assail it."

Shan looked into his gray eyes with a sinking feeling. He had hoped the Elf Lord would send a detachment of warriors along with them to guide and help protect them, at least until they were well on their way. But as he looked into Janerron's rigid face he knew that it would never happen.

"I wish we could do more than we have already done," the Clanlord said to them, "but I am afraid I cannot send a full team of soldiers with you as you had wished." Shan felt a knot in his throat fall down into his gut. "It is my solemn duty to protect my people and I must do so at times against my better judgment." The Elfling nodded in resignation before clearing his throat to speak.

"We thank you, my Lord," Shan managed to stammer, "for all you have done for us, for me." He looked down briefly at his right hand. "For freeing me from the curse of their trackers, for supplying us all with food and weapons."

"We will always remember your kindness, Lord," Kilgar spoke up. He looked at the others already mounted beside him. "Especially since we are not even from your own people." He bowed his head in respect. The others were quick to comply with his example.

Janerron held up his hand to them. "Are we not all children of Athiliel?" He managed a humorless smile. "Are we not all brothers?" The boys returned his tender expression. "As I was saying, I cannot provide you with a squad of warriors . . . but I can perhaps spare two of my men, for a short time."

Shan and the other boys looked at each other in disbelief. They beamed with a sense of reserved joyfulness.

"It will only be for a short while," Janerron went on. "They may ride with you at least until you can cross the river in safety." The boys' happiness was somewhat tempered by his words. Akthis was no more than two or three days ride away. What would they do after that?

"Many of our warriors sued to be able to accompany you," the Elf Lord continued after a moment. He looked down at Solonika. "Even my own daughter asked for permission, but I have chosen two who will see you safely to the ferry."

Two Elves clomped up behind them upon their own lofty thorka. Shan recognized them immediately from the council chamber. "I think you've already met," Janerron said. "These are two of our best guardsmen." Bohannon and Varian gave the boys a small nod.

Janerron came forward and kissed the Elfling on the cheek. "May Athiliel take care of you, my boy. May He ever guide and protect your steps. And may His will always be done in your life."

"Thank you, my Lord," the Elfling spoke quietly, moved by the gesture. Stiffly, somewhat nervously, Shan bowed before Janerron.

"May He protect all of you," the Clanlord intoned. Janerron stepped back and lifted his hand in salute to the boys as they sat mounted quietly upon their thorka. They all bowed to him in return, leaning stiffly forward in their saddles. "Fare you well," he said with an encouraging wave.

"Thank you, Lord Janerron," they each announced in turn.

Shan raised his own hand to bid the little gathering of Elves farewell.

Solonika suddenly rushed up to him. She wrapped her arms tightly around the Elfling and hugged him, pressing her cheek firmly to his. "I will pray daily to Athiliel for your safety,"she whispered. The beautiful girl stepped back quickly before he had a chance to reply. She turned and ran quickly off down the lane, wiping at a tear in her eye. Shan watched her go until she had sped around a large tree trunk and was lost to his sight.

Janerron looked deeply at the Elfling. "She's young," he told him with a knowing smile. "She's very much like her mother. They both feel things very deeply." Shan nodded after a moment then turned to join the others. Kilgar pulled the boy up behind him with a proffered hand. The riders swung to face the small circle of Elves. They raised their hands in farewell then rode slowly off down the lane. Bohannon led the way to the hedge entrance while Varian dropped back to the rear of their little company.

Elves within the village stopped what they were doing to watch the little party saunter past on their prancing beasts. Shan found himself wiping moisture from his own eyes as they approached the gate. Never had he seen such a wondrous city before in all his life, or such beautiful people. As they bounced easily along he found himself thinking constantly of the Elf maiden with the fabulous blue eyes.

After they had ridden through the hedge gateway they found themselves once again among swampy, close-set trees. Moss hung in tangled strings down from the gnarled branches. Shan looked back once to watch the mysterious seam in the boma come back together.

It took them the better part of the day to reach the edge of the dense forest trees. They twisted and scratched their way in a tedious column without talking. Shan watched warily for small clearings which might harbor one of the hideous Feldus trees. He shuddered softly as he remembered the horror of it. But he never did catch a glimpse of any of the dreadful growths through the wiry tangle of branches.

Once they had cleared the last of the trees in mid-afternoon, Bohannon turned them to the left to ride along the outside edge of the forest. They loped steadily over the lumpy turf, their teeth chattering with every stride of the great thorka.

"Wouldn't it be faster to ride along the road?" Doornig suggested. "We might get to the ferry a lot quicker."

Bohannon continued to jounce along on his mount. "Faster, yes," the Elf captain counseled without turning his head, "but there's a great deal less opportunity for concealment on the highway." He rode on for a few moments. "If we should come across anything undesirable, a party of gorguls, say, we could easily duck back into the woods to elude them."

"Oh," Doornig responded, "that makes sense, I guess."

They rode on for another couple of ahrin until the sun began to settle over a darkening line of trees in the distance. Shan caught a glimpse of a mighty river just this side of the rising mounds of a great forest. Varian spurred up beside Adrulax as they searched the outer edge of Darkwood for a good place to camp. He noticed Shan's gaze and swung in his saddle to stare off in that direction.

"The Tanalorn," he said. "Possibly the mightiest river in all of Ythira." Shan nodded in appreciation.

"I've never seen it before," he said, "not really. I mean, I saw it from a great distance the other day, but that's all."

Varian looked over at the elven boy. "You'll get a better look at it as we draw closer. And most likely the day after tomorrow you'll even be able to cross over it." His amber eyes were drawn back to the distant blue smudge. "And on the far side of that huge water course lies the great forest of Ban-Dolan, home to many of our people for hundreds of yehrin. Two full Clans of Elves dwell in there."

"Really?" Shan asked wistfully.

Bohannon had ridden on ahead for a short ways but had presently circled back with good news. "I found a cut in the trees just up ahead," he called. "The cleft runs back about forty kora and it's well shielded from the forest edge. We should be able to camp there for the night."

"There's none of those Feldy things around, is there?" Doornig wanted to know immediately. His eyes were wide with apprehension.

"No," chuckled Bohannon softly, "there are no blossoms in sight."

"Good," the redhead breathed out. He wiped at his forehead before leading his animal to follow after the elven captain.

They picked their way in the gathering gloom to the spot Bohannon had chosen. They climbed wearily down from their saddles. Shan moved gingerly around the clearing. He squatted and stretched, trying to relieve the tightness he felt in his body. In just a few days within the elven realm he'd completely forgotten how sore and stiff riding all day made him feel.

The night passed uneventfully. After a cold dinner of the flat cakes Mirithia had made for them and a couple of strips of dried meat they bedded down for the night. Bohannon took the first watch, followed by Shan, Kilgar and then Varian.

The morning dawned bright and clear. The travelers broke their fast with handfuls of toasted grain and some slices of *barma* fruit. They peeled back the reddish outer skin and popped sweet segments into their mouths with gusto. The thorka had been left to graze through the night and by morning had their fill of the lush grass in the clearing. Within thirty mira of crawling from their blankets the party was mounted up and riding off again.

They picked their way out of the trees, turning southwest once again, and rode easily along the forest's edge for a time. At several points throughout the day they could see dots moving upon the roadway some ten or twelve korads to the northwest, but could never quite tell who they might be. The Elf soldiers didn't seem to worry much about them.

"Gorguls tend to come out mostly at night," Bohannon told them at one point during their ride.

"That may well be your usual experience," Kilgar countered, "but we've had a couple of run-ins with them during the daylight."

"I said mostly," Bohannon replied a little indignantly. "Unlike some fell creatures which only come out at night for fear of the sunlight, gorguls *can* be abroad during the day. They just don't like it much because they cannot see as well in bright daylight."

"That's good to know," Gorian stated.

They halted once for a mid-day meal, pressing on soon afterwards. Towards the middle of the afternoon the little party drew near to the end of the forest they had been skirting all day. To their right they could see the dark line of the road several korads still to the west of them. Ant-like figures crawled along the packed earth in both directions. Shan could discern some larger shapes as well, wagons and carts of all sizes, being pulled along behind them.

Bohannon reined up on a small hill and looked down at the distant road. Still korads away from their vantage point, they could just make out the broad sweep of the Tanalorn River beyond the road as it sparkled in the sun's failing light. The unexpected beauty took the boys' breaths away. Varian smiled at their reaction.

Their leader turned and pointed more to the west, almost directly in front of them. Reluctantly they dragged their eyes away from the beautiful curve of the river to see where he indicated. "We'll continue on this course, due west, until we finally intersect with the road some korads hence," Bohannon remarked.

"I thought you wanted to stay off the road," Doornig challenged him.

"We have been," the captain said to them. He twisted in his saddle gracefully to look the redhead in the eye. "But once our present course takes us up onto the roadway, it's a direct shot from there to the ferry." The boys all nodded. Bohannon swung his mount around to look at all of them. "Once we leave the comparative safety of the tree line we'll have to ride out in the open the rest of the way. Stealth will no longer be available to us. Speed will be our best ally at that point."

Kilgar could see the sense of it. He nodded approvingly.

"With that in mind," Bohannon went on, "we'll camp here for the night, somewhere within the trees." His eyes automatically searched the edge of the forest for a likely spot. "In the morning, we'll make best possible speed for the ferry." He turned back to the others. "With some luck, and a little hard riding, we'll hopefully get to the crossing before sundown." He turned away from the view and swung his stallion into a walk down the back side of the hill. He worked his way slowly towards the fringe of the woods no more than a stone's throw away. The rest of them fell dutifully into line behind him.

They couldn't find any clearings within the forest this time but they did find a moderate niche along the border of trees. It formed a sort of cove or bower between the thick boles. It was shielded on three sides by the dense foliage, and only lay directly open to the northwest. They gladly made camp even though the sun hadn't quite begun to set.

They relaxed in the little alcove, leaning back in the shade of the spreading branches. The five boys joked softly amongst themselves. Gorian pulled a deck of cards from his pack and they sat around playing Riffin, a local Branby favorite. It took Shan several hands before he began to catch on. Doornig snickered at the Elfling's poor luck, until Shan got the hang of it and started to win occasionally. The redhead stuck out his tongue in concentration.

Bohannon sat with Varian a little apart from the others. They conversed in low tones. Every so often one of them would look back at the boys and nod.

Varian stood the first watch that night. He walked quietly across the grass between the boys and the picket line of their thorka. The six large animals huddled together under the lofty boughs, their long faces nearly touching. An occasional soft snort, the mild whisper of breath, or the swish of a long silken tail were the only evidences of their wakefulness.

The reddish-gold sickle of Kiara had risen much earlier in the day, drifting slowly across the sun bleached sky without anyone really even noticing. It followed the setting sun a short time after they bedded down, dipping lazily below the horizon in a halo of burnished bronze. A short while later, Sheera, the larger of the two moons, rose above the trees to the east in a shower of azure light. The silvery-blue orb was entering its last quarter and cast a soft radiance about their campsite.

Varian gave way to Gorian in a matter of two ahrin. The sandy-haired youth prowled the camp with a wary eye towards the darkness under the trees. At one point he thought he heard movement in the gloom, but the animals remained calm, and he soon abandoned his scrutiny. Sometime later, he was surprised to see the delicate face of a small deer poking its way out of the murky branches, its glittering eyes focused upon him. He watched it for a time as it munched on small leaves and the heads of recently sprouted forest bulbs. It backed away quietly under the trees and was gone.

Doornig took his turn to watch for a couple of ahrin. He yawned continually and his eyes were extremely heavy. He trudged around the little niche before settling down and leaning back against the thick bole of a tree off to one side. Before he knew it Bohannon had relieved him and he thankfully slipped back under his blanket.

Near dawn the Elf captain awakened Varian with a light touch on his arm. The soldier was instantly alert. "Gorguls," Bohannon whispered urgently. Varian got to his feet quickly and agilely.

"Should we wake the boys?" he asked softly.

The captain gave him a quick shake of his head. "We can handle them."

"How many?" Varian questioned as he silently drew out his sword. Bohannon held up three fingers in the moonlight. Varian nodded and followed quickly after his captain toward the left edge of the trees.

They had not gone far when they heard an odd crunching and stomping from not too far away. They concealed themselves behind the last two trunks on that side of the niche, just as the sounds of hissing and gurgling became readily discernible. The two Elves remained motionless, their drawn swords held down along their legs to keep them out of the moonlight. They watched as three hunched shapes skirted the outer edge of the trees.

"They have left the accursed Elf city," one of them hissed softly in their own foul speech. "They'll soon be heading this way."

"We must find a sign of them quickly," another rasped back. "The Black Eyes will want to know as soon as we do."

"Curse the Black Eyes," the first one gurgled in response. "I don't work for them; I work for the Master."

"Shut up!" hissed the third one in line. "We all work for the Master. Black Eyes included. Now just find the Elf boy."

The turf snapped softly as they continued to approach. Bohannon, using hand signs and pointing in turn to the three ugly brutes, easily conveyed his plan to Varian. They waited patiently for the first gorgul to shuffle past their hiding place. It halted after a few paces and bent down over the broken sod. The other two came a few paces behind, hissing and rasping softly under their breaths. At that moment the two Elf warriors sprang silently from their concealment, their swords coming up in a blur.

Bohannon dispatched the first of the trailing pair with a clean thrust of his blade into its back. The foul creature gurgled loudly in surprise as a glistening length of steel suddenly protruded from its chest. The scaly figure collapsed instantly as the sword withdrew.

Varian attempted to kill his opponent in a similar fashion but the clumsy oaf had stumbled on the uneven ground. Thrown to the side, Varian's whistling thrust made only a wicked cut to its ribs. The thing shrieked in pain as it sought to spin away. Blood sprayed the Elf in the face. The bulky form shouldered away from him, desperately clutching for the hilt of its own scimitar.

Bohannon cast a quick look at the two of them as they clashed together, their whirling weapons flashing in the moonlight. The first gorgul barked savagely at the captain, and instinctively the man turned in its direction. His blade came up in instant preparation. There was a quick sparkle of metal a moment before its powerful arm came forward. Bohannon dove to the side. A wicked dagger whistled past his face and skittered harmlessly off a stone. The Elf captain rolled lightly onto his shoulder. He quickly scrambled back up to his feet, cat-like, to face the creature's expected rush.

But the gorgul turned instead and pounded on its metal boots into the small alcove where the boys were sleeping. It took in the prone figures with a hasty glance, charging wildly upon them with a drawn sword. Bohannon sped off after it in pursuit, but he was already several steps behind.

The creature lifted its heavy scimitar over the first sleeper in line. A sudden snap from the darkness to the side caused it to stop, a feathered shaft appearing as if by magic in its chest. It gurgled ferociously as it tottered for a moment over Doornig. The boy stirred sleepily and looked up into the widened slits of the gorgul's eyes. It tried to raise its sword again, but the razored edge of an elven blade from behind took its head suddenly from its shoulders.

Bohannon became discernible to the red-haired youth just as the spewing carcass keeled over. The mighty scimitar flew out from its lifeless fingers.

Doornig scrambled up and away from the body where it collapsed less than a step from his bedroll. "Whew!" he whistled loudly. "That was close." The others had all bolted up from their blankets as well. They huddled eagerly around the fallen form.

Satisfied the immediate threat was gone, the Elf captain turned away and hurried back to help Varian. But as he rounded the edge of the trees, he found the elven soldier kneeling down on the sward, wiping the flat of his blade across the gorgul's body where it lay before him, face down in the grass.

"Sorry to give you a scare," Varian told his captain with a light smile, "but this big fella was a little clumsy." He chuckled. "It threw off my whole stroke." Bohannon shared in the laugh, then offered a hand to help lift Varian back to his feet. "What about the other one?" the junior officer asked as they turned back to the tiny clearing.

"It's dead," Bohannon stated. "Might say it lost its head." It was the captain's turn to chuckle.

Shan stepped out of the shadows, the recurve bow in his hands. Doornig's eyes suddenly went large. "*You* shot it?" he asked incredulously.

The Elfling gave him a little sheepish grin. "I couldn't very well let it kill you, could I?"

"But . . ."

"I heard them coming, I guess," the Elfling stated evenly. "I got up when I saw Bohannon and Varian hurry off in obvious haste." He shrugged as the two Elf warriors joined the boys by the reeking corpse. "I just wanted to be ready for anything," he added, lifting the bow.

"Well done," Bohannon told him. "I wouldn't have been able to get here in time. You probably saved your friend's life." He reached down and grabbed onto the gorgul's harness and started to pull the body away from their camp. Varian turned to help him.

"I guess I owe you my life, then," the redhead told him in a serious tone. "Thank you."

"Don't worry about it," Shan responded. "Before this is all through I can bet we'll owe each other our lives a dozen times over." He placed his hand on the boy's shoulder. Doornig gave him a solemn nod. "Besides, I wanted to see if all that practice Solonika gave me back in Avalar was going to do any good." He laughed a little uneasily and marched off.

The Elf warriors had dragged the three corpses together into a corner of the little niche, hiding them there from immediate discovery. They tried to erase any signs of their scuffle, yet didn't want to take the time to bury or burn them. The smoke would certainly attract unwanted attention, they reasoned. Instead, they just left them piled together for the scavengers, including the severed head. Shan looked back once before they'd gone very far to observe a string of jackards circling overhead.

They rode hard that morning for an ahr or more before slowing their thorka to a walk. They plodded along for perhaps forty or forty-five mira, picking their way along the tufted soil, and then urged the animals into a light canter. An ahr or so later they were running hard again for a short stretch. They continued to vary their speed as they traveled throughout the day, pacing the animals as much as they dared, yet leaving them with a little reserve for an all out burst should the need arise. About mid-day they finally joined up with the earthen roadway. They'd seen it angling towards them for the better part of the morning. Dozens of travelers passed them in either direction. They had slowed their thorka to a walk. Bohannon deemed it wise to appear as if they were in no hurry. They guided their animals through solid lines of carts and wagons. Some people even moved along on foot, clasping their few articles over their shoulders or piled up on knapsacks. Some of them rode laden thorros, and only a few people seemed to own thorka. The fact that they had six of the magnificent beasts gave them looks which revealed more than a passing interest. But it could not be helped.

The two warriors had adopted a couple of low, flat-brimmed hats to disguise their features and hide their elven ears. And once they had left Avalar, Shan had resumed wearing the head scarf Weeson had given him. Still, even with these precautions, they encountered many a curious glance.

Most of the people seemed to be moving eastward. They had come from Akthis with their bales and boxes, no doubt heading for various points up the road such as Falduin, Draydin or beyond. Many of them, perhaps those with very few possessions, were most likely fleeing the growing tensions to the south of Rangoor.

The westering sun was already beginning its slow descent to the horizon before they sighted the ferry in the distance. The city of Akthis stood on the far bank of the river. It was too far yet for Shan to make out many of its details other than the strong log palisade encircling the entire settlement or an occasional tower poking up over the wall. They crested a hill and came to a halt just off the road. They gazed down the long slope of the highway to the plain below. Teams of bathalisks pulled heavy wagons up the hill towards them, their broad padded feet practically filling the entire lane.

After a few swigs from his waterbag, Bohannon turned to the others. "Better be on our way," he called with a nod to their destination. "There's already a line waiting to cross the river." He eased his mount back onto the hard-packed roadway. The others came close on his heels, and together they wound their way down through the on-coming traffic.

Shan watched over Kilgar's shoulder as they maneuvered closer. The river just seemed to get bigger and bigger, its deep blue surface casting sparks from the fading sunlight like a blanket of diamonds. The winding cobalt band stretched from horizon to horizon. Its enormous power and majesty filled him with a sense of awe.

By the time they queued up at the ferry they had eight groups of people in front of them. The first four of them were simple knots of travelers making their weary way along on foot. They each had a few bags and packs piled high in their arms or strapped across their backs. The four remaining groups each had a few wagons or hand carts with them, but only two of those really had any heavy baggage. The loaded wains had a team of thorros to pull them.

Shan's party waited patiently for their turn. The thorka pranced a bit anxiously in the lane as two of the wagons and six groups of foot travelers filed onto the next large, flat barge. A rope was drawn across the front edge of the flat-bottomed craft by a young attendant to prevent others from boarding. Shan heard someone grumble toward the front of the queue. "This always happens to me," a man was mumbling.

"Sorry," called out the deep voice of an older man, probably that of the bargeman. "We're full," he said without the slightest trace of compassion. "You'll just have to wait for the next ferry."

They walked their animals forward into the now vacant slots. The sun was just beginning to set behind the city of Akthis as the barge got ready to push off from the little pier. A great bathalisk stood calmly off to one side, chained to a huge windlass. A thick quadruple braid of ropes ran down from its huge shoulder trace through a series of wooden eyelets on one edge of the ferry and disappeared into the sluggish depths of the river. At a low word from its handler the great animal started forward. The barge slowly began to pull away from the dock. A second large wheel, similar to the first, sat on the farther bank. It turned slowly to take up the slack. Another barge splashed simultaneously across the wide, turgid waters towards them from the farther bank.

The bathalisk's handler urged the mighty beast forward on its large padded feet with a flurry of dust. It snorted loudly and flapped its large ears several times. The heavy windlass turned slowly as the huge creature moved ponderously off to the side.

While they waited Shan took the time to study the city on the distant shore. It was easily the largest settlement he'd ever seen. Its walls were formed of large, banded logs, similar yet somewhat taller and stouter than Draydin's own palisade. The outer structure ran for a korad, if not more, on a single side. There were watch towers spaced periodically on the hefty wall, about every hundred kora or so. Perched atop the walls, these small observation huts were also constructed from sectioned logs with a series of rectangular windows facing outwards. As Shan watched, he could see men in uniform pacing slowly back and forth on an inner walkway between each of the towers.

From the ground level the Elfling could not quite see over the palisade, but he could make out several lofty towers, made of large yellowish-stone bricks. He could also see the tiled roofs of many of the buildings thrusting up into the air.

The alternating barges passed each other in the center of the rushing waterway, steadily cutting their long run across the swollen river. The approaching flatboat presently nestled up neatly against the pier with a clattering of wood. The handler dragged the great bathalisk to a halt in its ponderous progress. It scuffled to a halt in the dirt as the heavy braided rope grew slack on the windlass. A young attendant who had remained on the dock caught a stout rope cast at him from the deck of the large pontoon boat. He threw it over a heavy piling rising out of the bank to lock the craft in place. He then unhitched the rope railing and the occupants from the barge stepped out onto the wide pier in eagerness to be on their way.

After waiting a few moments to allow the dock completely to clear, one of the attendants on the barge beckoned to the next group of people standing in line to board the flat vessel as it bobbed lightly on the cresting breakers. He accepted coins from each cluster of travelers in turn as they scrambled aboard. The little party from Darkwood edged steadily closer. Bohannon leaned over to pull loose a saddle bag tie.

"This will have to be the last load for tonight," a burly voice proclaimed from the back of the barge. "It's already past dusk and we cannot run the crossing once it gets dark." Shan heard grumbling from somewhere behind them. "It's just too dangerous."

There were several torches already set aflame on the broad vessel. These were mounted onto heavy brackets along the side posts of the pontoon platform. The two remaining wagons in front of them trundled over the gangway and rattled up onto the gently bobbing craft. A handful of foot travelers were herded onto the decking as well, their few possessions held closely in their arms.

The closest attendant stopped Bohannon before he could walk his thorka up the planks. "There's not a lot of room left," the man said, eyeing all their animals dubiously. "We're not gonna be able to accommodate six of these beasts. They've got too many legs."

"It's urgent," Bohannon called down to him. "We cannot wait until morning to make the crossing. It could be a matter of life or death." He took out a purse from an opened saddle bag and jingled it meaningfully. The man licked at his lips as he watched the Elf captain swing the leather bag back and forth in front of him as an enticement. "We'll pay well," he said as the man hesitated.

"Well," he said slowly, reaching up his hand longingly for the bulging pouch.

"No!" called out the strident voice of another man from the back end of the barge. "We ain't got room." He shook his head emphatically. "Three's all we can take."

The first man looked over his shoulder at his fellow before pulling down his hand reluctantly. "Three," he told Bohannon. "No more." He grimaced, his eyes straying once again to the bulging purse.

The Elf captain leaned down from the saddle and spoke softly to the man at the gangway. "Make it four," he said with the lifting of one eyebrow, "and you can have it all." The man thought hastily, gave his partner a brief glance, then took the hefty leather bag into his greedy hands with a nod.

"Alright," he said slyly. "Hurry aboard." He stepped back to let them pass.

"Go," Bohannon said. He gave Adrulax a little pat on the hind end. Kilgar spurred his sleek mount forward. "Crowd all of your beasts together. Make them fit somehow."

"But what about you?" Shan cried out as they clattered up the wooden

Daryl Hanson

ramp. Their companions clomped up anxiously behind them. The attendant quickly ran the retaining rope into place.

"This is as far as we may go," the captain told him with a sense of disappointment. "Janerron tasked us with seeing you safely to the ferry, remember? And we have." He shrugged briefly. "I would have liked to take you across myself—but you can see how it is."

At a command from the barge master they cast off their mooring rope. The large ferry surged about in the waves, pulled forcefully against the guide rope. With a whistle and a tap on its great shoulder, the bathalisk handler slowly began to walk the beast backwards. It mewled softly in protest as the great wooden wheels creaked and groaned in reverse. The flat craft drifted slowly out from the dock as the slapping waters surged against its log pontoons.

The five boys climbed down out of their saddles. Just as they did several hissing objects sizzled past them overhead.

"Huh?" Doornig gasped as he nearly fell back onto the decking. "What was that?"

"Crossbows!" Kilgar snapped. "Coming from the shore!"

They all ducked down immediately behind the animals as another swift flight of steel barbs whistled past. One of the bolts struck a side post on the barge with a loud *crack* and it stuck there, quivering. Screams broke out from those huddled along the length of the large flat vessel.

The scattered groups of people left standing hopefully in their queues beside the dock cried in fear and bolted into the night. A troop of gorguls swarmed suddenly out of the darkness and spilled out onto the docks. They struck out viciously with their great swords at those scurrying for cover. One of them ran his curved sword through the chest of the bathalisk handler. The huge animal stamped to a stop without the encouraging voice and gentle touch to guide it any longer. The great windlass ground instantly to a halt. The heavy ferryboat was stranded in the surging waters just a few kora from the pier. Kilgar looked up in alarm, fearing one of the gorguls might try to leap across at any moment. He stepped forward and pulled his sword loose from its sheath. The young dock hand had cowered against a dock piling then darted off quickly into the growing gloom.

Shan watched Bohannon and Varian leap their thorka wildly about on the wooden landing to engage the precipitous enemy rush. Their blades carved through the surging ranks of gorguls with a whistling of steel. The captain cast a wild look back at the barge behind them.

The ragged flow of the river tugged and splashed at the large pontoon boat, frozen in place just offshore. With a powerful hack at the creatures pressing in on him Bohannon wheeled his mount for the stamping bathalisk. The clashing of swords and the close smell of blood only seemed to madden the huge beast. Two foul brutes were attempting to latch onto its thick neck harness but the Elf captain cut them down from behind before they could force the bucking animal to pull the barge back to the dock.

The occupants trapped on the rocking deck milled about with a growing sense of trepidation. They muttered nervously amongst themselves as they watched the pitched battle on the bank sweep around the two lone Elf warriors. The skillful pair sliced and danced about on their thorka. Many of the yellowish-skinned devils fell beneath their whirling blades. Some of the women aboard the ferry cried out fearfully at the spray of blood. They all knew if the savage gorguls succeeded in killing both of the valiant soldiers, the stranded passengers would be completely at their mercy. The frightened people on the sloshing deck all felt a sickening knot in the pits of their stomachs.

"The rope!" screamed Bohannon, all of a sudden, as he parried the awkward thrust of a scimitar near his throat. He circled around the clumsy thrust and slashed out with his own weapon. The keen, elven edge sliced the creature's arm clear off in a precise back-handed sweep. The bloody appendage flew past his face, the curved sword still gripped in its clawed fingers. He looked quickly back at his fellow soldier. "Varian!" the captain cried. "Cut the rope!"

Scrambling about on the dock, Varian slid under a gorgul's vicious over-hand chop. He flicked the heavy blade to the side, dispatched his assailant with a quick thrust of his own sword tip. He spun around on his thorka and raced for the heavy rope leading down the bank from the windlass. He had to fend off several powerful attacks before he could attend to his task. Even with the keen edge of his elven blade it took several powerful cuts before the thick, braided coils of rope parted.

The severed knob of the towline splashed vigorously into the surging river and raced quickly away. Unhindered, the flat bottomed craft was suddenly dragged out into the raging water. The thick cordage slipped through the last of the eyelets and disappeared under the dark waves. The barge was caught by the powerful rushing current and began to spin rapidly away in uncontrollable spirals.

24

River Pirates
[6th of Bellach, 4534 C.R.]

They watched the bank quickly slide away from them. The clash of weapons on the dock was soon lost to the lashing of the waves against their log pontoons. The large raft spun slowly in the rolling swells, spiraling further and further away from the shore. Before they completely lost sight of the pier, Shan thought he saw several of the gorguls break off their attack and hurry to scramble along the bank in pursuit of the drifting ferry. He breathed a silent prayer for the two Elf warriors as they spun away into the darkness.

"That was close!" Doornig cried out in relief. He crossed to the central rib of the barge, where there was a series of wooden benches, and sat down heavily. One of the torches crackled noisily over his head. Several of the other passengers took his example and found themselves places to sit. They plopped down on the heavy timbers, piling their meager belongings on the decking by their feet.

The animals soon became restless on the bobbing wood plating. The large wheels of the wagons had been chocked, Shan noticed, to keep them from shifting too much during the crossing. As it was, some of their cargo had slid about under the lashings. The four riders made sure their mounts were tethered securely to the side railings before coming together by the red-haired boy in the center of the craft.

"So what do we do now?" Gorian asked them as they stood in a circle near the bench.

"We'll have to wait until morning," Kilgar informed the others. "Unless they've got some sweeps hidden away somewhere there's obviously nothing further we can do tonight." The friends grunted in assent. Rimmy and Gorian pulled their cloaks on. A slight breeze kicked up off the river and it was quickly growing chilly.

The dark-haired leader gazed up at the stars for a moment. The night sky was relatively clear, with just a smattering of thin clouds overhead. Kilgar lowered his eyes to watch out in front of them as the untethered ferry continued to rotate slowly on the waves. He tried in vain to pierce the thick blanket of darkness surrounding them. The red-gold sickle of Kiara had been curving across the sky since mid-day and was about to set off to the west behind them. It hadn't quite reached its first quarter, so did little to illuminate their slow, rocking course on the water.

All around them people were settling in for the night. A few passengers pulled out light blankets from their meager luggage and curled up with them where they lay or sat about on the decking.

"Uh-oh," Rimmy called out softly in warning. "Look who's coming this way."

They all turned to see the heavy-set barge master picking his way among the wagons and animals, past sprawling passengers, on his way towards them. His glowering face appeared red in the flickering torchlight. He narrowed his eyes on them as he approached.

"He doesn't look too happy," Shan said through clenched lips.

"I don't doubt it," Doornig replied tersely, "would you be, if you were in his shoes?"

The man stopped by his attendant's side. He whispered something vehemently to him with an angry glare before turning back and stalking over to the boys.

"Who's gonna pay for this?" he bellowed heatedly, stabbing a thick forefinger in Kilgar's direction.

"Pay for what?" the dark-haired youth asked innocently.

The man spluttered in his face. "Pay for the barge!" he cried, gesturing wildly at the decking.

"I'm afraid I don't understand," Kilgar said calmly. "Pay for the *barge?*"

"Puhh! Don't understand?" the barge man ejaculated. He rocked about from foot to foot. He took in all the boys with his ugly stare. "Pay for the ferry, that's what!" His breathing was heavy and close.

"But we paid our fare already," Kilgar told him steadily. "More than enough for all of us, I believe. Even the animals." He indicated the attendant who had come up behind the man and hovered uncertainly at his shoulder. "Just ask your assistant."

The large man turned to level angry eyes on the attendant. The younger man cowered noticeably under his stare.

"I think you'll find your fellow has enough gold in that pouch he accepted to pay for our fares half a dozen times over." Kilgar blinked guiltlessly.

The barge master rumbled something under his breath. He gritted his teeth and stared menacingly into the boy's face. "But who's gonna pay to tow my barge back up river?" he roared. "It's gonna cost a fortune!"

"I don't know," Kilgar said roughly. "And frankly, I don't care." He held his ground. "It's really not our concern."

"Yeah, we were on the raft already, remember?" Doornig interjected.

"We weren't the ones who cut the rope." He smiled at the man innocently.

The big man rounded on the redhead with a vicious growl. Kilgar flashed his friend a look of warning as the boy shrank back a little on the bench. The barge man slobbered as his lips worked without speaking. He spun back to Kilgar.

"You tryin' to say it's not your fault we're adrift in the dark?" the man sputtered. But the boy held his stance firm. "It was your friends as cut the guide rope." He leered at them triumphantly.

Kilgar continued to look the man calmly in the eyes, then he shook his head slowly. "They didn't do it at our bidding," the youth told him. "It's really not our fault. They did it to save all of us." The big man stopped short, a startled look on his face. "There were some pretty foul creatures trying to get aboard the ferry," Kilgar went on, "or hadn't you noticed?"

The two river men looked at each other in surprise.

"You can complain all you want," said the boy from Branby. "But I would have thought you'd be glad to be alive about now." He let that thought sink in for a moment. "Let's face it, if those men hadn't cut the rope when they did, we'd all be dead right now. And then where would your precious raft be?" He blinked twice. "Think about that."

The raging scowl on the barge master's face immediately turned sour. He looked suddenly down at the toe of his boot. He kicked angrily at the decking several times. "I 'spose you're right," he mumbled unhappily. The younger man pulled awkwardly at his collar. His eyes wandered out into the darkness over the water.

"What do you suppose they were after?" the attendant asked idly. "The . . . the *gorguls*, I mean."

Shan gave the man a level stare. "Gold," he said straight faced. "And any other valuables they could get their claws on. Like all this cargo." He pointed towards the wagons. "Or these animals."

"Huh," the younger man said with an eye on the thorka. "Reckon you're right."

"So, where's that pouch, Ranse?" the barge man asked his fellow. The attendant reluctantly reached down and pulled the purse from a pocket in his cloak. It jingled invitingly on his open palm. "Gimme that!" the big man went on, snatching out and wrapping his greedy fist onto the leather bag. He spun instantly and stamped off with the coins in the bag jangling softly. "Now, let's see how much we've got here," Shan could hear the man muttering to himself as he moved away. Ranse hurried after him.

"Gold," Doornig said with a smirk. "And a bunch of blankets and tools. Hah!"

"It satisfied their curiosity, didn't it?" Gorian gave his redheaded friend a little poke on the arm.

Kilgar yawned. He looked up at the diamond studded night sky. "We should probably try and get some sleep," he suggested. "We don't know how long we'll be on this flatboat before we can get off."

"And in the meantime it's taking us in the wrong direction," Shan commented dryly. The dark-haired boy gave him a rueful smile. "But there's nothing we can do about that right now. Unless you want to take a swim in the dark." They nodded at each other.

"Guess we'll just have to wait, then," Rimmy said a little sarcastically, "and cross that bridge when we come to it." He flashed them a smug look.

All the other boys groaned softly and turned playfully to slap at their younger companion.

"Go to sleep, Rimmy," his brother told him. "I'll take first watch, but you can have the second."

"Do you really think we need to set a guard?" Doornig wanted to know. "I mean, way out here in the middle of the river? Who's gonna surprise us?" He snorted skeptically.

"I'm not sure whether those gorguls can swim, but I'd rather not be the first to find out," Kilgar replied.

"Fair enough," the red-haired boy said with a smacking of his lips. "I'll take third watch."

"Okay," Kilgar retorted. "That leaves last watch for you, Gorian."

"Right," the boy said as he pulled out a blanket and made himself comfortable next to Doornig on the bench.

Kilgar yawned again. Shan stepped up to him and laid a hand on his friend's shoulder. "Let me take the first watch tonight. You really need to get some sleep." Kilgar hesitated but the Elfling insisted. "You always seem to take the *corabent*'s share of the responsibilities around here and it's time you got a break."

Kilgar continued to balk, but the Elfling gave him a firm push towards a spot on the decking. "I'm not going to be able to sleep for some time, anyway," Shan told him flatly. "Really." Kilgar finally relented and slumped down against the central bench. It wasn't long before he was breathing slowly and evenly. The Elfling began to prowl the deck, stepping lightly over and around people where they lay.

A short time later Sheera slid up into view above the horizon. The large silvery-blue crescent moon seemed to fill the eastern edge of the sky.

Its pock-marked face was easily discernible and shed a dull blue radiance over everything. The peaks of each wave glistened with its sapphire glow as they continued to float lazily along. The river itself seemed vast, appearing to stretch endlessly across the whole world laid out before him.

He had never seen a river this size before, could never have imagined anything so incredibly wide. It seemed korads and korads across. And the large raft just bobbed along continually, helplessly adrift on an azure sea. The beauty of Athiliel's handiwork took his breath away. A sudden thought caught at his throat. *In the midst of such absolute splendor, how could there be such evil in the world?* He dropped his head sadly in consternation as he moved nimbly about on the gently pitching surface of the barge. People snored softly around him where they were sprawled on the deck planking.

After about an ahr a dark ridge seemed to grow in the center of the huge river. It grew steadily nearer, a kind of deep gloom that could not be avoided. It crept inexorably closer until Shan could recognize an enormous swath of dark trees which seemed to dominate the way ahead. Sheera's ominous blue glow gave the great forest a hazy outline, but it looked for all the world like they would soon be dashed on the ancient sentinels.

"Ban-Dolan," Shan whispered to himself. "It's got to be Ban-Dolan, that immense forest on Kilgar's map." He watched with a sense of disquiet as the huge trees seemed to rush ever faster upon them. "I think the Tanalorn must split up here," he muttered, "becoming two great rivers instead of just one. And the great forest must divide them." He watched in increasing fascination as the large flat boat dipped and rocked a little more strongly.

"What is it?" Rimmy asked him as he climbed up onto his feet. He latched one hand onto a sturdy side post and yawned. He blinked at the bluish glint of Sheera. "We seem to be moving a little faster now." The surging of the raft made his footing a little more difficult.

"The river's about to split apart, I think," the Elfling told him. "Once we get past the break I think the turbulence will settle a bit." He looked at Rimmy beside him. "I hope." The younger boy smiled back at him. "Only, I haven't figured out which way the current will shoot us." He shrugged. "I guess we'll just have to wait and see."

They didn't have long to wait. The raging waters grew a little choppier, but it was soon evident their craft would be swept off to the right. The growing dark wall of the forest began to slip away to port.

Sheera's waning glow played delicately off the tops of the trees, outlining them in a silvery-azure glaze. The powerful effects of the moonlight glancing off the boughs contrasted starkly with the deep gloominess beneath their arching branches.

"That's another home of the Elves, they say," Shan said evocatively. He grunted softly. "My very own people." He watched the limbs rushing past, yet his mind was far away. He wondered what Solonika might be doing at that moment. *Was she sleeping? Was she patrolling the outskirts of the city? Or was she sitting about somewhere in her room, thinking of me?* He shook his head in self rebuke. He would probably never see her again, yet he hoped, he prayed desperately, that wouldn't be the case. Those deep blue eyes seemed ever to haunt his thoughts these days.

The jolting roll of the water soon began to subside, as the Elfling had expected. They drifted onward for a time until the river's surface felt a little more like glass. Shan passed the watch to Rimmy, who kept himself wrapped in his cloak as he leaned casually up against the wooden side railing. "Night," he said to Shan. The elven boy cast him a dutiful nod before he curled up on the deck where Rimmy had been lying next to his brother.

The stars seemed washed out by wispy layers of cloud, so the Elfling found himself studying the pockmarked moon face as he lay awake, his arms folded back under his head. He sighed deeply several times, recalling another beautiful face hovering above him and just out of reach.

The next thing he knew it was morning. The sun peeked over the eastern horizon in a splash of golden bands. The river bank still seemed korads away, but the broad expanse of deep blue water didn't seem to fill the entire horizon like it had last night before it split into its two great arms. The twin torrents wrapped themselves around the rising mounds of trees which looked to thrust up from a long central ridge running between them. The great forest of Ban-Dolan tumbled along towards the northeast for hundreds of korads.

The people aboard the ferry slowly began to stir. None of them had brought much in the way of food with them except the drivers of the two wagons. They each had a single lunch packed under their steering boxes. It was a pretty discontented bunch who milled sullenly around on deck. The hungry passengers watched the boys nibble on some of their dried fruit and nuts with a few covetous glances in their direction while they tried busied themselves folding and stowing their blankets away. At one point Shan offered a little of his own food to a couple of small children traveling with their parents. Mid-bite Rimmy got up and crossed to another family and handed over his meager portion as well. The handful of adults thanked them for their kindness. After a while the two drivers also shared around what they could. It was a somewhat happier group who later moved around on the decking.

They drifted gently onward down the broad waterway. There was nothing they could do to alter their course. Apparently, at one time there had been a couple of long poles with crude paddles on the ends which they carried aboard the raft for just such emergencies. But when they asked the assistant about them, he turned red-faced. One of the poles had been broken some time ago and had never been replaced. The other one had been lost by the attendant's clumsiness a few days before.

"I tripped over the decking and dropped it over the side while I was trying to lash it to the railing," Ranse had confessed sheepishly.

The large, flat craft turned lazily around in circles as it coursed along. One moment Shan's side of the pontoon was facing west, toward the enormous sweep of the great forest. It almost felt like they were gliding backwards along the river at that point. But sometime later, they seemed to be facing more to the east. The land continued to rush by in a blur of green. Shan studied the bank and discovered he could make out the dark line of the road, and if he looked real hard he thought he could just decipher the smudge of Darkwood far to the east at the limits of his vision. His heart ached within his chest as he stared off wistfully into space.

His eyes roamed the bank in an unfocused stare. Suddenly his keen nose detected a trace of smoke on the air. He stood up from the bench where he'd been sitting and scanned the shore. Almost instantly he noticed a small, dusty cloud a ways up on their eastern side. He watched it for some time in idle curiosity before he realized it was the plume of a fire. The smoke rose in ragged billows from a small collection of buildings along the shore. Once the curling blossoms reached a certain height, the wind caught at them and stretched them out like dark brown feathers against the blue sky.

"Hey," Rimmy called out, "there's a fire over there!" He pointed off to the east. All eyes aboard the barge looked off in that direction. "I think it's a little town," he went on, "but several of the buildings arc aflame." People crowded to that side of the large craft to watch.

There were several dots on the river in front of the town. They seemed to skim the surface like birds, or perhaps a collection of water bugs, Shan thought. They were all studying the spot along the bank intently as they continued to drift closer.

After a few moments the darker specks resolved themselves into a handful of sailing vessels. They bobbed on the waves just offshore of the burning structures. Shan could not be certain what they were doing until he saw a flaming object streak from one of the ships, arc over the waves and crash onto a building at the center of town. The small structure burst suddenly into flames as smaller dark specks drifted out from the ships and floated over the waves to the village.

"They're under attack!" Shan raised his voice in alarm.

"Pirates!" the barge master called from his position at the prow. "They're raiding that village."

"Get us out of here," a man among the wagons called out fearfully, "before they see us and come to investigate."

"I don't have any poles, if you haven't already noticed," the big barge man called out truculently.

"Not that they'd reach the bottom here anyway," the attendant piped up, looking casually over the side.

"And I ain't got no paddles, neither," the master added with a sneer. He glanced meaningfully at his assistant. The younger man blushed suddenly before looking away.

"So what do we do?" another wagoneer begged querulously.

"Search me," the barge man offered peevishly. He shrugged. "Stay low and mind our own business, I guess. Maybe they won't even see us 'cuz they're concentratin' on what they're doin'. And then we'll just slide quietly on by without them even noticin' we're here."

"Fat chance of that," another man howled. "Pirates tend to notice everything, especially if there's a profit in it."

"Shut up, why don't you!" the master called through gritted teeth. He watched the shoreline nervously as they were pulled slowly along by the current. "Everyone keep your heads down," he hissed menacingly, "and shut yer traps. All o' youse!"

They all watched tensely for several agonizing mira, drifting, drifting, drifting. They held their breaths, scarcely daring to draw in air for fear the sounds might carry over the water. The boys froze on the decking, kneeling down on their knees, allowing just their eyes to peer over the wooden side railings.

In disbelief they watched the pirates brandish their shining swords to engage farmers with a collection of tools, picks, rakes, hoes and shovels. It was by no means a fair fight. Several of the villagers already lay sprawled on the shore, unmoving. Without any further resistance the bandits were able to drag bleating animals down the bank and thrust them into their long boats. Some of the men could be seen tossing bales of flour and other goods into the waiting hands of fellow buccaneers braced, sure-footed, between the thwarts. Once the small boats seemed stacked well enough with plunder, the rovers raced back down the sloping shoreline to their boats. They piled over the gunwales and quickly shoved off. The long oars struck at the waves like the legs of small water bugs. Smoke from the village continued to rise in thickening clouds behind them.

The pontoon barge slid slowly past the crackling blaze while the long boats skimmed over the tiny ripples to slap against their waiting galleons. Crewman began to throw parcels up over the ships' railings. The boarding party tossed item after item up onto the waiting decks.

The drifting passengers had begun to breathe a little easier once the burning village started to fall away behind them. "Steady, steady," the barge master called softly, eyeing the loading process astern. Parents still kept a hand clamped tightly over the mouth's of their youngsters just in case.

Their anxiety slowly began to ebb until one of the four galleys suddenly seemed to sprout legs. Long, sturdy oars slid out of their thole ports and splashed quickly into the water with multiple jets of spray. The vessel backed oars for several strokes before spinning nimbly on the current in a half-circle. The starboard bank reached forward and the port side oars stretched back, then both sets stroked in opposite directions at the exact same time. The result was a neat little turn almost instantly reversing the ship's position. Both banks of large sweeps paused momentarily in the air, parallel to the water. It gave the ship the look of a large bird poised on the water's surface, ready to take flight.

The sweeps came down simultaneously and dug savagely into the surging flow. They dipped greedily into the swells and then were raised, spilling glistening beads of water to both sides. They carved out a steady rhythm as the galley shot quickly forward. The passengers watched helplessly as the large vessel turned gracefully in their direction and rapidly bore down on them. The great ship drew readily nearer. Some of the women on the ferry cried out in fear, clutching desperately for their children and wrapping them fearfully in their arms.

The cadence of the booms slowed gradually as the galley came alongside of them. The long oars lifted out of the water and shot upwards like wings poised to fly. A cascade of droplets caught the sunlight which turned them into a shower of sparkling jewels. A sun-tanned face peered down upon them from the port side railing. The man wore a wide-brimmed hat which lay low on his head. He had donned it garishly in a sharp angle across his forehead. On one side the brim was folded up and pinned to the low cap, but off to the other it shot out freely to the side, a bright feather thrust into the wide band. Shan took in the man's appearance in an instant. He had thick, dark hair which fell to his shoulders, a neatly trimmed black beard and moustache, and he sported a golden earring dangling from his left ear lobe. He smiled a little avariciously as he gazed down upon the two wagons loaded high with cargo.

"Ho there," he called down in a friendly manner. "Where might you be headin' on this fine morning?"

The barge master cleared his throat and looked up into the man's dark eyes. "The name's Gaff," the man said, a hand shielding his eyes from the slanting sunlight, "Pember Gaff. I run this ferry and we were making a crossing at Akthis. Upriver a ways. Our cable was cut by accident and our boat got washed helplessly downstream." He peered up into the glaring light. "Can you help us out?"

The handsome man looked down from his perch and offered a broad grin. A glint of gold showed in his fine white teeth. "Well, Pember," he purred at the barge man, "it's not so much a question of whether we can help you—I can if it suits me—but it has to do with the *fee* involved." He opened his lips with a little *smack.* "You see, I'll have to charge you for it."

"Fee?" the barge master asked, still squinting up into the sunlight. "What kind of fee?"

"Well, let's see," the man at the railing had to say, "there's a towing charge, not to mention a hook-up fee."

"Hook-up fee?" Gaff wanted to know. He stood with his feet wide-spread on the barge.

"That's right. It involves having my men run a chain from the stern of my ship down to your *craft*," the bronze-skinned man returned. "That would take us a little time to accomplish, not to mention the danger involved."

"And how much does that cost?" the barge man sounded a little cynical.

"It depends," the sailor shot back. The look on the deck man's face told Shan he wasn't sure he wanted to hear the answer. "I can see you have no chain on your deck." He shook his head with a little *tisk-tisk-tisk*. "And that can be a problem." They all looked about the ferry to confirm the man's words. There was no chain, or even a rope of any kind, anywhere in sight. "No worries, though," he went on with a grin. "We can loan you one of ours. However, there is a fee—of course. Call it a rental charge."

"Of course," the barge master concurred dubiously.

"There's also a charge to compensate my men for the strain they'll have to exert." His eyes twinkled under the brim of his hat. "You know, the wear and tear on their bodies, as they pull at the oars for as long as it takes to drag you all the way back to Akthis. We can't very well use our sails to do that. The wind's just not right." The brigand smiled handsomely at them. "That will turn out to be a little expensive, I'm afraid. After all, labor is not cheap these days."

"No, of course not!" Pember Gaff's stomach tightened into a knot. He grimaced at his attendant. "You see what you got me into, Ranse!" he moaned softly.

"And then, as I'm sure you're aware," the seaman proclaimed with a little gleam in his eyes, "there is a cost for all the lost time I'll be incurring while I'm away from my business. For all the lost revenue, you understand." He licked swiftly at his lips. "Obviously, I will need to be compensated for that." He smiled broadly, his gold tooth sparkling brightly in the slanting sunlight. "What do you say?"

"So," the barge master drawled slowly, "let me see if I understand you correctly. You could help us out, as long as we have enough money to pay all the correct fees you require?" The pirate flashed him a playful smile. He pointed an index finger at Pember Gaff and nodded. "And the total amount needed must somehow include a chain rental fee, a hook-up fee, a towing charge, an exertion tax and a charge to cover all the lost wages for your business? Does that about cover it?" the big man asked sarcastically.

"I think so," the privateer stated with another grin. "After all, business is business."

"And what business is that?" Doornig couldn't help asking.

"Why, piracy, of course," the man on the ship called out lightly. His face split into an enormous grin. His eyes twinkled mischievously in the morning light. "I would have thought that was obvious. You did just seem to watch us sack a village, I believe."

The barge master cleared his throat. "Alright, bottom line, how much will it take for you to help us?" Gaff wanted to know.

The grin instantly became more of a leer. The pirate commander narrowed his eyes on the large man on the raft. "I'll need both of those heavy wagons, along with all their cargo, and these four beautiful animals right here." He pointed down at the boys' thorka. "That's all. You can keep the barge."

"But . . . but that's everything!" a man called out from the other end of the planking. "You cannot be serious!"

"Oh, but I'm afraid I am," the handsome pirate proclaimed.

"That's absolutely preposterous!" someone else shouted from the huddle of passengers.

The privateer's expression became severe. He leaned an elbow on the ship's railing. "That's my offer. Take it or leave it." He fiddled with the fingers of one hand before dropping them down onto the wide railing. He tapped them quickly in impatience.

"That offer is utterly ridiculous," the other wagon driver barked out. He tried to laugh confidently but it came out more like a tense cough. The men gathered around him abruptly broke into a verbal free-for-all, each of them raising his voice to be heard over the clamor of the others.

"Shut up!" yelled the barge master. The disruptive squabbling of the men behind him was completely silenced. Gaff looked back up to the grinning privateer, the sun still bright in his eyes. "And what if we choose not to accept your terms?" the man asked nervously. "What then?"

The handsome pirate leaned down over the railing a little, his dark brows narrowing on the barge master. "Then I'll just have to shoot you all and pitch you into the river." Instantly a dozen sailors appeared along the railing, heavy crossbows gripped firmly in their hands. They quickly trained the stocks of their weapons on the passengers below. "I don't think you want to do that," the brigand went on. "So, what's it going to be?" He tilted his hat back on his head with a bent knuckle. The long red feather curled softly in the breeze. "Come, come," he called after the people exchanged horrified glances. "Time is money."

The ferry master looked uneasily at all the people huddled together on his barge. "I'd say we don't have a choice," he told the wagoneers. "But it's your cargo, not mine. You decide for yourselves."

"Death or loss of a single shipment," muttered one of the drivers, "I'd say the choice was pretty simple."

"Yeah, I agree," another man said. "Give it to him."

By now the other three ships had finished their loading of stolen goods and had maneuvered out into the middle of the river to join their captain's galley. The ferryman looked back up at the leering pirate. "If you promise not to harm anyone," Pember Gaff called in a tense voice, closing one eye against the brightness of the sun, "we will accept your terms."

"Good!" the pirate crowed. "That's wonderful. There will be no more bloodshed today." He seemed pleased with himself as he turned to call out orders. "Dag, Tobbin, Rekki!" he bellowed to those somewhere behind him. "Run a chain to that barge. Make sure it's secure. We're bringing home an extra little prize today."

"Aye aye, Captain," a couple of husky voices hollered back.

"Alright," spoke up another sailor. "You heard the Captain, lads. Bring up a chain from below, and make it quick."

"Aye aye," came the loud reply. There was a clattering of feet on the deck plates as men raced off to do his bidding.

The brigand began to turn away from the rail, then abruptly swung back around. "Don't try and do anything stupid," he said with an engaging smile. "My men here will be watching you the whole time. And they can pin a coin to the mast at fifty paces." He laughed with a husky tone to his voice. "Oh, and one other little stipulation, if you please," he told them with a broad grin. "You'll have to pass all those nice weapons of yours up here." He pointed a ringed finger at the boys. "The swords, the bows, and any knives you may have concealed about your persons."

The five companions cast startled glances at each other. Their hesitation prompted the other passengers to gaze at them with disquieting looks. "Come, come," the pirate cajoled them. "You'll get them back eventually, once you're on your way."

"And when will that be?" Doornig asked with a ring of distrust in his tone.

"Sometime soon," the brigand smiled at them. The gold tooth glinted brightly out through his narrowed lips. "Very soon."

The boys still hesitated.

"Hurry up, boys," the thick voice of the barge master ordered. "Don't put us in any more danger than we already face."

In resignation Kilgar slowly unbuckled his sword belt. The others reluctantly complied. One of the sailors reached down with a long, wooden boat hook, and they all looped their belts over the metal barb. The pole was quickly withdrawn and then another was lowered in its place. They slid their bow staves onto it and then their belt knives.

"The quivers of arrows, too," a husky voice demanded.

It took a few moments to unstrap the slim leather carriers and then they too were handed off. Shan suddenly felt naked as they watched the long spars with the last of their weapons being retracted. ,

"Good," proclaimed the pirate captain as he watched the entire process with interest. He laughed again and finally strode off. The uneasy passengers waited to see what would happen next.

A short time later a dull rattling was heard as two men came forward with a long, rusty chain. One of them dropped over the side of the ship and landed on the deck of the barge in sure-footed style. The boys pulled back to give him room. He turned back to the railing above as the second man began passing the bulky links down to him a hand or two at a time.

"Hang on, Dag," he called up to his mate at the railing. "Let me secure this end first."

"Right, Tobbin," the other returned. He waited patiently while the man on the pontoon boat dragged the chain to the low side wall of the barge. The rusty links rattled noisily on the wooden decking.

Tobbin came to an abrupt stop just short of the stout post on the corner of the ferry. "Hey, Dag," he called back over his shoulder, "could you give me a little more slack?" A moment later the chain was played out a little more and the sailor was able wrap it around the post twice, before securing it with a lock he had pulled from his britches pocket. "That's good," he proclaimed. He backed up to the edge of the barge.

One of the long oars was lowered down to the pontoon decking and Tobbin scurried easily up it like a tight rope walker. He hopped over the railing to land next to Dag still holding a portion of the chain in his fist. Together the two sailors carried the chain in their arms toward the stern of the ship. In a matter of moments they had fastened it to the thick railing at the rear of the stern castle.

"Make way," a voice called from the deck of the ship.

"Aye aye," came the immediate answer, and it was echoed down the length of the ship in a series of relays until it was finally repeated on the rowing deck just below the main deck.

The galley veered slightly to starboard, allowing a little space to develop between it and the drifting barge. Once it had sheered away for about half a dozen kora the ship adjusted its course once again to match the pontoon vessel. A command was shouted and the great oars crashed back down into the river. Almost immediately a soft drum began to pound out the slow rhythm to the oar master's cadence. The oars dipped and swept forward in perfect time.

The light galley began to draw away from them. The sweeps dug into the sparkling water again and again, each time kicking up a light spray that splashed the passengers on the barge with beads of moisture.

It wasn't long before the ship had pulled completely past them. The heavy chain carved through the water between them as the ferry swung around behind. The slack slowly tightened until the entire length of the chain was out of the water. The ferry had been drifting side-on down the current for a time, but the tightening of the chain pulled the low craft around to follow the ship with its end point facing forward.

The sense of tension they all felt slowly began to ebb away from those gathered aboard the ferry as their journey dragged on for several ahrin. The sun finished climbing to its zenith overhead and still they plodded along. From time to time Shan watched the other three boats trailing along behind them, but there was little to see except when the sails were unfurled sometime after their outset and the great sweeps were raised up and drawn inboard, dripping with river water. The flapping sailcloth bulged with the light gusting of wind, and the great ships were hurried along. Little whitecaps crested all about them like a sparkling sheen of diamonds.

The rest of the trip, the passengers all settled themselves on the decking, shielding themselves from the harsh rays of the sun as best they could. A few of the people donned hats or scarves, while others tried to fashion make-shift umbrellas from the cowls of their cloaks or a light blanket spread out and tied to the deck posts above them with a little cord.

Shan watched the shorelines slipping by to either side. On their left it was an interminable stretch of dark green trees rising up from the water's edge to blanket vast, ruffled folds of land. Shan wouldn't have called them mountains, but the hills were fairly steep and the dense foliage made them appear intractable. Off to the right the land along the river bank seemed a lot more diverse.

In some places the ground was quite flat and displayed a variety of farms, orchards and vineyards. Occasional villages could be seen dotting the intervening spaces between them. At other times the land gave way to low, rolling hills with sporadic patches of trees. Every now and then the Elfling smelled the hint of a bog near the water's edge. These were fairly small, but their frequency seemed to increase as they moved further north-eastward. At one point Shan was almost certain he could detect a line of forest far to the east.

"Darkwood," he murmured to himself wistfully. He sighed several times before lowering his eyes to gaze forward. He caught Kilgar observing him with a sidelong glance. Their eyes met for a moment before the dark-haired boy looked away, taking in the incredible vista before them. The Elfling sat on the deck, his chin propped on one knee. He closed his eyelids for a moment, imagined a beautiful face framed with cascades of golden hair hovering somewhere just out of his reach. He sighed once again.

It was late-afternoon before anything changed. The sun had begun dipping toward the west, and shadows had started to grow long across the deepening azure surface of the river. Slanting rays still twinkled from the choppy crests of the water. Shan looked up to note a growing patch of green lying directly before them. The foliage seemed somehow different than what they had been staring at all day. The leaves ahead appeared a little sickly, much more yellowish than the great swath of Ban-Dolan upon their left. The smell even seemed rank to him, sort of like there were masses of decaying plants.

"Must be a swamp up ahead," Shan confided to Kilgar. He crinkled up his nose.

The dark-haired boy looked up. He sniffed at the breeze but couldn't smell anything unusual. He looked past the towing galley directly in front of them. With squinted eyes he could make out the lighter green and yellow foliage ahead. "Must be Watcher's Island coming up," he said with a slight pursing of his lips.

"Watcher's Island?" Shan questioned him.

Kilgar looked over at him. "It's a pretty big island in the middle of the Tanalorn," he replied. "Legend has it that it used to be an outpost of some kind in the dim past." He shrugged. "As for whom or what, I cannot tell you. I just noticed it when I looked at the map a little while ago."

"Think that's where we're headin'?" Gorian posed to Kilgar. The dark-haired boy shrugged once again.

"It would certainly make sense," the boy responded after a moment. "If I were a pirate, I'd certainly want a safe haven nestled in a place where no one would ever bother to go. A swamp would do very nicely for that, I should think."

All the boys turned to look where Shan had been gazing. Rimmy scrunched up his face distastefully.

"I think I can smell it now," he said with a grimace. "We're going in there?"

No one bothered to answer as they studied the unpleasant outline of the approaching bog. All four galleys cut through the water on a direct course for the large island in question. Shan could hear the ripple of the sails as they glided closer.

25

Suul'Rar
[6th-7th of Bellach, 4534 C.R.]

The little pirate fleet drew steadily closer to Watcher's Island. It wasn't long before Shan could distinguish the sickly jut of land which loomed directly before them. Just ahead, the great river split in two around the low, flat arm of swampland. The speed of the galley towing flatboat began to subside, the cresting waves along its prow diminished to a mere shallow arc. The sails were slowly being drawn up the yardarm and the thole ports began popping open. The great canvas sheets billowed softly in decreasing gusts as their shrouds were hauled in and tied off at the masthead.

The harsh voice of the oar master could be heard from below decks as the booms slid quickly out of their ports and hovered to either side of the ship like wings. They rested only for a moment before the oar master called them to action. A shouted command brought them slashing down into the river. "Stroke!" called out the blaring voice as the first blow of the drum was heard.

It wasn't long before a gap in the approaching foliage was discovered. The light galley slid easily forward between the close trees. On both sides over-arching branches, slimy with moisture, practically touched the yardarm as they glided into the slot. The surge and pull of the great river fell away behind them, leaving them to rock gently on the calm, greenish water. The barge was pulled quietly along into a broad-leaved jungle.

The boys looked up to watch the tightly packed stalks and branches pass by overhead. Torches and lanterns began springing to life on the ship plying its winding way before them. As the sun fell behind them, the darkening shadows gave the marsh a sinister feel. Sounds were amplified in the confining trees, and the drone of insects filled their ears with noise. Swamp animals swung about from branch to branch. Dark faces watched them in curiosity from their mossy perches in the trees as they drifted slowly along.

The three trailing pirate vessels slapped along behind them in single file. The twisting passage through the jungle growth was too narrow to allow otherwise. Lamps flared dimly from their decks as well, but did little to chase away the deepening gloom.

At one point Shan thought he saw something ahead, but the winding waterway made it impossible to tell. A few moments later he saw what looked like a tower, but it was dark and forbidding and it was quickly concealed in the rush of tall ferns and palm trees.

They broke out of the leafy defile and found themselves in a brackish lagoon. It was a couple hundred kora wide and nearly that long. The water here was murky and still and smelled of decay. The course of their passage sent lapping waves outward across the quiet surface. The lagoon bent slightly to the left as they moved slowly across it. They could see a growing glow surround the end of the curving inlet as they approached.

They skirted round a small finger of land and suddenly came upon a settlement. A series of fixed torches blazed over a long wooden dock where one other ship already rolled softly on its mooring ropes. Several men swarmed over the planking to prepare for their arrival. Shan could hear strident voices barking out orders as the four approaching ships eased up to the dock.

The oars of the lead boat came up with a practiced uniformity, dripping murky water from the tips of their paddles. The long stout poles disappeared quickly into the side ports with a scraping of wood. The ship slid nicely up to the bamboo bumpers. Several hands on the dock caught at ropes cast down from the vessel's railing above. They quickly moved to tie them off on the mooring cleats along the edge of the pier.

Shan took a moment to study their surroundings as the other three pirate ships packed with hooting buccaneers drew up to both sides of the worn wooden dock. The low structure was anchored in place with heavy pilings driven deep into the silt of the lagoon. The long wooden pier thrust out from an ancient stone quay that had been built into the shoreline. A tiled street ran alongside the lagoon where a number of ramshackle dwellings had been erected. These shabby hovels hugging the water's edge were fashioned from scraps of driftwood and other odd pieces of lumber, most likely cast-off from the wreckage of other ships. Just past the miserable structures, a row of palm trees ran down the far side of the road. And rising up out of the shadows beyond, the Elfling could make out numerous large stone buildings now tumbled into rubble.

Shan stared up in amazement at the sprawling ruins of a lost city rearing itself out of the jungle. He couldn't see much of it from his viewpoint. The shielding palms and the swiftly failing light endeavored to shroud the dark mass from even his keen eyesight.

"Hey," Rimmy called after a moment, "there's some kind of city back there." He pointed off into the darkness. The other three boys tore their eyes from the men who were working to off load the plunder from earlier that day onto the stout timbers of the dock. They turned their faces and squinted past the blinding glare of torches into the darkness of the swamp beyond. There was a hint of large stone walls, massive buildings and fallen towers.

"What is this place?" Doornig asked with a touch of awe in his voice. "It looks pretty old."

"I'll say," Gorian responded. "With the amount of vegetation covering those huge blocks, I'd say it was hundreds, if not thousands, of yehrin old." He whistled softly.

"What do you suppose it is?" the Elfling asked quietly.

"I've no idea," Kilgar told him. "It's not on the map." Shan looked at him for a moment. The dark-haired boy could only offer a shrug of his shoulders. "The island's on the map, but not this ancient city."

They had no time for further discussion. A section of the heavy railing on the pirate vessel had been removed and a wooden gangway had been raised up into place. Two of the brigands lumbered down the long ramp, approaching the barge. They latched onto the chain with a long boat hook and pulled the ferry up against the dock. The massive log pontoons scraped gently against the bamboo bumpers tied to the edge of the pier. The younger barge attendant threw a mooring rope from the deck of the ferry to the eagerly waiting hands on the wooden landing. They pulled the flat vessel up snugly and tied it off on another of the large cleats fastened to the wharf. A smaller gang plank was maneuvered into position and the passengers were quickly herded ashore.

The boys attempted to climb into their saddles, but they were instantly warned against it. "Don't you try that, laddie," one of the unseemly sailors called out with a quick wave of his hand. Shan thought the man's name was Dag, the one who'd held the towing chain at the railing of the ship earlier that morning. "You might be tempted to make a run for it on these quick beasts, but old Arak would have a royal fit if'n I let you boys do that. Might skin me alive, he might." He blinked fiercely at them. "Can't say as I'd like that much," he snickered cruelly. "So how's about you fellas walk yerselves down the ramp, slow like, and pull those magnificent creatures gently along after ya."

Kilgar shook his head softly to himself, but complied with the man's order nevertheless. He escorted Adrulax quietly down onto the dock with a calming hand pressed lightly against the stallion's long, sleek neck. Reluctantly he handed the leather reins to the grinning pirate in front of him. Another cutthroat stepped up to Kilgar, spun him about and proceeded to tie his hands tightly behind his back with a stout cord.

"Hey, is that really necessary?" Doornig snapped. "It's an island, after all, and it's already pretty dark out there. Do you honestly think we're gonna try and run out into the swamp?"

"Captain's order," Tobbin spoke up. His face was bathed in a smear of yellow torchlight where he stood waiting next to Dag. "We just do what we're told." He grinned at the redhead as he walked Ruggles down the ramp towards him. "Besides, you boys were the only ones who was armed. Arak thought ya might be a little dangerous." Doornig shook his head slowly as he offered up the animal's neck rope. Before he could make a snotty reply he was turned about unceremoniously and swiftly restrained. "No offense," Tobbin called to him as he was led away.

Shan stepped up to the next pirate and extended his wrists for binding. The man quickly slapped a cord over his arms and pulled his hands tightly together. He looked up at the Elfling's head scarf and grunted. "Been thinkin' yer already a pirate?" he asked with amusement. He didn't bother for an answer, but snagged onto the boy's bound wrists with one grimy hand and tugged him painfully along.

Rimmy and Gorian were quickly trussed up as well, and the whole group was led forcibly past the dilapidated huts on the edge of the stone quay and up the crumbling paved drive leading into the deserted city.

"Those broken down shacks won't be secure enough," one of the men was telling them. *Dag*, Shan thought by the gruff sound of his voice. The great thorka plodded along beside them as they picked their way over the fractured street tiles. Shan idly noticed the smooth stones had been finely carved, with a beveled edge along the outside of each one of the hexagonal-shaped pieces. Tangles of weeds had grown up through the interstices. He stepped carefully over these and the scattered bits of stone along the tiled path.

The pavement led them to the brink of the city, where huge carved blocks of stone formed walls and buildings of tremendous size. Writhing shadows from their torches slithered over the tangled moss and the creamy white stones in little fits and jerks. Light spilled out of one of the large structures on their right, along with howling bursts of laughter. Shan heard drinking vessels being clattered together amid the sounds of loud, unbridled revelry. A thunderous voice could be heard raised well above the others, excitedly recounting the highlights of the day.

"Come on," one of the pirates urged them on with a rough poke in the back, "the sooner we get you installed in one 'a the holding cells down here a-ways, the faster we kin join in on all the fun in there." He licked his lips in anticipation. "Sounds to me as Arak's telling a doozie, by all accounts."

"Arak," Shan spoke up. "I've heard that name several times today. Is that the captain's name?"

"You bet yer boots," another buccaneer spouted off from the front of the detail. "Arak's the captain, true enough. Arak Lazard. The wiliest scoundrel this side 'a Mindlheim."

They tramped on through the dark, expansive ruins, poked and prodded by Arak's men, until they came upon a fairly large building. The upper levels were completely in ruins, the heavy slabs had fallen in and many of the huge stone blocks of its walls were reduced to rubble. But the ground floor here had somehow remained intact. A small door fronting on the street appeared to be the only way in or out.

Their captors led them into the little doorway, stooping somewhat as they entered. One of the men carried a burning brand to light their way. The five companions ducked under the massive stone lintel and found themselves in a spacious apartment. Any original furnishings in the room had long since lapsed into decay, but there were a few stone benches and counter tops still intact, and the artwork on the stone walls was still relatively bright and captivating. They didn't have an opportunity to stop and dwell on the fanciful renderings or the unintelligible flowing script which connected many of the engaging panels together. The writing was incredibly graceful and Shan would have loved to study and ponder what they could see, but their guides led them brusquely down a long corridor to a small space in the back.

The privateers herded them eagerly inside. One of the men stopped just inside the doorway and freed them from their bonds before the boys moved on into the center of the room. Another man pulled an iron gate shut behind them as the brigands exited the room. Rusty hinges creaked loudly in protest as the grated metal frame snapped shut with a heavy *clang,* leaving the boys locked inside.

"You can't just leave us in here," Doornig yelled as the men turned to leave. One of them held a torch up and peered in at them. "What about food, water?" the redhead blurted out. "You took all our packs and supplies."

The man gave them a grim smile. "You had a chance to eat on that barge of yers, why didn't ya take it?" He showed rotting teeth between his open lips. When they didn't respond to him immediately he started to turn away. Another man stepped up and snatched the torch from him as he departed.

He held it out to cast a measure of feeble light into the room. They could easily see there were no other exits from the secured room. "Arak's in a pretty good mood after today's double haul, so maybe he'll be in a charitable mood to spare you boys a little food." He wrinkled his brow. "I can't guarantee how edible it'll be, but I'll see what I can do."

"Thank you," a couple of the boys said in unison.

"What's your name?" Kilgar asked him.

"Rekki," he said with a wink.

"Thanks, Rekki," the dark-haired boy called as the man turned and walked away. After that the small circle of torchlight dwindled off down the hallway then disappeared altogether out of the apartment opening. Kilgar slowly approached the barred door and peered out. He couldn't see much in the darkness but he was fairly positive the brigands hadn't posted a guard in the large outer room, nor even outside in the street. Gingerly he tried the bars. The heavy gate was firmly locked and did not yield. He rattled the door with increasing intensity but his efforts to pry them loose from the opening met with no success. Somewhat frustrated, he turned back to the others who all still stood in the middle of the room, regarding him numbly.

Shan could still hear the raucous cries of the marauders enjoying their dinner party. Many of them were still laughing uncontrollably and singing out boisterously into the night.

Very little light leaked into the outer compartment from the surface street outside, and even less found its way down the narrow passage into their cubicle. For all intents and purposes it was pitch black to the humans in the cell, yet the Elfling could dimly make out the sparse furnishings in their little prison. There were two small stone benches along one wall, with two low slab-like pieces along another. *Probably beds of some kind*, Shan reasoned. But their cushioned mattresses had long since withered away, leaving only a hint of color behind. A thick layer of fine dust covered the floor tiling throughout the room. It gritted softly under their feet as they began to shuffle around in the dark to find a convenient place to rest.

Shan instructed them where to find the heavy furniture and the four boys from Branby fumbled their way out from the center of the room. They cautiously held their hands out in front to keep themselves from colliding with anything in the gloom. Stumbling against the low, stone furnishings, they eventually managed to let themselves down wearily onto the large cool blocks.

"But where are you going to sleep, Shan?" Rimmy asked him as an afterthought

"I'm not," the Elfling answered, "at least not right away."

"You don't think we need to set a watch in here, do you?" Gorian wanted to know. He started to settle into a comfortable position on one of the stone slabs.

"No, of course not," the Elfling returned offhandedly. "I've just got a lot on my mind. I need some time to think some things out." He strolled over to the barred door and rested his hands on one of the metal crosspieces. "You get some sleep. There's no telling what we'll be facing tomorrow."

"That's for sure," mumbled Doornig, already half asleep. He yawned noisily from the other large slab. Kilgar and Rimmy curled up on the smaller benches. Shan glanced over his shoulder to see them all sprawled out on the meager furnishings.

The Elfling looked down the stone passageway and set his eyes on the small doorway in the outer compartment. Kiara had risen in early afternoon while they had been towed down the broad rolling swells of the great river. Tomorrow night would mark its first quarter appearance, yet now, as it drew closer to setting, it poured out only a feeble glow on the outside world. Sheera, on the other hand, was nearing the dark phase of its cycle and its lack of silvery blue radiance would make it especially hard to see out in the swampy terrain of the marsh tonight. *Especially for humans*, Shan thought with a smile to himself.

Even as he watched out through the doorway, the large face of Sheera must have lifted up into the sky over the broad leaves of the swamp. Sickly blue streams shone down over the ruined city and skimmed off the white stone walls. In the faint azure glow, Shan was able to examine the bars more closely.

The heavy gate had obviously been added to the room by the buccaneers in order to create a holding cell of sorts. They had been forced to drill holes into the stone floor and ceiling to house the door hinges. He inspected the mortar where they had filled it in and their workmanship was fairly shoddy. Given enough time Shan felt certain they could chip away enough of the dried mortar to twist their way out of the door, even if they couldn't wrench the heavy thing completely out of its sockets.

The soft murmur of deep breathing drifted over him as he turned back into the room. He prowled along the inner walls, trying to decipher the incised glyphs and pictograms running the entire length of the cubicle. He stopped in front of one panel where the figure depicted upon it was tall and graceful, yet strong. He studied it for some time. The handsome face looked like an Elf to him, but he could not be sure, for the character had a magnificent golden helm which covered his fair head. The thing which caught Shan's attention, though, was the incredible weapon he held out in his hand.

The device was obviously a sword, but it was unlike any other blade he'd ever seen before. It was long and sturdy, yet didn't look heavy or awkward at all. The helmed warrior grasped it easily in one hand. It must have been astonishingly sharp too, for it seemed to cut clear through an opponent's saber as if it were made of straw. Fascinated by what he saw, the Elfling sat down on the floor in front of the panel to study it further. The look of the metal was dark, almost black, unlike the silvery sheen of most swords. The marvelous blade appeared to glow of its own accord. Impulsively Shan leaned to the side to give himself a slightly different perspective. The dark metal seemed somehow to grow clear, almost like glass, but when he came back to an upright position, it had taken on a dark appearance once again.

The sudden change startled him. *It must be a special artistic rendering*, the Elfling mused. A trick of some kind, perhaps using a type of special paint or an unusual technique, to create such an illusion. He'd never seen an effect like that in any other painting before.

He rubbed stubbornly at his face as tiredness set in. He really should find a comfortable spot where he could throw himself down on the floor, right there or in a corner perhaps, to get some much needed sleep. But he just couldn't tear his eyes away from the beautiful artwork.

He looked up suddenly as he heard something stirring in the outer compartment. *Must be Rekki coming back with some food*, he told himself. But the sounds of movement were too soft and stealthy for a booted pirate. Intrigued by the gentle patter on the stone flooring, Shan climbed to his feet and turned quietly for the door.

The Elfling stopped at the threshold and peered out. He could see nothing at first, just the empty outer room down the narrow corridor. The low, clicking noises he heard sounded like delicate feet slapping lightly on the stone flooring. The toes must have had tiny claws, though, for their *tap - tap - tapping* came gradually closer.

All at once, a small shadow moved across the passage entrance and worked its way down the hall towards him. Shan could make out a little silhouette framed against the bluish-silver light which streamed in through the outer door.

The figure was relatively short, not much more than a kor in height, and walked with an odd swinging gait. At first Shan thought it might be some kind of ape, for it was low to the ground and covered heavily with hair. The little thing ventured inquisitively up to the barred gate and peered inside with wide slitted eyes. It blinked up at the Elfling, sniffing and cooing softly to itself. It sat down on its haunches, and stared up at him. Its feet, Shan noticed immediately, were exactly like its hands, with opposable digits, like thumbs, to grip and swing easily through the trees.

Shan wondered briefly if this creature had been one of those he'd seen hanging about in the sickly branches watching them arrive at the lagoon in their four large boats and a ferry.

The little thing looked up at him curiously, then swung its slitted eyes around the room, glancing at each of the sleeping boys in turn. And then it returned its gaze to the Elfling. It sounded as if it muttered something as it peered into his eyes.

"Keh-keh," it seemed to say to him. "Keh-keh."

Startled, Shan looked down at the ape-like creature. He smiled warmly. "You know, it almost sounds like you're talking to me." He gave the little thing a friendly smirk.

"Keh-keh," it responded softly, intently searching his face, his eyes. "Keh-keh." It sniffed again, as if it was trying to identify his scent.

Shan sat down on the floor just inside the gate. He crossed his legs and regarded the hairy little beast. "Keh-keh?" the elven youth talked back to it softly. "Is that your name? Keh-keh? Or are you just looking for some food?"

It perked up as he spoke, its tufted ears shooting up. It cocked its small face to the side, then proceeded to look him over with quick little snaps of its head.

"You are pretty cute, Keh-keh," Shan told him through the bars. He leaned forward to place his own face more squarely in the feeble light.

"Keh-keh," it offered to him once again. This time it reached a curled fist through the heavy metal crossbars and opened a stubby digit to point at him. "Keh-keh," it crooned lightly. "Keh- keh."

"If you're trying to tell me something, little fella," Shan commented slowly, "I'm afraid I'm just not getting it."

"Keh-keh," it said again, a little more emphatically this time. It withdrew its cupped hand and rubbed the back of it along one of its own ears. Shan frowned lightly in consternation. "Keh- keh," it repeated. It reached back through the door and touched its stubby index finger gently to the side of the Elfling's head. "Keh-keh," it told him again. "Keh-keh."

A slow realization began to dawn in Shan's mind. "Are you saying I'm Keh-keh?" he questioned the little creature. "Is that what you're trying to tell me?"

In response the small hairy form pointed at the walls of the rooms, at the paneled artwork. "Keh-keh," it said. "Keh-keh."

Shan turned his head to stare at the walls. Was the thing saying he was like those who built this lost city? Did it somehow recognize him? Was he one of them? He swung back to the hairy little creature, but it had scurried off suddenly. It shot down the narrow passage on its short legs, its longer forearms reaching down to the floor to help speed it along. Disappointed at its quick departure, Shan watched it tear swiftly out through the door, dash across the tiled street, and vault onto the side of another building. It hurriedly scrambled up the outside of the stone structure and was gone from sight in a flash.

He heard a whistle from outside that brought him back up to his feet. The slap of booted feet could be heard as the whistling increased in volume. Shan thought it might have been some kind of sea shanty, but it was so badly off-key he couldn't tell what it was really supposed to be.

Rekki tramped in from the street, ducking under the low doorway with a tray in his hands. A few clay bowls clattered dully together as he loudly marched down the corridor to the heavy iron door. "Ho there," he called cheerfully, stopping by the bars to peer inside. Everything must have seemed pitch black to the man, so he didn't realize Shan was standing there just inside the gate until he spoke.

"Hey, Rekki," the Elfling said to him out of the darkness.

"Oh," the brigand called out with a start, "didn't know you was standing there." Noisily, he blew air out through his lips. "I got some grub for all-a youse." He immediately started to pass small crockery bowls through the bars one at a time. Shan took them and placed them on the floor by the door. "Sorry it took me so long, but everybody was a little preoccupied with their own celebration. I had to dish it up myself."

"That's alright," the Elfling told him with a smile he was sure the man couldn't see. Down the street a ways he could still hear the sounds of merry-making, only the volume level seemed to have dwindled somewhat since they'd first walked past.

The man finished handing the bowls through the door and clapped the tray against his side. "It'll have to do until tomorrow. I'm sure Arak will want to talk to you a little more personally then."

"Thanks," Shan said to him.

"Get a good night's sleep," the pirate said as he started to turn away. "I'm sure you'll need yer wits about ya when you face old Arak Lazard sometime tomorrow." And with that he turned and stalked off.

"What was that?" Rimmy asked sleepily from one of the benches. "Did I just hear voices?" He yawned and peered around through the darkness.

"One of the pirates came by," Shan confessed. "He brought us a little food."

"Food?" Doornig groaned from his slab-like bed. "Did you say *food*?"

"Uh-huh," Shan said to him. "Looks to be some kind of stew." He sniffed at one of the bowls. "Can't be sure of the meat, though. And it's cold."

"That's alright," the redhead proclaimed, sitting up. "I could eat just about anything right now." He started to get up.

"Stay there," Shan offered easily. "I'll bring it to you."

"Well, isn't that sweet?" Gorian said with a yawn. "Bedside service." He rose up onto the edge of the stone bench as Shan brought two bowls over and presented one to each of them.

"Thanks," they murmured at the same time.

"Hey, where's the spoon?" Doornig complained.

"He didn't bring any," the Elfling admitted. "You'll just have to sip it, like soup."

"He probably had orders not to leave us anything we could turn into a weapon," Kilgar spoke up from his position next to Rimmy.

"What? A spoon?" Doornig was dumbfounded. "Some weapon."

"Shut up and eat!" the dark-haired leader told him.

Shan handed bowls to Rimmy and Kilgar, before taking the last bowl himself and sitting down in the corner. They chewed and slurped without talking for a little while.

"Where do you suppose the rest of those people on the barge are being kept?" Rimmy had to ask. "I couldn't see where they got herded off to. How 'bout any of you?"

There was only the sound of smacking lips for a few moments. Finally Kilgar grunted softly. "I'm not sure," he said. "They're probably being held in some of the other apartments scattered across the city."

"What do you think they'll do with us?" Rimmy questioned his brother. His eyes were wide, but the darkness hid his expression from all but the Elfling.

"I don't know," Kilgar told him. "If they were planning on killing us they'd most likely have done it by now."

"Yeah," Gorian observed. "Why feed dead people?"

"That's one way to put it," Shan said sardonically. He set his bowl to the side and stretched his back out against the wall.

Kilgar finished his stew and placed his bowl on the floor. He slid it back under the stone bench. "I suggest we all try and get some more sleep," he advised. "We can worry about tomorrow when it comes."

"Right," his brother muttered quietly. He draped himself out over the bench. The rest of them settled in and quickly closed their heavy eyelids. Within moments they were all asleep again, including Shan.

Dawn didn't immediately see the arrival of any guardsmen to collect them. As a matter of fact, the boys had to wait almost until noon before they were summoned. They simply sat around staring at each other in boredom and studying the curious designs on the walls. A few of them tried deciphering the flowing script displayed all over the white, stone panels. It wasn't any kind of dwarf runes they were certain, nor the blocky scribbles of the common tongue. It didn't appear to be the random scratches of the Uu-Keshi tongue, either, or any other language they might have ever heard.

The letters were beautifully drawn and flowed together in a very artistic fashion. There was nothing plain or vulgar about the way the script was written. The craftsmanship was precise and had hardly seemed to fade after all these yehrin.

Once they failed to solve the mystery of the unknown language the boys eventually lost interest. They scouted around the room to examine the paintings on the various wall panels and discovered several scenes depicting battles with a race of swarthy warriors. Some of the others portrayed foul yellowish-green skinned creatures with tusks, which they reasoned could only be gorguls. A few more displayed an incredible variety of monsters and demons. They saw the likes of three headed targs, an enormous rith, and what looked obviously like a kurgoth. Shan pointed at that mountain of fur with a shiver, the hair on the back of his neck rising stiffly.

"That's what attacked me in my room," the Elfling told them, shuddering violently with the sudden, intense memory. "A kurgoth," he whispered hoarsely. He swallowed at the thick knot in his throat. The others stared at the artwork in amazement, long after the Elfling had moved off.

Shan found himself in front of the panel he'd studied the night before. He sat down and gazed at it with great interest. For some reason it still intrigued him. The depiction of the helmed warrior with his startling sword was entirely captivating. But he couldn't have explained why. The unusual image of the sword seemed to burn itself into his mind as he continued to stare at the panel.

His reverie was broken by the arrival of a small contingent of buccaneers. They tramped in from the street and fanned out through the outer apartment. One of them continued down the narrow passage, his boots shuffling in the dust. He rattled loose a key from a small ring in his fist and fitted it into the heavy lock on the door with a dull *clack*.

"Come on, boys," the man said as he pushed open the door. It creaked solidly in protest. He stepped inside and waited for them, one hand still clamped lightly on the bar until the travelers filed out of the room. He pulled the heavy iron gate shut and followed them out into the street where he shouldered past them to lead the way.

The five companions trailed quietly along after the cutthroat. The other brigands fell into step behind, closing ranks around them, their hands loosely draped over the pommels of their blades as if in warning. The little procession turned to the right onto the tiled roadway in the early afternoon sun, picking their way over the hexagonal stones of the street. The party stopped only once in the middle of the street for the boys to stare about themselves. They marveled at the grand scale of the ancient city, crowing in awe as they craned their necks to take in the incredible view. Even in its ruins, the sight was spectacular. Massive stone blocks were toppled onto the roadway from the collapse of huge buildings and tall, graceful towers. Most of the structures were now covered over with carpets of moss and the thick creeping tendrils of dark-green ivy.

An annoyed pirate shoved them along. "You can gawk later," he said impatiently. "Lazard's waiting to see ya. Now shove off."

Obediently they trudged off after their guide. They were led past the large room where they had all seen the cutthroats celebrating the night before. The large room seemed vacant now and the opened window frames were darkened. They all turned left down a smaller street and found themselves in front of a two storey flat. It had a much more lived-in look than the place where they'd spent the last few ahrin.

The buccaneers prodded them up a half dozen steps onto a small landing. An open portal gaped before them. A trailer of silk arched over the doorway, delicately flapping in the light breeze. They ducked easily under the silken streamer and immediately found themselves waiting in a short hallway on the edge of the captain's apartment.

"Come in, come in," called a cheery voice through the arched doorway. "Welcome to Suul'Kar."

Suul'Kar! The name seemed to conjure up images from the distant past. It was a legendary name to the boys, much like Adonath, but the actual truthfulness of its existence had always been seriously doubted.

Gruffly the boys were ushered into the center of the large chamber by their detail of cutthroats and were left standing before a raised platform. A huge captain's chair sat solidly atop the dias. They stood for a moment gazing about, trying to take in their surroundings.

The place was strewn with paraphernalia from sea-going vessels. In fact, the whole room looked as if it had been torn out of a captain's cabin. There was a ship's clock situated in one corner. The time was obviously wrong, Shan noticed absently, but it *ticked* on nonetheless. A rope hammock was stretched out and strapped to a couple of pillars in another portion of the chamber. A block and tackle had been bolted to a side wall, with a series of ropes running through it to hold a large chandelier suspended in place over the main floor area. The chairs along the last wall were actually just a set of rowing benches ripped from the lower deck of a ship.

Not too comfortable, Shan thought.

Colorful swaths of silk and snatches of old sail cloth ran along the ceiling. These were nailed or stapled to the wood in various places, and gave the room the feel of a large tent. To one side of the living area, an arched doorway gave way to another apartment. Drapes could be pulled across to hide the spacious bed, piled now with bright red cushions.

The large, almost throne-like chair was perched on the front edge of three broad steps. Arak Lazard sat across the great wooden thing at an angle. He slouched back against one of the heavy armrests, his right leg draped over the other. His garish hat, with its long red feather, was thrust over a thick post on the high back of his chair. A dark-haired woman in a colorful silk dress hovered at his elbow.

"I'd offer you boys a chair," the captain said lightly, "but as you can see for yourselves, there aren't many around." He chuckled lightly and was quickly joined by the woman at his side. The substantial number of golden bangles on her arms jingled softly with her every movement. The pirate lord gave her arm a small squeeze then he lowered his eyes on the nervous quintet.

"I must compliment you, boys, on your choice of weapons," he said, with a twinkle in his eye. He cleared his throat. "They are very well made." He held up one of their knives he had resting in his lap. "Truly exquisite, I might add." He locked eyes with Kilgar. "I've never seen their equal before," he said, a tinge of respect in his voice. Lazard continued to examine the knife with great interest.

Over the man's shoulder, Shan noticed a long glass case lining the back wall of the room. Through the clear crystal cabinets he could see the rest of their elven weapons displayed behind the tightly closed doors. *Locked presumably*, he thought.

The handsome buccaneer dropped his leg down off the armrest and sat up. He drew the knife out of its sheath and balanced it lightly in his hand. "Very, very nice," he purred. "So where did you get them, if you don't mind my asking?" He tilted one eyebrow in curiosity.

Kilgar shared a quick glance with the Elfling. The dark-haired youth looked up at Lazard, his chin set. "They were given to us as a gift," he began slowly. "Where and how they were made I have no idea."

"Oh, come," the pirate captain replied. "I've already questioned the other people from the ferry, including that oaf calling himself barge master." He leaned forward in his great chair and narrowed his eyes. The woman beside him rested a dainty hand on his arm. "They all agree you were traveling with two men, very skilled warriors by the way they described them, who they also say had weapons exactly like your own." He made a few little noises with his tongue against the roof of his mouth.

Kilgar blinked in hesitation.

"Hum-m-m," Lazard drawled. "What do you say to that?"

"There's not much to tell, really," Shan took up the story. He glanced briefly at Kilgar. "Those men were our escorts, assigned to us as our guides." He swallowed somewhat apprehensively as Arak studied his face. "We're on a holy pilgrimage, you see, and they were . . ."

"*Pilgrimage?*" Lazard spit out with a heavy laugh. "Never heard of such a thing." He smiled at the little band of pirates waiting near the back of the hallway. "And just what might you be looking for, may I ask?" His grin took in the dark-haired woman standing at his left.

"We're searching for Adonath," Kilgar explained, picking up the tale once again. He tilted his face to the side and gave Shan a sly wink. He glanced back to the pirate lord who was sharing a disbelieving look with the bangled woman at his side. "Our, our guardians have tasked us to find the legendary garden where all life began thousands of yehrin ago."

"Really," Lazard was incredulous. "The Garden of Adonath?" he raised his ringed fingers to the ceiling, grinning broadly. "There is no such place in all of Anarra." He shook his head slowly. "And who would send five mere boys on such a foolish quest?" He scowled at them with a skeptical gleam in his eyes.

"You've probably never heard of him," Kilgar offered humbly, hesitating. Arak raised his eyebrows in anticipation. "The Sultan of Kananga," the boy said evenly.

"Kananga?" the pirate exclaimed.

"We are but servants of his son. We are not persons of interest ourselves, we have no recognizable status. And we don't have any money, as I'm sure you've already discovered. But the Sultan did provide us with the weapons and supplies we would need to make this arduous journey. And, as you've already indicated, he also appointed two of his trusted soldiers, men hand-picked from his own personal guard, to accompany us on the road." Kilgar dropped his eyes to the marble floor, his shoulders slumped. "We think they were killed trying to protect us at the ferry from the attack of those foul creatures of Kulnedra."

"Kulnedra?" The captain's tone was dubious.

Shan nodded. "Muurdra himself does not want our task to succeed." He gazed into the face of the pirate captain. "He has sent out his dark minions all over the land to thwart our discovery of Adonath. The truthfulness of the Garden's existence would spark people's awareness to his lies and schemes, and could almost certainly hinder his evil plans for Ythira." His leveled his eyes on the captain. "His insatiable desire is to supplant Athiliel as Lord of Anarra."

"Well, well, well," Lazard said as he rose to his feet. "You're talking about a religious holy war of some kind. Creator versus fallen creature, powerful though he might be." He stalked down from his great chair, down the three steps to the main floor behind the dias. He circled slowly to his right around the heavy wooden throne. After trampling back up the short set of stairs on the other side of the platform he stopped to wrap an arm around the woman's slim waist. "What do you think, Jadeetha?" he asked her. He cast a wary eye on the boys. "Sounds pretty incredible to me." He stroked at his neat little beard with his left hand.

The woman giggled lightly. The wild assortment of golden bands on her arms jangled musically as she tossed her cascade of dark curls behind.

She spun deftly on the ball of one foot to give Lazard a full embrace. "Their trip must be unbelievably dangerous," she said, looking back at the boys over her bare shoulder and batting her eyelashes.

"Unbelievable is the key word," Arak proclaimed sarcastically. He gave Jadeetha a soft kiss before playfully pushing her away. He strode back to his raised chair and sat down on the front edge.

"So you don't believe us," Kilgar stated evenly, looking intently at the pirate captain.

"Of course not," Lazard said with a ring of humor in his voice. The expectant looks on the boys' faces fell. "However," Arak spoke up, an index finger sporting a large jeweled ring pointed in their direction, "it was a very creative approach. I'll grant you that." He slid back into his chair, leveled a contemplative stare at Kilgar. He regarded the dark-haired boy for a moment before shifting his eyes to the Elfling. He tapped a fingertip on his chin several times. "Hmm," he murmured softly to himself, leaning against the tall back of the chair. *These two boys are obviously the key to this little group*, he thought.

"So what are you going to do with us?" Doornig piped up. His voice broke into a squeak. "Kill us?"

"Heavens, no!" the pirate lord exclaimed, leaning suddenly forward. "What do you think we are around here, a pack of murderers?" He almost looked offended.

"Well, you are pirates," Gorian reminded him. "You did just kill several people in that village yesterday. What else are we supposed to think?"

Lazard's eyes went wide suddenly. He bristled for an instant, and then his gaze appeared to soften. His eyes narrowed on them. "Oh, that!" he volunteered airily. "My men tend to get a little excited at times, a little carried way, it's true. But with the heat of the moment, the rush of a battle, you can hardly fault them. When you happen to find a weapon leveled in your direction, you'll do just about anything to survive." He blinked at them with a broad grin before throwing his right leg over the large armrest once again. "As for those villagers, most of them were simply knocked unconscious in the fray. We really try our best not to hurt anyone. It makes for a bad reputation, you know."

Jadeetha snuggled up to him at the side of the chair. He patted her small hand several times. "So," he said clapping his hands together sharply, "I don't intend to send you back with the others. But you've probably already realized that." He saw the unasked questions on their

Daryl Hanson

faces and went on before they could open their mouths. "Yes, true to my word," Lazard stated with a raised hand and a little gleam in his eye, "I have made arrangements to allow one of my ships to tow the barge men and the rest of their passengers back upriver tomorrow morning." He smiled, spreading his arms wide. "But as for you five," he stopped for a moment, eyeing each of them in turn, "I have something else in mind."

"And what's that?" Kilgar voiced the thought they'd all been thinking.

Lazard seemed rather pleased with himself. He sat back in the great chair and crossed his arms smugly. He cleared his throat softly. "I need a cabin boy for each of my five ships." The quintet of young travelers dropped their mouths open in amazement. "And you"—he counted as he pointed to each one of them individually—"one - two - three - four - five, appear to fit the bill most admirably." He grinned down at them from his raised platform.

"But . . ." Kilgar began, totally taken aback. He blinked several times. "But . . ." he tried once again. His mouth worked mechanically to articulate his thoughts, but he still suffered from a loss for words. Arak looked at him expectantly.

"I think what Kilgar's trying to say," Shan finished for him, "we really don't know anything about ships. We'd probably just get in the way."

"Confound it, boy," the pirate said with rising volume, "none of us was born to this life. None of us felt the pitch and roll of the deck under us until we were pretty much your age. And you can certainly all learn your way around a ship." His eyes took on an unusual gleam. "With you boys on those thorka of yours we could make an unstoppable force. Just think of the possibilities. We could hit our targets by land and from the water all at the same time." His eyes sparkled in his excitement.

"But . . ." Kilgar still tried to speak.

"Look," Lazard uncrossed his arms and propped them on his knees, "I really like you, lads. You're not like those other folk from the barge." He laughed mirthlessly. "You have a sense of adventure about you, and I can appreciate that. I can use that." His eyes narrowed on them. "You seem to be able to handle yourselves well enough. You're not cowed by the situation. Besides, you already know how to spin a pretty tall tale, by the evidence of what you've just told me, and that's fairly important around here." He grinned at them. "So, what do you say, boys? Will you join me?"

The five of them were completely astonished. They could only stare at the pirate captain in shock.

Jadeetha leaned in and spoke something quietly in his ear. Her bangles clinked with every movement of her arm. They couldn't hear what she was saying but she looked up at them frequently and pointed once or twice where they huddled in the center of the room. Arak Lazard nodded and she stood up again, one hand gripped on the heavy armrest.

"I'll not press you for an answer now," the privateer stated lightly. He patted softly at Jadeetha's hand. "You need some time to consider my offer. There's no hurry here." He nodded to his men who had remained standing quietly at the back of the room through their entire interview. "My men will see you back to your quarters. I'll make sure they bring you something a little more appetizing to eat than cold stew this time. Take your time and think about what I've said before you make any hasty decisions. We'll talk about it again tomorrow or maybe the next day."

And with that the men along the back wall shuffled forward to escort them back to their holding cell. Lazard turned away to engage the woman in light conversation. He watched them depart out of the corner of his eye as they filed noisily out of the room. Jadeetha laughed at one of her own comments and he turned back to her with a smile but his thoughts remained fixed on the boys. Something about them captivated him, but he just couldn't quite grasp what it was.

Established once again in their cell the five young men quickly grew restless. They took turns lazing about on the benches and pacing the room like caged animals.

"Seems like everywhere we go, we end up in some kind of detention facility," Doornig complained. He roamed the walls constantly, wringing his hands.

"What are we going to do?" Rimmy wanted to know. "Are we going to accept Lazard's proposal and become pirates?"

"Of course not," his older brother exclaimed with a meaningful glare. "We're just gonna have to find a means of escape," the dark-haired youth said matter-of-factly. Kilgar immediately started to look about the chamber with that thought in mind.

"And how are we gonna do that?" Gorian said with a laugh. "There's only one way in here and one way out."

"Not to mention that one exit is blocked by a heavy iron door," the redheaded youth offered smugly. He looked meaningfully at the imposing metal gate. "And we don't exactly have a key."

Before Shan could say anything about his discovery the previous night, another small contingent of buccaneers arrived with trays heaped full of steaming food. One of the men unlocked the door and remained standing there to block their way while the others swept into the room and placed three large trays on one of the great stone slabs. They were piled with platters of roast kuulo, grilled fish, boiled eggs, wedges of yellow and white cheese, and two steaming loaves of bread. Another tray bearing three pitchers of chilled cider and several wooden cups clattered and sloshed as it was plunked down on the neighboring stone slab.

The pirates hadn't even withdrawn from the room before the loaded platters were hastily being handed around. The boys tore into their repast with gusto. They clinked glasses together, filling the room with their sudden laughter. They hardly noticed the clanging of the gate as it was pulled shut behind the departing men. It wasn't long before the five hungry boys had quickly polished off all of the food. Soon after, they sank down on the stone benches or tiled flooring in contentment. Doornig belched, bringing snickers from all the others.

"With food like that, are we sure we want to escape?" the fiery youth asked.

"I can't stay here," Shan told them all solemnly. "Those gorguls will eventually find a way to track us down, and once they do, they'll manage to get out to this island. I'll never be safe here. It's certainly nothing like Avalar." He regarded them all with a genuine look of sadness. "I don't think I'm ever going to be able to rest until I'm dead—or this whole thing is all over."

Doornig nodded slowly in understanding.

Shan looked meaningfully at him. "I simply cannot remain here. I have to escape." The others were silent as he walked over toward the barred gate. "Which reminds me," he said with one hand gripping onto a metal crosspiece. The boys focused their eyes on him. "Last night I noticed the mortar on this door was poorly done." He tapped the toe of his boot against the anchoring bar. The others rose from their seats and moved over to join him. "I think, if we can find something we can use to dig with, a bar, a stick, a rock of some kind, we could scoop out this mortar and eventually pry the gate loose."

Kilgar knelt down and touched the spot with his fingertips. "Shan's right," he said, "I think we can dig this out. Everybody, look around and see if there's anything in here to do the job."

They scrambled around the room, looking along the dusty floor, searching under the stone benches and upon the walls for anything that might work. There wasn't much to be found except a small chip or two of stone from one of the large, flat slabs. Gorian brought them to the metal barrier to give it a try. He managed to scrape off a thin sliver of the mortar compound.

"Yeah, it'll work—eventually," the sandy-haired boy commented. "But it'll probably take a long time." He held up the tiny chip of stone. "We could find something a little bigger once we get escorted outside again."

"That's assuming they ever let us out of this cell again," Doornig muttered moodily.

"We could always play along with them for a time," Gorian pronounced. "About joining them, I mean." He drew questionable looks from the others. "At least until we can discover something to help us dig."

Kilgar just ignored him. "We should probably wait until dark before we start to work on that door too much anyway," he advised. The others all nodded their agreement. "In the meantime we should try to get some rest, conserve our strength. Sleep even, if you can. Who knows when we're going to need it?"

"Right," Gorian spoke up. He set the empty trays on the floor and stretched out on one of the stone slabs. Doornig was quick to do likewise. They both closed their eyes, and though it was the middle of the afternoon, they seemed to nod off almost instantly.

"Huh," Kilgar commented softly, "I wish I could do that sometime." He lowered himself onto a stone bench and rolled over on his side to face the wall.

Rimmy and Shan looked at each other for a moment. "Go ahead," the Elfling nodded at the remaining bench. "I think I'll study those frescoes some more. They really spark my interest."

"Alright," the younger boy acquiesced. He crawled onto the seat and flipped over onto his back. He yawned deeply. Propping his folded arms under his head, he closed his eyes sleepily and was out in less than five mira.

Shan smiled to himself as he regarded the sprawled forms of his companions. He walked slowly along the walls, puzzling over the curious artwork depicted on the stone panels of the room. One of them especially drew his attention. It was a beautiful map of Ythira, the eastern continent of Anarra. There was no writing upon it at all, no flowing script carved into it to mark out any of the different regions. But the shape of the land was unmistakable.

He knelt down to examine it more closely. Shan reached out to stroke the smooth surface of the panel. He lightly traced an index finger along the incredible length of what looked to be the mighty Tanalorn River until he came across a long, narrow island.

"Watcher's Island," he told himself softly. "Suul'Kar."

On the southern end of the long finger-like island was a seven pointed star. It piqued his interest immediately, for most artistic representations of stars he'd ever seen had only four or five points to them. He studied the thing with a growing fascination. It almost appeared to glow on its own as he scrutinized it thoroughly. His hand hovered for a moment over the spot, and the closer it came to the smooth stone surface the more intense the glow seemed to be. His fingers floated over the image, felt that it had a slight beveled edge to it. He ran the tip of his finger around the outline. It seemed somehow separate from the rest of the painting, like it had been inserted at some point into the polished stone panel. It moved slightly under the pressure of his hand.

The Elfling rested his left hand against the panel for balance and pressed down on the textured star with his right fingertips. He was sure he heard an audible *click*, felt it move slightly, but then nothing seemed to happen. He pressed a little harder. Abruptly, the star sank into the stone, and then the whole panel slid suddenly aside. He cried out in surprise as he fell forward into the darkness.

26

A Forgotten Crypt
[7th of Bellach, 4534 C.R.]

Shan slid face first down some kind of stone chute in the darkness. His forearms scraped against the roughened incline and his knees banged painfully upon worn seams in the rock. The chute leveled off onto a cool slab floor and the Elfling found himself sprawled in a thick layer of fine dust.

He scrambled hastily to his feet, choking on the swirling dust as he brushed himself off in the darkness. Only it wasn't completely dark. Dim beams of dusty light filtered down through vent shafts spaced periodically along the rocky ceiling. They reminded him a little of the scuppers on a ship, the narrow slits along the deck to allow raging water to run off. Here, instead of seawater, he saw dim beams of light drifting down through the thin holes from above.

He stood in a fairly small chamber, measuring perhaps only three or four strides across. A dim passageway led away into the yawning darkness before him. He looked briefly back up the small stone ramp into the gloom above. Apparently the secret panel had closed itself behind him once he'd fallen through the doorway because he couldn't see anything when he tried looking up into the holding cell above. He came to the quick decision not to try and scurry up that long ramp until he thoroughly searched the rest of the underground structure. Maybe he could find a way to escape.

Shan stepped across the little room and moved slowly off down the only passage he could determine leading away from the chute. He occasionally brushed at clinging strands of cobwebs in his face. He slid one hand over the wall on his left. It was flat and extremely smooth, and felt like cool marble. His boots rasped softly in the dust of the corridor. Sparse light, swimming with thousands of dust motes, continued to drift down from the floor above through those narrow shafts driven into the ceiling along both edges of the corridor. Shan could see the thick blanket of dirt on the passage floor had not been disturbed in a long, long time, perhaps even in hundreds of yehrin.

He counted fifty long strides before he came to an intersection. Another passage cut across his path at right angles. He looked in all directions before choosing the passage to the left. It seemed darker somehow than the first one, but he thought he could hear faint sounds coming from a long ways off. He couldn't quite place the noise, so he moved stealthily down the corridor to investigate. He had gone a long way in the dark when he realized the lack of light probably had something to do with the extensive ruins of the city somewhere above him. When they had first looked out at the city scape while they were being escorted back to their cell by the small pirate host earlier in the afternoon, they had seen the incredible amount of damage done to all the buildings and roadways in that direction.

The small circulation vents must have been blocked entirely with dirt and rubble. But it wasn't just a lack of light down here, there was a lack of ventilation as well. He coughed shallowly to clear his lungs of the close stale air. He continued to kick up the fine dust as he walked, and that didn't help the situation. He continued to trail one hand lightly on the smooth stones as he walked.

The Elfling had traveled about two hundred paces before he started to see a dim gleam far ahead. And it was perhaps half that distance again before he noticed a rise in the muffled noise from somewhere down the long corridor. He stopped for a moment to listen. It almost sounded like running water to him, but it was still quite a ways off.

The Elfling trudged on, the light puff of his breathing and the gentle scrape of his boots echoing in the confining space. Tiny patches of light filtered down every so often, but for the most part he walked along in the darkness. The droning noise ahead steadily increased until it was virtually roaring in his ears.

Shan had gone another hundred and fifty kora when he suddenly came out of the narrow tunnel and found himself on a small landing overlooking a wide cavern. The churning of a fairly good-sized river howled through the rocky hollow past his vantage point. It spewed from the rocks and gushed across the grotto in wild torrents before disappearing to his left through a large rough-carved channel.

Dim light slanted down from a rocky opening in the ceiling above, giving him a good glimpse of the rugged chamber. The tiled landing overlooked the raging flow from a height of about twenty kora. The long passage he'd been following must have been angling slightly uphill as he walked, but it had been such a gentle incline he hadn't even noticed. He swept his gaze around the broad chamber, the constant roar of water humming in his ears.

Shan discovered a slender stone staircase carved in the cavern wall to his right. It wound down to a stone dock on the water's edge. The Elfling skipped lightly down the mist-laden steps to the lower landing. A low wall ran along the edge of the stream to keep people from accidently falling into the current, but there was an open space off to one side to launch a boat into the current. He looked about the landing, then his eyes wandered across forty kora of rushing water to the opposite cave wall.

"Too bad we don't have any boats," Shan said to himself. "We could make our escape down this underground river." The current was probably too swift for them to try to swim, he reasoned. But as he turned back to climb up the steps in disappointment, a spot on the wall to his right caught his eye.

He sidled over to check it out and was surprised to find half a dozen small boats stored in narrow alcoves. They were upside down and nestled in shallow tube-like niches. He ran his hand along the curve of one shell, expecting it to crumble at his touch. Startled, he found it very solid and extremely durable. He easily pulled one of the boats out of its berth and turned it over on the landing. He tapped it and slapped at it but he couldn't seem to damage the smooth hull.

"Hmmm," he said out loud. "It's certainly not wood, and it's not made of metal, either." He tapped on it some more. "It's something entirely different. But I can't tell what it is." He pursed his lips. "It almost seems ceramic, but that would make it entirely too heavy." He shrugged.

Happy with his little discovery, he slid the narrow, canoe-like craft back into its stall. This certainly looked now like a viable escape route. He just had to retrace his steps to tell the others about his find. He started up the moist steps and stopped on the first rung.

"That's if I can get back up that narrow chute," he said to himself. "But even if I can manage to climb up to that secret panel, how will I get back into the room?" He pondered that for a moment, then shrugged in ignorance and continued on up the winding stairway.

Shan back tracked from the landing, heard the roar of rushing water gradually diminish behind him as he hurried along. Once he got back to the passage intersection he decided not to return immediately to find the boys. On a whim he turned left instead. This corridor sloped gently downward for a couple hundred kora until it came to a jumble of small rooms branching off the main passage. These were obviously too small for living spaces, most of them being only a few strides across. Each one of them had a small stone chair in the center of the floor and a few pegs driven into one of the walls. These little pins were made of that same mysterious substance as the boats he'd come across.

Shan scratched his head at these tiny cubicles. For the life of him he couldn't figure out what they were. *Preparation rooms, maybe, but preparation for what?* He shrugged and continued on, but before long he found the passage completely blocked with fallen debris.

He retraced his steps to the convergence of the two long corridors. He went left again and before long he came upon a heavy stone doorway blocking the way. This was not like the iron gate in their cell. It must have been placed here on purpose long, long ago. He studied it for a few moments. It was latticed with narrow openings throughout, which allowed him to look beyond it. But he couldn't see very far up the passage for it ran off at a sharp angle to the right after about twenty kora. Shan pushed on the heavy door but it would not yield. Just as he decided to give it up and turn back, he heard a clear rush of noise drifting around the corner. It was the unmistakable stir of many voices. They were muffled and dim, as if they were far off, and he felt like the large group of people all seemed to be chattering at once.

The Elfling couldn't make out any distinct words but the overall tone was genial. Was this a slew of Lazard's cutthroat guards, or could this be a pathway to the other prisoners? He couldn't be sure.

On sudden impulse he examined the stone door in more detail. He searched for a latch or a catch, or a spring of some kind, but all to no avail. There was absolutely no mechanism on the smooth door that he could see or feel. A thick metal bolt ran from the edge of the large door and was sunk deeply into the passage wall. He felt inside the lattices but could not detect any means to draw back the bolt. Finally, he tugged on the barrier again, but it resisted his staunchest efforts. Shan scratched at his chin and stepped back a couple of paces. He felt the back of his foot catch on an uneven spot on the floor. He stepped away from it and looked down.

There was a small curved area on the stone flooring of the passageway. It was about the width of his foot. The Elfling had seen several of them in his explorations but he hadn't thought them more than some form of decoration. Or perhaps they were some kind of distance marker for those who traveled about underground. He felt the raised circle lightly with the toe of his boot. It looked like a small stone ball embedded in the floor, and the top of it was just slightly higher than the rest of the paving stones. The boy depressed it slowly with the heel of his boot, and was rewarded by a soft *click* from the closed stone door. The heavy portal popped open stiffly and remained slightly ajar.

Gingerly, Shan pulled the door slowly open. He half-expected it to creak and groan after long yehrin of disuse, but it made no sound at all. It swung smoothly to the side on its hinges. He had nothing with which to prop it open, but it seemed to stay where he left it on its own. He let go of it cautiously and it rested smoothly against the passage wall.

The Elfling slipped through and stepped off quietly down the hall. He came to the curve in the corridor, peered cautiously around the corner. There was nothing in sight but an empty passage in front of him. He slipped silently around the corner and glided down the smooth passage to the next bend, about twenty kora away. He looked carefully around the edge with one eye. Another short jaunt of the passage ended suddenly in a blank wall. There was a short ladder attached there, solidly embedded in the stone. The slender thing was made from the same curious alloy, durable and strong, as the small boats on the river landing or the pegs in those tiny rooms. *What is this material?* he asked himself.

He grabbed onto the rungs with both hands, climbed up into a narrow shaft cut into the passage ceiling. The sounds of voices increased as he quietly pulled himself upwards. The smooth ladder ended after about twenty rungs, as well as the narrow shaft. Some kind of vent could be seen carved into the side of the wall there. Shan peered through the tightly latticed tile which was perhaps only a little wider than his shoulders.

He was pleased to discover all the passengers from the barge lounging about a broad room on the other side of the grille, and not a nest of notorious pirates. Similar to their own chamber, the large enclosure was sparsely furnished with only occasional stone blocks lying about. The people inside were huddled into several smaller groups, conversing animatedly with each other. They must have been content to know they would be going home soon, the Elfling reasoned. A handful of children ran about the chamber, playing some form of tag. At the edge of the room there was a large metal door barring them inside.

Shan reached his fingers through the grille and gently pulled on it. It wouldn't come loose, but it bulged a little in his grip. There were ceramic rivets in the corners of the plate to hold it in place. He was fairly certain he could force the grate or maybe pry the rivets loose if he tried harder. But now was not the time, he told himself. They should really wait until the people had been vacated from the room before they made any noise trying to escape in that direction.

He pulled his fingers out of the tiled grille and easily descended the smooth ceramic-like ladder to the passage floor. Shan followed his route back to the stone door. He was relieved to find the large stone portal still open and resting against the wall as he had left it. Confident he could open it once again with the floor switch he had discovered, he pushed on the heavy door. It swivelled easily on its hinges and closed itself with a light snap.

The Elfling turned from the barrier and jogged lightly down the stone passage. How long had he been gone from his cell? He couldn't tell. He hurried back to the main juncture, suddenly mindful his friends might have awakened by now. He imagined them panicking to find him unexpectedly gone from the cell. At the lone intersection he swung to the left and pattered quickly up the corridor.

The Elfling made short work of getting back to the little room where he'd fallen down the chute. He paused there for an instant, thoroughly examining all four walls and the floor, trying to discover a release catch of some kind for the panel above. But his fruitless search failed to produce any recessed stone catches or triggers that he could find. Perplexed, he stood with his hands on his hips and slowly surveyed the whole chamber.

The dim light leaking down through the vent shafts presently began to wane. Night was rapidly descending over the ancient city of Suul'Kar and Shan realized it would soon be extremely hard to see down there. A mild sense of panic made him hasten his exploration of every tile, every panel, of the stone lined cubicle. It was only a few strides across, so it wasn't like the area to search was tremendously wide. He felt along all the walls a second time, then dropped to his knees and ran his hands over the entire floor, but his urgent examination failed to produce a single likely pressure point. The Elfling coughed softly as he kicked up light clouds of dust. He continued to search long after the feeble light from above was totally extinguished.

Shan finally sat down in the darkness, a knot of dread growing within the pit of his stomach. How was he going to get back to his friends? He leaned on the bottom section of the chute, his legs bent, his feet on the floor to support his weight. He craned his head to look up at the top of the slide, hoping he might catch a tiny glimmer of light, an outline of some kind, from the edges of the sliding panel above. But there was nothing.

He dropped his chin on his clenched fists, his elbows resting heavily on his knees. He had a sudden thought that the release catch was embedded in the ceiling, but it was much too high above for him to reach. He sighed dismally with an expulsion of pent-up air. Then he closed his eyes in frustration, and prayed.

"Athiliel, Athiliel, what am I going to do now?" He actually said it out loud. "Has all Your protection brought me to this? Trapped here in the dark?"

He opened his eyes slowly to a world of darkness. He sighed once again before climbing back to his feet. He blinked a number of times, canting his head from side to side, searching for something, anything, he might have missed in his haste. He peered into the oppressive gloom for quite a long time, slowly turning on the balls of his feet to take in every hob of the room. He sank down at last at the bottom of the stone slide, crossing his legs on the dusty floor.

The Elfling couldn't tell how long he sat there, motionless in the dark. His mind seemed numb. Perhaps he slept for a time, but he just wasn't sure. All at once he became aware of a dim glow working its way down into the chamber from the narrow channels in the rock ceiling. It was a milky blue radiance which seemed to drift down and cling to the smooth walls. The stones themselves appeared to react to the tiny slivers of moonlight, filling the little room with a silvery-blue haze.

Shan lifted his head from where it had slumped against his breast and gazed about curiously. It appeared the stone panels had a natural phosphorescent quality when exposed to moonlight and the whole room was gradually filled with a subdued light. Yet it was more than enough for him to see once again and he scrambled lightly to his feet.

The long corridor stretching out before him developed an almost ghost-like outline. His eyes were drawn to a spot about halfway down the passage wall on the left. It was about the size of a large coin, and it seemed to grow brighter than the rest of the corridor. Somehow feeling pulled towards it, Shan drifted lightly down the dusty floor to investigate. His boots scuffed quietly on the layers of fine dirt.

The luminous spot burned with a cold, blue light. It beckoned him closer. He paced quickly down the hall, his eyes riveted upon the clean round mark. He stopped directly in front of it, and stared. It gave off no sound, but it pulsed somehow as he stood gazing at it. Cautiously he raised a hand to touch it, afraid that it might burn him or something worse, but it was actually cold under his probing fingers. He pressed at it, yet nothing happened. It was actually part of the wall, not recessed or carved into it as the star on the panel above had been.

He studied it in consternation. It was a perfect circle, a plain disk of radiance upon the stone wall, yet it had no other image or design to it. And no amount of pressure from his fingers could make it respond in any way. He stepped back and looked around. There were no other similar spots in evidence anywhere in the corridor. It did not look as if it were a reflection, nor did it cast out a beam of light in an effort to interact with any other corresponding marks on the floor or along the walls. Shan scratched at his head, baffled.

As he stared at the bright bluish-white dot he became aware of a warmth gradually growing in his britches' pocket. At first he thought he must have cut himself somehow in all his explorations, but he soon realized the source of heat was actually coming from *inside* the pocket and not from his skin underneath.

The Elfling thrust his hand down into the pocket and encountered a warm, almost hot, metal object. He cupped his fingers around it and pulled it up into the fuzzy blue light. He opened his fingers and discovered the medallion Ulfiir had given him the night of his escape from Draydin. It was the very same object he'd purchased and given to his guardian months before on his birthing day.

Shan stared down at the little metal thing in his palm. He held it lightly in place with the edge of his thumb. The long chain ran off his hand to dangle loosely in the air. The metal of the medallion no longer seemed dark as it usually did. Instead, it glowed with a dim reddish light. As he looked upon it intently, the stylized glyph, or whatever it was, grew steadily warmer until it almost seemed to sear his fingers.

On a sudden impulse the Elfling lifted up the small sign of the House of Korell and touched it lightly to the luminous circle on the wall. For a moment nothing seemed to happen, but then the radiant spot on the wall flared a little brighter. There was a sudden hiss of air as a large section of the stone panel pulled back and swung away from him, disappearing up against the ceiling.

Shan found himself staring into a very large room. Its walls glowed softly with the same dull blue light as the corridor. The farthest wall of the chamber appeared quite distant from where he stood at the edge of the passage, peering in. Carved pillars held up the massive stone roof. Dim forms of stone-like objects filled his field of vison, yet it was extremely hard to make out just what they really were in the murky light. Milky, shroud-like tatters of cobwebs clung all about them. It almost seemed as if someone had gone away for a extended absence, or had sold their home, covering all their furniture with light, loose cloth, but then had never returned to take up residence once again.

The small medallion in his palm had cooled considerably. When he looked down at it again, Shan saw that it had returned to its usual dark, almost black appearance. He thrust it absently back into his britches' pocket, stuffing the accompanying chain in along with it. Slowly, the Elfling stepped into the large room.

The air was cool inside, even more so than the outer hallway. A thick blanket of milky white cobwebs rippled softly over the scattered shapes as he walked reverently across the broad floor. Each and every step caused them to flutter and billow as he passed. He stopped at one point and scraped away some of the heavy webs from one of the many humped objects. It turned out to be a large stone sarcophagus. The lid of the coffin was intricately carved, with endless, interlacing loops and swirls like stylized knots of braided rope. The heavy lid itself was vaguely carved into the shape of a body. It almost appeared seamless as it rested precisely over the lower portion of the stone casket.

Shan pulled his hand back from the sticky veil of cobwebs and moved off down a wide aisle running the length of the crypt. Some of the other coffins he stopped to examine had complete likenesses of the deceased etched into the heavy lids. These only confirmed his suspicions about the people who had once inhabited this long dead city. The graceful lines of their faces and their delicately pointed ears told him they had been Elves. He wondered what had brought this great civilization into such ruin.

The magnificence of the chamber took his breath away. Each of the broad pillars was carved to resemble a large tree. They were all distinctly different, yet each of them had the familiar ruffled texture of tree bark, the knotted coils of twining branches, and dozens of intricately fashioned leaves. The wide, smooth floor showed through the scuffed traces of his footsteps in the finely grained dust. He could see a hint of the fine hexagonal tiles, all trimmed in gold, where he had walked.

He wandered slowly about the large chamber, stopping frequently to inspect some of the more curiously shaped shroud coverings. One of the largest tombs he discovered was nestled along the back wall. It had two full statues rising up off the elaborate golden sarcophagus. One imposing figure seemed to float on the air over the back of the coffin upon huge silvery-white wings. His fierce countenance was fixed upon a dark, shriveled form on the other end of the huge tomb. The demonic shape was enfolded in a sea of black robes and held one bony hand lifted up in defense. The enormous winged being was garbed in shimmering white apparel. He grasped a mighty sword in his upraised fists and appeared ready to transfix the foul thing cowering at his feet with his glowing blade.

Shan shivered as he gazed upon this vivid reminder of the on-going celestial battle. Here was the terrifying form of an Ilar warrior seeking to vanquish the misshapen sinister servant of Muurdra. The Ilyri were often only thought to be myths by most of the people in the world. But Shan actually knew better. Ulfiir had often talked with him about them, had made sure the boy had nothing but respect for these powerful beings, these Messengers of the Almighty. Perhaps they were totally invisible to all save a few chosen individuals, yet these incredible servants of Athiliel were often engaged in open warfare with the forces of evil. Their perpetual struggle would seek to shape the destiny of Anarra forever.

The Elfling looked down upon the large sarcophagus. There was no carved representation of its occupant on the heavy lid, just an intricate crest of some sort.

This is most likely the final resting place for some beloved king or mighty lord, Shan thought.

It had obviously been constructed here in reverence by his faithful subjects. The presence of the winged Ilar and its foul opponent could merely have been meant to indicate the elevated stature of the deceased or, as was perhaps even more likely, to illustrate his own personal beliefs regarding the eternal war between Athiliel and Muurdra, the Fallen One.

Shan contemplated the graceful writing across the flat surface of the casket. He sighed. It wasn't the first time he wished he could read the artistic gold script. He slid his fingers over the inscription until he encountered a low spot in the middle of the funerary box just below the last row of fine elegant lettering. The depression was circular and about the same size as the shining spot on the outer passage wall which had lured him to the large crypt.

"I wonder . . ." he said out loud, then reached down into his pocket and carefully pulled out the dark metal emblem. It remained cool to the touch, but it began to glow a soft crimson as he brought it closer to the stone coffin. He placed it lightly upon the depression and stepped back.

A seam formed immediately along the front face of the casket, near the bottom. It widened into a long straight crease, then slowly opened up like a drawer. A stone shelf slid smoothly out into view, covered with a white, velvet-like material. Resting upon the pure white cloth was a long, dark sword, and next to it a black ceramic scabbard.

Shan looked at the beautiful sword for a long time. His breath came in quick shallow drafts. Here was an ancient weapon he was sure, and yet impossibly, as he studied it with such intensity, it appeared completely brand new.

The Elfling slowly held out his hand and touched the wrapped hilt. A burning shock lanced through his palm and slithered up his arm. He recoiled instantly, snatching back his hand and blowing hard on his fist. He held up his injured member in the creamy blue light, flexing his fingers slowly before his face. Shan could not detect any physical damage done to his skin. And he would have turned away at that moment, to flee from the room in haste, leaving the elegant weapon undisturbed, but the sword somehow seemed to *call* to him.

An eerie chill ran up his spine as he swung back to look upon the saber lying in the velvet-lined drawer before him. It wasn't words exactly, yet he was sure the sword beckoned him, inviting him closer, urging him to snatch it up from its ancient resting place. The Elfling ran his tongue over dry lips and contemplated the weapon for a long, long time. It had somehow invaded his mind, tugging at his resolve. Thin lines of sweat dribbled down his face and sprang from his chin onto the gold trimmed floor tiles. Even the hair on the back of his arms stiffened as the long inert blade reached out to him, imploring and entreating him to draw closer.

Cautiously, against his better judgment, Shan stretched out his hand and lifted the thing slowly from its display cloth. It scorched a little at first, but not as severely as before, as he held it up before his eyes to inspect. But this time the sense of searing fire had entirely dissipated. It still felt somewhat warm on his palm but it no longer hurt to handle it. He rotated his wrist from side to side to look down the long dark sheen of the exquisite blade. The soft moonlit glow from the walls gleamed dully from its dark surface.

The hilt was rather simple but elegant. The handgrip itself was wrapped in a continuous strip of soft black cloth. It had the feel of leather yet seemed much more absorbent. The cross guard was gently curved where it swept across the tang and ended in short spike-like barbs on either side. These small spurs curled down slightly, like teeth, pointing towards the tip of the long, grooved blade. The pommel was a hexagonal piece of silver, smoothed and rounded off to resemble a knob-like button or flower and had been emblazoned with the same sign as Ulfiir's medallion.

The blade itself had a smoky, glass-like appearance. It was incredibly light and felt like it might be made of crystal. The Elfling was suddenly disappointed. It had the unmistakable look of a display weapon, for any edge made of crystal would certainly shatter at first contact with any real blade. He moved to place the sword gingerly back down on the white velvet cloth, but then he hesitated.

Shan debated with himself for a long time. The relic didn't actually belong to him; it was obviously the heirloom of a long dead king or Clanlord. And he really disliked the idea of disturbing the crypt any more than he already had. Reluctantly, he settled the blade carefully back on its cloth next to the black ceramic scabbard, and started to withdraw his hand. An intense whine instantly droned in his head. The Elfling cupped his hands over his ears, but it didn't seem to help. The shrill tone seemed more like it came from within his own skull than actually emanating from somewhere inside the large chamber.

The strange sword was calling to him, he felt sure, almost seeming to sing out in a long, piercing whistle. It beckoned to him, urging him to pick up the dark blade once again. He shuffled a few steps away from the open coffin, but the tones in his mind only intensified, driving him back to the edge of the drawer. Nervously, he wrapped his fingers gingerly around the hilt and the deafening siren sounds in his head immediately dissipated.

The peculiar blade felt good in his hand. His thoughts became unnaturally calm as he hefted the weapon once more. With a new sense of determination, Shan picked up the matching ceramic scabbard from the beautiful white cloth and drove the sword home. He thrust the dark sheath down into his belt. The blade sang to him in a soft melodic tone.

Shan scooped up the medallion from the little depression where he'd left it on the top of the sarcophagus. The drawer retracted instantly without a sound. It shut on its own, and within moments the narrow seam along the front had completely vanished. He stuffed the small thorka-shaped symbol into his pocket once again. He looked up for a moment at the startling visage of the winged Ilar towering above him. It seemed to smile grimly down at him as he slowly backed away. After a few halting steps, he bumped into another large stone coffin. The encounter sent a wave of jittery flesh across his back. He edged his way around the object and sprinted for the door. He weaved through a myriad of different tombs before he finally managed to exit the room.

He ran down the passageway, returning to the small cubicle with the long stone ramp. He looked back once after he skidded to a halt in front of the incline. The large door to the crypt chamber dropped down from where it had rested against the ceiling. It swung down quietly and moved smoothly back into place, flush with the passage wall. The luminous round mark on the passage surface had entirely faded away.

Shan cast a hasty look up the smooth slope of the chute and started to climb. He gripped both hands onto the raised stone lip on either side, much like a low railing, and scrambled his way up the dusty incline. He slipped and slid and scampered awkwardly up the long, steep ramp, but he finally reached the top. He rested for a moment on a short landing nestled up against the wall. He felt all along the inside surface of the hidden panel for a spring or catch. But none was to be found.

Quite by accident the Elfling came across a tiny raised bump on the far side of the small stone landing, near the edge of the wall. Only about the size of his thumb, it was much smaller than the other switches he'd already encountered in his explorations of the underground passages. Due to its location on the landing, the small lever hadn't been visible from the floor of the chamber. With a hopeful smile he pressed the little stone ball with the heel of his hand. It gave off a soft *click* and the panel slid silently open.

Shan tumbled back into the darkened holding cell and clambered quickly to his feet. The boys inside shot startled looks in his direction. They sat huddled tightly together on the two stone slabs. From the way they peered into the darkness Shan knew they couldn't see him.

"Who's there?" Kilgar called out nervously.

27

Che Underground River
[7th of Bellach, 4534 C.R.]

"It's me," Shan cried, stepping towards them out of the darkness.

"Shan?" Kilgar asked uncertainly. He rose up suddenly from the stone couch, searching the gloom between them. "Is that you?"

"Yes, I'm here," the Elfling confirmed. He held out his hand to touch his dark-haired friend. Kilgar grasped onto the elven boy's wrist and pulled him closer. The faint blue light of Sheera curled its way down the hall from the street beyond, giving the boy a fuzzy outline to embrace.

Kilgar wrapped his arms about the Elfling and slapped him on the back several times. Abruptly he pushed Shan out to arm's length. He peered at him closely in the semi-darkness. "It's good to see you," he began. "Well, okay, I can't really see you very well, but you know what I mean." Shan smiled and nodded before realizing the boy probably couldn't see him clearly enough.

The other boys found their way over in the dark and latched onto them. They hugged and slapped good-naturedly at the Elfling. They pulled Shan over to one of the couches and sat him down on the edge.

"Where have you been?" Rimmy wanted to know.

"We thought the pirates had come in and dragged you off," Doornig stated with genuine concern in his voice.

"Really?" the Elfling grinned.

"When we all woke up some time ago," Gorian proclaimed excitedly, "we realized you were gone. The door hadn't been forced open, so naturally we thought the cutthroats had taken you while we slept."

"Yeah, Kilgar was fit to be tied," Rimmy told him humorously. "You should have seen him." He clapped a hand on his brother's shoulder.

"Stop," Kilgar complained sheepishly. He brushed his brother's grasp lightly aside. "I was just afraid they'd come in here and carried you off without any of us even waking up. That really disturbed me to say the least."

"But when the pirates finally came back to collect the dishes," Gorian stated, "they never said anything. Not even to suggest you were off conversing with Lazard on your own or anything like that. They just didn't seem to notice. Even Rekki said nothing." The boys sat with their heads close together. "We figured if anyone knew anything about you being taken to see the captain, he would." He shook his head. "But he said nothing."

Rimmy leaned in. "I just hoped you had escaped," he said in a whisper. There was a glint in his eye from the stray moonlight. "But I couldn't figure out how you'd done it."

"So, when they came back to drop off more food a little while ago," Doornig went on, "Kilgar had a brilliant idea to keep them from sounding an alarm." Shan regarded their leader with interest. "He crumpled all our cloaks together into a ball to make it look like you were sleeping on the bench in the corner."

"And I curled up on the other bench," Rimmy pronounced, "to help make it more believable."

"The goons never even knew you were gone," Gorian finished in a rush of excitement.

Shan was impressed. His friends could be very clever when they put their minds to it. Kilgar looked over at him in the pale blue light.

"That's all well and good but that doesn't explain how you actually got out of here," the dark-haired boy exclaimed. "Or how you just got back in, for that matter."

Shan looked over his shoulder to the wall panels behind him. "There's a secret panel over there," he began. "It's within one of the walls."

"Secret panel?" Doornig's voice rose in pitch.

"Shush! Keep it down, will ya!" Kilgar rebuked him. He looked over his shoulder cautiously at the heavy iron door. "Someone might overhear you."

"Sorry," the redhead whispered stiffly, sufficiently chastened.

Kilgar swung back to peer at the Elfling. "So you found another way out of here. That's good. But why did you bother to come back? You could have been long gone by now."

"I'm not abandoning my friends," Shan spoke out adamantly. "I came back to get all of us out."

"Tell us about this way out," Kilgar entreated him with a hush to his voice. "Where is it? Where did it lead?" The boys drew in even closer in the darkness of the room.

"I was fascinated with all these artistic panels," the Elfling told them. "You all saw me studying them over the past couple of days." They nodded in unison. Shan licked his lips before going on. "One of them was a beautifully rendered map of Ythira. I bent down to examine it, and on the southern edge of Watcher's Island . . ."

"Right, which is where we are," Kilgar responded quietly.

"Suul'Kar."

Shan nodded. "Anyway, I found a star. It was the only marking on the whole island. It was kind of odd though, because the star had seven points to it."

"Huh, a seven pointed star?" Gorian interrupted. "That *is* odd."

"That's what I thought," the Elfling went on, "and it seemed to move a little under my fingers when I pressed it. The whole panel whisked suddenly aside and I fell down a long stone ramp into a series of passages below the city."

Kilgar immediately rocked forward excitedly. "Can we escape from the city that way?" he breathed. His eyes gleamed a little in the faint light.

"Yes, I'm certain we can," Shan was quick to announce. "There's an underground river down there, and even some small boats we could use."

"Wonderful!" Kilgar replied, his face beaming.

"Then what are we waiting for?" Doornig hissed as he started to rise. "Let's go!"

"Wait!" Shan responded to him. "I think we need to find the thorka first."

"Not to mention our weapons," Gorian offered. "We don't really want to abandon them, do we?"

"They're locked in Lazard's case," Kilgar stated. "We'll just have to go in there and get them."

"And how do we do that?" the redhead asked dubiously, settling back down on the stone slab in obvious disappointment. "We can't very well just waltz in there and demand he return them to us, can we?" He blinked scoldingly at them in the gloom. Kilgar looked up at him in a deliberate stare. "Don't tell me we need another diversion."

Kilgar just glared at him without saying anything. He turned to look at the Elfling instead. "Tell me, do you think the animals can swim that river?"

Shan thought for a moment, chewing on his lip. "I think so," he stated. "The water's pretty fast in that cavern, but I think they could handle it."

"You're forgetting one thing," Rimmy spoke up. The others turned to observe the young man as much as they could in the heavy darkness. "How do you propose we get the thorka down into that tunnel to begin with?" He blinked at them meaningfully.

"Oh," Kilgar confessed after a moment, "I hadn't really thought of that." He looked up at the iron door, a scowl on his face. The boys sat thinking in the darkness. Finally Kilgar looked over at them. "Unless perhaps there's another way into those passages," he said hopefully.

Shan thought briefly before responding. "There is another entrance, but you'd have to get through some kind of locked grille first. It leads out from the room where they're holding the other prisoners." He waved vaguely in that direction. "I'm not sure how to get there through the ruined surface streets, and they've got a locked gate as well." He turned suddenly glum. "It isn't much wider than my shoulders, not to mention there's a ladder running down from the main level to that underground passage." Kilgar's hopeful face fell. "I'm sorry," the Elfling finished, "but I can't see how the animals would be able to manage that route."

"What if we split ourselves into two groups then?" Rimmy wanted to know.

His brother looked over at him, a small frown growing on his face. "How would that help?" Kilgar asked him.

Rimmy cleared his throat. "Let's say one, maybe two people, go after the animals," he began slowly. "The rest of us follow Shan to the river and take a ride on some of those boats he mentioned." The others started to perk up a little at his plan. "We crash the thorka out through the swamp along the edge of the island."

"And eventually we meet up somewhere north of here, wherever that river comes out." Kilgar slapped a hand across his knee. He suddenly looked up to the door, mindful of the echoing sound. "Ooh," he hissed with a sheepish smile. He grabbed onto his brother's hand with a firm grip. "Let's do it. I like it."

"Not tryin' to burst your bubble," Doornig interposed with a slightly devilish grin, "but we still have to get out of here, *past* that locked door, before we can expect to try any of that."

"Let's put our heads together and figure it out," Gorian told him.

"Doornig's right. If we're going to retrieve our weapons, as well as the thorka," Kilgar told them flatly, "we'll need to find a way to get through this door." He got up from the stone couch and crossed to the metal gate. He slapped his palm on one of the thick crossbars with a dull thump.

The others moved over to join him. They huddled just inside the iron barrier and looked out. "The pirates haven't exactly given us much to work with," Gorian offered disdainfully.

"Right. They apparently think a couple of forks and spoons might give us an opportunity to escape," Doornig added sarcastically.

Daryl Hanson

"A couple of strong forks would be nice," Gorian responded lightly. "Then we might be able to dig ourselves out under the walls." He laughed sardonically.

"What's that?" Rimmy asked suddenly, pointing in the dim moonlight to the object hanging from Shan's waist.

The Elfling looked down to find the dark ceramic scabbard slapping at his thigh. "Oh, that," he said as he pulled it out of his belt and lifted it up for all of them to see in the murky light.

"Looks like a sword," Kilgar exclaimed with rising excitement.

"It is," the Elfling announced. "Well, sort of. I found it in a crypt down there, but I don't see how . . ."

"Maybe we can use it to dig out some of that mortar," Doornig interrupted. "Let me see it." He reached anxiously for the sheath.

"Wait!" Shan tried to tell him, but the redhead clamped a hand onto the sword hilt before he could pull the scabbard out of the way. Doornig screamed out suddenly in pain and instantly snatched his hand back. He blew on his fingers, rubbing them gingerly with his other hand. He flashed an accusatory scowl at Shan. "Look, I tried to warn you," the elven youth said in a placating tone, "but you never gave me the chance."

"What's the matter?" Rimmy wanted to know. He looked from Shan to the fiery-headed youth, still sucking on his fingers.

"It burns, that's what!" hissed Doornig. He glared across at the Elfling in the quasi-darkness. He clenched and unclenched his fist quickly. "The wretched thing must be cursed!" He continued to blow tenderly on his fingers.

"But if that's true," Gorian was puzzled, "how come it doesn't burn Shan's hand to touch it?"

"Oh, it scorched me, as well," the Elfling replied, "—at first. I picked it up from its resting place but had to let go almost immediately." The others looked at him quizzically. "I know this will sound strange, but I think it called to me when I was about to leave it behind."

"Called to you?" Kilgar queried him. "How?"

The Elfling shrugged. "It was like a high-pitched hum, a whine, really. I didn't sense it with my ears, though. I heard it in my mind." The boys gave him the oddest looks. "And the sword wouldn't stop whistling until I picked it up again. I could still feel some heat, but it was much more subdued, and after a few moments the pain just completely disappeared." He looked at all the others in the dim light. "At that moment I got the strangest feeling that it had accepted me somehow."

"Huh. Well, then you're gonna need to be the one to dig out this compound," Kilgar informed him. He pointed down to where the iron gate was thrust into a hole in the flooring.

"No, I don't think so," Shan told him. "I can't imagine it would do us much good." The dark-haired boy looked at him as if to speak, but Shan hurried on. "It's really not much of a sword," he told them. "Here, look." He slid the blade easily out of the scabbard. Doornig shied away as he did so. "It almost appears to be made of some sort of glass or . . . or *crystal*." The others leaned in, groaning in disappointment. "I think it's really only a display weapon of some kind. You know, for the crypt of the king, or whatever he was."

Shan set the scabbard against the bars and brought the blade up close to his face. "I don't even think it's sharp." He traced a finger lightly along the glimmering edge and was surprised to see a runnel of his own blood spread out easily and dribble onto his hand. "Huh," he said in fascination, "I guess it's sharper than I thought." He dropped his hand to wipe the trickle of blood on the side of his britches. "Anyway," he said with a look at Kilgar, "I'm sure it would just shatter if we try to use it on those heavy metal bars."

His friend nodded in resignation. "You're probably right," Kilgar said. "There's no use destroying such a beautiful replica." He started to turn away. "So what else can we use?"

The boys were at a loss, but they drifted all around the dark room, searching for anything that might help. Shan joined them for a time after he'd returned the nearly black blade to its scabbard. He shoved it back into his belt and turned to look about, but soon found himself studying the artistic panels around the room.

He stopped in front of the same one he'd noticed the night before. It depicted a helmed warrior engaged in single combat with a devilish foe. The man held an unusual, long dark blade in his hand. Stranger still, it appeared in the painting as if the unnatural blade could actually slice completely through his enemy's own sword upon contact. The Elfling slowly looked down at the odd scabbard hanging at his side.

A sudden thought tingled through Shan's mind. Was the sword he had just found in the underground crypt the same one he was seeing represented here in the artwork before him? He wondered. He brought his hand down onto the hilt, ran his fingers over the silver hex-shaped pommel. The other boys continued to rummage uselessly around in the dark. He spun on his heel with an immediate sense of determination and strode over to the heavy iron door.

Shan drew the long blade from its sheath. He stared at the smoky surface for a moment, felt the unbelievable lightness of the weapon. He really liked the balance; it felt good in his hand. Without thinking about it any further he slid the sword blade through the gap between the stone doorway and the outside frame of the metal bars. He rested the dark blade lightly on the thick metal latch buried in the stone doorpost. He increased his pressure slightly and he felt the heavy iron bolt give just a little.

Kilgar glanced up at that moment, saw what the Elfling was doing. He called the others together with a low whistle. They all converged on the doorway to watch the elven lad. Shan drew the sword out and examined the blade closely. There was not so much as a scratch on it where he'd forcibly pressed it against the heavy iron bar. He inspected the metal latch and discovered it had a crease in it, a light cut on the top of the bolt where the sword had rested. Shan looked up, finally realizing the boys were watching him, and shrugged.

"Well, here goes," the Elfling said. They watched him intently as he reinserted the sword. He poised it above the thick metal bolt, then chopped suddenly downward with it. The bolt snapped cleanly in half with a sharp *tang*. The boys all watched in complete shock as the heavy metal door swung gently open. They whooped softly in excitement when Shan stepped out of their cell and looked back at them through the bars. "Well," he called to them, "what are you waiting for?"

The four boys quickly scrambled out of the room after him. Rimmy was the last to leave. He wanted to make sure that he snatched up all their forgotten cloaks or any other articles they might have left lying atop the stone couches. Kilgar was patting Shan on the back. They both looked down on the naked sword in the Elfling's hand.

"I don't think that's a display sword," the boy from Branby told his friend. Shan looked him squarely in the eyes. Moonlight shimmered dully from the dark blade. "I'd say there's a lot more to that weapon than meets the eye."

The Elfling nodded slowly in agreement. He sheathed the unusual sword while the rest of them filed past him down the narrow hallway. They scuttled quickly across the outer apartment and pressed themselves up against the wall on either side of the doorway. Cautiously they peered out. Sapphire moonbeams flooded down over the empty walkway just outside the threshold.

"What do we do now?" Rimmy asked, breathlessly.

"I still think we need a diversion," Kilgar offered. "But where can we
. . . ?" Shan put a hand lightly on his arm. Kilgar looked at him
expectantly.

"Listen!" he said.

Suddenly they all froze, looking out into the hazy streams of
moonlight. But they couldn't hear anything. Not at first. The boys turned
questioning looks upon the Elfling, but he just lifted his hand slowly in the
wash of bluish light. He curled his fingers into a fist, yet left his index
finger extended. They waited for a few moments and then they could all
hear the clatter of running feet. They heard someone shouting from
somewhere down the street. Other loud voices quickly joined in, crashing
wildly together in the cool, night air in a growing swell of confusion.

"Fire!" they could finally make out the word. "Fire! Fire!" rang out
distinctly through the rising jumble of noise.

* * * * *

Torchlight blazed along the quay. Brackets were spaced every
twenty-five kora or so on the top of tall poles. Each of them cradled an
oil-soaked brand, set ablaze. They snapped and crackled in the still night
air. Two sentries strolled slowly back and forth between the torches. One
of them strode out upon the long wooden pier. The other one marched
down the stone embankment along the shore of the lagoon. They both
yawned as they paced slowly along. The rank waters were dark and still
behind them.

The two men nodded at each other as they came together at one point
where the dock met the quay. The first brigand turned about, a heavy
cutlass swinging from his hip, and retraced his route back out onto the
long wooden pier. The five light galleys were dark and silent as they
slowly swayed at their moorings. The oppressive silence was broken only
by the eerie groaning of deck timbers and the faint slapping of water
against their hulls. The railings creaked softly with the gentle rocking of
the vessels from side to side. Even the long, wooden planks of the dock
seemed to moan softly as the sentry walked past. To any but the stout-
hearted, the ominous sounds would have set tense muscles on edge or left
ripples of gooseflesh running down arms and neck.

The second lookout patrolled slowly along the great stone causeway.
He moved past the half-dozen ramshackle huts perched along the water's
edge. Yellow smears of light spewed out from the majority of them
through large cracks in their patchwork walls. From somewhere within,
someone could be heard singing an old sea shanty very loudly and off-key.

Daryl Hanson

The unmistakable sounds of clinking bottles and the dull clatter of tin cups spilled loudly out over the lagoon. Raucous bursts of laughter mingled with the explosion of angry voices over a variety of hotly contested dice and card games. Only one of the shacks remained completely enveloped in darkness. The heavy rattle of snoring escaped out through rents in its make-shift structure.

"That lot could sleep through anything," the watchman murmured to himself with a little wag of his head. "Even their own frightful snoring."

The bored sentry strolled down past the hastily constructed holding pens for the four great thorka. The large animals stamped and kicked in agitation as the pirate eased past. They lifted their magnificent heads and snorted loudly into the air. The man's bearded face swivelled to observe them as he walked along. He reached the end of the quay and looked up into the dome of the sky. The waxing crimson sickle of Kiara was setting to the west but the waning silvery-blue face of Sheera was now high overhead. The sentry sighed softly, wishing his turn at watch was already ended so he could join the others gambling loudly in the huts. *Who is there to guard against all the way out here?* he thought to himself. The snapping of a branch rifled through the air somewhere close-by and brought him to an abrupt stop.

He peered intently into the darkness under some nearby trees. A loud *twang* echoed on the night air, and then a sudden streak of light shot straight up no more than ten kora from his position. He tried to pierce the blackness but couldn't really see anything. Something hissed at him and charged out from the dense shadows. He managed to pull the cutlass from his scabbard before the thing was upon him.

The pirate fell back along the embankment as a hideous scaled creature with protruding tusks came up into the light. Its slitted eyes narrowed upon him and a whistling blur came down at his head. The heavy rush of air barely missed his ear as he continued to back away. Their weapons rang several times together in quick succession. The gruesome form coughed and barked at him in its pursuit.

By now the other sentry had been alerted to the clash of steel and had shouted an alarm. He came racing down the wooden dock and tore up the quay in the direction of the conflict.

The rattled buccaneer ducked and parried under the gorgul's relentless attacks, narrowly managing to keep the flash of the hefty scimitar from his throat. His own counter strokes were feeble at best, and were easily knocked aside by the long, strong arm of the ugly brute. It hissed and spit at him as he continued to back pedal. The other brigand continued to shout out an alarm until he could rush in to join him. Between the two of them together, hacking and slicing, they managed to check the creature's fierce onslaught. The savage thing leered horridly at them, its yellowish-stained tusks flashing sickly in the flickering light.

The sounds of running feet could now be heard trampling wildly out of the dilapidated buildings. The two sentries moved apart, trying to catch the thing in a kind of crossfire. It spun about continually, lashing out at them with its great sword. Its slit-like eyes glittered in the torchlight as it tried to engage them both at the same time. One of the two sentries managed to slip under its guard and drove his cutlass into the creature's armpit, impaling it in the heart. It screeched maniacally in anguish as it collapsed on the stones with a gush of dark blood. The scimitar clattered harmlessly aside.

A crowd of buccaneers immediately surrounded the two sentries standing over the fallen heap. "What is it?" one of the men called out as they hunched over it.

"Dunno," responded a second man. "Never seen anything like it."

"How'd it get here?" a third pirate blurted out, staring down at the blood-soaked creature.

Someone poked at it with a sword. He managed to roll the thing over. A gasp rose from the group as they looked upon it. Its slitted eyes were open and staring, its ugly face with its two great tusks caught the flickering torchlight and gave it a ghastly look.

Arak Lazard arrived at that moment and shoved his way into the center of the group. The pirates shifted to make room for him as they all stared down at the fallen thing.

"I still don't know what it is," said the first man who had spoken.

"I think it's called a gorgul," Lazard told them without looking up at the man. He studied the creature intently. "Here lies a thing out of legend," he spoke softly, "come to life before our very eyes."

"Don't you mean death, Captain?" one of the men asked. A few of the others sniggered at his words.

Arak looked up in irritation at the man who had spoken and fixed a stern eye on him. "If you weren't so dumb, you'd be stupid." The embarrassed man immediately dropped his gaze to stare down at the bloody corpse with all the others. The captain looked at each of the gathered men in turn yet they remained silent. Lazard returned his attention to the body. "Those boys were saying something about the foul spawn of Kulnedra chasing after them earlier this afternoon." He looked off in the direction of the boys' cell. "I wonder . . . ," he mused, but trailed off after a moment.

"What?" Dag asked him as he stood by his elbow.

"Oh, I just wonder how much of their absurd story was actually true." The captain continued to stare off through the rows of palm trees to the edge of the ruined city just down the lane.

"What do we do with this?" Dag asked him with a kick at the cadaver.

"Roll it into the lagoon," Lazard told him. "Let the swamp creatures pick its bones clean." He started to turn away. Two of the pirates stooped to heft the body in their arms. Arak paused.

"What do you think it wanted?" Rekki asked him.

"Perhaps it *was* after those boys, like they said," the captain mused. "I'll want to talk to them a little more first thing in the morning." He turned away, then swung back to look at Tobbin. "Let's make it after breakfast."

"Aye aye, Captain," the subordinate responded with a knowing smile.

"Did anyone see what it was doing before it attacked Skutter?" Arak asked suddenly.

"It got off a warning shot," Skutter told the captain himself. He pointed to the end of the quay. "From those trees over there. It sounded like a crossbow, but the bolt flared brightly like it was afire."

"I'd like to know how many more of those things are out there slinking around in the dark," the buccaneer captain exclaimed. To Dag's keen eye Lazard seemed to be a little unsettled, and he'd never seen that of him before. "Double, no, triple the guard for the rest of the night." He looked around warily into the veil of gloom. "And as for the rest of you roughnecks, I wouldn't expect to sleep too deeply tonight, unless you want to be awakened by one of those loathsome creatures with a knife in your gut."

The large ring of pirates gasped at his words and many of them squirmed uneasily.

"Keep your weapons handy at all times, lads." Arak Lazard pushed his way out from the center of the crowd. "I'm going back to my quarters," he said. "I want to know immediately if anything else happens."

"Aye aye, Captain," many of them spoke together. They watched him as he strode away.

"Dag," he called back when he stopped under the tall trunks of the palm trees. "Might also be a good idea to send a detail out into the bog to see if there are any more of those things lurking around." He resumed his march over the paved street.

"Aye aye, sir," Dag cried out. Arak lifted a hand to him but did not look back. The man turned to Rekki and Tobbin. "Form a detachment of ten men and scour the immediate vicinity for any more intruders. I don't like the idea of them hidin' out there in the bogs, waitin' to attack us when our backs are turned."

"Right," the two men nodded curtly in response.

Arak Lazard had just about reached his quarters when the alarm broke out. "Fire!" he heard someone shouting. "Fire! Fire!"

He spun instantly on his heel and sprinted back towards the quay. He could already smell the acrid tang of smoke on the air. He was puffing lightly for breath from his short run when he broke through the line of palm trees and slid to a stop on the broad stone embankment along the waterfront.

One of the rickety wooden shacks was ablaze. Bright yellow and orange tongues of fire licked greedily at the dry thatched roof, sending dark billows of smoke skyward. Streams of men ran all over the quay, scrambling around each other in confusion.

"What happened?" Lazard yelled at one of those rushing by. The man made a frenzied stop before the pirate captain, an empty wooden bucket held out tightly in his hands. Others quickly dashed past them to the edge of the lagoon. The disorganized mob commenced dunking an odd assortment of pans and buckets into the fetid water before racing back to the burning hut with them. They succeeded in wildly sloshing a great quantity of the water out over the ground from their mismatched containers.

"Those pesky luumin," the man spit out as he gripped the bucket in white knuckles. "One of them must have swung down from the trees and tossed a torch onto the roof over there." Lazard released him with a nod and urged him to resume his efforts with a curt flick of his wrist.

The captain scanned down the length of the causeway. He quickly confirmed that one of the torches was missing from its bracket. He frowned in consternation. Why would one of the arboreal creatures decide to do such a thing? They were extremely mischievous, he knew, often stealing anything left unattended, especially shiny objects. And once in a while they even snatched scraps of food, but since when did they ever get that close to fire before?

Lazard watched his men stumble around with their buckets brimming with lagoon water. They fanned out over the smooth stones, quickly forming a ragged line as they began to pass splashing bucketfuls. A few of them had finally stationed themselves by the growing conflagration and doused the rickety hut with each hastily received bucket.

Lazard watched the blaze from a distance. He could feel the heat on his face from where he stood, but he preferred not to get too close. He observed the organized chaos for a time as bucketful after bucketful was thrown onto the roaring flames, yet the fate of the little run-down shack was readily apparent. Lazard just hoped the fire wouldn't spread to any of the other buildings.

A movement from the corner of his eye caught the captain's attention. He swung to regard the prancing thorka in their hastily constructed corral. The proximity of the flames must have made them edgy and nervous for they stamped and raced anxiously around in their pen. Arak heard the timbers groaning behind him as the fire licked greedily at the glowing orange-red wood. The roof of the hut suddenly collapsed in a great roar, and fiery sparks were sent skyward.

The great animals kicked desperately at the makeshift wooden fencing in their eagerness to sprint away. As he stood watching them shift about restlessly, one of the little luumin dropped down out of the dark branches of a tree. It scurried up to the gate of the corral on its four limbs in leaps and bounds. Before Lazard could hurry over, the small creature hopped up on the fence and pulled the bolt free from the latch.

"No!" the buccaneer captain bellowed as he started to run for the pens.

The gate swung immediately open and the frightened thorka burst out of the small enclosure. They shot out over the open ground along the embankment, their hooves drawing sparks from the stones, and they bolted quickly into the trees. Lazard skidded to a halt in front of the open pen. He heard the dwindling sound of their furious flight across the marshy ground.

"Keh-keh," the ape-like form seemed to say to him. "Keh-keh." It scolded him soundly with a shake of its furry head before racing off on all its limbs, the thick calloused knuckles scraping noisily on the damp earth. It launched itself into the low hanging branches of a nearby tree, scampering off in an instant.

Arak Lazard stood motionless in frustration for several long moments. He stared off into the darkness under the trees. The captain knew they would be trapped on the island, and that his men could track the thorka down eventually, but his mind quickly tried to calculate the time and expense that might cost him. He sighed loudly.

As he stood staring into the night, a number of bulky forms crept up out of the gloom towards him. Wavering torchlight washed over the grim figures, revealing wide-set slanted eyes and large up-thrusting tusks. There must have been at least a dozen of them. The creatures coughed and hissed at one another as they quickly spread out before him. They looked exactly like the brutish soldier they had just killed, he realized with a tight swallow.

"Hey!" the captain bellowed over his shoulder without bothering to look back at his men. "Little help!" he screamed. He drew the sword he'd snagged from the case in his quarters. It was one of those he'd taken from the boys. He swished it back and forth experimentally. Already he liked the way it felt in his hand. Cries of astonishment broke out behind him as the pirates abandoned their buckets and rushed to his aid. They pulled out their weapons with a slithering of steel as they joined Lazard on the quay.

*　*　*　*　*

"Fire!" someone was shouting.

The boys waited just inside the compartment doorway. They shrank back after a pair of cutthroats rushed past. They waited for a brief span, yet the street outside remained deserted.

"Come on," Kilgar told them as he edged out into the silvery-blue moon glow. "This is the diversion we've been waiting for. Let's get our weapons." The others trailed along after him. They moved quickly from shadow to shadow, hugging the darkened edge of collapsed buildings, sliding under the dangling branches of scattered trees, until they arrived outside the captain's villa.

Lights poured out through the opened doorway, yet try as they might, they could not detect any sounds of movement from the depths of the house. Cautiously they snuck inside, stopping often to listen. They eased through the entry hall and stood at the threshold of the large room. A few lanterns blazed from the ceiling hooks but revealed no one in sight. Kilgar shared a look with the Elfling before the two of them scurried, light-footed, across the open tile floor. They skirted the dias with its huge, throne-like chair, came at last to the long glass case against the back wall. They could see their equipment spread out upon several of its shelves.

Shan tried one of the door handles quietly, but it was locked. *Just as I thought.* He moved to the next one and got the same result.

Kilgar gave him a shrug before smashing his elbow against the glass pane. Shards of shattering crystal sprayed everywhere in a loud chorus that echoed throughout the room. The boys kicked aside jagged fragments as they quickly pulled out their swords, bows, quivers of arrows and their knives. These they quickly handed off to Doornig and Gorian who'd moved across the room to help. Rimmy remained stationed at the hallway arch to warn them should anyone come running.

"One of the swords is missing," Kilgar spoke in a hushed voice. "Lazard's probably got it."

"That's alright," Shan told him with a slap at the ceramic scabbard in his belt, "I've already got a replacement." The dark-haired boy grinned at him. They found their packs piled in a corner. They grabbed them up and hurriedly pulled them on.

"Quick," Doornig called out, "let's get out of here." They turned hastily for the door.

"Who's there?" called out a woman's sleepy voice from the captain's bed-chamber. They looked up to see a robed figure standing bare-footed at the edge of the darkened room.

"Jadeetha," Shan breathed in a whisper. "It's just us, Ma'am," the Elfling called out as they skated over crumbling bits of glass. "We came to get our weapons back."

"But how did you get out of your holding cell?" she asked groggily. "I thought you were locked in tight."

"We're just sneaky, I guess," Kilgar responded to her. They hurried across the room, scattering sharp, odd-shaped fragments in their shuffling steps. The boys dashed into the hallway, but Kilgar paused at the arched doorway. "Tell the captain we considered his kind proposal to join his band of pirates, but we have regrettably decided to decline." He bowed to her slightly and touched a hand to his forehead in farewell.

And with that they were gone. They slid across the smooth tiles of the entrance hall and trampled down the steps outside. The boys bolted off down the street, quickly melting into the darkness. They glided as noiselessly as they could to the end of the tiled lane. Just as they huddled up against a ruined structure a wild clattering of hooves shot past them. They gasped in surprise as their four magnificent thorka streaked off into the darkness of the swamp.

"What do we do now?" Doornig hissed in exasperation.

"We could run after them," Gorian said.

"No," Kilgar was firm, "not in the dark." He shook his head. "We'd lose their trail in no time. And we'd never manage to catch them in the bogs anyway."

"Probably even break a leg out there in the process," Rimmy proclaimed.

"Our only hope now," Shan stated evenly, "is the underground river." He watched Kilgar stare wistfully off after the animals. He sighed and turned to look at the Elfling. He nodded quietly. "I'm sorry," Shan told him, clapping a hand on his arm. "I know Adrulax means a lot to you, but I don't think we have much of a choice at this point."

The dark-haired boy nodded again reluctantly. "You're right," he said, turning slowly away from their hiding place. "Come on, then," he called to the others.

They hadn't taken more than a dozen steps before the sounds of fighting broke out along the back side of the rock-strewn avenue. The boys froze for an instant as blood-curdling screams and the sudden wild clash of metal on metal split the coolness of the night.

"Either the pirates have gone totally mad and they're fighting each other," Gorian offered with a tense scowl, "or they've just gotten some unwanted visitors to the island." His eyes gleamed dully in the moonlight.

"Gorguls!" the Elfling exclaimed in a tight-lipped groan.

"Run for it!" Kilgar hissed. "Hurry! Back to the cell."

The five of them were off like a shot. They flashed swiftly down the street, careful to dodge around broken bits of tile and hop over clumps of weeds barring their way. The soft clatter of their boots on the stones mingled oddly with the frightened huff of their breathing. Sheera's muted brilliance seemed to dance from the milky white flagstones before them, enabling them to cut easily through the streets. They saw no one in their flight and the harsh sounds of battle died away behind them.

The boys found the entrance to their cell easily enough. They ducked quickly into the dark opening where it yawned on the edge of the street. They slowed their headlong pace abruptly as they groped around in the gloom. Shan moved up to lead them across the outer chamber, down the narrow corridor, past the iron gate they had left ajar, and into their familiar cell.

"Over here," the Elfling called out. He moved down the wall on their left until he came to the panel displaying the map of Ythira. The others huddled around him. As he bent down to press on the seven pointed star recessed in the stone, Shan noticed several other symbols he hadn't seen before. "Hmm," he said to himself. He ran his eyes quickly over them in the faint light. "No time now to puzzle those out."

"What's that?" Kilgar asked, standing anxiously next to him.

"Oh, just some markings on the map I don't remember seeing before," the Elfling announced. "It's probably nothing. Here goes." He depressed the image firmly. After a moment the panel whooshed open, only this time Shan had not been leaning on it and didn't tumble recklessly down into the darkness. The coolness of the passage below could be instantly felt.

"There's a long stone chute here," Shan instructed them, "just inside the panel. Follow after me, one at a time, and we'll meet up at the bottom. Alright?"

The boys grunted in assent. Doornig made sure he wasn't last this time, pushing himself ahead of Rimmy and Gorian as they queued up behind the Elfling.

"Don't worry, I've got a hand on the door to make sure it doesn't close prematurely," Kilgar said to the redhead as he pressed up close. "All of you follow after Shan, and I'll bring up the rear."

"Okay," Doornig muttered.

"Here we go," Shan said. He stepped through the open portal and slid down the ramp with a whirling of dust. "Next," he called back over his shoulder. They could hear his voice from somewhere far below.

Doornig wriggled past Kilgar and dropped onto the stone grade. He called out in surprise as he felt himself rushing downwards into complete darkness. Seams in the rock bumped uncomfortably against his backside. Shan helped him up at the bottom, pulling him off to the side as the next person came skimming down from above. Doornig rubbed at his tail bone with a low moan while the Elfling pulled Gorian to his feet. Rimmy came sliding down almost immediately, followed quickly by Kilgar. The two brothers scrambled onto their feet to join the others.

"How can you see down here?" Doornig mumbled. "It's completely dark."

"No," Shan told him, "not completely." He pointed up to the small slits along the edges of the stone ceiling, but then realized Doornig wouldn't be able to see his movement. "There are small vent shafts in the rocks high above. They let in air and enough moonlight for me to see."

"I wish I could see like that," Rimmy blurted out, obviously impressed.

"Come on," Shan told him as he turned to lead the way down the long corridor stretching out in front of them. "Hold hands if you need to."

"Good idea," Kilgar announced. "That way we can't get lost." He reached out and fumbled for his brother's hand in the darkness. Rimmy, in turn, reached out and clasped his other hand onto Gorian's.

Shan padded through the dusty corridor. He swivelled his head to peer at the spot where he'd opened the large crypt door, but he could see nothing now. He laid his free hand lightly on the pommel of the sword in reassurance as they plodded along.

They came at last to the cross passage and the Elfling smartly turned them to his left. "Turning left here," he called out to the others. They fumbled around a bit behind him, tangling their feet somewhat before managing to get their footsteps in sync. They trudged along in silence, only the soft scuffling of their boots could be heard on the dusty stones. Before long they could all discern a dim hum from far ahead. It slowly grew until they recognized it as the unmistakable roar of rushing water.

The boys expressed a sense of delight as Shan escorted them out of the tunnel. They stepped onto a landing overlooking a river cavern. Lazy streams of moonlight slanted down from a rift in the chamber ceiling above to bathe the rushing white water in a soft blue glow, which even the humans could see.

"Whoa!" Rimmy cried. "This is amazing."

"Yeah," Gorian agreed with him, "I'd love to see this in the daylight."

"No time to wait for that," Kilgar brushed past them with a shake of his head. He quickly followed Shan down the slippery steps. "Be careful," he called back to the others, "it's wet here."

They assembled on the dockside landing. Light spray from the river misted over them.

"The boats are over here," Shan stated, turning to the little niches along one of the walls. Kilgar helped him pull one of the light craft from its storage tube. They flipped it over and set it on the tiled landing. It canted to the side on its slightly ribbed keel line. They turned to study it for a moment. It was definitely hollowed like a dugout canoe, but had the long thin line of a kayak.

"Good," Shan exclaimed, peering into the shallow cavity in the wall. He reached his hand in and extracted a strong thin pole. The rounded shaft widened out and flattened to form paddles on each end. He held it up for Kilgar to see.

"A paddle, great," the dark-haired boy proclaimed. "We'll definitely need those."

They quickly pulled out two additional boats and four more double bladed paddles.

"Rather than try to cram three of us together in one of these little things," Kilgar advised, "let's put two in each of those." He pointed down at the two craft they'd laid off to the side near the low retaining wall. "Doornig and Gorian, you take one. Rimmy, you team up with Shan in the other. I'll manage this last one on my own."

"Right," they all offered in agreement.

They quickly set to lashing their packs and weapons down inside the small boats. They used laces from their boots to secure them to little hook-like projections they discovered along the inside edges of the gunwales.

"We're sure gonna miss the rest of our supplies," Doornig grumbled more to himself than anyone else. But the Elfling heard him.

"Who knows, maybe we'll run into the thorka somewhere else on the island," Shan told him. "Wherever this river comes out."

"Fat chance of that," the redhead complained.

"One can only hope," the Elfling shrugged. "I don't know," he said with a wry smile, "funnier things than that have already happened on this journey."

Doornig turned away, snorting in derision.

They set the boats down into the roiling water one at a time. Two of them held on while the first pair clambered aboard. Once Doornig and Gorian got themselves settled to their liking they allowed themselves to drift down a bit from the launching area. They held onto the retaining wall with a tight grip as they rose and fell with the surging swells. Gorian reached back with his other hand to steady the bow of the next boat with Kilgar as Shan and Rimmy stepped down carefully into the pitching little craft.

The first boat eased a little further along the low wall of the landing to allow the second pair a little place to grasp onto. The younger dark-haired boy clutched onto the railing while he tried desperately to help his brother keep his own craft under control long enough to scamper into it. Kilgar wobbled momentarily as he fought to maintain his balance in the shifting swells. He finally managed to plop himself down in the bottom of his boat. He gripped tightly onto his double-bladed paddle and thrust off from the landing with it.

The others did likewise, pushing off from the landing with their long oars. The three boats rushed away from the bank and merged quickly with the surging flow of the river. They all sped off down the channel and soon found themselves surrounded by darkness.

– 28 –
Crossing The Canalorn
[7th - 8th of Bellach, 4534 C.R.]

They bobbed along in the darkness of the passage. The roar of the open cavern soon fell away behind them. Spray from the choppy water moistened their arms and their faces. They didn't bother to paddle much as the surge of the river hastened them forward, but they used their oars to keep themselves steady as much as they could in the constant turbulence around them.

They bumped into each other occasionally in the overwhelming blackness, using only the tips of their paddles to keep from cracking their boats violently together. Their constant fear was they might collide with large rocks rearing up suddenly out of the darkness. If they struck against any boulders in the slapping waves they could be crushed into mounds of broken bones.

They seemed to ride the cascade for more than an ahr, climbing over the rolling swells and shooting down into the troughs in a never-ending rhythm. Trailing arms of roots and vines ran down from the channel ceiling above and dragged across their faces from time to time. The first time it happened, Doornig was completely unprepared and nearly toppled from the boat in surprise.

"Ugh!" the redhead hissed. "Watch out for the creepers," he called out, sputtering twisted bits of root and moss from his mouth.

A dim light eventually began to grow somewhere ahead of them, a sort of faint bluish sheen upon the water. They hurtled towards it until it seemed to fill the rocky channel with a dull illumination. All at once they shot out through a curtain of hanging vines into the open night air. Sheera was far off to the west, almost behind them, but the large, waning moon still gave out sufficient silvery-blue light for them to see fairly well.

The river rushed on through the swamp, shooting their little boats through tight arms of moss-enshrouded trees hanging low over the water. The night cries of birds and insects assailed their ears. Something large splashed into the river on their right as they hurtled along the ragged bank. Tree limbs and dense brush hung down into the surging water and scratched at their arms.

Kilgar guided them to the shore where he found an opening in the foliage. He drew his small boat out of the main current and slowed to a near stop in the shallows. He pulled himself up to the flat bank, negotiating a mass of twining roots with the end of his paddle. The others splashed out of their own boats and pulled them up easily onto the damp ground.

"Let's rest here a while," Kilgar said to them. "I think we've put enough distance between us and the ruins of Suul'Kar to deserve a break." He sat down on a thick tree root and regarded his fellows. "Besides," he offered with a wan grin in the moonlight, "I can't imagine they even know where we went."

"This river could be completely unknown to them," Rimmy stated as he sat down next to his brother. He grinned at Kilgar, who chuckled softly and gave him a little pat on the back.

"They might still be so absorbed in their fight with the gorguls that they haven't even discovered we're gone yet," added the sandy-haired youth. Doornig gave his friend a clap on the shoulder in acknowledgment.

"I'm sure Jadeetha knows we've run off," the Elfling informed them. "She heard us take the weapons from the case."

"True," Doornig interjected, "but I'm sure she couldn't tell which way we ran from there." The Elfling nodded in affirmation.

Something moved in the brush several kora way, and the boys all jumped. The small thing scurried off, leaving them all panting for breath and reaching for their belt knives. They relaxed after a moment as they hunkered down on whatever dry patches they could find.

"What's next?" the Elfling posed to Kilgar as he knelt down in front of him.

"Well," mused the dark-haired boy, "we're going to have to get off this island eventually. We should be able to use the boats to make our way ashore."

"Let's hope the farther bank of the Tanalorn isn't crawling with gorguls by now," Doornig cut in with a sneer.

"We'll have to take that risk," Kilgar replied. He shook his head sadly. "We haven't got any other choice."

"We certainly can't hide out on this island until the pirates come looking for us," Gorian interposed. "We'd probably starve to death before they even found us." He grunted softly to himself.

"Let's hold up here for a little while to rest," Kilgar went on, "then we'll drift down to the great river. We'll see then what we can find." He paused as he looked up at the night sky before glancing at the Elfling. "We may not have enough time to get across before the sun comes up. I'd really rather not be out on the Tanalorn in broad daylight."

"Yeah, we all remember what happened last time we did that,"

Doornig spit out in disgust.

"Which means we'll probably have to pass the day here in the swamp," Kilgar continued. "Hopefully, in the meantime, we don't run across any wandering patrols."

"Whether it's pirate or gorgul," snapped Gorian.

"We can make our crossing tomorrow night," the dark-haired boy continued, ignoring the interruption, "before the big moon comes up." He paused. "I kind of hope we can find our animals out there," he declared after looking out through the darkness of the trees, "—somehow."

"We could really use the supplies they're carrying in those saddle packs," Doornig chimed in.

"Exactly," Kilgar blinked at them all. "What do you say?"

"I think it's a good idea," Shan stated slowly, "as long as we don't encounter any signs of pursuit." He met eyes with Kilgar.

"That's a given," the youth from Branby proclaimed. "If we run into trouble we make a break for it immediately." He gave the Elfling a firm bob of his head, then looked at each of the others in turn. They all confirmed his plan with a slight tilt of their heads.

The remainder of the night seemed to pass slowly for them, huddled as they were under the drooping trees. They slept fitfully, managing to catch only scattered snatches of rest throughout the early ahrin, their backs touching. As usual, they took turns standing watch over the others, prowling about their tight little circle in a constant state of motion. Small animals continued to scurry around in the brush, rustling the leaves all around them

They were extremely hungry when morning found them. The only thing they carried in their light packs were their fire-making equipment and an extra change of clothing or two. Most of their stores of food were stuffed in the panniers on the backs of the thorka. Stiffly they rose to their feet and began to scour the boggy tracks under the tall, fern-like trees for anything to eat. They did manage to locate a few prickly plants with some overripe berries hanging down in moist clusters. They collected all they could find, suffering the stings from long, spiky thorns to produce a handful of sticky fruit apiece. It wasn't much, but it served to slake their immediate hunger for a time.

Kilgar insisted they take the day to roam through the marshy stretches south of their current position. They tramped along in a loose line, separated by about thirty kora, with the instruction to stop if they lost sight of their fellows to their left or right. In the event any of them lost contact they were instructed to hold their position and call out like a certain kind of bird until the line contracted in on itself. Shan laughed when Doornig and Gorian had a difficult time trying to duplicate the correct bird call. In the end Kilgar changed it to a whistle.

They made good progress through the reeking fen, only having to constrict their line of march twice. When they made contact once again, they moved off, gradually spreading back out to their full limit between one another. Kilgar whistled periodically for his lost animal. This was quite a bit different than their call to regroup, but it had taken Shan a few of Kilgar's distinctive high-pitched blasts before he could resist the urge to gather together again.

They trudged on through the brush for the rest of the day until it started to grow a little dim under the trees. The afternoon sun began to sink down toward the western horizon when Kilgar called them all together.

"I think we've come far enough for today," their leader told them. "It's beginning to feel pretty hopeless at this point." His shoulders slumped forward in discouragement. Gorian slapped him lightly on the arm.

"You know, it was only about one shot in a million we'd actually find them," he offered glumly. He gave Kilgar a little squeeze on the elbow. "I miss my thorka, too." The boys shared a sullen smile.

They turned to make the long, slow trek back to where they'd beached their boats, when Shan brought them up short with an upraised hand. "Wait," he called softly. "I can hear something."

"Pfff!" Doornig sneered. "In this incessant whine of birds and insects, *you* can hear *something?*" he snickered sarcastically.

"Hush!" Shan whispered tersely.

The boys halted in their tracks, careful not to make a sound as the Elfling strained to listen.

"Is it pirates?" Kilgar leaned over and whispered in his ear. "Gorguls maybe?" The elven lad wagged his head slightly from side to side.

"No, I don't think so," he muttered softly. "It's different." Then, after a long moment, he turned to Kilgar. "Try your whistle again," he encouraged hesitantly.

Kilgar obediently tightened his lips and offered up a piercing blast. They all waited for a long moment, holding their breaths. They searched the Elfling's face as he listened intently for a response. He tilted his head slightly to the side, his blue eyes gazing off into the canopy above them. The wait seemed interminable to Rimmy, yet he struggled to remain still.

Shan's vacant stare slowly morphed into a joyful smirk. "That's done it," he announced with a little smile. He looked off into the undergrowth. "They're coming."

"Who?" Doornig demanded. "What?" Lines of worry suddenly creased his forehead.

Shan's handsome face broke into a broad grin. "The missing animals," he said.

"Really?" Kilgar was incredulous. "They're coming this way?" The Elfling nodded gladly to him.

"I can hear their hoof beats very clearly as they're running," Shan said. His smile softened a little into a bit of a frown. "However, I can't be certain how many of them are still together." His eyes lost their focus for a moment and then he shook his head. He regarded Kilgar. "Whistle again."

The boy nodded and immediately complied, belting out a shrill blast from his puckered lips. They heard it echoing through the trees all around them. Then, after a moment, they all heard a faint answering whinny from somewhere out in the marsh. The unmistakable clomp of hooves quickly thundered closer.

The quintet watched with a growing sense of excitement as several dark forms seemed to materialize out of the gloom. Four large, sleek thorka darted through the mass of branches and bounded towards them. The great animals raced up to where they stood, their long graceful faces reaching forward with each thundering step, their long ears laid back. The boys stood breathlessly, watching their rapid approach.

The marvelous beasts pounded into a tight circle around them, nostrils flaring, their manes wild and unruly. They rose up loudly on their hindquarters before stamping over to the boys, their ears perking up. The large animals whickered happily and came to a standstill, blowing out air noisily in greeting and butting their owners affectionately with their great heads.

"Adrulax," Kilgar exclaimed in a joyful howl. "It's great to see you, boy." He scratched at the thorka's long cheeks and slapped lovingly at his damp neck. "Thought I'd never see you again, boy," he said emotionally. He hugged the great animal around the neck.

Shan stood watching as the other boys greeted their beloved animals in similar fashion. With calls of "Ruggles," "Thimba," and "Hoofnail," the trio of riders made their animals welcome with a variety of slaps, scratches and hugs.

After a few moments, Doornig tore open one of their panniers in his hunger and quickly doled out some of the packaged food. They wasted no time in scarfing down some of the dried fruit and meat, so hastily in fact, they didn't really even taste it. They offered the animals some dried grain out of one of the bags. Once they'd completed their hurried meal they mounted up and headed back to their stash of boats. It took them a fraction of the time they'd spent all that day on foot to make it back to the river.

Nightfall was settling over the swamps of Watcher's Island when they reined in at their temporary campsite. They hadn't bothered to pile stones together for a fire, which they figured was probably a bad idea anyway, nor had they taken the time to make any other adjustments to the area, save pull the boats a little further up the bank from the river and had tried to conceal them as best they could under some thick underbrush.

They dismounted near the small light craft. Kilgar drew them together. "So far we haven't seen any sign of pursuit, and that's good," he told them. "But we don't know how long that will last." The others all nodded in agreement. "I say we shove off immediately. We drag the boats down to the water and you four float downstream until you reach the Tanalorn. I'll ride Adrulax, leading the other animals behind us."

"Hopefully we'll all reach the edge of the great river together," Shan stated.

"Exactly," Kilgar replied.

"But who's going to pilot the third boat?" Rimmy asked, looking over at his brother. Sheera hadn't risen yet, so it was fairly dark under the branches.

"Tie it behind one of the other boats," his brother responded. "Or . . . or better yet, have one of you steer it along with the others." He shifted to look at Gorian and Doornig. "Are you two comfortable enough to manage your own boats?"

Both boys returned a look of confidence. "You bet," Doornig said a little too proudly.

"Of course," Gorian stated airily.

"Okay, you two split up then." Kilgar leveled his gaze on his brother. "Rimmy, you stay with Shan, and we'll all meet up together at the river's edge."

"Sounds good," his younger brother told him.

They hurried to carry the three small boats down to the water.

"If you try to stay in the shallows along the shore you won't likely get too far ahead of me," their dark-haired leader instructed them.

"Right," returned Gorian, "but if you should have to ride too far inland and we lose sight of each other, we can always stop along the bank and wait for you to catch up."

"Okay, good idea," Kilgar observed. He looked up at the sky. "Sheera will be coming up pretty soon and I'd like to be far out on the Tanalorn before that happens. Let's get to it."

The four boys thrust their small boats into the lapping current and shoved off with their long paddles. They kept to the shallow water, the eddies along the shore slapping softly against their light craft. Kilgar quickly mounted up on Adrulax, deftly snatching up the neck ropes of all the other thorka. He turned his mount and plodded off after them in silence, the chain of animals in tow. He picked his way along the bank beside them for some time. Only once did the boys have to pull their boats up to the shore when they lost sight of him. They waited as he skirted around a small cliff wall which rose up for a short time between them. Once he had maneuvered around the natural barrier, they pressed on.

It wasn't long afterwards before they heard the deep rippling of more water ahead. The island river splashed over some small rocks where it mingled with the mighty Tanalorn. They pulled up their boats along the level bank just as Kilgar rounded his last stretch of marsh trees. He walked the thorka up to them and slid down off the saddle. He studied the sky for a moment. Kiara, the smaller, reddish gold moon, had already set behind them and Sheera hadn't made its appearance yet above the distant horizon.

"Hurry," Kilgar told them. "We'd best shove off immediately."

He pulled lightly on Adrulax' reins, coaxing him down into the massive river. The other thorka followed timidly. They balked when their hooves splashed into the water, dropping their long heads to sniff at the gurgling flow. Kilgar finally convinced them to walk out into the strong current until the waters brushed their underbellies. They danced nervously around on their six legs but eventually allowed Kilgar to lead them further into the river. They panicked momentarily once their feet could no longer touch the bottom, but Kilgar swam with them and encouraged them with soft words and little clucks of his tongue.

The boys in their small boats launched out to join the swimming animals and they gradually moved out into the stronger current together. At one point Kilgar had enough of swimming and scrambled into a boat with Doornig. The redhead did his best to keep the little craft steady as

Kilgar slid himself over the rocking gunwale. The boy pulled his cloak out from under the bow strut where he'd tucked it and dried himself as much as he could with it. He looked over at the thorka swimming easily across the current.

"Good boy, Adrulax," Kilgar called out to his stallion as he tread his way alongside their little boats. "Good boy. Keep it up, Ruggles. Way to go, Hoofnail. And you too, Thimba. Easy now boys, keep it going. Keep it going." He ran a corner of his cloak over his soaking hair.

They were being swept quite a ways downstream as they worked slowly across the turgid flood. Their paddles dipped and scooped like water bugs but they soon began to struggle with each stroke. The muscles in their backs were feeling on fire by the time the azure disk of Sheera reared up over the distant hills. The larger moon cast its waning blue-silver light down over the peaks of the little waves like thousands of sparkling jewels.

They had gone more than three quarters of the way when Kilgar noticed the animals beginning to labor. No longer able to hold their heads high out of the water, they continually snorted spray from their nostrils. The strokes of their legs began to falter in the never-ending swirl of waves. Kilgar tried to encourage them from the boat. He called out soothingly as they fought to stay alongside the bouncing canoes. The boy clucked his tongue and the animals nickered weakly in return.

"Come on, boys," Kilgar said, "we're almost there." He looked anxiously at the approaching shoreline, but it didn't seem to grow closer nearly fast enough. He looked back at the struggling animals with a worried frown. "Almost there," he called out confidently. He kept encouraging them with the steady rhythm of his voice.

It seemed an eternity but they finally made it across the grand river. The thorka were almost totally spent when their hooves initially made contact with the edge of the riverbed. They stumbled weakly up onto the bank and stood on shaky legs, their long ears twitching uncontrollably. The boys drew their light boats into the shallows and hopped up wearily from their stiff-legged positions. Their muscles were extremely sore and tight as they dragged the little craft up onto the shore. They threw themselves down next to them in total exhaustion. Sheera's bright glow bathed them in a fuzzy radiance.

They lay there for some time. Shan was sure he had fallen asleep along with the rest of them because the position of the moon had changed considerably since last he'd noticed. The Elfling sat up stiffly on the lush grass and looked about. The boys were still flat on their backs, breathing deeply and regularly. A slight snore escaped through Doornig's partially opened lips. The thorka seemed to have recovered a little from their ordeal. They paced about slowly on the bank, cropping contentedly on the long grass. The muscles of their long legs still quivered occasionally in little spasms.

The Elfling stood up and stretched his stiff body. He knuckled a spot on his lower back until the muscles loosened enough to relieve the painful knots. He walked down to the river's edge in the milky light and gazed across the wide channel to the large island which seemed so far away now. He wondered what had happened in the ruins of Suul'Kar. Had the pirates beaten back the attack of the gorguls, or had they been completely overrun by the loathsome creatures, cut down in an avalanche of scimitars? Did Lazard survive the onslaught? And if he still lived, was he even now aware of their escape?

The Elfling smiled grimly as he pondered these things. He tried to imagine the buccaneer captain's consternation. The heavy iron bolt of their cell had been cleanly cut. But how? The boys hadn't had any weapons to cut through the thick metal, at least not until *after* they'd gotten out of their prison. So how *did* they get out and where did they go? He knew they couldn't have taken one of his galleys or the unwieldy barge, and yet they had somehow completely disappeared. His only assumption, Shan rationalized, was that they had run out into the darkness of the bogs. He could visualize the pirates combing the swamps with waves of search parties, hacking their way through dense underbrush with their broad cutlasses in an effort to find them.

He swung slowly on his heel to survey the vicinity. A small stand of trees was immediately to the east of them. The dark confines stood just forty or fifty kora inland. To the north he could see a series of low hills. There was a hint of a forest somewhere to the northeast, a long way off, yet the Elfling had no idea it was actually Draydin. And in the distance, beyond the swath of trees, there was the promise of mountains. They were now just a faint smudge in the darkness.

Shan pivoted to the south. Past the small stand of woods to his left, he could make out another long stretch of forest trees. It was hard for him to determine anything at this distance, to distinguish one grove from another. He didn't even realize he was looking at Darkwood once again. His eyes shifted from the distant dark line to the great curve of the Tanalorn as it wound its way up from the southwest. Sheera's dwindling light danced off the peaks of the rolling waves.

He started to turn back to his friends when a streak of movement and a flash of light from something metal caught his eyes. He focused in on the bank of the great river a couple korads away. It took several long moments for him to realize there were soldiers marching their way along the shore. His heart suddenly skipped a beat.

Shan turned quickly to his sleeping friends. He woke Kilgar and Rimmy with a fervent shake. "Soldiers!" he hissed at them. They rolled hurriedly to their stomachs and stared off in the direction he pointed. The Elfling gave the other two boys a solid slap on the legs. "Quiet!" he called in a tense whisper. "Soldiers coming our way." They all sprang up into a sitting position and desperately shook the cobwebs from their brains.

"Gorguls?" Gorian wanted to know.

"Can't quite tell just yet," Shan informed them quietly. "They're still too far away."

"Let's grab the animals," Kilgar said in hushed tones. "Nice and easy. No quick movements. Try not to attract their attention." He looked around quickly and spied the small stand of trees. "Let's hide in there," he urged quietly, with a nod at the little grove.

They came up slowly to their feet and pulled easily on the neck ropes of their animals. They moved off toward the tree line in a forced slow motion.

"Try to keep your backs turned to the moonlight," Shan advised them. "It'll keep our faces from shining out at them."

They reached the first edge of trees in agonizing slowness. They pulled the thorka in after them and moved back into the deepest shadows they could find. Shan hovered just inside the branches to get another glimpse of the approaching force. He breathed shallowly as he waited, his throat dry and tight. Suddenly he remembered the three small boats they'd left drawn up on the beach. He looked back towards them in desperation. *Too late!* he told himself.

He didn't have long to wait. Within a matter of a few mira the Elfling could definitely make out the bulky forms of broad shouldered, long-armed soldiers. Their distinctive metal stomp could just be heard as they topped a rise along the river bank. They were less than a korad away by that time.

"Definitely gorguls," the Elfling told the others when he moved back into the darkness to join them. They all crouched momentarily in the shadows.

"We should make our way deeper into these trees," Kilgar commanded tensely. "We didn't have time to conceal our tracks and they're sure to find them."

"Forget the tracks," the Elfling pointed out in harsh tones. "We left the boats down there in full view."

The lancing knot of fear seized them all in the gut. They moved off as quickly and as quietly as they could manage through the pressing branches. They hadn't gone more than a hundred kora into the trees when there came the loud bugling of a horn from the direction of the river.

"They must have found the boats already," Gorian wheezed.

"Right," Kilgar muttered dejectedly. "And those boats will lead them directly to our tracks. Hurry!"

The boys doubled their speed but the sudden thrashing at the edge of the trees spurred them on to even greater haste. The terrified boys tugged at the animals as they stumbled and grappled over the uneven ground. They could hear the regular chop and slash of metal as the gorguls hacked away at the confining branches somewhere behind them. Harsh, shouted commands rang out through the night.

No matter how hard the boys pushed themselves through the clinging undergrowth the sounds of pursuit seemed to grow steadily closer. At one point Shan caught a wild glimpse of a hideous face forcing its way through the dark weaving branches behind them.

"If we could break out of these trees," Kilgar was heard to say breathlessly, "we should be able to mount up and make a run for it." He swatted at a long, leafy arm that nearly struck him in the face.

Heavy feet stomped nearer through the tangles of dense foliage. The echoing ring of swords seemed almost upon them. The boys fought their rising panic as they twisted through the sheltering wall of trees. It was difficult to stay a step ahead in the overwhelming darkness. Only pale shafts of moonlight found their way through the thick canopy above, making the boys practically blind as they pulled anxiously at the terrified thorka. The animals neighed loudly in their growing panic.

The frightened companions broke out of the trees at last. Their rubbery legs felt numb as they stumbled over the tufted ground. Horrid faces with upthrust tusks were practically behind them. Almost at once a string of ugly creatures cleared the trees right after them with a last ringing stroke of their broad scimitars. With bloodcurdling shrieks, the gorguls scrambled immediately after them.

29

A Company Of Dwarves
[8th of Bellach, 4534 C.R.]

Kilgar tried desperately to quiet Adrulax as the large animal bucked and stamped. He struggled to get a foot in a stirrup as they spun about together in a tight circle. One startled look told him there would be no time for him to mount up. He pulled himself free of the saddle and swung to face the charge of the nearest foe as it quickly bore down on him. The scaly curve of its face was transfixed in a mask of hatred, its large, cat-like eyes narrowing upon him. Kilgar hurriedly pulled his elven-made sword from its scabbard and spun to face the creature's maddened rush.

At the same time the other boys released their hold on the reins in futility and frantically drew their own weapons. Freed suddenly of their restraints, the terrified thorka reared up and bolted away. The frightened boys were soon too busy to watch them run off. Neither did they have an opportunity to count the number of hideous faces scuttling towards them. They turned awkwardly about, bumping clumsily into one another, as they fought to keep their feet from getting entangled. Horrified by the angry line swiftly advancing to confront them, the boys sought to bring up their blades in whitened fingers.

The closest of the gorguls swept in to attack, but Kilgar clumsily batted aside the powerful thrust of the scimitar. Instantly, the dark-haired youth ducked under the clawed fist that swept past his face. The other boys nervously stood their ground in a tight circle, their eyes frightened, their feet constantly shifting over the lumpy soil. Tufted clumps of tall grass threatened to pitch them onto the rocky ground with each shuffling step. Soft beams of moonlight danced crazily from the bright elven blades which they brandished in white-knuckled fists.

The gorguls harried them with vicious thrusts of their wickedly curved swords. Backing and edging along together, the overmatched boys managed to keep the fearsome creatures at bay for a time without any sort of style or finesse of their own. They simply batted forcefully at the heavy blades each time one of them was thrust in their faces. The clatter of steel rang out ominously.

The two groups continued to shift their positions constantly, dodging and feinting, ducking and weaving. Unbelievably, the five friends managed to deflect a wild barrage of blows offering them little damage other than a few small cuts along their forearms. Their tactics were mostly defensive, but occasionally they retaliated in short, rapid exchanges.

The sword in Shan's hand had grown warm to the touch. The dark, shimmering surface quickly began to change until it had taken on an almost translucent quality. The gorguls hissed amongst themselves as the Elfling struck out at them with a weapon that was nearly invisible. They began to shy away from him as he cut clumsily back and forth at their scattered ranks in broad arcs of his mysterious blade. The thing seemed somehow to have a mind of its own, Shan felt, as it rang against the weaving net of scimitars facing them. It swept first this way and then that, effectively countering the terrible blows leveled at them by the gorguls. The fierce creatures barked and hissed angrily at the Elfling as they maneuvered crazily about.

Emboldened by the effect it was having on their assailants, Shan stepped out from the tight circle of boys to press their attack. The other youths looked on in amazement as the strange sword suddenly began to glow with an intense radiance. Kilgar tried hard to stay on Shan's heels, with the other boys following close behind. The scaly brutes fell back as the wondrous blade turned into a white-hot flame so near to their ugly faces. They hissed and coughed, their slitted eyes nearly blinded by its intense glow. The pitiful goons held up clawed fists to block the brilliant glare, while back-pedaling uncertainly away from Shan over the lumpy ground.

Growing steadily in confidence, the Elfling continued to advance upon them, the sword singing loudly in his ears. The blade had become completely incandescent by now, its startling white light pulsed brilliantly. Shan swung it out in front of him as he stepped forward.

"Don't be foolish," Kilgar breathed in his ear, struggling to match him step for step. "That may be a special sword and all, but don't get careless."

Shan looked over at him briefly, almost not seeming to recognize his friend for a moment. A fiery film of battle lust fell away from his eyes. But then he nodded and wisely slackened his forward progress. The sword was like a flaming brand in his fists. He could feel the warmth of it against his palms. He swirled it around in front of him with a little flourish and it looked almost like a barrier of light between them and the unexpectedly cowering gorguls.

The loathsome brutes remained nearly blinded by the sword's incredible brilliance. Their long, forked tongues snaked out through their yellowed tusks in near confusion. The narrow slits of their wide, slanted eyes blinked rapidly in apparent uncertainly. They had obviously never seen anything like this startling blade before and they didn't exactly know how to react to it. It seriously seemed to unsettle them.

The ten foul creatures now huddled tightly together in a knot. For several long moments they stood warily, muttering unintelligibly in their customarily raspy tones. The gorguls' long, batwing ears flapped excitedly against the sides of their elongated skulls. They lashed rapidly back and forward several times before finally settling back against their heads, and were still.

The quintet nervously eyed their scaly opponents across a few kora of ground. Shan couldn't tell how long their sudden stand-off would last before the gorguls stepped forward once again to resume their attack. He shot a quick glance at the other boys to either side of him. Breathing shallowly in fear, they all stood on the balls of their feet, their weapons held stiffly in nerveless fingers. They continued to shift anxiously from one foot to the other, intently studying the baleful looks the enemy soldiers cast upon them as they glared at the shining sword confronting them. Shan swallowed uncomfortably against the tenseness he felt in his own gut.

"What do we do now?" Rimmy asked in a tight whisper to his brother.

"I don't know," Kilgar replied through clenched teeth. "Shan seems to be holding them at bay for the moment, but we can't be certain how long that will last." Rimmy nodded with a stiff bob of his head.

"I say we back off slowly," Doornig interjected. Kilgar looked at him from the corner of his eye. The redhead tapped him with his elbow. "Whistle for Adrulax. He should fetch the other thorka with him. We mount up while Shan holds them off with that magic sword of his and then we all race off."

"It might work," Gorian said thoughtfully.

"—If the animals come back," Kilgar finished for him. He regarded the ugly brutes across from them. "Those things will probably get over their hesitation just as soon as we try to move." And even as he spoke, the surly creatures inclined their hideous faces together, hissing vehemently to one another in their foul tongue. Their topknots danced with each vigorous bob of their long heads. Through a series of angry growls from the one who seemed to be their leader, they finally came to a consensus. Leveling their cat-like eyes at the boys, the foul creatures broke from their huddled knot at last and stepped determinedly in their direction.

Just then, a loud whirring sound came from somewhere behind them. Something large whooshed crazily past Shan's ear and suddenly sprouted from the lead gorgul's chest. The startled thing gurgled loudly, spewing dark gore from between its tusks. It clutched uselessly at the great axe head buried up to its haft in its breast. The bulky figure pitched forward onto its horrid face as its fellows stared off over the boys' heads in sudden fright. A wild chorus of war cries erupted from behind them as a rush of steel-shod boots thundered up in their direction.

Not another squad of gorguls! Shan thought with a rush of panic. *We're surrounded!*

Kilgar risked a hasty look back over his shoulder. A company of stocky bodies was immediately discernible as they hurried up out of the darkness. Short, bearded figures charged through the fading moonlight towards them. They bellowed out a constant stream of challenges as they fanned out to sweep quickly around the huddled knot of boys. The gorguls started to scatter in all directions at the sight of so many armored warriors flushing past their quarry to engage them.

The boys stood their ground, still gripping tightly onto their weapons, as the tide of resolute soldiers brushed roughly around them. They appeared somewhat small to the Elfling, coming only up to his elbow, yet their strength and power were immediately apparent. Unable to spring away quickly enough, the gorguls were forced to engage the new arrivals. The short sharp clang of axe on sword rang out as the two forces clashed together in heated combat. The young lads watched in grisly fascination as the battle surged hot and heavy around them like a cascading wave. They maintained their ready stance throughout the fight but the circle of boys was somehow forgotten in the intense clash of razor-sharp weapons.

The tangled mass of combatants seethed over the damp, uneven ground around them. Many a foot slipped in the ever reddening muck. Blades shimmered in the moon glow as they were raised in broad fists and then came down in a blur of motion into the swirling tide of death. Powerful bodies surged wildly over the bloodied ground. Screams of intense pain were torn from gore-slimed lips as the skirmish raged on.

Yet the fierce battle was over in relatively short order. The thirty or so grim warriors who had come pelting out of the darkness made quick work of the nine remaining brutes from Kulnedra. In the passage of less than five mira the last of the foul soldiers had fallen to the ground in a shower of its own dark blood. Any movement from the mound of corpses was quickly met with a forceful dagger thrust from one of the bearded warriors. Then silence suddenly reigned.

"Burn them, lads," a husky voice called out from within the scattered ranks of soldiers. "Let the flames send their filthy spirits back to where they came from." There were hearty grunts of approval from his fellows. A few of them rushed off in obedience. The stocky figure pointed to one of their own, kneeling to the side of their company on one knee. He was holding a strip of cloth tightly to his muscular forearm. "Someone see to Heggel, there," he commanded brusquely. Unbelievably to the boys, he was their only casualty. "Bind up that gash until we can get home."

The short broad figure turned to the boys huddled anxiously behind him. They openly retained their weapons in their tightened fists, a little leery of the company of soldiers which had sprung up so quickly out of the darkness. The heavy-set figure tramped up to them with a grim smile spread wide on his whiskered face. "Never raise a weapon, lads, unless you intend to use it," he said gruffly. The fellow's eyes seemed bright and inquisitive as he took in their protective stances.

"You have nothing to fear from us, lads," the diminutive soldier called to them. He raised a massive fist up before his dark eyes, revealing his empty palm to allay their uneasiness. He nodded his large head as if to confirm his words. The bearded man dropped his own great bloodied axe to his side in thick sausage-shaped fingers. "We mean you no harm." His enormous bushy eyebrows seemed to move on their own as he regarded them.

The boys looked noncommitally at one another, their eyes somewhat guarded. They hesitated, rocking from one foot to another, before turning back to the short, massive fellow in front of them. They gripped their blades uncertainly.

Shan was the first to lower his weapon. The intense glow had faded from the blade and the long, keen sword had clouded over once again to its near black appearance. He inserted the tip slowly into his dark scabbard and drove the sword home. The broad figure in front of them watched his movements carefully, taking note of the unusual weapon, before looking up to meet the Elfling's bright blue eyes. He offered a good-natured smile, the heavy creases around his eyes appearing suddenly like deep fissures carved across his face.

Then Kilgar sheathed his own sword and the others reluctantly followed suit. The dark-haired boy nodded at his friends encouragingly, then swung to face the broad-shouldered little man.

"That's quite a sword you have there, lad," the muscular fellow rasped as he faced Shan across the narrow gap. "Lights up like a beacon. Probably wreaks havoc with those dark, slitted eyes of theirs, I'll wager." He nodded his shaggy head at the boy. "If it wasn't for that intense glow, we'd most likely never have seen you from our camp. Old Hengist over there," he pointed with a stubby finger at one of his men, but Shan wasn't exactly certain which one he'd indicated, "he has the best hearing in our whole troop. He called us all out of our bedrolls, said he could hear the clash of weapons somewheres close-by. Naturally, I listen to him most of the time, but I couldn't see anything in the faint light myself. And I'm usually pretty sharp-eyed." He grinned good-naturedly at them. "But then we saw what looked like a star fallen to the earth and we immediately rushed over here to investigate."

The boys studied him with fascination as he talked. His wreath of coarse brown hair, braided into thick rope-like coils, fell out from under a heavy helm to drape over his huge shoulders. A great beard dominated the lower half of his face. The tips of the long whiskers fell to his broad chest and were divided into four or five thick strands with jewel-like beads tied to the ends of them. The polished stones rattled together as he moved his big head from side to side. The broad knob of his nose spread wide to meet his jowly cheeks. Dark eyes peered at them with a soft glittering of moonlight from under a wide out-thrust brow ridge, complete with thick brown, unruly eyebrows.

The man was shorter than all of them, even Rimmy, but he looked as if he could wrestle all of them at once should he choose to do so. His great chest was like the bole of a large tree. It might even take three or four of them to encircle his powerful trunk. The rest of his body was massive as well, with thickly corded muscles on his arms and legs. His wrists and hands alone were like the banded logs of the palisade at Draydin. Shan was thoroughly impressed.

"A dwarf," Rimmy blurted out after a few moments. His eyes went wide in amazement as he studied the man. "He's really a dwarf." He turned to his brother in wonder. "Never seen a dwarf before."

"You're absolutely right, young lad," the powerful figure told him, looking up into his startled eyes. "I am a dwarf. We're all dwarves, and we're headed home to the Iron City. We've been away for nearly two cycles of Sheska, the greater moon." The massive dwarf pointed a huge finger skyward. "Even in the lush caverns Minthia we have long been hearing talk of marauding hordes of these foul creatures, roaming freely across the land. Scouting parties were sent out to put an end to all their nefarious activities." He looked back over his shoulder to the others with him.

The rest of the dwarves had finished dragging the mangled bodies together into an unruly heap. Several of them poured oil onto the grisly pile from a flask at their hips. One of the powerful warriors struck a spark from a piece of flint in his hand, and the whole mound burst instantly into flame. The little tongues of fire quickly engulfed the tangled bodies, turning them into a large, make-shift pyre.

"This is already the sixth bunch of those hideous devils we've encountered on our sacred task," the calm, husky voice of the dwarf leader told them. "That tallies up to more than fifty of those creatures."

"Great! That makes fifty fewer of these brutes to chase after us," Doornig muttered without thinking. He bit his lip as Kilgar swung a stern face to glare at him. "What?" he stammered. "I didn't say anything."

The exchange did not go unnoticed by the dwarf commander. He studied the boys for several long moments before speaking. Four of them were obviously human, but the fifth one he was not so sure about. The lanky one with the unusual sword piqued his interest. The dwarf could see for himself that Shan was tall and graceful, and his features were extremely handsome and fair. He harbored his suspicions, but the long head scarf the boy wore, perhaps to hide his undesirable heritage, made it difficult for him to tell for sure. The dwarf's dark eyes sparkled in the silvery-blue light.

Sheera had begun dipping toward the distant horizon. They would be left in complete darkness fairly soon and the rising of the sun was still a long ways off.

"My name is Gurvin," the massive dwarf said to them. "I'm commander of this company. Even now we hasten toward home. I beg you to join us as we travel." He licked at his lips. "We can offer you protection from more of these wandering patrols which have become so persistent around here of late." He looked pointedly at the redheaded boy. "Sounds apparently as if you have had several encounters with them already. Perhaps together we might determine why they seem to be harassing so many people these days." He inclined his large head to the side and focused his eyes on the Elfling. "And you, then, in turn, might enlighten me as to the nature of that *weapon* of yours." He smiled. His gaze flickered down to the sword Shan carried.

The elven youth turned to peer at Kilgar, one eyebrow raised questioningly. The dark-haired boy wriggled his lips around, glancing back at Gurvin waiting patiently in front of them. He dropped his eyes to the ground and kicked at a rock by his boot, considering. He looked up at the dwarf.

"Where exactly are you going?" he finally asked the hefty fellow. "Where's home?"

"Minthia," the dwarf announced, "the Iron City." He waved a massive fist towards the east. "It lies on the other side of the forest of Draydin, nestled at the foot of the Alkhorn mountains." He grinned broadly. "It's a beautiful city."

"Draydin?" Gorian muttered. "But that's in the wrong direction." Kilgar held out a hand to silence him.

The dwarf looked thoughtfully at the circle of boys. "Where are *you* heading?" Gurvin wanted to know innocently. He looked from Kilgar to Shan, then back again. He studied the two boys as they struggled to reach some kind of decision. *There's more going on here than meets the eye*, he thought to himself with a sly stare.

"Akthis," the Elfling finally said out loud. "We need to reach Donnor's Ferry." Kilgar nodded in agreement. "We're heading south."

"Ah," the dwarf exclaimed, with an exhale of breath, "what a shame." He smacked his lips together loudly. "And here I was hoping to enjoy the pleasure of your company for a time. I can bet you have a tale or two to tell about your travels."

The boys all seemed disappointed as well. The open and friendly manner of the man was inviting. Shan would have welcomed the protection of thirty fierce dwarf fighters to help them get back to the ferry. He seriously thought about asking Gurvin to accompany them on their journey, even actively contemplated trying to convince him in fact, as he absently stroked his sword hilt with one hand. But he couldn't come up with a viable enough reason to do so. *What would be in it for them?* he asked himself. *Just more time away from their families.*

"Well," the dwarf went on after a few moments, "could I at least offer you the comfort of our camp for the remainder of the night?" He looked at them hopefully. "You look a little tired to me. There you could get some much needed rest, and we'd be able to help you track down those frightened animals of yours." The boys looked up at his words in surprise. "We saw them racing away from here in fright as we came running up. I'm *guessing* those glorious beasts were yours."

"Yes," Kilgar had to admit, "those were our thorka you saw bolting off into the night. The sudden appearance of the gorguls scared them off before we could mount up. So we had to stand and fight, but we're not exactly warriors."

Gurvin nodded understandingly at them. "Of course," the dwarf commander replied. "We saw as much as we hurried over." He leveled his bushy brows on the boys.

Daryl Hanson

"Sure, we'd love to take you up on your hospitality," the Elfling added, as he realized the dwarf was still waiting patiently for an answer. "Yes, that would be great. We'd welcome a chance to rest without the threat of another attack."

"What I don't understand," commented the powerful dwarf, "is how those uncouth barbarians caught you on the ground in the first place." He blinked. "You should have been riding off as fast as you could on those swift mounts of yours, and leaving those foul things far behind in your dust."

Shan smiled uncomfortably. "Our thorka were utterly exhausted," he said, swallowing at a dry throat. "We were walking them for a while. I think we must have driven them too hard trying to avoid all those patrols."

The dwarf nodded his shaggy head. "That's certainly understandable," he proclaimed. "They are devilishly cunning. Foul lot of Kulnedra!" He spit contemptuously into the dust. "Relentless scum they are. Kind of like a sleeth when it sinks its fangs into you, they never want to let go." He shifted his dark eyes over them, noted how they looked sidelong at each other. There was more to them and their business than the boys were willing to admit, he felt certain.

"The gorguls came up on us suddenly," Doornig stated flatly. "Our animals were already spent, especially after swimming all the way across the river," the redhead declared. Kilgar kicked the boy sharply in the shins. "Ouch!" he cried, leaning away.

"The river?" Gurvin said in surprise. "What were you doing crossing the river at night?" The dwarf settled his curious stare on Doornig, but the boy dropped his head and stared at his boots. "Hmm?"

"We were just trying to get away from the pirates," Rimmy stated. "They captured us and wanted to turn us into cabin boys!" He thrust out his jaw defiantly, a sparkle of anger in his dark eyes. Kilgar flashed his brother a scathing look and then rolled his eyes skyward. Gurvin caught the interchange.

"Pirates now, is it?" the dwarf leader crooned, a bushy eyebrow cocked at an odd angle. "This tale gets better all the time." He gestured behind them. "Why don't you come back to our camp with us and we can sit down around a welcome fire. You boys can tell me all about your whirlwind adventures." Gurvin moved toward them, his arm still raised to indicate the way to their camp behind him. He hefted his axe and laid it along his thick shoulder. They gave way as he rounded their little group and trudged off in the direction he was pointing. "Hurley, Gammon, finish up here, will you," he called back over his shoulder. "Stay and tend that blaze. When it's completely burned itself out join us at the camp."

"Yes, Lord Gurvin," they said together.

"Come," the dwarf leader invited the boys as he marched off. He stopped after a few steps when they didn't immediately follow after him. He turned back to look at them while they simply stared at each other in hesitation. "Come," he encouraged them with a little wave of his thick hand. "I'll make sure we find your animals. Look, now the moon's almost gone." He pivoted and bore off into the darkness. He clapped his big hands together. "I don't know about you, but a fire would be most welcome about now."

The boys relented of their thoughts to hunt down the thorka immediately themselves and begrudgingly followed after the heavy-set dwarf one at a time.

The dwarves' camp was a couple hundred kora to the east. They'd thrown down their packs and cloaks at the base of a low hill. Tangles of hastily kicked-off bedrolls were scattered about. A line of thorro were hitched to a rope tied to a little pole driven into the ground. By the time the boys arrived with the majority of the dwarven host close on their heels, they found an inviting little fire crackling in a circle of stones. The five of them threw themselves down near the little blaze and gladly began to warm their hands. It really wasn't a cold night, but they hadn't had a fire in so long, it felt good just to soak it in.

The dwarf lord sat down cross-legged across the flames from them. He studied them silently from the pools of his dark eyes as they huddled close together. He coughed lightly and leaned towards them. The dancing firelight created moving shadows across his craggy face. The little stones tied to the ends of his beard tinkled quietly together as he pivoted his large head to regard them.

"I can see you don't trust me, lads," Gurvin announced to them. "I can see it in the way you hold your eyes." He brushed at his thick brown whiskers with a calloused hand. "I suppose I cannot really blame you. If I was in your place, and had gone through some of what you've experienced over the past few days, I probably wouldn't trust me either." He chuckled in a deep, husky voice. The wily dwarf sat back and watched them share guarded looks.

"Look," Gurvin went on, "contrary to what you might think, I am not your enemy." He cleared his throat. "In this day and age when no one seems to trust anyone else, I can see the hand of evil at work." The boys turned their faces to stare at him. "I am old enough to observe the seeds of distrust, the poison of racial hatred, as it seethes across our world in an endless tide. I can recognize the foul crops planted by the minions of the Evil One, sewing their seeds of discontent at his bidding, and I sense they are leading us all to destruction."

The boys found themselves enthralled by Gurvin's impassioned words.

"If any of us hopes to survive the growth of this pernicious disease," he called out in a husky voice, his eyes glittering in the firelight, "we must come together now, band together shoulder to shoulder with all of our brothers, regardless of race, and fight with all our strength to crush its diabolical and insidious head."

Shan looked down into the leaping flames. He studied the writhing yellowish-orange fingers for some time before finally looking up into Gurvin's watchful eyes. He cleared his throat. Kilgar laid a warning hand on his arm. But the Elfling just looked at his friend and gave him a wan smile. He cupped his other hand over Kilgar's, gave it a little tap, before turning back to the impressive dwarf sitting quietly across the little fire.

"The gorguls are after me," he said softly. "I don't know why, but they've been tracking me for almost a month. Sometimes I think they want to capture me, and at other times I feel they want to kill me. No matter where I run, no matter where I hide, they always seem to find me." He looked over at Kilgar. "I have been cautioned—warned really—time and time again to trust no one along the way." He looked deeply into the dwarf's dark eyes and swallowed. "Yet for some reason, I am inclined to trust you, a total stranger, with all I'm about to tell you." He finished speaking and looked down into the flames once more. Gurvin simply watched him silently, his large hands spread across his knees. After a moment the Elfling gazed up into his friends' faces. Their pale skin glowed somewhat from the flickering yellow light. Kilgar finally nodded at him.

Gurvin appraised Shan for a long while. "I'm gladdened," he said deliberately in his deep slow tones, "that you have found the heart to trust me." He scratched at his unruly beard with a bear-like hand. "Tell me more of your flight, that I may know how I might better help you. But first, please tell me your names." He blinked at them.

"My name is Shan," the Elfling told him. "I'm from Draydin village."

"The rest of us are from Branby," Kilgar stated.

"Neither one of those is too far from here," Gurvin confided in them.

"The forest itself lies no more than a couple days march to the east." The boys seemed a little surprised by the news. "Yet you say you've been traveling for a month?"

"I would have thought we'd have been carried further north in the crossing," the dark-haired boy said with a smirk. "Anyway, I'm Kilgar, and this is my brother Rimmy." The younger boy nodded his head.

"My name's Doornig," the red-haired youth announced with a touch of his knuckles to his forehead.

"And I'm Gorian," the sandy-headed boy relayed. "Good to know ya."

Gurvin inclined his head to them. He turned to the Elfling, a large hand lifted in invitation for him to recount his tale. "Please, go on."

Shan took a big breath and closed his eyes for a moment. "Let's see, what day is it?" he began. "I'm afraid I've lost count."

"Today, well, what's left of today is the eighth of Bellach," the dwarf told him patiently.

"It all started then, almost five hands ago," expressed the Elfling. He blinked in recollection. "It was the twelfth of Kaligath, I think, when a kurgoth tore its way into my room."

"A kurgoth!" Gurvin hissed in astonishment. "Are you sure?"

The Elfling nodded in complete seriousness. "That's what Ulfiir called it." He swallowed at the horrible memory. "It was huge and furry," he said quietly, "and it towered over me." His breathing became a little erratic. The dwarf listened intently to him as he went on. "It had glowing eyes and enormous claws. It nearly killed me. And it's really been one nightmare after another since then." He looked at his friends sitting quietly by his side. "If not for a little timely help from those I have been able to trust along the way," he went on, "I would have long been dead by now." The four boys reached out and laid their hands on his shoulders. Shan raised his own hand and patted theirs in gratitude.

"Well, you certainly saved all of us a couple of times, as well," Doornig said with a little sniffle, "with those keen eyes and ears of yours. Whew! That Feldus thing was sure nasty." He wiped at his nose with the edge of his sleeve.

"So," Gurvin leveled his dark countenance upon Shan, "what happened after the kurgoth attacked?"

For the rest of that early morning the Elfling recounted his flight into danger. Aided occasionally by timely comments from the others, Shan recited as much as he could remember.

30

Ⴀhe Ⴁooded Rider
[9th - 10th of Bellach, 4534 C.R.]

"Why Akthis?" Gurvin asked. "Why Donnor's Ferry?" He leveled a steady eye on the Elfling. It was daylight at last. The fiery ball of the sun had broken over the distant line of trees to the east. They had talked through the remainder of the night. The dwarves' encampment was astir with activity.

Shan hesitated. "Look" the shaggy-headed dwarf went on, "it seems to me if you want to stay alive you need to go to a place that's safe. Where people can protect you." He pulled thoughtfully on his great beard. "Come with me to Minthia. You'll be safe in the Iron City. It's impregnable. No amount of gorguls or targs or even kurgoths could get at you in there."

"I don't know, Lord Gurvin," the elven youth said slowly. "I think I need to keep moving. Akthis is just the next step of the journey for me." He looked off to the southwest.

The dwarf threw up his large hands in exasperation. He stood in front of the Elfling and looked up into his blue eyes. His great head came up to just above Shan's mid-section, hovering at about his breast bone. The craggy face was chiseled into a score of frown lines. The long braids of his hair fell back over his shoulders as he stared up at the boy. He squinted into the bright morning light.

Shan looked down into Gurvin's dark eyes. "I appreciate your offer to grant us asylum," claimed the boy, "but I don't think holing up in your city, no matter how safe it might be for me right now, is truly the answer to my dilemma." He looked down and rested one hand on the sword hilt. "I have to go," he said with sudden resolve. "It's like I'm being called—somewhere—and I need to follow wherever it leads." He met Gurvin's sober gaze with a resolute stare of his own.

The burly dwarf nodded slowly. "Well, I can see that you're determined on this course of action." He spoke in a slow husky voice. "So, in that case, I guess I'll be coming with you." He dropped his head firmly with his decision.

"What?" Shan was completely surprised at the dwarf's declaration. He looked around himself quickly. "But what about all your people? What about the home and family you haven't seen for months?"

Gurvin just blinked up at him. "What about them?" he said. "They'll still be there when I get back. I don't think my wife will run off with another while I'm gone." He laughed. "She'd better not, if she knows what's good for her." Shan joined him in his deep chuckle. "I won't be bringing all these men," the muscular figure told him. He looked around with a calculating eye. The enormous brows contracted in thought. "Perhaps just a couple of them would be fine. An entire company of mighty dwarf warriors would probably create too much of a stir." He nodded his shaggy head with the truthfulness of his remark. Shan grinned lightly back at him.

"I'm sure we'd welcome any help you can give us," the Elfling said with a joyful little smile.

The dwarf reached up and laid a huge hand on Shan's arm. "We'll gladly see you safely to this ferry of yours, if that is your steadfast course," Gurvin spoke huskily. The Elfling had a momentary stab of disappointment at his words and looked down. The wily dwarf observed the sudden change in the boy's demeanor. He lifted his great paw and touched Shan lightly under the chin. "As I said," the fierce warrior went on, "I'll accompany you to the ferry. More than that I cannot promise at this time." The boy looked timidly into the big dark eyes. "The course from there" Gurvin spoke up evenly, "will just have to rest in Durrock's capable hands."

The Elfling looked curiously down at him. "Durrock?" he asked in an odd voice. "Who's that?"

"He's the Creator, boy," Gurvin replied, a sparkle in his eyes. "Through His great power Durrock made the world as it is. With a wave of His mighty hand, He brought all of Anarra into existence. He caused it to be out of pure nothingness, and separated it from the Outer Darkness."

"Oh," Shan responded, "you must mean Athiliel."

"Athiliel is His elven name, yes," the barrel-chested dwarf told him. "Funny you should use that name for Him, lad," Gurvin offered with a curious look at the boy. "He is known by many names, but He is one and the same God. No matter where you may roam upon the surface of Anarra, He is still the same Lord. For example, He is known as Ka'Hanni among the desert tribesmen to the south. Te'Liira is how He's referred to across the plains of Kuria. Athalias is His name among the common folk." The scope of what he was saying slowly dawned on the Elfling.

"You're saying Athiliel—Durrock," Shan remarked, "is actually one and the same?"

The Dwarf lord nodded his great head. "Of course. There is but one

Daryl Hanson

Creator, only one ultimate Lord," Gurvin stated firmly. "Many pagan peoples try to make gods out of the rocks and trees, but they are all false, worthless. There is only one Creator who made everything. We all have different names for Him, yet we all acknowledge the same being."

"But not everyone believes in Him," Shan commented. "I've encountered many people who feel He's just a myth."

"No, sadly you're right," Gurvin retorted, "not everyone believes." He shook his head with a touch of sorrow. "Yet the beauty of His creation surrounds us all the same, it cries out to us. It is there each day for all of us to see. And it remains for us, when we cast our eyes about, to appreciate His handiwork, and all that He has done. We should acknowledge Him, praise Him for it, or else one day there will come a time of judgment."

"You are wise indeed," Shan looked at the dwarf with new eyes. "Wise in the knowledge of the world. I am glad to know you." He inclined his head in a little bow. The dwarf was obviously touched by the gesture. He coughed uncomfortably and looked away. Gurvin turned to study the other dwarves on the edge of the hills as they continued to break camp.

The mighty warriors were busy rolling up blankets, stowing all of their goods and cooking gear into packs, and loading these in turn onto a string of thorro Shan had noticed the night before. The sturdy little animals brayed softly as the parcels were strapped over their shaggy pelts.

"Armig, Heffy," the dwarf called out. Two of the stout warriors dropped their packets and trotted over. They came to a stiff attention before him. "I'm going to ride along with these boys for a while," he told them with a tilt of his braided head towards Shan and the others.

"I want you to accompany me." The two young dwarves nodded firmly. "It'll add another couple of hands 'til we can get back home to see friends and loved ones again, but I think you're both dwarf enough to handle it."

The two of them crossed their huge arms with a grin. "Indeed we are," one of them replied tersely. He had long, dark hair and dark eyes.

"As Durrock is our witness," the other responded, his tangled mass of red hair shaking with his firm nod.

Gurvin laid a large hand on each of them. "Good," he pronounced with a bone-shaking pat on their shoulders. The dwarf lord turned to the rest of the company. "I've just taken on another task, lads," he called out loudly to them. They all stopped their activities and gathered round their commander, some with burdens still clutched in their large fists.

Gurvin cleared his throat, yet his words still came out in a deep, hoarse voice. "I'll be taking Heffy and Armig with me to escort these younglings down the road a-piece," he said. He waved a bear-like fist at Shan and his friends. The circle of dwarves looked on grimly. "Hengist will lead you the rest of the way home." One of the dwarves looked up from the tangle of bearded faces and nodded firmly.

"But what of you, Lord Gurvin?" another of them asked gruffly. He was the one with a strip of blood-stained cloth wrapped tightly around his forearm. Heggel was his name, Shan remembered. "When will you return home?" The dwarf leader started to open his mouth but another dwarf cut in before their commander could respond.

"What about all the frequent attacks of these wretched creatures?" the hefty figure wanted to know. "Have we been hunting them in vain?"

Gurvin wagged his head from side to side. The smooth gemstones tied in his great beard rattled together noisily. He sighed deeply before speaking to his troops. "Shards no! I hope to learn more about all these worrisome raids," their broad leader told them in a gruff voice. He looked over at the Elfling. "I think they may somehow be related to these young boys here. How? I'm not sure. Yet, I pray Durrock guides our steps so that we may find out." He spit into the dust. "War is brewing, lads," he told his men evenly. "I can feel it in my old bones." He glared at them with a fierce stare. "Soon the whole continent might be stirred up in conflict."

"And what of Lord Berris?" Hengist asked him. "What shall I tell him?" The two dwarves locked eyes for a moment. It was a long time before Gurvin spoke.

"Tell him," the dwarf commander said, thinking carefully, "tell him that I deem it vital to do this for the good of all our people and the security of the realm." He stroked absently at his beard. "Muurdra's hand is at work in this, I am almost certain." He lifted his head and swung his gaze around to take in all those who stood there listening. "It has been a long time since the Dark One has reared his ugly head. Even now he rattles the bars of his cage in exile. And if Muurdra desires the destruction of these boys, then I must stand and oppose it. I must spit into his accursed eye." He spit loudly into the dust to emphasize his words.

The gathering of dwarves nodded their heads grimly. They raised their huge fists and roared out their challenge. Some of them even brandished their weapons with a rattling of metal. There was a look of smoldering fire in their deep set eyes, Shan could tell. He swallowed at a knot in his throat. The skin on his arms rose in stiff hackles.

"Now," Gurvin clapped his great hands together loudly, "let's all get busy. We break camp within the ahr."

The dwarves hastened away to finish their tasks. The fire was doused and the wet ashes were scattered. Bedrolls were tied onto the backs of their little beasts, supplies were rummaged through and some were reassigned to Gurvin's little team.

At one point early in the morning, Kilgar had walked out from the edge of the dwarves' camp to call for Adrulax. The boy whistled shrilly four or five times, his lips stretched tightly over his teeth. He waited for a time after each blast. Within moments of his last call a distant nickering could be heard. It drifted on the light morning breeze and then exploded into a thundering of hooves as the sleek black stallion came racing up to Kilgar. The big animal lowered his head to rub at the boy's outstretched hand. A few moments later the other three thorka scampered into view. They all neighed loudly in greeting.

In less than forty mira the two groups rode slowly apart. Both parties lifted their hands to each other in farewell. They wheeled their mounts in opposite directions and picked their way from the cluster of low hills where they had camped.

Gurvin never bothered to look back. He led them southwest, angling along the ridge of hills upon their left. The great sweep of the Tanalorn lay four or five hundred kora off to their right. They rocked easily in their saddles as they plodded slowly along.

The boys' troubled thoughts were often drawn to the great river. It was beautiful as it coursed majestically between its wide banks. Sunlight danced on the deep blue surface of the water. Their thoughts often drifted to the ruined city of Suul'Kar. The long stretch of Watcher's Island loomed directly across the rippling waves from their position. What had happened to the pirates? *Was that only just two nights ago?* the Elfling wondered. And what did they think about our escape?

Shan couldn't help replaying recent events in his mind. He grunted softly to himself in irony as he relived how he had stumbled upon the sword in the underground passageways. If they hadn't been captured by the bandits he never would have ventured to Suul'Kar, never would have found the spectacular blade in the underground crypt. He smiled lightly to himself as they rode along. He rested one hand protectively on the sword pommel.

The dwarf lord noticed the little movement. "Now mind you, you haven't told me all there is to know about that mysterious sword of yours," the gruff commander husked out. Shan looked down into the dwarf's dark eyes. Something held him back and he said nothing. He just smiled ruefully at Gurvin as they rode on.

They stopped twice throughout the day to rest the animals and to stretch their legs. "If Durrock had meant for us to ride all day," Gurvin muttered with a rub at his lower back, "He'd have given us hooves." His fellow dwarves snickered at him. Nodding their agreement, the two young warriors stretched out their brawny arms and rotated back and forth at their stout waists.

They also took those few opportunities to indulge themselves in a little food. Nibbling on cold meats and dried fruit, the eight of them satisfied their hunger. They washed the meal down with long drafts of water from their leather bags. While they ate, they left the animals to graze freely on the frequent tufts of long grass poking up out of the rocky ground.

After they had mounted up following their second short rest of the day, they started to turn away from the hills and moved out onto a wide tableland running along the great river. Sparse trees dotted the plains before them but they soon began to encounter occasional farms and small settlements, including a little village or two. These they avoided, circling widely to their left so as not to draw any attention to themselves.

Thirty mira out from the last village they had passed, Armig edged his thorro up from the back of their party and leaned over to confer with Gurvin. They rode slowly together, their small thorro stepping carefully through the rocky soil.

"Lord Gurvin," the young dwarf called out softly, "we've picked up a tracker." The older dwarf blinked casually. "A lone rider. He follows at a great distance behind us."

Gurvin swung his face calmly over to look at Armig. "You just now noticed him?" he asked, clearing his throat. "He's been with us ever since we left that last settlement."

Shan was the only other one of the group who actually heard their words. He stiffened automatically in the saddle behind Kilgar as they bounced lightly over the rough ground on Adrulax' long tawny back. He tried to look casually over his shoulder, lowering his chin and swiveling his head to the side to glance out of the corner of his eye. But he was unsuccessful. He could never see more than a hundred kora or so behind and the thorka's plodding gait jiggled his vision.

Armig dropped back to join Heffy at the rear of their little column. The rider continued to dog their tracks for the rest of the day, yet he held himself back expertly to keep from being seen. Shan watched the dwarves for some sign of agitation, but they just rode placidly on, seemingly not to notice. The Elfling kept his keen ears alerted to any more conversation between the three of them, only to be disappointed.

Gurvin did pull them up once under the thick shade of a couple of trees situated off the side of the road, using the pretext of stopping for a drink. The three dwarves watched the little track warily behind them. The five boys eagerly took the opportunity to quench their thirsts, unwrapping the straps of their botas from their saddle horns to swig deeply. The dwarves did likewise, only they seemed to keep a close eye on the spot where they had curved around a rocky outcropping half a korad back. Shan studied the spot once he'd realized what Gurvin was doing. The wily dwarf slowly drew on the spigot of his water bag and wiped the excess moisture from his thick whiskered lips with the back of one of his broad arms.

The four boys from Branby would have taken the chance to exchange in friendly banter, but Gurvin signaled them to silence. They were oblivious to the reason but they obeyed him nonetheless. The sudden thought that gorguls might be about brought them to a nervous state of rigidity. They scanned the land all around them for signs of danger, but after a while, when no actual threats developed, they eventually relaxed their vigilance. The dwarves seemed to wait patiently for an extended amount of time before they were rewarded with the light clomp of an animal's hooves approaching steadily. The almost imperceptible sound slowed as it drew near the outcropping and then stopped suddenly altogether.

Shan held his breath as he waited. Finally he detected the smallest of movements as a distant figure peered cautiously around the large rock in their direction. Even in the thick shadows under the small pocket of trees, the elusive figure must have seen them, for he pulled back immediately behind the large outcropping and remained out of sight for as long as they sat there.

Gurvin urged them out of their concealment at last. He tapped lightly on the thorro's hindquarters, exiting the coolness of the shade, and plunged back into the bright sunlight. The rest of them brought their animals' heads around with a gentle pressure on their neck ropes. A little kick from the heel of their boots sent them off in immediate pursuit.

Shan tried to look back once they were bouncing along the path again, but the wily rider remained hidden behind the rock and refused to show himself. The little party ambled along for a time with Gurvin leading the way, followed closely by Kilgar with the Elfling at his back, and then came Rimmy. Doornig and Gorian rode side by side, chatting softly together. The dark-haired dwarf, Armig, trotted next upon his thorro, with Heffy, the red-haired warrior, assuming the rear.

After a few mira Kilgar leaned back somewhat and spoke to Shan in a low tone. "What was that all about?" he asked. "The silent treatment during the water break, I mean." He swivelled his head to cast a sidelong glance at the Elfling. "What was Gurvin trying to do back there under those trees?"

Shan cleared his throat, trying to decide how much to tell him. "We're being followed," the elven youth told him quietly.

"Huh? Since when?" Kilgar was surprised. "I haven't seen anything." He paused to consider Shan's words. "Gorguls, you think?" The Elfling shook his head. "Then who?"

"Search me," Shan said.

"Not another assassin, surely," Kilgar tensed with the thought.

"No, probably not in full daylight," the elven youth pronounced. "He's been with us since about early afternoon, I think. A single rider, hooded. But he's very, very cagey. He wouldn't show himself back there when the dwarves tried to draw him out. I don't think Gurvin wanted to startle anyone, but I overheard him talking to Armig earlier. They've been aware of his presence for some time. At least Gurvin has." He smirked to himself. "He's a wily one."

Kilgar gave him a rough nod. "Let's not worry the others just yet."

They rode on in silence. The waxing curve of Kiara rose up over their left shoulders. Shan figured the smaller moon would be full in another four or five days. The sun continued to work its way down toward the horizon to their right when Gurvin casually called a halt for the day. He spied a little copse of trees which offered them a shelter of sorts. "I'd like a little something at our backs," the dwarf announced, "if we should have to stand and fight." He nodded sharply to them.

They dismounted wearily. Rimmy offered to tend their mounts and quietly went about settling them for the night. He proffered each of them a handful of grain as he went about currying them with a little brush from his pack. They nibbled eagerly at his kindly gift while he attended to their

Daryl Hanson

coats.

Doornig scouted the vicinity with Gorian and they discovered a small stream nearby, trickling down out of the trees as it hurried on its way to the distant curve of the great river. They filled all their water containers, everyone's personal drinking bags, as well as any extras they had strapped about the animals' saddle horns, before plopping down under the small cluster of trees.

Heffy started off to collect firewood, but Gurvin called him back. "Let's not kindle any flames tonight," the massive dwarf said to him. "I don't want to advertize our presence here any more than necessary."

The young red-bearded dwarf inclined his head before turning to help Armig with his task of concealing their camp. Between the two of them, using their belt knives, they hacked out an assortment of bushes from back within the trees. These they spread out like a fence wall in front of their site, anchoring them in place with rocks and clumps of sod.

"Huh," Doornig said looking at their handiwork, "that's a good idea. Makes for a nice little curtain to shield us from any unwanted eyes."

The young dwarves looked over at him. "It's only temporary," Armig commented. "The brush will be shriveled by morning, but they'll serve us well for the night."

Shan sat on a rock while they were working quietly. He gazed out over the lay of the land. It fell gently away from their small hill, tumbling down in an easy slope to the Tanalorn some three hundred kora distant. The Elfling could see the southern end of the island quite clearly from there, even in the failing light. Suul'Kar would have been just about even with their current position. He wondered again what had become of Arak Lazard and his rugged band of pirates. And then his eyes swept south along the great Tanalorn to where he thought Akthis lay. He chuckled mirthlessly to himself, realizing that they just seemed to be going round and round in circles. *Will I ever get to Redhaven?* he asked himself. He smirked faintly as he sat there on the rock, looking out. He dropped his chin onto a knee and sighed heavily.

Kilgar came over then and joined him, and the two of them just sat quietly, staring out, big eyed, at the world. The Elfling sighed again after a time, as the sun set in a blaze of glory to the west.

"You're thinking of her again, aren't you?" his dark-haired friend asked him.

"How did you know?" Shan responded.

"Oh, I don't know," Kilgar replied, "but whenever you get a moment to yourself your eyes take on a kind of faraway look, like you're wishing you were somewhere else." The Elfling looked over at him in the growing darkness. "Am I right?"

Shan could only give him a little smile. But it was a sad smile all the same. After a moment he sighed again loudly.

"She *was* extremely beautiful, I must say," Kilgar nudged him with his elbow.

The Elfling lowered his head, a terrible lump in his throat. He smiled ruefully. Here he was running for his life, hunted for reasons beyond his comprehension, and yet all his heart yearned for was to return to that wondrous elven city, hidden so cleverly away from the world in the depths of a despised forest, where a beautiful young girl strolled nimbly along through its wandering cobblestone streets. Her deep, beautiful blue eyes continued to haunt him.

His reverie was broken as Gurvin called them all to eat. They got up from their rock and made their way to where the dwarf commander had spread out broad leaves on the grass. There were lence cakes, dried strips of meat and some cheese in evidence. They all sat down in a circle and started munching gratefully on the meager fare.

Their talk was mostly subdued until Doornig looked over at Gurvin and cleared his throat. "Think there'll be another attack tonight?" he asked with a little tremble in his voice.

"Hard to say," Gurvin told him. "I haven't seen any sign of gorguls all day, but then again, they mostly come out at night." He chewed thoughtfully on a strip of meat. The boys looked at each other, their thoughts drifting to Bohannon and his companion Varian. A pang of doubt stabbed Shan in the heart.

"Those devils can be especially hard to predict," the dwarf lord went on. "Half the time you gear up for an attack with them and then they disappoint you. At other times they throw themselves into a fray even when they don't seem to have a chance of winning." He grunted softly. "It's almost like they're being controlled by someone else."

Shan looked up from his food, a hand with a wedge of cheese poised in front of his mouth. He half remembered an incident in the forest where he'd spotted another creature walking along with several gorguls. Even now he could recall its long white hair. "Maybe they are," he called out. The others swung curious eyes to look at him. "Being controlled, I mean."

"What are you saying?" Armig questioned him in a curious tone.

"One night, when we were still hiding in the forest of Draydin," the

Elfling began, "I saw a small troop of gorguls passing by on the road. They were being accompanied by a strange figure. He was tall and had long white hair." Gurvin leaned forward, keenly interested. "His eyes seemed dark as night."

Gurvin nodded slowly. "Sounds like a Morlung," the powerful dwarf replied. "Very, very dangerous."

"What's a . . . a Morlung?" Rimmy asked him in surprise.

"It's like a living corpse," Gurvin told him. The boys looked at him in horror. "They're actually still alive, they just look like they're dead, or so I've been told." He shrugged.

"You've seen one of those?" Doornig's eyes grew really large.

The dwarf shook his head. "No, I've never really seen one in person," he replied calmly. "But I've heard enough talk about them to stay far, far away." He rolled his great head around, and cracked his neck with a loud snap. Rotating his arms back, he popped his shoulders. "They're supposed to be Muurdra's field marshals," he went on. "Apparently they coordinate his forces, somehow directing their movements, and act as his generals on the battlefield."

Shan cast his mind back to that chilling encounter. "It moved with the grace of an Elf. Almost as if it floated across the ground somehow," he told them in a hushed voice.

"I've known those who have faced them in battle," Gurvin exclaimed. "They're extremely hard to kill because they don't seem to feel any pain. Perhaps it's because they have one foot in each world. That of the living and that of the dead."

The boys forgot all about the food in their laps as they listened to the chilling words of the dwarf lord.

Rimmy looked over at the elven youth. "You actually saw one, Shan?" he asked, his voice nearly a whisper. "In the forest near Branby?" The Elfling swallowed slowly and gave the boy an almost imperceptible nod. "Wow!" the young man blurted out. "That must have been a little scary."

"I've heard they can direct the thoughts of others," Gurvin announced. "It's believed they can control weaker minded individuals. They are also said to inhabit the minds of beasts at times. To turn them to do their bidding."

Shan shuddered violently. The words of Ulfiir lanced through his mind from that night long ago soon after the kurgoth's frightening attack. *"I merely severed the connection it had with its controller,"* he had said.

The Elfling blinked fiercely, startled by the sudden revelation.

"There must have been a Morlung outside the walls of the village that night, directing the monster's attack on me," he mumbled almost incoherently.

As the boys focused their eyes on the Elfling, they noticed Gurvin and the two young dwarves share a long, meaningful look. The wily dwarf lord regarded Shan with an intense stare. *What is it about this one?* he thought. *Unusual events seem to swirl about him like the eye of a storm.* He stroked thoughtfully at his long beard. The deepening darkness only seemed to kindle his sense of mystery. *And that peculiar sword,* he pondered, *what is it and where did it come from?*

Gurvin had gotten so wrapped up in his murky thoughts that he failed to notice the man as he stepped quietly out of the trees behind him. Shan looked up suddenly as the tall figure mysteriously appeared in their midst.

"Look!" he pointed, nearly falling back in surprise. He scrambled to his feet, bits of meat and cheese flying out from his lap in all directions. "The rider!"

Gurvin spun from his seated position and rose up quickly to face the intruder, a thick hand flashing for the haft of his axe. Armig and Heffy were not nearly as fast, but sprang up to stand shoulder to shoulder with their commander in a heartbeat. Their powerful hands hovered near their own weapons.

The boys from Branby were the last to rise. They came up awkwardly and huddled uncertainly behind the wall of flesh formed by the three massive dwarves. No one spoke for a few moments and the sudden intense stand-off was unnerving. The boys looked on breathlessly.

The tall man was hooded. His face was not discernible in the dark fold of his cloak. He stood motionless before them, his hands easily visible at his sides. He made no threatening motion towards them, but just seemed to regard them from the darkness of his hood. The two young dwarves slowly laid their large hands on the hafts of their weapons, their knuckles wrapping around them into a fierce grip.

"Don't," Gurvin advised them quietly. He waved a huge hand at them without taking his eyes from their unexpected guest.

"*Kimchuk,*" the tall man in the hood pronounced softly. Gurvin froze in surprise. "*Akki kahad dajurfik?*" came quietly from the fold of the cloak.

"*Kimchuk,*" the dwarf lord responded in a gruff voice after a long pause. "*Ha kahad dajurfik.*" With that Gurvin lowered his great axe to rest the double bladed head easily on the ground. He tilted his head slightly to the side. "I see you still have the axe I gave you long ago, old friend."

The hooded man reached up to touch the magnificent weapon strapped across his back. The two young dwarves tensed at the motion, but relaxed almost immediately when the man's hand returned to hang at his side. The rider's head inclined towards the dwarf a fraction. "And you," the faceless man's voice was low, "old friend, still wear the stones I gave you tied up so nice and pretty in your beard."

Gurvin reached up and absently tapped at the dangling gem stones. They rattled softly at his touch. "Please," he said amicably, with a gesture of one huge hand, "come join us." The dwarf stepped aside and indicated their camp. "We have no fire to offer you, but we have a little food and the company is somewhat enjoyable." He glanced at the boys and gave them a little wink.

"That would be satisfactory," the hooded rider told him. The big man stepped forward at Gurvin's bidding and reached out his hand. The dwarf clamped onto the man's wrist in a vise-like grip, bringing him closer. The boys retreated a pace to make room for the visitor. The two younger dwarves relaxed their rigid stance and swung back to their genial little circle.

The tall man reached up to brush the hood from his face. Shan's face lit up in astonishment as he looked into the man's green eyes.

"Altyrian!" he cried.

31

Ϲhe Ϲruth At Last
[10th of Bellach, 4534 C.R.]

"I've been looking for you for quite some time," Altyrian said, coming forward. "I see you're still wearing that same head scarf." Shan raised a hand and touched the dark blue cloth self-consciously. He pulled it slowly from his head to reveal to them all the pointed tips of his ears. He scratched thankfully at his itchy scalp.

"Hmm," Gurvin muttered, his hairy brows narrowing into a furry line. "Just as I thought."

Altyrian didn't seem surprised. The big man stopped in front of the Elfling and looked him over carefully. The clothes had changed a little, he could see, and the lad wore an unusual-looking scabbard at his hip, but the greatest difference the man noticed in the boy was a heightened level of confidence. He could see it by the look in Shan's eyes, the way he endeavored to hold himself. Altyrian was impressed with what he saw. Since they'd first met, his experiences had honed the boy. A little.

Gurvin stepped up to observe the interchange. "You two know each other?" he asked. He looked from one to the other.

"Yes," the big man declared, looking down after a moment at the dwarf standing somewhat between them and off to the side. "I ran into the boy some time back." He grinned wryly. "You might say he was a little stuck when I found him." Shan reddened a little bashfully as Altyrian swung his face round to peer at him.

"Stuck?" the dwarf asked with a raised brow. His face clouded briefly. "Chased by gorguls, or something?"

"Well, we did run into a few of those, as I recall," the big man settled his green eyes on the dwarf lord, "but I was referring to the web of a rith." Gurvin's bushy brows shot up in sudden surprise. "That's right," Altyrian went on with a light chuckle, "Shan had blundered onto the sticky surface of its great web and gotten himself helplessly trapped." His tone mellowed. "He was trying to cut himself free before the hideous occupant could enjoy him for breakfast."

Shan was sweaty at the memory. He could still almost hear the crack of those horrifying mandibles as they had closed upon the struggling targ next to him. He closed his eyes and shuddered. "I was being chased by targs," he offered in his own defense. "I really couldn't help myself." He spread his hands out. "They—it chased me over a cliff and we fell into the net together."

"Interesting," Gurvin said. He looked at the boy with a little smirk. "Chased by targs, almost eaten by a rith, narrowly escaping the jaws of a kurgoth," he swung his large head from side to side, "not to mention a few pirates and some gorguls thrown in. Why you've done more livin' in a month, boy, than most people accomplish in a lifetime."

Altyrian looked sharply at the Elfling with sudden intensity. "Wait, did you say a kurgoth?" He glanced quickly back and forth between the dwarf and the boy. Shan nodded his head in wide-eyed confirmation. "You're absolutely sure it was a kurgoth?" The Elfling swallowed at his own raspy throat. "When did this happen?" the big man wanted to know.

Shan hung his head and sighed deeply. "In my room," he said in a hushed voice, "back in Draydin. That's what seemed to start this whole thing." He blinked his eyes. They felt dry and gritty in the night air.

Altyrian laid a hand on the boy's arm to turn him to look into his eyes. "This happened *before* I rescued you? Before the web?" The Elfling could only nod slightly. "No wonder you seemed so afraid when I first met you, especially after what you'd just been through. I knew you weren't telling me the whole truth, but I never would have guessed a kurgoth. Why didn't you just tell me about it?"

Shan looked up into his eyes sheepishly. "I-I didn't know who you were," he stammered. "I was told not to trust anyone. Both Ulfiir and Weeson made it quite clear I shouldn't reveal myself to *anyone* under any circumstances." He thrust out his chin defensively. "Besides, how was I supposed to know you weren't just some total stranger walking down the road. I mean, for all I could tell you were another assassin sent out to kill me."

"The lad's got a point," Gurvin stated, crossing his huge arms.

"You're right," Altyrian looked at the boy with his deep green eyes. He smiled ruefully. "I guess I shouldn't have expected anything else. After all I had no credentials to present to you, no recommendations from someone you might have known." He shrugged fatalistically. "Not to mention I was a little late in getting to you all the way from Kulnedra."

"Kulnedra?" Shan exclaimed. "Why were you in such a foul place?"

Altyrian held up a hand quickly to forestall the boy. He looked around the meager campsite a little suspiciously. "Now is not the time or place to discuss the dark land. Talk of Kulnedra is best to be spoken of in broad daylight, when foul and evil things are hiding in their lairs. Let us discuss this another time." He stopped to stare out into the darkness for a while, listening. The boys shared uneasy glances. "It is also wise not to speak of such weighty matters out in the open, where anything might be listening."

"Agreed," Gurvin proclaimed, "but we don't seem to have much of a choice in the matter." He looked around dubiously. "I haven't seen any caves for us to crawl into. We don't have the time to travel back to the Iron City just now, to lock ourselves away in its heavy, steel palaces, or to have ourselves sequestered high among the trees of Darkwood. Nor have we been offered the opportunity to sit in council in the rocky vaults over Redhaven." He spread his huge hands with a careful grin. "This, my friend—*Kimchuk*," he said in deep tones, "is unfortunately all we have at the moment."

Altyrian smiled down at him. "And that's where you're wrong, old friend."

"Wait," Shan interrupted. "You two are friends?" he swung his head from one to the other. They both grinned at him.

"Unhappily," the dwarf said, rolling his eyes. "Altyrian saved me from an ambush a long time ago and I have been cursed with his friendship ever since." Shan took in Gurvin's sour face with a puzzled frown.

"Saved you?" Rimmy asked. "Saved you from what?"

"An enemy trap," the dwarf lord spoke gruffly. "I foolishly blundered into it in my youth." He turned his stern dark eyes on Altyrian. "I didn't have near enough skill to discern the signs on my own. But this tall oaf of a tracker did and if it hadn't been for him I'd probably be dead."

"Huh? What's so bad about that?" Doornig said. "You sound as if you're angry with him for saving you."

"I am," roared Gurvin with a bit of a rough laugh. "I mean, I was. You lads cannot imagine what it's like for a proud dwarf warrior to be beholden to a skinny, clean-shaven runt like this one here." He waved a huge hand toward Altyrian.

The boys all exploded into laughter. "But he's taller than you," Kilgar asked dumbfounded, "how can you call him a runt?" Try as he might, Gurvin couldn't maintain his angry facade any longer and lapsed into a broad grin himself. He threw back his great head and roared along with them. After a few moments the big dwarf wiped tears of mirth from his eyes. Gurvin looked over at Altyrian with a scratch at his beard.

"You were saying something about an alternate camp." He swiped at another trail of moisture on his cheek, then played idly with the stones in his beard. "Where is this place?"

Altyrian plunked a hand down on Gurvin's massive shoulder.

"Thought you'd never ask." He started to turn away. "Come on, I'll show you."

"Is it suitable enough for our animals?" Kilgar asked hesitating.

"Of course," the big man replied as he strode off. "Follow me."

They gathered up their things quickly and followed after him. Leading the animals by their neck ropes, the small party skirted around the little copse of trees. They found Altyrian waiting patiently for them on the back side where a little path led up to a crown of large rocks not too far away. Because of the trees the jagged rim of boulders could not be seen from below. Along the right side, a narrow defile snaked its way into the circle of rocks. The crease opened up into a tiny canyon of sorts, a natural bowl-shaped depression about forty-five kora across and surrounded by stones.

The new camp was open to the sky, but it was shielded well from all sides. There was plenty of room for the animals to graze on the wide swath of scrub grass. Loosened from their restraints, they trotted eagerly over to join a lone thorka already cropping quietly to the side. Scattered throughout the small gully the newcomers found tall spikes of rock thrusting up out of the hardened ground. These large stones offered the entire party sufficient places to prop themselves up against.

The boys were ecstatic that they'd be able to kindle a fire that could not be seen from any distance away. The two young dwarves quickly got a snappy little blaze going in the center of a rocky circle. They all settled down around the small fire with their blankets across their shoulders or thrown over their laps. The dancing yellow flames bathed their faces in its warm glow.

"Now," Altyrian said as he sat down cross-legged before them, "let's see if we can continue our conversation without anyone listening in."

The boys were curious as he took a small object out of his pack. It was about the size of his palm, and seemed a little jagged like a rock. He placed the little dark mass on a flat spot on the ground before them.

"Looks like some kind of meteorite," Gorian whispered to the other boys. They all regarded the dark object curiously. Even the dwarves leaned in to take a closer look.

It seemed like a hunk of dark metal to all of them, half-melted and misshapen. One end of it looked a bit heavier, thicker, almost like it had been thrown when it was still hot, and it had congealed in an unusual shape. They watched silently as Altyrian placed both hands on it and intoned something in a musical language. They saw nothing happen. But they could all feel the wave-like pulse it gave off. The hair on their bodies stood up suddenly like an intense feeling of gooseflesh rushing over them. The clicking of insects which had seemed fairly loud a moment before now sounded far-off and strangely diminished.

"What is that?" Shan asked Altyrian. He could still feel the hair on his arms crackling to the touch. The sword at his hip seemed to vibrate slightly and to give off a resonating tone in his ears. He looked around but no one else seemed to hear it.

"It's a small chunk of *sironath*," the man told them. "You were absolutely right," he pointed to Gorian. "It *is* a meteorite. It fell out of the sky a long time ago and it's blessed with some rather unusual properties."

"What does it do?" Doornig queried. He rubbed at his arms. "Other than make my hair stand on end, that is."

Altyrian regarded the redhead with a bit of a smirk. "I'm not exactly sure," he said, looking down at it. "I haven't discovered all it can do yet. But it should mask our presence for a time." He rocked his head slightly from side to side. "It acts like a cloak. Makes it harder for someone to find us with a casual glance or even to overhear our conversation." The boys raised their eyebrows at him. "I've had someone trying to follow me, so I've had to take precautions."

"Huh, you too," Gorian spit out.

"He's really not much of a scout," Altyrian went on. "I can slip away from him easily enough, but he's very persistent." He rubbed at the back of his neck. "Keeps turning up when I least expect it." He dropped his hands down into his lap. "He must be getting some help from other sources."

"What's he look like?" Kilgar asked him.

"Drives around in a big brightly painted wagon," the large man said. "Tries to pass himself off as some kind of bard or tinker."

Shan looked up with sudden interest. "His name's not Gravelle, is it?" He peered closely at Altyrian.

"That's the name," he said. "You know him?" When the Elfling seemed momentarily speechless in shock, he went on. "Such an odious little man."

"He wasn't so small as I remember him," Shan said, "that is, if it's truly the same man I've seen before. Sort of tall, with a broad brimmed hat and a long crooked nose." The man nodded. "Kind of greasy-looking, too, and has a repulsive little hunchback working with him."

"That's the one," Altyrian remarked. "What did he seem to want from you?"

"Back in Draydin he tricked me into getting a sample of my blood," the Elfling said with a grimace. He looked down at his fingertips in a half-memory. "I think that's how the kurgoth must have found my room, how it got my scent in the first place." He rubbed idly at a spot on his palm. "And besides that, Gravelle burned some sort of tracking mark in my hand. Thankfully Lord Janerron was able to remove it."

"I'm sure Gravelle must be sharing my movements with a Necromor," Altyrian spoke solemnly.

"A what?" Rimmy inquired with a scrunch of his nose.

"Another name for a Morlung," Gurvin told him off-handedly, patting the young lad on the leg with a great fist. The boy nodded with a trace of fear in his eyes.

"You mean there's one of those dead things close-by?" the boy gulped uneasily.

"Probably more than one, I'd say" Altyrian stated grimly. "I think they're beginning to gather somewhere nearby." The news sent chills shooting up Shan's back, and the other boys' faces were blanched white.

Altyrian reached into a pocket of his cloak and pulled out a sealed object. "Before I forget, Shan," he told the Elfling, "this is for you." He handed the folded letter to the Elfling.

Shan took the small paper and turned it over in his hands. There was no name scrawled across the face of it, nothing on it at all except a tiny splotch of red wax sealing it shut. He examined the little unbroken mark in detail. It had a single letter embossed in the wax. *"U."* The Elfling cracked open the seal and carefully unfolded the note. He read:

My dear boy,

I am so sorry I had no time to prepare you for what you have had to endure. I know everything must seem grim and hopeless to you by now. Have courage, even in the face of overwhelming odds. Athiliel has kept you alive for His own purpose. You are in His hands.

The bearer of this note is a friend. His name is Altyrian. You can trust him to help you. He will give you the guidance I cannot. All is not yet lost. Keep your chin up, my boy, and may Athiliel always keep you in His care.

Ulfiir.

Shan quietly folded the note and slowly handed it to Kilgar. He hurriedly read it before passing it to Gorian. Doornig leaned over his shoulder and read along with him. The Elfling turned to Altyrian as the boys passed the missive on to Rimmy.

Shan was suddenly overcome with emotion. He looked over at Altyrian, his eyes cloudy with moisture. "You've seen Ulfiir?" he asked. His lips quivered. "Is he alright? Is he hurt? When did you see him last?"

"He's fine, boy," the big man told him. "But he misses you terribly." His green eyes held Shan's expectant stare. "We had a long talk about you. He and I and Weeson."

"Weeson?" the elven boy interrupted excitedly. "He's alive?" He leaned toward the big man in eagerness.

"Yes, as well as the other two who accompanied you from Draydin," Altyrian assured him warmly. "They suffered a few injuries in your flight through the woods. Nothing a little rest won't heal."

"Thanks be to Athiliel!" the Elfling declared with a huge sigh.

"Weeson wanted to join me in the search for you," the big man went on, "but I knew I'd be able to travel much faster on my own. They did provide me with a fast thorka, thankfully, and once I knew where you were really heading, following in your tracks was quite easy. The places behind you are still buzzing with your passage." He laughed lightly. The boys all looked at each other with a sense of resigned satisfaction.

"I stopped long enough to speak with Lord Janerron along the way," Altyrian said with a grim twist of his lips. Shan's face lit up at the mention of the Elves. He wanted to ask about Solonika but figured now was not the time. "He told me of your encounter with the clumsy assassin."

The Elfling cleared his throat as he gazed into the man's steady eyes. "Thanks to a little help from Doornig and Kilgar," Shan had to admit, "I'm still alive." Firelight played from all of their faces as they stared into the small flames. "I guess I should have trusted you from the start, Altyrian," the elven youth said with a shrug of his shoulders. "But I have been so afraid to rely on anyone."

"I know, I know." The big man reached out and clasped Shan's hand. "Things would certainly have been better if we'd both trusted each other from the beginning." He sighed. "But that's water under the bridge, and cannot be changed now. Perhaps this is what I should have done from that first encounter with you." Altyrian leaned over and pulled the bandanna from around his head. Shan was startled to see the tips of the man's elven ears sticking up through his dark hair.

"You're an *Elf?*" Shan was astonished.

Altyrian grinned at him. "You don't recall that I first spoke *Keldarin* to you while you were pinned to that web?" Shan frowned at first but a vague remembrance slowly began to dawn on him.

"That's right," the elven boy said smiling, "I remember now. I couldn't understand you at all. I thought you were speaking gibberish to me." He grinned lightly then as he drew slowly to an obvious conclusion. "Then you must have thought I was an Elf, too."

Altyrian nodded. "Yes. But when you couldn't speak the elven tongue at all I was a little confused. I had expected to find someone who would easily recognize and accept me for my own elven looks. You haven't been the only one who's been hunted from time to time on account of his heritage." He rubbed his hands together. "I almost said something to you that night, but I couldn't reveal details of my mission without jeopardizing any chance for success. And I strongly felt the need to hurry on. Yet now, looking back, I was obviously wrong to conclude off-hand that you couldn't be the one I was seeking."

"And I was afraid to say anything in case you were trying to kill me yourself," Shan told him with a chuckle. "As far as being ignorant of my past, Janerron must have had some similar thoughts. 'How could there be someone who literally had no idea of what it means to be an Elf?' And yet I still don't know, really." He looked over at his friends who remained quietly listening. He sighed. "I would have loved to stay in Avalar. It was such an incredibly beautiful place. The most beautiful land I've ever seen, in fact. But I still wouldn't have been safe even there. Nowhere seems safe for me any more." He lapsed for a moment into silence. The others all looked at him, their eyes brimming with compassion.

"So, instead of sitting back and relaxing somewhere, we've had to be constantly on the run, fleeing from one close call after another," Kilgar said to him with a look of encouragement. "And we've survived—*you've* survived." The boy from Branby gave the Elfling a playful nudge in the arm. "Right?"

Shan nodded grudgingly to him.

"We've certainly been through a lot of tight scrapes together," Doornig confirmed. "And yet, somehow, we always make it through alive." He flashed the Elfling a crooked little smile.

"And don't forget that incredible sword you found," Gorian said to soothe the boy's nagging apprehensions. "Remember, great trials oft times bring great rewards."

Shan looked down at the unusual sword at his hip. "We have been through some pretty intense moments over the last month," he told his friends, "most of which I'd rather not have to repeat any time soon." The boys laughed softly at his declaration. He grinned wryly at them in return. "But I can honestly say I never would have found this unbelievable weapon if I had stayed locked away in Avalar the rest of my life, like I'd have wanted, no matter how long or short that time might have been." He blinked heavily in thought. He turned to the Elf warrior as he laid a hand on the hilt of his sword. "Altyrian, can you tell me anything about this unusual weapon?"

The tall Elf watched him with interest as Shan removed the scabbard from his belt and held it out for all to see. The unusual, black ceramic-like material immediately drew all of their eyes to study it. The Elfling slowly pulled the dark blade from the sheath. It glimmered oddly in the flickering yellow light of the small fire. A hush fell over the entire group as Shan laid the sword on the grass before them.

Altyrian leaned forward and looked at it with an expression of utter amazement. "A Sar'nathi blade!" he breathed in reverence. "One of the seven lost swords of Arias." He blinked his eyes in wonder and looked up into Shan's innocent face.

"I've heard talk of such a blade," Gurvin spoke quietly. "Legends and stories abound from long ages ago, but it has always been hard to determine the truthfulness of these things. Rumors were often spoken in secret of some long lost magical weapon of the Elves, yet never did I believe they truly existed—until now." He reached out a huge hand to touch it.

"Don't!" Shan and Altyrian said at the same moment. The dwarf's large fist hovered over it in mid-air.

"It cannot be handled by anyone save an Elf," Altyrian told him. "It will defend itself and burn the one who tries to touch it."

Doornig held up his hand. "I'll attest to that. I tried to pick it up when Shan first found it, and it burned me so badly I thought my skin would peel off." The others laughed softly at him. "Really!" he snorted in indignation.

Altyrian looked the dwarf squarely in the eyes. "It can only be wielded by one owner at a time. It somehow bonds with them and as long as that individual lives it cannot even be held by another."

The Elf looked down at the fabled blade once again. "The swords have been lost for over a thousand yehrin. Many of us even believed them to be destroyed sometime long, long ago, lost to us forever."

"Where did they come from?" Rimmy asked with a touch of awe in his voice.

"There were seven of them," Altyrian remarked. "One for each of the seven Noble Houses of the Elves. These swords are more than mere heirlooms, however. They are the initial means of defense for the seven different Clans. Wielded by a Clanlord or another specially chosen bearer, they have been carried into many a battle since their creation long ago."

"And when was that?" Shan asked, a glimmer of dull firelight dancing in his eyes.

"Long, long ago, a gifted elven-smith named Arias," the big Elf said quietly, "took lumps of *sironath* which had fallen from the sky."

"This same strange metal?" Kilgar asked, indicating the palm-sized piece resting on the ground in the middle of their group.

"That's right," Altyrian informed him. "The name *sironath* actually means 'heaven-cast' or 'star-cast' in *Keldarin*." He tilted his head back and glanced up at the night sky. "It is commonly believed among my people that Athiliel Himself tossed this strange metal down upon Anarra as a blessing to all the Elves."

He dropped his face to survey the hushed looks of those seated there around the little fire. Its small flames crackled softly as he looked into each of their eyes in turn.

"Arias somehow developed a secret process to meld the *sironath* fragments into an extremely hard, yet very light metal. He heated and folded the hot ore over and over again." He pursed his lips momentarily. "No one knows exactly how he was able to accomplish his difficult task and the knowledge of his special process has been lost since the time of their forging." He sighed softly before latching his eyes upon the Elfling. "With the death of Arias ages ago, the secret has been totally lost and no other elven smith has ever been able to equal his work."

The dwarf commander cleared his throat with a light cough. "Perhaps," Gurvin offered, "you need a dwarven master-smith to help you find a way. We are, after all, very skilled when it comes to the mining of metals and forging them into useful implements." He tapped his tube-like fingers on the blade of his great axe. The two young dwarves at his side grunted their assent. The mighty dwarf looked back meaningfully at his elven friend.

"No doubt, my good friend," Altyrian smiled at him, "dwarves are indeed incredibly gifted when it comes to the manufacture of metal objects." He shook his head. "But truth be known," he went on with a gentle wagging of his head, "there must have been another step, a special hidden process of some sort, which none of our people has been able to uncover." He wagged his head.

"Some even believe the master smith took the *sironath* and merged it somehow with shards of pure crystal," Altyrian continued. "The blades are said to be stronger than any steel known to us, yet are lighter even than any crystal. It is certainly a quandary beyond my understanding."

"I can vouch for that," Shan replied with a firm nod of his head. "The sword can cut completely through other metal, yet it almost seems as light as a feather."

"For that reason," the tall Elf told them quietly, "this special material has been affectionately dubbed *Crysteel* by its master."

"*Crysteel!*" Shan breathed out in awe.

Altyrian spread his hands wide. "In the end," he told them, "only seven of these wondrous blades were ever created. We call them the *Sar'nathi*, the Star-cast blades, the seven lost swords of Arias." He looked down and studied the dark, almost glassy blade on the turf. "There are some who even feel Arias poured a little of himself into each one of the swords, and that, perhaps as a result, they are somehow alive."

The entire party sat huddled in silence, staring down at the smoky black surface of the metal.

"I think you're right," Shan said after a long silence. The flames writhed in tiny, ever-shifting tongues of light. The circle of close faces looked up at him. "I think you're right, Altyrian," he said again, "about the blades being alive somehow." The dark-haired Elf narrowed his eyes on the boy. Shan fidgeted slightly with all the attention directed upon him. "It calls to me—*sometimes*," he said quietly. "Not with an audible voice maybe, but in my mind. At times it even sings to me."

The others regarded him in wonder.

Shan studied the blade for a long moment. He cocked his tousled head to one side as if listening. The little company watched his movements curiously. The Elfling finally looked up at Altyrian. "It's called *Skarbinger*," he said in a hushed whisper.

The tall Elf looked slowly around the small circle of faces. "I believe it is no coincidence that this blade has been found," Altyrian remarked with a tinge of excitement in his voice. "As Muurdra stretches out his evil clutches from the confines of the Outer Darkness, he seeks to terrorize and subdue all the people of Anarra. He strives to snatch at our hearts, and crush the joy of our lives, as he sends his foul minions scurrying forth from their dark holes in numberless droves. And even now, he is poised to re-enter our world in a blaze of destruction."

The on-lookers held their mouths tightly shut. Smoke kindled in the dark eyes of the dwarves. Terror tugged at the hearts of the young boys from Branby. The Elfling's face was a frozen mask of unreasoning fear. Shan finally managed to swallow against the rise of bile burning its way up from his gut. He turned his troubled eyes on Altyrian.

"I understand, now that we have the sword, one of the swords," Shan began falteringly, "the dark forces of Muurdra would seek to take my life. That somehow makes sense to me. Cut down an enemy before he can strike at you with a devastating weapon." He looked down momentarily to gather his thoughts. He gently stroked the hilt of the sword. "But, but they have been trying to kill me for quite some time now, long before I even found the mystical thing. And I still don't know why." He leveled his gaze on the tall Elf. "Who am I, Altyrian?" he asked quietly. "What have I done? And why is just about everyone trying to kill me?"

Altyrian looked across the little fire, his green eyes filled with sudden compassion for the Elfling. Shan's face pleaded with him to know the answer which had tugged at his heart for what seemed like ages to him. "Please, tell me."

The Elf warrior closed his eyes for a moment with a sigh. He slowly raised his lids and regarded the Elfling. "You pose a threat to Khairon," he said evenly.

"Khairon? Didn't Ulfiir call him the Usurper?" Shan asked, yet he foolishly realized none of those sitting around the fire was present during that conversation so long ago in the great hall of Draydin.

"Yes," the Elf warrior said. "He is known as the Usurper among the Elves. In his mind Khairon cannot afford to let you live," he went on with a grim smile, "and while you do his grasp on power will never be secure."

"How? Why?" the Elfling's face was clouded in confusion. "I don't understand. What am I to him?"

Altyrian reached out and placed one hand lightly on the boy's shoulder. "He's your uncle, Shan," the Elf warrior said firmly, looking deeply into the boy's eyes. The Elfling fell back as if struck.

"What?" Shan blustered. "How can that be?" His cheeks drained of color and his eyes failed to see Altyrian's face before him.

"Are you saying Shan's some kind of prince?" Rimmy blurted out. The dark-haired youth looked over at the Elfling in a kind of wonder.

"That's right," Altyrian told them. "He's the legitimate heir to the throne of the Elves." He looked at the elven boy, who was totally stunned by the news. "And that's why they're trying to kill him."

"How could I . . . how could I?" was all that Shan could mutter for the longest time. His eyes seemed glazed over as he sat motionless before them.

"I knew there was something about that boy," Gurvin mumbled to the two young dwarves sitting beside him. They exchanged looks of quiet surprise as they sat back in their usually stoic manner.

"But why would Shan be a threat to this Khairon fellow?" Doornig wanted to know. "Wouldn't an uncle take precedence over a nephew when it comes to matters of ascension?"

"Of course," Altyrian said with a grim smile, "in most circumstances that would be the case. But Khairon is called the Usurper for a reason. He seized the throne from his own half-brother in a jealous rage. And now mercilessly he seeks to hunt Shan down, the true and rightful heir of Vandikar, in an attempt to snuff out any possible threat to his reign."

Shan's eyes finally cleared of their mistiness. He turned to Altyrian with a faraway look. "What can you tell me about my parents?" he pleaded with the elven warrior. "Are they . . . ?"

"*Still alive?*" Altyrian finished for him. He leveled sad eyes on the boy. "I'm sorry to tell you this, but they've both been dead these past seventeen yehrin. Khairon killed your father with his own hand and when he attempted to snatch the Regent's wife, she fled. But she was heavy with child and must have gone into labor sometime in her dangerous flight into the wilderness. The child was delivered by an unknown mid-wife in a cabin somewhere deep in the woods, but sadly your mother perished during the birth." He looked compassionately at the elven youth, who just sat there numbly and listened. His ears seemed to burn with a suppressed anger.

"What were their names?" Shan inquired with a quivering voice. "Ulfiir never told me."

"Your father's name was Tanith," Altyrian told him in a kindly tone. "I knew the Regent well. He was a good man, a kind man. Yet he was not watchful enough, it seems, to notice the sly, secretive way Khairon lusted after power and plotted to steal the throne." The tall Elf waved a dismissive hand. "Your mother's name was Viridia. She was incredibly beautiful, and it was plain for me to see how much Khairon desired her. Tanith would always wave off my suspicions each time I approached him with such news. I tried to tell him what I'd seen in the Usurper's eyes each time he looked at her."

He paused for a moment, his face turning hard. "No one else ever seemed to see the same things I saw," Altyrian said. "No one else noticed the obvious flaws in Khairon's character, until it was too late."

"You called Shan's father Regent a couple of times," Kilgar pointed out. "Wasn't Tanith the King?"

"No," the big Elf swung about to look at him. "Ga'Larin is actually still King. But he rode off to war a long time ago with a great number of his troops. They journeyed far to the south and there fought a series of pitched battles in a valiant attempt to roust Muurdra's evil servants from their filthy lairs. And thus eradicate them once and for all."

"So what happened?" Gorian asked breathlessly. "Is Ga'Larin still alive?"

"Yes," Altyrian responded, "the last time I spoke with him, he was most certainly alive." He dropped his eyes grimly to stare at the small fire. "But that was several yehrin ago. Even now he languishes in heavy chains in some foul dungeon in Kulnedra."

The insidious name of that dark land seemed to steal its way into their hearts. They all looked down into the flames for a time. Gurvin fed the fire absently with small sticks and chunks of wood which had been piled up there for that purpose.

"Ga'Larin is your grandfather, Shan," the tall elven warrior announced, "and as long as he lives, he's still the King. When he went off to war long ago, he entrusted the leadership of all seven Noble Clans of the Elves, scattered as they were across the face of Anarra, into the hands of his son, Tanith. And now that your father is dead, Shan, you're next one in line for the throne. Since Khairon is Tanith's younger half-brother, he has no rightful claim to the throne so long as you're alive.

"The Usurper has searched far and wide for any sign of you for these many yehrin," Altyrian continued, "but all in vain. He truly hoped that you had perished along with your mother, but he could never really be certain. Yet somehow he must have recently learned you still live, and it has made him livid. Even now he's wildly bending all his will, all his assets, to find you—in order to eliminate the threat you pose to him."

"It all makes sense now." Kilgar looked quickly over at his friend. He clapped Shan on the leg. "At least now you know who you are and why everyone's been out to get you. That should be somewhat comforting . . ." Shan looked sullenly into his friend's face. ". . . At least a little."

Kilgar offered him an awkward grin.

Shan had a rueful look on his face as he turned back to Altyrian. "Why haven't they just killed my grandfather already?" he asked woodenly. "Wouldn't Khairon want to crush that threat as well, to keep his already shaky claim to the throne intact?" He smacked his lips loudly and thrust a hand into the air. "I mean, what would happen if Ga'Larin somehow managed to escape his foul prison?"

Altyrian regarded the Elfling with a little bob of his head. "Ultimately," he spoke up clearly, "Muurdra would have the final say in the matter, I would guess. The gorguls are his gruesome minions after all. They only appear to perform Khairon's bidding as long as the Usurper himself kneels down to serve the Evil One. In the end, Muurdra holds all the cards, and he must believe Ga'Larin still has a part to play in all of this." He shrugged his shoulders. "He's the only one who really has the power to do whatever he pleases."

"Within limits, I'd say," Gurvin spoke up in a gruff voice. He cleared his throat with a hoarse laugh. "Durrock will have something to say about that—*in the end!*" He grunted. "Mind you, Muurdra is extremely powerful, but the hand of Durrock is far mightier than the Fallen One."

"Amen to that," Armig said with a sharp exhale of his breath.

The entire group sat quietly around the fire. They all seemed to return their eyes to the small wreath of flames.

"What happens now?" Doornig asked after a long silence.

"Well," Gurvin said, rocking forward slightly. His eyes settled curiously on the Elfling as the boy tilted his head oddly to the side and stared down at the Sar'nathi blade. It seemed to whistle suddenly in Shan's ears, but glancing up at the others, the Elfling realized no one else had heard it. He listened intently for a couple of heartbeats as they all fixed curious looks upon him.

At the same moment Altyrian's eyes went suddenly vacant.

"Something's coming!" Shan declared all at once. They all leaped uneasily to their feet. The Elfling scooped up the strange sword in his right hand. The Sar'nathi blade already felt warm to his touch. "Something big!"

They looked around themselves in their darkened little canyon but couldn't immediately discern anything amiss. And then they all felt it. In the ground under their feet, it started as a light tremor, a dull vibration in the soil. It grew to a steady trembling until they could all feel it through the soles of their boots. They looked around themselves warily. Even the animals were suddenly spooked by it.

"What is it?" Doornig cried out. They instinctively came together into a tight circle with their backs nearly touching. They feverishly searched their dark surroundings, their hands reaching nervously for their weapons.

"We're about to be attacked!" Altyrian shouted over the rising clamor around them. He planted his feet firmly and brought up his great bow. He pulled an arrow from the quiver in calm determination and placed it on the string. "Brace yourselves!" he cried.

"Let's do this," Gurvin bellowed out as the sounds grew louder. He gripped his massive axe in tight fists. They could see a cloud of dust flying up as a hint of faltering torchlight played through the narrow defile in the rocks around them. "Make every stroke count, lads," he cautioned.

Shan held up the Sar'nathi blade and it began to glow from within.

"Here they come!" Altyrian shouted into the cool night air.

Here ends the first part of the Seven Lost Swords of Arias.

For more information visit:

www.vandikar.com

Glossary of ANARRAN Terminology

Alk - Large, antlered moose-like animal. Its massive horn-like antlers are prized for their hardness and are often fashioned into tools and household implements. The meat is also prized for its rich taste. These great animals are never domesticated but must be hunted in the wilds on a seasonal basis.

Anarra - The world. Consisting of several islands and continents, most of which is unexplored except for *Ythira*, the eastern continent.

Athiliel - God. The Creator of the universe, the One Who Is. All-Knowing and All-Powerful. He is called by many different names in different cultures, but is the only true God. Other names for Him are Durrock, Athalias, Ka'Hanni, and Te'Liira.

Avira - A cactus-like plant found in the desert climates to the south. The moisture it contains can help keep someone alive in harsh, dry conditions. The leaves can be boiled to produce a wax-like compound (*Avira butter*) which eliminates the adhesive effects of a rith's web.

Barma - Reddish-skinned fruit about the size of a small melon. It can be peeled like a banana or an orange, and yields sweet, juicy segments of fruit.

Barsilas Leaves - Large, almost translucent, vein-like leaves. When wrapped tightly around fresh foods, these tend to preserve the perishable products for extended periods of time.

Bathalisk - A huge domesticated draft animal. Similar in shape to a buffalo, only much, much larger and they have six great legs. They have a huge horned head and great shaggy shoulders. They range in color from a deep, dark brown to almost black.

Bork - A wild boar-like animal. These usually inhabit forests and jungles. Its meat is prized by hunters.

Bristleweed - A large, bush-like weed. It grows in large clumps with tangled vein-like branches. Once plucked off and dried, their branches form stiff, natural brushes used to curry animals. Sometimes the whole plant dries up, and its dried, snapped off husks roll interminably across the land.

Corabent - Large, predatory cats. They are strong and tenacious, with reddish-orange fur and wild, black manes. They are usually found across the great plains to the south of Ythira.

Cyr Nilth - The Fallen One, also known as Muurdra. Once the most beautiful of Athiliel's creations. Before his fall, he was second in knowledge and power only to the Creator Himself.

Ethulan - A meat-cake. Composed of flour and dried meat, these are cooked to produce flaky cakes which tend to stay well preserved for long journeys.

Fleef - Small, rodent-like mammals, similar to a mouse. They are extremely quiet, but can generally find their way into locked food stores.

Gorguls - An evil race of foot soldiers. Lightly scaled, with yellowish-green skin, these foul creatures were spawned by Muurdra long ago in imitation of Athiliel's creations.

Hand - An Anarran week. A period of time consisting of five days.

The *Ilyri* - Immortal, all-male race of angelic beings. Created by Athiliel to worship and serve Him, they are actively involved with preserving Anarra from being destroyed by Muurdra's foul agents. They protect the land and the water as gifts to mankind. They are also periodically engaged in actual open warfare with the *Neffeluur*, the Fallen Ones.

Jackards - Large, vulture-like birds. They are scavengers, and will feast on the aftermath of great battles. They are extremely ugly in appearance, with black feathers, red, beady eyes and wickedly sharp beaks.

Kabba - A root from low bush-like plants commonly found in forests or along streams. When dried and ground, the roots form a powder which is often poured into hot water to make a stimulating drink similar to coffee or tea. It has a faint, yet distinct cinnamon flavor.

The *Keldar* - The noble race of the Elves. They are graceful and immortal. They have a special covenant relationship to Athiliel, and as a result, they are hated above all other races. They are called the *Thuvan* by most other races.

Kiara - The smaller of Anarra's two moons. It is reddish-gold in color and has a cycle of twenty-eight days.

Kuls - Tuber-like vegetable grown in the ground. When baked or boiled they produce a starchy food highly relished by all Anarrans.

Kurgoth - A huge, hairy monster. Standing nearly ten feet tall, it is a blood hunter, or blood tracker, created long ago by Muurdra.

Kuulo - Domesticated bird, much like a chicken, commonly used to produce eggs. Its roasted or fried meat is a common dish. Many farmers and villagers maintain a healthy population of them for their own needs.

Lence - Tall, stalk-like plant. These produce large heads of tightly wrapped kernels, which can be boiled and eaten with a meal. When dried and pounded into powder, its kernels produce a fine yellowish flour. This is often formed into cakes, called *lence-cakes*, which stay fresh for a long time.

Luumin - Small, apelike creatures with large eyes and tufted ears. Their hands and feet are practically identical, with thick, calloused digits for grasping and swinging lightly through the trees. They prefer dense, moist jungle-like conditions. They are extremely mischievous.

Morlung - Tall, corpse-like beings with deathly white skin, long flowing white hair and totally black eyes. Although alive, they are often mistaken as walking corpses. Cunning and powerful in their usage of dark arts, they are also known as *Necromors*. They are Muurdra's corruption of the Elves.

The ***Neffeluur*** - The Fallen Ones. Once a powerful and immortal angelic race (see *Ilyri*), they fell with Muurdra long ago. They are still active participants in his rebellion against Athiliel.

Osk - Domesticated cattle. They are used to provide meat and milk for the needs of the people. Some of these powerful animals are even employed to do the heavy work of pulling plows and such things. Great herds of these horned mammals roam openly across the Plains of Kuria in the south.

Riffin - A popular card game. There are several different varieties and every town seems to sport their own rules.

Rith - A huge spider. They spin enormous webs across trees and canyons. They tend to have stiff, spiky hair all across their huge bodies. The are usually black in color, with flame-like streaks of red, orange or yellow running across their bloated abdomens.

Rogin berries - Large, dark-reddish fruit grown in wild thickets. They are about the size of a nickel and are somewhat crunchy on the outside like a nut, yet have a juicy inside which has a sweet fruity flavor.

Sar'nathi Blades - The fabled Seven Swords of Arias. Composed of *sironath* and dense shards of crystal, these long lost swords were created by a master smith of the Elves named Arias. With the elven smith's passing the secret to reproduce them was lost.

Shart - Long-haired, goat-like animal. These nimble-legged creatures have great spiraling horns. They are most often found running wild over high hills and mountain ranges, but are occasionally domesticated for their wool and their milk. Once sheared the hair is woven into a fairly cheap cloth called *sharcloth*.

Sheera - The larger moon. It is bluish-silver in color and has a cycle of thirty-six days. Its surface is deeply pock-marked.

Sironath - *Keldarin* name for an unusual meteorite material which fell out of the sky. The term means *starcast* or *heavencast*. This unusual substance was used by the elven master-smith Arias long ago to create a special set of swords for the seven clans of the Elves, called the *Sar'nathi* blades. There are only seven of them in existence and they were believed to be lost long ages ago in a series forgotten wars.

Sleeth (Watchbeasts) - Large, scaly cat-like creatures. They appear to be a cross between a great hunting cat and a large reptile. They have six legs and are extremely predatory in the wild. But they are more often domesticated, bred and trained to patrol the outer perimeter grounds of towns and villages, especially at night. They are mostly blind in the daylight.

Slor (Giant) - Large, lizard-like animals. They are strong and relatively slow moving upon their four heavy legs. With broad backs and long, powerful tails, they are frequently employed as draft animals in the far south, where occupants ride in large howdahs strapped across their backs. Their thick, mottled skin ranges in color from a pale green to yellowish-gold or even gray. Their smaller cousins can be found sunning themselves upon rocks and trees across most of Ythira.

Tanga juice - A dark blue juice made from the crushed berries of a tanga plant. Its flavor is a little tart, but is also very refreshing. The juice stays fresh for a long time in a leather bota, which makes it appealing for travelers to carry with them.

Targ - Large, three-headed wolf. They stand much taller than an average wolf and are extremely vicious. They are fast and relentless, but seldom hunt in packs.

Telm-wood - Extremely dense trees. The wood from these gnarled trees is very beautiful when polished. It is popularly used for carvings and for making tools and weapons. These items are especially strong and durable. It is the most prized type of wood for the fashioning of long bows.

Thag - An antelope-like animal. Smaller and more delicate than the *alk*, these animals commonly roam through forested lands and the lower slopes of mountains. They are especially swift on their hooved legs when spooked. The meat of the *thag* is highly prized for its leanness and its rich flavor. Leather from its hide is very soft and durable, and is often used for a variety of goods, including pouches, boots and other clothing.

Thark - A large flightless bird. Its meat is rich and savory in flavor and its long, colorful feathers are prized for ornamentations.

Theralon - A special unfaceted gemstone. About the size of one's palm, these smooth stones are often called the Tears of the Creator, or Athiliel's Tears. They can be used to make its bearer invisible and are a popular tool among assassins, but they are extremely rare and, as a result, very expensive.

Thisalant - A large, water fowl. These live around rivers and lakes, and all throughout marshy lands. Its call is like a wailing warble.

Thorka - Horse-like mounts of Anarra. They have six legs and can run like the wind. They are frequently used as mounts for warriors in battle, and often carry riders with dispatches and messages between kingdoms. Sometimes they are even employed for the sport of racing, where individuals wager on the outcome.

Thorro - A smaller beast of burden. They are a somewhat donkey-like in appearance, with long ears, hooved feet and a short, nervous tail. They are believed to be a distant cousin of the mighty thorka. They are often stubborn-natured but are a preferred form of mount for most people of Ythira, due primarily to their lower cost.

Timbercat - A large predatory cat. These cougar-like animals inhibit the northern forests and the lower foothills of the mountains. Upon occasion hunger drives them into the haunts of man in search for food.

Turth - Small, racoon-sized mischievous mammal. These curious critters often get themselves into tightly sealed places and containers, hunting for food. They are voracious, and will eat just about anything. They are cute with their bandit-like appearance, yet are despised by farmers and villagers for constantly getting into and spoiling their preserved foods. Their meat is eaten upon occasion when nothing else is available.

Ur - A small, marsupial-like mammal. They are especially timid and hop about very quickly on their long backs legs. They possess extremely long ears and can hear predators coming from a great distance away. They can be domesticated, for their meat is tender and tasty.

ADARRAD Table of Weights and Measurements

Item	Equivalent	Description
buhr / biri	1 second (s)	heartbeat of a standing thorka
mur / mira	1 minute (s)	50 biri
ahr / ahrin	1 hour (s)	100 mira
day	1 day	20 ahrin
hand	week	5 days
fist	1 month	24 days
yahr / yehrin	1 year (s)	384 days - or 16 fists
hob / hobbin	1 span (s)	distance between splayed thumb and little finger (apprx 8 in.) - 5 hobbin make up a kor
kor / kora	1 pace or stride(s)	just over a yard or meter
koreb	100 paces	also 1/10 of a korad
korad	1000 paces	approx 3000 feet or about 1 km (10 koreb)
league	5 korads	approx 5 kilometers
Se'Kora	Spring	96 days or 4 fists
Su'Villa	Summer	96 days or 4 fists
E'Dara	Autumn (Fall)	96 days or 4 fists
Stra'Mora	Winter	96 days or 4 fists

ANARRAN Table of Weights and Measurements

Item	Equivalent	Description
Mor'da	1st day of the hand	like Monday
Tohr'da	2nd day of the hand	like Tuesday
Kar'da	3rd day of the hand	like Wednesday
Fel'da	4th day of the hand	like Friday
Shar'da	5th day of the hand	like Saturday
copper bit	1/10th of a mark	small copper coin
copper mark	10 bits make up a c. mark	formed from a larger slug of copper, stamped with an image
silver penny	20 c. marks to equal a penny	small silver coin, 1/50th of a talon
silver talon	50 s. pennies to make a talon	larger silver coin
gold bit	10 talons to equal a crown	small gold coin, 1/40th of a crown
gold crown	40 g. bits to make a crown	larger gold coin
double crown	double weight gold piece	the largest Anarran coin

ANARRAN CALENDAR

4534 C.R.

(*Common Reckoning*)

KALIGATH
```
        1  2  3
 4  5  6  7  8
 9 10 11 12 13
14 15 16 17 18
19 20 21 22 23
24
```

BELLACH
```
    1  2  3  4
 5  6  7  8  9
10 11 12 13 14
15 16 17 18 19
20 21 22 23 24
```

HEPHNAUR
```
 1  2  3  4  5
 6  7  8  9 10
11 12 13 14 15
16 17 18 19 20
21 22 23 24
```

FARROK
```
                1
 2  3  4  5  6
 7  8  9 10 11
12 13 14 15 16
17 18 19 20 21
22 23 24
```

CAYLOR
```
        1  2
 3  4  5  6  7
 8  9 10 11 12
13 14 15 16 17
18 19 20 21 22
23 24
```

SA'RAN
```
    1  2  3
 4  5  6  7  8
 9 10 11 12 13
14 15 16 17 18
19 20 21 22 23
24
```

PELDYR
```
    1  2  3  4
 5  6  7  8  9
10 11 12 13 14
15 16 17 18 19
20 21 22 23 24
```

TEMMON
```
 1  2  3  4  5
 6  7  8  9  1
11 12 13 14
16 17 18 1
21 22 23
```

EDRA
```
                1
 2  3  4  5  6
 7  8  9 10 11
12 13 14 15 16
17 18 19 20 21
22 23 24
```

CHIRILLOH
```
        1  2
 3  4  5  6  7
 8  9 10 11 12
13 14 15 16 17
18 19 20 21 22
23 24
```

NIKLA
```
    1  2  3
 4  5  6  7  8
 9 10 11 12 13
14 15 16 17 18
19 20 21 22 23
24
```

G
```
          1
 5  6
10 11
15 16
20 21 22
```

DELFURD
```
 1  2  3  4  5
 6  7  8  9 10
11 12 13 14 15
16 17 18 19 20
21 22 23 24
```

MARAK
```
                1
 2  3  4  5  6
 7  8  9 10 11
12 13 14 15 16
17 18 19 20 21
22 23 24
```

DRAGELDA
```
        1  2
 3  4  5  6  7
 8  9 10 11 12
13 14 15 16 17
18 19 20 21 22
23 24
```

ZHADAR
```
    1  2  3
 4  5  6  7  8
 9 10 11 12 13
14 15 16 17 18
19 20 21 22 23
24
```